THE MARCH OF MAGNUS

BOOK TWO OF THE SPARK CITY CYCLE

ROBERT J POWER

DEPAOR PRESS

THE MARCH OF MAGNUS
First published in Ireland by DePaor Press in 2020.
ISBN 978-1-8382765–4-6

Copyright © Robert J Power 2020

Available in eBook, Audiobook, Paperback, Large Print and Hardcover.

www.RobertJPower.com

For Rights and Permissions contact:
Hello@DePaorPress.com

CONTENTS

For Jan, the better writer of us both.
Just let me be better at one thing in our life.
Just once.
You are my soulmate, my muse.
My one for life.

1

THE FROZEN ALPHALINES

"We have to move now, Erroh," Lea hissed, shaking him. She thought it strange to hear her own voice aloud again. Too long since she'd spoken to another person. *Too fuken long.* She pulled him from the snowbank and to his unsteady feet. A harder task than she'd expected, but it didn't matter. He was weak and ruined and none of that mattered either. Her Erroh, only hers, nobody else's.

Her lungs struggled from the water. Perhaps it was the running too. How far had she sprinted? A mile? More? Did it matter? *Not at all.* What mattered was this moment. *And the fuken cold.* She was exhausted, far from home, and frozen to the bone. For a cruel moment, she wondered if she was asleep, huddled in a little shelter with a driving blizzard raging around her, bound to wake any moment and continue her silent trek. Bound to watching her love wither away under the watchful eye of a whore. Or else a blizzard had finally caught her, and she was drifting towards darkness now.

No. She pushed those thought away. This was no dream, no grace from the absent gods. She'd earned this luck herself. She had been careful. She had been patient. She had walked beside them long enough that good fortune might fall upon her.

Lea stifled a tear and shook him again, her thoughts frantic and exhilarated and delirious. She'd waited for this moment. Prayed for this moment. Doubted this moment. She should have lost him in Keri. She should have lost him in the storms. She should have lost him at the gates of the city of Conlon, when an army had stood between them and silently mocked her. She should have lost sight of him a thousand times or more. But she hadn't, had she? She had risked it all, and somehow, he was in her arms right now.

The mountains' glow stood out against the night. Why wouldn't it? Though she didn't know why, every other building these last dozen miles had been long-abandoned and lost to the unforgiving southern winds. It had been so easy to follow tracks, to follow a glowing light high in the mountains. Harder believing there was hope at all. Just another night sitting lost in desolation. Unsure how to act. Unsure *when* to act.

She remembered the inhuman screams and believed them to have been Erroh's. Primal and awful and echoing across the valley as though wailed by a god. Terrifying and familiar. Lea knew well the terrible sound of torment, and she hoped to never hear screams like that again, but she knew better: war was in the wind. The absent gods knew what terrible things were coming, and they knew the cost.

So many months. So close to Erroh. *Waiting, waiting, waiting. Failing.*

She had watched disbelievingly as he fell. Cried out, seeing his body dashed against the rocks, tossed like a rag doll discarded by the world. She had almost reached him at the first bend. But she was too slow, too ruined herself. Too unsure of anything. She had never stopped running along the river's edge in pursuit. He had never been alone.

She took Erroh's frozen form in her arms and hugged him with all her might. *Welcome back, Erroh. It's time to go home.*

He wavered, but followed her urging. "I'm cold, Nomi," he whispered, and her heart broke. She recovered her dry pack and cloak, and helped him away from the river's edge. The snow crunched beneath their feet, and every deep step was arduous with his weight upon her, but it was glorious.

"We'll walk a while, my beo, and then we'll warm ourselves," she whispered, and willed a sudden drift of snow to follow them from the water's edge. Every step seemed impossibly pronounced. Who knew when the Riders would catch up? With gloriousness came terror and denial. Perhaps his keepers would believe he'd perished in the fall, she thought, but doubted there was any more good fortune to call upon. Be strong, she told herself. She'd evaded capture for months; she just needed a few more steps.

He tripped and fell in the snow, taking her with him. Fresh shards of freezing daggers struck her body and she almost yelped. Instead, she willed herself to rise.

"We need to clear the valley, Erroh." She spat snow from her chattering mouth. "Take my hand." She pulled herself and him to unsteady feet, and though he followed, he fought her, struggling against every step. In the light of the shattered moon she could see the shell her Erroh had become. "Oh, what have they done to you, my beo?" she whispered, pulling him forward. She could see the cold take hold. He would die soon enough if they didn't find cover. She would likely die soon after. She'd felt this cold before, many times, yet it never prepared her. Each breath whistled through protesting lungs.

She was tougher now, but the wilds of the south were unforgiving and she'd had time to get to know them well. Getting to know the land had become one of her routines these past few months. What else was there to do in the fading hours, watching a slow thundering line of murderers? What else was there to do, waiting for Erroh to return? Tonight should have been no different. From her little nook below the home of glowing light and echoing screams, she knew the distance to the falling man, the best route to recover him, the best place to take cover in a vast open valley.

"Come on, my beo."

Every frustrated step was filled with panicked gasps until they found salvation in a deep cluster of evergreen trees. Again, she prayed for snow to cover her reckless prints from the river's edge to the deep trail they left now. Two sets were harder to conceal than one. She counted the steps they took. Over five hundred in total, and eventually they reached the edge of the forest and staggered further in. He was so beautiful and so fragile and so heavy in her grip. He wavered, but she refused to allow exhaustion bar her way after coming so far. She'd take aching and fatigue, for they were familiar. As was freezing to the edges of death. She looked into his glazed eyes; he was closer to hypothermia now than she'd ever come. The valley rumbled with the low threat of thunder. Thunder of a chasing pack. *Just a few more steps, my love.*

Erroh's head spun. This wasn't real. He was dead, or dying, and still he leant on the girl. Carried in a frozen march. It looked like Lea, and he cursed his dying mind's thoughts. His Lea was lost to him forever. Dead, most likely. He coughed and his lungs ached, constricting tightly; he was drowning upon dry land. Each gasping breath was a terrible labour, and his stomach filled with an awful gelatinous substance. It swirled and churned, and the taste reached his mouth.

"I can't."

He fell to his knees and threw up, and the bile warmed his mouth and chin pleasantly. The rest of him continued to ache and freeze. *Where am I?*

She stroked his frozen cheek again and helped him back up. None of this is fair, she thought. The rumbling grew, and she cursed the absent gods, as she had for so many months.

"Will you fail me again?" she demanded, and Erroh answered by plodding forward as though controlled by an invisible puppeteer. His limbs obeyed, yet no movement was assured. Somehow, he didn't slip again as the Riders appeared over the hill, on the other side of the river.

Their torches illuminated the world and sent out terrifying shadows across the snow. She pulled Erroh behind one of the spindly trees, long dead to the ever winter. They watched the line of Riders race along the water's edge, roaring as they went, and she held her breath as they passed. She searched her memory for the crossings the brutes would take. How far from here? A mile? Two? Less? Perhaps they'd dare to face the frozen waters as she had? It all depended on their desperation, she thought. When Erroh spoke coherently, she might understand better how any of this had happened.

"Let's go," she whispered, leading him by the hand through dry, leafless branches into the darkness of the green. The moon gave her just enough light to see. The Riders did not return. She never knew the distance they scrambled through the forest; only that no step seemed far enough. Time became nothing but a shambling scramble in freezing wet garments until, without warning, he fell against a tree trunk, coughing heavily. She knew that cough, and it filled her with a coldness far icier than the shards attacking her body. *This isn't fair.*

They hadn't made it far enough; there was no other way. She slipped her cloak free and spread it out and began stripping him of his filthy, ruined garments. Exhausted from his coughing fit, he didn't fight her, only muttering a few times in a strange voice how cold it was as she pulled his undergarments free, before removing a blanket from her pack and placing it across his battered and beaten body.

"So cold."

"I know, Erroh."

The rocks she chose were perfect. A good height, masking the sparks of the kindling as the flames took hold. Months walking the frozen road had returned to her some skills she had learned from her father in the cold few years before the city had called. *Not called – dragged. Alone.* They were the few memories she had of him. Walking the frozen south had added further understanding of what had become of her line. Any suggestion he still lived was long gone. She was an orphan in her entirety now. It hadn't bothered her at all.

"This will warm you, my beo." His naked body shook in reply.

The fire took a life of its own, and she took a few moments to warm her aching fingers. After stripping her own wet garments free and pulling a thin gown over her own battered body, she began the last of her preparations. She found a gentle slope away from the fire and stabbed into the soft snow, scooping it into a fine shape with a little hand spade. She attacked the snowbank with the skill of a female that had completed this task a thousand times before. No, not thousands, but at least a hundred.

Though the cold never ceased its onslaught, she continued until she had dug a fine little gouged hole along the snowbank, wide enough for two frozen Alphalines to lie along. She swiftly pulled a few bushy shrubs suitable to the task and left them near her diminutive ice cave before returning to the fire and her broken Erroh.

Erroh wondered whether he would ever feel warmth again. The delicate crackle of the fire at his side suggested as much, but despite its flickering attempts, the cold was deep in his bones like the very river of ice he'd escaped in, slowly surging through him, inviting him into oblivion. He liked this summons and drifted towards it willingly.

"Nomi?" His throat croaked painfully, and again he wondered if he'd lost his mind at the hands of a mad god. He didn't mind this madness; he didn't mind lying down and drifting into death. He'd prefer to do it in a warmer place, though, maybe with the cry of battle in his ears. That would be a fine enough death.

She lifted the cloak and slipped into the delicate warmth beside him. She nestled her head against his shoulder and willed him to fight the shock. She could still feel the shaking. She looked into his crazed eyes and loved him. She said nothing and neither did he. For just a moment, she allowed herself a smile. The road was so very lonely. Against all odds ever played in a terrible hand, she had bet, won, and stolen away with her prize. She had beaten the entire world. She had found her mate. Her Erroh. Only hers. No one else's. Watching him in chains had almost broken her. Watching him with the beautiful whore had been worse. Watching the whore take him to her tent was... She shook her head. *Not now.* There was enough time to ask questions. Fine questions. All of the questions. Perhaps when he had breath to answer. *We have all the time in the world.* She reached out and placed the driest log on the fire. It sparked nastily in reply, but after a few moments began to burn brightly. Good, she thought, and above, a few flakes of snow began to fall around them. *Even better.*

"I love you, Erroh."

"Thank you, Nomi," he whispered back.

———

Crack. Lea leapt from her coverings at the sound of heavy boots. Shaking the sleep from her mind, she looked into the night and spotted the torches coming through the forest. How long had they slept? Long enough that the cold shocked her warm body to its senses, and long enough that the Riders were now here, searching the forest.

She pushed a mound of snow across the fire before pulling a bleary-eyed Erroh to his feet. He protested, but she hissed him to silence as only a mate could without alerting eager ears. The boots became searching voices, and the Riders drew ever nearer.

Don't panic.

She'd been here before. A few feet from a marching horde that was unaware of how closely they approached a secret sanctuary. She grabbed her pack, bedding, her slow-witted mate, and threw them all into the hole. It was a fine hole. Smooth, secure, and spacious. With her mate lying flat and wedged against the back, she lay beside him and pulled the shrubs in front of the slit of an entrance. Moulding snow at their roots to hold them upright, she covered both Erroh and herself in her black cloak. Only a keen-eyed tracker might find them in this light. She slid her blade from its scabbard. If they were discovered, the seeker would be the first to die. A small consolation.

The walking flames swirled in the darkness. They spread out in a long line a few feet apart. She could see they were not tracking. Instead, they were simply walking through, hoping to come upon a battered warrior, dazed from misfortunes. Could Erroh even fight? Perhaps if she placed her second sword in his hand, he might emerge from the stupor. Sometimes, the only thing needed was a sword.

The hunters trudged right through their camp without hesitation. Hurried, driven, and oblivious to the signs of their prey, they missed broken branches here, deeper clefts in the snow there. Lea began to believe, until one hunter tripped on a jutting rock that had housed the flames and cursed in brutish, unknown words. She clenched her teeth, held her breath, and waited for death. He shone his torch down upon the ground, stepped over the rocks, and dismissed them as part of the landscape, choosing his steps a little more carefully. His light passed over their camouflage. It lingered for a moment, and all she could see was dazzling brightness as he neared. *They've seen us.*

The world went suddenly dark again as the hunter climbed up the slope, his foot passing only a hand's distance from her face before continuing on. When her racing heart began to settle, the Riders' sounds were already fading to the gentle breeze and the call of the forest.

"We have to find some proper shelter," she whispered, pulling him close, kissing him upon the forehead. Worryingly, his body had not warmed as hers had. Warm enough to walk a few miles more come daylight, she decided.

"Leave me here." His words sounded like a brook forming in his lungs. Just some water from the river, she told herself, knowing better. She closed her eyes and recalled what she knew of the land. They needed little, just a few warm walls with a roof and a locked door. Maybe a fireplace to pull him from this edge.

"I'll never leave you. Rest another few hours," she hissed.

"Thank you, Nomi." Erroh fell still and slept again. His laboured breathing was worryingly feeble. Around them the snow continued to fall, and she pulled him closer, willing her warmth to serve them well. The hunters' sounds had diminished completely, and Lea allowed herself to weep as she waited for dawn.

2

MAGNUS

T*hirsty*. So very thirsty. The good thirsty. Earned from a night's fine activities. Fine enough to take a year off a man's life. Magnus was no mere man, though. He was a legend, wasn't he? Wiping his bleary, legendary eyes, he dared a stretch, but the nubile brunette strewn across his body held him fast. There were worse ways to wake up, he decided. She looked so peaceful.

Still thirsty.

His bedchamber was dimly lit, and it was a blessing. The only light came from the glowing embers in the old stone fireplace. After the night's entertainment, it had been a smart move on the girl's part to close the curtains. What was her name? Rienna?

He discovered only empty wine glasses by the bedside locker and he stifled a curse. A wise general knew the value of pre-emptive strikes, and a headache was brewing. Rienna twisted, draped a flawless arm across his chest, and adjusted herself for comfort. He ran his fingers through her hair and then caught himself. This was not Elise. It would annoy Elise to catch him running his fingers through the hair of such a sweet young maiden. Running his fingers through wonderful hair was for Elise's pleasure alone, and Magnus would do little to annoy the woman he loved.

He eased the girl from her resting place, placing her head gently down on the thick feathered pillow without rousing her from her dreams. He did so with the skill of a man versed in such frequent manoeuvres. *Only on special occasions.* He felt old, despite his age. Maybe he was old. Rienna hadn't thought so.

The ruined legend slipped away from the luxurious four-poster bed and began stretching his stiff, powerful muscles. He stood taller than most and was sturdy enough across without too many unwelcome bulges. His long, greying beard matched his hair, and though he believed his eyes suggested he was a kindly older man, most people thought them cold and brutal. Elise loved his eyes; she said they were the strongest part of a well-sculpted face. Aye, there were more and more creases appearing every year, but they complemented his appearance. She had insisted as much, as she did every year.

Opening the curtains to let in the warm sunshine, he glimpsed himself in the long wall mirror and again felt old. He wondered if Rienna found his appearance alluring, or was it just the prestige? The scars across his body were too many to count. He'd felt every single blow. His eyes trailed down along the scar from a deep gash that ran from his shoulder to his sternum. Girls always liked that scar. Rienna had. She'd spent quite a time running her fingers down the indentation, her tongue soon after. He smirked, thinking he should have died from the wound. He knew that somewhere out there, a blade carried his name. *Hopefully not an arrow. No legend should ever fall to a coward's arrow.* Magnus knew he would die in war. The world hadn't yet found one big enough to kill him. He had a few years yet, but the world usually found a way. The sleeping girl rolled over, searching for a new body of warmth. It was a large bed, but she soon found her place and Magnus smiled.

Donning a warm robe, he crept along the long corridor separating their bedroom from the rest of the mansion. Another turn, down some grand stairs and on towards the kitchen. He had many rooms in his home, but the kitchen was his haven. It was large and comfortable for a man his size, filled with pots, pans, and metallic hanging utensils – more than an old warmonger could ever need. The white walls were reassuringly sparse but for a few shelves filled with every spice a real cook might call upon. The large, open stove was a fine place to while away the time thinking of glorious days, glorious nights, some of them the night before.

He fell to easy prepping as he did most mornings, even the mornings honouring his birth. In the distance he heard the mongrel horde stalking the perimeter of the Manor of Magnus, searching desperately for predators foolish enough to step foot into their territory. His pack of hounds did more for security than any patrolling soldiers could ever do. Easier to train, as well – until they smelled their master's delicious workings in the air. After downing a glass of water, he tasked himself to prepare food for their guest. It felt like a morning for eggs.

Rienna entered the kitchen uneasily, searching for the nearest escape route. She bowed to the legend and wondered could she avoid the awkward conversation of the previous night. *Fine night too.* Magnus stood over the little flames, looking impressive while attending to banal duties. He was lost in his tasks; slowly slicing a loaf of bread, turning each egg and sipping on a steaming cup of tea. A far cry from the wild animal, larger than life only a few hours previous. Her body ached; there would be bruising. *Wonderful bruising.* She bit back a smile.

"Good morning..." She wasn't sure how to address him. "Sir" seemed formal, considering recent events. She would leave once it was polite to do so. It wasn't him, it was her; she'd tell him that. Best he knew she just wasn't that type of girl.

"Good morning, Rienna. How did you sleep?" He turned slowly from his cooking, looking her up and down with stunning hazel eyes. She eyed the door and he read her thoughts, shrugging gently. She realised she'd missed a button and swiftly recovered her appearance.

"I slept well... Magnus?"

"Please stay for breakfast. I fear I've made more than enough for two," he said in a gravelly voice that had once commanded thousands during the Faction Wars. A voice used to taking charge, be it on a great march, in the bedroom or offering breakfast. The eggs smelled nice. As did sizzling meats.

"Thank you for a lovely night... sir, though I should probably make my way home." She eyed the door and his face darkened ever so.

"I hope I have caused no problems for you?"

"None, sir," she quickly reassured him as he cracked a fresh egg into the pan. Perhaps breakfast wasn't the worst idea at all, she conceded. He stood over her, and she felt meek in his presence. Most of his victims did, she thought.

"There's no unfortunate young man out looking for his betrothed?" he offered with a smile. It was a good smile, one she remembered from the night before, and she shook her head. *No suitable male for Rienna.*

"But you're so beautiful..." He stopped cooking, showing astonishment, and fuk him but he was so charming. Maybe she'd stay for the eggs. He'd scrambled them and added butter and pepper.

From above them, the sound of footsteps broke the silence. He poured steaming tea into a mug and set it in front of her. She took a seat at a long oak table near the stove, placing her bag at her feet. It seemed a strange thing to sit in a grand kitchen, waited upon by a legend. She looked through the window to the growing morning. It would be a fine day to answer questions from her father as to her whereabouts. Within a flash, Magnus had placed a goblet of spring water down to accompany the steaming mug of tea. He brushed his fingers across her cheek and returned to his cooking. She enjoyed the shivers that ran up her back from his touch. She remembered similar shivers from the night before. *Too much alcohol.* The footsteps grew louder, and Rienna prepared for the awkwardness to come.

He placed the meal of eggs, meat and toasted honey bread in front of her. "Forgive my crudeness, but thank you for a magnificent night."

She blushed, liking the authority in his every movement, even when doing menial tasks such as talking, cooking or seducing.

"Thank... you... too?" It still hadn't struck her. And then it did. She thought it a nice blow, too. Everyone in this region knew the legend of Magnus, the Master General of the Rangers. The man who should be king. If the people could, they would kneel at the sight of his crown. However, these same people believed he'd never don a piece for any price. The people of the east answered to his orders, answered to his peacekeeping, answered to his justice, and they answered willingly above the Primary. Though he forwent a title, he settled disputes in the great manor hall, and both parties invariably accepted his ruling. He was fair, wise and decent. She'd seen his Rangers answer many worthy causes in her young life. They dealt with groups of bandits roaming freely. Their presence in this part of the world kept the brutes from the Savage Isles from getting ideas above their station.

However, it wasn't just through keeping the peace that they served the common folk; for after the stormy season, Magnus and his warriors were first to appear at the door of the unfortunate victim, laden heavily with tools, supplies and good cheer. He was no stranger to scaling the roof of the decrepit barn her father refused to knock down. Thinking on this drew a smile. The east had flourished well under his many years ruling. He wasn't born on these shores, yet it was his home. A good man. She looked across his shoulders, down his powerful arms, and remembered his grip from the night before. How had she possibly considered leaving before breakfast?

From his seat in the tavern corner he'd jested how much he was looking forward to scaling the barn's roof come next season, and his laugh had been contagious. Of course, she'd accepted the offer of an ale instead of leaving early with her sisters, and she'd sat among legends at the finest table and found it pleasing. *Legends.* A few drinks and many laughs later, having a few glasses in a more comfortable setting seemed like a fine idea. Rienna chewed the delicious food and watched his mastering of breakfast. Behind her, the old oak door creaked open and the other member of the homestead emerged from her slumber.

Elise was a goddess, and it had been Elise who had whispered the suggestion that she join them in their bedchambers. She was a furnace of burning energy, and she had unleashed it in all her wild glory when the bedroom door shut, the curtains were drawn. Rienna had felt like fair game among two fierce birds of prey. It had been terrifying and exhilarating as each worked upon her and she upon them and every other way between. She felt her heart quicken and her mouth fell silent. *Not that type of girl?*

Elise appeared with only bedsheets around her thin body and had never looked grander. The years only showed in a few laughter-lines around her eyes and mouth, and Rienna thought her unimaginably beautiful. She supposed any female worthy of Magnus would need to be. Walking was beneath her; she glided across the floor, letting her hand brush across the younger girl's neck as she took a seat at the table. Smiling, she closed her eyes in exhausted fulfilment when Magnus kissed her cheek and placed her own mug of boiling tea down in front of her.

"I should have cooked for you this morning, my love," she scolded. "You both looked far too peaceful sleeping."

She winked at Rienna. "Who wouldn't sleep after the games?"

As far as uncomfortable conversations went, this could go worse.

"Perhaps we might have her over more often?" Magnus chanced, and Elise touched Rienna's hand and there was a wonderful warmth to her. In her own diminutive way, she was just as impressive as her mate. Every movement of her seemingly frail body was taken with such deliberateness; she intimidated. Everyone spoke of her beauty; everyone spoke of her prowess. Aye, she was more famous in the City of Light, but in the east they treated her as they should treat any queen.

"I'm sure Rienna has more aspirations to her life than bedding down with aging fools like us. Besides, what would her father say?" She squeezed Rienna's hand. Rienna returned the gesture. *As charming as her mate, too.*

"If it helps you sleep better at night, I'm sure we could work something out." Magnus laughed and took his seat at the head of the table. In the courtyard, his hounds began to bark maniacally. "Whisht," he roared, as the cacophony of howls hit a crescendo that pierced through the open window. *Too early for that.*

One brave beast managed a final yelp before falling into

disciplined silence. The largest of the dogs stood at attention at the doorway, awaiting instruction. The rest followed their pack leader's behaviour. They knew good behaviour resulted in important things like breakfast. They knew their place in the world. It was a good place. Any of Magnus's pet monsters could fell a man in seconds, no matter the armour. A dozen in all, reared for blood, yearning for war. A wise warrior could go into battle with these creatures and return victorious.

"Oh, shut them up. My head is aching," Elise muttered.

"Ah, they've settled." Magnus put more eggs on and wondered about spending the day hunting boar with his boys. A fine day to mark a tragic year's passing. Elise's sudden coughing fit took his enthusiasm, and he turned around to see Rienna offering his mate her goblet of water. His fading mate declined and caught the heavy cough in a weak breath. One hound whimpered, for they knew. When it passed, Magnus embraced her in his arms. *She's too young.* Another season had passed and she was still denying the paltry time left given by every healer who'd seen her. *Healers? A stupid fuken word.*

Erroh had suspected her ill health, and Magnus hadn't wanted him to watch her fade away into nothing. The time had been right for the boy to leave. However, he could have returned by now. He missed his son, as did she, but Erroh had no place in this dying house. If nothing else, Magnus would maintain her dignity. Discovering she had a daughter-in-law would be wonderful. *Maybe he'll write?*

Erroh would survive Elise's passing, but how could he tell Lexi? He couldn't even tell her how sick her mother was lest she sacrifice her place in Spark and come home. She was like her mother. Alexis might never forgive him, but the burden was his to live with.

"Are you okay?" He released his beloved mate and kissed her hand. Her beautiful eyes sparkled in reply. Defiant and unstoppable. Sometimes he almost believed her legend. Until the end, she would smile and play and suck every sweet drop of juice from the fruit of life while she still could. One day she would close her eyes and never open them again and go to wait for him from beyond. Until then, she had a fine breakfast to eat and a strong cup of tea to drink in such enjoyable company.

———

Rienna accepted the passionate kiss from Elise, and with Magnus's suggestive remark ringing in her ears, she bowed and left the Alphalines to their privacy. She was only a little disappointed that he didn't kiss her goodbye. Though, he had offered to walk her home. Regretfully, there were certain ways a young female should behave once she drew the curtains. A gust of wind caught her hair as she left the grounds and she wondered if a storm was in the air. Perhaps she might loosen a few planks of wood in the old barn just in case.

"I liked her," purred Elise to her beloved, and hugged the sheet around her body as the beautiful young maiden disappeared through the gates of their manor.

"Thank you, my darling."

"Happy birthday, beo." She blew him an invisible kiss.

"She was a wonderful gift."

"I enjoyed myself just as much."

"Yes, you did." Magnus chuckled.

Elise stretched out dreamily as he placed a second helping of scrambled eggs down in front of her. From outside, something alerted the dogs and they took to rapturous barking. Magnus recognised those barks. *New guests.*

"Perhaps we might invite Rienna around again for another night before I pass on."

He hated when she joked like this. It was her way; he would play along. "I think that's a fantastic idea," he said, walking to the window, watching the four figures approach in the distance. Two Rangers escorting two mysterious figures. A young man in far too much black with a long, flowing ponytail, accompanied by a striking young woman with interestingly coloured hair. The girl's hair was an easy giveaway, and he heard himself growl. *Guests from the city.*

"Perhaps she could comfort you when I go?"

Magnus broke his stare and turned back to Elise. He hated her breaking his heart like this. "As you wish, my love." He kissed her delicate fingers. "But I wouldn't go to war for her." Elise liked this and accepted his touch as he ran his fingers through her hair.

"We have new guests. I think you might need to get dressed, and I might need my sword."

3

UPSETTING EPIPHANIES

"No, Lea, this tastes terrible. Have Nomi cook something else." Erroh knocked the wooden ladle from his mouth. The spoon returned a few moments later and settled again by his lips. The liquid poured into his mouth and he swallowed, and he wasn't happy about it.

"What is this?" he demanded, turning his back and pulling the warm sheets over his head. The room didn't spin in complete darkness. Free-flowing mucus gushed from his nose, his throat was raw as though he'd spent a week screaming, and a phantom hand held his chest tightly. His body ached to the bone, and he remembered little apart from Uden vanquishing him. He pulled the bedclothes tighter, but the shaking wouldn't stop. Was the chain holding him? he wondered. *Nomi will set a fire and take the cold away.*

"Where are you, Nomi? I'm so cold... Can't get warm... I'm too warm..."

The room was dazzling. He dug further in under the covers. Who'd brought the covers and placed him in this bed? *Lea.* He started to cough again. Whipping the bedclothes free, he sucked what air he could, but the light brought blinding pain. Someone pushed him gently back into bed. Why was he naked? How was he warm and freezing all at once? Suddenly, he met the Woodin Man's eyes and he pulled away from his killer, screaming what profanities he could. Uden embraced him and it was familiar and comforting.

"Magnus will avenge me."

"*… something unintelligible…* Erroh…"

"He'll tear the rest of you apart." Erroh swung and connected and saw blood pouring from the giant's face. He looked down and remembered eating the gelatinous substance in his hand.

"You can't have this back," he cried, leaning over and throwing up for a while. *Lea.* "I love you, Lea." With a colossal effort, he lay back in bed. "Please close the curtains, Uden."

"You'll feel better tomorrow, my beo," Lea whispered, taking the damp rag and laying it across his forehead.

"Thank you, Mom."

After a short time, he fell back asleep, snoring loudly as he did. Soaking another rag, she tended to the waste sliding down the side of his bed. Surely her broth wasn't that bad? Scavenging supplies in the abandoned settlement was proving difficult. The shack they hid in was the smallest of the dozen buildings in the area and that was fine with her. To any passing hunters, the larger structures were more enticing targets.

She threw the rag into the dying embers and stretched. The shack was a furnace and she was sweating herself. Good for burning away the fever, though. It didn't take a healer to spot the improvements in Erroh. Another day and he might recognise her. She felt her chin where he'd punched her. It ached more than his punch yesterday; this was good. Soon, she'd need to dodge his strikes. Careful not to wake him, she crept out into the bright frozen light of the south. She needed to wash away the bile and sweat from the last few hours' nursing. She began wiping the tears from her eyes and cursed her jealousy. She knew Erroh loved her, and through his bizarre ramblings of Uden, wooden men, and the flavour of eyeballs, he'd never said he loved Nomi. *Whore.* That was something at least.

She glided through the abandoned fishing village. The houses she passed were built from the surrounding trees, and they did a fine job concealing them from passing search parties. The little houses were spread out across a valley slope overlooking a massive lake covering its basin. The lake met great mountains on the far side; to gaze upon such peacefulness in the middle of hostile lands was a strange thing. She could see ripples from fish-hunting insects gliding across the calm surface and she relaxed. Who knew what had become of the inhabitants? Likely conscripted into the great southern army.

"Thank you," she whispered into the wind. To nothing; to the absent gods who might have gifted them this reprieve. As usual, there came no reply. She stepped up to the edge of the lake and closed her eyes, dropping beneath the icy surface. All agonies lost in the refreshing embrace. She'd never realised how much she missed the cold when living in the city. To them, cold was a blanket of snow a few days a year or a biting wind between changing seasons. She'd once believed a rainstorm could freeze the life from her. This, though, was cold and this was incredible. She washed the stains from her clothing before ambling back up the slope, sensing the air changing and the snow beginning to fall. Happy knowing the fresh layer would conceal her footprints, she lifted the latch of the old creaking door and disappeared inside.

That first horrible night, the fever had taken hold and she'd walked him further than she should have. It was while searching for another temporary campsite in the light of noon that she'd discovered the path leading to this haven. With Erroh tucked up in a warm bed, it hadn't been difficult removing any sign of their tracks. Walking invisibly in this land of brutes had become second nature to her.

She could feel the warmth in the room already drying her long hair. She sat down on a little bed frame and took her journal out. Her only friend throughout her journey. Her companion that would never betray her nor love another.

Near day's end, the light faded. She peered out through the tattered curtains to look upon the gentle snowfall. Too bright for a fire, but if a blizzard hit, she'd take the chance. Any fool out in a storm would have greater worries. Erroh stirred and began muttering again and she steeled herself. How much more could she take?

"Is that you, Nomi?"

Lea said nothing. She watched the sky instead.

"I'm sorry I hit you. Can you put the fire on soon?" He opened his eyes and sat up.

"I will when it gets dark, my love." Her jealousy bit at her. *Don't ask, Lea.*

He curled back up and coughed deeply. "Thank you, Nomi." The net of mucus was breaking. If she didn't ask now, she knew she never would—or, worse, she might ask and he might lie. *Don't ask, Lea.*

"Do you enjoy sleeping with me?" she asked, gripping her journal, hoping he hadn't fallen asleep.

"It's warm."

No, no, no.

"Do you enjoy kissing me?" she asked, and shook her head. She didn't want to know. She needed to know. *Do not answer.*

He answered in their brutish language. It could have been a yes. Or a curse. It could have been anything.

"Do you want me to kiss you again?"

"Kissing is nice." His words devastated her. Apparently, his part of the conversation still had miles to walk. "No kissing, Nomi. Remember?" His voice was strong in his delirium. *Wait, what?*

"Why no kissing?" Lea knew how pathetic she sounded. She had braved the south alone; she could survive this.

"Lea."

"You love Lea?"

"Always."

"Could you love me?" *Shut up, shut up, shut up.*

Silence.

"Erroh?"

"Lea dressed in yellow," he said, falling unconscious.

————

The fever finally broke and Erroh returned to the waking world, bleary-eyed and confused. Everything felt familiar, like memory seen through the haze of a drunken charge. He remembered forests, an awful battle and a ridiculous drop from a mountain. He remembered letting himself fade to the bottom of a river, and it was a fine death. He remembered sleeping with Lea in a hole. *Something like that.* Erroh stretched limbs that hadn't moved in many days and discovered his mate asleep in the little cot opposite. He knelt down in front of her and ran his fingers through her long dark hair, and he remembered a little more. *Safe.*

"Thank you," he whispered, and her dazzling eyes blinked open. He leaned in and kissed her perfect lips. She reciprocated, but swiftly pushed him away.

"You should bathe," she said dreamily. Strange greeting, he thought as sleep crept back up on her again.

Erroh made his way down through the town. Its silence unnerved him, but still, this place felt safe. He stood by the water's edge and vowed to tell her everything of these past months. He walked to the water and took a few deep breaths and it felt like an eternity since he'd inhaled painlessly. He waded out from the shore and by the time the freezing water reached his waist, his entire mind had collapsed. As though the icy grip tore all joy from his body. He stumbled, and fear gripped his chest like a fever tenfold to the one he'd beaten. He should be dead. He knew this as he knew the sky's colour. Luck had kept him alive these past months. Nothing else. Everyone else had died, but he had fallen upon unlikely fortune. He splashed back towards the shore, gasping, and part of him didn't want to struggle any more. He should have died; he deserved to be dead. *Dead, dead, dead.* His will fractured, he wailed aloud for his failures, for his miseries, for everything. Life had finally beaten him. He reached the shore and fell where sunken pebbles met melting snow and he wailed again. Why fight anymore? His soul was empty. His hope had diminished and his will had abandoned him.

"Erroh."

Lea was beside him, carrying a warm robe, but he couldn't rise to her warmth, couldn't pull himself a step further. He tried to speak but his mind was lost to horror. To guilt.

"I am lost."

"Shush, Erroh."

"It is all my fault."

"Shush, Erroh."

"No, you don't understand." He could have ended the war before it began. Thousands would die because of him. The world would end. The Woodin Man would march on the city, burning it to charcoal, and all he wanted was to hide away and forget. Let his father march into war for him. Let legends do what Erroh could not. He thought of his lost swords, Mercy and Vengeance, and knowing they would go to use killing innocents brought fresh hopelessness.

"It's not fair," he screamed, and she pulled him from the water. He knew he was freezing but he couldn't feel the cold. He could feel only empty misery. She held him as she always did, and he dared not look into her eyes, for he knew her shame. She knew the measure of him and it was unimpressive. He heard her hushing in his ears as she gently rocked him. *I love you too, Lea. I'm so sorry.* You shouldn't have come for me.

Lea held him until he stopped shaking. She held him until he eventually rose from the water. She coaxed him back to the shack and set him down by the fireplace and the embers' glow. Erroh stared into the glow and began to weep.

Something in him had shattered and she rose above jealousy. She would pull him from this misery as she had pulled him from the Cull, from the river, from the fever too. She recovered a liberated bottle of local sine and poured two generous portions. He took the mug without taking his eyes from the embers, downing the liquid in a few desperate gulps.

"Come back to me, my love," she whispered, and he looked at her and revealed all the anguish in one desolate glare, and she embraced him as he wept anew.

After a time, when the sobbing had fallen silent, she drew away and met his beautiful broken eyes.

"I'm beaten," he said.

She began refilling his mug. "Tell me everything."

Though the words tore him and her apart, he did. He spoke of watching Aireys burn in the pyre, and Lea wept herself. He spoke of learning the language and of the Hunt themselves. Of their customs, their wildness, their blind devotion to their mad god. And he told her of Nomi.

Whore. She held her tongue, though the temptation to strike out was fierce.

He told her how the female adored him and how, in desolation, he'd loved her warmth and needed her company to stave off madness. He told her how she'd kept him alive, fought for him, fed him, shared a bed and nothing more. Lea asked if he'd desired her body and he confessed her beauty, and though it stung, she held his gaze. He told her of Nomi nearly dying as she recovered a little bag clinging to his wrist, and Lea remembered. He told her how the girl had kissed him, declared her understanding of love for him; he hadn't stopped her. He showed her Nomi's ribbon holding the pouch to his wrist, and this stung as well. Lea reached out and touched her mate's knee as he told her about the mad god living in the mountain. His collection of ancient relics with scriptures of lost history. She felt his fear as her own, and she denied him his failure. She knew the rest of the tale.

There was no spark in his eyes when she took him to her bed. There was no witty remark at her expense. She removed her blouse and lay across his chest, listening to his heart, and he did not play; instead, he kissed her forehead, closed his eyes and let sleep take him. There were better ways to finish emotional evenings.

At dawn they rose and faced the bright morning together. The last of the infection had burned away, but his mood was one of defeat. He followed her like a hound, lost in thoughts, and she doubted him ready for the road's severities. At noon, she opened her pack and removed two sets of sparring swords. A lifetime had passed since they'd swung them in anger. She started to stretch and waited for the warrior in him to resurface.

"I think I'll rest today," he said, watching the fish jumping up at the first of the warming season's insects. She didn't like that feeble answer, not one little bit.

"No, no, let's spar," she demanded.

"I think I'd prefer to walk around the lake instead."

"Just one contest, or are you afraid of your little mate?"

Her mocking stirred his competitiveness and it pleased her. He picked up a blade and held it ready. Without warning, she leapt forward and swung viciously at his arm. Just as quickly, he blocked the strike but allowed the weapon to fall from his grip, then retreated away before falling to a deep bow.

"Well won, Lea."

He turned around and began walking around the lake, leaving his mate behind with nothing more than frustration as company. At least his wit remains, she thought dejectedly.

4

THE WRETCHED HEALER

The land below the cart's wheels was uneven. Rough and stony and perfect. Less chance of an attack on uneven ground. Above him, Emir could see the dazzling rays of sun breaking through the small holes in the tattered sheet acting as cover; he hated the mornings most. Mornings were the furthest from sleeping and forgetting. The little beams of daylight bounced around as the cart overcame a bumpy ridge, and Emir bounced with it. This would have been dreadful hungover, but now it was merely uncomfortable. He used to love drinking, but now he hated sobriety. He missed the numbness of dreamless slumber, and he missed silencing mournful thoughts. He also missed his friends, but they were dead now.

Get through today, he thought, as he did every morning. The convoy wasn't far from Spark. Soon his charge would finish and his final debt would be paid. When it was, he'd climb into a bottle and drown. Beside him, Lara bounced as the carriage broke free of a stubborn obstacle. She moaned and curled up in a ball. For a month now, she'd climbed into his bedchambers while he slept and people were talking. Even a wretched convoy needed a little scandal. He doubted she cared. Did he? Every morning he'd wake up with her at his side. Just close enough to feel his presence. She hadn't spoken since the first attack. Hadn't spoken, and took strange company to bed. Maybe power attracted her, he thought bitterly, though the bitterness was less for her need and more for his miserable station in life. He was the most powerful fool in a travelling convoy of idiots. Any convoy relying on his leadership were idiots.

The carriage pitched again and she rolled up against him.

"This is my bed. You would be happier out of it," he whispered, hoping to add the suggestion to her slumber. He'd said it to her face more than once, yet still she made her midnight pilgrimage. At least she hadn't tried to kiss him. That would be soul crushing. She'd had it worse than any of them. Perhaps there were worse things than a mute bed-mate, he supposed, patting her head delicately.

Slipping away, he dressed quietly and dropped to the mud track below. The steady ground immediately caused him to stumble, as it did almost every morning. From the back of the line he could see the despairing refugees of the convoy and thought them all wretched. So many battered carts; an entire town searching for salvation. Creaking, rattling, diminishing, and they were all his to care for.

He walked up the slow line, meeting the eye of every driver, sharing a word or two where needed, listening to word of the road; he was their acting mayor, for what it was worth. As it did every morning, displeasure united them. Resting only in the hours of darkness was crushing morale, but they couldn't argue with the miles covered. Though they showed their teeth, they answered to him like desperate children eager for any reprieve from terror. Most in the convoy had tasted horrors, and when Emir had suggested action, they had answered willingly. So far.

Idiots.

Emir couldn't see Stefan's horse, and he cursed under his breath. The long-haired fuk hadn't slept again. Instead, he'd taken to the road, determined to kill himself searching for ambushes. What good was a sleep-deprived second-in-command? How Aireys would laugh seeing both men keeping this pathetic convoy trundling on. His stomach rumbled loudly. The rations they survived upon were pitiful as it was, but game was scarce and they had depleted the stocks. He wondered would near starvation cause a revolution among the Keri wretches? He'd gladly lead the revolt and happily dethrone himself. *No, you won't.* He'd lead them, and he would do it well. For a few hundred miles more. When they reached the City of Light, let another idiot speak for them.

He passed the warrior's cart and wondered about climbing up to see about Azel's ruined ankle. He only answered to "warrior" these days, since the fall of Keri, and Emir thought it a strange thing. Half dead from exhaustion, those few surviving defenders had tracked the slow convoy. None of them had been his friends. Aireys and Quig had left him all alone in this world without a drink to keep him company. Azel had spoken of the carnage, the blood and the heroics, and the tragedy that had befallen each brave man. *Each brave woman.* Quig had died trying to save Aireys. She had not died alone. Emir had handled the tragedy in his own way. His rationed alcohol never had a chance. Three days of drunkenness and sorrow. Alone, and the only person whose opinion he valued was—

The sound of approaching hooves snapped him from his thoughts. The former champion of Keri had appeared from the wildness of the Wastes. Stefan slowed his white stallion and brought it alongside Emir. A few seasons back, the fine beast would have suited his grandeur. As it was, Stefan looked as Emir felt. Broken, exhausted, worthless. He hadn't shaved in an age, his eyes sat deep in emaciated sockets and his pale skin looked closer to death than ever. He needed to rest; he needed to eat; he needed to let go of despair. Ever since the first attack.

"There's a dip in the land a few hours ahead. Be a tight squeeze to ambush there." He dropped to the ground and walked alongside his mayor's cart, wrapping his mount's reins around a rung on the side of the cart. His hands shook, and Emir could see the weight upon the man's shoulders. *The attack wasn't his fault. It wasn't anyone's fault.* He'd nearly eliminated his lisp, a flaw earned a lifetime ago in a warm inn. It that old life, Emir might have revelled in his torment; challenging times brought the worst out in people. Sometimes it brought out the best. Even in deserters.

"And the ground we're travelling on is no good for a charge

28

either," Emir said, and they fell silent for a few moments. Counting their steps, unsure of what words to share. The town called Stefan "coward" now. A name given to him by his once-friend Azel, who'd spat in his face for refusing to stand during the town's defence.

"Should be a good day's march," the coward muttered.

Emir grabbed the long-haired fuk by the shoulder and tugged his head back. "All right. Let's take a look." The carts kept drifting by, and Stefan never argued as Emir began inspecting the wound.

"Maybe the scar will attract a pretty Alpha in the city," Stefan mocked, wincing at Emir's rough prodding.

"As long as she has a friend. Ah... Come on, Stefan. Have you been at this wound?"

"... No."

"Because I told you not to touch it."

"I haven't been at the fuken wound."

"I will not lose you to a stupid infection," Emir snapped, and Stefan nodded sheepishly.

He'd been at the wound. In his defence, it was an impressive wound, spanning all the way across his forehead, just beneath his hairline. Stitched carefully but prone to itch in this dry climate. He had earned it defending the convoy. Saving lives. *Just not all of them.* Whatever people said, he didn't deserve to be called "coward."

Emir took hold of Stefan's collar as though he were about to strike the fuker down. His second-in-command didn't argue. Didn't flinch. "We can't lose any more of us... We just can't." He held the collar a moment longer and almost allowed tears of frustration to flow before releasing the grip and patting the man's cheek. *Not a coward.*

Stefan ground his teeth and held the healer's gaze as though his own tears would escape if he let go. Instead, he nodded in appreciation; in agreement; in solidarity. They continued to walk for a silent time and then Stefan eyed Emir's cart. "Did you wake up with her again?"

Emir nodded.

"How is she?" He watched the cart like a mourner beside a loved one's grave.

"If you spoke to her, she might tell you."

Stefan shook his head and Emir could see him eyeing the Wastes. The broken fool was itching to get back out scouting for food.

"She's latched on to you, Emir, and I'm just a reminder of what she lost." He hopped up on his mount and began releasing the horse's reins.

"Go get some sleep, Stefan."

"I'm good for now, Mayor."

"That's an order."

"One more hunt for food," he said, kicking the beast hard and escaping the confines of the great convoy. Emir didn't bother to call for him. The man would run himself to ground until he died. Or until they made it to Samara. Emir couldn't save everyone, and he wouldn't bother trying to save everyone, either. As he watched Stefan ride away, he knew that some just didn't want saving.

The first ambush had come from the rear, just as sunset had settled, and Stefan believed himself to blame, for he had led the march. The raiding party had concealed themselves, and anyone could have missed them in their hiding spot as they passed. Lara's family cart was the last in the line. As she'd shuffled along slowly with the rest, lost in fatigue, lost in thoughts, the first silent arrow had pierced her mother's heart and she had fallen to the ground below. Lara's scream had alerted the rest of the refugees. Her father had dropped the reins and jumped down to rescue his wife without a moment's hesitation, and another arrow had struck him in the chest. They lost ten defenders to one deadly barrage of arrows before the bandits escaped with her family's cart into the darkness. After the attack, Emir had tried for an hour to stop Lara' father bleeding, but there hadn't been a chance; there hadn't been the tools. Lara, weeping beside him, hadn't made his attempted surgery any easier.

As they'd buried her parents side by side, Lara kept whispering that they'd "only shared a meal an hour before," repeatedly, as though it were a prayer to the cursed, absent gods. Stefan had marched up and down the pathway searching for signs that should have warned them.

Screaming his innocence, condemning his foolishness, begging for forgiveness, cursing the killers. The following morning Emir had declared that each man, woman and child must carry a blade or crossbow. Complacency would never happen again under his watch.

A few days later the attackers had returned. As before, they'd attacked from the rear, but this time the town of Keri had stood firm and made them pay. There had been a couple of dozen of them, and led by Stefan's ruthless charge, the refugees had slain every one. He'd charged straight into the attackers with swinging blades and screamed his hatred and guilt into their faces as he took their lives. Many of the younger cubs grew up that desperate evening. Stefan, most of all. The former champion of Keri had emerged from the battle with just a scratch and the experience of being a killer. He hadn't been the same since.

Still, they call him a coward.

A few days later, Azel and the few battered survivors had tracked the convoy down and crushed the last embers of Lara's fragile mind with grave news. She'd cried for her "big man," and so had he.

Emir clenched his teeth and tried to fight the desolation creeping up on him. He wanted to scream until it hurt and then scream a little more, but this wasn't how a mayor behaved, so he held his tongue and counted the miles, waiting for the end. He took out the scribbled map. The closer they got to the city the more sense it appeared to make, but there were still a few inaccurate markings on the brittle yellow paper. A previous owner had circled a little blotch with the words "just a fuken stain" underneath. He always smiled when he read those words. He ignored the stain-like marking and ran his finger along the map's route a few times.

"For you, Aireys," he whispered to the wind.

5

CAGE

F *uk this.*

Lea sat up, grabbing her undergarment to cover her chest. "Maybe it's Nomi you want?" She slipped away from the bedclothes and stood up in the cold darkness. Dressing swiftly, she cursed him with every effort. Trouser leg—fuk him. Other trouser leg—fuk him too.

From his bed he offered a self-deprecating comment, and she cursed him again. Just come back to life, she thought. She laced each boot, then grabbed her coat. She wasn't sure where she was going, only that she wasn't coming back for a while. She stopped in the doorway and looked back at her mate, willing him to stop her. Erroh lay on his back, staring up at the grand sight of the ceiling rafters above. She kicked the door shut behind her.

"Fuk you, Erroh."

Great plan, Lea. Point made. You really showed him, she thought, hugging herself against the cold. *Well done forgetting your cloak, too.* The shattered moon shone bright; the land was stunning, and she was leaving Erroh. She'd tried her best with him. Oh, how she'd tried. She'd taken what little progress he'd made and held it closer than she should have. Yesterday he'd smiled. He hadn't smiled today, and neither had she. That wasn't Erroh. Erroh had died a long time ago in Keri. Aye, she'd had her moments of despair. Her pain had been a different misery to his, but he was born and bred for this. He should have bested this affliction. When he bothered to speak, his voice was dreary and indifferent. At first, she'd believed confiding in her was part of his recovery, but he'd slipped further from her grasp. Too much time had passed. Instead of rising to the challenges to come, he'd lost himself in daily lake walks. Where was her petulant, perfect mate? Where was the legend who had stared down an entire army without blinking? Where was the hot-blooded male who desired her body?

"Dead in Keri," she whispered into the wind, and hated the unfairness of the world.

She walked farther down the slope, rubbing her arms to stave off the bitter chill. Her footsteps crunched loudly in the night air. In another life, this would have been a fine place to live; she hated this settlement now. She hated her mate, and in the same breath, she loved him. He didn't love her as he'd once proclaimed, and knowing this cut her deep. He'd demoted her to fondness. *At most.* She'd waited long enough and received little; she would wait no more. Weeks of desolation, all for nothing in this place. Not to mention the months before. She would have walked for years for him, for her hero, for her champion, for her Erroh. What a fuken waste, she thought.

Throwing herself at him had seemed like a fine naked idea. His passionless kiss and unenthusiastic touch had been more those of a man struggling to finish a tasteless meal than of one dining upon a lavish feast. She'd believed herself quite the delicacy, but he could fuk off now. She could have cried, but her anger and frustration bolstered her resolve. She walked for a time around the lake and hid from the wind beneath a large boulder as far from the shack as possible. Lost in thought, spinning rocks into the tranquil dark water, she did not hear him approach.

He passed her the cloak. "Sorry," he said wrapping his own heavy cloak around his shoulders, waiting for her to accept his apology and offer her own. He hid his irritation. She knew what pain he suffered; she should have allowed him this. Admittedly, he could have shown enthusiasm, but why bother fooling her? There were worse ways to behave, he imagined.

"I'm losing you," she whispered.

He felt he had lost himself. "I'm just struggling with life… my beo."

"I don't want you to call me that anymore."

Erroh knew well the games of females, and he had little interest in playing along. "As you wish." He stifled a yawn and felt sleep call. Perhaps she would take the other cot again tonight and allow him to stretch out in comfort.

"We need to warn the city, Erroh. We can't stay here any longer," she said, finding a fine rock worthy of skimming. She whipped it across the water and cursed as it disappeared in the night.

"We are two lost little Alphalines. Samara will know the attack is coming long before we ride the distance." It wasn't his fight anymore; it wasn't hers, either. They'd been through too much; they'd been apart from each other longer than together. Best they stay here a while; there was such a nice view. "This is where we need to be."

"I'm going back home to Spark City."

"It's not your home anymore, my be—Lea."

"I'm leaving in a few days."

"I'm not ready to leave," he said, turning away. The shack was warm and it was late. Bed was calling.

"I'm leaving you, Erroh."

He stopped walking and faced the only girl in the world he'd ever loved. He didn't know how to feel. It was just another obstacle the world threw at him. He knew he should argue, but felt numb acceptance. He imagined a cage in his head where all his hope, confidence and love now dwelled.

Nothing could make him leave. Not even her. "You will offer a final kiss and be done with me?"

"Aye," she replied. He almost reached for her, but the cage held him in place. In the cage he was safe from terrible things. She was movement, she was terror, she was anywhere in the world other than this place, and if she were playing no game to make him leave, well, so be it.

"As you wish, Lea."

He trudged up the slope, crawled into bed and closed his eyes, but sleep eluded him and he thought this an act of cruelty by the absent gods. Some time later, his mate returned and warmed herself by the fire. He watched her undress and he felt little anger or sadness. It was rare that any female returned to the city. Rarer still that a female gave up a mate, but these things happened after a weak culling. He'd believed they'd walked far since the Cull; perhaps not. She slipped into the bed opposite and he listened for her breathing to change. When it did, he followed soon after. He had settled dreams. He felt safe.

The following morning, he spent the day throwing up anything he ate and he did not understand why. It felt like the first days after their coupling. They became strangers again, living in the same room. Outside, fresh layers of snowfall covered the area, winds thrashed their walls and both Alphalines were silent as they endured the storms. They spoke little in that time, but she told him a few more days and he agreed. Eventually, boredom drove her out to face the cold. She began practicing her routine daily, and he watched her brave the cold from the warmth of the doorway with a cup of tea as company. He thought her beautiful, watching her body twist in the gentle breeze, but he said nothing. Never asked to play along. She twirled gracefully with a wooden sword in each hand, and her feet were steady in the trodden snow beneath. Thrusting forward with divine agility, spinning across the ground, felling all invisible foes standing against her; she was a goddess of war, a vengeful wraith of fierceness, an Alpha in all her glory.

As the days of freezing waiting continued, he braved the cold to stand closer, and she answered by performing for longer periods.

"Will you spar with me, Erroh?" she asked him each day, and eventually boredom drew him from his silent observing and he took up arms.

He was no match for her. Each strike she aimed was measured and proficient. She carried her left a little low, but he couldn't take advantage. He never knew why, but he tried. He spent most of the skirmish blocking her assaults, until he slipped beneath her guard and searched for the killing blow only to receive a sharp snap across the knuckles for his troubles. It was familiar, painful and almost welcome. His body felt awkward but embraced the movement.

"You've lost your speed, Erroh." She circled him like a wildcat hunting an injured pigeon. He almost dropped his weapons in protest but then gripped them tighter. She smiled in answer to his frustration. He met her next attack and tried countering again, before retreating a few seconds later with fresh welts across his body. There was cruelty in her smile. *Fuk off, Lea.*

She tried to hide her smile as they fought. He was trying. His movement was laboured, but he'd recover like she had long ago outside the city gates.

"Your left is low."

"So take advantage." She swung wildly, excitement getting the better of her. He countered and landed his first bruising blow across her cheek. Leaping away in a defensive pose, looking every bit the Alpha his bloodline suggested, he brought both swords up and watched her movements. *He wants to win.* Within a breath, she left her own mark across his cheek, and once again they continued their dance.

They fought until sweat covered her exhausted body, but neither yielded and she began to believe in him. The snow fell heavily around them and the light dwindled, but all that mattered was the fight; the competition. If nothing else, she willed his competitiveness to pull him from this nightmare. *Last chance, my love.*

Darkness fell and with it, both Alphas. Erroh took a knee first, gasping loudly. One of his weapons fell and disappeared in the slush. After a moment, he dropped the second too.

"Enough, Lea." His breathless voice was weak again.

She knelt on the freezing ground herself. Her body ached. It hadn't ached this much in months.

"Well fought, Erroh."

"I could do with some sleep."

———

Lea sat opposite her mate and felt her heart shatter. More days had passed and she could no longer delay. She knew it; so did he. She watched him play with her sword absently.

"I'll need this one for myself," he said, as though perusing a stall for wares.

"They're a set," she replied, but he was right; he would need a blade down here in his solitude.

"You can find another one on your journey." He tossed the blade onto the bed. *His now.* "Perhaps when I make the walk myself, we can reunite them."

His words felt false, and she tried to control her heartbeat, her misery, her fuken temper.

He watched her separate their supplies on the bed and he searched for words he could never speak. *Please don't go, Lea.* He wouldn't say it, but he could think it. He struggled for breath. She took the cofe pot and the empty bag of cofe for herself.

"They're mine," he snapped, and she placed them on his side of the bed. It didn't matter that there were no beans to brew. Outside, the wind began to howl, and it carried heavy waves of snow in each gust. They battered the side of the shack mercilessly. Erroh felt a strange calmness in the storm. *Snow keeps her here.*

"This is no longer mine," she said, passing her bow across.

"It was a gift."

"You'll need 'Baby' up here with so little to hunt," she insisted, gently severing the last tie that bonded them. She let the tears free of their restraints as she prepared the last of her provisions, and he could only watch on. He took the pieces of the great weapon and assembling tools and placed them gently on his side of the bed. He wished he

37

could love anything as much as she loved that bow. He'd never come close. Apart from her. He adored her, but she was slipping away and he couldn't form the words or act upon them. Deep down he could feel his need for her screaming for release. It battered the cage in his mind and challenged him. Erroh, the Hero of Keri, lived in that cage. He struck fiercely at unbreakable bars and vowed to tear the entire world apart if Lea desired. But the bars were too sturdy. His fears too many. Erroh of the cage was heartbroken. Erroh of the South was unmoved.

6
———

MEANWHILE, BACK IN KERI

He held his breath and squeezed tighter. The roar of the river pulled both grappling enemies further from the raging storm of battle into a different war altogether. This will be a final task finely done, he thought. Cass's lungs burned, but all that mattered was the kill. They spun in circles beneath the water in a demented dance of death. His fingers dug deeper into the flesh; his nails broke through skin. He saw nothing. His vision blurred; perhaps it was the blood. His victim swung wildly, thrashing Cass's face, and that was fine. Two heavy gloves formed up around Cass's neck and that was fine too, because he had begun strangling first. Besides, he had nothing to live for; he'd no fear of death. He'd accepted his inevitable death carrying Jeremiah's headless body back up the slope.

The grip across his throat faltered and searched for his eyes. This was good too. He ignored the pain and finally the grappling, scraping claws ceased their struggles before going limp. *Not yet.* He held on until his lungs could take no more; only then did he release his victim to the gushing river's flow. For an absent breath, he thought he would not resurface. He sensed his fallen friends and they welcomed him, until his head broke through and he sucked in precious air.

His battered body fought the current, but it pulled him swiftly downstream, away from the great defence, away from his dying friends, away from Keri. He could still hear the barbaric war cries as he flowed by, and he fought no more. *Escape.* He could have struggled more and reached for the water's edge, but he didn't. He could have stolen up behind them, a one-man counter-assault, but he didn't. He gasped in the water's pull and fled the battle.

The final wall of defence had crumbled beneath an unforgiving downpour. Such bravery, punished by the absent gods' design. Thrashed up against rocks, dragged backwards over rapids, and swallowed deep by undercurrents, he stubbornly kept his head above water, and as the miles passed, the water's grip on his body lessened.

Eventually, miles from home, nestled in the deep green's safety, he swam to the river's bank and pulled himself ashore. Lying among the reeds, he cried for his friends and ran his fingers through his thinning hair. Surviving, he had betrayed them. He knew Erroh would have climbed from the water and charged into battle. All of them would have, but he couldn't rouse himself from the river. He'd never felt as much hatred as he did in that moment. Hatred for the city, hatred for the Primary. Keri had answered to the city's law; to her laws. How dare she allow such horrors to occur? Safe behind the city's walls. He thought on this matter for a time and hated the world a little more.

Pulling himself from the water, he concentrated all his hate and sorrow into imaginings of vile sedition. He thought of the female's life he'd taken while dragging Jeremiah's body back home. *Killing a female is the Primary's worst crime in the world.* In times of war, however, everything changed.

The last Regulator of Keri crawled onto the riverbank, consumed by hate. For days, he made a home by the water, eating what he could forage, sleeping troubled dreams, and each day he grew a little braver. Eventually curiosity drew him from under his rock and back up the river's route towards the remains of the town. When he arrived, the monsters were gone.

He entered through the gap where they'd stood their defence. He thought his fallen companions brave and beautiful, and he loved them in death as he could not in life. He walked through the ashes begging for forgiveness, counting their ruined bodies and weeping for each one.

Keri was still beautiful. It always had been; it always would be. Even with the unnerving words scrawled upon the largest wall at the far end of the town. *Who is the Woodin Man? Why will he burn the world?* It didn't matter. This town would always stand. The people would return; a century from now, any horrors would be long forgotten. He looked at those painted words and formed a beautiful image in his mind.

Later, he returned to the wall with a little art pad he'd recovered from the house of the greatest champion the town had ever known. He doubted she would have minded. He planned his own message and scribbled down his sketches. When the light finally died, he made his way home and slept in his lonely bed, steeling himself for the miseries to come.

———

"Goodbye, Quig. You held firm and won the day."

The big man would have liked that. The big man could have held his head high, stepping into the darkness. Cass placed the great battle scythe against the massive mound of earth. It was the final grave. They'd buried most of his comrades long before the final attack in the town's graveyard. Now, he buried the last few warriors upon the slope. Each grave boasted a headstone and a delicately-painted inscription. He rubbed his thinning hair and said a few prayers for each. The brave warriors would forever stand guard at the entrance and hold the line, and Quig would lead the defence. He wondered if their ghosts could ever forgive him. It was a small matter.

Aireys and Lea had met their end in the pyre. He knew this because Erroh had spoken of their barbaric behaviour. He vowed to never speak of their fate again. Both warriors deserved better. He had not found Erroh's body, and deep down, Cass wondered if the mighty Alpha had pulled one more great feat from nothing. He wanted to believe. He knew better. Again, the anger flared up inside and he cursed the city.

. . .

He painted for days. He'd always been a fine artist; easier to pour a life of frustration and guilt into something beautiful. Those who knew him best, knew of his skill, suggested he court a potential wife with his majestic impressionism. He would just smile; those who knew him best didn't know him at all.

He'd never displayed his work in public. He'd feared ridicule, for this was a town of fighters. He'd still earned a few pieces and a little careful pride providing the Sickle's interiors with artwork; the sloppy glances of drunken art connoisseurs were the closest he'd ever come to exhibiting and it was enough. Now he had one more anonymous creation to offer.

He used some of Aireys's supplies. He mixed them with his own and finished his masterpiece. Those cruel words would be lost. Instead, he would leave something worthy so the next generations would always know. He did not sign his name.

He took one last look around the Sickle and took a few moments to admire his handiwork. He knew he could never return. He ran his fingers across the rough brushstrokes of the "Tower" piece. He'd never liked that work; the sun had set and he hadn't caught the colours in the sky swiftly enough, but no one had taken it or the rest of the pictures from the walls to burn in the flames, and this had secretly pleased him.

Cass slipped his pack onto his back and set out for the City of Light. He carried the weight of their deaths on his shoulders. He felt as if he were a man walking to his doom.

7

A GOOD DAY

E rroh opened his eyes and stretched. The last three days he'd
barely moved, and had spoken even less. The light shone
brightly through the ragged curtains and he could see the deep blue in
the sky. Today was a good day to walk the Wastes. With so few clouds,
there was less chance of freezing in a wayward drift. He stood up,
craning his neck until a pop took the stiffness away. His stomach
turned seeing her empty bed. He didn't feel sick when he slept, so he'd
been sleeping more. He had no appetite, but he ate some dried salted
fish anyway. Indifference afflicted him. He was afraid to live but not
wanting to die. It had been three days since he'd washed, too. How far
had he fallen from grace? He imagined the taste of freshly brewed cofe
as he dressed. Maybe some cofe was all he needed to rouse himself
from this stupor. *Maybe.*

He faced the morning with a brisk stroll down towards the edge of
the lake. He thought about Lea's bow. His bow now. He really didn't
want her bow. He'd tried so hard not to take it. It was the only thing
they'd passionately spoken about through the three-day blizzards. The
snow had stopped, though, and the skies were clear. It was early and
she'd packed her bags.

He watched her bathe. She didn't seem to mind the cold as much as he. She hid her modesty behind a thin gown, and though it did not conceal a great deal, he felt little desire. There was a wretched burning in his stomach, and he almost doubled over. *Sleep.* Sleep would ease the pain. He shuffled back up to the shack, slipped behind it and emptied his stomach. Shivering, he struggled over the threshold and into his bed. He pulled the sheets over his head and waited for sleep to numb the pain. Deep down, the Hero of Keri ran his fingers along the unbreakable bars and sang a melancholic tune of an unvanquished brigand.

She had to leave. He'd given her nothing, but now she delayed. The blizzards had been a fine excuse. As though she hadn't faced blizzards on her lone march. During the worst of the snow, if he'd stated his intention to come with her, she would have grabbed her pack and walked out into the white without hesitation. Anything to leave this prison. Her pack was ready. *No last kiss.* It would be easier that way. She embraced the freezing water and let her mind relax. She didn't hear the storm brewing.

Thunder. From far away. *No, something else entirely.* Something familiar.

Erroh twisted under his sheets and opened his eyes, hearing the Riders approaching. He gripped the sheets and pulled them tightly around him. There was safety in the dark. They were closer now. *Outside.* A few dark shadows passed the curtains. Great beasts sitting atop greater beasts. They took the light from the room as they passed, but he was safe. Hidden within his prison. They would not find him and they would move on. He counted seven as they rode by. He could never take on seven alone. *Not now.* The shadows never noticed him, and that's all that mattered. His heart hammered out of time; his hands shook violently. Deep down, the Hero of Keri opened his eyes, relished destruction. Relished their death. He struck at the cage, but Erroh of the South dug his head into safety.

. . .

In the gentle wind and the splash of a delicate wave, Lea's mind was elsewhere. Dipping her head beneath the water, she held her breath and scrubbed the last of the soap from her long black hair. Rising and breathing in the crisp southern air, she discovered all seven Riders spread out across the shoreline, watching her.

They were dressed in heavy animal leather with metal plating; she felt defenceless in her damp gown. None made any attempt to speak or move. Instead, they just watched the beautiful girl out in the lake. Erroh had always insisted she master the art of cards at the table. It was a gift for life, he'd always said. She held her breath and played a bet. She waved at the group of Riders. Apparently, she was skilled in the art of waving, as a few returned the gesture. One of them even turned his mount sideways and began cantering his way back towards the little cluster of houses. The rest watched her bathe.

She rubbed the soap in the water and began washing her hair again as casually as she could. She tried to stop her hands shaking. Where is Erroh? she thought. *Sleeping again.* She brought the soap to her arms and scrubbed, all the while searching for plans, any plans; the simpler the better. Her soap smelled of honey. A few more Riders moved up the opposite side of the shore, leaving two sitting atop their horses, staring and arguing under their breaths. What to do with the half-naked girl in the water? she wondered.

Shit, shit, shit.

She could swim, she thought, knowing well that by the time she reached the other side, they could have walked around the lake at least twice. Panic struck her; she scrubbed harder, smelled more honey, and they watched on, regardless. She whispered to the absent gods to assist her. To save her. To do anything.

The gods answered in a way that she didn't expect.

They were searching for him. Uden was searching for him, and it terrified him. He knew Lea was out in the water but he couldn't rouse himself. *Is the door locked?* She was probably scared, and he tugged the blanket over his head more. It was nice and warm. He heard a male shouting from some distance and his heart hammered. He imagined cage bars shaking deep down, but it was too far away. A few words repeated in his head and he ignored them. Covered them over with blankets.

Save her.

Such simple, terrifying words. He liked simple things like words. He also enjoyed staying hidden. *Save her.* He heard her scream. His hands stopped shaking and he felt the need to remove the blanket from his head. *Save her.*

One Rider called out to her. She looked back at him and nodded and immediately resumed scrubbing. She wished she had her weapons. Armour or not, she'd take them all on if she had her weapons. If she had weapons and an Erroh behind her, then she'd kill them all.

The Rider called out again. Everyone at the table was waiting for her final play. If only she had the ace of queens. If only she knew their language. If only she could place another bet. She gestured to her dress and snorted angrily before scrubbing vigorously at an invisible stain. He must have believed her dress was clean enough, as he roared again, far louder.

Save her.

Save her.

Save her.

He imagined a cage bending to his will and felt the familiar fear take him. *Save her.* He took that fear and embraced it. Fear made him a better warrior. *Save her.* He remembered that feeling of standing at the wall with his fallen warrior comrades. *Save her.* In the corner, her two blades lay side by side. They were pretty blades. *Save her.* He suddenly wanted to give them both back to her. After he'd finished using them. *Save her,*

Erroh. He could feel the anger rising above the terror, the indifference, and he could taste vengeance on his lips. Bitter and godsent. His stomach settled. Nothing else in the world mattered. He needed to save her.

Shit, shit, shit.

Lea walked towards the shore carrying the soap. She steeled herself for the storm to come. She acted meek; she acted pathetic. She pledged to take at least two of them into the darkness. As she waded through, she tapped her mouth as though mute. It was all she had. She imagined the coming battle; she imagined that the third Rider, now moving along the shore with the battle axe, would probably be the one to kill her. As she drew close to them, the second Rider dropped and rummaged through her clothing while the first Rider reached out to her. He muttered something incomprehensible and she nodded noncommittally. This was the end.

She held the bar of soap tightly. *Let them die with honey in their noses.* In her nose too. Unsatisfied with her answer, he muttered something and his comrade chuckled. The other Riders must have sensed the threat in the air as they too left their half-hearted search to meet with the pathetic, unarmed little female in the transparent dress. He treated them to the same jest and laughed loudly. She noticed one remove a fine and sturdy rope. She ignored the Rider's help, playing the unimpressed mute as best she could. Let them jest again and she would use the moment to leap at the nearest, she thought. Her eyes fell upon the man's sheathed sword and…

His outstretched hand turned into a fist, which shot out and exploded across her chin. The world went slightly dark as he dragged her to land. *Not the plan.*

The second brute left her pack and pushed her assailant away, shouting brutish profanities before allowing her a moment to gather her wits at the shore. Spitting blood from her mouth, she screamed out, warning Erroh. An impressive scream. They argued with each other about her fate and she had a strange thought: perhaps not all of them were brutes. It's no way to die, she thought. Better to die with a sword in hand or with grandchildren at the bedside.

Erroh burst through the wooden door of the prison shack. He could have roared. He should have roared. Returning from the brink deserved a roar. Instead of roaring, he sprinted down the slope with her swords in his hands. He had a plan, a simple plan. He would kill them. All of them.

The world slowed and he saw everything. He could see brutes surrounding his mate and they scared her. He felt the rage of so many anguished months turn to ashes in the fires of vengeance. He felt himself reborn in fury. He remembered Keri; he remembered killing; he remembered everything.

The nearest Rider turned his mount and met the silent charge, pulling his sword free and kicking his horse's ribs, he charged up towards Erroh. Perhaps he thought he was something unspectacular to be slaughtered in one charge. As it was, Erroh sidestepped the charge and leapt at the unsuspecting Rider with both blades raised. The unprepared Rider tried to block and fell from his saddle, gasping his last few breaths. The rest of the Riders kicked their massive steeds and charged back up the slope, seeking immediate retribution. All but one.

The panicked Rider gestured wildly, and she considered taking his sword and then his head. It took her a moment to realise he was begging her to run before his comrades returned with her companion's head. *Oh, poor little Rider. Do you not understand whom you Hunt?* She almost smiled at the absurdity of it. He still believed she was in danger. Perhaps they aren't all evil, she thought again. She stood and watched and ever so loved his violence. This was his moment. She would have hers.

·   ·   ·

Erroh was having a good day. A very good day, in fact. The first good
day in months. He was unchained, liberated, and his plan was working
splendidly. *As usual.* His blades slashed across the throats of the next
two Riders in the same perfect swing. After everything he'd put her
through, he would save her, and he would do it with style. Like the
Erroh he was.

Both bodies fell behind him as he charged on the last three. The
next to fall believed he'd broken Erroh's guard, only to see the second
sword swipe down through his own defence. He saw nothing after that.
Erroh left the dead man where he fell, facing the last two attackers. He
never stopped moving and felt alive in the motion. He roared a
challenge. It was a fine roar. He took his time killing them. As he'd
moved down the slope, he'd seen her rise. He'd seen the mark across
her face, the blood dripping from her mouth, and he wanted to impress
her more. To win her back.

The last Rider fell to his knees, clutching his ruined stump of a
wrist, and Erroh finally fell still. He felt the fear of before emerge and
he spat it away, along with the man's blood which marred his face. He
spun around and removed the brute's head, kicking the head messily
into a snowbank. It was brutal; they deserved it. He turned to the last
Rider, still standing with Lea.

Brin, for that was the Rider's name, dropped his sword and prayed to
Uden that the demon show mercy. He raised his hands skywards as he
had seen many of the victims do throughout their great cleansing. He
walked backwards towards the female. Maybe she would show the
mercy he'd tried to show her.

No mercy, Erroh thought. They had shown Aireys little mercy. Why
should he? He recovered Lea's second blade from the skull of one of
his victims and wiped the blood on the corpse's sleeve. He walked
down to the water, watching the man gesture, understanding his pleas.
If he let him live, they could be tracked, but to tie him up was a

freezing death sentence. The man shook but fell silent as Erroh came upon him. He accepted his fate as though condemned by a god. He wasn't much older than Erroh.

"He tried to stop them hurting me," Lea said.

"It means little now."

"Perhaps you might keep him as your captive here in this cursed place, Erroh."

"I will stay no longer. May I walk with you again… my love?"

"That would be fine, Erroh," she said.

Erroh spun on the doomed man. He wanted to hate him, to kill him and be done with the matter.

"Go to Uden, the mad god, and tell him Erroh will take his other eye if he marches north," he shouted in a terrible southern accent. He stood on the man's toes and applied a swift kick to the side of the Rider's knee. It popped and there was screaming. A few seconds later, there was a second pop and more screaming. A few seconds after that there was a punching sound, and no more screaming.

They dragged the unconscious man back up to the shack and dumped him in Erroh's bed beneath the blankets. Erroh left some flint near the tinder, some fuel, and enough food to last until his discovery. Erroh fashioned two splints and left them beside the doorway. It was all he could do. The man would live. That was enough. He thought it a godly act. With that done, he looked to the blue sky above.

"It's a good day to ride."

"It's a good day," Lea whispered, more to herself.

8

ALL ALONE IN THE ARTH

Something had happened. Something terrible. There had been whispers, followed by wailing, and soon enough rumours spread like fire across the Arth. These rumours had reached their pinnacle behind the walls of Conlon, where they had festered and grown gloriously. Within a handful of hours, the Hunt nearly collapsed upon itself. What wonderful and beautiful hours they could have been, lamented Nomi. She had seen none of this and believed even less.

She had been in silent mourning, licking her wounds with the rest of her warring clan, when she'd learned of the tragedy. Today, she felt less mournful knowing Erroh lived. She would not smile; anyone could be watching. *Perhaps Uden?*

Everyone in the city knew Erroh's name now. They whispered it, revering and cursing it in equal measure. Her Erroh had become something divine. *My Erroh.* Except, he wasn't her Erroh. She had accepted this and accepted she would never see him again. She had also accepted her fate, and last of all, she had accepted that her life would end soon.

But it will end well.

She sat beside the cart brushing her blonde hair for the second time that morning. It was difficult keeping perfect hair out in the Arth.

Erroh's one for life no doubt managed the task. She tugged at a stubborn knot and painfully emerged victorious. She smiled in satisfaction. Brushing her hair was something to do while waiting for death.

She could count on one hand the number of times she'd walked beneath the fallen city of Conlon's menacing shadow. This would be the last time. She thought it an ugly place against the beauty of the march. The walls were ancient and spoke their tales of age. Millennia-old scorching had scarred the many structures within. Its outer wall rose into the clear blue sky at its sturdiest, but some sections were crumbling and some had collapsed altogether. Uden might claim to know the reason why.

Uden had been her god ever since she was a child, and she had believed in his words. They all had. However, as though someone had pulled a hood from her, she could see everything now. Uden was a man. An extraordinary one but a man nonetheless. He had earned his place and status through fierce acts of violence, for that was how southerners did it. Even those not born upon its frozen lands. He'd twisted her people's will to his own by instilling fear. *Boundless fear.* She knew his legacy, and it was unique among her people. He'd been a clanless warrior with a greater knowledge of the world than any other. Knowledge was a gift, and from what she'd learned, he'd risen higher than all others—so high, he'd soon proclaimed himself beyond the fate of ordinary men.

The god took us all in.

She had been a believer her entire life. Her sister Riona also, at least for a time. She still loved her people despite their flaws. She wondered would they come back from the brink? Could they come back? Perhaps all they needed was to share sacrilegious conversations with a beautiful man for a few months. Just enough to stir some doubt.

Her people favoured embellishment; they always had. She wondered which rumours held most truth. It was said that the Woodin Man had offered food and drink to the challenger, and as they sat and ate, the challenger had attempted to assassinate their god, a deed without honour. But a god couldn't die at the hands of a demon, it appeared. Some claimed he had taken flight as his means of escape. Others suggested he'd summoned great flames. The stories grew in magnificence with each retelling; this was the way of the Arth. She tried to imagine Erroh sprouting wings of fire. Were she not about to die, she might have smiled.

Many days they had camped and done little more than wait. Finally, this morning had brought word of the assembly. Uden would speak with his followers: to reassure, to lead, to be godly. So, she brushed her hair and tried to look her best, for she knew he would punish her crimes.

One less in my clan will make no difference.

Her clan had once been a mighty fighting force under Oren's rule, but now its ranks were thinned to less than half and their leader was missing. It had suffered a terrible culling at the hands of Erroh. Enlisting some fresh youth from the training camps was such a time-consuming operation, she thought, and almost laughed aloud. Even on her last day, she worried about her finger's welfare.

The great battle horns drew her from her thoughts. She knew they would play this day. Ever since his arrival. The god was calling his flock. *Hail, hail the lucky ones.* They bellowed out, and with each deep note Nomi fought an urge to flee this place. Such thoughts were folly. Menacing eyes were upon her. They had been these last few days. Ever since the whispers of Uden's injuries had reached her comrades, they had not left her alone. If she fled, she might make it to the nearest treeline before the crossbow wielders took her out. Dishonourable practice in battle, but killing a runaway was a task well suited to them.

She replaced the rough wired brush in her hand with the smooth little dagger. She ran her finger along its perfect edge and winced at its sharpness. She could cut any knots of hair free with this fine piece. She kissed the steel and returned it to its scabbard along her waist. She had a nice waist. Not as shapely as Lea's, she suspected. *Those lucky ones in love.*

Around her, many companions answered the horn and roused themselves from the great wait. She allowed herself a moment's hesitation before accepting her fate. If Riona was here, she wouldn't be frightened. Riona might have made it to the treeline, she imagined. She had not seen the deed done. Sighing, Nomi followed her brethren, her former bed mates and those she called friends, through the archway of the city gates. She couldn't help but notice the space between her and everyone else. They knew her fate for caring for the heathen as she had. She was part of the Hunt, but for how long? She thought these to be fine rambling thoughts, suitable for walking towards death. She had never questioned the world and its ways, but now her people's actions filled her with eternal doubt.

The wrong side.

She allowed herself a few moments to think of Erroh. Childish thoughts like love. *Love.* She wanted no man but Erroh. *Lea's Erroh.* Nomi smiled sadly, thinking of lost opportunities. She said a prayer to his gods and asked that he find his one for life again. He deserved happiness, even without her. She walked with the packed crowd through ancient streets. She could feel the tall buildings closing in on her as she walked deeper within. *Poor little Nomi, alone in the world.* She wished she had a crossbow on her back, but they forbade such dishonourable weapons behind the city walls this day. She knew there were other voices of dissent but she had no way, no will or desire, to seek them out. Let her final act speak loudly to them. Who knew how significant an assassination upon a leader could be?

She took in the final warmth of the sun and walked the last few side streets to her last destination. She feared crucifixion. She couldn't face such a terrible end. This act would see to that, she reassured herself even as her bravery deserted her. She could have fled sooner, but this life was all she knew. Would ever know. The crowd were boisterous and they took each step as one. Closer and closer they marched, for Uden was calling and all would obey. All except for one little insignificant girl with blonde hair. She turned into the city's centre and met the sight of Oren hanging limply from a whipping post. His face was a demented grimace as he held desperately onto consciousness. Loose strands of hair matted in dried blood clung to his skin. He took strained breaths through a shattered nose. He hung high above the crowd on a recently constructed wooden stage. His knees were bent so that he appeared to be worshipping his god, the Woodin Man, who sat upon a throne.

Terror.

Nomi's shaking fingers touched the dagger's ebony handle. A few of her god's generals were among the crowd, shepherding them into a fine dignified assembly of acolytes. One of the tall generals took a special interest in her. He looked her up and down a few times before guiding her smoothly through the throng. He smiled warmly and she wanted to wail aloud and the great man above her drew nearer.

The god had made no grand entrance to rapturous applause and trumpets blaring. Instead, he waited for his flock to gather around him. For such an inspiring god, he liked to keep himself hidden from his disciples. Perhaps he feared overly zealous infatuation? Perhaps he feared those with similar intentions to hers? Perhaps he did not love his people as he claimed? She'd never seen him as close as this. A mere whip's length apart. He was magnificent, imposing, and terrifying. *Godly.* How could she accomplish such a task?

Uden stood up slowly from his throne of black metal and pretty jewels. Each movement impossibly restrained, as though he saved himself for the precise moment he could erupt in a terrible wrath and kill them all. He faced the crowd in all his magnificence, and despite her terror she was mesmerised. A long black cloak hung loosely from impossibly wide shoulders. His armour lay thick and formidable underneath. At best, her blade would scrape him, and in that dreadful moment, she believed in him anew. Believed in his immortality, believed in his words, and she hated herself for it. He raised his arms to the sky and she almost expected lightning to erupt from his fingers. He wouldn't need lightning to kill her. His massive hands could crush her skull with little effort. Even the imposing stature of Oren was diminished in this god's company.

Uden silenced the crowd of hundreds with a deep, croaky voice and Nomi imagined Erroh standing against this deity. She marvelled that her beautiful man had survived. More than that, she saw the devastation inflicted upon their meeting.

"I still see all," the god declared, tilting his head so all might gaze upon the intricate stitching on his eye-patch, and somehow this too was impressive. His audience was enthralled, but his blindness pulled her from her own awe. She felt like an outsider as the surrounding crowd gave a little more space where she stood.

All alone in the Arth.

The god scratched at his patch and smiled. He took a few steps closer to the edge of the stage and let everyone take in his godliness. She stepped forward unmolested and searched her will for steel. For anything to keep her strong. She thought of Erroh. Uden was closer now. All that stood in her way were a few lines of eager acolytes and some wooden staging. She'd always been nimble. If she leapt up, she could take him by surprise. She waited for him to turn to her, to gaze upon her with his one remaining eye and glare into her soul and condemn her for her sins. If he did, all was lost anyway.

Attack him.

He held the crowd in complete control. It was little surprise his few appearances still caused great echoes to filter down to all that marched in the Hunt. When he spoke, it felt like his words carried for miles. When he roared, it felt like the world shook in fear.

"Do any of you believe I am less than I was?" he cried, and she took a sudden step back at his outburst. Her fingers dropped from the handle. She hadn't noticed herself take hold.

"Did you believe me slain by a false god?" He wanted an answer. He waited. The gathering went eerily still. The congregation tried their best not to meet his eyes. *His eye.* He glared at Oren, kneeling before him, but his voice became softer. "I have met our enemy."

Another general stepped towards Oren with a whip raised skywards, and the crowd watched in delight.

Uden spoke again, above the piercing crack, the grunts of exertion from the torturer, and the low moan of the fallen general. Nomi jumped every time she heard leather ripping flesh. She despised the brute, but he was part of her clan and this made it harder to watch. She allowed herself the indulgent thought of flight one last time; the faint hope that, at this late hour, so close to the fire, she still might slip away.

"Oren brought forth the demon and he came as a man delivering fire." The whipping ceased and Oren collapsed in the roped hold. Blood trickled down his shirtless back and collected in a little pool of mostly red beneath. Uden knelt down beside him and took his face in his godly fingers. "Smile for me." Oren smiled weakly through his tears and this pleased Uden. He nodded to the torturer and the torment continued.

Attack him now while the crowd is distracted.

Uden suddenly spun back to the crowd and it was godly pantomime and she missed her opportunity.

"Oren will return to my embrace, for I am a forgiving god," the forgiving god proclaimed, and the crowd cheered in agreement. "He will still march with me, for I love him so."

The crowd loved Uden so and cried out again. The last crack was loudest. It sent a stream of crimson droplets across the stage, and Oren finally broke and wept aloud. This must have pleased Uden, as he gestured again and the broken general was released with a splashing thud and finally lost consciousness. It seemed like the smarter thing to do. Two more generals carried him from the stage, but not before Uden took hold of the man once again and kissed his victim's bloody forehead. Oren had earned his favour once more. The crowd erupted and Nomi could see how greatly they desired similar punishment to receive similar love. She wondered momentarily whether she had ever been that far lost from reason. Her breath caught in her chest. She'd never known fear as vibrant as this. Not even in battle, with a wild warrior standing over her with a swinging blade.

The tall, smiling general appeared at her side once more and Nomi wondered if he'd ever left at all, or had merely stood statuesque as the surrounding crowd separated further apart. She suddenly felt naked, exposed. She felt left out in the open, on show for all to see.

"I forgive those unknowingly misled, for they cannot see as I see. But those who betray will endure no mercy, no kindness, no reprieve." There was the slightest murmur of disapproval that filtered through the zealots, and Nomi desired concealment more than she desired her next breath. She thought about the blade at her waist and it felt too far away. Uden stepped across the stage and stood over her, and she shook.

"You are my children, and a betrayal from a child is the worst pain I could ever feel." He touched his patch. The torturer dragged a bound child onto the stage and Nomi's heart dropped. *Mish. No.* It wasn't fair. He was an innocent. He was no disciple of Erroh. He was a good little Uden devout.

Mish was pale, and he shivered from fear as they dragged him in front of the god. His god. They threw the child to the wooden floor, where he lay at the Woodin Man's black boots. *Do something.* She turned to flee, for the child was lost, but the smiling general must have read her intentions and laid an arm around her shoulder. There was little force in his grip. It was just there. *Resting.*

"Erroh corrupted this child." The torturer grabbed Mish's hair as he tried to speak. To plead his case. To beg his forgiveness? After a yelp, the child went silent.

"There is no hope for such an innocent creature," warned Uden, running his fingers through the boy's hair. Mish closed his weeping eyes at the god's blessed touch. He smiled blissfully. A believer until the day he died. She wondered would he accept his life as nothing more than scripture in his god's holy sermon. Uden leaned down and kissed his forehead, for he was a loving god, and she prayed in silence for mercy. "I have met our enemy, and he has powers of corruption that even I cannot overcome." The crowd booed in hatred. He silenced them all with one placid wave of his powerful arm.

"He tore one of my fingers apart, and he took my eye." He paused, surveyed the gathering. "These wounds are a beautiful thing, and I am greater for them."

Nomi tried turning away again; she could take no more. She knew the measure of herself, and her cowardice disgusted her. His strength and power were too much.

"Erroh of Spark City is our quarry, and when we extinguish his fire, our war ends," Uden roared, and the crowd cheered in renewed belief and the arm on her shoulder tightened. She reached for her dagger.

"He flees like a coward. He left his whore behind."

Around her, as though awaiting the inevitable punchline to a finely told jest, the crowd erupted as one, and their eyes fell upon her, watching gleefully as Uden leaned over the stage to stare into her soul. The grip upon her shoulder felt like a claw upon beaten prey. The tall general's warm smile now appeared like a demented grin displayed to a crowd of howling maniacs. Her mad god was quite the brazen showman, and yes, she understood her part now in his pious performance. A second general placed a hand upon her other shoulder, holding her securely. She almost collapsed under this terrible fear. All hail those without hope. With nothing to lose.

Do it.

She lashed out with all her might at those who held her. Swift, fierce strikes. The generals faltered in their hold for a breath, and she leapt. She heard the crowd scream in excitement, in terror, in disbelief, as she scaled the stage to face an overwhelming force. Much to the amusement of the god, she continued her charge down on him. Pulling the feeble blade from her belt, she swung wonderfully and wildly. With impossible speed from one so large, Uden evaded the assassination attempt and she tripped and fell over the child. Blood was in the air and the mob screamed for it. Uden was happy to oblige. She met the child's eyes and thought them wide with fear and awe. They pleaded for rescue, they pleaded for understanding, and then they looked away in disgust at her blasphemous behaviour. Mish looked upon his god, and his eyes loved the giant receiving the war axe into his powerful grip.

Nomi fell to her knees and let the dagger fall from her grasp. She held out both her hands in submission, and the crowd were rapturous.

"I have gifts for Erroh," Uden said, testing the weight of the axe and the sharpness thereof. It looked like a good axe.

"Mercy for the child?" whispered Nomi through silent tears. *Perhaps for me as well?*

Those that heard her voiced their disgust at such a plea. They let Uden know as much and he started to laugh loudly, and Nomi closed her eyes. At least her hair looked nice, she reminded herself.

"There will be no mercy." The crowd waited for blood. He rewarded their patience.

9

HOW IT WOULD BE

Lea stared at the journal. *No, not just a journal.* Following the lines on the little diagram, she counted a few numbers in her mind. Little numbers, many miles. She checked the sky again, but it didn't matter. Making good time mattered. Clear sky or not. She ran her fingers along the sketches and thanked the absent gods with whom she'd occupied her time while alone. She studied her artistry. *Rough, clumsy and priceless.* Her cartography skills had improved as time went on, but she could see when the cold had bit harder, when her pen had slipped in quaking fingers, or when boredom and misery had driven her to sketch more detail than necessary. In the glow of a tiny flame, huddled in whatever secluded nook she'd taken for shelter, she would scribe all that she had seen. For weeks on end she would memorise and copy the vastness of the great land into delicate scrawls on crinkled, cream-coloured paper. It was something to do and it had kept her mostly sane. *Mostly.* These sketches were priceless now.

Lea slipped the journal into her pack and double-checked the restraints on the two mounts that she led. All carried small packs of scavenged supplies in equal measure. Behind her, Erroh waited with his three mounts. They were fine charging beasts. They could make great time swapping between these animals. *Waste not, want not.*

"Let's ride," she said, and he nodded. Killing had done him the world of good, but she feared he might relapse, or even change his heart in the last few moments. Once they'd broken free of the sanctuary's valley, she hadn't slowed the pace.

They took off, and their mounts destroyed the ground beneath them. The sharp wind caught her hair; the icy gusts shot down through her spine, spreading coldness right through to her bones. She'd never felt better; she was determined to get them home.

The first days were both the hardest and easiest. The clouds held no threat of snow and the path was clear. The world was vast, but with her sketches guiding them they raced the wind, and they raced it magnificently. Within a breath of waking, they rode until the night fell. They sacrificed little time where they could. Throughout, they rested only long enough to eat a few mouthfuls of dried fish before changing mounts and resuming their hasty charge. They stayed away from rivers lest they stumble upon marching brutes; they paid heed to markings left by wandering armies. For the briefest time, it was good. It felt as it had before. Erroh and Lea together again; what could go wrong?

The absent gods might have suggested a great deal.

It drew on him like an itch. Something slight, barely noticeable, yet, as the days passed, it grew to a maddening desire. *Violence.* He wanted to spar. He needed to. The silent hours upon the galloping steed had given him plenty of time to think and regret and oh, he had much regret. As if his mind hadn't taken enough of a battering, his months captive had left his body a devastated ruin. His muscular arms had diminished away to nothing. All those years of strenuous training, lost in the clinking of dragging chain, the wrath of elements, and the slow march into madness. *Weaker.* Magnus would be disappointed in him. Imprisonment was no excuse for giving up. He needed to find the savage that clawed at his mind; he desired combat.

Whenever the cutting wind allowed, he watched her in the saddle. He thought her changed; he thought her as battered as he, and he thought her incredible. She led fiercely, leaping across small streams or breaks in the land, through the ever-thick forest, never easing up, and he followed. His Lea. His beautiful Lea. He wasn't ready to earn her forgiveness and this was strangely reassuring. Was it not a tale all too familiar to them? They had faced each other when they hated and loved each other most. They had found a way through violence.

Miles to go.

Lea dropped from her mount and began undoing the saddles. The mounts had performed their duties admirably and she patted each one before leading them to a break in the trees. They grazed like kings where the frozen grass broke through the white. The cold would be little trouble to them; nestled together, their body heat kept them from the chill. However, the Alphalines had no such natural defences. Erroh dug a hole deep enough for them both, should they have need of it, while she set a small fire as the day's light diminished and the darkness hid them from the rest of the world.

"We made fine time today," he said. She thought he sounded humbled, unsure of himself. She wanted to comfort him, reassure him, but no words came. Out here in the frozen white, pandering to him would serve neither of them. Besides, they had all the time in the world to rediscover their desires.

"Aye, we made fine time," she said.

"Do you think it will snow tonight?"

"Aye, my beo," she replied, and she caught his smile. *Beo.* Aye, she desired his warmth, his love, and his touch, but all that would come in time. *Not yet.*

"Though I'm tired, I'm not ready for sleep," he said, looking to the night sky above. She thought on this for a moment before opening her pack and removing the sparring blades. She faced him, and he didn't hesitate, and this pleased her greatly.

There was no playful introduction to what they needed most. No tentative strikes like before at the lake. They tore violently into each other and there was only one master. He was laboured in everything he did. His manoeuvres were apprehensive; his actions were slow as though trudging through water. She spun around the slippery ground, striking freely, delivering painful raps to his knuckles, arms, stomach and everywhere else, and why not punish him? Had she not suffered months of bruises on her porcelain skin when first they had taken up the blades against each other? She punished him, and he smiled each time, and this pleased her greatly too.

Pride. He could feel its stinging reminders every time she neared. *Crack.* He felt another stinging portion of pride, and he accepted each reminding strike. She was a vengeful, dancing goddess and it hurt his pride understanding just how far he'd fallen below her standard. Below his own standards. The night came alive with the wondrous cracking echo of reparation, and she came at him again and he parried the first strike before leaving himself open to the predictable follow-up across his nose. She followed through with a kick to his shins and he stumbled backwards, feeling warm crimson droplets land on his whiskered lip. He realised he needed a shave and he loved this.

She charged his retreat; her body felt alive in violence again. Unrestrained. She giggled and delivered more torment upon his wretched frame, and, to his battered credit, he took it well. Like any Alphaline should.

"You fight like a peasant," he mocked, holding his nose and falling away from his punisher. She allowed him a moment to stem the flow. She thought the drops of red looked pretty on the white ground.

"I'm sorry, Erroh."

"I had it coming."

"You still do." She cracked her wooden blades together loudly, and he spat more blood away. Without warning, he charged her again, intending to draw a little blood of his own, and this pleased her most of all.

———

The first marching finger they came upon was at night. Long after they'd finished a gruelling sparring session and sleep was calling, the sound of marching shattered their solitude. They heard them long before they entered the valley, and early enough to allow them to conceal their presence completely. From atop the valley wall, concealed among the trees, they watched them. Only in those first few moments, seeing the collection of Riders, warriors, and captors below, did Erroh understand just how close Lea had been to him these past few months. How painful and lonely she must have felt. So close, yet so far. He wanted to take hold of her and whisper his gratitude for what she had done, but he didn't. Instead, he remained mute and wondered if Nomi was one of those marching beneath the glow of torches.

The Hunt moved without urgency, but they took each step with determination. They followed the centre of the valley until it led them off into the next. Snow fell lightly, but there was little chance of a blizzard. Erroh suspected most southerners recognised the blow of the wind and the change in the air when they walked. *As did Lea.* How far Lea had come since fearing a little rain and wind out in the Wastes. At least as far as he had fallen.

"They will need to camp soon," she whispered in his ear, and her warmth was a comfort.

"Sometimes, they are content to ride through the night," he countered. He thought of the night marches and remembered them as the worst. He thought of other dreadful horrors: of the constant pulling chain; of a cutting, scraping belt of metal upon bruised skin. He thought of sorrow. Terrible sorrow. He thought of the cold. The terrible, terrible cold.

"I am aware of this, Erroh."

Eventually, the line of fire faded into the night, the silent dark world returned, and Erroh breathed easier. She exhaled slowly before stoking the concealed flames and placing a log gently on the embers, wherein the warmth returned. Sitting on opposite sides of the fire in silence, they watched a few delicate snowflakes meet a fiery end in the heat. It was almost cosy, and Erroh wished he had the words to share with her. Words that would come easily. Words shared between a happily mated couple. *Any words, really.* Since their decision to part ways and dissolve their mating, neither had spoken on the matter. *Why talk when time can heal?* She deserved more than a silent, humble wretch. He searched for the words and found something worthy.

"I love you with all my heart," he said, and she smiled into the flames. They flickered in the breeze and highlighted her features. She was perfect.

"I thought we were finished," she whispered.

"I wasn't myself."

"Who are you now?"

"I'm your one for life."

She liked that term and hid it beneath some elaborate stretching. *Fuk him and his charm.* She wasn't ready yet. She needed to take a breath. Though she hid her excitement, she could see a spark in his tired eyes. She was weak for that fuken spark and weak for him. Weakness had allowed her to delay longer than sanity suggested, but that same weakness was a gamble that had paid off spectacularly. He was half the male he'd been, in need of a bath and a close shave, but he was still perfect in her eyes. Truthfully, he had impressed her these last few days. Even seeing the Hunt, he had not shattered on her. Aye, she could also see the pain hiding beneath his grin. The same pain whispering in his ear to give up. Perhaps Erroh needed something more than just fighting pain? Perhaps she did too? She looked upon her broken, beautiful Alphaline and wanted him closer to her. It had been so long since she'd felt the comfort of just another's presence, and she wanted his touch above anyone else's. They had slept on opposite sides of the fire these past few nights; some things were still too far from their grasp. Still, though…

"What are you doing?"

Without warning, she slid across onto his lap, and planted both knees into the soft ground on either side. Facing him, she ran her fingers slowly across his cheek. *A little reward.* He closed his eyes at her touch and tried to embrace her, but she pushed his arms back down by his side. He stopped struggling, as she was still leading. She moistened each cheek with a little water. He shivered in the cold but smiled curiously. Swiftly, she took her pack and removed what utensils she needed to complete the task. The first was a small bar of soap, which she rubbed in her fingers before spreading it into a thin layer of foam across his face. This task she took her time with. He sighed loudly in complete surrender, and she pulled her little blade from its casing. She checked its thin edge in the fire's light and, satisfied, she went to task.

She was better at shaving than he, and Erroh thought this a curious, wonderful thing. Her rough, calloused, hands sent shivers down his spine every time she positioned his head at the ideal angle, and the gentle scrape of the deadly blade swiping the soap clear was an incredible thing. She could slit his throat with ease, and Erroh thought there were worse ways to die. She knelt in close enough that her breath touched his lips. Her eyes focused upon a stubborn tuft of hair beneath his chin, and she adjusted her rear slightly on his lap and it tested his resolve. Behave, he told himself. Until they had escaped the south, he pledged. The cold struck his skin and, to his misery, she completed her task. Their eyes met, and he thought her so very warm and firm and kissable, and oh, how he wanted to do many imaginative things to her. He reached up and ran his fingers through her hair, and she closed her eyes. She missed him too.

She leaned forward and blew on his skin to soothe any raw pain. "I love you too, my beo," she whispered, and despite herself, she bit his lower lip before sliding away from his warmth. She slipped into her bedding on the other side of the fire. They were no longer what they had been; they could become so much more. She knew it would work out. It had to. *Miles to walk.* This was how it would be. Anything less, and they would crumble to nothing.

10

THE FLAGSHIP

W rek ushered the two wretched men through the archway of the city gates before any further awkward questions emerged. The blond wretch reeked of sweat and the march, while the smaller wretch hid his odour beneath alcohol. *Cheap sine.* What else were refugees to do? Wrek wondered. What could Wrek possibly do to help such rampant misery? Not much, but ceasing an assault was something.

Lost in pain and misery, they were silent. Viewing the Spark in all her splendour usually silenced even the most boisterous. Neither man showed enthusiasm, regardless. Perhaps meeting locked gates after a long march was difficult to take. The smallest man nursed a bleeding lip. He probably didn't know how much worse it could have been. A lesson learned—to be careful with words and actions when walking in the city. Wrek wasn't used to playing the peacemaker, but times had changes and he had changed with them. Simple curiosity had turned to something more. Watching the daily incidents outside the gate was a fine way of learning appreciation for one's place in the world. He had believed pockets heavy with pieces would make up for having no soul, but standing watching the city's front gate had created a desire to do more in this life.

Fame had changed him. Everyone knew his name, his dealings, his threat. Even the Black Guard nodded respectfully as he waltzed through the gates unmolested. Perhaps, had his life panned out differently, he might have made a fine Wolf. *Worse ways to earn a piece.* As it was, he was rich and renowned in this city, and yet it wasn't enough for him.

They passed winding, narrow streets, barely wide enough to pass a horse through.

"This way, lads," he called to his entourage, all the while wondering if they would appreciate the gesture such a venerated bouncer had willingly given them. He'd pledged for them. It was no small matter. Perhaps they'd flourish, perhaps they'd flounder, or perhaps they'd stab him in the back for his efforts once they turned this next corner. It was in the laps of the gods. *The gods—ha!* People found faith easier these days. Wrek imagined it was probably the oncoming war. Well, Wrek believed only in his sword; it was as good a god as anything. He hated the thought of a deity controlling his movements and actions. But if there were gods, best they stay the fuk out of his way and concentrate on everyone else.

The absent gods approved of this.

They rounded the corner and attempted no assault. "I can't promise you very much, friends."

"We'll take it anyway," muttered the smaller man, wiping the blood on his sleeve, and Wrek wondered if such an unimposing wretch spoke for the entire contingent of refugees. He wore expensive clothing that had faded to blandness. His hair was unkempt and knotted. He shuffled along as though each step was a dreadful effort upon the stone footing. He was quiet now; at the gates he'd had more to say. Wrek almost smiled at the absurdity of such a battering.

Welcome to Samara. Clench your fist.

"Your people look a little thin. I'll wrangle up some supplies. Best I can do."

"How about shelter behind the walls?" the blond man asked. His long hair was at least brushed, but his handsome face was hidden behind an anxious glare.

Wrek could hear the pity in their voices, could see it in their walks, and he hated that he could. Hated that he cared.

"Primary's rule," he growled. *No space at this inn.* They left the wretches needing most help in the great glowing city's shadow. Better that than wandering the Wastes and succumbing to the murderous barbarians. Wrek halted and placed his hand on the battered man's shoulder. "There are others with far less than you. The nights aren't cold yet, my friends. You have a fine number of carts that you can break down, and I'll try to get a few tents for those who need shelter now… Might even get a few bottles of proper alcohol to ease the pain." It felt like a weak bid, but the smaller wretch removed his hand from his pocket and shook Wrek's gratefully. Wrek ignored the stench. "I'll find you after," he said, leaving them by the office of the Primary with instructions for what to say.

It's all I can do.

These wretches had troubled words from the road, just like the thousand other refugees singing the same song. Every day brought whispered truths; every day, the identity of the culprits became clearer. Wrek didn't believe that Magnus was marching; he didn't believe lunatics from the Savage Isles had tired of neutrality either. He believed it was the fuken south. Up to no good all over again. Like cancerous tendrils corrupting a greater beast, the southerners were trickling out from their frozen lands, killing every settlement they came upon. Had he and Sigi not almost fallen like the others? Had they not fled to the city ahead of those pathetic others? It wasn't as though they could return to the salt mines. Better to face a marching army than return home.

"Fuk," Wrek muttered to the wind. Thinking of the salt mines always stung. Wrek had no friends. He used to have friends. Close friends. Trustworthy friends. Friends he could call brothers. Now, he had none. Well, he had Sigi. Sigi was a friend of sorts, although he wasn't sure Sigi knew the value of friendship or completely understood the term. He was a business partner. Truthfully, it was less Wrek's resourcefulness and more Sigi's understandings of shrewd dealings that had led to their successes. Sigi was a simple and subtle genius. A man driven to attaining wealth beyond reasoning. He lived for the profits, and these were fine times to understand economics. No, more than mere understanding; Sigi was fearless in his endeavours, and ruthless like a brother's dagger in the back. At least with business dealings.

Wrek walked past a group of dwellings and tried to remember if he and Sigi had recently acquired these plots or if they were still in discussions. It was hard to follow his partner's plentiful dealings. He caught sight of a young lady brushing her hair in one of the hovel's doorways as he passed. She offered a warm, grateful smile and Wrek supposed that yes, it was likely they held the deeds. And what reasonable landlords there were too. Sigi understood this economy. He always had. In fact, he did more than just understand it. He took advantage of it with ruthless efficiency. He controlled Spark City now and was paying a fortune for the honour. Wrek walked past another little cluster of dwellings he knew they held the deeds to. How many now? *More than enough, at least.* A few more months of this profiteering and he'd struggle to remember which plots were not owned by the illustrious partners.

In the first few months Wrek's expertise in keeping Sigi alive had been key to their rising star. His skill at guarding the door of The Rat's Nest, the flagship of Sigi's massive fleet of property, had begun the flood of money. That should have been enough for anyone; it was for Wrek.

Sigi is a different monster now.

Though he no longer needed to, Wrek still worked the door of their flagship tavern. They could afford more than enough able-bodied doormen to work every inn they owned, but Wrek's activities were renowned throughout Samara and truthfully, he liked the attention. Women flocked to him; men sized him up, backing down more often than not. Moreover, the atmosphere was boisterous and wonderful for distraction. There was revelry, jests, humour and sometimes spectacle. Though he'd never admit it, sometimes he felt like friends surrounded him without the worry of betrayal rearing its inevitable head. He understood why the people of Samara adored him. In any establishment where Wrek kept peace, only honest decadence was allowed. There were no safer places to drink. Who desired an unexpected chair in the head during a brawl, or to have a pocket picked by wandering hands when the senses were numbed?

Perhaps it was also his way of dealing with events that drew customers in, too. Very few bouncers had such a way with violence; fewer bouncers could offer such a sense of humour while dealing said violence, too. There was a charm to his aggression, and perhaps some citizens of Samara needed a nice taste of violence mixed in with fine laughter to make the perfect night. His forgiving nature the following evening with his contrite victims was also well renowned. He was an attraction; he was effective, and Sigi did the rest. Sigi's sine had become the single most valuable commodity in the city. Granted, that wasn't hard when the competition was likely to gift a regular customer a case of blindness or poisoning. A man with a flowing income and a willingness to reinvest everything he owned, was likely to fail spectacularly or find himself elevated higher than most.

Wrek reached the old oak doors of the tavern and stepped inside.

Sigi thought war to be a beautiful thing. As beautiful as war was, though, he thought this war improbable. Aye, there would be battles, there would be losses; sometimes the world just needed to stretch its muscles. After a little stretch, shrewder minds would prevail. Word from the road suggested the southerners were coming, and he always trusted the road. *Well done, them.* He had no issue with the southern faction stamping its feet. Didn't they have a few valid complaints? Had they not been reduced to a wandering group of freezing nomads these past few decades? He'd learned to keep his political views to himself. Such things were bad for business.

Sigi caught sight of Wrek entering and waved him over. He thought Wrek a fine weapon to wield in many nonviolent ways. The people loved him, but more than that, he'd earned the respect of the city's guardians. *Closer to an army these days.* Sigi needed a man to deal with the city's Wolves when the time came.

The Black Guard. Few ways to make pieces in Samara these days, but the Black Guard were hiring and growing in number every day. A fine manoeuvre by the Primary to swell her defences. The Spark was where the southerners would stop their march. Everything suggested as much. Two great armies meeting. Sigi thought this most beautiful too.

Wrek neared his table in the far corner of the tavern and Sigi winked for silence. There was still business to do. He offered a smile to the young couple who read over the contract one more time. Wrek knew Sigi's doings and kept his common tongue from breaking the moment. Sigi loved the moment right before they struck the deal. He allowed no one else to conduct business apart from himself. How else could he enjoy these moments? Even if it was a simple rent arrangement. He relaxed his head back against the wooden wall and caught sight of a drunk man at the other end of the tavern suddenly taking notice of Wrek's appearance, and he smiled at this too. He looked back to the young female sitting across from him, mouthing the words slowly to her nervous mate. *Search for the catch, little ones.* He added salt to the yellow soup still steaming in front of him and wondered if he should have had eggs for lunch instead.

"There's no catch, my friends. I wouldn't be where I am without doing fair business," he offered, dipping some bread in his soup before daring a taste. *Should have had eggs.*

Wrek had found himself a pint of ale, but the frothy head was untouched; Sigi suspected another request. Whenever there was money involved, Wrek was humbled; he loathed asking for funding. *For the wretches again.* Wrek's generosity was becoming recognised throughout the city, and Sigi approved somewhat. Small acts of kindness helped build a good reputation, and Wrek was welcome to continue his charitable acts for now. It was a small matter, as Sigi held the depthless pouch of pieces and there would be no ill-spending.

The female signed the contract. *Excellent.* Sigi smiled and shoved the two pretty bags of pieces across the table. "By all means, count them, my friends."

The concerned young male appeared as though he'd signed his soul away to a demon. "You give your word you will not evict us?"

Sigi tapped the fourth line on the second page. "Only if you miss your payments. Three missed payments in a row." The catch they'd searched for did not exist. Hence their apprehension to sign such an attractive agreement. It was more than attractive. Ten pieces a month they had to pay him as rent. The Primary had charged them twenty. With their rental agreement in hand, he would deal with the Primary's rent collectors from here. He was willing to take a loss. For now. He was happy to take chances.

"When the Black Guard come for the taxes, show them the seal and send them my way," he reminded them. They were a nice couple. They frequented the bar. Now they could afford to visit more. Like all the others.

Wrek watched the deal being struck and nodded politely as the now slightly wealthier couple departed the inn. The bags they carried were a drop in the ocean to the pieces their taverns earned every night. If Sigi was happy to buy up the rental agreements of every household in the city, it was his prerogative.

Sigi placed the deeds and contract in the massive safe behind the bar. "Can you deal with the Black Guard when they come for her taxes tomorrow morning? And explain that we've expanded... again?"

"Not sure that I can, Sigi. I have to ride out to the farm and speak with Jeroen."

"New shipment already?"

"Aye," said Wrek, scratching his beard. Sigi never enjoyed dealing with the tax collectors personally. Perhaps it was the monthly fortune handed out stinging his pride; perhaps Sigi didn't trust himself, or perhaps he just needed to make Wrek feel as though he brought more to their partnership. Whatever the reason, whenever he could, he had Wrek deal with the Black Guard, and Wrek had fewer issues with them than most. Ever since the robbery.

It had happened in the first few weeks, and it was Wrek who had taken care of everything. A group of fiends had stolen their entire stock of sine. Wrek had offered a group of Black Guards half of what they recovered as an incentive, and he and the Guards had worked together to recover the goods. When they'd apprehended the three foolish criminals, Wrek had persuaded the men that stealing from any of their properties resulted in consequences. One of them still hadn't recovered full use of his right hand yet. Much to Sigi's dismay, Wrek had donated the entire stash of sine to the Wolves. A shrewd move, earning favour among the marshals of the city. There had been no further incidents. More than that, Wrek now had as much freedom as the Primary throughout the city.

Sine.

Wrek didn't drink much sine these days. He spent so much of his time assisting in the brewing and moving that he'd lost the taste. He was in the minority. The Rat's Nest had been their flagship and they had sailed the sine seas upon it. They owned every tavern in this city now and the people weren't losing their thirst.

"More trouble at the gate," Wrek said.

Sigi shrugged and left his bread to die in his soup. "Terrible times for the wretched people altogether." Wretches had little currency when they first arrived. Those wily few who earned their way and cleared their tab, well, Sigi had all the time for them.

"We could help?" Wrek suggested.

Sigi nodded uninterestedly and Wrek wasn't at all offended. He knew to play it humbly. "We need to better staff the taverns."

"I suppose we could use a few more," Sigi muttered. "How many need to gain entrance?"

"A few hundred."

"We can't save everyone, Wrek. The wretches are well enough down by the wall."

"They deserve better than what they've received."

"Primary's orders."

Wrek sipped his ale and cracked his knuckles loudly. This act usually terrified any sane person. It even caused Sigi a moment's pause. He normally did it before punching someone very hard. Wrek

74

was not without his bartering skills. Wrek could see Sigi calculating the numbers in his head.

"We could find a use for fifty willing wretches," Sigi said at length. "Pretty and handsome. They bring in more patrons. Make sure they are pretty... get a few blonde girls too." Wrek smiled. He'd hoped for only twenty. "They'll need some tents, I suppose?" Sigi added, eyeing the safe holding the funds reserved solely for Wreck's charity.

"Don't worry, Sigi. I'll find time to meet with the Black Guard in the morning before I head out," Wrek offered, and Sigi smiled at this. Another successful transaction completed.

Excellent.

11

LOST IN THE SNOW

Where was a welcoming Nomi with a warm fire and warmer bed when he needed it? He'd been in better places in his life. He'd been in worse. Not too many, if truth be told. At least Lea was with him. At least she was no stranger to this nightmare. He trusted her and she was beside him now, calm as a lake. She didn't smell like she had before. Before the fall of Keri. Not that she smelled bad; in fact, she smelled rather wonderful. It was more that she smelled different. He remembered her scent from before. He even had a little pouch still attached to his wrist that reminded him of her. *Tied with Nomi's ribbon.* Perhaps Lea had run out of her perfume these past months. Perhaps she'd cast the little bottle aside one lonely day on the march. He might have asked her, but he didn't. He thought it best to hold his tongue on matters like aroma. Especially when the enemy surrounded them.

Above their heads a nest of irritated crows cawed contemptuously. He hadn't seen a crow in months. Miles had raced past in silence these last few serene weeks. Most without hazards, but the valleys were closing in as they neared the warmer lands of the north and more recognisable wildlife were appearing on their march. It was just a shame a fuk-load of the Hunt had appeared at the same time.

Erroh watched his breath in the air and missed the feeling of warmth—when his fingers didn't sting with every clench; when his feet didn't suffer eternal dampness, like walking in a marsh. He missed warming and drying in a fire's glow, but the fingers of the Hunt were too close, so they sat in the cold hugging each other for warmth. Just another struggled day in the Wastes. At least he was free; at least he was feeling like himself again. He could have told her this, but conversation was still strained. *As usual.* She hadn't tried to bridge the distance with revealing, spoken words, and neither had he. Conversation would return when it was ready. When they were ready. He was sure of it.

He rubbed the thickening stubble on his chin. He needed another shave. A line of cavalry walked a little below them, close enough that he could make out the faces of each Rider. They trotted along with little haste despite the difference in air pressure. They would finish their march long before nightfall; long before any snow, either. They weren't the first line they'd seen this day, nor the second or third. He doubted they'd be the last, either.

Fuk it. Fuk it. Fuk it all. Lea ran her finger across the scribble their route had taken as if it would help. *This isn't fair.* They hid in a small cluster of trees atop a valley wall between two nasty-looking mountain ranges. There really was only one route to take for at least a hundred miles either way, and so they had taken it. So had everyone else in this cursed land. Their route through a thinning valley should have been an hour's ride on a clear day, but the enemy were crawling everywhere, like little stinging insects upon a hive just waiting to frenzy all over them. Worse than that, beyond this area, stretched out across the lands afar, were thousands of settled Hunt who'd now set themselves to one great gathering. Waiting and preparing for war. *Fuken everywhere. Fuk it, fuk it, fuk it.* There was no safe path to take, so both frozen Alphalines waited.

Her father might have been proud that she'd mastered these lands so well. That she'd evaded capture, avoided freezing, eluded ambushes. Perhaps the child left alone in Spark would have cared that that bastard Wiiden cared, but Lea, mated to Erroh, did not. She wondered how Wiiden would have felt about her leading them into a precarious position without an escape route. *It's not my fault.* Speed in the saddle had granted her great daring and carelessness, it would appear. In her defence, they were certain to come upon larger forces at some point. It was just a shame they'd come so far that turning around would bring the same disaster as creeping another step forward. She'd felt this panic before, outside the southern city, watching helplessly from far off. She suddenly remembered the shared kiss. *Concentrate, silly girl.*

She looked at her scribbles from a few pages back, finding little success. *Maybe a turn through this range? Or following this river here?* Aye, it might be possible to find another route, but southerners took the same routes for good reason. They could sacrifice their mounts and all their speed, hoping to slip past, or they could try something else. She only needed to discover what that something else was. Erroh wasn't ready to offer any suggestion, and she dared not let him believe they were in as much danger as they were. She did not trust him. *Yet.*

He knelt beside her with unblinking eyes, watching as they marched below. This group would pass soon enough and find their place among the hundred other camps. Smaller armies, all gathering, all preparing. *Terrible times to come.* She could have burdened him with such worry, but she'd earned her right to lead unquestionably. He stretched out his freezing arms and she could see how much better his clothes fitted now. He was improving every day, and improvement was an Alphaline's obligation. He probably needed another shave, but sometimes she liked a little grizzle in her mate. She looked at his lips for a few breaths longer than she realised, before looking away. Did fear like this draw a desire to procreate? Admittedly, riding with him these last few weeks had stirred temptation. Sparring was satisfying, but it couldn't quench every urge. His arms looked better these days. After so little time, he already matched her speed with the blade. He was becoming magnificent again. Looking at the enemy scurrying below, she reflected that this was no bad thing.

She watched as a couple of Riders unexpectedly separated from their comrades, left their horses behind and began frantically climbing the slope. Lea held her breath. Beside her, Erroh silently drew one of her swords from its scabbard. The thicket of bush and tree they'd chosen suddenly didn't appear in any way thick enough now. *Oh, to have the time to dig a big hole.* She pulled Baby from her back and watched. Perhaps they climbed the mountain to see as far as Erroh and Lea could? Perhaps they were hunting their nightly dinner? Or perhaps they'd spotted the hidden Alphalines and this was the end. She'd almost forgotten this feeling of terror. Almost, but not quite.

The ascending Riders were clumsy. Each deep step was precarious, and it became clear they had little idea that Erroh and Lea were nearby. She heard their grunts and curses and silently she notched an arrow, only for Erroh to hold her draw with a steady hand. His eyes were cold, his mouth clenched tightly. He looked like he wanted to kill them brutally. It was reassuring; she thought of him charging the Riders at the lake.

A few feet from the summit, the nearest Rider slipped and slid a few feet down the slope. This halted the second man's climb; he roared triumphantly as the first slid past him. She recognised the tones without understanding their words; the southern mood was light as they gathered for war. The fallen Rider allowed himself to slide a few more feet before sitting up and accepting the hand offered by his mocking comrade. They both skidded back down the slope together to find their place back among their marching parade, wiping clumps of snow from their clothing as they did. She thought she heard laughter from the line, but it was muffled beneath the drumming of her heart. Another duo dropped from their horses now and began to climb the slope further up the path.

"They were wagering who could reach the top before slipping," Erroh whispered, returning his blade to its scabbard. "Sometimes the march is boring."

"I know this, Erroh."

"It makes them appear almost human."

"Almost."

Every few hours another line of southerners passed them by, but thankfully no more were interested in scaling the slope for entertainment. She wondered if it was the subtle changing of the wind. She watched the sky and hoped for nightfall. More than that, she hoped for snow.

"Any idea, beo?" Erroh whispered, and she began frantically running her fingers back along her scribblings. A few pages, and the world opened up. *So close.* She grasped the journal as if it kept her afloat. As if it would give her an answer, having failed thirty times already. "I'm sorry. I don't know what to do. It's the only path."

He took her hand. "I would have gotten us killed already." Sometimes he said the right thing. She squeezed his hand in hers, and he bent and kissed it.

Erroh could feel it in his bones. Some things one couldn't forget. He'd learned more about snow than he'd thought. He felt the weather turning. Aye, he'd been battered and broken with barely sensible thoughts as company, but his body remembered the cold. His body remembered when a fine storm was in the wind. He sat in the freezing snow and placed his arm around her shoulders.

"Let's just wait here a little longer," he whispered, closing the journal in her hands. She was watching the sky through the branches above. Perhaps she could feel it too. The sharp wind caught her hair and he could see her breath much clearer in the bitter air. They couldn't survive a snowfall without a fire. They couldn't light a fire without being seen. *Fuked.* Far across the landscape a wave of darkness began to cover the land ahead of sunset. *Less fuked?* Erroh knelt, watching the world. He thought of a plan, a simple plan that couldn't possibly work.

"It will snow all night," she whispered.

"No, it will *blizzard* all night," he said, grinning.

It was a fine storm of snow. Capable of killing a person. Capable of killing a group of people. An entire army, in fact, if they didn't take proper shelter. Erroh had little interest in shelter. He was far more interested in doing stupid things. It was probably a smarter move to face an entire army alone. The first delicate flakes fell around them and the wind began to rear its nasty head. Erroh went to task, tying all the horses together. His fingers immediately began to stiffen in the cold as he twisted each knot securely. She understood his plan immediately and began assisting in the arduous task.

The snowflakes began to fill the air, and vision beyond a few feet was lost to a white wall of nastiness. Below them, another line of southerners that had entered the valley were now settling down for the storm, and this both pleased and unnerved Erroh. Little lights began to appear all around the valleys, each flickering flame a bright warning of where not to tread. If he really thought about it, it wasn't even a plan. It was a little walk that would probably kill them both.

"Are we doing this?" he asked.

She wrapped her hair up in a ponytail. "Let's go for a little wander."

The snow worsened in moments. It came in unforgiving waves, battering them as it fell, and the wind cut them to the bone. Visibility lessened, and every frozen breath heralded the disappearance of another distant, flickering flame in the thickening haze. Shivering and half-blind, they began moving the beasts down the great slope. They moved as one entity. A few ropes attaching each beast in an enclosed circle, with Erroh and Lea in the centre, taking what protection and warmth they could. They held a rein in each hand and slowly walked the living shelter down towards probable death. The slope was slippery, but the beasts held their footing. Hissing orders to the horses under their breath, the two Alphalines inched down towards enemy territory, careful to keep wide of looming encamped shapes in the darkness.

The wind must have taken offence that they had denied the natural way of things, for it howled its outrage. A piercing, shrill cry that rose in volume the closer towards doom they marched. They reached the bottom of the slope only a hundred feet from the nearest camp and continued onward. Already Erroh could feel the dampness seeping through his many layers and immediately freezing in the bitter air. Was this what frostbite felt like? he wondered. It was more painful than he'd expected. *Worse than walking in chains.* Despite the horrible conditions, the mounts did not resist their masters. They suffered with them but kept moving. Each hoof dug deep into the ground, and both Alphalines matched their pace.

Without warning, he felt the desolation come upon him. He heard chains in his ears and felt the drag around his waist. He felt alone, terrified, wretched. He caught sight of a flame in the distance and for a moment thought about releasing his mount and scrambling towards it. *I'm not ready for this.* He stumbled, and Lea reached out instinctively and steadied him. She didn't notice his panic. Why would she? He felt the grip of panic give way to shame. Shame for what he'd become. How easily he was shaken. The horse suddenly pulled in his grip as he slowed his step. The world would turn, snow would fall. The horse was marching on, regardless. He took hold, gripped tightly, and took the panic and locked it away. He bit that *fuken* shame and swallowed it in fury. *Walk on, and worry about the rest later.* He clenched his teeth and upped the pace, and Lea stumbled and he reached for her.

They would never make it. Her path into darkness would be paved in white. She pulled the horses forward, fighting the inevitable, and one mount whined in torment. They were suffering, and somehow, this made it so much worse. She battled with her hood. The wind kept pulling the garment from her head and leaving it hanging uselessly down her back. *It's not fair.* After a time, she gave up altogether and stopped pulling it back up. It felt like hours since they had started the horrible trek, and it might have been. It might also have been moments. Who could tell in this nightmare? This wasn't the first time she'd been out in a blizzard, but never had she faced one as fierce, nor without some cover in reach. She couldn't see anything beyond the leading horse's head, and she now realised their folly. They'd had no choice, but this would lead to doom. They could not survive this nightmare.

She stumbled like he had, and he reached for her. Tragically, he was not swift and she fell, taking him with her. The horses did not halt their march, and she relinquished her grip. She lay in the snow and the pain immediately lessened. The wind was less fierce in the growing mounds of soft, white flakes. *It's not fair.* She knew she would die this very hour. She'd walked them into a nest of vipers without escape. This was not the first time she'd lost hope in these freezing lands. It would, however, be the last. It was amazing how swiftly the touch of cold took breath and hope.

Erroh grabbed her fiercely and dragged her to her feet. He called for her, but his voice was a whisper in the growing gale.

She matched his step; her face shook like his had, moments ago, and he took her hand and dragged her onward as she had dragged him.

"We can do this," he cried, and she nodded. She was paler than he'd ever seen her, and fresh fury overcame him. He needed to walk it off. *Too much caution.*

"Are you okay?" he cried, and she didn't reply. She struggled forward as though led by a chain. Since she'd rescued him, she'd appeared dominant. Assured. Now she resembled the scared little waif from the Cull. Only then did he see the terrible toll this solitary march had taken upon her. *She has her own traumas, too.* There was only so much a weary mind could take. Did he not know this? Had he not almost shattered?

Fuk this. He grabbed her hand and began jogging. Immediately the snow at his numb feet stuck and fought him, but he roared like a wild warrior upon a battlefield. She ran with him and the horses; grateful for the increased pace, she matched it. His muscles screamed in agony; his mind reeled. Through the roar of the blizzard he heard the whisper of *Retreat, surrender,* and it enraged him further. He howled, and the horses broke into a trot, and the going quickened and became more demanding. She gasped, and he led her until they ran their fastest, each step agile and determined. Every suggestion of giving up strengthened his will again. Magnus would have approved.

At such a pace, she suffered a terrible torment, but his stubborn drive suppressed her own doubts. Is this how one faces one's own suffering? she wondered. Running it out until night fell and dawn followed. As if in answer, the night drew darkness down upon them and she didn't care. She kept running. Exhaustion, panic, all lost to painful salvation. All lost to unlikely hope. The mounts thundered through the valley where the enemy had marched earlier. She worried, beyond the cold, that they might blindly fall upon encamped southerners, but in that moment all that mattered was the race. She held the vision of her sketchings in her mind and trusted their course towards a pitiful forest somewhere ahead. They rushed through valley after valley, never slowing, never taking breath; holding each other's hands, racing death.

———

Beric knew well it was never wise to stray from camp during a blizzard. It was the first lesson they taught a child when out marching. A lost fool might stray and their body never be recovered. It happened every season. He'd lost a lover or two in his time. A brother or two as well. It was on nights like this that fools wandered out and never returned. Even with the great gathering underway and many of Uden's fingers nearby, a man might become so lost that Uden himself mightn't find him. But Beric needed to relieve himself, and even nights like this couldn't stop him. A few feet from safety would suffice. Any nearer and the smell would earn the vitriol of his companions at the fire. It was precarious to undertake such an act in this weather, yet the second lesson Beric had learned was this valuable art of relief. As he finished (and with still some feeling to his nether parts), he caught sight of some movement in the breaking waves of snow.

The movement drew nearer, a handful of feet from any light and safety's touch. It was a large mass of movement, and as he finished his task and buttoned his trousers, the dark outline charged past. He could see the outlines of horses. *Horses loose. Can't have horses loose.* He followed in pursuit for a dozen steps before common sense got the better of him. He was too far from the fire. Too far from his comrades. The storm immediately began its assault, and he shuddered under its cruelty. Through the blinding, stinging drifts he could just make out the outline of two figures leading the horses forward. Had they no sense about them?

"Are you crazy?" he roared, and his voice bounced in the wind. They gave no answer; they barely stopped. There was a flash in his eyeline as a wave of snow flew past his face and blinded him. "Ah, you'll lose your life out here," he roared, giving up on them. *Let them risk death.* He wasn't willing to step further into the great white. They had ideas of their own, he imagined. Besides, the third lesson he'd learned was, if in doubt, keep running until you outrun the storm. He waved them off on their way, and they appeared to wave in reply. Perhaps they desired excitement, as so many younger soldiers did. Perhaps they marched to ease the boredom of slowness. He knew well some younger Riders just couldn't sit still. The prospect of war brought out the impatience in the young. More so than others. Perhaps they believed that reaching the edges of the first wave would somehow hasten adventure. Poor fools did not understand how slow marching north would really be, how long it would take. A few weeks waiting would cool their tails, no doubt. Boredom on the march was never spoken of, but it struck the youngest and oldest.

They disappeared from his sight, and Beric made his way carefully back towards the warm glow of the fire. He looked to the darkened sky and wondered would dawn break before or after the storm. *Small matter.* He took a moment to catch his breath beside one of the great wheels of the wooden carts and discovered, much to his irritation, an arrow embedded deeply in the wheel just above his head. Another comrade must have thought it amusing to fire an arrow blindly into a storm as a game of chance for the unsuspecting. He pulled the arrow free and left it in the snow. Perhaps he'd speak with Oren on this matter. Too slow a pace was driving their people to complete idiocy altogether.

———

"Take the shot," Erroh cried in her ear. Even in the darkness he could see how pale the cold had made her skin. Slowing was bad, he thought. Stopping was suicide, yet here they were, delaying. She hissed him to silence and released the arrow. It was a careless shot that flew a few feet wide of its intended target. Around them the mounts began to rear in their hold. They could feel the cold too.

"You missed," Erroh spat, and heard her growl in reply. Truthfully, even a master of the bow could not control this wind, this visibility. Her quarry didn't notice the attempt on his life. The ignorant brute waved them on and began to turn away towards a little glowing flame a short distance away. Instinctively, Erroh waved back, grasping most of the southern words. In the brute's defence, he could never have expected the enemy to stroll right through their territory. Lea cursed under her breath, returning the bow to her back.

"You never miss!" he chided her.

"Well, it's windy."

They linked hands, took up their reins once more, and returned to their running, knowing well that slowing down, especially when nearing a camped finger, was pushing their luck even further. Perhaps it was stubbornness, perhaps it was desperation, perhaps it might even have been hope, but they ran with the storm's wrath, through the valley and on into the next valley and the next after that. They ran without respite or stealth. Their vision was nothing more than the darkened wall of eternal drift, yet they never faltered. Their map was avoiding any nearby flame that flittered into their sight and nothing more. They ran for miles under the cover of beautiful, incredible mounts until a dark shadow met them in the form of the small forest. Despite the bitter wind easing off, they still took no respite. They pushed on, for that is what frozen little Alphalines without alternatives were inclined to do. They took the pain regardless of how unimaginable it was.

That last night, trailing behind the Hunt's great march, was the worst night of their lives. Had either been alone they would have perished, they would have given in to inevitability and lain down in ruin, but together, they drove each other forward. In the desperate moments when their screaming muscles begged for relief and they slowed to a shuffle, they willed each other on. Sometimes with a heave, sometimes with a curse, and sometimes with a mate's desperate plea. They took turns inspiring each other and eventually, they bettered the night.

Then, with no warning, the sky cleared and the cruel wind tipped its hat. The relentless blizzard released its hold upon the world and the way ahead became easier. Many miles north of the nearest campfire, they hid themselves beneath white, laden branches in the forest. Erroh dug a shallow hole, while she gathered fuel for a fire to burn away the pain. Sitting side by side in front of the little flame, they warmed their weary bones, took easier breaths, and counted the absent gods' blessings. They ate sparingly and settled down to sleep.

With his damp clothing drying by the fire, Erroh lifted his sheeting, revealing all that he was, and invited her in. She stripped her own garments free and joined him, pressing herself tightly against him. They kissed once before she closed her eyes and nestled in against his chest. Weakly, she reached out and tugged his hair before allowing slumber to take her.

Erroh listened to her breathing and his own for a while as exhaustion began to overtake him. He enjoyed the feel of her warming skin against his own, and he dared a sigh of relief and delicate contentment. Out here, braving the Wastes was natural. This was life, and surviving such a night was simply part of it.

Though he was giddy with exhaustion and relief, he could not draw his thoughts from the numbers the gathering Hunt were amassing. There were enough of Uden's fingers already gathered to sack Spark tenfold. Who knew how many wandering brutes were still to arrive? Or worse, were already attacking the city. Uden had promised war, and war was coming.

His last few thoughts were of hope as he fell to slumber. A few weeks before and Erroh could never have braved this night. He'd twisted his agony into triumph. They both had. Miles had been walked, and the road ahead felt clear. There was still time, and both he and Lea were back in the fight. They might even play their part in the battles ahead. He just didn't realise how great a part.

12

ALLEGIANCES

Magnus held his blade tightly in slightly arthritic fingers. *Pain is in the mind*, he reminded himself, gripping the pommel tighter and accepting the punishment. The blade's tip dug into the gravelly ground and he stabbed absently, waiting for his guests. His hounds' agitation grew and he let their low warning growls fill the quiet morning air. *Good little beasts.*

He gestured for their escorts to return to the barracks, allowing the visitors to approach alone. There was Primary business to discuss, and his warriors didn't need to suffer the boredom of words with city rats. *Alpha rats at that.* How far they had fallen, answering to the queen bitch's will, he thought. He sighed, spinning his blade in the ground a little more. *What does Dia think I've done now?* He hissed the hounds to silence before the growls turned to more. His war hounds would tear them apart long before they reached his doorstep if he didn't control them. They brought their mounts to a stop in front of the waiting legend. The boy spoke first.

"I am Wynn," he said. "I bring words of Mydame from Spark City."

Of course you are, and of course you do.

Alphalines or not, dropping and speaking at eye level was the polite way to discuss things. Perhaps pulling the ponytailed fuker from the saddle would teach him a lesson, thought Magnus, but instead of violence, he twisted his blade in the little stones some more. They looked a young couple. Probably culled only a year or two. Perhaps making an example of the young man would be unnecessarily cruel. Then again, there were times to educate. Wynn looked like a man needing educating. The girl, less so.

Wynn slid from his horse and took to one knee in the same motion, like a man suddenly remembering his place in the world. The hounds surrounded him immediately and began their customary great smelling. Committing his scent to memory. To know him as a friend, or how to hunt him down should Magnus decide.

Magnus just spun his blade in the dirt. "That's better," he muttered after a time.

Idiot, Wynn chided himself. A simple mistake was enough to lose the great man's respect. Magnus was a great man in Wynn's eyes. Once again, he'd allowed stupidity to impede intention.

Behind the insulted legend appeared another legend. She carried herself with grace, beauty and fierce power despite her small frame. Wynn recognised Erroh's features in both parents. Magnus's nose. Elise's jawline. Both intense in every movement. Like old gods in tales, they were more than simple humans. They'd come to the right place; would they be welcome? The stronghold's lands were vast. Fitting for a king. Even a king who denied his rightful throne. Around the large whitewashed mansion were fields of grain, gardens of growing vegetables, all separated by neatly manicured lines of evergreen trees. It was a small wonder Magnus rarely left this haven.

"Guests from the city? And here you are making them kneel in the dirt?" Elise said gently, and Wynn wondered if the blade's tip might blunt under such abuse.

"I'm Lillium," Wynn's mate said from atop the massive horse. She did not bow. Elise bowed for her.

"Another fine northern girl, I see," she said, as Magnus pulled Wynn to his feet before shaking his hand painfully.

This is going splendidly. They'd spent many weeks travelling east, and with every settlement they'd passed through he'd grown used to the admiration their presence demanded. It was a strange thing to feel their every movement and words scrutinised now.

Magnus released his grip. "Wynn… Wynn… Why do I recognise that name?"

"I am line of Marvell and Lyanne."

Magnus must have thought this wonderful news. "Marvell of Colo?" he cried, and Wynn's face lit up at the mention. He tried and likely failed to disguise the pride he felt. It was known his father told many tales, most of which barely touched upon truth and every one of them for his own entertainment. Marvell proudly claimed to any who would listen that he had the beating of Magnus; he also claimed to have saved Magnus's life three times in one day. He proclaimed to have inspired the weapon known as the Clieve, and one drunken night after the first season's festival, he'd claimed to a tavern of fellow drunkards that he'd been there on the day when the king of the south fell. Admittedly, he'd later denied such a statement, when sobriety reared its unwelcome head. *Who wanted to be known as a king-killer in the chronicles of time, anyway?* Wynn's mother had suggested that his father was merely a charming storyteller, skilled at engaging his audiences. Wynn had argued differently; he thought the man a liar, even if he loved the lying bastard.

"Last I heard, the man met a wild girl and had a little cub. Truth be told, I didn't believe it until now. Tell me, is he well?" Magnus asked.

"He is well."

"Still telling stories?"

"Still telling stories."

"It's been too long since we spoke. Time has no interest in distant friends," Magnus said, and strangely enough, placed his hand upon Wynn's shoulder. Wynn could only nod in agreement, having little idea as to the influence of time upon friendships. He thought Magnus's hand was very heavy, and for a moment he wondered if some of

Marvell's tales held more truth than he'd believed. Perhaps there was some truth to his mother's suggestion that Marvell's scars cut deeper than his ruined body, that he hid the pain in jests and tales instead of thinking quietly on them. Wynn had assumed him to be lying when he'd spoke of his close friendship with the great man before him.

"There are whispers of troubling things," Wynn said.

Magnus thought it a pleasant surprise to meet his oldest friend's impressive-looking cub, but Wynn's presence here swiftly took the smile from his face again. Every few months Dia would have her finest shimmering messengers appear at his gates with pressing word from Samara. Aye, it was his right to learn of city things, but more often than not it was to remind him who controlled the world. This arrangement was of his own making, if he was honest with himself. Seeing Wynn stirred memories, as was inclined to happen with the old. When the war of the Four Factions had ended and only the wild King Magnus remained, relinquishing his entitlements and delivering to Dia the entire world was the right move, and he had done it willingly. After that, he had done his own part to ensure peace would endure. A younger Magnus might have thought differently, but he'd felt old even twenty years ago; two wars fought were enough for anyone. Ruling a second kingdom was equally unwelcome. Royalty had their time, did little with it. These last few years Dia had shown less fear for the warmonger than she should have. Perhaps it was old age swaying her better judgement. He felt the pain return to his fingers. *Growing old is a terrible thing.*

Lillium slid painfully from her mount. She had not yet adapted to life in the saddle, and she was reminded of that now. Elise embraced her as any sister of the city would, and Lillium accepted but offered no warmth in return. Why should she? This was not her land; these were not her people. She doubted she could ever feel comfortable in these lands. *These serene, peaceful lands.* Meeting Magnus had confirmed her suspicion that their great mission was a fool's errand. Though she should have felt relief, she felt fresh frustration. She hid it in a clenched jaw. So many miles travelled with her mate. *For life.* Her stomach turned, as it normally did. *What a waste.* Any fool would see that the legend had little intention of marching and slaughtering innocents. There had been no sign of brutality on their entire journey east. No stories in the wind, no terrified words from the road, and certainly no towns deserted.

Even this morning, as they passed through the small, wretched-looking army base, there had been no sign of warmongering. The Rangers had looked fit and ready to fight, but like their leader, they looked comfortable in this peaceful setting. Again, she thought of the wasted months. *No, not wasted.* Just months of her life gone to waste. She wondered if these two would offer them a bed for the night. She could do with time away from the saddle before turning right fuken around and returning home. *Home?* She had no home, she thought miserably. She looked to her chosen and wondered if he'd choose his words carefully or just come right out and accuse a legend of murder. Or perhaps, as he sometimes did with matters he considered important, he might show restraint, might show deference. She couldn't help notice the features in Magnus's face.

Like Erroh.

There was a flicker of excitement in her mate's face at this meeting, and for a moment she warmed to him. He'd been so nervous upon meeting his hero. She might have reassured him that Magnus would not take offence at Dia's questioning as they rode side by side these last few miles, but she hadn't bothered.

"There always are worrying things," Elise said, unexpectedly sliding her arm into Lillium's and drawing her away from her mount. "Come and speak of Samara as guests, young ones," she said, and despite herself, Lillium answered to the older woman's gentle insistence like a dog following the suggestion of a meal. There was power in this female's casual movement. Subtle allurement in her gentle words. "I have not spoken to a city girl in an eternity. I desire to know many things. We shall talk while the males hobble the mounts."

As before, Lillium was helpless to resist Elise's charms. She liked her immediately. A strange thing, as Lillium rarely liked anyone upon first meeting. *Apart from Wynn.* The older woman led her through the lavish manor doors, asking excitedly of Spark City things as though they were friends of decades gone and eager to know the latest drama among a close-knit group of squabbling friends. Lillium couldn't help but engage her, even if speaking of her home brought tears to her eyes.

Lillium soon found herself and Wynn sitting across from the two legends at a large kitchen table, all with steaming mugs of tea in their hands. Lillium wondered how long the hospitality would last, as Wynn had a habit of saying the wrong thing at the worst of times. He must have read her mind, for he set about ruining what little cheer there was now by being himself.

"I have questions... for you both," he said, addressing only Magnus, who seemed bemused.

"Does Mydame have a fresh issue with me... with us?" the great man said.

Aye, she fuken does.

Lillium sat in silence, sipping her bitter tea, listening to Wynn insult the legend at his own table. It started with obvious questions as to his wanderings, as to his potential marching, as to his thoughts on her leadership, and admittedly, Lillium found Magnus's disarming replies wonderfully charming. She could see his attractive face remain calm, obliging and overly understanding as Wynn's questions turned to suggestions of dissent emerging from the east, followed by a blatant insinuation that Magnus might know more of the slaughtered villages than he let on. The only sign of offence were the white knuckles in Magnus's clenched fist, and before she realised, she'd been staring at them a little too long, wondering how fiercely they could strike a man down. Were Erroh's as impressive? *Don't think about that.*

She knew Wynn despised himself for querying Magnus as he did; she knew Wynn believed every word the legend said, but the young idiot was painfully self-righteous and just bursting with delusional honour. Wynn would blindly follow the Primary, for he was a good little Alpha male.

And then matters worsened.

"Though it pains me to ask, I will need to see your journal, Magnus," Wynn said, when there were no more insulting enquiries to make. Elise had remained silent throughout the questioning, but at this she reached out and took Magnus's fist in her calming hands. Wynn was oblivious to the unease, because Wynn was oblivious to most things. "It's not that I don't trust you, sir. It's that I have a duty to enquire on such matters."

Magnus allowed the irritation to show on his face. He leant across the table and the room appeared to shrink around them. "It is never good to ask a man for such a thing."

"I do not enjoy this, sir."

Elise was equally unimpressed. There were fewer things more sacred to any higher-lined person than their journal. Aye, there were some, like Wynn, who rarely scribed thoughts and experiences within their pages, but to most, a journal was the closest thing their people had to scripture. It served them and kept them sane out on the road. It was their life; it was their experience; it was a reminder of how far they'd come; it was theirs and theirs alone. To seek entrance into something so personal was an insult at best; at worst, it was a call for blood. Wynn should have known better. Should have told Lillium his intentions of making such a request, too; Elise could see her dismay. Perhaps he'd wanted to avoid another heated argument. Perhaps it was a fine move on his part. That said, some things were worth arguments.

"You should not ask such a thing, little cub," Elise hissed.

"I will do what I must."

Lillium drained her tea. "Wynn... my mate, I think you should trust our hosts. There is no sign of murder in this place. There is no need to insult, nor to demand a sacred thing," she said quietly, and Wynn seemed to wilt at her words.

He faced Magnus while addressing her. "Regardless of how I feel, I have no choice. Mydame demanded I read these past few months' entries, and fuk it, but I will answer to her, as much as I hate to commit such an act."

Magnus shrugged. "It's a shame. I don't have a journal. Lost it. In a river a few years back."

Wynn recognised the lie for what it was. His eyes fell upon a tattered old journal lying guiltily at the side of the stove. "If you cannot provide me with what I desire, I shall ask for your mate's journal in its place."

If Magnus was displeased with this request, Elise's fury was tenfold. Her face turned from a serene pale to a tempest's red. "Oh, I don't think you should do that, little Wynn. I don't think you should do that at all," she warned, and the threat in her voice was terrifying. More terrifying than the prospect of returning to Dia having not exhausted all avenues of enquiry. *Poor, stupid Wynn.*

The table fell silent but for the act of Elise refilling Lillium's mug and then her own. She offered nothing to Wynn, and Lillium thoroughly enjoyed this.

After a time, during which Wynn's misguided sense of honour must have dissipated beneath his common sense, he straightened up in his chair and spoke. "Perhaps I should apologise. I should have been prepared to face the Primary before requesting such a thing."

Lillium narrowed her eyes, thinking him weak. Magnus must have thought so too. He stared through the younger male, and Lillium imagined the wrath of the legend upon the battlefield. *Taller than Erroh.* Elise coughed gently. It might have been a hint. Magnus spoke and the room appeared to shake.

"If I marched, the world would know my step. Be thankful that I owe your father my life. Be thankful I know him to be a good man, too. Be thankful I'm assuming the absent gods cut you from the same gullible cloth," he growled. "I understand you are doing the queen bitch's bidding, and I'd even admit we've all had to bend to her will at some point, young Wynn, but this is the east. This land is ruled by me." He eyed Elise; a silent moment passed, reserved for only them. "And me alone."

Wynn nodded. "Yes, sir. I appreciate that now, sir." *Anything you say, sir.* The blood had left Wynn's clean-shaven face, and Lillium thought again how much he'd been looking forward to meeting them. If it called for it, she would have sniggered. He dared not meet the eyes of either legend. Instead, he reached for his mug, but tragically discovered that somewhere along the way he'd drained its contents. After a painfully long inspection without reward, he placed the empty mug back on the table, and this made him appear pathetic. It was the highlight of Lillium's day.

Elise poured a fresh cup for him, and Lillium found her smile impossible to conceal.

"You can't possibly believe you'll get away with this lightly, though, do you?" Elise whispered seductively, and this was far scarier than veiled threats.

Magnus started to laugh again, a wonderful and terrifying noise that sent shivers down Lillium's spine.

———

Wynn was losing. That was an understatement. "Losing" gave the impression that he was in this contest. Nothing could be further from the truth. The old Ranger had given him the option of steel or wood. Steel and the drawing of blood would have ended the contest, and Magnus would have had his reparation. Wary that the cut might be too deep, Wynn had suggested the wooden sparring swords instead. He regretted that decision now. That, too, was an understatement. "Regret" didn't seem any way strong enough a word. "Lament" was far more fitting. He lamented that decision. It didn't make him feel any better, though.

Magnus hadn't even broken a sweat as his blade attacked from impossible angles, impossibly fast. Wynn parried and felt the blade clatter his senses, and he stumbled backwards. Another unexpected strike sent him into a full spill to the ground. He spat away a fresh mouthful of blood and sat for a moment in the middle of the sparring ring. There weren't very many signs of war in this peaceful stronghold other than this arena. Wynn had expected to discover a castle dedicated to the clashing of steel, decorated with fine trophies, all lorded over by an old man, ravaged by time and injury. What he'd got was Magnus. Older, but still a terrifying force.

"I yield," he gasped, holding out his hands in submission.

"No, you don't." Magnus wasn't finished; therefore, Wynn wasn't finished either. Wynn nodded dejectedly, climbed to his feet, and raised his blade. His arms were already bruised and he was certain at least one bone was broken. *I had this coming.*

Deserving or not, they'd fought for over an hour, and he'd never felt weariness as potent as this. Sweat streamed down his back and forehead, his eyes stung from kicked-up dust, and his chest felt as though every breath was drawn through a vice. A groan slipped from his lips and rose above the gentle whisper of the cool afternoon breeze, and he felt Lillium's gaze burning through him. He wouldn't face her, couldn't bear to see the smile on her face. *I had this coming.*

Magnus showed little fatigue, and it was disheartening. Though Wynn tried to counter and save what face he could, he could not adapt to the master's manoeuvres, no matter how hard he tried. Every strike was a killing blow. Or at least an attempt at a killing blow. Magnus favoured fierce power over tactics. Perhaps the Ranger didn't like to delay a fight longer than he needed to. Wynn did not understand why; he had the stamina of a god. *Absent or no.* They met again, and the great man battered Wynn to the ground for the tenth time at least. He gasped for air and Magnus leaned over him, bemused.

"You need to control your breathing, little cub. Take short breaths to recover; hold them when we strike." He spun around and bowed to Elise. "You are worse than my mate, worse than my son—dancing around, avoiding getting hit, countering where you can." Without warning he spun back, struck Wynn across the chin and left him dazed in the dirt. "Don't expect anyone to relent."

In this moment Wynn understood the ways of Magnus: this wasn't just a beating; this was testing. This was a lesson from a legend. With his mind reeling, he climbed to unsteady feet, watching a fresh stream of blood drip down from his mouth. Might have been his nose. Many places to bleed on a face.

"I enjoy dancing," Wynn muttered, before he could catch himself.

"You sound like my son. Let's go again." The older warrior charged forward and wooden blades clashed loudly as Wynn fought with all that he had, holding his breath, determined to earn a modicum of respect. Within a few defensive strikes, his blade was knocked clear before Magnus's forehead striking his cheek ended the fight and Wynn fell in ruin to the ground one last time.

"You aren't bad, but you lack guile. My son has guile if nothing else. Learn it," Magnus said, and Wynn couldn't rise. His head spun and his vision was dark.

"Thank you... sir?"

Magnus felt wonderful. He'd felt old before, but now he felt rejuvenated. He looked at the battered cub in the dust and felt guilty. Wynn was so much like his father it was like having the fool around. *Nice man, a little dim.* There were worse ways to be, he supposed.

Watching in silence no more, Elise grasped Lillium's arm in hers. *Sisters from the city.* "You both will stay as guests a while," she declared, and it was no question.

Magnus thought it a fine idea. Disturbing news of savage attacks was one thing, but for Dia to believe them his work was worrying. Something was in the air, and for a strange moment, Magnus wondered if the absent gods weren't at play with his destiny. Having two young Alphalines to call upon should they march was no small matter. Wynn was wild and unrefined, like a shard of diamond. There were ways to shape something tough into something striking. There was also something striking about the girl Wynn was mated with. He would have liked to challenge her in the sparring ring, but something in her eyes suggested violence would bring him nothing but misery. Elise had likely spotted it too, and as Magnus tended to the battered Wynn, Elise led her away.

"You look like you could do with a few days out of the saddle, Wynn, line of Marvell," Magnus said, his tone softer than before. Wynn almost smiled in reply, and Magnus wondered just what it would take to understand the obvious coldness between the couple. Perhaps in time he might speak of such matters. Magnus would not push; Magnus would wait.

————

Every room they passed was as lavish as the next. Each was decorated with art, silks and mirrors. There were lots of mirrors. Each room was glorious, with a king-size bed in the centre. All but the last. Elise suggested they stay here; it was the finest guestroom, and the farthest from her own, and to Lillium's eternal joy, two small beds sat against the walls on either side. Elise insisted it had "the finest view of the green countryside," and Lillium smiled gratefully as they spoke of finer things.

She even laughed when accepting the violent embrace from the older Alphaline, upon learning that her son had gained a mate.

13

COLOURFUL CONVERSATIONS, REMATCHES AND A DEAD GIRL

It was beautiful. It was ugly, brown and horribly wet. It probably had a terrible smell, but the muddy path was the purest vision of beauty either Alphaline had ever seen. The feel of the stable ground beneath their mounts must have been just as welcome. Their loud, echoing hooves were an elegant symphony to both riders after such a long journey either way. While the land showed signs of a warmer climate, there were still white layers along the higher slopes, in the evergreen trees, and on every hedgerow in between. Miles to go, but the path ahead was improving. They'd faced no storm since that great and terrible walk, and the sky remained clear. The change in temperature brought fresh game, and Lea now treated them to kills of pheasant or quail every night. For a precious few days, they believed the needless punishment was over, for now. Perhaps it was all in their imagination. Whatever it was, it was better.

Her maps had served them well. With the land becoming vaster and the deep mountain ranges disappearing into the horizon behind them, they moved with more freedom than ever. They travelled as they had a long time ago, holding hands, growing closer, before everything had gone wrong in a little dead town called Keri. They felt like the only people walking the Wastes, slowly falling in love all over again.

Though he was a lot better at it this time, Lea could not fully trust him yet.

Mud gave way to colour, and with every mile they drove their mounts, richer grassland appeared. Eventually, one innocuous afternoon, with a lazy sun warming their faces after the biting breeze, they passed the last slushy mound of snow and left it behind. They barely noticed the spectacle and didn't miss it, either. They followed the tributaries of the Great Mother, knowing well their beasts would carry them all the way to the city, eventually. Erroh behaved more like himself, taking the lead frequently, and she allowed him.

For every mile away from the southerners they travelled, Lea thought she'd feel better, but instead she became more restless in her thoughts, in her actions, in her absent words, and she couldn't understand why a growing anger overcame her any time they sparred. It was bitter, nasty, and it unsettled her. She could have spoken to him of this, but she didn't. They should have spoken of things, but they didn't. Erroh pushed his body to its limit every time they fought, and she matched him. More than that, she punished him. She was never satisfied until she'd drawn blood. The fresh welts and bruises she wore daily were a constant reminder that Erroh's fierceness was returning. His body had filled out impressively. The exercises he'd performed vigorously these past weeks were bearing delicious fruit upon his arms and chest. He was improving, but so was she. She saw things quicker now, particularly in battle. She saw each manoeuvre in her mind: the openings, the feints, the counters and the killing blows. The world slowed around her, and like him, she became incredible. She took the pain he delivered and delivered her own. She had once considered herself a fine swordswoman; now she considered herself one of the finest. She craved to become better. She craved to be the best.

They loved their life on the road. It was almost perfect. Almost, but not quite. And then, one afternoon in the rain, she realised exactly why.

It was still bitterly cold, but he desperately wanted to let the rain cover his body. He released the reins from his grip and held both his arms out in the air, taking it in. The mount continued walking, regardless. It knew its direction through the routine. The reins slipped silently to the ground and Erroh looked into the sky and closed his eyes. *Wonderful, freezing rain.* It never rained in the south. At least not in the places he'd visited. Rain felt like home. It also left a shimmer upon the land; the world was radiant in this downpour. He sat contentedly, enjoying this moment in the saddle, until she brought her entourage of beasts alongside his.

"Tell me all about that beautiful whore."

Erroh opened his eyes. He'd been expecting this. "Don't call her that. Her name was Nomi." He knew she had unanswered questions. Questions that wouldn't help either of them in the short term. Questions whose answers would make her stomach churn. Questions she'd probably feared would drag him back into his cage again. She needn't have worried. He would be honest, much to his own detriment.

"I need to know everything."

"Aye, you do, my love."

Lea knew what he'd said while under the fever's spell, but it was time to put matters to rest. It wasn't just anger that consumed her thoughts; it was her instincts. She was finding it difficult stopping herself from tearing his clothing free and taking what was hers. *My Erroh, nobody else's.* She was no delicate flower. She knew they loved each other. She was certain he had not taken the whore to bed. *Still, though.* She just needed to know his heart. She just needed to know the full truth. They needed to address the whore in the bedroom.

"It's a stupid name. Don't you think it's a stupid name?" she asked, and he smiled warily. Perhaps he thought it a pretty name. She wanted to hit him with a sparring sword. Just once, across the nose.

"I think it's a name."

"Why did you kiss her?" He did not smile. He appeared as though he'd returned to a life in chains for a moment, and she almost retreated, wary that he'd crumble, but leaving this meal unfinished would help neither of them.

"We've been through this."

"And I might need to hear it a thousand times before I'm satisfied," she said.

"She kissed me, and after all we'd been though, I allowed her."

"Did you like it?"

"Not at all. She was hideous," he snapped, then immediately realised his misstep. "I'm sorry. I shouldn't have said that."

She said nothing and watched him squirm, for that was what an angry female was inclined to do when her mate mis-stepped, when he needed to be made to understand what it felt like to have walked in her boots these past months. What endless torment it was wondering what their beo was doing with a "hideous" girl in a tent when no one was looking.

"I was lost, Lea, and it was nothing." His face was flushed. Was he lying? Was he embarrassed? Was he lovesick? Her stomach turned in knots. *Whore, whore, fuken whore. Like Dad with his whores.* "I'd fought her advances so long; it was nothing. I only loved you. I only love you."

Better, but nowhere near good enough.

"What does she mean to you?" Lea asked, and Erroh fell silent, as though he didn't know what she herself meant to him. As though the whore meant quite a lot to him.

"I owe her my life," Erroh muttered after a moment's pause. He'd been enjoying the rain and all. He wanted to kick the great beast forward and cease this talk of the other female. It hadn't taken a great deal to sour his mood. He'd been true to Lea even with the greatest temptation sitting beside him. Why speak of this again? What more did Lea need? He fought his annoyance. They hadn't argued in weeks. *Fuken females.*

"She held you captive. You owe her nothing!" Lea cried, and it was a good point.

"What could she have done?" he countered, delivering an equally good point.

"She could have set you free."

There was a great fight in the air. They probably needed it. He clenched his fists a few times and tried to control his temper. It was easier than he expected. He stared across at his perfect mate and he could see the hurt in her face. "I would have been dead within a day, and they would have killed her for the act," he said, and wondered what he might have thought were it him in her place.

"I would have kept you alive, Erroh. Besides, what matter is another dead southerner? ... Unless you care for her," suggested Lea, and Erroh knew the danger.

"She didn't know you were tracking us. She would have released me had she known." He reached across and took Lea's cold hand and kissed it gently, hoping to calm the tension between them.

"You idiot, Erroh. She would never have released you. She sacrificed nothing for you. She is a whore. Tell me, did the whore open her legs to you?"

"Don't call her a whore," he mumbled, kissing her hand a second time, then releasing it and kicking his horse forward. There was no safe way to continue speaking with her. Let her vent her frustrations; let her cool herself after. Let her do whatever she needed to do, really.

Lea wasn't finished, though he tried to flee. "Was she good?" she screamed, letting months of pain surface. *Fuk you, whore from the Hunt. I'll call you anything I want.* "Were you as protective of her honour when she offered you her body?" she cried out, and this release was incredible. *Fuk him, too.* She caught up to him and grabbed the reins. "Tell me what happened!" she demanded.

"I desired her, Lea. I thought her kind. I thought her beautiful!" he screamed right back at her. "But I never touched her, and she never offered me herself like that."

"Liar!"

"She accepted that I loved another." This shut Lea up for a moment. A short moment.

"Why do you dream of her?" she hissed, and Erroh's face dropped. In shame? In defeat? *In confusion?*

"I don't," he replied, more to himself.

"I know the whore's name. You speak it while sleeping." It was a half-truth, laid down like bait to learn more. He was confused, and she wondered if she had pushed too far.

He looked around and searched for the truth in her words and for words of his own to offer. "I'm sorry, my beo. Oh, I'm so, so sorry. I didn't realise."

He couldn't meet her eyes, and she could see the shame. *The perplexing shame.* Admittedly, he'd only spoken her name a few times in his sleep. He called out for Lea many more nights, but it was Uden's name he whispered, mostly.

Dreams. In the dreams, Erroh remembered pain and blood. Nomi's pain and blood, to be exact. He remembered the green eye of Uden. The dreams were never the same, but they involved her demise and *oh, it hurt something fierce.* He could have explained this to Lea, but he didn't have the words. He was indebted to Nomi; he always would be. *As indebted as he was to Lea?* Besides, there was something different to these dreams he'd dared not face in the light of day. Something he'd dared not think about; something he knew as truth. Brought out by his mate's accusations. Something deep within whispered that Nomi was dead. More than a whisper. It was a knowing, and his only proof was in a dream. How could he mourn a dream? How could he reveal his devastation at the girl's demise?

"She did everything imaginable to keep me alive. I owe her a life debt that I can never repay." He faced Lea. "You owe her a life debt, too, a debt that we are now arguing about in the rain, while she…" His voice faltered, then grew hard. "While she is dead upon an ashen pile or a vacant husk in the ground." He turned away again, gripped the reins and kicked the beasts forward. The muddy path was slippery, but the horses accepted the pace. He never looked to see if she followed. He didn't care. He wanted time to think of the little blonde barbarian lying somewhere in the ground, a thousand miles behind them. She would be forever cold.

Lea never followed. After a few hours he found a fine glade with a hot spring. Finally, a bit of luck after a miserable day. Their words burned in his mind, and he wanted to scream his own frustrations away. Why couldn't it be easier, he thought. This wouldn't be their last argument, and it probably wouldn't be the last about the dead girl, either. He released the mounts to graze in some damp, lush grass. Leaving his pack under a tall evergreen tree, he set a fire and stripped down to nothing. He slipped into the warm water beside the camp and began to wash the road from his body.

After a time, he heard the light thunder of her mounts. Watching the path, she walked the beasts to their rest spot for the night. She didn't look like she'd been crying. He supposed that was a good thing. Or else a terrible thing. She went through her own routine of setting camp. Releasing the beasts to graze, she set a large chunk of meat to cook across the little flame. Doing her best to avoid him, she prepared her bedding deliberately slowly. He didn't rush his bathing, either. She set her bed as far away from his own as she could without it seeming petty.

Hours alone had done her mind some good. She knew she had overstepped her bounds, but she would offer no apology. They were Alphalines; they could do nothing with measured restraint. It was limitless emotion, or it was nothing; it was their lineage; it was their way. Sometimes, when calmer heads should have prevailed, it was a curse.

He was right about the whore. *Fuk him, but he was right.* The loneliness, the cold, the fear brought such terrible anger. Born in the snow, it had grown every day and it wore her out. How easy to direct it all at Nomi, all nice and neat. To be unable to control her emotions was maddening. Life had dealt them a terrible hand, but a hand strong enough to continue playing. She was afraid to allow herself happiness lest the gods or the world itself turn on them again. Nomi had kept him alive, she told herself, and the anger stung anew. Was it really so terrible that Nomi had desired what couldn't be hers?

Was it really so terrible imagining Nomi as more than a brute from the south?

She smiled. Erroh was incredible and Nomi had wanted him. How could Lea hate her for that? *Because I fuken can.* She decided she could be angry; she just didn't need to show how much until she didn't really feel angry anymore. It was a plan, a simple one, and it made her feel better. She even smiled before shuffling over to where he bathed. She was patient; she would wait for him to speak. He didn't, so she tried another tactic. She picked up the heaviest rock she could find and threw it into the water right beside him. It was an effective way to instigate both action and conversation. The splash soaked her a little bit too. He waded over to her and stood waist high in the water, looking up at her.

"Are we fine?" she asked with her eyes.

He splashed her with the skill of a man who had splashed in rivers before. It was a fine splash. Impressive height, and the direction of the water ensured it collided satisfactorily with her body. They were growing as a couple.

"I'm sorry."

"I'm sorry too."

He reached for her and she hopped into the water beside him and kissed his lips. Their first kiss of desire in weeks. Their first kiss that suggested their urges had grown. In the gentle sway of the water, he pinned her against the bank and she allowed him. She wrapped her legs around his waist. Without words she willed him to proceed. She clawed at his naked back as he ripped her garments free. This pleased her greatly. He kissed her naked body and she moaned. Buoyed on by her pleasure, he lifted her in the water as passion overtook him. Staying afloat against the side of the river, she gripped nearby reeds and closed her eyes at his touch, and he touched her in many ways. She reached for his manhood and loved him.

She was incredible; her taste, her touch, her warmth, her everything. She embraced him and kissed him as only she could. He returned her

kisses, as only he could. The world stopped for them and only them.
Terrified and hesitant, they locked eyes and she allowed him closer.
More than that, she invited him to her. He held her in the sway, entered
her, and she moaned loudest at this. There was no war, no worry, no
fear of death. There was only the gentle pull of the river and the
swaying of their happiness as they found their rhythm. He believed
himself skilled at many things, such as facing armies and lighting fires.
Sometimes he could hold his drink and play a mean game of cards. He
wasn't certain he was skilled at this act, though. He wasn't even sure
she was skilled in the art, either. Not that this wasn't the finest moment
he'd ever experienced in his short life. He hoped she was enjoying it
too. She looked like she was, and she sounded like she was.

She really was.

He didn't know how long time stood still. Long enough that she cried
aloud as though stabbed and perhaps, wonderfully, she was. She
screamed in his ear and bit down hard upon him and he screamed with
his own passion as he spent himself inside her and it was glorious.
Finally. He held her as they panted for a wonderful few moments more
before he fell away from her and found himself weak in the knees.
They smiled, they kissed, they laughed, they adored and whispered
delicate words for each other and each other alone. So quietly that the
gods couldn't hear. The air was thick with the scorched remains of
their meal and he didn't care. In a shorter time than he thought
possible, the urge for a rematch was upon him and, climbing into the
cool night air and feeling terrific about himself, he assisted his lady
from the water. He led her to the covers of his bedding and she slipped
underneath to begin battle once again.

With his one for life asleep in his arms, Erroh smiled contentedly, for
he had no energy to do anything but. At first, their coupling had felt

ROBERT J POWER

like the most natural and beautiful thing, shared between soulmates; a perfect pair. However, their hunger and their animal instincts had soon taken over, pushing all gentleness aside. Desire and rage and lust and power. There had been a glorious violence to their furrowing, and he loved it. His body hurt, and they were both covered in bruises. He'd taken out all those many months of frustration and focused them on that one beautiful act. So had she. She had moved with him, like she always had before. Like she always would. He felt less burdened now. He felt free of the Hunt's clutches. Running his fingers through her hair, he closed his eyes and finally felt bonded to her forever.

14

EMIR'S GUIDE TO PEACEFUL RESOLUTIONS

I t was hate at first sight, and it grew to something worse.

"Get the fuk out of my fuken way, you fuken cow," Emir hissed to the redheaded bitch standing in his way. He'd never been smooth with females on his better days, but this afternoon he was spectacularly unpopular. He didn't care in the least. He had places to be, and a nasty piece of work wearing a stunning red dress was blocking those places. The dress matched her hair.

"Well, you can just fuk yourself, you ugly little worm," the fiery witch countered, standing firm. It was easy to be brave when two Black Guards with weapons drawn were standing behind you, he thought.

"I'm not ugly—you are," Emir spat, knowing how feeble his lie was. She must have known it too. She raised an eyebrow, and her smug disdain suited her. This wasn't the first time he'd approached the gates and received nasty threats. However, it would be the last time. As mayor of a fallen town, he had one last declaration to make before he relinquished his post. *Then I can die in peace.* He'd led the convoy to the Spark. He'd done her bidding. Weeks ago, granted, yet still, he could not allow himself to slip away into drunken insignificance. When they'd settled, when they could care for themselves, when they were safe, well, that was when his charge finished.

Upon their arrival, the gates had remained closed, and Wolves had swiftly escorted them away to a drearier place, with only the city's weak pledge of support as any form of reassurance. He'd believed the pledges of aid and all. He should have known better. He'd waited so very long, and nobody had braved the walk through the shantytown along the outer city walls nearest the Great Mother. It wasn't just the Keri survivors, either. There were over a thousand refugees tucked in, trying to survive in their despicable little shacks and tarps, taking what shelter they could from the blazing heat. They suffered in silence. *No more.* All desperate, all anguished; they were a new race of people. A new community of wretches that were dying out already. Nobody spoke for them, nobody gave a fuk, and today, after downing a half bottle of awful sine, he'd decided that they'd waited long enough. It wasn't simple goodness on his part. It was a desire to be free of responsibilities. Those he'd arrived with still looked to him for answers. It didn't seem to matter that he and Stefan were younger than most other adults there. *A drowning fool will grasp at a floating splinter.*

"And another thing," he roared, continuing his tirade upon the unimpressed gatekeeper. He stepped closer, each word giving him drunken courage, his worn feet kicking up an impressive cloud of dust in the dry heat. And she, well, she stepped forward herself to meet his aggression. He took a breath and she tried to counter, to cut him off, to state the same shit he'd heard a dozen times over, and he was having none of it; he shouted louder. It became a wonderful release of venom. He didn't know what he said, only that he criticised the city, the Primary and, strangely enough, his aching, bootless feet. At some point he felt a delicate tug from his second-in-command, but Emir would not relent. Instead, he began waving his fists in exasperation, and the two Wolves pointed their blades at him. In that moment, he wondered if he would be this day's whispered incident. *Nothing like a spike in the ribs to calm the masses, to send them scurrying from the gates.* These were violent times. Few would blink an eyelid in surprise. *Welcome to Spark City. The city of life and hope.*

It was a little girl, Linn, who had finally sent him over the edge, and she took this perfect moment to cough delicately from where she cowered behind Stefan. She was covered in grime and disease, hiding while the angry little man fought the black giants for her—how could any heart not melt? Linn's needs were greater than most, and Emir had taken it upon himself to intervene. She needed a few doses of a nasty green medicine and a stocked healer's bay in which to recover—no more of his ineffectual remedies, of gasping in her bed within the flea-bitten pit serving as his clinic.

"It's okay, little one," he muttered, calming himself before turning back on the redhead, hating her anew. Hating her matching dress as much. Hating how grand and stunning she was. As if anyone had the time to appear as impressive as she. "I'm just speaking with the nice lady with the keys, here."

Let me have some of that delicious city life, you witch!

Admittedly, Emir had it better than the others. He had a shack all to himself where he could sleep in relative privacy, which was a godsend in this wretched place. Aye, Lara still made her nightly visits, as there were no herbs to remedy a broken heart. *Or a broken soul.* He had lost Lara to misery, but this little girl might have a chance.

The two Wolves made to poke him a little, but the beautiful redhead dismissed them with a casual gesture.

"You think because you studied here, you can waltz right in?" She stood with impossible confidence, with her hands upon her shapely hips. Behind her, the cold grey intestines of the city and its endless possibilities mocked him, tantalising him. He *had* studied here. He *had* earned a little grace. Had he earned a right to return? *Yeah, bitch, I really have.*

"I imagine you are a man of influence in wherever it is you hail from," she went on. "However, you are not in your little village anymore, are you?" She took another step and towered over him. A fine act of dominance. He smelled her perfume. It smelled of riches and privilege.

"Why do you deny us dignity?" he muttered wretchedly. "Do you think I'm likely to steal enough bread and boar for the hovels' population? Do you believe me an assassin bent on taking out your precious Primary?"

Without warning, her face softened. He had little idea why, until the shame of a solitary tear slipping down his grubby cheek enlightened him. Why had she mentioned his home? Home was gone, like his friends. *Dead. Alone. Forever.*

"Talking gets a male much further in Samara," she said, sending her Wolves away to watch the gates for other refugees attempting similar argument. Turning back to him, her face still soft, she introduced herself as Roja.

He sensed a change in the wind. He introduced himself as cordially as he could and stated that he spoke for Keri. She said she knew the place. That was as pleasant as things got. She offered him an opportunity to state his case, so he begged for help; she countered that the city had little to offer. He demanded to speak to someone of greater importance who could help, and she appeared insulted at this request.

He said he spoke for hundreds.

She said she spoke for the entire city.

He conceded that as a fair point and offered his services for a few healing ointments, minimal supplies and free passage for himself and Stefan.

She said no, a little too swiftly.

He called her a bitch.

She leaned in, sniffed him and suggested that "smelly lowerlines" could offer very little to the city. Even if they were prodigious healers. He hadn't recalled mentioning just how good he was, and chose to take it as an insult.

It was at this humiliating moment that a petite Alphaline blonde appeared at the gate, attempting to get Roja's attention. The blonde then looked beyond Emir, smiled, and Stefan finally entered the conversation, albeit with an elaborate bow. To her detriment, the young woman appeared rather taken with him from the off. Smiling and batting her stunning eyelashes and silently he charmed her. Only Stefan could form an instant bond with a girl so swiftly.

Emir didn't believe Stefan had ever been a good man, but these past months, he seemed to have found a soul. He'd imagined Stefan would disappear into insignificance once they'd landed in Samara, but he'd never left Emir's side. Friends through adversity? Maybe so. The town looked to them for everything. *Absolutely everything.* Marching to the City of Light had broken most of them. The sight of the locked gates had destroyed the rest. Perhaps Stefan was broken like them. Perhaps Emir was too. Perhaps Stefan might charm the blonde and earn them entrance.

Go to task, my good man.

"I don't smell that bad," Emir muttered, turning back to Roja. He sniffed under his armpit and then drew back sharply. "Well, I can't do anything about the smell, but perhaps if you allowed me to enter, I could purchase soap," he offered. Alas, no matter how many times a man bathed in the Great Mother's raging water, the smell always lingered. Everything he owned reeked of sour milk and human waste. It clung to his clothing and to his skin beneath. There were moments when he woke up nursing the pains of a night's drinking and was reminded of the fetid destination his miserable life choices had led him to. He hated those moments. Roja could never understand the misery of his world. Of all their worlds. To her, he was a hindrance to her day.

Emir took hold of the child, Linn, and pulled her forward. She wasn't even from his own tribe. Apparently, there wasn't enough to be doing without caring for all the nomads outside Samara.

"How about I arrange for you to be given some soap? I feel that would be a service to the world," Roja growled. She was too close to him. Close enough to reach out and touch him. His screaming in her face so openly was a dangerous thing, though. Despite everything she felt, or had ever felt, she had spent far too long earning her reputation for him to berate her as he had. Inside the city, everyone knew the authority she commanded and the respect she demanded. In the city she was happiest. In the city she was Roja of the red. *Queen bitch.* She should have been above this task, but her grandmother had insisted she know the people's plight. Insisted Roja speak for her, utter the few helpful words that she could.

Truthfully, Dia's hands were tied, and therefore Roja's hands were tied. There wasn't the money anymore. They had spent it on the wages of a growing army that might never need to raise a weapon in anger. *A foolish yet needful gambit.* Any support they'd offered to the first few refugees couldn't be offered now. Truthfully, she understood Emir's frustrations, understood his wretched goodness, but it was a small matter. His unexpected shouting had shaken her. Worse, it had drawn the attention of a few other wretches camped nearest the gates. *Never good.* Perhaps his boldness buoyed them on; perhaps they simply desired entertainment. After all, there was little to do by the river but sit, be hungry, and cast blame. *Or go sit on a rock and be mysterious.* She could see the contempt in his eyes, and it bothered her. This bother made her angry. A Primary was supposed to be above caring. He said he spoke for hundreds, yet he carelessly proclaimed their faith in him as though it were nothing. She knew well where he came from; perhaps, then, when the supplies finally made their way here, she'd make sure that Keri was served last. She thought on this threat and held her tongue.

Threats are bad with witnesses around.

Threats aren't a great way to have first conversations, either.

He continued speaking, and she allowed him. "You think you are special because you furrow in silk, bathe in warm milk, and overly paint your face to look even more beautiful, but still, you are no different to any of us. You were just born with a golden platter at your lips. Walk a fuken day among us and you'd smell as bad as me, appear wretched like me – you might even learn the value of charity. Of humanity."

These last words were spat; the spittle took flight, and she wiped her face as though it would infect her. Eventually, he stopped speaking and she searched for composure. In truth, his sudden appearance had unsettled her. Perhaps, had she taken a moment to compose herself, she might have handled his outrage better. They might have spoken cordially. *That would have been nice.* But instead, he'd pissed her off.

"You are not welcome inside the Spark," she declared loudly, so all around would hear, and there were low murmurs of dissatisfaction from the crowd. They'd heard this speech before. Seen her stance. *Task done.* Some began to walk away. *Not quickly enough.* "Be glad the Black Guard don't move all you wretches from the walls." She leaned in closer to his unshaved face. "Take your child away before she spreads a plague throughout these walls," she whispered into his ear. These words were not for the crowd. They were personal and meant only for him. *And whatever whore you made the child with.*

He pushed her away. He shouldn't have pushed her, and certainly not so harshly. It wasn't a very gentlemanly thing to do. If questioned later, he would have admitted that he immediately regretted the action. That, and his accidentally brushing her right breast with his hand. In his defence, it was her powerful stance that had caused the travesty. Had she allowed herself to step back, he told himself, to succumb to the force of his shove, the unfortunate incident involving her chest, his hand and the ensuing punch might have been avoided altogether. Perhaps Emir's life might have been different had this event not taken place, but it did, and it was.

The world exploded as she whipped her fist out impossibly fast, and his vision went dark. His head shot back and he felt himself floating in the weightless morning air. He regained consciousness right as his body crashed to the ground. *Beaten up by a female.* He could hear the taunts already. He lay sprawled in the dry, dusty mud. Climbing unsteadily to his feet, he couldn't help noticing the amount of gravelly blood he spat from his lip. Not at her, though. Despite the ringing in his ears, he had just enough sense left to know that such an act would make things infinitely worse. He let the thick drool of crimson and light brown dust dribble down his vest. *I want to go home.*

"You broke my jaw," he slurred, and fresh blood spilled down his front. *Alone forever.* Female or not, he never ran from a fight. It had been a cheap shot on her part, though. There was little honour in cheap shots. His head spun. He saw three of her and went for the one closest.

"Leave him be," Stefan roared, drawing one of his blades from his scabbard and facing the two Black Guards as they charged Emir. His fearlessness impressed the blonde, who was watching from the gate, a subtle smile on her face. She stepped out, barking orders of her own. Orders that slowed the Guards' haste yet not their intent. They circled around Emir and Stefan, and the crowd cheered at the prospect of violence, at the prospect of rebellion, at the prospect of taking the city this very day, once they'd cleared the gates. They declared bravery, they shouted threats, they made no move to help at all, and Emir stumbled towards the redhead with violence on his dazed mind. He never made it. Quig caught him before he could strike out at her.

What the fuk is Quig doing here in the city?

Was Quig not dead?

Maybe Emir himself was dead? *Ooh, that makes most sense.* He wondered had some other Wolf snuck up behind him and gutted him, or had Roja killed him with a second devastating blow? He didn't want to die at the hands of a pretty girl. He wondered briefly if his lifeless body was now lying in the dried mud outside Samara's gates. Maybe he'd never made it to Spark at all. Maybe he'd died with his friends in Keri. That made the most sense. *Dying doesn't hurt.*

Maybe I'm dreaming this.

"Be still, or you'll get yourself killed," Quig hissed, holding him in a powerful grip, pulling him away from the beautiful, vengeful goddess. "Lads, we need not kill anyone today," he roared, and the Wolves begrudgingly withdrew their assault like bickering siblings answering to a disapproving father.

He doesn't sound like himself, Emir thought, and spat more blood from his mouth. After a moment, he realised his nose was seeping blood as well, and he wondered if she'd had time to recover a hammer from beneath her dress and struck him with it.

"We're all fine here, lads," the big man added, eyeing Stefan, and Emir began to notice subtle differences—the hair a slightly different shade, the beard a little wilder. *A killer's eyes.* They were not his friend's. His friend was still dead. He experienced tragedy all over again.

"That smelly little worm needs some time in chains," Roja hissed.

"Are you into that?" asked Emir, recovering some of his senses. The senses used for mocking. The important ones. Pulling away from the grip of the giant, Emir felt his jaw and wondered if it wasn't broken at all, but merely dislocated. Roja glided towards him, her threat clear. Before she could attack again, though, the big man stepped between them. His shadow loomed over her, but she was anything but intimidated.

"Just a mere misunderstanding between citizens of the city," hushed Wrek, holding out both his hands in the most neutral gesture he could muster. It was quite an effective technique he'd learned some time ago. "I'm sure we can all just calm ourselves and enjoy the morning." He stared at the warriors, who took this moment to retreat fully. *Never mess with the man holding the bottle of alcohol.* It wasn't worth the repercussions.

"Emir is no citizen of this city... not anymore," Roja countered, folding her arms, tapping her foot in the dirt and looking suitably petulant, so Wrek answered in kind. He sighed aloud, theatrically so. He shook his head in perfect frustration.

"Well, I think we could rectify that. I could use a man like this." He corrected himself immediately. "Two men, in fact." He smiled, daring her to argue. She too knew the value of his alcohol.

"You have no business here, Wrek," she challenged.

"Come on, Roja. This one is on me. Nobody needs banishment from certain establishments... I mean to say, nobody here needs banishment from the city," Wrek countered, and Roja diminished visibly.

· · ·

"The child needs healing," muttered Stefan, and Roja took the little girl's hand in hers. She did this with more gentleness than Emir had supposed she might.

"Fine," she said briskly. "I'll see to her, and you have your way with the wretches." Emir saw a flicker of warmth in her face when the orphaned girl looked into her blue eyes. That warmth vanished as she eyed Emir one last time, and he wondered might she be considering having him killed. He'd be wary of walking into dark alleys for the next while.

"Thank you, sir," Emir offered, watching the two impressive females lead the little girl Linn away. He shook Wrek's outstretched hand. His grip was fierce.

"So, you are Emir from Keri? I've heard your name whispered among the wretches. Good deeds are not always left unnoticed." He pulled Emir in close. "I know she's pretty, but attacking her is hardly a way to earn the heart of an Alphaline," he mocked gently.

"I had her right where I wanted. Charmed, she was," Emir muttered, releasing Wrek's hand and attempting and failing to stem the stream of blood with his sleeve. *Flowing too freely.* Perhaps he was drinking too much these days, he thought blearily, and pledged to redouble his efforts so there could be no doubt at all.

"I'll walk you both through the gates, boys, and I'll find you after you've registered with Seth. Use my name and it'll rush matters." Wrek's relaxed features now turned serious. "I'm vouching for you, so don't go around starting shit with anyone. You do that, I'll settle matters myself." With the terrifying threat delivered, his face warmed immediately. He led them through the gates and explained how he knew who Emir was, and that he'd been searching for someone these past few weeks to act as an ambassador between hovels and city.

As he spoke, Emir felt a deep, sinking sensation. He had little interest in becoming a voice for those outside the walls. He represented too many as it was; how could he speak for the entire collection of refugees? What could he say?

"What would it be worth to us?" Stefan asked.

The dense crowds separated around the trio as they walked, and

Emir couldn't help noticing how people stared at the big man. *Who is he?*

"Free travel between the gates isn't enough?" Wrek asked.

"We need to home a couple of hundred people," Emir said, looking around disbelievingly at the inner parts of the city. Since he'd last been here, it had changed a great deal—and not for the better, either. Was it just the threat of war? he wondered. It had always appeared eternal before, but now, it felt older, as though invisible cracks had appeared and diminished it, though not on the surface. He'd remembered it being alive, but now it had little vibrancy. The people looked as miserable as those in the shantytown; there was uneasiness in the air, a whiff of danger, and there were far more guards in black than were strictly needed. Perhaps it had always been like this? Perhaps youth remembered only so many things. Perhaps he had a concussion?

"A couple of hundred? I can work wonders, but even that is beyond my reach."

Stefan tugged Emir's shoulder and, looking around carefully to avoid the notice of any onlookers, pulled the second blade from his scabbard. He did it slowly.

"Will this help, friend?" He handed the broken blade across to Wrek. It wasn't even a proper sword. It was half a sword. Shattered in two along its shaft. The pommel was pretty, but they had tempered the blade with no skill or love. The unnatural black finish summed up its value. Or lack of. It was a very weak piece to barter with. "Scratch the blade."

Wrek did, and discovered the golden glimmer underneath. In this economy, this blade was almost priceless to the right buyer. "A fine bartering tool in desperate times. I might even have a buyer. However, let's keep this a secret for now," Wrek suggested, testing the weight of the golden piece. "Clever concealing. I knew I'd found the right men," he added, handing the magnificent blade back to Stefan, who swiftly hid it back in its scabbard. "Trust me, this will work out spectacularly."

It really wouldn't.

15

2827

Wynn opened his eyes and regretted it immediately. Blinking a
few times, he ventured some head movement. Nothing
special—a tilt to the right, a little to the left. It was sunny; he could tell
because it burned his eyes. He closed them again tightly before braving
a glance to the occupied bed across from him. Her long hair hung
down the side, drooping lifelessly just above the floor. Each slow
breath she took made the little fading blue strands quiver slightly. Most
of her hair was brown now; only the tips alluded to the vibrant blue
goddess she had once been. A lifetime ago now, it would seem, when
they first met. When he had first fallen in love with her and she
with him.

"Are you awake, Lillium?"

Nothing.

It felt impossibly early. Noon? No. Closer to dawn. It had been well
after midnight when he'd burst through the doors and declared himself
the "Great Warrior Wynn" to his slumbering mate, hoping to earn a
reaction. *Any reaction.* He'd thought unexpected levity might be the
way forward. He'd planned to share what was left of his bottle of wine
with her. She might have joined him, and they could have spoken about
things. About opportunity and destiny. He had called to her a few

times, and when no reply came, he had settled down to drink alone in the bed opposite. He didn't remember finishing the bottle or letting it drop from his grasp to the carpet below. *Another opportunity lost.* He'd hoped a little drunken courage would help; as per usual, it hadn't. Since they'd arrived in this haven, she had slept more than usual. *She likes it here.* That was reason enough to stay here, he supposed. Liking something was a good look to her. They were on speaking terms, which was nice, but they had mastered the art of indifference to each other's needs these last few months. If their hosts realised this, they said nothing on the matter.

"It's time to get up."

Silence.

"I'm sorry if I disturbed you last night," he whispered, and still she did not stir. *Why should she?* Admittedly, he'd had better ideas in his life than trying to keep up with the pace of Magnus, but there was reason to celebrate. *Have I even decided yet?* He rolled himself out of bed, stretching what pain he could from his aching limbs, neck, and everywhere else, and discovered his head had begun to thud. He drained the goblet of water by his bed.

Did Lillium leave this?

He knelt down beside her, kissing her on the cheek. She stirred, winced, then rolled over and lost herself in a nest of silk and satin sheets. *I love you so much. I just don't have a fuken clue what you need.* He could have sought advice from Magnus and Elise last night, but the mood had been light, the cheer as intoxicating as the evil beverages they raced each other to drink.

You didn't give Magnus an answer either?

"Magnus has offered me a seat at his side," he whispered, and she made no move. He decided it was just exhaustion after so many months travelling. "At his war table."

It was an unlikely honour and thoroughly undeserved. He would be the only Alphaline in their corps. Magnus had said that several times; he'd said it would be a fine life. Even if Lillium left him. *When* she left him.

Wynn sighed and considered stealing her goblet of water. She wouldn't need it as much as he. Just a mouthful to take the headache's edge off. It had been over a week since they'd last lain beside each other in his smaller cot. Yes, she'd kissed him when his lips touched hers; yes, she'd allowed him to enjoy her gifts, but she had never writhed in ecstasy as he'd believed she would. *Ever.* Instead, she had simply lain there, staring up at him as he thrust himself inside her, looking into his eyes, into his soul. Never blinking. Was this act not his right as her mate? He had needs; had she none of her own? She'd been the first to initiate their furrowing out in the road. She'd been the first to remove her garments, her fingers quick and eager. He thought her incredible. Beautiful. *Uninhibited?* And now he thought her cold. He reached across and downed the water. She would unlikely suffer the same headache as he.

As usual, Magnus was already downstairs when Wynn entered, wiping his mouth and craving more water. After being force-fed some salted meat and eggs, Wynn followed Magnus out into the morning's burn, allowing the sleeping females the comforts of emerging dishevelled from their beauty sleep at their leisure. This had become part of their routine these past few weeks. At first, Wynn had been unsure why Magnus was treating him to a Ranger's life. Now he understood, as he warmed to the calling of a lifetime of servitude. Besides, a legend could only lead a legendary army for so long.

They rode down towards the army camp. The echo of their hooves upon the pebbled path was relaxing to his ear. The excited hounds bounded along below. Only Magnus could find a balance between semi-retirement and warfare, all within a mile of each other, Wynn thought.

Magnus's Rangers were a different breed of men and women altogether. Not Alpha, but more accomplished than most other traditional combatants. They were no mere army and would not fight like any mere army. They were not faceless units moving across the game of battle, led by faceless leaders who believed holding ground was more important than seeking victory. They numbered only three hundred in total but could defeat any army ten times their size. Magnus respected each warrior and knew each by name. Though most had never known a war, when needed, they would fight spectacularly. They would know victory. One could not simply walk into the ranks of the Rangers, either. It was said that the trials and testing were fierce.

Magnus had offered Wynn a life in the corps and felt cautiously optimistic about it. Perhaps with harsher training and a little character growth, Wynn might become the protégé he'd hoped would succeed him. Battering him around as he had once done with Erroh made him feel younger every day. *Nothing like broken bones to get the juices flowing.* Aye, it had always been Magnus's hope for Erroh to lead the line, but as much as he desired a son following in his footsteps, he also wanted a peaceful life for him. He wanted peace, but he felt something brewing.

Watching Wynn in action reminded him of Erroh's wildness, his carelessness. In many ways, Erroh resembled Magnus, but he was also like his mother; he had her daring, especially. But did he have her ability to slip out of everything thrown his way when that daring threw him into impossible things? He really hoped so. Elise insisted that Erroh would surpass them both, and Magnus had his worries. Well over two years without a word of accomplishment, apart from losing three bouts to Alphalines in the city. Magnus wanted to be wrong about Erroh more than he wanted to be wrong about the unsettling feeling he had. *You always have a feeling.* Aye, that was true too, but mostly his feelings proved to have merit. Mostly.

Perhaps Erroh needed the opportunity to discover greatness. He'd lived a brutal, sheltered life. All violent play, never for real. On the other gnarled hand, Magnus's youth had been nothing but treacherous violence. He'd never wanted to be a legend, earn a crown, dominate the world. He'd picked up a blade and a few years later had put it back down with nobody left alive to challenge him. Admittedly, Erroh was the finest swordsman he'd ever seen. At least for one so young. He missed his son more than he could ever admit. Few people challenged, argued and bested him as Erroh did. The day they faced each other with sharpened blades would be the true test of the measure of them both. They would clash and the ground would shake underfoot. All masters and apprentices clashed, eventually. Just to know for certain. It was the way of their kind. That day would not be soon.

Magnus dropped from his horse and surveyed the sky. The clouds looked darker on the horizon. Maybe there would be a wind and a barn's roof needing repair. Alluring young ladies to bow courteously to afterwards, perhaps? Wynn dismounted and followed. Around them, Magnus's hounds charged through the line of tents in search of kindness and scraps, their excitable barking alerting the waking army that the Master General had arrived. Each Ranger he met, he greeted with idle chat. They warmed to Wynn, however, as a quail would to an Alphaline's arrow tip. They would struggle to answer his orders, but it would be a swift struggle once Magnus intervened.

That said, Magnus believed it best for Wynn to earn their respect himself. It might be good for all involved. Theirs had been a life of heavy lifting and marching. Wynn's life was one of study and entitlements. Besides, there was always the honour of challenging for his position. Magnus didn't fancy any challenger's chances, though a battle would be good for morale. He looked at the clouds passing over the horizon again. Were they throwing off his mood? Something itched in his mind, gnawed restlessly through his paranoia. He spat in the dirt and muttered a curse under his breath and caught sight of a distant rider nearing. More bad news of bandits, he thought, but his uneasiness spread. *Something is stirring; that's why you want Wynn beside you. That's why you want to open the safe.*

"The more Alphalines, the better," he whispered to himself.

"Sorry, Magnus?"

"Nothing, Wynn. Just thinking aloud."

Beyond the tents, they passed the straw archers' targets and stepped through the tall inner gates. A whitewashed wall enclosed the camp's centre, where a few sparring circles were marked out in the ground. There were weapons everywhere. Most hung from wooden stands beside the massive furnace that had given them life. Even in times of peace it remained prepared and well stocked. This was a warmonger's camp; Wynn felt at peace here.

The Master General's quarters were the only fully constructed building in the massive compound. It was built of solid stone with a finely crafted oak door; the door always remained locked. Magnus's treasures were hidden deep inside. *Good to be the king.* Magnus unlocked three heavy-sounding locks and gestured to Wynn to follow.

"So, tell me, did you speak with Lillium as you pledged you would?"

Wynn shook his head and could see the disappointment on his new master's face. That look suggested he should talk with her soon. *To face her.*

The old Ranger ducked his head under the doorway as he stepped into his quarters. He was a simple man in warfare. The room smelled of sober age. Of steel varnish, heavy mustiness, and polished leather. In the room's centre stood a circular table with ornate carvings along each leg. Its elegant surface held a plethora of hand-drawn maps, some torn, and some marred by age and bloodstains. Some as old as the age the world found itself in. None from before this age, however. Others were recent scribblings, discovered on the bodies of hunted bandits only a year past, each one as inaccurate as the next. Magnus would readily admit that knowing the exact geography of the world was an obsession. Without a great ladder to climb high into the sky, it was near impossible to get a truly accurate picture of the land and their place in it, but by looking to the larger maps pinned to each wall, a man could at least discern more than he could by simply riding or by staring down from the hilltops. Nowhere near good enough in the legend's eyes, of course. A man could go mad staring at maps attempting to earn true sight, Wynn thought. Magnus had a greater idea of the world's shape than any other living being, but Wynn knew the man thirsted to know yet more.

Standing in the corner was an old steel safe with a strange, numbered dial in its centre, and Wynn imagined it could take a man a decade to break through, at the cost of a thousand sharpened blades. Along the walls, between each pinned map, hung little burned-out candles upon brass holders. Behind them deep marks, scorched into the walls, suggested just how many years Magnus's war council had met in this place. Wynn thought it incredible that they had formulated plans to conquer the entire world within these hallowed, draughty walls. There was an unusual energy to this darkened room.

Marvel, his father, had stood here too in years past, and lately Wynn's turn had come. Though he hadn't understood why at the time, he had attended a few meetings with some older Ranger generals. All had tasted war in the Four Factions conflicts; all had been unwilling to retire to a peaceful life, too wary yet to commit to earning a living upon the land—land that was rich, fertile and gifted to them by Magnus himself. Though they appeared haggard and weary, their knowledge was vast, and Wynn had listened intently as, in voices barely above whispers, they discussed matters of a brutal army marching toward the north.

However, each meeting had resulted in a similar stalemate. With no solid intelligence to call upon, there was little action to take beyond waiting for more news or, worryingly, for another terrible event to occur in the Wastes. Though neither general said it, the men knew something was amiss.

Wynn's first lesson was learning the act of patience, and he thought it a fine skill. Instead of adding frustration, they focused on recent trivial eastern matters, such as bandits' wanderings, or flooding threats. This was how it was done, according to Magnus. From the grandness of war, to petty roving thieves, or offering aid for desolate farmers, the council exchanged words, arguments, and suggestions before deciding what various plans of action might be taken. Magnus listened as a man among equals and welcomed all voices. He alone decided what action to take. They wasted no time after and went to task immediately. It was efficient, effective, and Wynn desired to be part of this world.

Now, he watched the older Alpha kneel in front of the impenetrable safe, grunting with the effort as he did.

.   .   .

"So, what do you think? Will you be enlisting, Wynn?" Magnus growled, more to the safe and its combination. More to himself for forgetting it. There was a three in there somewhere. He was certain a three was in there. And a seven. Was it a seven? He liked seven. Seven was a trustworthy number.

"Aye, sir," Wynn said, turning away from the safe, and Magnus thought this to be fine manners. He himself would have looked. Knowledge was worth rudeness. Knowledge was worth everything.

"Speak with Lillium about it today." It was the first order given. That would be Wynn's life. It would be a fine life.

"Sir, why offer me such a high position?" Wynn asked.

Magnus shrugged, thinking on the combination. "I feel a march coming. Better to have an Alphaline leading the line with Elise and me."

"Surely I'm not the first Alphaline to tread this path," Wynn countered.

"Does it matter?"

"Aye, sir. To me it does."

"I'm wary of the Primary and her withering mind. I'm worried about things I don't know. You don't live the life I've lived without questioning everything. Something is happening, young Wynn, something dreadfully unsettling. Go talk to Lillium and tell her of my generous offer. Make her believe it is an offer that you will both accept. Truth of the matter, it doesn't really matter if you accept or not. You are a Ranger now, regardless."

"And why is that, sir?" Wynn asked carefully, and Magnus almost smiled despite his darkening mood.

"Because I own you." The room fell still as he continued working with the dial. Click, click, pop, nothing. Within, he kept the treaty. The Primary's reluctant signature. *Has she forgotten?* Click... click... nothing. Elise had the code hidden away somewhere. He hoped he wouldn't have to ride back home and get it. There was no three, but there were three numbers. Was that it? he wondered.

"How do you own me, sir? No man owns me."

This was not the first time an Alphaline had learned the hold

Magnus had upon them all. He enjoyed watching them struggle with his words and learn of their divided allegiance: Answer to the Primary in all matters, but come war, they would be loyal to the Master General.

"Fine words, Wynn. It isn't as bad as it appears."

Magnus knew the dangers of any Primary with an army of Alphalines gathering behind the city walls. No individual deserved that power. He'd seen what complete authority wrought upon any individual. He would have included himself. Choosing to step away was the smarter part; ensuring his dominance, even in silence, was possibly his finest tactical manoeuvre. Click... click... pop... creak. *Perfect.* To the world, it appeared that he'd formed an army to protect himself if needed. But the world didn't know he had the power to conscript every Alphaline old enough to wield a sword into his Rangers. *Now that was a fuken army.*

"I don't understand, sir," Wynn said, taking the ledger of records Magnus kept on hand. Strange that Dia still sent accurate records on demand. Perhaps she knew exactly what might send him marching towards the city gates.

A fierce hammering at the door disturbed them both.

"Sir, I have an emergency dispatch from the city," announced a young warrior from outside, and Wynn granted him entrance. His hands shook as he passed the sealed message from the Primary directly into the hands of Magnus.

There was a deathly long silence as Magnus read the text. From outside, Wynn listened to the stirrings of a hundred warriors rousing themselves from sleep. His head still thumped painfully and his stomach was close to unsettling him, but he remained motionless. Wynn's mind reeled from the cryptic declaration and the reasoning. He had questions, many questions, all the questions. He held his tongue, however, when Magnus folded the piece of paper into a pocket in his cloak and took a long breath.

"The world is about to change." His voice was strange; heavy, melancholic, fierce and vengeful.

"Sir?"

"Prepare the Rangers for a march to Spark City," he growled, lost in deep thought. "They depart tonight."

"Sir, what about the council?" Wynn gasped, as Magnus thundered past him.

"This course of action is the only recourse; besides, I don't give a fuk for delay." Magnus was deathly pale, as though someone had drained the blood from his body. *Pale like Elise.* Without warning, he stumbled against the doorway as though struck unawares in the stomach, and the room appeared to shake under his great weight, but he did not fall. Instead, he took a breath and punched the wall supporting him before recovering his balance.

"The threat is very much real. It's from the south." He clenched his fist. "Mydame has ordered me into war... As though... as though I could stay here."

"What has happened, sir?" Wynn asked fearfully.

"They have declared Erroh to be a coward."

Oh fuk.

"He stood with a group of farmers and tried to hold a southern charge. She said he fled from battle but was captured while everyone else stood firm to the end." He took a few more breaths. "She said he allowed his mate to be burned to death."

The two Rangers climbed atop their mounts and rode back towards their soon-to-be broken-hearted mates. Behind them, an entire army began the swift process of packing up and preparing for a great and final march at a moment's notice. A march that would gain momentum as they traversed the Wastes at terrific speed, growing in size as each absent Ranger discovered their intentions. They addressed each task with competence, as if they'd prepared these last twenty years.

16

HAVEN

S he sipped the black cofe. Her third already, and it was just after dawn. Roja didn't know what she'd do without the beverage. She'd be a right nasty bitch, she supposed. Close to scalding was best. An aged, cooling brew was a terrible thing. It needed to be fresh and perfect. She took her cofe addiction seriously because… well, because she hadn't much else. Her grandmother was exactly the same. In this shitty, painful world, one had to control at least one thing.

She sipped the full-bodied potion and reclined in her seat. The aged leather creaked under her weight and she found this oddly comforting. Mydame was a little late this morning. Dealing with economic matters again, no doubt. Worrying about the city economy would kill her grandmother. Better that than a vengeful assassin with a grudge, she supposed. Or else a brute's arrow from a thousand feet against the wind. Or else burning with the city as the southerners reached their gates. *Or else. Or else. Or else.* Or else Magnus, once he learned the truth of his son's actions. *Got him marching swiftly, though, didn't it?* She knew it had. It was a clever enough manipulation of the truth for it not to be a complete fabrication. It didn't make it right, though, did it? Dia always suggested Roja's faith in the nobility of people was misplaced. Perhaps she was right. Magnus might have behaved differently had they not compelled him to honour his son's shame. Some matters couldn't be left to chance. Roja inhaled the cofe steam and forced these thoughts from her mind. She needed her wits about her; she needed to be strong.

"Come on, Roja," she whispered to the old room. She'd never really liked this room. It wasn't the room's fault. It was dimly lit and it smelled of carbolic soap and crushed lavender. Pleasant things normally, but when she sat alone it suffocated her. This would be her red-carpeted office, eventually. Her cage. *When Dia passes into darkness.*

"Get your thoughts together," she snapped, pouring a mouthful of black fire down her throat, its sting quieting the panic in her mind. She squinted her blue eyes, reading one of the many scrolls of historic scripture decorating the black wood panelling around her. Her grandmother adored words from the past and kept them near. Most collectors did. How far might the world have come if people shared their knowledge? When she became Primary, she would donate each piece to the city's tiny library. Each forgotten note deserved to captivate others as they had her. Words written by the dead, centuries ago. Cataclysms ago. All dead. *Leaving us behind, unprepared.* Desperate words penned as the night closed in, now just decoration.

She sipped another mouthful and thought about the great metal machines. Something about mechanisms always soothed her. She had a strange affinity for their workings and often spent longer than needed down near the great turbines of the city. She always had. The constant loud humming silenced her thoughts. She hadn't visited the machines recently because of the wretches. It wasn't the thing the world's future leader should be doing. She almost smiled at her complaints. People were dying and she was recoiling from her privileged life.

At least I'm not as alone. She thought of Linn and fretted more. Bending ancient law was proving more difficult than she'd assumed. A few sisters whispered about her intentions for the little one. Would she have behaved any differently? Rules were rules, but if Roja couldn't bend them to serve her needs, what was the point in holding power?

Shitty bloodline, shitty destiny.

"Fuk all of this," she spat, wondering how she would make it through the day ahead. It wasn't even a special day. It was just another day in the city, and as much as she disliked this room, she felt safer here than in her chambers. Within this cage she could weep with her grandmother without ridicule; without showing weakness. It was a haven from her persona. A place she could shed the "queen bitch of the city" skin. Every day seemed harder than the last. Things that had merely bothered her before now crushed her spirit. She could feel the people's open hatred every time she walked the city streets, hear thinly veiled jests whispered under breath as she passed. She'd seen the crude remarks scribbled along back walls in side streets. Only a couple of nights before, she'd entered a tavern to hear the last verse in a rather suggestive song performed by a worryingly skilled group of troubadours. They'd had the good sense to muddle a few of the more sordid details and they'd changed the names, but the sentiment was there. The embarrassment too.

Worst of it was that they were fair criticisms. There wasn't a single meeting where Dia and Roja didn't squeeze a few pieces from the shattering budget into assisting the wretches. She could have shared these thoughts with Silvia, but the girl couldn't keep a secret at the best of times. Still, all best friends had their foibles. She was her only friend, really. And growing up, Silvia had matched her lack of inhibitions; their days together had been full of silly, salacious, mostly harmless fun. Roja sighed into the silence; she knew those times had passed in the wind. She was getting old herself, despite her few seasons. Now she needed to behave like a Primary in waiting. It was her duty. *Grey, glowing walls surrounding.*

But what was the point of griping? Ask any person wandering the streets, or the wretches beyond, and they'd snap up the opportunity Roja would inherit. Some even worked for such an opportunity. Sigi came to mind, as well as his lesser partner, Wrek, for whom she had a grudging fondness.

Fuken Wrek and his ideas.

The colossal bouncer wasn't the same animal she'd first encountered when they took over the inn many months before. It was only a slight betrayal to her grandmother drinking in their establishments regularly, but a girl needed her vices; the atmosphere was forgiving and their sine was incredible. It was little surprise they'd risen to glory so quickly. Some said they were the lifeblood of Samara these days. Let them own the city, for all she cared. She'd had a few clashes with Wrek, admittedly, but then again, she'd clashed with quite a few people since Dia had stepped from the public eye. Hidden away, leaving Roja to face the uproar.

The behemoth wasn't above a fine idea now and again, and his suggestion about easing tensions between the city and the hovels was compelling. She only had to endure another few meaningless meetings in chambers. Chamber meetings were below Dia, but Roja would do the needful.

She heard the handle turn, and the Primary glided into the room as though she were half her age. A vision of Roja in fifty years, even if they shared no blood.

Dia brushed her wrinkled fingers through the hair of her granddaughter as she passed her. Such incredible hair. *Like her mother's.* The red hair sometimes reminded her of the southern massacre; it struck her anew and almost took her strength. In this room she could show emotion; to her granddaughter, she could be a caring old woman with a bad knee. *Old before her time.* She almost leant across and hugged the beautiful young Alpha, but instead she settled upon a world-weary smile, taking her beverage before sitting down opposite her most trusted companion.

Roja took on much and asked for little. She would be a strong ruler, like she herself had been. *Had been.* She was too old for a war. *At least a decade too old.* Roja was far too young, but with Magnus in her ear, perhaps they could prevail. His time of hiding in the east was finished. As was her time arguing with him. Habits were hard to break. She was tired of her life, but she was not yet done. Thoughts of stepping down were delicate, fruitless dreams. She wouldn't relinquish leadership until Gemmil and the south were burning. She could feel the rage of revenge burn inside her. *Good.* This rage would help her with the difficult decisions. Most decisions were difficult, she noted absently. She meant the more ruthless decisions.

She looked at her granddaughter, who sat waiting for her to speak. Dia knew it would be rude not to at least enquire, and she wasn't happy with the new arrangement, but perhaps it was love that made her wary.

"How is Linn?" she asked. She had long wondered if Roja would ever find a mate, and now it seemed even less likely with this additional load weighing her down. It was clear the fiery redhead would take no male despite Dia's wishes. Erroh's Culling had convinced her of that. Perhaps had Dia not manipulated the apprehensive girl into putting her name forward, Roja might very well have gone into the Cull in search of a mate. Line of Magnus and line of… Dia would have been incredible. There would have been interesting family gatherings, at least. She wouldn't have sent them south to meet their death, either. Dia regretted other things too. Like delivering word of Erroh's fate to Magnus and Elise.

Roja smiled. "Linn is doing well now."

Dia wanted to offer supporting words, but caution won out. "When is she returning to the hovels?" She almost apologised for the hateful tone in her voice, but held her tongue.

Roja stopped smiling. "She's staying with me a while, Mydame."

"She is no pet."

"She has nobody else."

"What about the healer you spoke of?"

Roja blushed and Dia raised an eyebrow. She'd always had a thing for healers. Ever since she was a wild young thing in search of desire.

Fuken Wrek. Wrek had arranged for Emir to represent the wretches from the hovels. Roja hadn't argued, had she? She'd had the beating of him; she could intimidate him as well. He wasn't as impressive as she'd remembered. Still, though, he'd saved the child's life. From Stefan's whispers, she'd gleaned that Emir had found the little crying cub holding onto the cold bodies of her parents in a small shack at the far end of the hovels. At first, Linn's stay was to be for just a few

nights; a few good meals and sleep to aid recovery. A few nights had
soon become more. No, like her grandmother said, the child was no
pet. She would be so much more, regardless of Dia's disapproval or her
many sisters' whispers of outrage. Linn would receive the same
entitlements as Roja. *Fuk the bloodlines.* The little girl was her
responsibility now.

"The healer has no ties to her. She is alone," Roja muttered, as
though addressing a lowerline and not her grandmother. "He hasn't
even bothered to check in on her since he passed on the responsibility,"
she added. His lack of interest bothered her. *He should have tried.* She
thought it typical behaviour for a wretch. She could take it up with him
in chambers.

"Typical male," Dia tutted, but her thoughts were unsettled. Roja had
shown no real warmth to anything or anyone in her life, and at first Dia
had feared Linn was just another idle plaything countering her
insecurity. A balance to the misery she faced every day. But would it be
so bad for Roja to bond with a child? she wondered. Perhaps it might
even stir the fires of maternity deep down. Better than spending every
night draining goblet after goblet of vile poisonous sine in the enemy's
camp. *Fuken sine.* Rousing the city in the same breath as it strangled
the life from it.

"How many more recruits?" Dia asked, changing the subject lest
the festering disappointment in her granddaughter's face find a voice.
It was easier to discuss the business of the day, anyway. Easier, but
more depressing.

"Twenty more, and Wrek has more filtering through every couple
of weeks."

"I suppose that's good news," muttered Dia unhappily, mentally
counting the cost of another twenty warriors pledging themselves to
the city. Twenty new sets of ill-fitting armour. Twenty beds to supply.
Twenty new meals a day. Twenty new payments. Every week their
treasury lessened. *Maybe they'll fight for sine?* She felt her age today.
She looked at her wrinkled hands and then towards the perfect

porcelain skin of her granddaughter and fought the urge to embrace her and beg forgiveness for the pain she'd placed upon her. Roja desired warmth, love and reassurance. Things a grandmother should give freely. All she could offer was silent concern. Even in this little hidden room in her tower.

"I'm sorry, Roja," the Primary whispered into her cofe. The redheaded girl never heard the words. She was brewing a fresh, steaming inferno for them both.

17

FADED GODDESS

L illium closed her brown eyes and let the light haze of rain brush against her face. It was hard finding a moment's peace atop such a massive galloping beast, but in the dwindling light she found a way. The light rain was a wonderful relief from the aggressive ride. It refreshed her. Drove her onward. She felt alone out in the Wastes, lost in thought. *Not alone.*

"How was he last night?"

Beside her Elise struggled with her horse. After the struggle came the taming. The desperate beast countered and Elise moved with each motion, her body smooth in the saddle, calm, and blissfully sure like a spider upon a fragile web. Neither animal was broken in yet, but subservience was in the air. Elise rode like a wild warrior as she charged towards the horizon, chasing the sunset. For a dying female, she lived like a goddess from another world. She had her bad days, frequently. Today was not one of them. There was something in the air.

"The same as usual. Nothing changes; he won't speak. I've little interest in trying," she countered, attempting to slow the pace a little more.

"Then let me," Elise said, grinning. Lillium knew that dangerous grin. Before she could argue, Elise had kicked her beast forward. She wasn't finished racing, so neither was Lillium. They chased each other through the heavy green, the loud, roaring hooves covering the sound of thunder miles behind them. Thunder from an army. The legends were marching one last time.

Lillium couldn't count the weeks since the Primary had torn what happiness she'd had left from her wretched mind. Time healed, but she could never recover. Nor forgive herself for being relieved that it hadn't been her. Each dawn brought fresh despair. Traumatised by life and not a year out of the city. *Pathetic.*

Elise finally slowed, and the grateful beast took the reprieve willingly. As did Lillium. "Life is tragic, and unfair. The greatest crime the city commits is not preparing young Alphas for the desperate unfairness they must face. As a child, you should learn pain, embrace it and cry and recognise it. Then fuken beat it the next time it comes around. All this energy spent demanding things to be fair is wasted. A fine warrior can get crushed by brooding on injustices." She coughed a little and caught her breath. Patting the horse, she tugged the reins sharply. Love and dominance, all in a simple gesture.

Lillium had watched her many times upon the road already. She attempted to break only the fiercest and proudest animals. They were the best, she'd said, and the best horses are capable of incredible things.

"You had a rougher start to a mating than most," Elise told her. "A bad mating doesn't define you."

She wished she'd loved Wynn from the moment she'd seen him, but she hadn't. He'd grown on her, endeared himself to her. She'd succumbed, mostly out of her own desperation. She remembered watching Wynn indifferently before Erroh had entered, and she wondered if she should have followed her instincts. Even if those instincts would have dragged her life in an entirely different direction. It was in the dark, above two fierce warriors, that Lillium had finally let go of whatever desires she had and gifted Lea something she'd never received her entire life. *Kindness.* Lillium had always thought it cruel that Lea suffered because her Alphaline parents were insignificant, while Lillium's grander pedigree guaranteed her every entitlement. They were the same age; they were equally skilled; they were as pretty as each other. *Almost.* Could she have gone against her own word, denying a desperate, tragic girl a chance at happiness? *Easily.*

"I'm defined by my choices, Elise," Lillium countered. She could feel her face flush in irritation. If Elise spotted it, she said nothing. Elise knew everything. Every day she prodded for action. As though it was Lillium's task to manage.

"You didn't choose badly. Wynn isn't a terrible male; he's just... an idiot."

Lillium laughed at this. And why not? It was probably true.

His behaviour with the fallen Erroh had charmed her somewhat. He'd flicked his hair back; his jaw had caught the light just perfectly, and something had stirred in her. Something to hold on to, at least until she stepped away from her first Cull, and oh, it had seemed easier. She still thought him beautiful. She might always. *Fuk him.*

In the Cull he'd been unable to keep his eyes off her, and a girl liked that type of thing. It didn't take long for her competing Alpha sisters to understand, for his attention was obvious. His boldness at desiring only her was wonderfully reckless, and they'd dared not go against her the way Lea had attempted to go against Roja. *I could have blinked more.* She regretted her absent restraint. She wished she'd pushed him like she had Erroh. She wished they all had.

Wynn had bowed gratefully upon learning of her choice, had taken her hand and kissed it, and he was beautiful and charming and Lillium had been deliriously happy. She'd felt like the most important female in the city. *Apart from Lea.* She remembered so many things about the first night they'd kissed. Mostly, she remembered Erroh in his misery and fuk him, but he'd been funny and kind and forgiving, and incredible, and witty, and beautiful, and oh, so wonderfully oblivious to everything. Including females. Especially females. Erroh had charmed her that night. She just hadn't known how much. It had been difficult to see anything above Wynn's shimmering charm, and she hadn't wanted to look any other way after they'd become mated.

And for a time, it was wonderful. Erroh, Lea, and her entire life, forgotten in a newly mated journey east. Wynn had presented himself as everything she desired and, truthfully, a little more. He'd been kind, warm, and attentive, and she had longed for him as much as any female would. He was a fine kisser, and he made her believe she was a good kisser, which was probably more important than being a good kisser. The first few nights coupled were perfect. Beneath their blankets, hiding from the wind and the turn of the season, with only the night and its hidden animal wanderers for company, they had tasted each other, writhing closer, giving in to desire, and she remembered falling for him completely. How many nights had she and Lea spoken about their future mates? Terrified, excitable conversations about childish true love, happy families, and everything in between? Too many to count. Wynn had appeared worthy of so many imaginings.

"Magnus is far from perfect, Lillium. When we first met, he was wild, and me, well, I was even worse."

"Wynn is not wild. He is tepid."

This time, Elise laughed. It was only in her laugh that Lillium could hear how damaged her lungs were, how close to shattering. How short a time there was left. In almost everything she did, she was a goddess. In some things, though, she was as fragile a human as anyone else.

It rained the night he'd ruined everything. The first wave of droplets had extinguished the flames in the campfire, and soon afterwards the embers had fizzled out and the warmth had disappeared altogether. A harsh wind had blown through them, and they'd huddled in beneath the cover of an overhanging oak tree, wrapped close like soulmates. She'd laughed about the fire dying while passing the bottle of sine across, and they'd drunk to the weather and kissed a little more.

When the sharp wind had blown the rainstorm away and the moon began to shine down upon them, she had looked on his drunken features and felt the urge to push their wonderful union a little further. She had kissed him eagerly and let her hand explore his body. He had moved with an animal's hunger and she had let him. It was a gift for only him. She had wanted to please him with all of her heart. She had also wanted to be pleased by him. She'd suspected it could be an awkward and embarrassing act for them both, but she hadn't cared. She'd only cared for what would bond him to her. They were mated; they were in love. Besides, they could always just practice until they became masters.

She'd spent all her life waiting for this moment, and then the moment had passed. Unspectacularly. It was a terrible thing to endure a selfish lover. He was rough; he was clumsy; he was swift. She felt him spend himself inside her, heard his moan in her ear, and within moments his weight lifted, leaving her cold beneath. He sat up and drank deeply from his tankard.

"Incredible," he had said, before stretching out and waiting for sleep to come. That wait, too, was swift. Lying there listening to his snore was heartbreaking. It hadn't been awkward; it hadn't been embarrassing. It had been nothing, really. Had he held her after, had he kissed her more, had he said sweet little nothings in her ear—that might have been something. She had lost her virginity in anti-climax. She'd almost wept, but instead, she'd wrapped their blankets around them both and held him for warmth.

The following morning, he'd been his charming self and she'd smiled despite the crushing disappointment. She should have said something, but she was uneducated and unsure in these awkward matters. As night fell, he took her again and she opened herself to him. Truthfully, he took a few moments longer to rid himself of what desire he had left, and then, for a second time, he left her cold and unsatisfied. However, he had whispered that she was "beautiful" before stretching out in the campfire's light and, on cue, slipping into a satisfied sleep.

She had not warmed to his charm the following morning. She tried to voice her grievances, but it took a half bottle of sine before she'd had enough courage to say the words. Damning, he thought they were, and admittedly, they hadn't been delicate. It was their first fight. It had taken only a moment for Wynn's calmness to disappear in a torrent of outrage, and she saw him for who he was. They'd argued, and looking back, attacking his manhood might have been the wrong approach on her part, but for him to gather every one of her annoying habits and throw them in her face was not the finest defence on his part, either. He'd declared that her snoring could wake the dead. That consuming so much of their water rations would get them killed. That spending so much time applying paint to her lips and keeping her hair so blue was a needless pastime. Fuk him, but she'd allowed the tirade, knowing well that once he'd calmed, there would be apologies, there would be regret. There would be a way to settle matters. But after he told her he hated her accent, he'd drunk deeply from his bottle before muttering that she was the worst female he'd ever taken to bed. That's when she'd slapped him and he'd disappeared into the forest to drink alone.

He'd woken her up with his drunken fumbling at her dress. She'd grabbed his wrist and held him fast. A warning, he understood.

"If you want me to last, I'll last," he countered, and she could smell the drunkenness upon him.

She remembered that it had rained again, and the surrounding forest was loud with its glistening crackle. His muddy clothing was soaked through, his pale skin was scraped, and his eyes were bloodshot from tears. She had released her grip and invited him, and he'd entered her one more time, and though he performed better, it was passionless. He stared down upon her for a longer time than she'd ever thought possible, his stubborn face grimacing in cold determination, his rhythm constant and predictable. Eventually, and despite herself, she stirred and climaxed and despised herself and him as she did. Only then did he spend himself in a sweaty grunt before rolling away, clutching his stomach as though in pain.

"Better?" he'd asked, gasping the cold air into his battered lungs, and she'd hated him, hated herself, too, for believing in love, in warmth, in happily fuken ever after.

"That was fine," she'd hissed, wiping away cold beads of sweat, cursing the pain, and cursing the dissipating ecstasy. They spoke little in the days after and the days after that. They made excellent time upon their mounts and became little more than travelling companions. Their days were of the road ahead; their nights were little more than indifferent mutterings until, every thousand miles or so when the urge was uncontrollable, he would climb atop her and she would allow him. Every time they did, they grew closer for that moment, but further apart. To his feeble credit, he now waited for her to reach climax. Her thoughts were elsewhere when she did. As each week passed, their bond severed a little more, until, by the time they reached the domain of Magnus and Elise, she could barely stand to be around him at all. And he? Well, it seemed she scratched his itch and little more.

Better than being burned alive with your love watching on.

Any delicate flickers of resentment she'd held towards Lea about the choices they'd made were quickly lost when Magnus brought word of her fate. She remembered collapsing on the floor and feeling the warm touch of Elise's arms surrounding her, taking away what misery she could. She remembered Wynn standing in the doorway, unable to offer any comfort as both females wailed their heartbreak to the world. She remembered Magnus standing above them, clenching his massive hands into fists, looking out towards the horizon towards the Spark.

The Rangers had marched immediately, and Magnus had waited behind for a few days. To mourn, to console, to accept. Then, to declare Elise unfit for travel, drawing her rage down upon himself. She wasted little time convincing the man otherwise. Lillium had been the one to clean up the broken glass. Wynn had announced that he would march with the Rangers. And Lillium? Well, she had declared herself to Elise, no matter the outcome. It hadn't taken both females long to become close, and Lillium would have stayed with her until the very end.

"We can rest down across the bridge," called Elise from up ahead. *Oh, thank the gods of respite.* Lillium wondered, could she face her own mortality with as much confident grace? How powerful had Elise been in her heyday? *Legendary.* They crossed an ancient keystone bridge, untouched by time, with fast-flowing water below. The path opened to a clearing, and both females took shelter under a willow that hung lazily out over the rushing waters. Lillium was soaked through, with splatters of mud across her face, while Elise appeared fresh and ready to ride through the night. A light mist was accompanying the drawing darkness, and the low rumble from the thunder behind was slowly catching up with them.

"Sometimes, when you don't notice, his eyes burn with regret," Elise said.

"Is regret good enough?"

"Probably not, but regret is fiercer than anger."

"I think the stone is set on our mating." She'd never said it aloud before. It felt strange to say aloud. It didn't feel liberating.

Elise thought on this a while. "I'll have Magnus talk to him."

"No, please don't."

"Tell me, young Lillium, what harm could it do?"

The thunder echoed loudly across the land. Lillium looked to the clear sky above. It would be cold tonight, no doubt. Elise lit a fire effortlessly. Catching a spark, she added a little kindling, and Lillium felt the warmth as she removed her small pack from the mount as it grazed by the green grass. As good a place as any to make camp.

The thunder exploded over the hill as the first rider raced towards the waiting females. The clatter of three hundred heavy iron- and leather-armoured Rangers filled the evening air as they eased for the day and came to a stop along the riverbank. Without haste, each soldier dropped from their beast and began preparing the camp for the few hours' sleep they would take. The first tent erected was always the

Master General's, and soon enough Magnus appeared from the crowd in his heavy armour, looking impossibly impressive. He creaked loudly with each step he took, and Lillium enjoyed the pride on Elise's face as he approached. Now, *they* were a match, she thought. He took Elise's hand, kissed it as though they'd been apart longer than a couple of hours.

"Were you worried?"

"Never, my love."

"We broke in the two stallions. It was rather easy. Barely an inconvenience at all. Males are easier to break," she said, eyeing Wynn, who appeared from behind Magnus, leading his own mount. He too wore battle armour and looked equally appealing. Armour suited Wynn just fine, Lillium thought. The women would flock to him when he entered the Spark. It didn't bother her in the slightest.

"Well, I think it's time to relieve ourselves from the harshness of the day," Elise decided, watching as the finishing touches were applied to their tent. She took Magnus's hand and led him away. "Lillium, would you like to join us as we… discuss things?" she asked loudly, and Lillium froze. Elise's eyes were upon Wynn, studying him for a reaction.

Magnus was as surprised as Lillium, yet allowed his mate's words to shake him for only a moment. He knew a game was afoot and watched for Wynn to rear like an aggrieved stallion, to fight for what belonged to him. Perhaps Lillium did too. Instead, Wynn occupied himself by hobbling his horse for the evening's graze, his eyes everywhere but on his mate.

"I'm sure Wynn would object," Magnus said, eyeing the younger man tensely now. Still, Wynn's indifference spoke louder than any retort, and Elise led Magnus away while Wynn went on preparing his horse for the evening.

Surrounded by an army of comrades, Lillium had never felt more alone in her life.

18

HOMESTEAD

Lea recognised these lands. She believed she'd locked everything deep in the faded, lost thoughts of childhood, but no; she recognised more things than she expected to, than she'd wanted to. The breaks in the surrounding hills elicited unexpected emotion. Something terrible; something hidden; something irrevocably lost. Some of the far-off shadows brought visions of youth and of family. Erroh is your family now, she thought, and felt better. Well, no; she merely felt less alone.

She knew she'd endured a forgotten few years before she lived in the city. Flickers of a child following in her father's footsteps, grand and swift, up a frozen hill, battling a bitter southern wind travelling north, its chill cutting through her clothing. *Tears.* A tall father's disapproval. Even in these last few steps, these last few miles, she'd wondered if there were warmer memories. Anything beyond gruff instruction.

Cruelty.

She recalled little beyond blurred, unreliable moments, but walking these last few miles had brought something back, like a flavour she'd once loved that was now bitter to her tongue. Her father, the apple of her eye. Whenever she thought of him, she thought of a bastard. *A bastard.* Fragments. Lost. She couldn't remember his bearded features anymore. She couldn't remember his eyes, either. She tried hard, but found nothing. And her mother, oh, her mother had been beautiful. *Hadn't she?*

Brothers, lost. Hateful of the Spark. Keeping the family traditions. These last few miles tore at her nerve, and the urge to flee struck her. Why had Erroh willingly agreed to her half-hearted request?

Because he is your family.

"Perhaps it isn't as it appears," Erroh said from beside her. Their pace was slow. Erroh could whisper and she would hear. This was a place for the dead. She knew. She'd always known, but remembering was a savage torment.

"Perhaps," she whispered, but Erroh was distracted with the path and the surrounding signs, ominous and abandoned as they were. They'd seen the first signs of terrible things a day before: fields of crops left to grow unmolested. They could have sought homesteads throughout the lands, but they had not. Thoughts of neighbouring settlements both stung and brought relief. They could have turned around and continued north, but home was where the heart lay and Lea needed to know how broken it was.

I know now.

"We've diverted for long enough as it is, my beo. May as well stay the course another day and know for certain," he'd said, and she'd agreed. What type of daughter would she have been, were she not willing to make at least one pilgrimage? To say a proper goodbye.

They dropped from their horses, walking the last few steps to the house. She remembered this homestead as a mansion. She remembered impressive walls of stone, turrets and buttresses, and perhaps a moat? Really, though, she remembered its grandness. This was not the memory she'd created in her mind, and oh, it stung. It stung like a spark in her belly and grew as though given life. A sting became a burning effigy, and Lea fought her beating heart lest it shatter her chest.

"I knew this," she whispered, as Erroh placed his hand upon her shoulder. "I've always known this." She could feel the spark rising through her like fire that destroyed. Why speak aloud?

Destroyed.

Her family home was no impressive thing at all. To be accurate, the *shell* of her family home was no impressive thing. Destroyed and burned to a charred ruin.

"We don't have to go any further," he said.

"I've come this far."

She let go of her mount's reins and stepped toward the iron gates, rusted and bent. Then she wondered if the attackers had caused this destruction, and as she stepped through the gates, she stopped wondering about them altogether. Her mind was on other things. Tragic, unfamiliar things.

The blackened shell of the house still stood in part, while all else was rubble. She mistakenly remembered an iron portcullis, but saw now that they were only modest iron bars. Strange the things an unwanted child would imagine from the safety of her bed, with entitled sisters all around her. Stepping through the frame, she wondered about the old door's original colour. *Blue? Aye, blue.* She thought its size unimpressive. Her house had been closer to cottage than castle, and things made greater sense now. Tears streamed down her face and she wiped them away in disgust. Her feet crunched on the rubble she stepped upon. She spun around the main hall and remembered it being far bigger. Had she truly been that small?

"I didn't want to leave," she screamed, and outside, along the path where nightmarish things had never happened, she could see Erroh clumsily tie the last horse to a nook. She could see the simple uncertainty on his beautiful face and she wanted to hit it. She also wanted to hold him, or be held by him. But mostly, she wanted to strike out and hurt. "Why didn't I want to leave?"

If she could have, she would have climbed the stairs in search of further memories, but the wooden steps and the ash they'd become were long since lost to the wind, to the storms, to fuken time. Buried beneath weeds and growth. After fire, the world found a way. She had learned the impressiveness of this many years ago. It had taken only a few short years for the Wastes to recover the lost ground. *Years.*

"This is a shitty little home. Why wouldn't I want to leave?"

Glimpses of the household filled her vision. Fresher hidden memories returned in a terrible haze. Days and nights of joy, terror, sorrow, relief. Muffled laughter, muffled screams. Candles burning the darkness away as they dined upon salted meats. All of them. Sitting around her, everyone more impressive than little Lea. Loud voices, fists upon wood. *Fear.* She felt it anew in wretched darkness and warm tears streaming down her five-year-old cheeks as they did right now. She remembered a frozen, desperate flight through the snow. *Alone, alone, searching for distant light.* She felt the terrible pain of separation as they took her away. *Taken away in a carriage.* Her father had not waved goodbye. Her mother had not kissed her. Her brothers? As the fire grew within her, she saw their faces more clearly. Why had no one seen her off?

"This is not my home," she screamed again, spinning away and catching sight of a long beam of charred wood; it was as thick as the oak trunk it had been shaped from, hardened and sturdy, running the length of the house above her head. Such a beam could fully support a diminutive homestead like this. It could take the weight of a dangling body just fine. A fine, treated beam, capable of outliving the burning fires all around it. The beam was held in place by the charred remains of the front and back walls, with only one support standing in between, and it was this near-ruined support that Lea fell upon. Her own fire erupted from within and exploded. She should not have come; should not have remembered. She cried out, louder than before. Loud enough to scatter a few nesting crows in the remnants of the chimney. Loud enough for the dead to take notice. It was all she could do.

Erroh watched her spin around the ruins of her home, and words and gestures failed him. He remembered when all he'd expected was some awkward conversation at a rather uncomfortable table and a roof over their heads for the night. His uneasy attempts to charm his mother-in-law, and enduring the cold scrutiny of his father-in-law towards the strange male bedding his only daughter. When Lea had suggested they travel back to her home, how could he argue? Every mile since had told them the familiar story. He could have insisted they return to their route, but he hadn't. Perhaps he should have.

He watched her reach the charred ruin of the support beam in the centre of the house, and he left the horses where they were. He had no answers to her questions.

She struck the beam fiercely, her fist cracking loudly as chunks of charred splinters took flight. Her accompanying scream was agony to his ears and worse for her. Whatever pain she endured was not enough to satisfy her. She struck again and screamed again, and Erroh reached for her.

"Get away!"

He did for two more fierce strikes. Each wet thump sent bloody chunks of wood into the air, each strike weakening her and infuriating her further.

"Lea, my beo," he cried, but she turned from him, striking this time with her other fist. Erroh could see her misshapen fingers where she'd dislocated a bone. He knew that pain, knew she could control it.

"It's not fair!"

Thunk.

"So long… so fuken long."

Thunk.

Erroh took hold of her. She didn't appreciate it. She fought his grasp. "Get your fuken hands off me, you piece of shit."

"Shush, my love," he countered, gripping tightly, holding the furious Valkyrie tightly. Holding her as only a mate could. *For her benefit.*

"All you put me through. All I endured. You'll never know. Fuk you, Erroh. Fuk everyone. Fuk the absent gods." Like an eel, she squirmed from his grip and knocked him away, her power disarming him. He did what he thought was right. It probably wasn't. He spun her around and slapped her fiercely across the cheek. Just enough to distract her, just enough to break through the furious daze consuming her. She didn't appreciate this either. She took it rather badly, in fact.

"Don't you dare touch me!"

Undaunted, he tried to take hold of her again, to calm her, to bring her back to him. Her arm swung out and the world went dark.

Falling.

He landed in a heap among the ruins, and his senses betrayed him completely. His head spun towards darkness once more. "What the fuk was that?" he gasped, and she fell still. Her ruined hands fell by her side and through his blurred vision, he thought her godly even in her manic, panting state.

"I didn't mean to do that," she said, and he could see her anger festering beneath her instinctive guilt. He'd struck her first, but still, her strike had been fiercer. He shook his head, struggling to unsteady feet. She struck the beam once more, weaker this time, and fell against it, panting deeply.

"I'm so angry, Erroh. I'm sorry," she whispered, and this time, she allowed Erroh take hold and embrace her.

"If I could take your pain," he offered weakly, taking her injured hand in the evening's fading light and inspecting the damage. Blood trickled from her fingers to his, and he drew in a breath. He'd seen his own misshapen, ruined fingers like this. Though perhaps without the blood and from a different angle.

"I never endured the task of resetting a bone before; I have endured far worse though," she said. The tears flowed freely from her eyes now, and she allowed them. This was unlike her, he thought. Though surrendering to tears was sometimes an agreeable thing.

She winced at his touch and eyed the unnatural angle of her middle finger.

"Do you want me to…?" he asked, and she shook her head.

"You've already done it?" she asked, and he nodded.

This confirmed her decision. She took hold of her bruised and battered hand and, with a swift pop, returned her finger to the correct position. She tried to form a fist, but the pain was too much.

"Take it," he said, and she hissed.

"Taking it!" After a few moments, she clenched her fist a few times.

"Well done, my beo."

"I'm sorry for hitting you."

"I had it coming,"

"Usually, but not this time," she said, and kissed him. "I... it... just all came out. I have my horrors too, my beo. I carried them so long," she whispered. She clenched her fist a few more times, and each time she grunted with the effort. Only then did he release her to collect some rags to wrap her wounds, a treacherous task he attempted as delicately as he could.

"Somewhere among the ruins my family burned," she said, her voice barely audible. "I can't even bury them. I know I should mourn them, but that rage was not for their demise. You are my family, Erroh. You always have been."

"We'll rest here tonight, my love," he said, fastening the bandaging and testing its strength. "It might be a painful ride tomorrow, but once the swelling subsides you can—"

"I will not stay here. We have wasted enough time."

"As you wish, my love," he said. He got to his feet, walked over and released their mounts.

19

ROJA THE BEAUTIFUL AND THE WRETCHED COMPANION

Emir knew his problems had begun with a kiss. *Isn't that how it always starts?* For him, it was a kiss shared between Stefan and Aireys. He hadn't even seen it; he'd been a thousand miles away in the city enduring the horrors of a brutal education. Perhaps had he realised it was little more than a fleeting event between energetic, curious youths, he might have taken it better, but back then, it had seemed so important.

Emir knew it had been her first kiss; she'd told him as much the summer he'd returned. His fledgling desires for a childhood friend were crushed in that moment. *Only friends.* Aireys wasn't to know that Stefan would make Emir's life difficult forever after. Who knew Stefan's longings would match his own? Who knew it would take a wretched conversation between two wretches in the witching hour, when sorrow grew monstrous and the tongue was looser, to bring it to light? When people had nothing else, they had words; they had confessions. Emir wondered if friendship through tragedy was a tentative thing. Tentative, unexpected and appreciated. These last months in Samara had been difficult, but at least he had a companion he trusted. So, when this comrade had a request, who was he to deny him a few hours of insufferable tedium? No, not tedium: far worse than that.

Emir drank carefully from his glass. Just enough to taste, just enough to slip closer to numbness. He performed this task as any desperate man would when there were only a few drops remaining and no spare piece for refill. His role as diplomat between both sides of the city wall paid nothing, and healing those from the hovels paid even less. He watched the crystal-clear sine disappear, savouring the last drops of its wondrous flavour, and somehow he resisted draining the lot. Instead, he swirled what remained in the glass. One sip more? Two?

Counting the moments between bouts of drunkenness was far better than addressing his companion, he supposed. *Stefan needs a night like this.* Roja had had little to say since they'd found themselves alone in this cosy, welcoming tavern, and this suited him perfectly, so he savoured the taste of the best sine he'd ever tasted and thought miserable thoughts of the only female he had ever loved.

"Should have died," he whispered suddenly, gaining the redhead's attention. He shook his head and avoided her gaze. How much had he drunk this evening? Enough that loose thoughts escaped his lips. He dared not think on further dark matters lest his feelings surface with a deafening roar. She didn't need to know his pain. She didn't need to know that every day was a nightmare, that today was no different.

Truthfully, sitting at this table had made this day far worse. The atmosphere in the smoky little inn was irritatingly boisterous and tragically familiar. Conversation, however, was strained at their cluttered little wooden table hidden snugly in the far corner. *Quig would have liked it here.* Trying not to catch her attention and endure forced conversation, Emir tried to signal Stefan on the dance floor. A tricky thing, for Stefan was playing with a goddess tonight. Or, at least, attempting to play with the goddess. It was almost comforting, seeing him charm an Alphaline woman. Sometimes ignorance was a gift, he supposed. Sometimes ignorance made a male attempt impossible things. Sometimes ignorant manoeuvres resulted in improbable outcomes.

.   .   .

Stefan could feel Emir's burning glare, but dared not meet it. Instead, he looked into the blue eyes of Silvia and tried desperately not to smile. He had a fantastic smile—or at least, he use to have. Tragically, a drunken and rather undeserved mishap had robbed him of one of his smoothest tactics. He ran his tongue through the gaping hole where his front teeth should have been and remembered better, less painful times. Silvia bit her lower lip in reply, and Stefan knew her own game was now in play. She was enjoying the attention and well used to it. His father had warned him of females capable of such tricks. Stefan had learned to leap headfirst into engagements with women like this. Still, though, there were many miles to walk before he charmed this one's dress off. A girl like this would require more than soft whispers and extravagant compliments. Could have used that smile, he thought. *Fuken Alphas.* He took hold of Silvia's hand and spun her around; the sight of her white dress, twirling majestically in her wake, took his breath away. He'd never known lust like this, and tonight he would embrace this feeling of normality.

They're all dead.

He almost stumbled as she spun a second time and a tragic memory of a grand champion surrounded by friends struck him. Instead, he forced the guilt down—futile, he knew, like trying to drown a beast that could hold its breath eternally—and he took hold of the girl and almost smiled in the reprieve.

They will always be dead, but tonight I dance.

"You are divine," he whispered, and she giggled wonderfully, and he was charmed and he forgot himself even more.

"I'm pleased we can play. All we do is talk of serious matters," she whispered, and her breath was warm upon his ear and her lips brushed against his cheek as she spun away.

"I aim to please those most beautiful," he said, and she liked this. And why wouldn't she? It wasn't too long ago that most women had swooned beneath his charm. Swooned beneath unoriginal words of courtship.

"I'm aiming for distraction," she whispered.

"As you wish."

He was single-minded these days. Not through choice, but through bare necessity; for his own survival, for his own sanity. A single-mindedness to keep him in place. Should he deviate from this, he risked succumbing to the misery of his life, of his choices, of his fuken luck. Whatever tasks Emir demanded of him, he completed. Perhaps it was a desire to repent for his cowardice; perhaps it was a will to help those he called comrades; perhaps it was simply his terror at choosing his next step. It was a sobering thought to know every step taken had lead to calamity, but in Emir he trusted. They all did.

He gripped the girl, fought a smile and enjoyed this moment for what it was. Distraction for him, and for Emir too. Perhaps if the wretched healer looked up from his melancholy, he might see something more beyond the end of his own nose; he might even see the value in himself.

And if Stefan fell in love for tonight, well, that was a fine way of forgetting single-mindedness.

"Their happiness would disgust anyone, really," Roja muttered, and Emir knew that tone. Mocking, irritated, and indifferent. Uttered to stave off boredom for another few moments when silence fell between them once more. As usual, he did not offer agreement, though she made a good point. She made many good points, admittedly, but as the speaker for the wretches, he could never offer her an inch. As the killer of those he cared for, he would offer her even less. Instead of offering anything, he tried to catch the barman's eye. A difficult task in such a crowded room, full of good cheer and flowing movement. He wondered absently if he could convince Roja to allow him to bring in a few more people from the wall to tend table. He thought about asking her, but held his tongue. He could address this matter the following morning as they sat in battle, spitting vitriol each other's way while their companions fluttered their eyelashes at each other.

"At least he washed," she said, an edge of danger in her mocking tone, and still Emir did not react. He could feel her burning glare as she played absently with her hair, and he ignored her. He knew her all too well. It hadn't taken more than a few weeks. She was ready to explode all over the table and anyone sitting at it. Namely him. She was about to behave as most emotional Alphalines did.

Unable to display any restraint.

Always over the top.

Incapable of calmer thoughts.

Able only to strike out. And hurt. And maim. And kill. *Kill.*

Aye, he knew Alphalines, all right. As human as everyone else, only slightly better at it.

With nothing else to do, he glanced up at Roja and the half-empty glass sitting lifelessly in front of her. "This place needs better staff," he muttered, eyeing the drink and then his own empty glass.

If Roja heard, she said nothing. She continued pulling on a few of her stunning red strands, inspecting them as if seeing them for the first time, then releasing them and reaching for fresh, new ones. He could have asked her why she did this, but that was against the rules. That would have been a conversation.

Down at the dance floor, where Stefan appeared to be successfully charming the ever-irritating Silvia, the band finished up their jig and broke into another song without taking breath. A few cheers broke out as more dancers took to the floor, and Emir reminisced about nights at the Sickle. He closed his eyes and imagined a festival's evening when fights were in the air and those he loved were nearby. He liked this song. He remembered Aireys liking it too, and the wretched pain began to surface. He heard Silvia laugh loudly and he opened his eyes, and for a wonderful moment saw Stefan as the arrogant cur he'd once been. Strangely enough, it made him smile again.

"Better staff? Let me guess—you have someone in mind," Roja said, pulling him from the false merriment. "Tell me, Emir, why do the people like you?" she added, when he did not rise to her bait. She'd let her hair fall down along her perfectly sculptured cheeks and was staring at him with cold, dangerous eyes. Boredom had brought out a boldness in her.

He wanted to whisper that they weren't battling wits in session. Really, though, he knew better. Instead, he shrugged carefully. What type of question was that, anyway? *One without a safe answer.* Was she jealous? he wondered. It was a strange thing to be liked, something he'd never experienced throughout his life, but the wretches in the hovels had taken to him fiercely.

"Perhaps it's because I don't charge a great deal for my services. Generosity goes a great distance… Mydame."

"Sometimes generosity is misspent charity. Yes, the lowerlines would likely hold aloft a likeable idiot, I suppose," she countered. She'd said harsher things in session. Her dazzling eyes flashed from the two dancers back to him, and he could see her knee gently tapping with the song. Though she was mocking him, her jest lacked her usual bitter cruelty. He knew her better than he would have liked, thanks to their near-daily meetings and their heated conversations. He knew she loved cofe, dancing, and the workings of unusual machines. He didn't know when she'd spoken casually of such things, only that she had, and he'd listened.

She swayed a little absently, and he realised that if he asked, she would join him on the floor. He almost laughed at the absurdity. Was she that desperate to win him over and ease the tensions between the two warring factions of the city? Those with health, cheer, and full plates, and those without.

"Careful, Roja. It's as though I'm getting under your skin, leathery as it is," he mocked, and she laughed, swishing the alcohol in her goblet. It was clear, it was bittersweet, it was room temperature, and it was all a drowning man could ever need.

She caught herself weaving and stared at him. "Don't think us sitting under a truce earns you favour. I'm here by request."

So, you don't want to dance?

"You think I'm enjoying your company? This is fuken painful," he countered, enjoying how easily words came once the mind was at play with the finest sine ever brewed. "As if it's not frustrating having to sit and discuss matters with you every morning, now I have to sit and endure your company during my leisure time? Oh, do fuk off, Roja…

you… whore." He hadn't meant to add that last part. She despised that word; this he also knew.

She tipped some sine from her glass onto the floor beside her. Just enough that it cut him up. Just enough to show she'd noticed his gazing. He almost screamed at the waste, but he held his tongue. "Don't call me that," she said, her voice strangely calm; he'd have preferred an outburst. There was something positively terrifying in the cold tone. The type of voice that came from behind you in the dead of night as you walked a fog-laden alleyway. That voice never meant good things.

"Are you going to beat me up again?" he countered, and wondered did his voice sound as slurred to her as it did to him.

"Wrek's not here to save you if I do." That same tone.

"He'll be along when he hears my heroic squealing," Emir joked, and thought again how closely Wrek resembled his dead friend.

"I'll have you bled dry long before that," she warned, a playful lilt to her tone now, and he wondered if she was enjoying this contest of threats.

"Not at all. I am a master healer. I'd just steal someone else's blood before my heart gave out. I have the tools and all. I could explain how, but it would only confuse you."

She laughed again and tipped a little more sine onto the dusty floor below. "I am a simple female, I suppose. I only understand ruling the world."

The band finished the song and immediately moved to the next, a slower piece with less percussion and more vocals. Some would call it a beautiful piece, suitable for the more intimate moments, and Stefan and Sylvia slid closer together. The night was young and the young were falling in love, it would appear.

"We could talk about the wheat rations, I suppose," Roja said, admitting the same defeat as he, upon seeing both their friends embrace on the dance floor. One more dance to endure.

"This will cause one of our deaths," Emir warned. Their argument from earlier that morning was on her mind, it seemed.

"I'm intending to have you killed regardless, so I am happy to argue a little more," she said, and for a moment Emir feared her wrath. For a moment.

"When you do, will you put Wrek back in charge?"

"He's too hard to kill. You are… unimpressive."

"I think I'd prefer to talk about the wheat rations. So… um… can we have more?" He nodded to his almost-empty glass.

"No," she replied, and he rolled his eyes.

"I think I preferred when we were sitting here in silence."

"I agree," she said, drinking her sine, savouring the taste, and he hated her a little more.

"Also, sorry for calling you a whore. It's probably not true."

She looked away into the distance, grinding her teeth. Perhaps the sine was more bitter than she'd expected. "Oh, what they say is all true."

He thought on this a moment before finally drawing the attention of the harried barman. He'd mastered the silent language of tavern orders. An excitable smile, a few fingers raised, followed by a subtle bit of pointing. "Four new glasses of sine please," he said with a wink to finish. *Perfect.*

He watched as, without warning, Silvia reached up and touched the gap in Stefan's teeth, then smiled and kissed him. This kiss lasted the rest of the song and beyond. To their credit, the band sensed desire in the air and played another romantic tune, this one even slower. The two dancers swayed with the easy rhythm, their bodies in unison, their lips never separating; to most of those watching, it seemed perfect. Emir and Roja, unmoved, exchanged another glance of frustration. Yet another song to endure.

"I thought Alphas only played with their own kind," announced Emir suddenly.

"We can play with whoever we like, healer. The wretched and the beautiful."

"Can you become mated for life?" he asked, watching the tray of jingling glasses, full of loveliness, carried down to them by a flustered barmaid. Next was the tricky part: he was without a piece to pay for them. Regardless, he was careful to note that the third glass on the right held the most sine. The barmaid's route, weaving through the noisy, crowded tables, would bring her to Roja before him, denying him first choice. He offered a silent prayer to the absent gods for the third glass, for a drunken patron to step in her way and send her along a different path, resulting in her reaching him first. Oh, how he prayed to those damned absent gods. *You took everything; give me this.*

Roja didn't even blink; she answered as though the words were intrinsically embedded beliefs. "Occasionally, though why anyone would mate below their station is beyond me. It is our right, our duty, to mate with the strongest. For this world to recover, we must—"

"Spoken like a zealot in the church of ignorance," he interrupted.

"Probably," she said easily. "But there is worthy logic to good breeding."

"Mixing a little blood here and there between the people is no bad thing, Alphas are simply educated and skilled. I could be just as impressive as any of you, had I the advantages you had," he countered, and he thought it a fine argument.

"Aye, I would agree."

He hadn't expected that at all. He had more to say; he always did. Before he could reply, she spoke again.

"Is this your fascinating attempt at seduction, Emir? Wondering about mating with me for life?"

He didn't like that tone, not one bit. "If I attempted seduction, you would know it, my dear," he countered smoothly.

"Apart from the smell, you aren't overly unattractive, Emir—I will give you that. But surely you must feel a little foolish attempting such flirtation with me."

"I wasn't flirting with you."

"If you say so."

"I wasn't flirting with you!" he snapped, and she was thoroughly amused. He felt his fury rising, but before he could defend himself, the sine arrived. Naturally, and much to his despair, she took the largest glass without taking care to see which held most. He hated her anew in this moment. "I am but a pauper," Emir muttered, waiting, looking away from the tavern girl tapping her finger against the edge of her tray a few times, awaiting payment.

"Most healers are," Roja said, reaching for a couple of pieces to pay. As she did, she caught Emir's sleight of hand as the large glass in front of her appeared in front of him. Their eyes met as he tipped the contents between his lips. "You have a chivalrous soul," she mocked as he drank.

"Ah, leave me be, princess. You have enough coin to buy the city's storage of the stuff. Allow me the larger glass," he hissed.

"Maybe if you paid your way, you'd be entitled to more."

"I've paid my share," he lied, grinning at his absurd claim, for Silvia and Roja had paid for all rounds but the first. That round had come from the collective pockets of Emir and Stefan. She'd seen them double check the price and all.

Two little boys, counting their pittance.

"What made you as wretched as you are, Emir? Did you fall in love with the wrong girl? Did you kill the wrong patient?" she said sneering, and immediately cursed her loose tongue, for she knew the insensitivity of her words. This was not banter along the wall with a soldier she intended to play with; this was not loose jesting with a rival sister; this was not even camaraderie among close friends. "I didn't mean…" she said, and fell silent.

He was already looking away, draining the glass as though it were nourishment to a starving rat. There were things a decent person never mocked, never enquired about, never spoke of, and she'd done all three with careless mockery. She saw the pain on his face and the accompanying anger. *Murderous anger.* She recognised it; she'd seen the same look on the faces of many other wretches. Sometimes, when she sat in her little haven with Dia, she allowed their agony to affect her. "It was a nasty jest…"

She liked Emir. She'd always liked him, and she had a fine memory. He had changed. He was no wild apprentice, charmingly boisterous and completely oblivious to an awkward princess hoping to catch his eye. No, he was truly wretched and broken. Yet still, his pride shone through the misery, and this she liked even more. His company was refreshing; in this city, few people spoke their mind openly. Least of all to her. Even those scattered at the gate were wary of challenging her, yet Emir had little hesitation. There were moments when she saw beyond his aggression, and they made her long to tear away the veneer of wretchedness.

Many were broken in Spark; many were ready to hide within themselves and never emerge. She could see he was beaten, shattered and inevitably doomed. Like a crustacuus in a fisherman's trap; he was alive, but the surrounding water was bubbling. Displaced in this world, as though the absent gods had plucked him from a chosen path and gifted him a dreadful burden instead. She saw all of this, yet still, she knew of his wretched goodness and despite herself, was inspired by him. He cared deeply for the pitiful. He fought for the smallest crumbs and he did it for no gain of his own. She suddenly thought very little of herself for mocking his refusal to pay.

"It's a small matter," he hissed, and spat in the dirt at his feet. His hands shook slightly. She'd never seen them shake before. *Bad affliction for a healer.* If truth be told, there were fine moments when he argued in session and she saw the passion in his eyes and a hidden pride in himself. She saw none of this now, and she suddenly felt the desire to reach out, take his hand and offer him a few additional wheat rations. Just as suddenly, she realised she'd been staring at him too long, but he didn't notice. He was thinking of whatever horrors her jest had invoked. *Nice move, Roja.*

Wrek walked through the crowd accepting compliments, jests and handshakes in his stride. Business was good. Business was always good. He caught the eye of the bartender and offered a questioning nod. The man returned the gesture subtly. No patrons up to no good. It was early in the night. Plenty of time still. The crowd parted as he walked, and he accepted a freshly brewed pint of ale, which he sipped tentatively. It wasn't just sine they held control over these days. Every time a different brew appeared within the city, Sigi was swift to meet whichever artist had created the draft and strike some deals. Wrek had been present at these "meetings." This was life in Spark City, he supposed. It was the cost of staying on top. Deals were better for all involved. Safety under Sigi's watch was an enticing offer. No further harassment to face, either, and a lick of the profits was better than starving completely. Sigi had Wrek manage the welfare of the many in their employment, and Wrek had discovered it a difficult yet most rewarding position. Who knew he'd have a knack for such things? Who knew he could protect those he felt responsible for? *Again.*

He held the tankard up in the air, testing its colour in the smoky light. *Not perfect yet.* Perhaps a dozen master brewers combining talents to create a couple of different beverages was not enough. He sipped again and swished it around his mouth before swallowing. *Too sweet.* Perhaps they'd used one too many master brewers. He left the tankard on the counter and returned to this evening's probing march. This was his favourite part of his day. Before the hours watching exhausted him. Before his throat became dry and cracked from boisterous engagements. Before anyone began stirring a brew of trouble.

Despite his size, he glided through the patrons easily enough, his pace swift and direct, imposing and unnoticed by most. The sign of a good tavern's peacekeeper and a terrible leader of a warring bandit tribe. For a moment the stuffy air became cool and rich. The tavern's door slammed and he caught sight of two brutes entering and cursed under his breath. One of the nasty-looking fukers was as big as he. The other was smaller, bald as the shattered moon and likely just as dangerous. He wondered just how well he'd fare against two Alphas in a fair fight, and he doubted his chances. That didn't mean he wouldn't destroy them, were they troublesome.

He left them to settle and continued his circuit around the room until he spotted the two beautiful patrons engaged in their own dance of intimacy upon the dance floor. He smiled beneath his beard. His eyes searched for their likely companions and he found them swiftly enough, sitting in uncomfortable silence away from prying eyes and eager ears. They tried desperately not to look each other's way, and he thought about sitting down as though among friends.

"Nice to see the two of you out of session, playing nicely," he said, coming up behind them.

Emir shook his hand warmly. "You haven't been in the meetings for the last while, Wrek. We've been missing your company something terrible."

To Roja, he offered a bow. Again, he wondered about joining them and thought better of it. There was still a room of boisterous fiends with emptying pockets and full tankards. There was potential for mayhem yet. As if the gods of chance had overheard him, he heard the bellowing laugh of one of the Alphalines as he cracked a jest at the expense of the tavern keeper. Wrek clenched his fists.

"Ah, sure, you don't need me these days. You are positively friends now," he said, eyeing the two dancers. "In fact, some of you have bridged the gap between city and hovel rather spectacularly."

"It'll likely end in tears," Roja pointed out, clinking Emir's glass. Emir was drinking from it at the time and drew back his head in annoyance.

"Or with someone getting knocked out," hissed Emir, tapping the chair beside him for Wrek to join him, as though inviting a friend. *Tempting.*

"There have been fewer incidents at the gate since you chose diplomacy. I would take that as a fine thing," Wrek said. "Next round is on me," he added, ignoring with only a little sting the offer of company and cheer, before bidding them an enjoyable evening. He'd caught sight of one of the Alphalines starting an argument with a table of drunks.

The song sped up, and so did the dancing couple. Their bodies spun and turned in perfect unison with the beats, and Emir worried he would never get home tonight. His belly was empty and he wondered if he could wrangle some free bread and cheese out of Wrek's generous offer. Perhaps Roja could cover the balance?

"How is the child?" he asked her, wondering how best to manoeuvre food into the conversation. The first task was disarming his opponent with casual distraction; the next was asking for food. Roja smiled at the mention of the girl, and then the smile turned to a scowl. That was more like her.

"Her name is Linn," she hissed, and Emir wondered about that tone.

"I know. So... how is little Linn?"

"You could have checked on her at least once after dumping her in my lap," she growled.

"I didn't want you to..." he struggled for the words, "return the problem back onto me."

"She's not a problem. You must think little of me to imagine I would just send her back to the hovel as sickly as she was," she snapped.

Here we go again.

"Don't worry. I think little of all people, but it's good to hear that she is cared for and... well... um... Send her my best, I suppose," he offered, eyeing Stefan's glass. As he did, Roja drained her own and reached for Stefan's, downing it impressively. She coughed only slightly. She slid Silvia's glass across to Emir before raising her arm and signalling four more glasses. The barman immediately accepted the order, pouring four drinks and sending the stressed barmaid their way swiftly. It was good to be the queen bitch of the city, apparently. She placed a few shiny pieces as obviously as possible in front of her place. She was paying the next round despite Wrek's offer. Emir's stomach growled loudly and he caught a wretched bile-filled burp in his throat.

"We'll have some soup, and a few buttered rolls," she added, sliding the pieces into the girl's fingers. Emir offered a delirious wave of appreciation. The sine was kicking in. Admittedly, there were good things about Spark.

"That's very generous of you, Roja," Emir said, offering his soberest bow, and she appeared to like this.

"See? I can be generous. Remember that the next time you claim anything to the contrary, my wretched little friend."

"So, we are friends then?" he slurred, wiping his mouth. This was a more difficult task than he'd expected. *Potent sine.*

She thought on this for a breath. "Haven't I always made that clear, healer?"

"Well, I suspected differently when we first met and you gave me a concussion." He knew he probably shouldn't have said that.

"You put your hands on my chest when we first met. I think it's remarkable that I allowed you to live the night." This had been coming; it had taken only a few drinks to finally bring it out in the open. Truthfully, he'd thought about apologising every day they met, but how could one form up such words? So be it. In his growing drunkenness he tried to reply, but she took his hesitation as a rebuff.

"At least my breasts have given you a gift for the lonely nights in your little shack. Again, I am generous to the wretched."

A wounded Alphaline was a dangerous thing, he knew.

Apologise for the benefit of the wretches you serve.

Apologise for the regret you really do feel.

Apologise, because it's the right thing to do.

All sobering, honest thoughts. Unfortunately, Emir looked at her chest again, noticeably, and shook his head. Her gown was silk and extravagant, with a slightly low-cut neckline that hinted at magnificent treasures within. She was stunning, naturally so. A healer could tell such things. A healer could also cut deep when needed.

"I tried to please myself at your expense—honestly, I really did. A few times. It's a frustrating thing to fail as a muse for desire, but there really wasn't enough to grab my imagination." He mimicked a grabbing motion. "A healer can tell these things. A healer can tell what is flesh, what is… padding. Tell me, oh goddess, how much padding do you use? Your shape is impressive in that gown, but we know better." He downed his drink, offered his most charming wink and waited for the slap. He had it coming and it would be worth it.

. . .

Silvia leaned in tightly and kissed Stefan passionately. Her meaning for the night was crystal clear. She thought him a wonderful distraction for the now. He stroked her hair and pulled gently at her waist, his enthusiasm as clear as hers. She loved this moment before the first real dance. And then he was gone. Torn from her lips by a savage brute.

Roja didn't slap Emir. She didn't even appear like slapping him, and this was worse. Instead of lashing out, or returning his jest, she reached for her drink and appeared rather hurt. Emir liked this hurt. He liked it a little too much.

"Oh, laugh, you silly whore," he said, unable to stop himself. "It was a joke. I don't even remember what your breasts were like," he offered, and, strangely enough, this didn't seem to make matters any better. His head spun, and he looked at his glass and realised he'd reached the distance his sanity would allow before the night disappeared from his grasp. He wanted to drink more, say more, hurt more. Oh, he wanted to hurt her.

"Fuk off, Emir," she muttered. The hurt in her voice sounded delicious. He had more to say, but the sight of Stefan flying across the dance floor distracted him. Stefan landed with a heavy thud upon a table and kept going, taking every goblet and platter with him.

Puk.

A terrible rage engulfed Emir. The aggressor was a big bastard, and despite his impaired vision, his painful hunger and terrible drunkenness, Emir leapt to his feet. He had little skill conversing with beautiful redheads, but in tavern brawls, he felt alive. It was the Keri blood in him. *All hail the Puk.* The big brute had an accomplice, bald and menacing, and his eyes upon Stefan's partner. He took hold of Silvia's wrist and attempted to dance with her. Emir knew he'd get a hiding, and this thought troubled him less than he expected. He only wished Quig was at his side and maybe Aireys a little further behind, getting ready to rescue him when he was knocked unconscious.

"What are you doing?" demanded Roja, taking hold of his shirt, holding him fast; denying him the opportunity to save a fallen comrade. *Denied again.*

He felt dizzy, as though a deluge of blood untainted by poisons had rushed into his head. "Get your fuken hands off me," he snarled, pushing her away, but still, she held him fast. His body wavered as the many drinks took hold. It tore his sanity from him. Such things happened when those as miserable as he drank too much.

Denied again.

"Wrek will sort this. You'll get yourself killed, idiot," she growled, and he shoved her hard. Harder than the day they'd met. Hard enough to break the hold, and the world and all its cruelty struck Emir anew like Aireys's denial all over again.

Denied, denied, denied.

"I don't want to live!" The words felt as though they were torn from his chest.

All he felt was a depthless anger at his misfortune, and he cursed and spat and Roja was beside him again, trying to hold him, trying to deny him the right to stand with his friends, and he hated her for trying to win his favour, for trying to befriend him, and for being more beautiful than Aireys could ever have been. "I owe everything that I am to you," he mumbled, so only she could hear, and she heard, and she said nothing. "Some would say you are beautiful; what I see disgusts me." She stopped struggling, and he took this as a sign that there was no return. The rage overcame him, and why not? He hated her. As soon as he had learned who she was, he could only hate her. He had wanted to scream, but he was a clever little wretch, so he had condemned her quietly, for that is how diplomats condemned each other.

"You do not understand the world, or pain, or loss," he cried, the words tumbling out of him now. "Your indifference towards the suffering of the lowerlines is disgusting." If he'd had a piece to throw at her in disgust, he would have thrown it. As it was, he was a pauper, he was wretched, and his only weapon was a venomous tongue. He heard his voice break and she just stared at him as though nobody in her life had ever torn her soul apart. "Nobody warned us about what moved in the shadows. Yet, you knew. You and your whore of a grandmother." He poked his finger into her chest and pushed, and she stepped back as though shoved by a behemoth. She looked as though she would cry, and this pleased him. "Aireys, Quig, Jeremiah… all of them!" He caught himself there. Better few saw this outburst. He waved his hand in apology for raising his voice. It was insincere.

She shook her head, and he hated her more than any other before.

"We… thought…" she began, and fell silent. This was likely a finer tactic on her part.

"You ruined my life, Roja." It was all coming out and he couldn't stop himself. Too much sine. Too much misery. Tomorrow he would step down from his position. Let someone else carry the burden, he thought, eyeing the dance floor. Silvia had disarmed her assailant with a kick to the groin, much to the hilarity of the cursing brute's comrade. Stefan was rolling in the rubble; the band were, unbelievably, still playing despite the ruckus; and Emir dearly wanted to be in the middle of it, getting his head kicked in, just like at home. Instead, he was a terrible distance away, and his only relief was tearing apart the soul of a beautiful girl.

"We are trying…" Roja began again, before finding no substance to her argument.

He could see her drunken unpreparedness, and it was almost endearing. Almost, but not quite. He shoved her again, knowing well the crime of striking her. Wondering if life in chains, without responsibility, would be such a terrible fate. Aireys would want him to strike her.

"Every day I bow and beg for your charity. I squirm in the mud, grateful for anything you place into my wretched hands and… and…". He could see the pain in her face and knew no further words would have any effect. *Fuken good.* "I'm bored with your company."

Feeling wretched and unfulfilled, he spun around, almost collapsing in the process, and sauntered through the obstructing tables and chairs.

. . .

Roja fell back in her chair, watching the drunken healer weave through the tables. She saw him grabbing a heavy ceramic mug, long since emptied, and her limbs felt impossibly heavy, as though she'd been struck fiercely in a sparring bout and was taking a moment to find her breath. Emir casually strolled up to the bent form of Doran, who was nursing his tender groin. He appeared to be offering help before he suddenly smashed the bald beast across the head with the mug. There was a haze of blood splatter as Doran collapsed to the floor. Emir managed one defiant swing before succumbing to the raw power of Aymon's thrashing fists. The fall through two wooden tables knocked him out cold, and Roja caught her breath in dismay. The crowd roared their approval, surrounding the open dance floor, enjoying the return of the good old times to this once notoriously dangerous inn.

Aymon roared in victory until Wrek entered the fray. Appearing from the far side of the room where the tables were most densely clustered, he cleared the last line of the watching crowd, using a table as leverage. She thought him impressive as he leapt upon the unsuspecting Aymon, fists like hammers meting out concussive blows as though Alphaline blood was nothing to fear. Roja knew, as everyone else knew, that stepping upon Wrek's hallowed ground with malicious motives was invitation to war. He lacked grace and finesse, but he battered Aymon as though he were a mortal lowerline. The crack of his fist across Aymon's chin, sending the Alpha reeling across the floor, just added to his impressiveness; to his legend.

For all that, however, Roja was drawn to the motionless body of Emir lying awkwardly among the splintered table and shards of glass. With the crowd intent upon Wrek's continued punishment of the beaten Aymon, she sauntered down towards the ruined dance floor, carefully trying to conceal any suggestion of her inebriation. A difficult task with each uneven step she took.

Aymon's struggles ceased, and Wrek dragged him from the tavern and threw him out into the night. After a few breaths, he shoved his way back to the dance floor, seized the bleeding Doran and did the same to him, though not before inspecting the wound running along the man's crown. As nonchalantly as he could, he slipped a few coins into the hand of one of the bouncers and sent him away in search of a night healer. A difficult task to find one, Roja imagined.

"Everyone out. Tonight is done," Wrek declared. Most of the revellers began to disperse, grumbling, but a few stubbornly argued with him, for there was still a danger in the air.

Silvia took hold of Stefan, and Roja heard his dazed apology about covering her dress in blood. A shiver ran down her spine, though she didn't know why. They stumbled out into the night to tend to whatever dancing they still intended, and Roja left them to it. Around her, the tavern was nearly empty now. The legend had spoken; the night was done.

Roja, however, had little intention of leaving. Wrek must have seen the grim expression upon her face, for he allowed her to stay.

She knelt over the drunken healer and found him breathing lightly. She brushed a few broken pieces of glass from his chest and around his hair, and she thought how content he looked now, lying unconscious among the debris. As if bar fights were a natural thing to him. She sat with him until the tavern was still and silent; until most of the destroyed furniture had met a glorious death in the fireplace; until she'd washed the last of the dried blood from his face; until the damp cloth had slowed the coming bruising; until he looked beautiful again.

She'd no clue why she did any of this. *Guilt?* His revulsion at her had stung worse than any lurid graffiti or muttered jokes ever could. His condemnation was testament to how foul their world had become.

When he opened his eyes, her work was done. She gently slid his majestic head off her lap and placed a cushion under it instead.

She didn't like the bemused look on Wrek's face when he unlocked the massive bolt and sent her off into the cool night.

"I think I fuked up," muttered Emir as Wrek helped him to his feet. He looked around at the mess of the dance floor, the splatters of blood, the shards of glass and the many signs of mayhem.

Wrek laughed loudly. "No, Emir. I think you did just fine tonight, my friend."

20

ADAWAN

Beneath the waving shade of leaves, Lea stirred. Her hand lay in the dry dusty undergrowth and she never felt more relaxed. She didn't want to rise from her warm bedding. To rouse herself and face the morning. She desired this warmth, this comfort, this embracing arm around her. *The little things.* She loved waking up like this every sunny morning, with a rested body still suffering the bruising from their night's activities. It was her turn to prepare breakfast, but she considered feigning sleep until he rose first and instinctively began preparing. A devious plan, if truth be told.

She stretched slightly and felt the ruined parts of her body anew, and she loved him for it. Some pain was wonderful. Finishing her stretch, she caught her fingers in the bedding, sending a sharp sting down her arm. *Take it.* Her hand had improved these last weeks but there were moments when she remembered home. Like the sharp reminder, though, the pain faded away swiftly. Time heals every wound eventually. The absent gods had gifted them these last few weeks. The further north they'd travelled without incident, the more their sense of optimism had grown, however tentatively. It was, she knew, the sort of optimism that flattened a person when its deceit was inevitably revealed. Still, though, the desolate lands they now travelled appeared peaceful. Vast, undisturbed, serene. Were it not for the reappearance of tracks indicating a large pack of Riders, Lea might well have believed they had earned this optimism. As it was, they were hunting.

Erroh still spoke of horrors in his dreams, but most nights a gentle embrace or a delicate whisper usually silenced his agony. She wondered if he slept lighter would he hear her own nightmares, nightmares of horror and death and constant running through the snow. It was a small matter. She kissed his cheek and climbed free of his warmth, and immediately regretted the decision. Staring at his bare chest in the dawn's light, she somehow stopped herself running her fingers across the curves and ridges. His muscles had become more defined. Firmer. A few weeks of joy, a few weeks of comfort, a few weeks of strenuous exercise outside of the saddle had rewarded him wonderfully. Rewarded them both, to be exact.

There were some fine new curves and muscles to her shape, too. She could have said that pleasing him with her alluring body was not a delightful thing, but that would have been a lie, for she loved his lustful gaze. She liked the muscles she had toughened; she liked the strength she had earned. Every mile nearer drew war a little closer. If painful tasks such as lifting her chin above a hanging bow twenty times a day improved the chances of survival, it was little cost, and if it kept them looking pretty for each other, well, that was fine as well.

"You ruined me," he groaned, sitting up from the blankets, catching the strip of dried meat she threw before chewing heartily. *A breakfast of kings.* He took a deep breath, enjoying the air. Easier to breathe in this warmth, he thought. "I would kill for cofe."

"We'll buy a keg and a cart to carry it in when we reach Samara," she promised. "Can you see in this light how much fresher these tracks appear to be?" she asked, and he glanced around their transient campsite, wiping sleep from his eyes. He climbed from his bedding and stretched the night's aches away. *Worth it.* He felt the scratches on his glorious ruin of a back. The thin welts rose up from his skin and he wondered had it hurt as badly as they'd played? He wouldn't complain. She might scratch harder next time. He thought on this and decided he felt fine about her doing that. Sometimes they were gentle, caring lovers. Other times they were beasts of instinct.

Perfect.

"Fresher, all right, but harder to track," he said, and she nodded in agreement. A fine move, resting the night instead of losing the scent to darkness. The group they tracked used every concealing trick. Occasionally the clefts in the dry ground disappeared in the rushing flow of rivers, only to reappear a mile upstream; sometimes the Riders doubled back on themselves altogether, and it took both their keen eyes to follow this curious route. The smarter manoeuvre may have been riding on towards Samara to deliver word of the road to their precious Primary instead of hunting these phantom tracks, but Erroh had done that before, hadn't he? The city could wait, and Lea agreed. If the Hunt camped themselves less than a hundred miles from the city with nobody the wiser, a quick charge could be catastrophic.

When he thought of the city, his mind stirred with tactics, violence, and heroics. He knew such thoughts were foolish. He was no general; he was no legend. He would fight under orders of greater minds than his. They both would. It was a slow lesson he'd learned these last few weeks with nothing but peace and reflection to occupy his thoughts. He could accept it now, think openly of it and survive the crushing shame. He had failed the world, but there was redemption in denying that terrible doubt. Vowing to continue on. He had learned what knowledge most Alphalines were denied; he'd have little say in this war's outcome; he would merely stand upon the walls with Lea at his side and inflict what horrors he could upon whoever stood in front of him. No single person could affect immense things. Not even mad gods.

"Do I have time before we leave?" she asked, testing Baby's give. Unhappy with whatever she discovered, she turned to tighten it slightly before oiling the piece. She tested it again and grimaced before flexing her fingers. There were deeply sheltering trees in this area, plenty of quail to hunt. *No pigeon.*

"We have plenty of fresh kills. We are probably eating too much as it is."

"You're probably right. I suppose it's habit," she muttered, disappointed not to be practicing with Baby.

He drank from his water tankard and grimaced at the tepid, flavourless liquid. "Unless you could hunt some cofe." He thought on this for a moment. "We have no cofe in the east. When this war is over, I will build a nice cofe farm. We'll be wealthier than Dia herself." He drank the water again. "I'll also have a sine brewery."

"It sounds like a simple plan," she said, watching a bird in flight a hundred yards away. It looked like a pigeon. She held her arms out as though Baby was still in her grip. Drawing back on the invisible string, she followed the bird for a moment before releasing a phantom arrow into the sky.

"You pulled the shot a little left," he mocked.

"Inane conversation distracted me," she countered, drawing a second invisible arrow and releasing it. "Direct hit," she muttered as the oblivious bird disappeared into the blue. "Tell me, Erroh, as you build us great, exciting things, what shall I be doing?"

"You can do all the cooking, because you are a female." He offered a charming grin to counter her glare.

"Nice to know I'll be of value."

"Oh, yes, and we will have nine children. All of them boys. Do you want a girl? You probably want a girl. Very well, we will have ten children, so. We could teach them to be troubadours and live off their earnings."

"I would like three. That's enough," she warned, removing the sparring blades from their baggage. With optimism had come a greater frequency of sparring. Sometimes they battled three times a day, each skirmish more brutal than the last. Fully recovered from his misery in chains, Erroh was probably still the finer swordsman, but as both surpassed their supposed peaks, the difference between their skills was becoming smaller every day. She twirled both battered blades menacingly in a fine arc, waiting for him. "One quick battering before we leave?"

. . .

For a few more days they tracked the phantom Riders and their attempted concealment east of Spark City, until they reached dead lands where the path became dry and miserable. He'd seen this type of land only once before, and it had not been nearly as menacing. He'd also never dared to travel through it, for it was land directly touched by the great fires many centuries ago. Unlike most regions in the Four Factions, nature had not yet reclaimed the wilderness here. It felt like walking through the graves of an entire race, silent but for their horses' hooves clattering upon the dead ground and their snorting in the wind's dusty embrace. Spread out before them was nothing but deathly expanses of brown and orange. The tracks were unwavering, though, and led them across a massive open plain; no life ran through its sandy, desolate heart. The dead ground cracked underneath them, and he could feel his mouth drying as the wind battered them as they tramped grimly on. He felt too exposed with nothing but open dunes around them, where any half-wit keeping watch might spot their shapes against the landscape.

"Only a fool crosses the Seas of Adawan," Lea said, looking to the horizon beyond. "Unless they know it well," she added, making no attempt to cease her march.

"What lies beyond this dreaded heat?"

"I've heard bandits, murderers… those banished from the city, but who knows?" She wiped dust from her eyes. His own stung with painful tears. "Truthfully, I don't know, but I would wager more problems," she added.

"They sound like my type of people," Erroh declared, testing his water canister and discovering it only half full.

"I warn you, I think we should return to the path."

"We have a marker to follow; we have time to search. Who knows the value in knowledge?"

"Well… I suppose we've come this far. Why make any sensible decisions now?" She attempted levity, but her face was serious and driven.

. . .

They pushed on along the miserable path in pursuit of an unknown enemy with the sun burning down upon them, their fatigued beasts panting, and the carrion birds flying overhead. It was a foolish trek, yet Erroh had long ago learned to listen to his gut feelings. There had to be value in knowing what lay beyond. Only a fool tried to ignore insignificant things.

On the second morning, with their water disappearing at an alarming rate, they saw a distant speck in the mounds ahead. They followed the tracks for a few hours more until they came upon an unlikely oasis in the middle of a hidden nothingness. An island of green; a half mile wide and as deep. *Fine place to hide from war.*

She heard it first as they rested under the first suitable cover of leaves and soft earth: the low hum of activity in a solitary valley deep within a green forest surrounded by scarcity. He looked back to where they'd come from, wondering if the Hunt would consider a march. They had carefully eased themselves across this terrain in a day and a half, but the Hunt might traverse it in a harsh day's ride. For a breath, Erroh imagined staying and hiding from the world, the war, the everything. He thought of a cage and he cursed his resolve. He would never be chained again; would never fail again. He would willingly die first.

They left the magnificent beasts to graze in the grass and continued the last of their journey on foot, following the hum further in.

What they found was a town, a very strange one, hidden deep in a massive quarry. It was crude; it was aged; but it was a town nonetheless. Its construction combined the designs of the ancients and those following after. Iron structures littered the sunken landscape, rusted and crumbling, held together by wood and rope. Their uses were beyond Erroh's understanding.

"Please tell me you have little intention of going down?" she asked from beside him, taking Baby in one hand, an arrow in the other. She knew well his intentions; more than that, she knew her part to play, if needed.

"Maybe they have some salt I could borrow," he whispered, trying and failing to reassure her. It was no gathering of southerners, they discerned; however, it was just as precarious a place to stumble upon. At the far end of the sunken town the path led deeper into a tunnel lined in walls of white, and Erroh wondered as to the value of such a hidden place. Anyone could see the inhabitants of the town were no innocent salt miners. They were a fledgling society, and they wore their threat openly. As Lea had suggested, this was no place for civilisation. It wasn't the first time Erroh had seen such a nasty group of inhabitants, though at least he had no journal to lose this time.

A few males emerged from the depthless cavern rolling a couple of barrels of raw rock salt. He knew this because they left a trail of white dust behind with every heave. Each barrel held enough salt to finance most settlements for a few seasons, and the men left both barrels stacked with dozens of others, before batting clouds of white from their mouth wraps and returning to the task of mining. Erroh suspected Spark had little idea the salt mines lay at its doorstep. Perhaps the entire world's fate might have differed had the city known of such riches.

Throughout the town itself, at least a hundred dwellers went about their business as the afternoon sun warmed the world around them. Only a few dozen shacks stood intact, without shattered glass windows, collapsed roofs, and rotten wood; the rest had been abandoned. Erroh imagined a thousand people might once have lived here working the mine. Bandits were brutal, but surely a massacre on such a grand scale was beyond even their wickedness.

All the way from his hiding place among the green, he could smell the stench of waste. There was likely to be a rushing water source deep down in the cave or in the surrounding green, but wherever the source, the bandits had clearly decided against any type of sanitation. Perhaps they believed the thick flavour of salt in the air, or the thin white layer that had settled upon almost every surface, was enough to keep their home sterile. As it was, discarded waste littered the ground. From above, Erroh could see rats running freely through the muddy pathways, avoiding eager hounds also searching for a meal.

At the centre lay the largest structure, and Erroh immediately recognised it as a tavern. It bore the weight of time, its roof and walls warped and discoloured. He imagined a harsh breeze flattening it, yet the ramshackle structure still stood. Perhaps the salt preserved more than just the dried carcasses hanging by the open-air slaughterhouse standing next door. For a moment, Erroh remembered teasing a healer in the days before Keri fell.

What else can salt do?

A small group sat on its porch at a wager table. An older female with darker skin and Erroh thought her exotic. A younger player with knotted blonde hair who wore his youthful mediocrity openly. But it was the third player—a hulking commanding brute—that drew Erroh's attention. Even sitting he was impressive. A man ruling brutes would need to be and this man was king. Just once in his life, he'd have liked to challenge someone smaller than himself. *Is that too much to ask?* The man wore a jet-black sash, tied majestically like royalty, and he appeared to be winning at cards.

Erroh started to move, and Lea gripped his arm, shaking her head.

"They are not part of our world," she warned.

"They could be." He could see her concern turn to anger. Perhaps with the city so close, the shrewder move would be to slip away with their new, secret knowledge. Surely scouting was an admirable task? *Fuk that.* All would be fine if they allowed him to speak. It was just a matter of getting that allowance. He felt the nerves in his stomach.

"I must speak with them, Lea."

Her eyes were prettiest when she was angry with him. She appeared positively beautiful. "There is nothing to gain from this risk."

"They need to know of the Hunt. Moreover, they might offer something to the fight."

"This is not your task. Better with a battalion of Wolves behind you," she hissed.

"Well, you go and get them at Spark. I'll wait right here, shall I?"

"I'm wary, Erroh. What's stopping them killing you the moment you step down into that cesspit?"

"You are," he said, taking her hand and kissing it lightly. "Unless you are off finding a pack of city guards, of course." He removed his pack and the cheap swords he'd taken from the Riders. He would choose only one, preferring to greet these black-sashed bandits as a simple wanderer of the road. It usually worked. Like the southerners, these brutes favoured the honour of melee weapons over the practicality of arrow or bolt. Perhaps they shared Erroh's skill. Still, he donned his armour.

"Stay in clear sight," she warned.

"As you wish."

"Ah, this shit feels all too familiar," she grumbled, stabbing a few arrows into the soft earth in front of her before drawing one.

"And we lived through that, didn't we?"

She made no reply.

He looked at each blade he'd recovered from the Riders many weeks before and christened them "Cheap" and "Shit." He tested the tips and settled on "Cheap." Finely crafted swords were priceless out in the Wastes. With the proper materials so difficult to come upon, having two magnificent weapons was a godly thing, and losing both was a tragedy worthy of a bard's cutting tale.

He stretched himself a few times and prepared for battle. Or just conversation. *Whichever, really.*

"I am alone and offer little threat," he declared loudly, stepping out from concealment to descend the sandy slope into the pit. Raising his cheap sword in both hands above his head, he stopped at the bottom, allowing the bandits their surprise. The foul air was worse down here, and he felt his stomach turn. He didn't have to wait too long for the loud stirrings of commotion to surround him. Hushed whispers filled the air, menacing threats, collective curses all grew and suddenly fell to silence as their leader stood up. He was a big man when standing. He would have towered over Quig. However, had they faced each other, it would have appeared like a behemoth challenging its image in a mirror. It was a small world; perhaps they were brothers. Perhaps big hulking men with imposing glares just reminded him of his fallen comrade. No, Quig had been a friend, while this menacing brute had a treacherous look to him.

The brute stood away from the group, with his glass of sine, and his hand of cards and took Erroh in—as Erroh had hoped—as being no threat.

"One doesn't stroll into Adawan, little one," he called out, and the gathering crowd agreed. A few muttered threats, a few challenged Erroh's manhood, others accused him of being from the city.

Erroh ignored all of this and bowed deeply, and it appeared to work. With a wave that seemed like far too much effort, the brute gestured for the crowd to part for the newcomer. Perhaps they thought Erroh a willing bandit cub eager to join the clan, or a careless trader intending to strike a futile deal. Perhaps they thought him a random wanderer, foolish enough to stumble upon this oasis, and any of these suited Erroh just fine.

Sensing that no challenge was at hand, the crowd began to return to their duties, though half-heartedly; there was salt to refine, meat to slice. *A world to turn.* They stared coldly as he passed, all of them silent, all of them armed, all of them donning black sashes upon their armour. They were legion, this bandit group. A small army. All they needed was a cause. *Or payment.* Erroh's heart hammered; his arm itched. He was ready to kill.

"Hold your step right there so I might decide how well the day treats you," the bandit leader said, as though serving drinks in a quiet tavern. As Erroh played the unimpressive wanderer, this man played the unimpressed warrior. There was likely a boisterous threat coming. Those townspeople who had begun to disperse now stopped and turned back, looking from their leader to Erroh. Some murmured their own thoughts on the matter, and Erroh imagined he was standing in an arena with a mob hoping for blood.

"What payment do you bring to earn my favour?" the leader asked.
"My words."

The crowd fell silent as the leader drew his sword. *Boisterous threat, indeed.* Erroh scratched his arm.

"There's no need for violence, sir."

"There's always need for violence," countered the brute, stepping down from the porch and stalking him with sword raised. With every step his pace increased, and Erroh stepped back, playing the part of terrified messenger just right. Magnus had once told him that even a king should take a knee if it served his greater will.

"I bring a message of warning," Erroh cried out, dropping to his knee in subservience. Far above, he imagined Lea muttering curse after curse. He hoped he knew what he was doing; it was just like cards. He kept his grip on Cheap but kept it low. *Not yet, Lea. Not yet.*

The brute moved nearer, almost close enough to strike. Almost close enough for Erroh to dodge the strike, remove the attacker's blade and shove it up a place that endured little sunshine. Even on a day like this. "Speak up, or I'll have your pelt," he growled, slowing suddenly and likely saving himself an arrow through the neck.

"Sir, my name is Erroh of the road, and I've heard and seen very worrying things," Erroh of the road said quietly. He watched the bigger man's movement, searching for signs of a sudden strike. The blade's perfect tip hovered intimidatingly above his sweat-covered forehead. He'd been here before. It would be fine. He thought it a nice blade. "War is in the wind. An army marches on Spark."

"Are you alone?"

"I am."

"Come on, I'm in no mood for any wanderer's whispers from the Wastes, but fuk it, I've had a dreary morning. I could do with a laugh." The man turned away, muttering something about his name being Ulrik and motioning for Erroh to follow him. Erroh got to his feet and went over to the tavern; Ulrik had stepped back up to the porch, and he bade Erroh sit at the card table opposite before offering the little pile of pieces stacked up neatly in two perfect towers.

"I'll likely kill you, but, until I decide the matter," he gestured to the cards, "do you play?"

Somewhere behind, Erroh heard a muted curse as a warrior lost his gambled wealth to an interloper. The defeated man kicked the dust a few times before someone ordered him to preform sentry duty along the ridge between green and pit.

Muttering to himself, the bandit accepted the charge and marched up towards Lea's hiding place, his curses growing louder until he disappeared into the treeline and suddenly stopped. When discovered unconscious later, he would declare that he never knew who knocked him out, but that there were at least three fiends brandishing clubs.

Erroh spoke of the Hunt and the marching menace, and Ulrik appeared unimpressed. As Erroh spoke the bandit eyed the dark-skinned female but she gave even less away. Though there might have been a glimmer of recognition when he mentioned the Riders.

Eventually Ulrik heard enough. "Admittedly, pickings have been slim. There have been plenty of convoys travelling to Spark Shitty, but they have provided precarious pickings at best." His grey eyes studied Erroh intently. Still, though, despite his threats, there was something likeable about the brute. Perhaps there was something behind the bravado? He offered Erroh the cards, and Erroh dealt from the bottom.

"Erroh... Erroh... That's an interesting name," whispered Ulrik of the Adawan.

"I've always thought so, sir."

"Few with that name. And there might be one less a few breaths from now, what with walking into hostile territory with no regard for himself or his hosts." Ulrik opened his bet with a few pieces and Erroh met them tenfold. To play any more would be a rather expensive task for Ulrik. Harder to play a humble hand when playing at being humble.

"It seemed like the right thing to do... sir," he added, losing the quiver in his voice. The giant poured a small glass of sine and pushed it in front of the cub. *Fuk it.* Erroh drank deeply without breaking eye contact with the killer. He hadn't tasted sine in so long. He felt the burn hit his stomach and he knew the familiar warmth would soon surround his entire being. It felt like sitting at a table with old friends. He coughed.

Ulrik matched him and then poured a second and sighed, looking at his hands as any gambler would, knowing the inevitable next play. "Erroh... Erroh... Eeeee... row... Air... oh... Not too many Air-ohs at all. We live in a small world upon vast lands. Do we need another war wiping out whatever's left of us? Tell me, Erroh, is the butcher Magnus marching to slaughter some of us and save the rest?"

"Magnus does not march."

"Are you sure?"

Erroh wasn't sure at all, so he over-bet and threw his winning hand down before Ulrik could match his bet. A foolish gambit. The mention of his father had unsettled him.

Ulrik placed his cards down in defeat and shoved the winning pieces over to Erroh's large pile. "Why is it always southerners with a bone to pick? Still, though, the east is quite a distance away." He took the cards back and began shuffling. His fingers were a blur, the fingers of a man who spent most of his days playing. He began dealing from the bottom, obviously, for all to see.

"Distance doesn't matter. They number enough to take Spark City."

Ulrik's hands were still for a breath and then he continued to deal. "The city and its bloodlines have never approved of my... lifestyle. So why should I care?"

"War is bad for business, even for bandits."

He laughed. "That wasn't exactly what I meant, little Erroh of the east. The city has little issue with bandits; we keep her blood moving. Saying that, I agree war would be bad for all."

"If you join our effort, they could make allowances for your... lifestyle." *Whatever that means.* "You know this land; you know the paths better than any scout. We could use your knowledge," Erroh said, dropping his cards at a lost bet. He dropped all pretence of the lowly wanderer. His voice was assured now, his stare as cold as chains in the snow. "You command hundreds in this pit. All skilled, all hardened. War is coming and you must play a part."

"Look around. There's little reason for this war to spill over into

my territory. No, little Alphaline, we will play no part in the days
ahead."

"You and your people are cowards so," Erroh hissed.

"Watch your tone, little cub. You don't know who you play with."

He leaned in close now, and Erroh downed his sine. He had a
feeling there would be no third drink offered. The bigger man was
intimidating and used to disagreement. Begging, pleading, pledging
would do little to sway his mind on the matter. Spitting into the ground
at the larger man's feet, Erroh eyed him coldly.

"I've said my part, Ulrik. If you cannot serve a better calling than
this, I will be on my way." Scooping up his unearned pieces and
pocketing them swiftly, he stood up from the table and turned to leave.

"A legend's kin would earn quite a ransom," Ulrik warned,
standing up himself. "The Hero of Keri would also be some coup."

Hero of Keri?

"A bandit leader's head would earn just as much," Erroh said
evenly.

"I'm sure it would. I think we've spoken enough."

"I came here under the banner of peace. I came here to warn you,"
Erroh argued, hiding his frustration as best he could.

"You came here to recruit for an army of your own. I followed your
father once. I have no taste for such butchery again. Now…" Ulrik
reached for his impressive-looking sword and held it casually over the
table. "How can I trust you to keep this fine sanctuary secret?"

Oh, Lea would not let him forget this misstep soon. He would
suffer her mocking all the way back to the city. Worse than that, she
would be right in mocking him. In his defence, he would try anything.
How many of his dreams involved endless crushing numbers marching
towards himself and Lea. Aye, this insignificant collection of bandits
might have little bearing on the war's outcome, but they would need
every hand. Erroh raised his own hand as though stretching, as though
pointing to the sky above.

"I give you my word."

This didn't appear to appease Ulrik, who laughed and held his
blade out in front of Erroh. This was going wonderfully. His sword arm

The March of Magnus

rested on the grip of his cheap sword. He had more to say, but sometimes actions spoke louder. He dropped his arm as though beginning a fair fight between two contestants in an arena.

Thunk.

An arrow from somewhere above embedded itself in the playing table, and Erroh immediately raised his arm again, stepping away from the shaking table and its unsteady contents.

"Hold!" roared Ulrik to his bandit brethren, who had immediately taken up arms. "The next one will go through my eye, yes?" he said, looking uneasily at Erroh.

"Oh, no. If it goes through your eye you'll just keel over and die. No, better it goes through your neck. Far more dramatic." Beside him the exotic female reached for her drink and Erroh thought her nerve impressive.

"A sound tactic," admitted Ulrik, eyeing the arrow and looking up for the offending archer.

"You won't find them," Erroh hissed, backing away from the table and dropping from the porch. He had questions about Keri and his father, but keeping the same number of Errohs in the world took precedence.

"Ah, fuk it—would you look at that?" spat Ulrik, sliding a card up the shaft of the arrow. He tore the ruined ace of queens free and flicked it away. "Threaten a man in his home, but don't kill his fuken cards."

"My apologies. If you come see me at the city, I will purchase a new deck for you," Erroh declared solemnly, backing away, watching every fiend around him. They stood tense, ready to strike, ready to destroy. It was only Ulrik holding his arms out that stopped them from attacking.

You once took on an entire army single-handed. What's a little group of bandits?

"You may have earned an enemy this day, little Erroh," Ulrik said. He followed Erroh cautiously down the steps, as much to escort him from this pit as to ensure no arrow struck him down.

"All my friends think as much, when first we meet," Erroh replied, reaching the pit's slope and hurrying his retreat. With a mocking bow, he spun around and charged up into the treeline, hoping Ulrik would give no further chase. Fortunately, the bandit leader must have believed he was still in an archer's sights, or perhaps simply that killing Erroh would fail to make his day any less dreary. Whatever the reason, he gave no further pursuit.

"Don't say a word—just run," he said under his breath upon reaching Lea in the green's cover. She looked like she had several words to say. "Just... don't say a fuken word."

They disappeared into the green, listening for the sound of riders in pursuit. Erroh couldn't relax until their mounts had carried them far from the green oasis, deep into the burning deathly lands. Only then, without a sign of following dots on the horizon behind them, did they slow their pace.

And only then did Lea bring her mount alongside his. She had the tact to conceal her smirk, but it was there, just beginning to upturn her exquisite lips.

"So, my beo, that simple plan didn't work terribly well, did it?"

21

THE MAGNUS WAY

"I think any good beginning is saying sorry," Magnus said. "You have incurred her wrath, you have earned her anger, so embrace it and perhaps in time, she might let you embrace her again. Though, do not hold your breath."

He looked upon Wynn as any disapproving father would, upon hearing of dreadful behaviour. Wynn had had not yet grasped the extent of his misstep; perhaps, with education and a touch more wisdom he might. For now, his usual reliance on charm would do little until he'd mastered the art of goodness. Magnus knew people well enough and was worse for it. People weren't inherently good. Any fool believing that believed in fairness in the world and the value of opinions—particularly their own.

He took a breath and Wynn waited, watching him as though every word was golden, and perhaps to the little cub, they were. Wynn was a good man without a fuken clue.

"Winning her back might takes years." He was tempted to allay the boy's worries, but what good would protecting him accomplish? Marvel had trained this cub poorly, and it was no surprise the cub was volatile, immature, unprepared for the grit of this world. He had a poet's soul, and poets without steel beneath their skin were crushed.

And Lillium? Well, any person could see she was a right fuken mess altogether. Truthfully, Magnus had never met a less suited couple than this. Regardless, there was hope for them. It hadn't been a stroll for himself and Elise. Their missteps had started a war. And ended it.

"I appreciate your advice, Master General, but it is not your affair to discuss… and… she was just as cruel to me as I was to her." It was a fine argument, and one whispered from a child who believed the world was fair, and that his opinion mattered.

"Avoid sleeping with her, Wynn. At least for a time," Magnus continued, ignoring the younger man's words. From two sources he'd learned of their downfall. Admittedly, Wynn's own explanation was less condemning than Elise's account, but it was enough for Magnus to understand Lillium's growing desolation and understand what needed doing. It would start with words, followed by entertaining things after.

The wind rapped itself against the tarp and the fabric shuddered loudly. Though the weather had improved, today's march would be bitterly cold. It was days like this that he missed his home the most. When a thin layer of sheeting was not enough to stave off the cold; when his muscles ached constantly; when his mate's breath was a dull, aching rasp. He longed for days when awful matters were discussed upon comfortable chairs in front of roaring fires and a goblet of wine to numb the embarrassment. And these conversations were embarrassing. As it was, he had to make do with a freezing tent flapping in the wind, tight muscles and the offer of a wooden stool to his guest.

"Surely you can see how little she values herself, Wynn?"

Wynn just shook his head in puzzlement.

"How do you see her?" Magnus asked, watching Wynn closely. The boy squirmed like a cantus eel upon a line. He was unprepared for conversations like this, and silently, Magnus cursed the cub's father anew for not preparing him.

"Well, she is a goddess," whispered Wynn, lest his mate hear his compliment, lest he show his warmth for her; lest he show anything beyond frustration.

This pleased Magnus, who stood up. "Aye, she is a goddess! That is the first thing you've said all day that hasn't made my skin crawl or my stomach turn in disgust." As he spoke, he stood over the smaller man and began stretching his limbs. His tendons popped loudly, his joints crunched, but the relief was immediate.

"If I were younger, there would be any manner of things Elise and I would do to her. Things that would make the girl smile all night." It was only half a jest. Perhaps in peacetime when he didn't feel responsible for her, when her mind wasn't as fragile... Wynn needed to remember just who he'd mated and how much a man should fight for precious things, for if this went on much longer, they would slip further apart. "You must remind her why she chose you."

"How?"

"Start all over again, little cub. Start before desire separated you."

"But, where to begin?" Wynn muttered. "How can we undo what occurred?"

"Oh, that is rather easy, and something you probably should have known before walking the Wastes with any mate. Do not take her to your bed until she invites you... if she ever invites you, that is."

The old Ranger flipped back the tent flap and beckoned for his protégé to follow him out into the fresh morning air. He spoke as though discussing tactics, which in part they were. Fine tactics, to save a mated couple. Wynn looked around for any sign of his mate, a difficult task given the bustle of activity as the Rangers prepared for the day's march ahead. All around them, campfires were being covered and concealed, tents were stripped and packed, horses were brushed and saddled. Despite the cool breeze, he could feel that the warmth of the north and the dryer nights were drawing nearer. Soon enough, they wouldn't need tents at all when simple bedding beneath the stars would suffice at the end of each day. A better thing; more rest meant more marching. *Not far now, not far at all.*

Though the march had been swift and without incident, the last few days had been tough on Elise. He could have halted the charge or, worse, left her for a few days to rest, but war was stirring and a legend couldn't show weakness. Even for Elise. No, she was tough and the path was clearing. Better to keep going and recuperate in Samara. Besides, she'd never allow him to leave her behind.

He spoke low, for he had golden knowledge to share. Knowledge that ensured any girl he lay with left his bed with a tale to tell. Knowledge he'd learned under the watchful eye of the first goddess he'd ever known. Knowledge a father should pass on to a son.

"If you earn her desire again and she asks you to her bed, go with only one thought: to pleasure her."

Wynn raised an eyebrow, much to the bemusement of the bigger man. Behind them Lillium appeared from somewhere in the surrounding forest, and Magnus thought this perfect timing; it was almost as though she had arranged it. The last of the faded blue in Lillium's long dark hair was gone. Magnus knew she had stopped colouring her hair, and he approved. Wynn, however, sighed for the loss. Elise followed with scissors in hand. Both were engrossed in hushed conversation, and Magnus offered a silent prayer to the absent gods. Lillium had been the source of Elise's comfort and strength in these trying times.

"Look at her, Wynn. Isn't she the most desirable girl you've ever seen? Don't you want to make her scream in pleasure?"

"I tried."

"You pleased yourself."

"She enjoyed it."

"Did a wiser man than you not take you aside and explain a woman's needs?"

Wynn shuffled his feet. "I know where everything goes." His face was crimson in embarrassment, and Magnus almost relented, almost left it, for these were words rightly shared between father and son. Between master and apprentice. Marvel had a lot to answer for; allowing his son to walk into the world without preparation was just cruel. No young cub would master the art of bedding a lady from the beginning, for that took nearly a lifetime. However, being skilled in the act once you found yourself there was something else entirely, and something to learn at any age. He cleared his throat and kept his voice low, as if these were eternal secrets to be taken to the grave—and they probably were.

"If she invites you to her bed, do not allow your manhood to touch her. At least, for a time."

"That doesn't sound like—"

Magnus interrupted him by clipping him across the head. Better he listen and understand. "Wynn, we are strange, amazing creatures with far too many appendages that go to waste. Use them all, and use them upon her entire body. Use them until she wails, use them until you satisfy her beyond reason, use them until she comes for you. For she is your goddess and worthy of such things."

"But what if—"

"Whisht! Aye, you never shut up!" Magnus resisted the urge to clout him across the head again. "Start with your tongue. Start by kissing the most pleasing parts of her body. For the entire night, if need be, until…"

"Until?"

"Until only you are left unsatisfied."

"Every time?"

"Every fuken time. And when she reaches for you, well, make sure it is memorable." Wynn appeared relieved at this advice, although nervous, to be sure. And why not? It wasn't every day a young man learned that his prowess beneath the blankets was less than impressive. He had taken his humbling lack of knowledge well, however, and his instruction better. Unfortunately, the lessons were far from over. Mere words could never return the distance between the couple. The truth was, Lillium's crimes were insignificant compared to Wynn's unintentional nastiness. Words and apologies were a fine start, but sometimes it took a little more.

Wynn's pride was stung, but there was a relief to revealing everything to Magnus. In fact, the older man's words made his responsibilities appear simple. He would do better, he told himself.

I can't do any worse.

"When this is over, tell Lillium you had it coming." Magnus said, leading him through the mass of movement up towards a long-abandoned shack around which they'd made camp. Whoever had lived in this shack had chosen wisely; the path was clear and the forest surrounding it was likely to gift any hunter a lifetime supply of meat.

"When she asks, tell her exactly why you had it coming, too," the Master General added.

Beyond the shack was a lake stretching out for miles either way, and Wynn imagined that if hunting was too difficult a task, anyone could live off the fish they caught.

"When this is over," Magnus finished, "tell her this was a gift."

Wynn understood nothing of what Magnus was saying, but he nodded regardless, hoping to catch the meaning in some words. They drew nearer the shack and Wynn noticed that when there wasn't an entire army settled, the land was damp and green. He imagined a farmer growing all he needed in this soil. It was a fine place to make camp, but it was a finer place to build a shack and live. He looked back and was surprised to see Lillium and Elise following. Their voices had fallen silent. Elise's pale face wore the smile offered when you've just bought a useless map from a devious tavern keeper. He didn't like that smile, not one bit. And Lillium, well, she wore her misery openly, and a pang of guilt struck him. Perhaps he really was as naïve in the ways of females as Magnus suggested.

"When this is over, tell her your blood is contrition; that this is just the start. Tell her you are sorry," Magnus told him.

"My blood?" Wynn asked, and Magnus punched him through the shack wall. Admittedly, it wasn't a very good wall, it smelled of dampness, but it was still very much a wall. Now it was kindling.

I had this coming.

Wynn felt the blood stream from his nose. Crawling on all fours as wooden planks fell around him, all he could do was count his front teeth. He'd lost none, but his face stung something terrible.

"What the fuk, Master General?" he rasped, scrambling from the ruin of a wall before crashing through the makeshift door, hoping to escape the next assault. "Ouch." He stumbled away from the wreckage as the shack around him crumbled. A hundred years it might have stood, and Magnus had ruined it in moments.

I had this coming.

He repeated the mantra in his head and fought the growing darkness as Magnus fell upon him, battering his reason. He scrambled from the behemoth's grip, kicking out as he did, and slid in the wet muddy ground. Stumbling, he caught Lillium's eye and, humbled as he was, he was glad she watched. He spat away some blood, and a pair of hands took hold and battered him a little bit more. The world spun and he was falling and he caught sight of Elise standing beside Lillium, her eyes fierce and cold. This was likely her doing, and he had it coming and it was all right because he had been wrong and Lillium deserved more than he'd ever given.

"Stupid little cub," Magnus roared, and took hold of him again, slapping him with an open palm. The crack sent a few birds flying from a branch above. Wynn watched them go as his head flew back and hung loosely in the big man's powerful grip. Magnus held him upright for a painful few breaths, deciding if he'd received enough of a beating. It turned out that he hadn't, because a moment later he was flung like a child's doll back through the rubble of the century-old shack. Once again, Wynn climbed to his feet and even managed a weak block against the charging Magnus. Unfortunately, one block wasn't nearly enough to diminish the beast's charge, and he swiftly received a fist-shaped hammer to the stomach, before he could counter. This strike took his breath and he fell to his knees, trying to avoid throwing up all over himself.

"Give me a moment," he gasped, and Magnus took hold of his hair and shook him fiercely.

I had this coming.

"Fight me," Magnus demanded, shoving him to the ground in disgust, and Wynn could only spit the taste of bloodied mud from his mouth. With as much force as he could muster, he tried to trip the bigger man with a sweeping kick. Magnus easily outmanoeuvred his attempt by skilfully taking a step back, laughing aloud at the pathetic effort, and Wynn's humiliation was complete. "My youngest could do better."

I had this coming.

197

"Of course she could do better. She's my daughter," Elise said, and dimly, Wynn saw Lillium snigger; this stung worse than any battering. Still, though, he had it coming and he would take this battering, because… well… because Magnus suggested he should. Wynn had tried for so many months, but now, in this bloody moment, he understood his failures. He wanted to cry out. He wanted to beg for a reprieve. Part of him imagined her leaping in between them and pulling him free. Saving him like a good mate should. The rest wanted to take the pain tenfold and show her he could change.

Magnus's fists hurt terribly, but that wouldn't stop the onslaught. Besides, he was enjoying himself. And why not? This was a fine way to relieve a great march's stresses; to relieve himself of the terrible rage he felt every day. And, perhaps, attempting to heal the wounds of a foolish young couple was good for the soul. He couldn't sit down with Lillium and offer comforting words. He had them to offer, for he was no mindless brute, but words like his were better coming from the mouth of another woman. That was how it was.

He charged through the camp, battering the younger man who stumbled before him. His Rangers had the good sense to ignore the beating. They'd seen many skirmishes and had likely been part of a few themselves. An army was no place to hold silent a quarrel, and Magnus approved of such events. *Better for morale.* This was a Ranger's life, and it was brutal. Though nowhere near as brutal as the life of a young Alphaline.

The one-sided fight brought both combatants towards the centre of the campsite, and Magnus decided Wynn had had near enough. He swung wildly and missed by quite a distance, allowing Wynn an opening for a decent counter. Enough to get a lick in before the knock-out blow; enough to give the younger man confidence. Wynn, however, attempted no counter; instead, he opted for a stumbling retreat over redeeming his pride, and Magnus was thoroughly disappointed. Fearing one more blow over the chance of victory was no way for any Alphaline to behave. *Marvel has not trained the boy properly.* Wynn managed a full three steps before Magnus took hold of him, spun him around and cracked his fist upon his chin, knocking him out cold. When he came to, Elise and Lillium carried him to his tent.

"I'll take no bed. Roll out a rug for me," the cub muttered dreamily, and Magnus approved.

————

Lillium sat by her battered mate and counted with silent satisfaction the bruises on his shirtless body. She laid the cold, bloody cut of steak across his beaten face and sat back to write in her journal. Outside, the Rangers were disassembling the camp. They would leave them behind for at least a day, and though Lillium thought it a small matter, she knew she would dislike the quiet hours alone, for she had grown rather accustomed to the rumble of the march. She had never believed she would favour a life in the corps, yet these months had been curiously rewarding. If nothing else, a hard day's march allowed for even less uncomfortable conversation with her mate than usual. She enjoyed the duties of a soldier's life, and sparring had become a wonderful pastime again. Oh, how proud her parents would be were they to know her calling towards this life had stirred something fierce in her. How bitterly disappointed they would be to know she marched under the Rangers' banner. She was a city girl, was she not? Her allegiance to the city should have prevailed.

"I'm sorry, Lillium," Wynn whispered, and she shrugged as though she'd heard this a thousand times before. She had. The steak slid from his face and she caught it. "I had this coming," he whispered, taking the steak from her hand and seeing to his own wounds.

She looked at him curiously and thought on the shame he would doubtless be feeling after such a beating. Seeing him humbled had pleased her more than she'd expected. More than Elise had suggested it would.

"Aye, you had it coming. It was brutal."

He didn't reply. Instead, he closed his eyes and fell back asleep as the concoction they'd given him for the pain stole his consciousness.

She watched him for a while as he took shallow breaths and allowed her mind to wander. In this light, with such vicious injuries, she thought he could have passed for a dead body, crushed by a wagon or struck down by a dozen arrows. Strangely, she wasn't troubled by this vision and thought on it a little while longer, until his snoring killed the illusion and she returned to her journal.

22

THE VISIT

R oja could hear her breath in the driving rain, gasping and
desperate. Her feet clattered loudly on the cobbled ground but
their echo was lost in the deluge. *It's too late.* At this lonely hour of the
night there was no one in the city willing to answer her call, or their
door. She knew where the city healers healed, just not where they slept.
Great leader you are. As she sprinted beneath another arch in this
endless city, her dress ripped and she willed herself to push harder. She
was soaked to the bone, all warmth lost in the bitter cold, but she
would endure it all for as long as it took. Ahead of her, the monstrous
figure of Wrek lumbered doggedly on. For a man his size, he could
move with swift feet; she struggled to keep his pace, but somehow, she
did. The grey and hazy electric glimmer of the night was lost to the
agonising rush of the chase. She became nothing more than the
constant drumming of feet in a terrible race. Rhythmic and anguished,
and so fuken exhausted. Another arch, another side street, another
silent charge.

"Open the fuken gate," Wrek roared, and his influence prevailed,
for a gap into the world beyond appeared, allowing them through. His
white shirt was soaked through; he hadn't taken a moment to grab a
coat when she'd appeared at his doorway. Begging for help was not

below her now, for greater things were at play. Power struggles in the city could wait. A life was in the balance. Possibly two, for she would slit the throat of the absent healer charged to stand this night.

"Move!" she hissed, passing both bewildered gate guards. They did not try to calm the passing storm, and she sprinted through, almost tripping as she spun left towards the hovels along the wall. *Desperate times.* The gentle glow from the city walls lit up the dirty pathways through the little shacks, but still, every step was near calamitous. How fine a sight it would be to see the queen bitch of the city humbled and stumbled, collapsed in a ruin among the debris, for there was debris everywhere. She'd never walked this part; she'd never seen such dreadfulness. Aye, she'd known of it, but it may as well have been a thousand miles away.

Wrek, however, knew the path well enough, stopping only a handful of times to catch his bearings and then taking off again, swerving left of a flimsy wooden structure, ducking low beneath a tarp support, or charging straight over a dead campfire as he went. She followed each step of his, tripping only once on a nasty bucket of waste. The air was thick with foulness and she found it hard to breathe. How could anybody live like this? *Linn had.* As had her parents, for a time.

Finally, Wrek reached a little hovel door in the heart of the slums. It was a fine door, the only one in a strangely snug little shack. It looked like it had been constructed purely to lock out the outside world. Wrek battered the door as though he were battering a drunkard unwilling to leave the premises. Each strike was as loud as a war drum, and by the third beat he apparently decided it wasn't working. Without warning, he stepped back and charged straight through the finely-crafted door, and everything went to hell.

Quig crashed through the door and Lara leapt from her bed in fright. He stumbled through the ruin of a doorframe and she almost fell upon him, weeping. Her big man had found her, her big man still lived. Deep down, she found something she'd lost. She felt a whisper stir. It leapt from her breath and birthed into the world, the first words she'd spoken in months: the beautiful name of a boy she'd loved, bursting forth in a wail.

"Quig!"

Before she could take a second breath, Emir knocked her back into the bed they shared, standing in front protectively. This made no sense to her. In the dim light she could see Emir raise a fist and throw it at her Quig, and this made less sense, but she trusted him, for Emir was her only family. Everyone else was dead. *So was Quig.* Except he had just broken down the door and was roaring incomprehensible words at her. She screamed even louder. Her big man. Her Quig.

The deafening roar of a mostly naked young lady screaming her heart out filled the room. Roja stood stunned, her eyes wide. Amidst the curses, the threats, the outrage and the wailing, a candle was lit by an equally topless figure, and calm returned. As the flickering flame took hold, Emir threw some sheets to cover his bed-mate's shame, and Roja ignored the turn of her stomach. She leaned against the unsteady wall, gasping for breath, and the roof creaked under the weight. The damp room smelled of eucalyptus, sweat and stale alcohol. There was enough space for a double bed of cheap sheets and blankets and little else. Upon the walls were various labelled jars of healing oddities, most of which were empty. In one corner lay an old crossbow and a handful of bolts. In another sat a few journals and books stacked as neatly as possible. She didn't know what she'd expected, really; he had always claimed he and everyone else had nothing. Somehow, seeing it for herself brought his desperation closer. Still, though, he had a lover, didn't he? That wasn't nothing at all.

"Quig…" The blonde female slipped from behind Emir and took hold of a thoroughly confused Wrek. She repeated this name again and again until Emir took her shoulders and hushed her gently, like a kind father to a terrified child, and Roja's own frantic panic was lost in a strange, tender moment.

"This is not Quig," he whispered. "Quig died with Aireys in Keri.

They died together," he added, and eased her from Wrek. "They died together, little one. They died together."

The girl's voice faded to a whisper. Emir held her tightly and guided her slowly back to the side of the bed. Her eyes never left Wrek at the doorway, but some realisation took the strength from her knees. Roja didn't know why Emir spoke to his lover as he did, but she thought it a touch unsavoury. *Does he whisper like that as he furrows her?* She shook that thought away. He was welcome to do whatever he wanted. *Whomever?*

"This is Wrek," Emir said, "and he ruined my fuken door."

The girl shook as though she, too, had spent far too long sprinting in a night's cold downpour. She couldn't take her eyes off Wrek, though. "I'm… sorry," she said, and her voice was broken, like that of a child rather than the impressively chested female she was. "I thought you were…" Whatever words she'd attempted failed her, and Emir stroked her cheek as she fell silent.

"It's fine, lass," Wrek said, shifting guiltily from foot to foot. In the candlelight, Roja could see his face blush. "I'm sorry for causing you such a fright," he said. "It wasn't any way for a beast to behave." He looked at the door apologetically. *Big man see door smash.* Any other night it might have been funny. She remembered their mission: Linn needed a healer's touch, and the shock of catching Emir on top of another girl was wearing off now.

"She hasn't spoken—" Emir began, but Roja interrupted.

"I need your help, healer. I need it now," she demanded. "Linn is dying." She tried to make it sound angry—to threaten him, to make him come with her and fix little miss Linn. It sounded desperate instead.

"Tell me what happened."

Emir had heard that tone more often than he liked these days. It didn't matter the issue or prejudice; that tone was instinctive and universal. Usually, the matter was nowhere near as serious as the loved one suspected, but it was impossible convincing them otherwise. Besides, allaying their fears was energy misspent. He'd fix their loved ones; that was enough.

"Do you know how long it took to get a fuken door with locks in this wretched place?" he grumbled. "Most people just scream until I answer. Could you not have waited a moment longer?" He pulled a shirt over his bare chest. Most nights now, Lara climbed into his bed, and so he'd taken to wearing his trousers to sleep, with a thick cord wrapped tightly in a knot where a belt should have been. It kept his trousers up, but mostly, it kept them on. *Even when drunk.* Stefan referred to them as "Emir's belt." He'd like to say he would be a gentleman, that he could control his urges, but he was well aware of the beast in men, driven by desire and a moment of thoughtlessness. She would allow him, he knew, and that temptation was the terrible thing, for she was not herself. *Not anymore.* So, he tied that knot really fuken tight, and avoided destroying something lost and beautiful. The shirt, however, had had to go. Most nights were too warm, especially when he woke up to her wrapped against him and the only thing to cool him was her silent, sleeping tears.

Looking into the rain through the door-shaped hole, he shivered. "It was warmer earlier," he muttered, as a means of explaining why there was a mostly naked girl in his bed. He could have explained to Wrek, but what did it matter? And would Roja really care?

He dressed swiftly while Roja explained Linn's sufferings; he recognised the girl's plight and knew how swiftly he needed to act. They'd found no real cure for the affliction; only treatments, and most never worked for long. They called it "heavy lung," and he'd studied it as a youth in the city. Perhaps, with the proper time and the most brutal of experiments, he might have understood this illness better. As it was, he understood enough about the harsh concoctions used to treat it; there was only so much room inside a fragile young healer's soul before looking in the mirror became too much. He knew heavy lung to be a cruel sickness. Spread not through touch or breath, but by the bloodline itself, it drowned whomever it touched, from the wildest Alpha to the lowliest child. It didn't matter, really. What mattered was finding the right concoction to clear the clogged airways.

The child was young; she would panic without a calming presence at her side. He suggested as much, and only then did Roja lose her harshness. Instead, the blood left her face and Emir regretted his words.

"Lara, I have to go," he whispered, but Lara only had eyes for Wrek. In her defence, the resemblance was eerie; he himself had believed his old friend had returned the first day they'd met. Perhaps a shock like this was all she needed, he thought hopefully.

The sheeting covering her naked chest slipped down, and Wrek swiftly pulled one of the fallen blankets from the ground and offered it blindly. She took it for the gift it was and nodded slightly, her voice lost again. *But it had been there.* Emir had attempted so many things to drag her out from misery. Who knew all it took was a big hulking brute crashing through the door in the middle of the night?

Emir picked up his medical bag. "I have little to treat her." Another consequence of the slums was the limited supplies. His former master, Old Jun, was never one to share from his stock, and even though Emir had begged for the meekest scraps of healing herbs and any spare tonics, Old Jun's heart was about as open as Spark City's gate. He gave little, saving his finery for the citizens of Samara. Those with pieces in their pockets.

"Roja will show me the way. As for you, Wrek, and your destructive abilities..." Emir looked at the door. "Anybody can stroll in here now and take what paltry riches I have."

"You want me to wait here until you return?" Wrek asked, unsure of himself. Unsure of the mostly naked girl's intentions, but wanting to undo whatever ruin he'd caused.

Emir spotted Lara gripping the blanket a little tighter around herself. Being alone with a stranger was a different beast altogether. She looked ready to fall to pieces. He knelt down beside her and touched her hand tenderly. She blinked back tears, and she stared at Wrek and did not cry and Emir was so proud of her. He spun away from the girl, stepping close to Wrek, who, up close, was even more impressive. Not that it mattered.

"She's been through terrible things." He trusted the massive warrior, but their friendship was only a few months old. How well could you know anyone in that time? He dug his finger into the behemoth's chest. Bigger or no, his meaning was clear. Were something unsavoury to occur, Wrek would not see dawn.

Wrek bowed deeply. "I give you my word, sir. I will watch the door. Go, save the child."

"Thank you Wrek… and keep talking to her."

It would be only a little stealing on his part, Emir told her, and Roja had nodded without argument. More than that, she suggested that she be the one to break into the abandoned healer's quarters, lest he knock himself out trying. Before she could, however, he gripped her shoulder softly.

"It's a nice door. Let's use the window instead." He hopped up onto the frame with surprising grace and put his foot through the glass with no regard for the noise of it, cleared the frame of shards and hopped inside. Two of the Black Guard, alerted by Emir's voice and the smashing of glass, had come running up some side steps with weapons drawn. But one threatening stare and a dismissive gesture from the Primary in waiting sent them on their way.

If questioned about the break-in the following morning, they would report nothing out of the ordinary.

After a lot of rummaging and loud cursing, Roja heard the flip of a bolt and the fine old oak door creaked open. Emir's bag was packed to the brim, as were his pockets. As was the little sack on his back.

"She might need more," he assured her in that same tone. It wouldn't suit arguing his motives. She gamely carried the healer's bag as they jogged away towards the great chambers of the Alphalines.

This building was one of the few original structures still standing. Its walls matched those of the surrounding city wall and felt just as eternal. It towered over all the other rooftops around it, and a pair of sleepy guards stood at its entrance leaning upon their pikes. They immediately straightened up as Roja led Emir through the main doors. She hadn't attempted to explain why she'd charged from this building less than an hour before, and she offered less explanation now as to why she returned bearing the sound of a thousand chinking trinkets followed by a scruffy wretch as her night guest. *Just more rumours.*

The hallowed building was always cool, and tonight was no different. Their footsteps were silent in the thick carpet, and they swept through dimly lit corridors, up creaking staircases, climbing level after level until they reached the top. It was here that Roja's steps were swiftest, each filled with trepidation of the great unknown. One question ran through her head in a dreadful mantra, hammering along with her heart.

Does she live? Does she live? Does she live?

"How is she?" she gasped, falling through her doorway as the dreary, low light of melancholic grey and black gave way to the warmth of light and vibrant colour.

Roja lived well. That was the advantage of having cleaner, richer blood, Emir supposed. He looked around her quarters and saw that they resembled his own, and he immediately felt a pang of sorrow for Keri. Pictures adorned the walls, and soft silken fabrics padded the furniture. Rugs covered the varnished wooden floor throughout the five-room palace, lit by many little bulbs of stinging electric light; they cast shadows upon her many treasures and all the shades of colour accompanying them. How many wretches could inhabit these lavish accommodations? he wondered.

A young girl, fifteen at most, led him through the main room into an unnaturally warm bedroom. Inside, the young Linn lay in a bed of silken sheets and woollen blankets. She lay on her back, wheezing; her eyes darted from side to side in panic and he could hear the blockage in her lungs. Her forehead had a nasty bruise from where she'd collapsed, and her face was deathly pale but for rosy cheeks. It was little surprise Roja had been convinced she was dying. He laid his treasures aside and, careful not to disturb her, examined her swiftly.

"Shush, little one. You remember the healer. All will be well now," Roja whispered tenderly, and Emir could hear the relief in her voice.

"She has calmed somewhat, but the attack is getting worse," Roja's younger companion offered, leaving him to his work. "I tried to get her to control her breathing, but she barely listens to me."

"Thank you for staying with her, Lexi," Roja said.

Emir recovered a few ingredients from his bag, and the room filled with a bitter stench. He could feel their impatient eyes upon him as he ground them to a pulp with his mortar and pestle, but he would not be rushed. This was his arena. He added the ingredients to a clear fluid and the stench became aromatic. Immediately, he felt his own breath come easier. Linn must have sensed something too, as she took a deep breath and hacked violently, and he shushed her to calm like a father would a child. He promised that the aromatic sludge he massaged across her chest would fix her right up, and soon enough her breathing quietened. After a time, her blinking, watching eyes settled and at last, she fell asleep, snoring lightly.

"See? No problem at all. I will stay a little while longer, but I believe she'll be fine," he whispered to Roja, who still stood in the bedroom's doorway. Leaving a jar of the potent elixir by the child's bedside, he wiped the eucalyptus smell from his hands onto his shirt, its potent aroma covering his own. Better than nothing, he supposed, thinking how badly his own stench filled the room.

"Thank you, Emir," Roja whispered. She turned to the young girl and embraced her. "Thank you for everything you did, Lexi… You were right."

"Ah, it was a small matter. I've just had some experience," Lexi replied, turning to leave. Before she did, she looked Emir up and down just once, and he expected a sniff of disapproval, for, despite his deeds, he was still just a wretch. "So, you are the famous Emir, then?" She smiled before bowing deeply to Roja and slipping out into the darkened hallway. "He really does have a nice jaw," she said mockingly, as Roja slammed the door behind her.

Roja caught a look at herself in the mirror and almost laughed at her absurd appearance. She looked less the queen bitch of the city and more a wretch from the hovels. Her dress was near ruin, torn and muddied. Her painted face was smeared and faded, with tracks of shade where her tears had fallen. Worst of all, her usually stunning hair hung lifelessly down her back. She was wretched. While Emir sat with the girl, she crept into her own bedchambers and slipped on a more appealing dress, then washed the smears from her face. *He's with another.* Aye, he was; but there wasn't harm in innocent flirtation, was there? Brushing her hair was the only major improvement to her appearance she made. He'd know her game if she made too great an effort, for males noticed these things, did they not?

"He is a good man," she told her reflection, and then, without warning, collapsed against her bed, weeping uncontrollably. She knelt as though praying and dug her face into her silken covers to mask her moans. The more she cried, the greater the release. The stream became a deluge as all the pain she'd stored released itself. Pain of the city, of her sins, of her fears and of her jealousies. She couldn't say how long she cried, only that it was fierce. When she eventually stopped, she felt better than she had in an age. As swiftly as she could, she dried her eyes and attempted once more to make herself presentable.

"Could I get a mug of... cofe?" Emir asked when she re-entered the child's chamber. He had left Linn to sleep propped up on pillows; her snores were settled and steady now, her colour better than before, and Roja's own fluttering heart settled.

She led him to her kitchen table. He was hunched low, his face drawn from exhaustion; every step was an effort. He sat down at the table, and in the brighter light she could see fresh stains of blood on his shirt cuffs. He seemed to notice them for the first time too. He crossed his hands over them, as though it would improve his appearance. He was a wreck, and, in that moment, she knew she cared deeply for him. *Beyond childish imaginings.* His goodness, his warmth, his nobility. *His naked chest?* She thought of the blonde bed mate grasping his naked chest, and she bit her upper lip irritably.

He hadn't addressed their first terrible night, which was typical of men, really. Instead, they'd met in chambers and argued as violently as before, and she'd enjoyed it. The meetings had continued as Stefan and

Sylvia grew closer. At least twice a week they'd danced, drunk, and kissed before disappearing away for livelier activities, leaving Emir and Roja behind. He never left the table first. He was a fine drinking partner as long as she paid, and she did pay. And why wouldn't she? She had the pieces to spare. Better that than sitting in a dark room worrying about the world every night. They hadn't argued in a few weeks.

"Cofe? Certainly." She thought of what he really desired. She had a hidden bottle of sine somewhere, if Lexi hadn't stolen it.

"You have a fine place here," he said, looking around the room, and she felt embarrassed, remembering the squalor he lived in. Because of his position, she could have offered him a home of his own within the city, but he'd take too much relish in rejecting her. They based much of their relationship upon besting each other; he would use these chambers against her, she knew, and she, well, she would use his against him.

Finding no sine and cursing Lexi and her tendencies, Roja began preparing some food. It was something to do. "What is the charge for this visit?" she asked, noticing that sitting seemed to exhaust him even further. As though stopping was worse than pushing on through exhaustion. He rubbed his eyes with grubby fingers, and suddenly she wondered about drawing him a bath. She caught herself imagining climbing into the water with him. *To do his back.*

"I'll take four extra blankets per shack," he muttered, and had she believed him, she might very well have agreed out of gratitude. As it was, this argument could continue at the next chambers, where she would reaffirm that two additional blankets were enough for the wretches. There were fewer and fewer refugees appearing at the gates, anyway. She had fewer supplies to call upon, but what she could offer was offered freely.

"Nice try, healer."

He laughed, and it turned into a crude yawn, and she felt her own adrenaline dissipate after their frantic, panicked race. He tapped the medicinal bag at his feet.

"I have enough payment, but a man can try." He winked and

offered his most wretched grin, and she imagined drawing hot water and his naked chest and other naked parts of him. She dropped the pot a little too loudly over the little hearth. Stoking the flames with shaky hands, she tried to compose herself. He was with another, he was lowerline, he was a drunk, and he smelled terrible, and even if they were drinking companions, she knew, he still hated her.

By the time Roja had brewed the steaming beverage, he'd gone and applied a fresh coat to the little one's chest, and returned to his chair.

"Do you think Stefan and Silvia will make it?" he asked, accepting the mug of black liquid.

She took a neutral seat beside him. Not too far and not too close. It was a fine choice of seating, and it allowed her to stare into his wretched, beautiful eyes. A strange nervousness had come over her, and she fought a smile at her own childishness. She was no stranger to late-night rendezvous with beautiful males, but Emir was a wonderful challenge and a wonderful distraction. In this moment, her worries slipped away. It didn't matter that war was in the air. It didn't matter that they had a pathetic army to counter the southerners' march. It didn't even matter that a brewer of alcohol had more influence over the lowerlines than her grandmother did. That the city's economy had collapsed altogether. That everyone hated her. In this moment, she was every bit her age. She was a nervous young female sitting with a young man who had sneaked into her quarters.

"It's not like Silvia to stay with a man longer than a few days. Stefan seems to have charmed her," she said, keeping her voice light.

"I enjoy your company," he said suddenly, and she eyed him warily. His gruff, bitter tones were hard to decipher at the best of times. He was normally mocking, so she just sipped her cofe and thought about a bath.

Don't ask. Don't ask. Don't ask.

"So… who was the pretty young thing in your bed?" She bit her tongue. Stupid thing to say. Stupid way to say it. *Stupid Roja.*

"Oh, yes. She is rather pretty, I would suppose," he agreed, rubbing his eyes again to stay awake. "She is just a friend."

He had more to say. She was sure of it. She hoped he had more to say. After a moment, when he said nothing more, she ground her teeth but couldn't hold her tongue.

Don't say it. Don't say it. Don't say it.

"Could you trust Wrek with her?" She bit her stupid lip again. *Stupid Roja.*

He shrugged his shoulders, but she could see the worry on his face.

"Can you trust her?" she asked. *Why do I continue?*

Again, he shrugged, and she cursed her cruelty. It wasn't enough to drag him from the bed of his love in the middle of the night; now she had to go and question his mate.

"We don't have that type of relationship." He yawned again, and she felt nasty and cruel. What right did she have?

"She is your female of pleasure, then?"

Shut up, shut up, shut up.

"I'm not sure I know what that is, but she isn't that either." He laughed. "Her name is Lara, and she is my shadow." He reached for his belt, which was actually a rope, and tugged at it. After a few moments the laugh fell away to silence, and he told her who Lara was and why she was his shadow. He started by apologising for not mentioning her sooner, and then he told her about a wonderful festival called "the Puk." He spoke of his friend Quig, of a girl called Aireys, of an Alpha named Erroh and his mate named Lea. And though she knew some of his wretched tale and the dreadfulness of it, she listened quietly and understood the true depths to him.

As the first flickers of dawn lit up the palace, he finished his tale, breaking from tragedy to join in with the goddess as they laughed at Wrek's expression upon facing the little blonde screaming incoherently at him. Knowing that dawn brought less chance of another attack of breathlessness for little Linn, Emir grabbed his ill-gotten treasures and vowed to return in the evening to make sure the child would continue to recover. He walked with Roja down the stairs of the hallowed building in silence and in far less haste than they'd climbed them so many hours before.

After finally escorting him out through the guarded entrance, she took a breath and a leap of faith. "I enjoy your company too. Perhaps we could talk again some evening soon. Just us alone?" she asked in an unrecognisable voice. It was a wonderful question, and to her astonishment he gave a fine reply.

"Aye," he muttered, shrugging his shoulders, rubbing his eyes, yawning, and thinking more of his bed than who lay with him in it. The dawn was blinding him. He bowed half-heartedly to the most beautiful girl in the world and turned on his heels to walk down through the quiet city streets, leaving her behind. He allowed himself a moment of regret, then remembered the shattered door of his shack and made his way grimly home.

To his relief, Wrek lay in the far corner with a blanket propping up his bushy-haired head. He got to his feet as Emir stepped over the threshold. Lara was wrapped up in the bedsheets, sound asleep, a comfortable distance away.

Hearing word of Linn's recovery, the big man patted him on the shoulder and eased what remained of the door across the entrance, with the promise he'd return that very afternoon with nails and good intentions.

With dawn brightening the wretched hovels, Emir climbed wearily into bed and Lara opened her eyes, leaned over and hugged him. She still wore no shirt to cover her finer parts, though Emir was becoming rather used to such a sight.

"How are you feeling, Lara?" he whispered, closing his eyes.

"A... um...," she whispered back, releasing the embrace and putting her head back on the pillow. Her voice was weak, and Emir found tears streaming down his cheeks. He'd missed that voice, weak as it was. He draped the bedsheets over her and she smiled.

"Did Wrek speak with you?" he asked, placing his forehead to hers and releasing her hold.

"... Yes."

"He's a good man."

"... Yes..."

"Just like Quig?"

"You too." She rolled over away from him and wrapped her arms around herself. After a few moments, he heard her weep until she fell asleep, and he allowed himself a delicate, hopeful smile. Perhaps she was not yet lost to the darkness. Ensuring that his belt was tight, he drifted off and dreamt of red hair.

After what seemed like only a few moments, the sound of a panicked voice jolted him from his slumber.

"I need your help, healer!" Someone kicked at his door, and Emir rose from his bed with the skill of a man well used to interruptions. He patted Lara gently; she cowered beneath her blankets.

"I need it now!" an older man demanded from outside, poking his head into the gap where Wrek had broken through. He was panicked, gasping, and Emir wiped his eyes and reached for his shirt.

"Tell me what happened."

23

BANNER OF SAMARA

Magnus wouldn't miss the dreary amble of the march. Riding atop a mount in the dead of night was one of the more exhausting moments on any march, yet here he was in the rain, doing exactly that. He flicked a tassel from his bright golden cuff, which glowed in the flickering flames of the torchbearers on either side. It had been Elise's idea to wear his garish ceremonial armour the last few miles; it was also her idea to march through the night. She had been right on both counts.

The city knew of their impending arrival. Arriving a day early might disrupt the city's best-laid plans, for there would be ceremony. Petty as it was, arriving early would irritate Dia, and getting under her withered skin was a good start to the storm to come. Usually when visiting Lexi, Dia offered little in the way of formality, and why would she? He was only a father visiting his daughter. Now, however, he brought an army, and Dia would do everything in her power to inflict her dominance upon him, and likely deny their agreement too. *At first.* Aye, he was well aware of her treachery and well aware of her hold upon her precious Alphalines. It was a small matter; the Alphalines, the Rangers, even the fuken Wolves would all march under the Master General's banner, eventually. He would play the

part, eat a little of Dia's shit, but hold his temper until the right
moment.

Beside him, looking equally ridiculous in his own dress uniform,
was Wynn. He carried himself better now, and Magnus thought this
telling. The boy desired heroism, stature and honour, but he had not yet
tasted brutality. He would under Magnus's watch. He wondered how
much the young Alpha would take.

"Feeling foolish yet?" Magnus asked.

"Feeling fierce," the young man replied, and he sounded it. "You'll
be the one standing out, sir."

Magnus could only laugh, looking down at his golden plating. This
was how legends entered the city. In the dead of night, looking fuken
fierce. How impressive a sight for the waking citizens, to glance out
and come upon a camped army and a golden god eyeing them down.
That's how you impressed. That's how you earned recruits. From what
he'd heard, there would be plenty to recruit.

"How are you feeling, Garrick?"

Just ahead, leading the procession and thoroughly unhappy about it,
was the old Ranger Garrick. He was lead scout and had been for three
decades. He was far happier out in the Wastes, training a young
apprentice how to track and trap, than marching with his comrades. Of
all his advisors, Magnus respected Garrick above all others, even if
Garrick was not built for open warfare. Give him a sword and a deep
forest, and he'd slay any battalion without being spotted once, but he
went to waste on the battlefield. He'd taught Magnus, and Erroh after
him, almost everything he knew about surviving the wilderness.
However, as with all legends, Garrick's time of glory was long past.
Not that the old Ranger would have cared about such things. He'd
never settled; he'd left no legacy but his teachings. Some might argue
that his was a life ill spent. Magnus thought differently.

"Journey's end," the old Ranger said bitterly, as though the sight of
the stunning electric light and eternal grey was an affront to the green
of the Wastes. "Ugh… I'll see to matters," he added, kicking his beast
on towards an open plain not far from the city gates.

Magnus almost smiled. As soon as they settled the camp, he knew,

Garrick would request he be allowed into the undergrowth to go to task scouting the enemy. It was little surprise he'd had more women leave him than any other lonely man. And he was lonely; this Magnus knew. But for all his loneliness, he could not sit still for long, could not endure the mundanity of casual conversation, could barely stand the company of people.

"Of course you will." Magnus flexed his fingers a few times, kicking his beast forward. It hated the additional weight of the golden armour, and he felt for its struggle.

They walked the path through the last break in the tree cover and met the full, beautiful glow of civilisation.

"Welcome to Spark City," Wynn said.

"Get ready to bleed for her," Magnus countered. He looked back to Elise, hoping she'd share his enthusiasm, but she barely acknowledged the sight. Slumped in her saddle, looking decades older than she was, she gripped her reins tightly, and his heart dropped. *So weak.* The last few days they'd pushed harder, and she'd pushed with them. She looked broken, beyond repair. She bled for Spark in her own way. As ever, he wanted to forsake duty and take her in his arms and bestow curative rest upon her while the world around them trundled onward. Instead, he watched Garrick set the Rangers to task, his body a blur of movement as he ordered them to assemble and begin the unloading. The man might have been uncomfortable around people, but he could certainly drag impressive routine out of them.

The low hum of hundreds marching turned to a thunderous rumble as the arduous process of unloading got underway, followed swiftly by the pitching of hundreds of tents. Magnus was always impressed by the speed with which they attacked their duties, and tonight, at journey's end, it was no different. They began erecting the Master General's tent, and Magnus vowed a medal to the soldier who made it windproof and warmest. Stopping at the crest to savour the victorious relief of a successful march, he watched Wynn bring his horse down towards the cluster of movement. In the bitter wind, he heard the Alpha bark out a few orders, and this pleased him; the young general hadn't yet convinced the Rangers, but he was winning them over. *Not so much with Lillium.*

Elise knew well she had chanced her life by marching this pilgrimage, and tonight was the first moment she understood her fate. The last few miles, she had barely seen the path ahead. Her weak grip had been the only thing keeping her in the saddle as her mount followed the march. She could have called out for Magnus, or failing that, Lillium, but determination had suppressed her weakness. Her vision had faded as the evening drew in, and now, as darkness surrounded her, she could just about see the raindrops falling, stealing the warmth from her body, stealing the last of her breath. She willed herself to stay afloat as her wonderful Rangers went to task around her. The city's glow was a sight she grasped as long as she could. She was home. It was beautiful. It was worth it.

She fell.

The moment lasted forever.

It was an awful sound. A hollow thump as her body hit the ground. Few people noticed it, but Magnus was already running for her. He'd seen her waver as she attempted to climb from her horse, and then, without warning, she simply fell. Worse than that, she did not break her fall. He took hold of her freezing body and cursed his own breath for how strong it was. If he could, he would have given her every one that he had. As it was, she took dreadful, weak gasps, her beautiful eyes fluttered and closed, and she felt so very fragile in his arms.

He fought his panic, and Rangers appeared all around him, eager to help, eager to see. He cursed them all away, lest she pass in this horrible moment. She'd suffered from heavy lung her entire life and, as with many similar afflictions, it was a younger goddess's game. Sometimes she choked, sometimes she coughed, and sometimes her body betrayed her altogether.

He called out for a healer. Someone better than a field medic. The shell of their tent was thrown up around them now, as hastily as though they were facing an unexpected blizzard, and Magnus lay with his fading mate, stroking her hair, willing her to rise again. Her moan was weak and distant as he slid her into her cot. Her gasps were strained as he draped some blankets over her.

"Don't worry, sir. It's a bit of warmth she needs," Garrick muttered in his gravelly voice. With a dip of his head, he stepped into the tent, followed by two of his scouts carrying a heavy iron stove. He patted Magnus on the shoulder and had the eager soldiers drop the weighty stove down at the far end of the tent. "This will help," he offered, taking his knife and cutting a hole in the tent's fabric above his head. He slid a small empty pipe through the gap and attached it to a little hole on the top of the stove. "It'll be stuffy, but it'll be a furnace," he said, then set to work lighting the rusty old piece. Within a breath, he caught a spark; his old hands moved swiftly now, and he puffed gently on the tiny flame, building the kindling around it, and within moments the room lost its bitterness. He stood and swiftly stitched the tear around the little opening he'd made in the tent's roof, and the rain above their heads faded to little more than a delicate, reassuring tapping.

"Thank you, Garrick. But how will I calm matters when Cook comes looking for his stove?" Magnus whispered. *Always the general, never the mate.* Worrying about his soldiers, never enough about a goddess.

"Fuk him. You are the Master General. You can do anything I suggest," the old Ranger replied. He knelt down beside Elise and slipped his fingers beneath her nose. Magnus would have allowed few people to attempt such brazen familiarity. "Aye, a weak breath, but a breath."

"You've always told me to follow my gut, old man. My gut tells me worrying things."

Garrick laughed, removing his hand from Elise's face and placing it back on Magnus's shoulder. "Ha, you say that enough times and she'll arise stronger than ever, just to prove you wrong. She will not die tonight. She will outlive us all."

"Do you hear that, you stubborn bitch?" Magnus whispered. "Garrick predicts unlikely things."

"Her legend is not yet done," Garrick whispered. "Her mighty halberd will swing once more in war, decapitating all who stand against her. Fate's sick sense of humour would not have her make it this far, just to kill her off."

"You aren't making me feel any better, old man," Elise whispered distantly. The effort to speak took its toll, and Magnus wiped away his own silent tears, then some spittle from the side of her mouth.

Garrick, taking her words as victory, bowed and turned to leave. Before he stepped away, he quietly assured Magnus that he would tend to what matters needed doing, and Magnus offered no argument.

With the gentle rumblings of a hundred tasks lost beneath the delicate tap of the rain and the crackle of the stove, Magnus lay down on the cot with his beloved. "I thought you slipped from me, my love," he said, gently stroking her long black hair. He dared a kiss across her forehead, noticing the fever immediately. *She'll not survive a fever.*

"Silly Magnus. I'm not done yet." She gave him a weak smile. "I just need a little rest."

"Aye, that's good to know," Magnus whispered, holding her tightly lest she not make the night.

It was dawn before the old city healer appeared at her tent and late afternoon by the time he departed. After a gentle examination Old Jun suggested there was little to be done, save offering a few different tonics to ease her breathing. When this failed, the old man lit aromatic candles that thinned the air. He said it was "a strong and safe remedy," before hastily departing the stuffy tent. Magnus cursed his every step, knowing well it would offer her no relief. He had read of great healers in tiny scribblings by long dead forefathers, and he wished yet again that the scribes had taken the time to write less about themselves and their inevitable woes, and more about actual formulas to advance this dark age. Particularly concerning medicine. He knew there was an answer to her affliction, but he also knew there

was little time to discover it, for her final dawn drew closer
every day.

In a voice barely above a whisper, she insisted Lexi learn her fate
from her own lips, and Magnus would not argue. Though he longed to
see his daughter before anything else, there were pressing matters that
could not wait another day; dawn had also brought word that Dia
demanded his presence. War was in the wind. Matters were urgent.
Nothing else mattered. *Anything you wish, Mydame.* Had Magnus not
needed a distraction, he might well have returned his true feelings on
such matters, but instead he accepted her invitation and took his
protégé with him, hoping to instruct Wynn on how to control
precarious things and how to learn the art of patience. Leaving Lillium
to sit with his fading goddess, he led Wynn through the settled Ranger
camp; each Ranger offered grim nods and anxious salutes as he passed.
He offered little in reply, instead keeping his eyes towards the city, his
expression neutral lest he fracture and break. This is how legends
behaved; this was how Master Generals led and taught.

———

The crowds of wretched wall dwellers slowed their daily ambling in
the filth to watch the two figures walk on the city gates. Wynn
struggled to contain the pride he felt on his glorious return to the city.
Walking with the legend Magnus, his hero, his master and also his
friend. *Bruises included.* The world slowed, and then seemed to
completely stop its turning. Nothing else mattered but the two Rangers
leading the way, and Wynn felt ten feet tall. Standing atop a giant while
hiding in his shadow. Neither Black Guard at the gate dared interrogate
the two approaching warriors. They gave the order; the gates opened
and both Alphas marched through without awkward questioning. The
wretches lining the outer wall, hoping to argue their own entrance, fell
silent as the Rangers walked past. They too recognised greatness and
its march.

Once inside the gates, Wynn couldn't help but notice the change.
The city's glimmer had diminished. The air was musky and bitter.

Debris lined the streets. Previous discreet cracks now stood out noticeably, as though a century had passed rather than just a few months short of a year. Mostly, though, he noticed the people. There was a dreariness to them. Conversation was muted and cautious, as though speaking raucously might bring unwarranted attention from the many Wolves patrolling the streets. During these last months of marching, they'd heard different whispers, outlandish rumours, but now that he was finally returning to Samara, Wynn was eager to learn exactly what the truth was. Seeing the wretches along the wall was an unsettling omen of the threat, but stepping behind the gates was something else entirely.

Magnus must have noticed it too. He said little, but watched the world with cold, calculating eyes until they reached their destination.

"Of course she'd pick this fuken place to speak with us. Hold your nerve, Wynn," Magnus muttered, stopping Wynn with a casual grasp to the shoulder. He leaned in close so no eager ears could hear, and Wynn thought what a strange sight the golden pair must have looked, plotting under their breaths outside the hallowed halls of the Cull. "Recognise when further words will do little good; know when retreating is the only option. No matter what happens, I sincerely doubt we will leave this meeting satisfied."

Wynn could only nod in agreement as he followed his Master General into the building.

The officious Seth, tasked with the running of Alphaline things, led them through the long hallway into the chambers, where no test awaited them this time. The room hadn't changed in the many months since he'd last stood under the female's glare. The memories seemed a lifetime ago. Lillium had glimmered in the darkness. She still did. And there was no grand, illuminating show of power this time.

Dia was already waiting as they entered the cold room and met neither man's eye. Beside her stood a stunning redhead whose name Wynn couldn't recall. On either side of the females, in an attempt at displaying strength, stood two Black Guards, and Wynn took a fine dislike to both. Months of travelling with Magnus had influenced him somewhat. *Not to be trusted.*

"I hope Elise makes a swift recovery," offered the redhead formally.

"Elise is dying, Roja. There will be no recovery," Magnus countered. Wynn thought it strange Magnus knew the girl, or that he offered such knowledge openly.

"I'm so sorry," she offered, and Wynn also thought it strange just how distraught she appeared. She took a step from her side of the podium into the shadows to compose herself. A subtle tug from the Primary coerced her back to face the two Rangers below. "My deepest sympathies, Magnus," she said, recovering.

"Tell me of the southerners," Magnus growled. "Tell me of my son. Tell me absolutely everything." He addressed the Primary and the Primary alone. It was the opening shot in an encounter likely to have ramifications, and Roja took the hint and stepped aside for the Primary, who stared down at Magnus coldly. When she spoke, the tone she used was even colder. Her voice echoed in the dimly lit room, adding to her impressiveness.

"You aren't the same beast you were, when last we spoke of war," she spat. "And I am not the same waif who brought you to your peaceful knees. You may make demands on anyone else, but you hold no rule over me."

Perhaps Magnus's suggestion that the years had been unkind to her mind held merit, Wynn thought, keeping his face carefully neutral. Or perhaps, despite her appearance, she had grown fiercer.

"Look, I'm tired. I've come a long way," interrupted Magnus.

"And for that we are thankful," Roja offered. To Wynn's surprise, the Primary nodded in agreement. She was clearly grateful, but could not offer the words nor offer Magnus an inch. *Precarious words indeed.*

Magnus softened his tones, now playing the part of humbled peacemaker—and playing it well. "I gave my word I would march if needed, and here I am. Better I know all so I might plan. For the good of the Four Factions; for the good of Spark."

His words must have worked, for she began to talk now of the warring southerners. She spoke of the Woodin Man. She admitted to the betrayal of Gemmil, and Magnus cursed his name. She suggested an army greater than any before, marching north. She told him of the slaughtered settlements, of burning females, and then she spoke of a little town called Keri. She mentioned the term 'Hero of Keri,' and Wynn thought her rather skilled at talking. Then, with gritted teeth and a slight incline of the head, she leaned over her podium of influence and apologised for keeping secret Erroh's heroism. Taken aback, Wynn wondered if Magnus might leap up to the balcony and dispose of the two bodyguards before tearing the Primary apart. Some might argue his actions would be justified, but Wynn prepared to leap upon him before he did something the world would regret.

"So, I dragged Elise across the Wastes under false pretences?" Magnus asked, shaking with rage. Reaching that ledge and hauling himself up would be no problem for a man his size; the greater question was whether Magnus had the strength to pull both himself and his Wynn-shaped burden onto the platform. *Just slow him down and don't get killed.* The price of being at the table of a legend, he supposed.

The two Black Guards exchanged nervous looks. Perhaps they wondered if they were enough to stop such a behemoth. If Dia was nervous, she showed little in her face.

"I needed you to march, and my tainted words assured it. You've done far worse yourself… savage," she hissed, looking across to her granddaughter. *Next question.*

"We are desperate," Roja said. "We were wrong in suggesting cowardice in your bloodline. Please know that we have depthless regret that Elise has come into harm's way. Whatever your needs, the city will provide."

"It would be better if you knelt at my feet and begged for forgiveness, instead of hiding up there in the shadows. I am no true Alpha, begging for a scrap of flesh from one of you. I am not intimidated by your little Wolves either," Magnus countered, staring with the same animosity that Dia cast upon him. They were cracked pillars of the old ways, forced together in uncomfortable peace, and Wynn now fully understood just how perilous conversations between both parties could become. Their bitter words could shatter the Factions more than they already had been. He suddenly understood why Magnus stayed as far from the city as he could. They weren't simple stubborn allies; their relationship was far more volatile than that. Perhaps they had laced previous visits with sweet cordiality, but come time of war and heightened emotions, things could take a terrible turn.

Roja must have understood this too, for she allowed her hand to brush her grandmother's arm before addressing Magnus. "If it will earn a reprieve, I, the Primary in waiting, will kneel."

Dia's face flushed at this. "I will not bend to you, Magnus. I will meet you face to face, but I bow to no male. Would you demand Roja bow at your feet?" She spat the words with such venom that Wynn fought the urge to step back. "Like a fuken dog?"

Wynn overstepped his boundary now; he reached out and grasped the old Ranger's shimmering golden shoulder. He gripped it tightly. He dared not stare up at either female lest he stumble away in terror, lest he make matters worse.

"No, I would not have you answer for another's sins, dear Roja," Magnus said. "I would not jeopardise your legacy, just to appease my own taste for retribution. You need not bow at my feet... ever."

Roja bowed deeply in reply, and after a moment Dia followed. Her face relaxed ever so, and Wynn felt a storm blow itself out.

Magnus took a breath himself. With the rush of blood dissipating, perhaps he too understood the importance of calm. Besides, knowing your son had done a great deed was something to hold on to, Wynn supposed. *Nice to have a dad who cares.*

"If what you say of the Southern Faction is true," Magnus said evenly, "these are worrying times indeed. Such an army will not be fought with Rangers and Wolves alone. You know what I will need, Primary."

Roja appeared confused. Her gaze moved uneasily between Magnus and her grandmother.

"You want my Alphalines to fight, don't you?" Dia hissed.
Your Alphalines?

"We need every one of your Alphalines."

Dia sighed. She gripped the podium and, despite her fragility, appeared strong and resolute. Stubborn. "You really believe agreements, brokered amidst fire and wars and tragic desperation, should still be kept two decades on? Oh, Magnus, we are allies, but you may not take ownership of those under my watch." She did not blink, did not shy away; instead, she stood firm high above. It was a fine place to conduct meetings. Wynn was certain Magnus would take that moment to attack. To his surprise, Magnus offered nothing more than a deep sigh of his own.

"I believe we will speak of this matter again... Dia." Offering as insincere a bow as he could, Magnus spun on his heels. "Fuken bitch," he whispered, loudly enough that everyone present could hear, before beckoning Wynn to follow him from the freezing room. *So much for a warm welcome.*

"I look forward to our continued discussions, Magnus of the Savage Isles," hissed Dia as Wynn bowed and followed his hero in an unlikely tactical retreat.

24

THIS IS NOT HOW IT LOOKS

M agnus looked around the street for something to kick. Something that would make a loud crash. He found an easy target in his golden armour. Lifting the cumbersome cuirass above his head and kicking it against the office door resulted in a satisfying clatter, perfect for what he desired. He kicked it again, feeling better about the world.

"She brings out the best in me," he muttered, picking up the armour and giving it a cursory glance for dents before donning it swiftly. He knew he should have held his temper until they returned to the camp, but some petulant outbursts couldn't be helped. He'd expected resistance and downright betrayal; he would have been wary of Dia giving him everything he desired from the outset, but what he hadn't expected was how easily she'd manipulated him. Aye, he might have marched without the honour of his line at stake, but Dia had denied him that decision. *Easily.* Worse than that, she knew his anger would crumble beneath duty. He couldn't ignore this threat, even if he wanted to. *Well played, Dia. Go fuk yourself.*

He wiped a bead of sweat from his brow and cursed the late afternoon heat. He never understood why some nights were so cold in this region while the days could be sultry and blistering. It was worse after standing stationary in a cold room and all. He took a deep breath and tasted the foulness in the air. He'd always hated this shithole of a city. The City of Light and Hope, many called it. If that were true, why had the city not shared its knowledge of electricity with the rest of the Wastes? Probably wouldn't seem so mysterious and whimsical, he supposed.

"At least Erroh's honour is intact," Wynn offered, and this almost made Magnus feel better. Almost, but not quite.

"He should have held the town. He should have found a way," Magnus countered. The cub was his father's son, destined to be more. Hearing Dia's words had stirred some hope as to his son's fate, as Magnus too had suffered a time in chains before returning the anguish tenfold. Dead was dead, but capture was opportunity and Erroh was smarter than he had ever been. It was a faint hope, and he held that hope for a beautiful moment before crushing it for what it was. A man could go mad relying on hope.

"Come on. Let's get back to safer territory," he muttered, eyeing two passing Wolves. They offered no second glance. Their march was casual, indifferent and wholly unlike the gait of any usual Wolf. Magnus recognised them as enlisted men. A dangerous thing to accept every hungry recruit that came running, he mused bitterly. He'd never accepted a pledge from a recruit he hadn't looked straight in the eyes. If a killer stared back, they were welcome under the Ranger banner. It was easy enough spotting a killer, and easier spotting a runner. If Dia's army held enough of these desperate men, it would be down to the Rangers alone to defend the city. *No problem with Alphalines to call upon.*

No longer trying to make an impression, their pace was easier on the return march. The sight of so many emaciated refugees down along the wall was sobering, yet somehow calming. He could feel their desperation as he passed and almost hear their bellies growling. Such were the silent costs of brutes marching, no doubt. The refugees watched Magnus and Wynn pass with cold enthusiasm. Their spirits were battered, but the smallest vestiges of hope remained. No doubt many had cursed his name these twenty years, yet now, he was to stem the tide. He was the wild storm they so desperately needed. Magnus clenched his fists, thinking of what was to come. His head spun with visions of battle, tactics, and oceans of blood. None of these visions were unfamiliar to him, for his dreams were heavily laden with the horrors of war and the weight of victims. His victims. He'd have liked to say he could remember each warrior's face at their last bloody breath, but he couldn't even remember the face of the first he'd ever killed. Aye, he remembered moments; he remembered bodies, and he remembered the dreadful silence after. This silence was worse than anything else. Without fear, hatred and the thunder of violence to distract him, he was cursed to face what his brutality had wrought upon this world, and he did so in silence. A man with depthless regret may as well search for futile things like redemption and faith, believing they could redeem a ravaged soul. Magnus, however, believed only in the gods of his own actions and the goddess who lay beside him. He could feel the burden of remorse creeping into his soul as the realisation of inevitable war struck him raw, like a shard of ice down his back. He would speak later with Elise on these matters, as he always did, when such burdens became too much. But how much more comfort was she capable of offering now? Whatever would he do when she had no strength to embrace him as he whimpered for all that he'd done? For all that he would do? Tough to be a legend. Tougher to be a widower.

They reached the camp, and without duty now blinding his thoughts, he noticed just how far apart each Ranger tent stood. At least a few feet more than needed on either side, in a vain attempt at privacy. The land was little more than an ocean of white, flapping tents spread out across an entire field. It was impractical and ill-disciplined. Ordinarily this would have irritated him, but the grandness of Spark City was now marred on all sides by wretches and Rangers, and this pleased him somewhat. Dia would be furious. Besides, Garrick had assured him no crop was planted where they settled; let the bitch rage all she wanted.

From the first tent to the last, spreading out in a great secluded square, a few dozen shirtless Rangers had already begun hammering poles deep into the dry ground, while another few dozen were attaching long wooden beams. In only a few hours they'd fenced off a quarter of the encampment already. Another fine suggestion from Garrick, no doubt. Easier to keep the Rangers and Wolves apart with the appearance of segregation. *This is fuken Ranger territory now.*

He passed through half a front gate, ignoring the muffled curses of three Rangers attempting to align each gate perfectly. Wynn scampered along with him, his eyes darting from one sight to the next, marvelling at their collective efficiency. *Play it right, young cub, and it'll all be yours.* Already the simple ploughed field resembled less a place of the Wastes and more a bastion of warmongering. Sparring rings were marked out, their red and white paint standing out against the brown, muddy terrain. Straw targets attached to heavy poles were hammered into the ground for archery and swordplay practice, and beside each range stood large, locked wooden cases holding the Rangers' entire armoury. Within each one were battle axes, long swords, daggers, hammers and every other weapon favoured by Magnus's warriors. The largest of all the cases stood outside his own tent. He alone had the key, but no fool would dare attempt to open the case anyway, for inside hung his mighty Battle Clieve. Beautiful and barbaric. When he donned those beasts, a hundred enemies would fall. Or so the song went.

"Should we organise a hunt?" Wynn asked, and only then did he notice the empty fields surrounding the camp. The guests at the walls were spreading Samara's resources thin, and now, with another army at the gates, the rations would be even thinner. Magnus was never one to accept charity, and the last thing he desired was to take a single grain from the city.

"Aye, take whoever you want. Kill everything you can—enough to feed ourselves, enough to share with our brethren by the walls." Visions of the wretched faces came to him once more. The need to recruit had become more than pressing, and filling a starving belly helped garner true loyalty. *To the killers within the hovels.* Moreover, feeding the helpless was the right thing to do. The first clash shattering the world's peace was some time away. In the meantime, a daily hunt was a fine way to keep his Rangers sharp, entertained, and fed.

Lexi came running from his tent with arms raised. With all the gracelessness of a young girl learning to grow into herself, she leapt upon him and he caught her and she giggled with joy. His wretched mood faded, and he hoisted her high in the air as he always did. She laughed, for she knew this ritual; sliding her arm free, she swung her elbow across his face and kicked him in the chest and he dropped her again. He gasped at her unexpected strength and felt his armour for damage.

"I've missed you so much, Magnus," she cried, embracing him one more time before he could catch his breath.

"Call me Dad, for fuk's sake… Also, your hair is too short," he gasped, shoving her away. She was growing to be quite a young lady. Quite an Alphaline too, according to the city.

"Maybe so, but at least I took the time to brush it, you scruffy-looking farmer."

"I'm no farmer," he cried. "Farmers breed sturdy children with strong jawlines. Whereas you—well, you are a little waif with freckles."

"The boys in the city like these freckles just fine," she warned, bowing deeply at Wynn, and Magnus's smile wavered ever so. That might not have been a joke, he thought. She was as tall as Elise now, and her body was tragically fitting itself into all the right places. Her features had sharpened since he last saw her; her eyes had grown colder, more beautiful. Aye, she would break many hearts, once she grew a little more. *A lot more.*

Her face darkened ever so. "I spoke with Elise. She's not in a great way." She took his hand and squeezed it, her eyes suddenly glimmering in hopeful excitement. A daughter's enthusiasm was a beautiful thing. He'd missed her so fuken much. "So, I brought the gift of the finest healer in Samara."

Her words almost broke Magnus's heart. She was becoming such a fine young lady, yet still so childish. Elise's fate was sealed, and still Lexi hoped for something impossible. She spun away as though it was no matter they hadn't seen each other in nearly two years.

"I don't wish to see the healing process," she announced. "I think it's best if I go torment Garrick for a while." She turned to walk away and then stopped herself. "I think she drank a little too much healer's serum, or else she's been taking those strange mushrooms, like that time when I…" Swiftly, she hugged him once more, kissing his cheek before walking away.

Magnus watched her leave, smiling at how easily she dragged the bad mood from almost everyone she met. Feeling a little lighter than before, he stepped through the flap of his tent and was dismayed with what he discovered within. A little rat of a man was clawing at his mate's naked chest. He charged forward with fist raised. Somebody was about to die. Somebody was about to get his throat ripped out, and then the real punishment would begin.

Elise felt pure, delicious air surge into her lungs for the first time in months. Her mind spun in delirium, and she stretched her naked chest out as the healer rubbed harder, and fuk it, but it felt good.

"Lie still," he muttered, and she giggled and gasped. It wasn't just his wonderful, calloused hands upon her quivering skin that was divine, although that helped. No, it was a strange feeling of hope that came from this young male's touch. The serum Old Jun had given her was potent, and the bottle was almost empty. She wondered if she could ask for more; perhaps the healer manhandling her chest had some to spare. He was not completely grabbing her in all her glory, but she'd allowed the sheets to fall away, allowing him to see what she had. He was half her age, but she knew she was stunning. She loved to tease; loved to torment; loved to make males feel as uncomfortable as she could.

Distantly, she heard murmurs, but everything was a wondrous, naked blur and she wondered was this how death snuck up on the living? She didn't mind. What mattered was the massage and the air filling her tired, broken lungs. She rolled in her sweat-soaked bedsheets and tasted eucalyptus in the air and sucked it in deeply. Her nipple brushed his fingers and he leapt away and cursed, and she giggled again.

"Can you please hold still, Elise?" he whispered, and she felt delirious tears stream down her face and lose themselves in her damp hair and she wanted to sing. She hadn't sung properly in years. She thought of a few notes, but her voice was a whimper, so she fell silent and swayed with his godly touch.

"Oh, this feels terrific," she wheezed, then coughed and tried to speak again. "Never stop… Emir?" *Aye, Emir.* She dimly recalled her daughter's shattered expression, how the girl had struggled to reach out to her, fighting back the tragic words. Then she remembered Lexi muttering about a gift, and then a smelly wretch grabbing her chest. *Wonderful, smelly wretch.*

"Save your breath, Elise. I've no intention of stopping as long as you stop your squirming."

She stretched again, wanting to rise. He cursed again, and she stared beyond the stubborn healer, who was doggedly massaging life back into her, as a shimmer of bright light disrupted their moment together. *Stupid light. Leave us be.* She vaguely recalled Lexi vouching for him. She also recalled his foul mouth and thought him oddly charming.

"You have sad eyes," she whispered, and the daze fell away as she stared into his soul and found nothing. *Nothings can get filled, though, can't they?* She heard the slippery slither of fingers upon the sticky salve, and as he lathered her again, she reached for his face to soothe the dreadful pain in his eyes. For only pain could batter down the thrill of touching a goddess as he did.

"Save your strength, Elise. You have a long fight ahead," he muttered, as her hand scraped loudly down his stubbly chin.

"You need a shave; I have a knife. I also have soap. Am I beautiful?" She giggled and took in yet more air. Her throat was dry and painful, and she had never been happier.

"You are exquisite. Tell me, what have you taken to ease your discomfort?" he asked, and she took her hand from his chin to point at her medicine. She heard him curse again as he inspected her little brown container of white ambrosia. It was her turn to curse as he pocketed it.

"That's mine! No shave for you!"

He laughed and rubbed a small amount of his salve above her upper lip, and the sweet smell of eucalyptus hit her senses anew. With it came the seductive call of sleep. *Life is good.* She felt herself flying and breathing and it was beautiful, and she wanted to sit up and tell the young male all about everything she knew about everything in the entire world. Even though they'd barely spoken, he seemed like the type of person who enjoyed conversations about everything. Conversations about flowers and honey. And string. She loved string. And suddenly he was gone, torn from her naked body by a wonderful, wonderful god. Her god. She watched her god assault Emir and thought this delightful. Well, that's what anyone got for putting their hands on her, she supposed. Even those trying desperately not to be charmed by her. She could have said something to defend him, but Magnus was awesome when enraged, and besides, Emir had told her to save her breath, hadn't he?

"Leave the cub. He's had enough torment as it is. He needs a shave, though," she declared, and summoned enough air to sigh loudly before collapsing wonderfully back into her bedclothes. *Nice touch. Sleep now.*

"What the fuk are you doing to my mate?" Magnus roared, and Emir allowed the bigger brute to drag him from his seat. Little point in struggling, really. Magnus struck him once, a fine uppercut from a standing position, just beneath the chin, and Emir's counter was to fall helplessly from his seat into the dirt below. The legend allowed him an entire breath before he picked him back up, only for Elise's delirious words to hold the assault.

"Whisht, you fool! She's finally settling," Emir hissed, as only a healer could when dealing with emotional mates. "If you want to batter me, do it outside," he added, feeling for a break around his jaw. All he found was a dull numbness; he'd been struck by giants before. This was no special thing. Magnus released him to look upon Elise, his eyes terrified and hopeful. Truthfully, the man had a right to be aggrieved, discovering a nasty wretch rubbing his mate's naked chest. Emir wondered if it would help if he'd said that he didn't really notice such things as beauty when healing the sick. *Mostly.* Elise might have been twice his age, but she was indeed like a fine vintage, as they said.

"She's wheezing less," Magnus said carefully. Perhaps saying it aloud might shatter the illusion. She *was* wheezing less. Gone was the desperate grimace, as though she were climbing an impossibly snowy slope; in its stead was a contented smile, like she'd been sated by a fine meal. She suddenly opened her stunning eyes and waved weakly at Emir, before closing them again. Magnus leaned over her and covered her shame, but not before inhaling the balm the healer had placed upon her skin. He shook his head as though kicked, and perhaps that's what it felt like inhaling this potent mix for the first time. Enough to shake the senses, enough to clear the airways, enough to break a fever's sticky clutch.

"I've applied the balm once; I will apply it again. You can sit and watch my intentions when I do, or you can fuk off out of here with your swinging fists." Emir knew the legend of Magnus; he also knew the temper of his son. He watched as Magnus gingerly inspected the jars of stolen ingredients, sniffing each with uneasy distaste as matters appeared to settle in his mind. Suddenly a delicate snore sounded, and both men turned to watch the patient sleep. One candle flickered in a slight breeze, casting shadows over the two men as they sized each other up.

Finally, Magnus sat down and gestured Emir to do the same. "You will sit and watch over her." It wasn't a question.

Emir took her hand and felt for her pulse, counting absently. It was stronger than it had been when he'd arrived an hour earlier.

"She's seen a thousand healers and never had such a swift reaction. What is this concoction?" Magnus asked, dipping his finger into the little brown bowl of the horrible green substance. It stuck to his finger and dripped onto his trousers, but the behemoth didn't appear to notice. Instead, he sniffed it a second time and shook his head as though he were tasting sine. *Bad sine, at that.*

"Just something for clearing a clenched lung."

"Does it work?"

"Sometimes."

"Is it working?"

Silence.

Emir returned to examining the sleeping legend. Beside him, Magnus reached down to recover a rag from a basin of water. He wrung it out twice, but before he could place it across his mate's burning forehead, Emir reached out and caught his wrist, holding him fast.

"If you want to help, put another few logs into the stove," he hissed.

"Listen, you little—"

"Whisht, legend," Emir spat, interrupting him. Still, he held his wrist fast, gently tugging him away from the sweating Elise.

"She's burning up, healer. I will not have her suffer in this way."

"I cannot tear away her heavy lung, but I can get her through this fever. Aye, she's burning up, all right—burning the nastiness from her body. You want to kill her? Cool her down. Let that nasty little fuk of an infection tear her apart. You want to help? Then keep the furnace burning until her body kicks the shit of that which attacks her." With that, Emir ripped the cloth away and wiped it across his own brow. As he did, Magnus stared at him intently, like a peaceful cat watching a large crow stroll off on its merry way; he could kill him, or he could save the effort needed to strike.

After a moment Magnus got up, opened the furnace hatch and stuffed in a fresh log. He left the hatch open, and the loud crackle filled the room along with a fresh surge of dry heat. Taking a seat, he stared at Emir once again, his expression clear. *This had best work, for your own sake.*

They never spoke more than a handful of words, as though offering conversation might somehow relinquish ground. Magnus sat staring into the flames, thinking warmongering things, no doubt, while Emir spent his time crushing various ingredients into a horrid pulp and mixing them into differently coloured mushes, after which he would scribble a few thoughtful notes into a journal. It was something to do while waiting for the fever to break, while fighting off exhaustion, while attempting to repay a debt to a friend.

The fumes in the sticky heat wrought havoc on Emir's sinuses. He counted it two full days since he'd properly slept. Though he'd left word with Stefan to send for him were there any emergencies, he'd resigned himself to a few long hours in this wretched room. Watching over a legend took precedence over anything else. It shouldn't have, but it did. He could see how strong she was, and not just from the many scars tainting her porcelain skin. Magnus had told him she had suffered the ailment all her life, and he thought her impressive. He'd always believed himself skilful at healing, but really, it felt as though he had miles to walk through a burning desert before he could ever hope to discover a cure for this sickness. His concoctions could break the mucus, granted, give a temporary respite, but he could not tear away the shadow that gripped her permanently.

After a while, exhaustion took hold and Emir's mind wandered. Sometimes, when silence whispered to him, he allowed himself to drift away to another place where friends still lived. As he often did at such times, he imagined what life could have been like if the world itself had been fairer. Recently, though, some other thoughts had begun to emerge from beneath his wretchedness. They came to him in moments when he became distracted, when he saw Roja for the goddess that she was. Beautiful, incredible. Unattainable.

"Very few people speak to me the way you do, healer," whispered Magnus suddenly, pulling Emir away from his thoughts of tearing a red dress from a redheaded girl.

"I'll speak to anyone that way… even a legend." He wiped his eyes and they stung terribly. "That said, I am sorry for speaking as I did."

"A master never apologises," Magnus sniffed, leaning over to touch Elise's hand, which lay draped over her chest. "Will she be well?" He'd lost the bitter tone from before, and his temper with it.

"She will survive this fever. She will recover until the next, but sir, there is no cure for her affliction. I'm sure you know this." His voice betrayed the helplessness he felt, and Magnus must have noticed this too, for he bowed his head. They could hear that Elise's breath came more easily than before. Gone was the deathly, wet rattle. Her body was drenched in sweat, but she looked calm, as though a great fight had ended.

"Just how good are you, healer?"

"No one has asked me that in years. I would say I am skilled enough."

Magnus shook his head as though this was no answer, and perhaps it wasn't. "Well, I'm asking you now."

"I was once the finest apprentice healer this city has ever known."

"So why aren't you sitting at Old Jun's table, fleecing the citizens of their pieces?" Magnus spat.

"I'm not city material," he lied. Magnus stared through him, and Emir burned with shame. He rarely spoke of his apprenticeship. Of the mistakes he'd made. "Look at these concoctions." Changing the subject, he gestured to the jars of stolen ingredients. "Old Jun never had the foresight to push beyond what he already knew. He's a fine healer, I suppose, but much of what I've learned is through study and… experimentation. I've made grand leaps, but I live with my mistakes." He tapped one particular jar, then looked to another. "When a dying man is slipping away, what bastard wouldn't attempt unlikely things? Sometimes it worked. Sometimes I made mistakes."

"You made a nasty concoction and the city wanted little more of you?" Magnus asked.

"This city would welcome me in a heartbeat. Especially Old Jun," Emir muttered, fighting the memory of a foolish child condemning a soul to torment. "Truth is, after sitting watch over a dying man, whose pain is multiplied tenfold because you attempted an unproven remedy, you too might be a little shaken."

"You created something terrible. That would shake any man."

"Well, if you ever want to send a brute screaming into the darkness, you come to me," Emir said. He packed away his belongings and Magnus looked at him strangely.

"So you fled the city, gave up searching for progress and accepted mediocrity?"

"I know what you desire: you desire me to heal Elise of her

affliction. As though a cure for heavy lung isn't something I've spent years attempting to discover."

"That's exactly what I want you to do," Magnus growled, as though he challenged death to a battle of wits and Emir listened despite himself. "Whatever you need, I will provide. Whatever you need from the city, I will also provide." He spoke not as a desperate man offering all that he had for a loved one. He spoke as a commander discovering a strategic point and claiming it as his own. "This is no mere request; you have the weight of the Master General behind you. You did nasty things; redeem yourself."

Emir stood uneasily, wavering. He was intrigued with the Master General's offer, yet distraught at the idea of further responsibility, further errors. Still, though, something in Magnus's tone gave him strength. Enough strength to forget about his wretchedness.

"Where are you from, healer?" asked Magnus.

"Keri," whispered Emir, and Magnus said nothing for a few moments. He stood up and took a bottle of sine from one of his unpacked satchels. He poured the clear, violent liquid into two goblets, handed one to Emir, and took a seat. The cure for exhaustion was hardly in alcohol, but it was a more enjoyable way to battle weariness.

"So, you know my son."

"He was… is a friend."

"He is… was a good son. Tell me about Keri," Magnus said, and his voice was quiet and gentle.

Emir took a seat with the eagerness of the alcoholic he was and told the legend all about Keri and what his son had done for them. When he'd finished, Magnus spoke of his own tales, his own legend, and it was impressive. They drank the bottle, and as the first glimmers of the city lights burned to life, Magnus spoke to Emir more as an equal and less as the grubby little wretch who deserved a painful death.

Satisfied with Elise's improvement, Emir stood, bowed, and made to leave. Beside Elise's bed, he set a pot of his balm and gave Magnus awkward instruction as to how to massage it into her skin until she was strong enough to do it herself. That done, he packed his bag and stepped out into the evening's hazy light. Magnus stood, stretched, and followed him.

"You've earned your rest, healer," Magnus said, walking him through the camp. Each step was an effort, dogged by the dreadful exhaustion and wonderful inebriation. At the swinging front gate, Magnus stopped him. "For what it's worth, you've earned my gratitude."

"Elise still has a few miles to walk, but she needs to rest," Emir cautioned. "In the meantime, I'll think on what you asked." He looked down through the hazy morning light towards the hovels. "But I will not leave those who've suffered alone."

"There isn't enough violence in the world to make up for the horrors the south has inflicted. There will be recompense," Magnus muttered, following the healer's gaze.

"I hope you kill them all," Emir said coldly.

"That's what I intend to do."

Emir turned to leave, but Magnus caught his shoulder. "I'm sorry for striking you as I did."

"A master never apologises, sir," he countered, grinning.

25

HEART

Dia sat in her silent sanctuary, waiting for her granddaughter to arrive. *Late again.* That was fine; there was enough on the young girl's plate. Dia preferred these quiet moments to herself sometimes. Moments to look around the stuffy little room, to gaze at the art upon the walls, to take in the scent of age, to calm her rising panic, to form action for the day ahead. Mostly, though, in this little haven she could steel herself for yet another meeting with Magnus. Every day she could feel her grip lessen. The city grew weaker while he gathered strength. He was popular among those with empty bellies, and Dia thought it a fine political move. But would this support last when the forests ran dry of beasts, or when they picked every tree clean of fruit? Magnus didn't know the meaning of rationing; he and his Rangers were relentless in their gathering. She had given what she could these many months. *Kept them alive.* She would continue to do so, despite their lack of gratitude. *Lowerlines.* Oh, how swiftly they forgot as they gorged themselves on succulent meats night after night, none of them believing the well could go dry—and it would go dry soon enough. Well, apart from one wretch, that is. At least one of those lowerlines saw the greater picture.

She winced, suddenly hearing the heavy thump of her

granddaughter running down the corridor towards their sanctuary. Running like that was not behaviour befitting the Primary in waiting, she thought. Even at desperate times like this. *A Mydame should never run under any circumstances; she should walk with the grace of a leader and expect the rest of the city to run for her. A Primary arrived when she saw fit, and arriving late was a fit enough time.* Roja was mastering the art, she supposed. She knew why the girl was late. The city liked to whisper and Dia liked to listen, and she had heard quite a lot about the drunken healer.

The door crashed open and Roja fell through, looking every bit as dishevelled as Dia had expected. *When you play with wretchedness, it rubs off.* It must have been some night.

"I'm sorry, Grandmother," she said, closing the door and attempting to straighten the picture frame behind the door, which she'd just cracked. The paint on her face was smeared and running, her hair was a tangled mess and she smelled of sweat, alcohol, and vomit. Overall, Dia was not overly pleased with her granddaughter's appearance, yet she said nothing. She offered a welcoming smile, and she held that smile, even when Roja threw up in a small bucket usually reserved for previous weeks' economic figures. It was a fitting end to such miserable reading.

"I'm so sorry, Mydame," Roja whispered hoarsely.

Wordlessly, Dia offered a cord with which to tie her hair back, her sense of duty melting away as her maternal instincts took over.

"Are you about to break some news to me, little one?" Dia asked. Seeing her misery, she stroked the girl's cheek before moving to the table to prepare a little cofe.

"No, Mydame. I drank too much last night."

"My dear, you can be as hungover as you want. Just try to appear a wreck in these chambers alone. Next time, walk."

Roja nodded guiltily. She was shaking, and Dia frowned.

"What pressing matters do you have today that cannot wait? Perhaps a few hours in bed might serve the city best."

"I will recover by noon." Each word was an effort, and despite herself Dia almost laughed. How long had it been since she'd ruined herself like this? "Oh, why do we behave so irrationally?" Roja asked, wiping her mouth with quivering fingers. "Why can't we just show restraint when something unexpected happens?"

"What did you do, my dear?"

"I hurt someone. They upset me... I just... did what any good little Alpha female would do."

Dia knew well who she spoke of. She poured the cofe and offered it to her granddaughter. Slicing a few chunks of honey bread, she lathered them with butter and placed them on a plate in front of the wretch. Naturally the girl refused, knowing better. She slid the plate away and Dia slid it right back, eyebrow raised, her meaning clear.

"They can accuse us of irrational behaviour, but tell me, my dear, do you think Magnus is any less reasonable than I?"

Roja thought on this, and the effort appeared to cause her a great deal of pain. "I think we should work with Magnus," she muttered, taking the bread in silent defeat. "He is our ally."

"Next you will say the enemy is at the gates and we must band together as though history is nothing?"

"Is that so bad?" Roja asked, suddenly finding a taste for the bread. She ate hungrily, swallowed the first piece, burped gently and reached for another. Her face was still as pale as before, but she no longer looked like she'd taken a bolt to the chest. She probably felt like she had, though; perhaps even two.

"There is time to bend. Magnus knows this. Nothing will change when he comes begging for those loyal to me. He chose his wealth over his rights."

Roja sighed, no doubt as frustrated with Dia's answers as Dia was with her questions. Every morning they argued this point in some form or other. Roja trusted Magnus far more than she should have, the result of Lexi whispering in her ear.

"But Mydame, you pledged the Alphalines to him. Surely the word of a Primary is worth gold," she challenged, and this time Dia sighed before refilling her empty mug.

"Surely the word of Magnus is as worth as much, yet still, he broke his first. I rule over a fractured nation, and my grip is loose." Dia's voice broke, and she caught herself; Roja reached out and took her hand. Such gestures could crack even the sturdiest façade—and it was a façade. The world was crumbling because of Magnus. Yet still, she allied with him. She'd built him an army of Wolves to fight alongside. It was enough.

"Mydame, the east pays more taxes than any other faction. It always has. He has camped at your gates and will fight when the time comes. Is that not the sign of a man who has kept his word?"

"Why do you continue to fight for him? He has paid a fraction of what he can afford. The east grows rich while the other factions struggle. He enjoyed two decades of ignorance, while I gathered the wretches together and rebuilt what I could. It's easy winning a war when you know nothing else, but undoing the horrors after—that is the true test of will. They say Magnus relinquished control, but really, he was incapable of rebuilding the world under new laws. A true legend would have supported Samara; a true legend would have supported all of the Four Factions; a true legend would have policed all of the world instead of just his precious east." She slammed her fist down on the desk and Roja pulled away. "He has weakened the world, weakened me, and still returns with his army and demands I surrender my legacy. I would rather die than allow a savage like him to have it all." She took a breath and eyed Roja with every ounce of sincerity she could muster. The young female was a queen in waiting, a true leader if she took a moment to believe in her own ability. "When Magnus learns the whereabouts of every Alphaline, what then?"

"He desires rule in the east alone," Roja countered, and Dia patted the girl's cheek for the childish reply it was.

"If they march under his banner, can we really trust him to relinquish control after?"

"He did before."

"Look at what I've built, Roja. Only a weak leader would allow a treacherous warmonger to continue his legacy. You have known only peace in your time; you do not understand brutality. The unfairness of it." She took her granddaughter's hand and marvelled, as she always did, at their contrasting skin colours. Dia's blood was northern; her skin was golden and smooth, where Roja's was pale and rough. It burned in the sun. Roja squeezed back with her pale, shaking hand. "When Magnus meets with us today, we will resist his rage, resist his charm, resist his intentions, until the hour is late. Though perhaps I might soften my tone with him, if that would satisfy you?"

"Whatever my feelings, I will support you, Mydame," Roja whispered, and Dia nodded in approval. Regardless of the girl's apprehension, she would do her duty, Dia knew. And when she eventually replaced Dia, Magnus was unlikely to bring doom under her watch; such was the vastness of the debt he owed her.

"Thank you, little one," she said. Truthfully, she'd long thought the answer to uniting the factions lay in Roja and Erroh. What a magnificent match that could have been. Though she praised Roja's indomitable will, she wished there were a little more manoeuvring to the female. He had been ripe for the plucking, and Roja had stepped away. Instead of the son of the greatest warrior that ever marched, her granddaughter favoured the company of a wretched pauper, clever and resourceful though he appeared to be.

"What news of the Wastes?" Roja asked after a time, and Dia shook her head, for it was a dreary topic. Refugees continued to be drawn towards the city lights these past weeks, but, worryingly, the numbers were falling. Settlements were going silent across the Wastes, and even Dia's own runners were disappearing. It was becoming a precarious thing walking the road these days. Granted, during wartime, it usually was. Though no swords had clashed, nor any discussion brokered, they were very much at war.

"Little has changed. The first wave has marched beyond the border; they say three thousand at least."

"We can hold three thousand," Roja said.

"Aye, but Magnus will not wait behind the gates. Not if there's fighting to be done."

Roja picked up her journal and read aloud as though Dia was unaware of their misfortune. "We lost Keri, we lost Cathbar, we lost Nioe... and..." Her fingers ran down the parchment as she listed town after town and Dia thought it dreadful reading. "What of Raven Rock?" she whispered warily, and Dia spat in disgust.

"To the fires with Raven Rock. It can look after itself," Dia hissed, as though its name were an affront to her. It was not the largest settlement by any means; it was merely the largest settlement at odds with Spark. They had chosen their place in the world. They had a wall; let them man it, she thought bitterly.

"We could use the wealth of Adawan," Roja countered, flinging the ledger away as though knowing Dia's response. Dia shrugged. *Leave those bandit bastards to their own devices and their depraved leader.*

"Let us care for ourselves first, my dear. This isn't the first time the city has struggled financially. We will be fine," Dia said, attempting and failing to convince herself otherwise. Truth was, the city was balancing precariously on the edge of ruination. If Magnus appeared at her gates with a chest or two of paid back taxes, they wouldn't risk outright mutiny every week. At least they were no longer accepting recruits. Let Magnus add to his smaller ranks. Let Magnus pay their way.

"What about loaning some pieces?" Roja suggested, and Dia cursed at this suggestion. There was only one man rich enough to offer support in this city, and Dia was disinclined to go running to him for financial aid. Sigi would take advantage, she knew. He had demanded an audience these past few weeks, and Dia suspected he aimed to elevate himself higher than he already was. Truthfully, despite his mediocrity, he had become rather important. It was always rats making fortunes in times of war. Such was the way of things. His vile brew was the toast of Spark, allowing him the ability to buy into almost everything flowing in or out of the city. His greasy little fingers dabbled in every pie in every sector. In less pressing times she would have exterminated the pest for what he was, but she had missed the opportunity, at least for now.

One positive note to his risen star, however, was his control of all payments for most of the houses in Samara. She still didn't understand his actions, but one nice easy payment had allowed the Wolves to be paid outright. It was a delicate blessing not having to chase those few hundred citizens every few weeks. Still, though, she trusted him as little as Magnus, though the two could not be further apart.

"The economy will flow as it always does. What we need is something to kick it forward," Dia said thoughtfully.

"What do you suggest?" asked Roja, releasing the cord around her hair. It was adding to the headache. A small price to pay for stupidity. Her head was still spinning from her dreadful morning, but this room had a fine ability to dredge the wretchedness from her. She merely *felt* like death now, and no longer desired death. Her hand still stung and her heart continued to race, so she downed more cofe to calm herself. Emir had fuked up, she'd fuked up more, and now, she needed to apologise. It was easier realising these things in the calming presence of her grandmother and the rituals of responsibility. She could see her grandmother's side to the argument and accepted it. That said, she thought better of Magnus than Dia ever had, and since Magnus's arrival, the city felt safer. There was greater cheer in the streets; even the wretches appeared happier. Though, perhaps that was because of Emir's actions. Her stomach turned, just thinking of him. *I fuked up.*

"Yes, we need something to rouse the city," Dia declared, her eyes glimmering in excitement. She glided to the grubby window and looked out over the wakening city. "Tell me, Roja, how goes the wretch's little vegetable patch? How soon until they harvest?"

"How did you know of this?" Roja asked, and Dia smiled her all-knowing smile. As though she hadn't been aware of the funds Roja had donated to Emir and his ideas. What else did she know? Did she know how best to apologise?

"It's a good idea; your little friend has had quite a few," Dia conceded. "Perhaps, when their little harvest comes in, they might finally have something worth bartering with; a reason to enter the gates."

"A matter of weeks, I would think. I will speak with him on this matter, though they had only a paltry few seeds to plant."

"Perhaps you could find him more bulbs, seeds—whatever he

needs, really. We have fertile land but no willing hands to work it. It is a sound plan. We may as well have the wretches work for their stay here."

"As you wish, Mydame," Roja said, still reading through her notes. Her head was thumping, but her stomach had settled nicely. Her mind was a blur of the previous night's activities, but she remembered the tavern. "There were more skirmishes again last night in the old quarter between Ranger and Wolf," she said carefully, lest her grandmother question her further. These scuffles were happening more frequently. The Rangers were testy and raring to fight, and if the southerners couldn't be found, well, the Black Guards were willing combatants. Especially those who knew their history. There was no real harm— nobody had lost more than a few cups of blood and a little pride—but tensions were growing.

Dia smiled strangely, sipping her cofe. She looked out towards the largest building in the entire city, a relic of the ancients. A tomb of history. Roja hadn't seen an event in the massive stadium since she was a child.

"We should have a tournament," Dia said suddenly. She turned to the younger Alpha. "We can charge one piece for entry for the day, and one piece for entry into the arena. Even the wretches have that to spare." Her eyes gleamed at the prospect of the additional funds. "The Wolves can sink their teeth into the Rangers to settle the tension. Nothing like some spilled blood to calm the masses." It would be a memorable day.

"Aye, that sounds like a fine idea, Mydame. I shall make preparations. Is there anything else to be discussed?"

Dia turned her full attention to her granddaughter now. "Yes, my dear. What did you do to Emir?"

Their discussion concluded, Roja took her grandmother's advice and bathed, then set about making herself as appealing as possible. She practiced her speech ten times over until she was certain it would echo forever as one of the more graceful apologies. They would do it right.

He would accept all she said and then kiss her, just like it should have happened that very morning; this was how these things were done. She applied a few drops of her finest perfume, and at last, after a far longer time than she would ever admit, she was ready for her meeting in chambers with Emir. The man she might have fallen for.

She arrived early, unable to contain her nervous excitement. She'd rarely apologised for anything in her life. Today, however, with a serenity to her thoughts and a frisson of amorousness affecting her every move, she would happily take the blame for her behaviour. She might even offer an explanation. It was her bloodline; it was how they did things. They were wonderfully irrational warriors, unable to control themselves at either the worst or the greatest of moments. If he wanted to love her right back, it was best he learned such things.

She reached the old mahogany doors of the ancient debating halls and pushed them open with little effort. The creaking echo filled the chambers within, and she stepped through to find him already waiting there, sitting with his back to her upon one of the padded leather seats at the long oak table used to separate such anguished arguments. He'd sprawled countless scrolls of notes, in barely recognisable yet familiar handwriting, out in front of him, and he did not greet her; instead, he read in silence. He did not turn to face her as she walked through. She drew nearer, and a terrible dread filled her. The gravity of her actions struck her cold.

"Where is he?" she whispered, taking her place on the other side of the table. The ever apprehensive yet charming Stefan stared back at her. Through her. By now, she called Stefan a friend, yet his stare in this moment was cruel and malevolent. And why wouldn't it be? His gaze struck her as violently as a fist, and she nearly collapsed.

With no preamble, he struck her again with cutting words.

"He has resigned. I will speak for those along the wall from now onward." With that, Stefan straightened up and began reciting the notes of a lost man.

Devastated.

26

THE DISTILLERY

Mea held the scissors with calm, steady fingers despite her searing anger. She grasped Jeroen's head in her hands, tilting it towards the light. She wanted to kill him. Or at least graze him a little. She took hold of a tuft of his tangled hair and snipped it mercilessly, and it fell silently to the floor, joining the rest of the damp clumps. Perhaps a foolish-looking cut would suffice. *Who'd accept a stupid-looking Alphaline into their army, anyway?* Usually she found cutting her mate's hair a soothing thing: cutting equal lines, running her fingers through the long, wet strands, making him pretty. *Only for me, not for Magnus.*

"Fuken hold still," she warned through gritted teeth. He wasn't moving, but still, fuk him. It had been a difficult year of weariness and argument. *And wealth.* With success came dissatisfactions, she supposed. He supposed the same, and that's why he desired to leave her. She adjusted his head once more and her scissors flashed ruthlessly. A cut level with his jaw was what he'd asked for. *As you wish, my fuken beo.* "All you males are the same—warring and whoring, no doubt."

Jeroen jerked his head around to face her. "You think that little of me?"

She sighed. There was another fight in the air. It was something to do, she supposed. There were other things they might have done, but their desires were less than ever before. How long had it been since they'd lain together in passion? Weeks? Months?

She pushed his head back angrily. "I think you're an idiot, searching for heroics." The early morning sun caught the blade and sent a shimmer of light above their heads. They were excellent scissors. Sharp and clean. *Just a little cut.* Truthfully, she loved him no less than ever, but it was difficult to keep her head when fatigue and overwork drew on her last threaded nerve. Sometimes, instead of leaning over and saying meaningful nothings, it was more rewarding to strike out bitterly. Sometimes, she just couldn't help herself, and sometimes he couldn't either. Today was the worst. Today was delivery day. Afterwards, they would earn a few days' respite before the process began all over again. Perhaps after a few hours of rest she might accept better his argument that death was an honourable thing.

"You know it's not just that, Mea," he said, moving his head slightly again, causing her to nearly clip his ear.

The distillery was a fine thing, and their wealth was growing, but it had taken more work and effort than she'd thought possible. Aye, they were merely labourers upon their own land, but the haste to build and brew had taken a heavy toll. Sigi was no simple man, but he had ideas above his station. She'd seen the ruthlessness in his eyes, the greed, the vanity. She had once believed that she would never endure anything harder than the first few months with a newborn. Turns out running the most profitable distillery in the Four Factions under an aspiring bully was far worse. She cut awkwardly at Jeroen's head, ripping a few strands of hair from his scalp, and he flinched.

"Sorry."

"No, you're not."

She ran her fingers through his hair and checked the level. It was a fine cut so far. Only a few more delicate snips and he'd be the prettiest Alpha male in all the Wastes. She knew him well, and knew his frustrations. More than that, she forgave his frustrations, but she could not surrender without at least fighting the matter. Perhaps motherhood

had taken some of her wildness, but for Jeroen, his desire had aged like
a barrel of sine into a potent brew. He was a male, born ten years too
late. As the Faction Wars had fallen away to an uneasy peace, he had
come of age. It was a strange thing to deny a frenzied warrior
everything he'd trained a lifetime for. It was a precarious thing to store
such disappointment within a happy life, too. Ever since she'd chosen
him, he'd been attentive to her needs and been a dedicated master to
their cub. He'd asked for little in the world and gladly taken what was
given, and now he desired to reach out and take something only for
himself, and it tore her apart.

"I just don't want you to march to your death," she whispered, and
kissed his cheek, and he sighed. Magnus was his idol, and what
happened when an idol spoke loudly of war? Males like Jeroen just
couldn't help but dream.

She tidied up a few uneven strands and he looked less the
dishevelled farmer and more the magnificent warrior who would lose
his life in battle. For not every Ranger became Magnus. Not every
Ranger returned home from war, and sometimes not every legend,
either. Truthfully, she'd wondered how a life of violence might suit her.
Aye, in the beginning, before their forest became known as a
precarious place to stroll, she had proven herself an excellent
markswoman. The itch to test her ability still lingered when she
thought about it for too long, so she rarely did.

"I'll ride a mount, so," he offered, and she almost laughed.

These past months, they had forgotten what a fine match they were.
Easy to fall into a life of comfort while raising a cub, she supposed.
Perhaps Jeroen had perceived that his work with the child was done;
Tye had little to learn beyond walking the road. He would be a fine
Alpha male. *Once he gets a little wiser.* A true Alphaline accepted
everything as a test, and the opportunity to test his primal instincts dug
into his soul. More than that, without much distraction, such
opportunities gently pulled him from his comfortable life.

"I must do this," he whispered. He faced her and wiped the tears
streaming down her cheeks. She pushed his head back towards the
good light. She couldn't cut his hair when he stared up at her.

"Just think on it more, my beo," she whispered.

Jeroen kissed her hand. "As you wish, my love."

Truthfully, he did not desire battle like a drunkard craved sine with the popping of a cork. But what type of male allowed others to march when a threat loomed? Aye, he feared battle less than most warriors, but he was no foolish cub willing to bleed for a worthless cause, all in the name of heroism. He had met with Magnus, he had heard his words, he knew his own value. How could he ever meet his son's eyes, having turned down his duty to march?

He sat up as Mea displayed her skill and took a quick glance into the mirror at the fine job she'd done before patting the loose hairs down and stepping out into the morning light. His ears pricked up at the subtle sound of a wheel rolling down a nearby path; it was faint but constant. Another day, another shipload.

Mea gazed out through the kitchen door, hearing it too.

"Time to go to work," he said, trying to conceal the bitterness he felt. Aye, a tough, profitable year was the worst thing any happily mated couple should suffer.

"You look beautiful," she said, and he stopped in the doorway.

"You will argue all the way to my Ranger's pledge, won't you?"

"Until I win," she whispered, and his heart broke for her.

"I will pledge only if there is no alternative," he whispered. It was all he could offer. If Samara came under attack, she was just as likely to pick up a blade. Two, in fact.

He turned again to leave, but she glided over and caught hold of him and shattered the burgeoning fight. Her lips met his and they kissed and forgot their quarrels for a moment. It was just them both, without wealth, without influence to chase.

"I love you," he said, and again heard the rolling wheels draw ever nearer. It wasn't all work, though. There were some better days.

"I love you, too. Now go play with your friend." She gave him a playful swat.

Jeroen stepped out into the cold morning air, stretching as he did. A swine beast marched past, and he cursed the previous night's wind. He'd ordered Tye to secure the paddock. As usual, the little shit had neglected his responsibilities. He was getting older and more reckless. Had he been any different at his age? Yes, he really fuken had been.

The cart drew nearer and Jeroen recovered his weapons. Though Wrek would have driven the cart through the night, no steaming hot beverage awaited him. At least, not at first.

———

The four horses pulling the wooden cart breached the far end of the hidden sanctuary, and Wrek pulled the reins once before leaping from his perch, searching for prey, be it master—*hopefully master*—or apprentice. Landing gracefully in the soft soil, he lifted his wooden blade and watched the world with suspecting eyes. He gripped the lead horse to slow its pace with one hand and let the loud creak and rumble of the little convoy come to a silent halt. Satisfied there was no surprise attack in the wind, he waited. Friend or not, he was wise to the world. There was no insult greater than approaching an Alphaline's home unless one was greeted first. Who knew what an incoming stranger might be up to? Sigi would have marched right through the farm towards the sine-shed and begun filling those barrels right to the top. He would argue that he paid for the right, and perhaps he would have a point. Saying that, there were better ways to conduct dealings. The older Wrek became, the more he learned this knack. The richer Sigi became, the less respect he showed to those around him, even Wrek.

These past few weeks, Sigi had spoken less and less about his simple plans. If Wrek hadn't known better, he'd have believed Sigi was avoiding him altogether. It might have made Wrek nervous, but he was well used to seeing how influence and power corrupted. Few were immune to its seductive clutch. Had Wrek himself not changed these past months? *Fuk it.* Whatever Sigi was up to would happen with or without his knowledge. Why worry about the unknown? *Philosophy of an unprepared man as doom draws in.* Still, though,

Wrek was climbing out of Sigi's shadow. He was finding something in the world again, something he'd believed a long time lost: a belief in people.

"Hello," he called out, twisting his neck to the side until it popped; relief surged through his tired body. Night drives were difficult and trying, but he trusted no one else to make the trip both ways safely. Besides, it was always nice to get out into the darkness and count the stars as he passed underneath. Usually, he enjoyed these trips, but like any great things, they were destined to end; he would miss these morning excursions.

He almost smiled as he saw Jeroen step out into the clearing. Wrek intimidated most people, but not Jeroen. From their first meeting, Jeroen had matched his steely gaze as if in answer to some uninvited challenge. Unsurprisingly, they had become friends almost immediately.

"I don't wish to wait in this shithole farm all day."

Jeroen spun a sparring blade from each hand. He cleared the distance in moments, and Wrek met him with his own sparring sword, and the loud wooden clatter of their thrashing weapons suddenly filled the sharp morning air.

As usual, Jeroen used a neutral form, battering methodically down upon the taller man's loose defence as though he were threshing wheat. But Wrek was no ordinary fighter. *Not anymore.* He beat back Jeroen's hammering combinations, meeting them and driving them back. There was probably no better time than now to be proficient in the blade, he knew. Here, as always, Wrek took what lessons, what practice he could.

Early in their partnership, when the arduous task of building had required a modicum of distraction, they'd sparred. At first Wrek's style had been brutal and fearless: wading into battle without thought, trusting in his own brute strength and sheer stubbornness to attain victory; this tactic had served him all his life and had only ever failed him once. However, his flaws had been quickly exposed and, under Jeroen's instruction, he had learned patience, defence and fine ways to bring down heavy swelling. After a time, even though the Alphaline was still a superior fighter, sometimes Wrek snatched victory. Not bad for an uneducated brute from the Wastes.

"You're far too slow today," mocked Jeroen, ducking underneath a wild swing from his opponent and spinning away from the inevitable left jab that would have floored a lesser man. Wrek muttered a curse as the spin's momentum resulted in polished wood slapping his face, leaving a thin line of stinging red across his features. *Foolish.* He'd left himself wide open, and his opponent was never one to allow error. Wrek charged forward, putting everything into each blow. Swinging left and right, battering at Jeroen's stubborn guard.

To anyone out in the forest, it might have sounded like thunder. To the combatants, it was merely the first round. They sparred through the open compound, neither giving ground, avoiding collisions with the homestead's beasts, who scurried away from the melee. The two men fought on, hopping fences, charging through vegetation and desperately trying to use any part of the terrain as an advantage; this was their usual behaviour, and today was no different.

At last, Wrek's own mood got the better of him. He struck too violently, spending too much energy, slowing his strikes a fraction with each flurry. Recklessness had him searching for the killing blow too early. It was a terrible thing to be aware of these errors, he reflected, panting, to be unable to stop himself. Each attempt was parried and countered, usually painfully, and soon enough Wrek felt the missed sleep catching up with him. Frustration drove him onward, like a creeping cart in the night, and he parried a fierce strike, bringing his weapon down with all his temper, and the forest shook with a crack as the blade snapped.

"Ah, fuk this oaken piece of shit!" screamed Wrek, throwing the broken piece of shit sword away in a rage. He dropped to a knee, gasping for air, the need to conceal his tiredness no longer required.

A few feet away, Jeroen dropped his own blades from a defensive cross and took a few heavy breaths of his own. "And that's why I carry two blades. You are not yourself today, my friend."

"Had I a shield, it would be different."

"Then you'd be far more predictable."

"Aye, I know." Wrek began inspecting his face for stinging welts. Though there were fewer than usual, those he touched stung something fierce. He struggled to his feet and the two men retired to the well in the middle of the homestead, where they took turns dousing themselves in buckets of cool water before drinking from a steel ladle.

Refreshed, quenched and having little interest in getting to task, Wrek sat on the stone lip of the well. "I bring bad tidings, friend," he began. *How exactly do you form the words that ease the crushing blow of ruining a man's livelihood?* He searched his mind for gentler words, but knew that only the truth would do. "Sigi is moving the distillery." He couldn't meet Jeroen's eyes. "One fuken year, and he wants to move again." He shook his head and spat in the dirt. This was not his doing, but it made it no easier. They'd only now mastered the art of their routine these past few months, only now climbed above the slog —and it had been a terrible slog. It had been no small task building a distillery in the Wastes. It had been no small task finding honest partners, either. Jeroen was discovering this, too.

"To where?"

"Someplace in Samara. Somewhere safe, behind the gates." It was one thing betraying his business partner by speaking of future dealings; it was another thing entirely revealing everything to a soon-to-be ex-partner. It would be a dangerous thing indeed if Jeroen and Mea felt aggrieved, and Wrek knew beyond all doubt that they would. He spat into the dirt again.

Jeroen sighed and counted a few numbers in his head. An old dead friend had suggested it calmed the mind. "There's a far greater risk of being robbed in the city," he said levelly. "Better to have it a distance away, under watch from our kind. Tell me, do you agree with this?"

One, two, three.

"Oh, I agree with you, Jeroen, but you know him. Once he decides something, it is done."

Jeroen looked at the large shed they'd built, housing the precious distillery. Truthfully, they'd hated the work, hated the routine, hated the unease of watching the turn of alcohol, hoping the recipe stayed true, all the while desperately fulfilling the ever-increasing orders placed upon them by Sigi. It was no life.

Four, five, six.

"Why?" he asked coldly. "What does he know that we lesser lines don't?"

Wrek shrugged. "I'm sure he knows a lot more than me. Maybe he believes the southerners will march right on through?" That shrug again. "If I'm right, perhaps I could get you accommodation within the walls."

Seven, eight, nine.

"And what becomes of the distillery? What becomes of his word that he gave?"

Nine, nine, fuken nine.

Wrek shrugged for a third time, before gesturing to the shack and the current barrels needing refilling. Jeroen could see the anguish in his face. Up to now, he'd believed Wrek a good man, believed that only Sigi was a greedy bastard. He should have been relieved to know the truth, now, but sometimes it was the principle of the matter.

"I don't think he'll want another distillery in working order," Wrek warned. It wasn't a threat. The truth was that there was only one brewery to serve the city. Jeroen almost sneered. Just who would dare come collecting?

"Is this formal exile?" he demanded.

"I wanted to give you a warning to save your next few payments," Wrek said. His face was pale; he looked like a man convinced that revealing the truth was never the right move, but a man who revealed the truth, regardless. "It isn't respectable what he's done. You aren't the first he's pulled the rug from; you won't be the last." He shook his head and grew angrier as he spoke. "It won't cost Sigi a fortune to replace the parts needed for a new distillery. If he sends some fools searching, I'll be standing at the gate with you both. You have my word." He shook his head, not at Jeroen but at his own thoughts.

"A class gesture, my friend," Jeroen said, and Wrek appeared to appreciate this.

Both men turned their heads as, without warning, Mea sprinted by. Wrek attempted an awkward wave, but she'd already passed.

"It can't be," she howled.

They saw Tye clearing the outer fence, and Mea's howl turned to manic wailing as she sprinted towards the two figures following him.

"Look who I found!" roared Tye, pointing to the unmistakable figures of Erroh and Lea emerging from the forest.

27

BROKEN

The highlight of Emir's day was in waking up. In the moments between sleep and consciousness, he imagined his life a marvellous, wondrous achievement; a gift from the absent gods. The brief few breaths, before he remembered where he was. The moments before the crushing realisation struck him anew; the moments before the thumping headaches emerged; the moments before his wretched life took him aside where no one could see and beat the ever-living shit out of him. It was usually around his first or second stretch that the rediscovery of his wretched life in a wretched hovel struck him below the belt and broke him. This occurred most mornings, and today was no different.

Well, except for the weight across his chest. That was new. *Lara?* She'd been absent a few weeks; she was doing better than ever. She could now hold a comfortable conversation most days without giving the suggestion that her spirit had been crushed. She'd even laughed at something witty Wrek had said, when they'd stolen entry into the city a few mornings before. *Aye, improving wonderfully.*

He stretched beneath her warmth, and the dawn's early rays crept through a break in his hovel wall making him squint. The burning shards of light had appeared through the open door, carelessly left to creak in the morning breeze. *A fine new door.* Wrek was quite the generous handyman. He'd attached a sturdy door to the shack next door where Lara had slept these last few weeks. Lara had watched him as he worked. She'd even offered him water for his trouble.

Emir covered out the burning dawn with his grubby hand, and as he did, Lara moved across him. *She's grown taller.* He felt her warm breath in his ear and a few locks of red hair brushed over his hands. *Red hair?* His headache whispered its nasty intentions, but he didn't recognise the warning because Roja was lying on top of him and he couldn't comprehend any thoughts beyond the notion that Roja was lying on top of him.

What would Aireys think?

Aireys is dead. He felt her death anew for a second before sliding the sleeping Roja from his chest and rolling her to the other side of the tiny bed. Though her garments were crumpled and unkempt, they were still upon her, and his rope belt remained tightly around his waist. Unsure of what else to do, he stroked her hair gently to wake her. As he did, he spotted the half-bottle of sine by the side of the bed and caught a memory of kissing her.

In the dark?

In this bed?

He remembered her touching his chest, tearing giddily at his shirt and falling upon him. He remembered laughing; he remembered kissing.

"It's time to wake up."

She stirred at his touch and the sun eased her from her slumber. She stretched, and Emir recognised that look of serenity, right before the hangover ambushed her. Things were about to turn awkward, but he had a simple plan. Stored away were some gloriously overpriced eggs he'd gained a few days before from the grimy hands of a grateful patient. Saving them for the right moment had been a touch of foreshadowing genius on his part. Even the wealthy suffered rationing in times of war; even the wealthy enjoyed cooked eggs for breakfast. Along with the half-loaf of honey bread, there was a glorious feast to share. It was all he could offer, and he would offer it all.

With a girl who isn't Aireys?

He ignored the guilt and something stirred deep within him, as though an unbreakable veneer of cold misery had cracked slightly and allowed a sliver of warmth to creep inside his soul. Not enough to return him, but enough to build upon.

He recalled sitting across from her in the tavern; it had felt strange, exciting and wonderfully familiar. And why wouldn't it? There were only so many things friends could do when falling in... lust? With her pouch full and a wildness in her eyes, she'd proposed a game and he had met the challenge openly, though he couldn't recall the rules. Something involving many questions and the sipping of ales. At some point it had become downing sine with each question asked, and beyond that, it became rather blurry. Perhaps she had enjoyed his company, for she'd jested and laughed more than ever before. Spoken more openly of her true beliefs and even voiced her fears and worries. He couldn't remember now all that they'd spoken of, but he would never forget how her alluring smile had masterfully captured his desire. There had been an energy; it had felt like Puk. Like home.

She'd spoken of leadership, obligation and forgoing love and desire for the benefit of the city.

He'd spoken of the sickle, the cheer and his old life of freedom.

"Roja," he whispered, stroking her cheek like he'd done the night before. When they'd been so close. Before they'd become closer. Her eyes opened and fluttered a few times, and she smiled up at him. He almost kissed her, but as awareness crept over her, her smile dropped away to horror.

"Where am I?" she screamed, sitting up and pulling away from his embrace. He immediately felt the absence of her comforting warmth. "Oh, no, what did you do?" Her voice was brittle and hoarse. Before he could offer water, she shoved him away, her body a whirlwind of turmoil and regret. "No, no, no!" she screamed, and he wondered just how bad her hangover was.

She struggled out of the bed and fell awkwardly against the wall, as though her body was still asleep. Somehow, she stayed upright, though she wobbled precariously, and Emir imagined she was still as drunk as he. Especially when she knelt suddenly and threw up all over his floor. He leapt from their bedding, took her long hair in his hands and laid it down her back.

"To the fires with me," she said hoarsely. "What have I done?"

Roja's head spun in horror. The same horror any higherline felt on waking after a drunken night of debauchery in a friend's grubby grasp. *He's more than that now.* She shoved him away, cursing her stomach, cursing her aching body, cursing fuken everything. This was not how a Primary in waiting should behave. Not even one in love. *Stupid, stupid, stupid.* Her instinctive prejudice asserted itself: he was everything the Alphaline sisters would frown upon. *Should* frown upon. He was everything Roja wanted, and waking up beside him in this horrific state was the worst fuken thing she could have done. She threw up again and stumbled on her bandaged ankle.

She'd loved the night with him. She'd taken what pleasure she had in his company, wary of pushing their friendship further. *Not now. Not him. Not fair.* She fell against the wall and the morning light blinded her. It was late, far too late, and Dia would know what had happened, the city would whisper... again. She panicked. A fist of cruel anxiety took hold and shook her to her soul. Waking up wrapped in the arms of Emir of Keri was the worst thing she could have done.

"Are you okay, Roja?" he asked softly, and she wanted to strike out. To hurt him, to punish him, to tell him how much he tore her apart. How much he'd always torn her apart.

"Let go of me," she hissed, whipping her ruined hair away from him. It fell down on either side of her mouth, taking some rancid, bitter spittle with it. *Wonderful.*

. . .

He'd offered to walk her home, and she'd loved the gesture. She'd tripped up and fallen on the stone steps near the gate, because that was what foolish females did when charmed by wretched males. She'd had the grace and quick-wittedness to pull him over with her, and he'd laughed in her ear, and she'd joined in despite the pain. It wasn't serious; she knew this now. She'd known it then, and played along with his game of concern. Any female might have done as much, when wanting more time alone with a man. *More distraction.*

At his home, even though she'd known the next sine would be the poison to destroy the following day, she'd had one last drink with him, regardless.

"I'm not that wretched," he mocked gently from behind her, and she couldn't face him. She'd known this would happen, known she couldn't trust herself. She could not do this. Should not do this. She formed a fist and struck the side of the doorway. Better that than him. Fresh pain ran up her arm, and she hissed it away.

"How did I get here?" she growled, knowing the answer.

"You hurt your ankle and I treated you. We had a few drinks. My mind is a blur."

She hated his reply. Hated how she felt. Hated what she needed to do.

"Do you bed most of your patients?" she demanded, and caught the foulness in her breath. Despite herself she covered her mouth, and despised his beautiful eyes studying her. Trying to understand. She hated him. She'd always hated him. Because no one else did to her what he did to her, ever since the first day she'd caught sight of him standing on a rock. *On a fuken rock.* He, a wild ingenious pauper and she, a young queen in waiting. It was a small enough world.

It wasn't until they were at the gate that they first spoke; he'd looked so different, so broken. She'd seen his wretchedness and her heart had skipped a beat and then it had sunk when she'd believed him a father. She was no angel of virtue, swept up by the first charmer. She'd loved men; she'd enjoyed loving with men. But Emir shook the fuken ground she walked upon. *He always has.* It wasn't fair being unable to take him for her own. She loved Emir, and she hated him for it. She threw up again, and he allowed her to. Somehow, this angered her more.

He hadn't been strong enough to lift her into his hovel, but he'd carried much of her weight. She remembered collapsing on his bed as he lit a candle, and she'd never wanted to leave the place. He'd begun examining her foot gingerly as she'd drunk from the bottle of sine, enjoying the shivers running up her spine into her head at every touch. She could have told him she'd used to watch him as he studied. She could have told him she'd never had the nerve to approach such a reckless, beautiful apprentice.

She spat the last of the bile from her mouth. Her stomach was aching and unsteady, but at least it was emptier than before.

"This should never have happened. Another time, perhaps, but not now." *Not when your heart pines for the dead saint.*

"I'm not that bad a kisser," he mocked gently, and reached for her with a smile and a shrug.

Of course he did. He looked charming as he did, and she could feel only a terrible rage fall upon her. At herself, at him, at the female who had died in Keri, and at opportunities lost in this life and the one before.

"Do not treat this as a small matter, healer," she warned, and hated him for not loving her back. For being unable to love her back. He tried to embrace her again and she shoved him away.

"It's no matter, Roja. We fell asleep is all. I doubt you caught anything, either," he joked, pulling at his trousers and the double knot on the piece of rope around his waist. She didn't know what he meant, and then she knew exactly what he meant and felt a little better. And a little worse.

"Give me your word: you did nothing as we slept?" she demanded.

"I drank enough that I'm not sure my body would have been up to anything, my dear." He patted the bed and its crumpled, disgusting blankets. They weren't even silk. "Sit down and enjoy a little recovery. I have some food; it'll make you feel better."

At some point she'd squirmed free of the upper part of her dress, and it hung limply down against her legs. It was ruined. Or in need of skilled repairing. She fastened the buttons as swiftly as she could. Her mind spun, trying to recall the duties she'd already missed. Her breath caught in her chest, and the room appeared to darken.

"I'm so late," she gasped. "I'm so fuken late. I can't believe I spent the night here with you. This shouldn't have happened. Why didn't you just walk me home?" She wanted to scream, to shed a thousand tears, to shake him violently, to leap upon him and steal away into the Wastes forever. Instead, she cursed her misfortune and tried to catch her breath. He just watched her dumbly, and she hated him again for not understanding how unfair life was. *It's not fair. It's not fair.*

"I have everything to ease the pain," he offered, slipping past her to rummage among some boxes in the corner. "If I had the world, I would offer it to you, Roja. But for now, I have something special squirrelled away. Trust me."

She hated his condescending tone. It was the same tone he used for calming patients close to breaking. Well, she was close to breaking. The world was going to war. Thousands would die and she was gallivanting around with a wretch.

"Oh, fuk off, Emir," she spat, and felt better casting vitriol his way. She found her shoes tucked neatly under the bed. She remembered him doing that, and her panic began to give way to the terrible anger.

"Calm down, Roja. It's a small matter."

"What would you know of small matters?"

"Well, I know it's a beautiful morning, we had some fun last night, and now, we can have some nice food and suffer a wonderful hangover together."

. . .

For a brief, terrible moment, she remembered passion and desire overcoming her. In the flickering candle's light, she remembered kicking her foot away from his grasp and sliding from the bed to where he knelt. He'd thought she'd fallen and tried to catch her and she'd allowed him. She'd stared into his eyes and told him she loved him with no words, and then she'd kissed him. They'd fallen to the floor, lips together as though they were one entity. She remembered his delicious taste and his sudden vigour—wanting her as much as she had wanted him. They'd rolled in the ruin of a floor and she'd giggled and bitten and he'd bitten back, for that is what foolish friends did when they were falling in... love? She'd desired him, reached for him, and they'd swayed into bed where the warmth and comfort were overwhelming.

As dawn neared, he'd been the first to lose the fight to sleep. He'd rolled away, his mouth an unflattering grimace, his snore as wretched as the pillow he rested upon, and her heart had burned openly for him. It should have been beautiful. It should have been perfect. It should never have happened. It could never happen again. It wasn't fair.

Leaving her to her little outburst, Emir began rooting in a cabinet. His pride stung at her overreaction to waking up with him, but he ignored it as best he could. He'd never known a girl who hid her agony as Roja did. Beneath some concealing rags he found a half-loaf of honey bread. It crunched wonderfully in his testing grip and he set it aside and recovered the three magnificent eggs. He hadn't had eggs since Keri, and his mouth salivated at the thought of frying them.

Laying them on a swaddling of rags, fit for any queen, he held them out to her and her face turned a furious red.

She regretted it the moment it happened. She knew the value of each lightly spotted egg on both sides of the wall. She couldn't help herself. She grabbed them from him and slammed them on the dirty ground below. The sharp crack was enough to waken the dead and silence the wretch. She dropped the rags and they fell into the ruined mess of egg white, yolk and heartbroken shell. She watched him stare at the floor in disbelief, and she was suddenly ashamed. She knew the true cost of her cruelty. She almost hoped he'd crack a joke and allow her the dignity of offering an apology, but he said nothing and so neither did she. Instead, his arms fell limply to his sides and she turned away and reached for her shoes.

"How far I've fallen," she hissed, knotting her laces. She stood and turned to leave, but a rough hand took hold of her arm.

"You aren't a patch on Aireys," he said flatly, and his words shook her to the core. She was not Aireys. Aireys was a saintly ghost of virtue and honour, while Roja was a cruel bitch of nastiness and wrath. She tried to shrug his hand away, but he held firm and her fury returned upon her tenfold. None of this was fair.

"It's not fair," she cried, spinning around and striking him away with a fist. She felt her knuckles split as they cracked against his cheek; his head whipped back and his body followed. The world suddenly slowed to a crawl, and her body with it. Her mind, however, was sharp, and she watched helplessly as he fell against the far wall and continued right on through. With a sickening crack, like eggs upon a floor, Emir's limp body came to rest against the wall of the neighbouring shack.

For a moment she believed she'd killed him, until she saw his chest move up and down slowly. He blinked his eyes but did not try to move. Instead, he lay there, in a dumb, broken stupor. In that pathetic moment her rage dissipated, leaving her to her shameful guilt and her depthless regret. She could have fallen upon him and wrapped him in her shaking arms and begged his forgiveness, cursed their ill choice of words and pledged her love for him there and then. But her tale was not one of hope and love and endings. Hers was a struggle of injustice and sorrow, and many unsaid things. She turned away and walked into the morning's burning light. After a few moments of ducking between the hovels, she ran, hoping to make the meeting with Dia.

. . .

If Roja said anything as she left, Emir didn't hear her, nor did he want to. For he was broken. Broken by cruelty, broken by sorrow, broken by three fuken eggs and an Alphaline's intrinsic calling to violence. With an effort, he pulled himself to a sitting position and wondered blearily if Lara had heard the commotion. If she did, she did not try to assist him and this was fine. He needed a few moments to compose his spinning thoughts and maybe bleed on himself a little. So this is what he did. A thin stream of blood from somewhere within the scruffy clumps of hair dripped down onto his chest. He counted the drips and felt sleep calling. Mustering all his will, he reached up and felt the large gash at the top of his head. His vision darkened and his stomach churned cruel bile. He tried to move his feet but such a task seemed beyond him, and only then did he realise half his body was still in the shack, wedged against the hole he himself had made. Distantly, he heard people, and he thought about calling out to them.

"I will need another wall," he whispered instead, and fell unconscious.

Bad dreams, Emir?

He shot up from his sleep in dull alarm and found his pillow soaked in a rather impressive-looking puddle of blood. His thoughts were hazy and disjointed, and he wondered if he had slept or maybe died a little. He couldn't see the sun, nor tell if noon had passed. He was in no fit state to see anyone today. *Especially Roja.* He thought again of kissing her and spat into his hand and began scrubbing his face of dried blood. The last thing he wanted her hearing was how badly she'd battered him. Not that he had intentions of speaking to her again. Midway between seeing those eggs shattered and flying through the wall, he had finally realised his place in the world, realised the foolishness. He'd fought his wretchedness for long enough. He'd answered his pledge to Aireys a hundred times over. His watch had ended; his task was fulfilled. He was done.

The ruined wreck of a healer pulled himself to his feet cautiously. His vision kept darkening and, from experience, he suspected he had a rather impressive concussion. He climbed back through the hole in the wall, sparing a moment of sorrow for the ruined eggs cooking slowly in the rays of the sun. He grabbed the quarter-bottle of sine and his journal and stuffed them into his pockets, then grabbed the honey bread and relinquished all responsibility. *And why not?* No one had helped him as he'd lain unconscious in ruins.

Fuk them all.

He was done speaking with her, and he was done speaking for them. Aye, Wrek would have issue, and if they revoked his rights to entry, well, so be it. What would stop him wandering back home to Keri? Aye, he'd probably be struck down, but he was a solitary wretch and there were many paths. Truthfully, he knew he couldn't leave. Though his heart was a torrent of rage and grief, Aireys had known he'd willingly sacrifice his happiness for helping those in need. She had damned him to a miserable life of servitude. In another way, she had damned him to survival. But not today. Today, he was taking for himself. He was a step away from tragedy. Who knew how many more steps he could take before they led him into the Great Mother and the great sleep after, or to the top of the city wall and the wind beneath his flying toes?

"I've had enough," he muttered to no one, and no one argued.

The river.

Walking through the thin, claustrophobic pathways, he met the eyes of no man, woman or child. He answered no calls for his skills, nor did he provide news on supplies. He kept his gaze ahead and ignored the muttered curses as they faded behind him, lost in the hum of the hovels. He continued until he reached the great river's edge. There had been no heavy rainfall these last few days and it purred tranquilly, as it did most warm, sunny days. Its clear water rushing swiftly along was enough to keep him wary, but was not precarious enough to sweep him away. Holding his precious treasures above his head, he waded slowly out into its depths.

The coldness took what remaining dizziness there was, and each step became assured. The purr of the water was replaced by the hum of the turbines a little further upstream, and he enjoyed the privacy offered by their shadow. A superstitious fear of unknown electrical things and the lack of fish in this part of the Great Mother meant fewer people, and this was exactly what Emir desired. The hum soothed him, though he'd never known why. It felt ancient and it felt like the future. As a careless youth learning the city, he'd always found time to come to the river. It had settled his racing mind and whispered inspiration, all in the same moment. He'd imagined both his finest and most terrible remedies out along the river. Only now, with misery as his only muse, did he return. The water reached his chest and he remembered the struggle as a youngster when he'd been at least half a foot smaller. He almost laughed and waded onward.

The last few steps were a struggle, taken in excitement and carelessness. Then, halfway out into the river, he came upon his prize. It was no blessed harbour or sun-dried oasis. It was a rock. It was a fine rock, because it was large enough to sit upon, and large enough to elevate him high above the crashing, bubbling, breaking waves beneath. It was over a decade since he'd sat upon this rock, and he smiled for the memory. It had seemed larger back then. But wasn't that the way with memories? Greater than they were? More terrible than they were?

"My rock," he whispered over the gentle rush of water and the delicate breeze. No fuken bitch in a red dress and expensive shoes would wade out here.

This far from the river's edge, he couldn't smell the hovels or hear the collective murmur of a thousand lost souls. Scrambling up to the top of rock, he laid his treasures aside on the warm surface. The sun shone down its heat upon him, warming him through, and for a wonderful moment, Emir forgot himself. A fine place to recover from hopelessness. A fine place to spend a day.

Sitting cross-legged with his back to the city wall, the slums and *her*, Emir opened the little cork on the bottle and drank deeply. Alcohol was no answer, but he had found no others along the way. Like the skilled ruin of a man that he was, he battled through the first retch as his body fought valiantly against the poison.

"Whisht, and take it," he warned his body, and drank a second mouthful; this bitter amount went down a little smoother. It was the light to guide him through, and he didn't care if it led directly into a fire. He thought of Roja one more time, of her touch, of her warmth, of her love, and tears coursed down his face. He granted them safe passage and wept openly. Nobody could see him, so it was fine. He drank, he cried and he thought about his miserable life because that's all a wretched healer could do when sitting atop a rock in the middle of the world's longest river, when their entire life had fallen apart. *Again.*

Eventually, after a few hours, someone came looking for him. He heard the splashing and cursing and saw the form of Stefan wading out to see him. He reached down a hand to help him up and offered the sine. Stefan eyed him curiously, and Emir could only shrug in silent reply.

"A man is looking for you."

"Is it serious?"

"He dislocated a finger."

"Is he an Alphaline?"

"I don't think so."

"Tell him to fuk off and pop it back in himself."

"Eh… Okay so. Eh… are you okay?"

"No, my friend, I'm pretty fuken far from okay."

Stefan put his arm around Emir's shoulders, and fuk him, but fresh tears came streaming down his face. After a moment Stefan joined him too. Perhaps Stefan understood their terrible plight; perhaps Stefan's anguish matched his own; perhaps Stefan was just as broken as he. Emir had never felt closer to his once-sworn enemy, and never further from the child he'd been, than he did in that awkward moment.

After a while both collected themselves enough that their whimpers faded beneath the gentle rush of water below them. Wiping the last tear away, Stefan shoved him gently.

"Come on, tell me what happened or I'll knock your teeth out."

He wasn't certain what Stefan might know from Silvia, so he said it all, beginning with his guilt for desiring another over Aireys. As he spoke, his sadness gave way to stubborn anger and disgust. It matched

Stefan's, though his second-in-command attempted to conceal his own feelings, perhaps to serve his own corner.

"I could talk to Silvia on the matter," he offered, and Emir shook his head.

"I'm done with words… Too many words… Not enough actions…"

"Sometimes many words are needed, so we can better understand actions and behaviours," Stefan countered, and despite himself Emir thought it a fine point. *Still though, fuk off, Roja.*

"She has the world on her shoulders," Stefan went on. "She barely speaks to anyone but you. Not even Silvia. I know she beat the shit out of you, but I believe she loves you, Emir. I believe she's loved you for quite a time. You love her right back. You wear that same goofy 'hit you in the fuken face' expression whenever she's around. I remember that expression from when… Aireys was around." He shrugged and fell silent, his argument offered.

Emir believed him honest, but still he shook his head. Words were words, and he was finished with the bitch. He turned to Stefan, his face solemn. "Sit the meeting, Stefan. Try on the title of leadership for a while. See if the role suits you."

To Stefan's credit, he could have argued, but he didn't. He took it as the order it was, and obeyed, and Emir realised he was a changed man from the vain shell he had once been. Perhaps Stefan desired a little leadership of his own? That would be a fine thing, but he doubted it. Stefan had tasted life on the road. He was happier in the shadows.

After a while, Stefan plunged back into the water, likely to steel himself for the meeting to come, and Emir once again found himself alone upon the rock. A profound sense of relief overcame him at his release from leadership. He had spread himself a little thin these past few months. Sometimes it took a rock to centre the mind, to help a man find his soul.

He lay down the near empty bottle of sine and reached for his notepad. With a careful sigh he opened a new page and inscribed the words "heavy" and "lung" at the top. Nothing immediately sprang to mind, and he listened to the rush of water, the hum of electricity and the distant brushing of trees around him. Despite himself, he relaxed. He allowed himself to think beyond his own wretchedness for a while and dream of greater endeavours. A little while after that, he wrote a few notes, beginning with the word "salt."

28

AND NOW, A BRIEF RESPITE FROM THE ROAD

"It would have felt wrong not returning here," Erroh said, struggling in Mea's lung-bursting embrace. He returned the gesture and felt the great weight of a life's rough march dissipate in a homecoming.

As the friends embraced, a behemoth of a man shuffled his feet patiently, waiting for the formalities to finish. When the last excited hug was released, Jeroen introduced Wrek, and Erroh offered his hand. They sized each other up. Erroh thought he saw a flicker of recognition on the bearded man's features, and it likely matched his own. There was something indescribably familiar about him. Even his name seemed appropriate in his mind, and then he realised he was the spitting image of Quig, though older and less jovial. He was taller, too —no small feat. Perhaps seeing him in one too many strangers' faces was Erroh's way of accepting his friend's death. *Why only Quig, though?*

"Wrek is our business partner, and a friend," Jeroen said. Like Quig, there was an impressiveness to him. He towered over all others and appeared at ease with being so intimidating. He had warm features, suggesting kindness, but behind those cold, scrutinising eyes, there lay a fighter. If Jeroen pledged for the man, that was enough. A pledge was no small thing.

"Good to meet you, friend," Erroh offered, and suspected the taller man was deciding whether to trust the smaller Alphaline. He must have had as much confidence in Jeroen's word as Erroh did; after a slight hesitation, he took Erroh's waiting hand and shook firmly.

"You must sit with us," Mea declared, shuffling both worn-out Alphalines back up towards their home. "Tye," she called, "see to their horses and tend to them before they eat our crop."

They'd needed a breath. Just a breath. Just one solitary moment of peace before making that last pilgrimage to the Spark; before informing it of coming horrors; before everything changed forever. It had been Lea's suggestion, and he hadn't argued.

Sitting in the shade cast by the sun, Erroh couldn't remember the last time he'd felt so at ease. Well, so at ease with his clothes still on him. Platters of meats, trays of steaming vegetables and cool water jugs filled the table, and Erroh's mouth watered at the spread. The seasons have been good to them, he thought, looking around the homestead; new buildings, larger groups of livestock, tenfold the patches of vegetables than before. In fact, most of the farm not used for grazing was covered in massive square patches of corn. He could smell the distinct aroma of bitter alcohol in the air, and Erroh wondered about the steam coming from a large shack at the far end of the farm's boundary fence.

Sine? From experience, he knew sine merchants were tricky. A dangerous thing to have a sine brewery sitting out in the open, just waiting for thieving. No better place than Alphaline territory, he supposed. Wrek had found an opportunity here, it would appear. Erroh could see the man's eyes upon the herd of mounts they'd dragged from the south; Tye was busy hobbling them in a lush grass patch. From his outfit of fine cotton and smoother cloths, Wrek looked like a man who could pay a satisfactory price. It had been a long time since Erroh had needed a full pocket of pieces, having lived off the land so long. Perhaps a little generous negotiating was exactly what they needed before returning to civilisation.

As was usual with Mea and Jeroen, the mood at the table was welcoming and light. The food was delicious, and the two hungry travellers gorged on everything in reach. After their usual diet of charred quail and boiled mushrooms, it was a wonderful shock to their systems. Their hosts had the good grace to offer a second and third course. Erroh ate until he could barely move, and then he continued on, regardless.

Mea spoke of failing markets, a weakened Primary and an upcoming tournament. Wrek and Jeroen boasted about their prowess and suggested entrance, and Erroh thought again of a little dead town in better days.

His duties completed carelessly, Tye left the mounts to graze and sat down beside Lea, eager to enjoy any spoils offered. His eyes were alight with excitement and boldness, and Erroh delighted in his company and his lack of diplomacy.

"I knew the southerners couldn't kill both of you," he declared, as though many months of turmoil were no small matter. He received a hefty slap across his head from Jeroen, who understood that many months of turmoil were a great matter.

"I am glad that you both survived, though," he whispered, glaring at his father before offering his most charismatic grin to Lea, who laughed delightedly at his charms. The boy had grown older, as was likely to happen where time was involved, but still, beneath his youthful features there burned a fierceness that hadn't been there before. He knew he was better than before. He knew he was dangerous. He wore his emotions openly; Erroh suspected he would walk the road by the turn of the season. Might not be a bad idea. *Walk east, ask for Magnus, mention me.*

"Forgive him; he's just being Tye. He doesn't understand decorum. If you wish to speak of your journey, you are among friends," Mea said, glaring at her cub, who shrugged away the uneasy silence his statement had created. "You look like you have been through enough, without having to relive it for casual discussion."

You have no idea, Mea.

Erroh sipped his cofe and played with a few forgotten morsels on his plate. One may have been an entire piece of buttered potato chunk. He scooped it up, bit once and swallowed. *Just parsnip.* Moments passed, and finally Lea spoke for him. She told them what she could, and she told the tale well. Beginning with the threat on the horizon, she recounted the tales of Keri and beyond. To any listener, it appeared heroic and magnificent, but really it was just a slow, agonising way to tell of the butchering of comrades.

"Those from Keri made it," Wrek blurted out, and offered a gentle apology for the interruption. Unnecessary, too, because Erroh had heard no finer words spoken these past few months. "Led by a very interesting young healer, too." He felt Lea take hold of his shirt in excitement, in relief—in hope?

"Emir?" Lea asked warily. "Are you talking about Emir? He made it?"

Wrek laughed loudly and it was a magnificent, booming laugh; like a sword struck loudly upon a table, it echoed through the gathering. "Ha, so he wasn't shitting me when he claimed to have befriended the Hero of Keri. He and Stefan will be glad to see you."

Erroh's eyes met Lea's before she continued on. She spoke of chains, of marching and snowstorms. She omitted the tale of a certain dead girl, and Erroh was grateful as he took over. He was no great teller of tales. He spoke of fire and death, of duels and failure. Hearing his recollection of Uden, Mea placed her hand upon his. It was all too familiar, and Erroh remembered such a gesture a lifetime ago, before he'd become the war-beaten warrior that the tales told of; before he'd found a mate of such fierce strength, she took his breath away. He spoke of great numbers marching; he spoke of inevitable war. Last of all, he spoke of an eye torn from a mad god, and of freezing to death in a river.

"You followed your mate to the ends of the world," Mea whispered, and Lea shrugged as though it were no great distance. As though she hadn't almost perished. As though she carried no scars from it.

"I would be dead were it not for Lea. No better mate, no better warrior, my beo," he whispered, taking her hand and kissing it.

"I told you they'd make it," Mea declared, eyeing Jeroen, feigning innocence.

"I never said they wouldn't."

"You thought it, though."

He had more to argue, but fell silent, grinning. Perhaps he had thought it. Almost everyone at the table had thought as much.

Stuffing as much salted meat as he could into his mouth, Tye chewed just enough that he could form words. "Why do they only speak of the Hero of Keri? What of the beautiful goddess Lea? Seems to me, you should be part of the songs sung in the hovels." He swallowed, smiling goofily at Lea. *No decorum at all.* Had Erroh been any different a handful of years ago? Probably not. It wasn't every day the most beautiful female in the world sat down for a meal.

Walk the road and return to find one. It's worth the effort.

It was a rare thing to find levity in conversation. To this very moment, it had been nothing but a struggle between them since their journey back north. He knew he had a sense of humour. He knew she did, too, but they had fallen out of the habit of making each other laugh. A dangerous affliction for a young mated couple. As if they hadn't faced enough already.

"They only speak of me, young Tye, because I am a hero, and Lea... Well, she hid away with her little bow, didn't she? A shrewd move on her part." He smiled weakly and found it strange to jest of serious things. He felt little guilt. Moreover, he felt better about himself. In his mind he imagined Quig laughing at his words, and for the first time in months he remembered his friend fondly, and not as the tragic vision of his final moments. Perhaps humour was a finer way to take hold of traumas. Take that which offends, upsets, and downright cripples and shove it back down with humour. Quig would have been proud.

"Perhaps I cowered. It was the smarter move. I could have returned months ago, but idiot over here was stupid enough to get caught," Lea countered, daring a smile. Amazing that after being burdened so long, it took only some friendly faces to ease their misery. "At least I saw first-hand the numbers marching," she said, and the cheer left the table.

Jeroen eyed Mea warily, and Erroh could imagine why. This sanctuary might not remain a sanctuary for very much longer. The city could offer little protection this far out, and the forest could offer little concealment, even this far in.

"I think we could use something stronger," muttered Wrek, getting up from his chair. He returned a moment later with a glistening bottle of sine and poured a glass for everyone at the table. Erroh decided he very much liked Jeroen's new friend. When he spoke, it was with an uneducated commonness, yet he drenched each word in authority. He was a leader, no doubt.

"Not going to lie, I ran from the southerners once," Wrek said. "Reckon I was the lucky one too." His face darkened. "I'll not run from them again though." Erroh did not push for the tale. Wrek offered it anyway. "Lost a pair of friends to them another time, too. At the time, I believed another group of bandits were marching. Once me and my business partner reached Spark, well, we heard differently." He drank from his sine and Erroh could see the festering anger. Wrek held up the glass of clear liquid in the sun's rays. "When they come knocking at the city gates, I'll be waiting with a bottle of sine alight and my finest sword. I doubt I'll be alone." He drank the full glass. "Here's to battle and the taste of revenge."

"War is in the wind," Tye said, and Jeroen cursed under his breath. Mea just looked towards the horizon, and the table went quiet.

"What does your father believe?" asked Mea finally, breaking the stony silence. She stared at Erroh, who thought this a strange question. *How would he know?*

"I'm sure Magnus will rip the second eye from the Woodin Man," Jeroen declared, sounding like one of Magnus's Rangers. Jeroen caught Erroh's surprise.

"I assumed you had come from the city and had seen what happened there," Jeroen said, and Erroh shook his head.

"We wanted to come here first. Who knows what will happen when we return?" He eyed Jeroen uneasily. "What has happened?" he asked, wary of learning of an attack; wary of horrors; wary of anything, really.

"Forgive me—we should have told you when you arrived, Erroh. Your father has marched. He's camped on the outskirts with the Ranger army." Erroh smiled at this. Suddenly, he felt less alone in the world. He'd assumed Magnus would only become involved if they threatened the east or the Savage Isles. If Magnus marched and led, Erroh would kneel to his leadership. *For now.* An unproven warrior desired victory and honour, but Erroh knew better than that and desired something less. He knew well they would all likely die, but not before they tore the fuken hearts from their vanquishers' chests.

Mea offered even better news. "Elise made the trip; I would imagine it will thrill her to meet the female who stole her cub's heart."

Erroh's heart skipped a beat in shock. He'd kept silent about his fears of her passing. He'd expected never to speak with her again, and as time passed, he'd almost accepted it. Almost, but not quite. Knowing she'd made the trip yet again was a miracle from the gods.

A foolish belief.

In that moment, looking around the table, he felt lighter. He tried to imagine no storm was coming; that no death would touch this table. He willed it to be true, but he knew it to be a foolish belief. The moment passed and turned upon itself, like being caught in a vicious tide, dragged further from the surface. A chill ran up his spine, for terrible things were coming; far worse than he'd ever imagined. And sooner, too. He sipped his sine and thought about grabbing the bottle and downing it in one; about hiding from his fears.

Climbing into a cage and never emerging.

Lea watched her mate stir in his seat. He looked off in the direction of Samara. She could see his trepidation. His entire family was less than a day's casual ride from here. They'd only arrived, and it was time to leave. Lea would have happily stayed a night, but she would not deny Erroh a moment less with his family. Besides, how bad would meeting her in-laws really be? Perhaps they would become the family she'd never really had. Perhaps they would fill the aching hole she'd felt her entire life. Help heal the wounds she still carried. Visions of her homestead struck her, and a terrible anger came upon her. She took a breath and sought calmness.

Climbing atop their last two mounts with pockets filled with pieces, they waved to the family of Alphas. This was not a goodbye as before. This was something else entirely. Turning back once, Lea watched Tye face up to the tall, bearded warrior in the middle of the sparring arena. They turned the corner as the loud clatter of wooden blades and mocking insults filled the air.

Their horses picked up speed as Erroh led them through the last few miles of their epic journey across the world. Eventually nervousness gave way to enthusiasm, and Lea imagined the cold city stone and the bright lights of home. Her old home. For a moment she was back in the frozen south, huddled inside a hollowed tree trunk, long dead from the cold. She remembered listening as the storm blew in around her, and the snow took hold. She hadn't expected to live until dawn. She hadn't expected to see the city again. She'd lost her faith in the gods that awful night. She'd found them the following morning. She'd never felt further from this place of hope.

She took the lead along the last mile, through a beaten path she'd travelled many times in her younger years. It opened up to reveal the dark grey shadow of Spark City.

Journey's end.

No. Journey's true beginning.

It was turning dusk as the clear sky above gave way to bright, shining stars and the unmistakable glow of the shattered moon. Erroh slowed on the last slope before making the final push to the gates. He could see the slums all along the wall. Somewhere within was a drunken healer he wanted to embrace. There were so many huts. So many lost souls. So many victims of a war brought on by a madman with delusions of grandeur. Further from Samara's closed gates were the Rangers' tents. They were readying themselves for death, misery and mayhem. Preparing themselves for their complete annihilation, most likely. He shook those thoughts from his mind, instead choosing excitement at reuniting with his family.

"I look a wretch," Lea whispered from beside him.

"You look incredible."

Lea looked beautiful. At most, she needed a fresh coat of paint upon her lips. Female-type things. He, however, did look a wretch. Sweat and dried mud clung to his face, his hands, his clothing. He needed a shave. He needed to brush his hair. He reached over and took her hand. They slid from their saddles and walked their mounts towards their destination.

———

Somewhere in a little wooden room, separated from the city, just above the roaring scream of the river, a bored worker stretched and thought about eating the bread and cheese he'd brought with him for supper. Deciding he could catch a quick nap before his shift ended, he absently pulled a long metal switch down and a loud hum filled his ears. He'd performed this task a thousand times before with no issue, and this evening was no different. Above his head a little bulb glowed, and he paid little attention. He paid even less attention to the two figures walking the last mile, hand in hand, watching in exhausted silence as the city's glimmering lights illuminated the evening.

29

TEARS

He'd done this once before, a lifetime ago. Though back then he'd been a nervous young Alpha male, coming to claim an unwanted prize. *No, not unwanted. Unwilling.* How many miles walked since then? *One would say more than enough.* Half with Lea beside him, half without. Months apart from each other. The evening air was cool, with no bite. His heart beat in excitement and disbelief. Fear. He squeezed her hand as they came upon the fence encircling the encampment of his father's army. It wasn't home, but home was where the army was.

"This place has changed," Lea said, stepping through the Rangers' gates. She bowed a greeting to the sentry, who waved her through without question. To Erroh, he offered a cursory glance and deemed him little threat. Perhaps he believed him a wandering wretch in need of a little recruitment. Magnus had always been wary of a static march, and the inattentiveness such stillness drew. A perfect example was a careless sentry. Erroh recognised many Rangers as they went about their duties, but none gave him a second glance. He wasn't surprised. He had changed a great deal since he'd begun his walk so long ago.

This anonymity didn't last long. From a distance away, he heard the deep, thunderous barks of two massive hounds as they bounded down through the camp towards him. *The boys.* Behind them followed the rest of the fledgling horde. Rangers had the good sense to clear a path for the beasts as they went hunting.

"Ah, my boys," Erroh cried, and they both leapt upon him as one magnificent tag team, dragging him to the ground. The hounds of war had their first victim felled. *There would be more.* They licked, scratched and nipped in excitement, and he was overcome in a sea of fur, saliva and massive teeth. Three years meant little to their memories. The younger hounds, equally monstrous, caught them up now and bounced around the newcomers eagerly, adding to the explosion of energies and movement but unsure of what to do next. The commotion drew attention to the new arrivals at the entrance of the camp, and suddenly a name cut through the noise in the form of a piercing shriek.

"LEA!"

Hearing her name, Lea spun around in time to see a familiar female sprinting towards her. Her hair was a dull brown, matching the faded beige of her uniform. It took Lea a moment to recognise Lillium before she answered the call with a high-pitched scream of her own, for that is what close females were known to do when unable to contain their happiness. She dropped her horse's reins and met the embrace, and tears were already flowing.

"You're alive!" Lillium cried. She spun Lea roughly and Lea allowed her, realising in that moment just how much she'd needed her only true friend this past year. They separated to wipe their tears and took a breath to scrutinise each other's appearance with swift subtlety, for that is what females were also known to do.

"I've missed you so much," whispered Lea, and Lillium's face darkened. Her hands tightened around Lea's shoulders and she knew Lillium was no longer the same girl. Lea wasn't either. Lea had faced horrors and risen above them, yet Lillium appeared broken. A best friend could notice these things. Lea shook her head and grabbed Lillium in an embrace again. "What happened to you?"

"We will talk on it soon," came her friend's careful reply. She eyed Wynn, who was assisting Erroh to his feet.

Around them, a crowd gathered as Rangers recognised the scruffy wanderer as their Master General's kin. They battered Erroh with welcoming hands and uncertain salutes. Lea less so. Perhaps they were wary of city females; perhaps they knew their place.

Though Wynn had offered Erroh only a handshake, Lillium embraced him eagerly. "You brought her back," she said.

"It was Lea who brought me back," he countered, and accepted her polite kiss upon his lips.

Wynn took Lea's hand, shaking it. His grip lacked strength and conviction; it matched his stance.

"That's what good mates do," Lea said, and he shrugged as a few more Rangers offered their welcomes. She wasn't sure what had awaited her on their return home, but she hadn't expected such warmth. She looked beyond the growing crowd to the daunting walls and thought them beautiful. *Home.*

Fuken home.

The air was alive with excitement, and news of their arrival spread fast. Both warriors were cheered as returning heroes; haggard, battered and victorious. Erroh wondered how joyful the crowd would be when they learned of his opportunity to end the war—and his failure to do so. His own cheer faded away. Every compliment, every pat on the back and every firm handshake stung him. How many would die because of him? These were his father's brave warriors. Erroh's brave warriors were lying dead in the battlefields of Keri. They surrounded him and threw words he could not reply to, for they were many and he was but a failure.

"Welcome back, Erroh. We heard you were dead."

"You've grown into a fine young man."

"Is it true about the town?"

"They call you a hero."

"A pleasure to meet you, Erroh."

"Your father will be so proud."

"Your father will be so happy."

"Your father…"

"Your father…"

"Your fuken father…"

Though it was pleasant to be among people again, the sudden step from silence to chaos was bewildering. Lea must have thought so too; she stepped closer to him. The cheers and congratulations reached their zenith when Magnus and Elise stepped from their tent.

"Am I dreaming?" Magnus cried, and the crowd parted as though he were a mongrel horde charging. Erroh was released from the grasps of a hundred different hands. Suddenly he felt heavy and he searched for words. His mind was awash with thoughts of struggle, of loneliness, of joy, of fear, of anguish, of sorrow, of relief. No words came. No cry of triumph, that, despite it all, he'd returned as a greater Alphaline than before.

"Father, mother!" he cried, and Magnus ran to him, for that is what a loving father was inclined to do when discovering his son alive. The crowd immediately fell away, knowing their place. This greeting was for blood alone. Magnus fell upon Erroh and hugged him, and both males sobbed openly in front of the world. Neither cared, for this is what males were inclined to do when joy and relief overcame them.

"Where have you been, you little shit?" Magnus whispered, and for a moment Erroh felt like a wild youth comforted by his master standing over his first victim.

"To dark places, Father."

"You are in the light now, little cub."

"My cub," Elise wailed, tearing Erroh from his father's grip with surprising vigour. She too had tears streaming down her face. She held his face in her hands for a moment to meet his eyes, before locking her arms around him and squeezing the wind from his lungs. *Missed you too, Mom.* After a moment, she released one arm and dragged Magnus towards them. "The boys are back again."

He was overwhelmed and he embraced it. It was three years since he'd walked from their gates. Three years of wondering if they would meet again. *Three fuken years.* He couldn't stop crying. He never wanted to stop. He wanted to hold this moment with his parents before the cruel reality of the coming storm struck them. And then he did let go. For there was one other task that bettered a parents' embrace.

"I would like you both to meet my mate, Le—"

Elise leapt upon her like a bird of prey before he could properly introduce her. "I have another daughter," she cried, dragging a smile from her victim.

"It is an honour to meet you," Lea gasped, struggling politely. A fine skill.

"Lillium told me of you, of the Cull, of so many things," Elise said, taking Lea's face in her hands as she had with Erroh. Without words, they spoke of things unknown, and Erroh wasn't sure how he felt on the matter. "I think we'll get on wonderfully," she said, kissing Lea's forehead.

"Lillium told me nothing, but it is still an honour to meet you, Lea," Magnus said, bowing deeply. "Welcome home to the Spark."

"The honour is... mine, sir," Lea said carefully, and Erroh knew her struggle. For a wonderful moment, he remembered the arguments they'd shared in their first few miles. It would be hard for a girl from her region to warm to Magnus, but she would. The bastard was far better with females than he'd ever been, and Erroh heard him whisper, "Welcome to the family, little cub," as they embraced.

There was plenty of alcohol. That was an understatement; within an hour, they'd carted the first barrels of ale and sine from the city. As the last of the little electric orbs came to light in their full glory and the city worker in charge of their maintenance closed his eyes and chanced a quick nap, word spread through the slums. The filthy side streets

between each rickety wooden shack came to life as each wretched
dweller offered their own piece to the growing rumours that the warrior
had returned from the frozen wastes bearing unthinkable scars and
injuries. A few suggested he still wore the scars of four arrows. Others
suggested he'd lost an eye. Some suggested he was alone and the
goddess with the bow had been slain.

Whatever the tragedy, the wretches from the wall could hear the
sounds of the revelries in the camp growing louder. After enduring
unending misery of their own, it became too much to bear. With nerve
on their side, a few wretched dared the walk towards the camp, some
out of curiosity, others hoping for an invitation. They knew well it was
a celebration for the Rangers, but regardless, they walked the short
distance towards the sounds of great cheer. The aroma of sizzling, fatty
meats filled the night air, and a few musicians struck a few notes. They
couldn't help themselves. At the gate there was no willing guard to
stop their entry, and each wretched soul stepped through the entrance
and into the writhing mass of joyful celebration, and it was Magnus
who welcomed them the last few steps.

He could see the pain of the last year of their lives. They needed
levity, if only for one great night, to ease the daily monotonous
suffering. Though he'd believed it a foolish idea at first, Dia's
tournament was a fine idea. He decided this could be the prelude to the
event. And why not? His coppers would do little sitting in chests. Best
to do some good, earn goodwill and pick up more followers.

As the wretches neared, he bade them enter, patting a few as they
passed, offering his most charming grin to some of the prettier women.
The night's young, and Elise is sprightly. He called for his runners and
made a plan. It was a foolish, generous plan. It worked.

————

Sigi almost shed a tear in joy when he received the late order. The
swift trade sent him far beyond his highest targets. *Weeks ahead.* As
they loaded the last barrel of expensive alcohol, he retired to his
quarters with his ledger and a bottle of wine. Scribbling a few

illegible notes that only he could decipher in the light of a flickering candle, he counted the newly-gained funds and added them into his untidy columns of numbers. It wasn't just the payment, for he was richer than the wealthiest warmonger ten times over; his delight was in knowing the mountains of pieces offered in exchange for his reserve might well have emptied the warmonger's chests. Workings were afoot. Discussions were happening between those in elevated positions. When he withheld payments, no one would step in. *Could step in.*

He sipped his wine and ran his figures through a third time, each time feeling more assured. Yes, he was in touching distance of greatness. *No, not greatness.* He didn't care about greatness. He cared about absolute power. Ever since he'd poured his first glass of sine into a grubby bottle and passed it across to his first citizen, he'd owned the city. It was only a matter of time until he staked his claim. He was a rising star. He sipped his wine, raised his glass to a doomed legend, and thought about eggs for supper.

———

"We must speak of worrying things," whispered Erroh, leaning in towards his parents, who were seated across from him. He was sitting through his second feast of the day, and his stomach was already churning at the sudden influx of rich flavours. On his plate lay a sizzling piece of seared deer steak, but he'd already eaten his fill. In front of him was a half-empty glass of wine. It felt as though he hadn't tasted alcohol in a lifetime. His vision was already blurring. He knew to pace himself, but the night was young and the celebration hadn't taken off.

"There will be plenty of talk," Elise whispered, taking a moment to smile at her cub. "Not tonight, not when we are celebrating. Not when my family is back together… larger than before."

She's right.

What would one night cost them? he thought, forcing himself to chew another mouthful. They sat for more than an hour, as still more and more wretched wanderers flocked into the Ranger camp in search of food, alcohol and humanity. *The Woodin Man can fuk off tonight.*

Elise couldn't keep her eyes from Lea, and Erroh thought this was approval. "Praise the damned absent gods, you are beautiful."

Lea blushed at the compliment but offered a smile, and Erroh laughed at her discomfort. A few days before, she had been a wily warrior, capable and terrifying. Now she appeared as more the meek, nervous girl who had once shuffled appealingly across the balcony of the Cull. It was strange, the effect a mother-in-law had upon a mated female.

"She's pleasing enough, I suppose," he mocked, and Lea punched his shoulder. This delighted his mother altogether.

"Right, Wynn, move yourself," Elise declared, gesturing to the ponytailed Ranger to vacate his place. Wynn's face dropped as she shoved him away from his steaming plate of deliciousness. "You as well, Erroh. Fuk off away, so we females may talk of real matters," she added before sliding in between Lillium and Lea. A panicked look shot across Lea's face at this new seating arrangement, and Erroh laughed again. *Show fear and you are dead.*

"I suppose the males must speak of manly things, so," Erroh offered, but the women had already begun speaking in low, conspiratorial mutterings. Even Lea's initial panic was lost to an unheard jest that brought the three laughing loudly.

After a few moments, Lexi joined them, and their little feminine army was complete. Lea whispered something unknown, and all four girls laughed again. In unison, they looked at Erroh and laughed even louder. Lea blew him a kiss amid the outburst and he bowed theatrically. Seeing his mother with the younger Alpha females was a wonderful thing. It drew out the city in her, instilled life into her bones. She looked even younger than when he had last seen her. Perhaps there was something to the warm air in this part of the world? Perhaps it was being back in Samara? Magnus and Erroh despised Spark, but to Elise and Lexi it was still home. Perhaps it would always be. For Lea, too.

"Come join us, Erroh," Wynn said from the far end of the table, digging into some unfinished food left behind by Elise. "It's probably safer at this end." And this time Magnus laughed and clinked the young Ranger's glass. Any fool could see that Wynn and Lillium were uneasy. *Perhaps he threw her in a river?* Whatever had occurred was not his business. Besides, Lea would tell him.

All around them the party grew in size, in drunkenness, in noise. He looked to the nearest cart and caught sight of a familiar girl tending to the barrels. He watched her for a moment and thought of Keri and Puk. *Tara? Clara? Something like that.* She was working as if in a makeshift tavern. Standing high above the crowd, she poured glass after glass of ale and sine effortlessly. A few others stood atop their own carts and delivered the potent liquid to those in line. Few as smoothly as the girl, though. She did not smile or speak, but she poured each glass as though it were the most important task. She appeared to be in charge too. *Lara?* He tried to wave at her, but if she saw, she did not acknowledge him. Perhaps having survived when Quig had not was too much for her. That guilt struck him anew. He sipped his glass and shook melancholy away, pledging to suffer no guilt tonight.

Eventually the massive form of Wrek and his own cart appeared at the gates, having returned from Mea and Jeroen's. His appearance drew Lara's interest and she dropped gracefully from her cart mid-pour, leaving a dozen disappointed hands behind. One more so than the others. Climbing up beside him, she shared a few words with the giant before they set to splitting the shipment in half. Wrek sent another server back towards the city and went about controlling the queues with expert precision. Erroh waved and again was reminded how similar he looked to Quig. *Stop it, Erroh.* He shook the thought from his mind. Thinking too much of his dead friend might send him down a darker path. Magnus had once warned him of the devastating trauma suffered by warriors who obsessed over battles fought. Better to talk when needed and rise above it when not. *Fine advice.*

The wretches soon outnumbered the Rangers, and the party truly sparked to life. *All in honour of a failure.* A few faces were familiar among the masses, but there was only one he desired to speak with. The man he was still indebted to. Facing Emir would bring renewed joy and guilt, he knew. They called him the Hero of Keri, yet how could any hero face Emir, having watched Aireys burn as she had?

How do you broach the subject?

Emir did not appear. It was the fool Stefan who approached Erroh first. It took Erroh a few moments to recognise him beneath the wretchedness. His blond hair was tangled, his chin was grizzled, and his shoulders were slumped. Mostly it was his dead eyes. The last time he'd seen him was from behind as he'd skulked away. He was a damned coward, and Erroh's knuckles turned white as he knotted his hands into fists.

To Stefan's marginal credit, he didn't shirk away from the humiliation of facing Erroh or Lea in public. He bowed down deeply to Erroh first and offered a knee. From his scabbard he pulled a broken blade and dug it into the ground at Erroh's feet. He offered the same deep bow to Lea, who eyed him as coldly as did Erroh. Knowing he had earned no right by apologising was a better move on his part; he knew his worth as a man when in the company of the Alphas who had stood the line those terrible days. He was a pathetic sight, and Erroh said nothing.

"All I have to offer," he whispered, standing up swiftly before disappearing back into the mass of Keri survivors.

Erroh did not call after him. He lifted the broken blade from the mud and placed it across the table at his plate. *A strange gift.* A few of Stefan's comrades stepped closer and thanked both warriors before shuffling away to enjoy a taste of their old life. Erroh offered a smile and a few words to these wretched souls. Everything they said tore him apart, for this was known to happen to an Alphaline who'd failed the world.

"The Heroes of Keri…"

"Thank you for all that you did…"

"Without you, we would have perished…"

"My son fought with you. Do you remember him...?"

They kept coming, and Erroh could not settle. Every time he did, he felt a gentle pat on the back and heard another whispered word from a Keri refugee. He tried and failed to meet Lea's eyes. *Praise for failure.*

Eventually, the interruptions ceased and he could resume his celebration. Only then did he fully notice the relationship between Magnus and Wynn. They spoke as master and apprentice. He shouldn't have felt jealous of their bond, but still, listening to their easy camaraderie stung ever so. He'd never had an easy conversation with Magnus in his life. Perhaps that was the way of things. Perhaps Tye, in his turn, resented the relationship Erroh and Jeroen shared, and theirs had been a fleeting apprenticeship. *Invaluable one, though.*

When he could eat no more, he turned to drinking ale and found his tongue unaccustomed to such bitterness; thankfully, with the skill of any fine drinker, he swiftly remembered the art and began honing his craft. He forced himself to relax, but as he did, thoughts of the shack in his frozen haven came to mind. The crowd grated his nerves and the cheerful mood set him on edge. Surrounded by those he cared for most, he'd never felt as alone. No, that was not quite right: he'd felt more alone once before; this was a close second.

He tried to engage in conversation. He listened as Magnus argued the effectiveness of war hounds in battle, while Wynn countered that the use of beasts was a waste of training and unnecessarily cruel. Erroh could have argued that Wynn had never seen Magnus's beasts at war. He could also have added that perhaps there really was some cruelty involved, though not for the killers who went upon four paws. He could have spoken these thoughts aloud, but instead, he stared off into the night, his eyes dancing from glimmering light to glimmering light upon the imposing wall, and suddenly it occurred to him how needlessly ostentatious the lights were.

Why hasn't Spark shared this miraculous gift, anyway?

Though he didn't know why, looking at the absurd beauty caused a sudden sense of panic and he reached for his glass again, only to find it empty. He looked across the crowd to the serving carts, and the distance felt too vast. His limbs became cold, his body became statuesque, and he wanted to scream. He felt fear take hold, and the desire to hide beneath bedsheets in a little frozen shack became overpowering. *Fuk that, fuk that, fuk that.*

He suddenly felt the urge to grab his mate and lose himself in the forest forever, only to return when the city was about to fall. That sounded far more enjoyable than receiving any more praise from strangers who were unaware of his failure. Tomorrow his father would know that he could have ended the war before it began. How many joyous revellers here would die?

All?

"Are you okay, Erroh? You look as though you've just taken a beating in the Cull." Wynn grasped his arm and steadied the shaking, empty mug Erroh held. Upon his tired friend's face was concern, and Erroh felt pathetic for the jealousy he'd felt. "Worry no more, Erroh. You'll only be famous for a few more days, after which I'll be the centre of attention," he mocked, and strangely enough, Erroh calmed.

"What are you going to do? Cut your hair in public?" Erroh joked.

Magnus reached across and took his son's hand and held it. "Aye, little cub, best you calm yourself. You are among friends. If you need a moment, there is a tent already waiting for you," he said warmly, and Erroh shook his head. He'd hidden away in a cage beneath sheets once. Lea would kill him if he started cowering again.

There's only so much she'll take before she leaves me.

"It's a lot after such a journey," he offered, shrugging. It was all he could say. If they learned of his failure at this moment, it would turn into a right shit party. "I'll be fine." He turned to Wynn, feigning a smile. "So how are you going to steal my thunder?"

"There's a tournament being held, and I will fight for the Rangers," Wynn declared proudly. Magnus patted him on the back as he did.

"For the Rangers? You'd better win or Magnus will kill you," Erroh said, and Wynn laughed.

Magnus leaned in to both young Alphalines. "What are you laughing at, Wynn? Erroh speaks no lie."

"I'd better get some sparring in, I suppose," Wynn muttered, and the weight of responsibility seemed to strike him. *Now he understands what it is to apprentice under Magnus.*

"It'll be a grand day altogether," Erroh said. He looked to Lea and immediately she saw his distress, but he waved her concern away. It took mouthing words of love tethered with a smile before she relaxed.

Magnus and Wynn argued again. This time, they spoke of the arena. This discussion Erroh could be part of. He looked at the empty mug in his hand and steeled himself. "I'm getting some ale. I'm not yet drunk. The night is slipping away from me."

"No, Erroh, the night is only beginning."

30

PAYMENTS

The girl in red played with her hair; she did so to fight the urge to yawn. Her hair was still damp, but already the red strands were warming in the morning sun. Despite her efforts, a yawn broke through her guard, so she took that moment to stretch her arms before leaning back against the wooden shack. *What's an early rise during penance, anyway?*

He'd repaired the wall, she noticed; more likely, Wrek had repaired it. Wrek spent a great deal of time down the hovels these days. Probably as much as she. *It's where the popular people play.* She rubbed the last of the sleep from her eyes that her bath had missed and listened for any sign of movement inside. He was sleeping in longer today. She'd heard him snore a little while earlier. She could have knocked. Could have woken him. But that would have defeated the purpose. She'd knocked the first morning and he hadn't reacted very well. She discovered a smudge of unpleasant dirt upon her cuff and wiped it off swiftly. An hour from now her dress would be covered in similar muck, but when he met her, she would look her best. The first hour was Roja's; every moment after was fair game. Poor Emir had little idea how determined she was.

She heard the rumble of movement as he roused himself. His routine began with a few muffled curses as he fought a hangover before stepping out to face another arduous day. Further familiar noises emerged from behind the door. She held her breath and waited. This was her favourite part.

He opened his door and looked to see if his guest waited. He was not disappointed. She offered a beaming smile every morning, and today was no different. He understood her game, yet he did not understand her tactic. In one way, it was nice. In another way, it was unsettling. She slid away from the shack and he noticed she wore blue silks today. *Stunning.* She always wore silk. Soon, she'd look as wretched as he. Soon, she'd be scrambling in the muddy depths with him. There were worse things, he supposed.

"Good morning, Emir." The shack's wall creaked loudly as she drew away from it.

"So, you are here again?"

"It's something to do," she countered.

"Well, that's a better reason than mine," he said, slipping past her to make sure her leaning had done no damage to the structure's stability. It hadn't, nor would it have, but sometimes, Emir liked to be an asshole.

He hadn't responded well to her advances at first. Truthfully, she had gone about it all wrong and paid for her mistake. She had offered gifts. Nothing spectacular, just gestures to make him smile. She'd quickly learned of his lack of interest in trinkets or treasures. Her attempts at buying his forgiveness went down like eggs to the floor. Her next attempts involved shouting, and at first, she'd believed that bore fruit. He'd listened politely and nodded in agreement, and when she'd finished her tirade, he had simply walked away. *Fuker didn't even shout back.*

Eventually, she'd begged forgiveness and, strangely enough, the words had come easily. After the apology, she'd asked for opportunities of redemption. He'd laughed to himself, accepted her apology and walked off with no further words.

She'd tried shouting at him again, and it didn't work... again.

So, she had taken to crushing his spirit with her presence. A fine plan, if truth be told. Every day she appeared outside his shack before sunrise, willing to accompany him on his rounds. The first week, he hadn't even acknowledged her presence, but now, well, now they sometimes spoke. Come the evening, when exhaustion struck her and his hands shook from toil, they parted ways. Sometimes he wished her a good night, but mostly he closed the door on her. A lesser female might have walked away from him with pride intact. A better woman might have done the same. As it was, this dreadful penance served her soul. Aye, it was for him, but it was also for herself. No distressing day was ever the same. This was why she loved the man. This was why she allowed him to behave as an asshole.

Naturally, Dia had argued as to duty, but her arguments were weak, and eventually she'd given up the fight on the matter. Roja suspected Dia saw the truth with her old eyes—that Roja was ill-prepared for the grand task of Primary. *Ill-suited.* Or maybe Dia understood that Emir was worth the fall from grace. Roja attended the futile meetings with Magnus, and that was enough. She left every other duty in Silvia's hands. A warier person might have suspected Silvia had her eyes on greater things.

So be it.

The world had halted for a moment in precarious time. The people waited with bated breath. The brutes were not yet at the gate. The river of refugees had stemmed their flow. And the coins? Well, the coin pieces were just as scarce. So, what was wrong with a dalliance? What was wrong trying to find her soul in a wretched hive of misery? So, like a little hound awaiting scraps, Roja followed Emir every morning.

She'd seen blood before, but when he worked with the gorier injuries, she became faint. Struggling with her balance and holding down her breakfast, she tried to assist him, and sometimes succeeded, as he stitched up open wounds. Who knew the hovels were a place of such clumsiness? Stomach bugs, fevers and broken bones did not faze her; in fact, she was a helpful distraction, sometimes uttering calming words or offering conversation with the patients or their emotional kin as Emir mended what needed mending. It was in these moments that he nodded approval. Only the day before, he'd thanked her for calming a brute of a woman who'd stood guard over her sickly husband as he gasped for air. An hour later, Emir had called Roja a "stupid whore" when she'd dropped a bottle of dream syrup, but she was a tough girl and took the name-calling on the chin.

She knew some people crumbled upon hearing nasty terms.

She knew some people screamed ill-informed outrage just for effect.

She knew some people were offended by words. *By fuken words.*

She looked around at the misery—of the hovels, of the world, of everything. She had been wrong about many things; it was acceptable to be wrong. What mattered was rising above offence.

It wasn't until she chose to rise above words that she realised how easy it was to rise above words.

By the second week, he had accepted her help. As angry as he was with the world, the wretches, himself and especially her, he would still take help with the sick and dying. Where healing was concerned, she was the least effective healer he'd called upon, but she tried and that went a long way with Emir. While he gave the appearance of being lost in the moment of cleaning and sealing up an infected tear, he listened to her gentle voice talking reassuringly with his present victim. In those moments, she brought value to their partnership. In those moments, she didn't act like she was queen bitch of the city. She didn't even act like an Alpha female. It wasn't much, but it was something.

"Something new today, Roja," he said, as she fell in line with him. "Today, we collect payments." He pulled a large metal tankard from his satchel and shook it to show it was empty.

She played her game, too. She wanted him to elaborate but said nothing. Instead, she looked to the unmarred sky above. "It will be a hot day."

He nodded in agreement but made no reply. Even if she made a fine point. The hot days were the worst in the hovels. On hot days, people were carelessly active. Nothing worse than active people to a set of ill-equipped healers. She was learning quickly, and that also mattered.

"So... what's the canister for?" she asked eventually. She used the same tone she had taken to using when seeking a reaction. Humble, respectful, strong. A tone as far from queenly as she could make it. It sounded natural. It sounded like a female who wouldn't smash three eggs all over his floor.

"Like I said before, payment for services." His face hardened. "My services, to be exact. You bring little to this... endeavour."

"Oh, you love my company," she countered, and he almost smiled. Well, he looked as though he almost smiled, but then he hacked deeply, spat up some phlegm and stamped it into the ground. This too was progress. She was getting to him. They both knew it. Any month now and he might share a meal with her. *Perhaps some eggs?*

He was a man possessed, and she matched his pace. Every few moments he glanced at a grubby sheet of crumpled paper with badly written names scribbled on it before adjusting his route, until eventually they came upon a shack using the city wall as one of its outer walls. Roja thought the wretches who'd built it were rather clever. Fewer materials used and evenings spent with free lighting. Desperate times brought out the best in people.

Putting his notes away, Emir coughed once and began knocking furiously at the door frame. There was a nasty stained blanket covering the doorway, and inside she heard hushed whispers.

"I can hear you."

Muffled mutterings.

"Open the fuk up, you cheap bastards," he shouted, and she was taken aback at his sudden outrage. She recognised that tone. He used it when he was getting the upper hand. Usually that tone edged the argument in his favour. *I hate that tone.*

The blanket opened swiftly. A grubby young woman covered in week-old filth looked out and smiled hopefully. "Ah, healer. How are ya?"

Roja recognised that smile. She used that smile every morning when greeting Emir, and it had the same effect.

"I want the payment right now. If not, I'll not help with any more ailments… you cheap bitch," he growled. Unsure of how this might go, Roja found a nice crack in the wall to gaze at. She stared at the lines of wire, with lightbulbs attached, as they disappeared in behind the transient wall. *Clever little lowerlines.* She did not remember this place from any earlier visit. Perhaps he had tended to them a long time before. Perhaps he had been called in the middle of the night by a frantic guardian.

There was movement behind the woman, the clinking of bottles and the discreet sound of nervous, shuffling feet, a few more whispers that Emir pretended to be unaware of, and then the smiling woman smiled once more and bade them enter.

She pointed to a patch of grubby cloth and flattened hay. "Please take a seat, healer." Her equally grimy mate sat over a makeshift cradle with a young child sleeping inside. He looked both nervous and protective. The child looked new to the world. Emir declined the offer of the chair and tapped his foot impatiently.

"All we can offer is some sine," countered the father, lifting a half-full bottle of violent alcohol for their aggressive guest to peruse. The unnatural yellow glaze to the substance was likely the worst thing Roja had ever seen, and she fought the urge to step in and demand Emir leave the wretches be. In that moment, she felt ashamed to be standing silent, but stay silent she did. Was she that pathetically eager to earn his approval? It was ugly and unfair; but this was how things worked. She held her tongue.

Emir did not.

He took the bottle and held it to the light from the doorway. Shaking it a few times, he uncorked the top and inhaled. "Aye, I suppose this will do." He unscrewed the top of his own flask and poured a dollop of the fluid into it before passing the crude sine back to the father. He leant over the child, his piercing eyes scrutinising the mouth, the nose, the ears. "You didn't spit in the bottle, did you?" he asked, setting his flask to one side before prodding the little one under the jaw. "Doesn't matter. It'll be drunk, anyway." He placed his ear against the child's chest. "If she shows the symptoms again, come find me." He stood up, eyeing both parents. "Day or night. You've paid your dues. Don't fuken hesitate next time."

The child's mother took his hand and kissed it gently. For the briefest moment, Roja thought Emir would show emotion. He gave the hint of being moved, but perhaps it was just the shock from being touched unexpectedly. He pulled his hand away and nodded quickly. With the transaction for his services completed, he turned and walked back out into the early morning sun.

"If you don't have a name yet, Quig is a nice girl's name," he offered, as the curtain was closed over.

They spent the rest of the morning filling his tankard full of sine or whatever bitter homebrew the wretches offered, and the routine was the same. He shouted for payment; they offered poison, and he accepted every drop. Every time he opened the tankard, the mixture of bitter aromas stung her nose, yet he seemed unaffected. *Shows the depths of alcohol dependency.* There were no coin pieces offered. Just alcohol. Sometimes there would be jests, and sometimes aggressive arguments between both parties, but always the payment was made. They would hand a bottle over and a mouthful's worth would cancel the debt. After each transaction, he would engage in a quick inspection of wounds or ask questions and advise how to avoid further visits. No matter the hovel, by the time he left, neither party seemed aggrieved. In fact, most visits ended with a handshake and a kind word offered his way.

By the time the afternoon sun burned their skin, Emir had reached his goal. He screwed the cap on the full canister and hid it in his bag. Their march had brought them to the furthest reaches of the hovels.

"I have one more stop to make," he told her as they approached a rickety shack. "This is where we found Linn's parents." The shack lay along the river, hidden from the warmth of the sun in the shade of the city walls. A fine view, but bitterly cold. Roja's heart dropped. *They thought themselves safe here.*

"Superstitions stopped anyone dwelling in it, but we found a use for it," the healer whispered.

He knocked and entered without waiting for an answer, and Roja followed. It was bigger than most shacks, built in the earliest days when the first refugees had arrived. Roja remembered Dia ordering the shacks to be erected as far from the great gates as possible. Roja hadn't given it a second thought. They'd thought themselves superior and generous. *Slum it for a time.* There weren't enough condemning terms to describe Roja's mistake. *No, not a mistake. Negligence.*

Roja had learned this walking the desolate pathways with Emir.

The fetid smell of sour milk mixed with human waste almost brought her to her knees. The air was thick, and breathing came harder in this chamber. She wanted to flee the moment the door shut behind her; she felt entombed alive. It was dim but for a few slivers of light streaming through the cracks to penetrate the murkiness. A palace of nightmares, she thought. In the corner rested a small bed of straw covered in ancient bedsheets. Along the walls hung various pieces of dented armour and stained weapons. A small table sat in the centre of the room with discarded empty bottles lying strewn across its stained surface.

In the far corner, a hunched figure was sitting with crossed legs, sharpening a tiny dagger. She could see its sharpness in the dimly lit room. The light scrape of blade against whetstone was the only sound to be heard. Its dry, grinding pitch rhythmically pierced the air. The man didn't look up. He kept sharpening the tiny little piece of steel. Roja felt stirrings of fear down her neck. Something about this man was off. She'd seen broken wretches before. This was different. She felt terror, and wondered uneasily why Emir had brought her here.

Emir leaned down beside the man. "Hello, Cass." His voice broke the scraping rhythm.

Shaking fingers touched the tip of the blade and, satisfied, the man placed it aside. "Hello, Emir. How are you?" His voice was tired and tragic.

"I'm well, my friend. How are you today?"

Cass ran his fingers through his thinning hair a few times and massaged a few strands before replying. "I didn't sleep again."

Roja couldn't be here anymore. She looked to the door, but Emir shook his head.

Cass picked up the little blade and began sharpening its edge once more. "A blade like this can't penetrate armour; however, it can go through skin easily."

"It's certainly sharp. May I look?" Emir asked, and Cass passed it across. As he did, Emir patted his hand in gratitude and pulled a loaf of honey bread from his satchel. Its enticing, sweet aroma was foreign to this stench. He set it on the table, then held the dagger up to a beam of dusty light that had crept through a break in the ceiling. He examined it as though it were a bottle of cheap, poisonous alcohol. "It is a stunning thing indeed." Emir swished the tiny dagger in the air as though it were a toy. "I'd like you to meet a friend of mine. Her name is Roja." He passed the dagger back to the waiting hand. Cass leaned forward and stared into Roja's soul.

"You are right, Emir. She is beautiful. Though not like Aireys." Cass rubbed his hand through his hair again. "Not that I care for such things. You won't tell, right?"

"She's no Aireys, but she's pretty enough," Emir countered, and Roja felt their combined sorrow. She was not part of their melancholy, not part of the tragedies that had brought them to this terrible shack. She wanted to speak, to share words, but she said nothing. If this were another of Emir's cruel manoeuvres, that was fine. She could take it. She suspected this was another education, Emir's misguided way of reaching out to her. *Not misguided at all.* Of course, she would tell no one.

Emir looked at Roja strangely before facing Cass. "I know you have questions for the Primary. Perhaps Roja might answer them for you," he whispered.

"Does she speak for the Primary?" Cass's eyes opened wide and Roja felt that fear again. He was tall, well built, but she was swift. Besides, if he were dangerous, Emir wouldn't have allowed her to enter. Still, she watched his shoulders, leaving his hands to continue sharpening.

"I speak for the Primary... If I can, I will help." Before she could stop herself, she glided over to him. Closer than caution might have preferred. Close enough that he could swing that blade and cut. She knelt down to meet his eyes and all she saw was a lost man. The blade tightened in his hand before he placed it down.

"Who are you to the Primary?"

"She is my grandmother."

He accepted this and took a long breath before releasing it. "I hate her, you know. She failed my brethren in Keri."

She'd heard these grievances before, and, usually with the weight of armed Black Guards at her side, she had engaged them openly. This was different. This was dangerous. This was tragedy. This was terror. This was the world outside her sanctuary.

"Tell me," Roja whispered, and placed her hand on his. He didn't seem to notice. His eyes were a thousand miles away.

"Why were they silent? Why not warn us of the threat?"

She had no answers, for there was little to ease this poor broken man's suffering. "Tell me of Keri," she said softly.

He looked at her strangely, and only then did he appear to notice her hand. He took a deep breath and released it and began telling her about the battle of Keri. He did not weep, but behind her she heard Emir sniff once and Roja's heart broke for both of them. It was so easy to hide away and make important decisions without the taste of real life to burn her. She knew the tale, but not from this man's mouth, and only after he'd finished did she realise he held her hand tightly.

"I'm so sorry, Cass. I'm so very sorry," she whimpered, as tears fell from her cheeks and the guilt over so many damaged lives struck her. *Not only from Keri.* She kissed his hand and he released her.

"Thank you for your words, Roja. They have served you well today," he whispered, and returned to his blade.

"It is a lovely blade, Cass," she said quietly, and he smiled.

Behind her, Emir roused himself from his silence against the far wall. He gestured to Roja that daylight was but a breath away. "Do you need anything, Cass?" he asked, making to leave.

Cass shook his head, returning to sharpening his knife. "Azel said he'd come by when his watch ends."

"He's a good friend. Get some rest, eat some food. I'll be back again."

Emir led her back into the light and closed the door behind them. "Thank you," he said, walking out towards the edge of the riverbank. She looked to the sky and realised many hours had passed. Her stomach was empty, and a terrible weakness had overcome her. She tasted the air and found it unusually sweet after such a stench. "I'm unskilled with afflictions of the mind. I try my best," he said, shrugging. She could see how deeply he hid his suffering.

"Will he recover?"

"Perhaps in time. Truthfully, this vacant state has overcome him. At first, he was merely beaten when he found us on the road. Now, though, he's just slipped further into the darkness."

"Can I do anything to help him? Perhaps we could arrange for better accommodation?"

"He won't leave that damned shack." Emir shrugged again. "No one else wants a shack where a family died. Nobody wants to see a rambling man walk the hovels, sharpening a fuken dagger, either. It's not ideal, but it is what it is."

"I hope I helped."

"If there was more to learn of mind afflictions, I would study. I never thought Lara would pull herself from such a state, yet she thrives now." Emir reached the river's edge. "Perhaps speaking with you might stir something deep. He is still a good man somewhere deep within. He must be."

Emir did not stop walking; he lifted his satchel above his head, dropped into the river and began wading out towards a massive boulder some distance from the bank. She remembered seeing him upon this rock a lifetime ago. She hadn't joined him then. She didn't hesitate now. She wondered what Dia might have thought and felt liberated dropping into the water. It was something to do. The water took her breath, and she gasped aloud. He spun around and smiled for an entire heartbeat before reaching the boulder, where he climbed up and sat waiting. She struggled in her blue dress but dared not show it. He offered his hand and she batted it away. With water streaming from both their bodies, they sat side by side upon the barren island. It was a fine rock.

"I'll only follow for so long," she warned.

"And then you will leave me be?"

"Would you really care?"

He took out a little piece of cloth from his bag and unwrapped it to reveal a few slices of fresh honey bread and two eggs. *Hard-boiled.* He cracked the shell on one and offered the second to her. As the sun set around them, she felt the heat of the boulder dry her soaked dress. Sitting beside each other facing the endless river, they shared the food and ate in silence. She felt the purr of the gentle flow ease her into relaxation and she thought this moment perfect.

"Wine would have added to this feast," he jested. It wasn't a hilarious jest, but she smiled. *A thank you, a meal and a joke in one day?* He was spoiling her.

"You could always drink from the tankard," she offered, swallowing and savouring the last morsel of the finest meal she'd had in her life. He reached into his satchel and took out the flask. Unscrewing the cap and inhaling, he tipped the lip and allowed the contents to drain into the waters below. In the little stream of clear fluid, she could see the first of the city lights begin to illuminate, shimmering in the pour. It was rather eye-catching, but all she saw were the fruits of the entire day's efforts flowing away forever into the dark water below.

"What are you doing?" She grabbed for the canteen, but he held it out of reach like a bully with a stolen treasure.

"I am friends with Wrek. Do you really think I need this foul concoction?" It was a fair point, but it was the principle of the matter. The last of the liquid fell from the bottle and, after a quick shake, he returned the cap and put the offending canteen back into his bag. He said nothing for a few moments. She could see he was watching the little glowing orbs come alive in the water's surface; they danced across the great expanse like fireflies taking flight for the first time. It mesmerised him, for it was an awe-inspiring sight.

That said...

"Why the fuk did you have us walk through that cesspit all day screaming abuse at everyone?" she demanded. She thought him vile and almost shoved him from the boulder, back into the river where he belonged. *Almost, but not quite.* Instead, she thought of her line, she thought of eggs, she thought of control. "They have nothing. And still you took from them." She shook her head and muttered a few curses under her breath, and Emir just watched the water serenely. "It just seems shit," she whispered, more to herself. She just couldn't shake the desperation in their faces. *Mean Emir, coming to collect his dues.* She couldn't forget their relief when he accepted payment. They had nothing.

Nothing nothing nothing.

"I'm sorry," she said for the umpteenth time that week. "It's your payment and you can do with it whatever you see fit."

He placed his hand on her leg and patted it gently. He hadn't touched her since that horrific morning. "They need to be able to pay something," he mumbled. "It gives them pride, a sense of worth."

Confused silence.

He continued on. "They've lost everything. They can't afford a healer, but they can afford me." He took a deep breath and broke away from staring into the water to stare at her. He smiled again, and she melted inside. "They argue the price of payment out of pride. They pay the price in the end and feel no further debt to me. Did you see their faces as I left?"

"They looked happier."

"Aye." He moved his hand from her leg and took her hand in his own. "Besides," he said with a laugh, "I think a fair bit of water is disguised as payment, anyway." He glanced over at the Rangers' camp and heard some dogs barking manically. They sounded joyous. He might have said more, but Roja couldn't help herself.

"I am foolishly and completely in love with you, Emir."

He didn't react the way she expected him to.

31

THE PARTY

Lea excused herself from the table. Her mother-in-law's laugh still rang in her ears as she left, and Lea believed it wonderful; kind and infectious, putting its listener at ease. *Welcomed.* She'd charmed Lea as she had Lillium. If royalty still ruled, Elise would make a fine queen.

Her feet were a little wobbly beneath her as she strolled and sipped her wine. Ahead of her, Erroh wandered aimlessly through the crowd, and she followed. Lillium sprinted by them both with two empty jugs in her hands. Her destination was one of the great carts. Behind her, Elise and Lexi cheered her on and Lea smiled. Hours had passed, but it felt like tonight would never end. It was strange being around so many bodies; it would have been easier with him at her side. *Duties of a hero.* It felt strange being apart from her mate. It felt even stranger to suffer dependence. *Not dependence: devotion.*

She glided towards him and wrapped her arms around him from behind, crossing her hands over his chest, pulling him from the growing crowd of revellers threatening to surround him and demand he regale them with tales of heroism. Like excited beasts, they craved his words and attention; she just craved silence with him, the chance to breathe a moment and remind him they'd made it. Remind herself, too.

The noise, the jostling crowd, seemed surreal, and she expected to waken somewhere out in the Wastes with a thousand miles still to charge. She led him by the hand and he followed. Without warning, she spun around and kissed him, and for a moment, they were alone in the Wastes once more. In the distance, a few musicians struck the first chords of a song neither wanted to hear again. Wordlessly, they stepped quietly away from the masses, taking in the cool night air, walking along the barely lit outskirts of the camp.

"Quig sang it well," Erroh said, inclining his head back towards the far-off music.

"We all did."

"Thank you, my beo," he said, taking her hand and holding it to his heart. She could see the anguish of the months of travel on his features, dimly lit in the city's glowing. She watched a smile break through the pain and felt the need to kiss him once more. "You saved me."

"It was something to do." She shrugged, tipping some of her drink into his glass. The ultimate act of love. He leaned in to kiss her and she tugged his hair and he yelped. The blaring music suddenly faded. The musicians struck a few loose notes mid-crescendo and then, one by one, the instruments fell silent. She strained to see through the gathered crowd.

"Something has happened?"

"Something always happens," he muttered, allowing her to lead them back towards the gathering.

A dozen Black Guards walked through the gates and on into the centre of the gathering. The crowd sensed violence in the air, and the Rangers grinned at the prospect. The numbers were favourable; this was Ranger territory. The Black Guard, however, had always walked wherever they wished. Tonight, they carried no weapons or shields, displayed no open aggression. But there was still intent. If there was violence, they would throw only fists.

All in good fun.

The leader removed his helmet and walked towards the table of Magnus and Elise. "We wish to offer our welcome to Erroh of Keri. We also wish to speak with Lea... also of Keri."

Magnus glared at him from his seat. *Perhaps he likes that song.* Lea recognised the voice; Erroh probably would not. She increased her pace through the crowd, her heart in her mouth, her hope rising.

Azel of Keri bowed down on one knee in front of Magnus, and the crowd went deathly still. The whispers had already begun; people were well aware that the Primary would be annoyed at such deference. On either side of Azel, two other archers broke rank and also knelt down. The wretched guests once again found their voices and enthusiasm, realising the Black Guard were not stirring a brew of trouble. The Rangers remained silent, remained hopeful. Further back, two other Black Guards left the formation altogether. Stripping off their helmets, they went about demanding a couple of mugs of ale from the pouring attendants. As they did, Wrek walked up and stood casually at their sides.

She saw all of this as Erroh met the kneeling archers first, and she fought to contain herself. *My boys made it.* Azel spoke for the three. Guillem pulled out a solitary arrow. He tapped it three times before handing it to Patir, who placed the tip against his forehead before passing it forward to Azel, who kissed the tip once. Lea recognised the arrow and the honour they'd bestowed upon it. They had taken it from a quiver used in the battle of Keri.

How many similar arrows had she fired?

How many had struck down brutal invaders?

She could recognise the distinctive white feathered flight even from a distance. The shaft was smooth and straight, and the steel tip was sharper than most. Fine arrows made by a warring town. Azel passed it to Erroh.

"All I have to offer."

The cub accepted the gift and went to shake the archer's hand, but Azel was already turning away, distracted by the real reason they'd knelt. Erroh might be the Hero of Keri, but Lea was their champion. *Their real leader.* She had led by example and led them to survival. She hadn't let them down. When all was lost, she had ordered them to safety. She'd been the last to leave, staying behind and further delaying their pursuers.

Their joy at seeing her alive was overwhelming. With the honourable formalities concluded, they bounded around her like faithful hounds reunited with their kin after a long time apart. She shouted for "her boys," and they embraced her as one elite unit once more.

"It's lucky you are prettier than most of them," whispered Wynn, taking the arrow from Erroh and inspecting it. "Come on, let's get drunk while your mate sees to all those males." Erroh could see his grin, and he cursed the cur. *I am prettier.*

The three Black Guard took her to a private table and set about adoring her loudly, and Erroh was struck by a pang of jealousy. Not for the attention they showed her—that would have been petty, beneath him—but for her having living comrades. Every brave warrior who'd stood the line had died under his watch. Still, though, it brought him warmth seeing all four so deliriously happy.

"That sounds like a plan," he told Wynn. *A simple one.*

Lillium ambushed Erroh, albeit clumsily, before he could make it to his seat. She fell drunkenly against him, nearly knocking them both to the ground.

"I agree—Erroh is far prettier than them," she slurred. "Although everyone looks attractive in that black, shiny armour." She regained her feet and, using Erroh as leverage, straightened herself. "Oops —sorry."

"Those two by the cart aren't particularly appealing," warned Wynn, seemingly uninterested in the drunken state of his beautiful mate. "Now, why would any self-respecting Alphaline join up with the Black Guard when there's a perfectly acceptable army already willing to take them?"

Lillium grinned. "At least we can agree on that one, my darling... love."

Erroh touched the scar above his eye absentmindedly. It seemed so small now, and he couldn't even remember how painful his broken ribs had been. *Fuk the Cull.* Usually, he was bad with faces and worse with

ROBERT J POWER

names. But these fuks he remembered all too well, though their names escaped him.

"Let's ask them to leave," suggested Wynn. He slurred his words like Lillium.

"Nicely," she added, her face mischievous and dangerous. It wasn't unlike one of Lea's expressions. Both she and Lea had inherited the distaste for the Wolves expected of any Ranger. Erroh just thought the brutes needed a good kicking, but looking at Lea speaking with her comrades, he thought it a little cruel to deny her this release.

"No, I think we should leave them to it. It is a joyous occasion, after all."

"Fuk it—the Hero of Keri has declared peace," said Wynn, raising a glass. "Until I'm Ranger Champion, I'll adhere to your better ruling."

Elise played with Magnus's hair. She felt alive in the surrounding energy of the gathering. More than that, she felt youthful, vibrant, ready for war. To Emir, she thought, quietly raising a toast to the healer. His enthusiasm for experimentation was nothing short of legendary, and a little unsettling. And she had been a willing candidate for his vile tonics. He hadn't killed her yet. That was a fine start to their partnership. Tonight, when she needed it most, she felt well. She might never recover, but there were moments when she could breathe more deeply than she had done in years, and without suffering a coughing attack. She leaned across her only man and stroked his thin beard gently. Though Magnus was relaxed, he stared intently at Erroh. He was feeling the same sense of pride and relief as she. *A fine look to him.* Few things aroused her more than his parental instincts. They'd brought up a fine little cub. *A fine Alpha male.*

"Bored now." She rose from her seat and slid across the table as though she were a wild youth, before landing gracefully upon his lap. Around her, people turned in surprise as half the dishes and goblets took flight beneath her reckless manoeuvre. If they stared, she cared little. They were king and queen at this table. *In this fuken city.* They behaved as they wanted to, and she aimed to misbehave this very moment.

"We made a fine child," she whispered.

"He looks older."

"He looks less the little cub," she agreed. "And more one of us."

A legend.

Magnus took hold of her rear with a firm grip and she sighed. Even after this long together, she still felt electric pulses shoot up through her body when he touched her. Especially when she could breathe. He squeezed and her muscles ached from his strength, and she loved this too. Around them, people found better conversations elsewhere. *And why not?* Such beauty was a godly, blinding sight.

The absent gods agreed.

She kissed him and bit his lower lip playfully.

"Now that you breathe, you want to make a scene, woman?"

"Don't you want me to make a scene, my king?"

"I'm no king," he hissed and bit her back, digging his fingers into her skin. She knew there would be bruising where he held her, and this pleased her. The best nights resulted in bruising on both their bodies. *A scrape or two as well.*

"You're the king of the entire fuken world, and me, well, I'm in charge," she warned, and took hold of his hair. A warning, a declaration, a little bit of play.

"I think I preferred having you without vigour, my beo," he whispered, and they both laughed.

"I can't watch this anymore," cried Lexi from somewhere down the table, and both legends laughed, kissed and bit a little more. This moment in time was precious. Elise could feel it in her brittle bones. They'd conquered the worlds and behaved like legendary gods; they'd beaten terrible odds, vanquished supposed heroes, and torn apart wretched, imposing brutes. *Torn families apart, too.* But this... This felt different. Dia was not shifting on her decision. The Rangers were no longer the force they had once been. The warlords of the Savage Isles had vowed to never march again, not even if given a royal decree. Magnus might argue, but this felt like the end of the world.

At least for the aged legends.

"You have to yield to Dia. You have to do it tomorrow, Magnus," she whispered.

He said nothing for a time and she was satisfied to wait. Truthfully, she was as aggrieved as he, but the days were slipping from their grasp. The enemy was nearing and still they had made no preparation. Best take what they had and get to task. It wouldn't be the first time they were outnumbered. It wouldn't be the first time they would kill them all.

"If I bend to her will now, who else will stand up to her?"

"Teach her the value of fear," Elise suggested, and he was quiet for a moment.

"I'll think on this, my love."

She shifted into a more comfortable position, and he hooked his arms around her in an embrace as though she were a babe in swaddling. She was fierce, she was unvanquished, but in his arms she felt safe and sheltered.

"Set things moving in what favour we can, but truly, this will be Erroh's war, not ours," she whispered, wrapping her arms around his neck. "When it's over, tell him I was proud."

She looked over at her son, who was engaging in conversation with Magnus's two newest Alphaline lieutenants. From his gestures and jests, it looked as though he were entertaining them greatly. They hung on every word. Lillium was smiling. *Beautiful.* Wynn was laughing too, and this was pleasing to see. *And rare.* Elise knew it was the leader in him. Whenever Erroh tried, he was capable of greatness beyond his parents' shadow. She knew it, because she had taught Magnus how to lead. Before her touch, so to speak, he had been merely a wild brute with charm and delicious aggression. Afterwards, well, he was godly.

Magnus kissed her cheek, his eyes still upon their new daughter. "Not just Erroh's war, my love. I find myself staring at the girl. Beautiful, aye, but there is such strength beneath that veneer."

"She is a perfect female for our little Alpha male. Keep your eyes to yourself. There are plenty of others to look at." She could see his irritation at her teasing, and she approved. Lea was beautiful and spoken for, and besides, Elise was the real goddess. *Best he remember that.*

"First you ban Lillium? Now you ban me from all the young—"

She slapped him and he laughed. "Take me tonight; only me. Remember everything," she whispered, and he clutched her tighter.

"As you wish, my beo."

———

"Stop laughing at me," Roja cried, but Emir couldn't. It felt wonderful releasing pent-up emotions. It was a fine compliment, even if her feelings were misguided. *Poor little Alphaline.* He tried to catch his breath, but the absurdity of her words made it funny. Her outrage was even funnier.

"You're a fuken pig!" She picked up a rock and threw it into the deep, black river. The ripples brought the reflection of the glowing wall to life again. It was a good throw and went further into the darkness than he expected. She looked at him again, her brow creased in dismayed anger, in embarrassment, and again he found it hilarious. She didn't hit him, though he had it coming. *This time.* She was growing as a hot-blooded Alphaline. He tried to catch his breath; his laugh turned to a snort and tears streamed from his eyes.

"I'm sorry," he gasped, searching for distraction. He found it in the growing cheers from the Ranger camp. He was certain they were cheering.

Roja played with her hair again. "If someone tells someone else that they love them, it's cruel to laugh." She crossed her legs, and his laughter ceased. He reached out and stroked her cheek. "I was happier before I ever met you," she added, and he could tell it was a lie. She shrugged as though she realised her lie too. "Before I fell in love with you," she added, to cover her embarrassment.

"I always believed your kind were exactly the same as us lowerlines," he said, as if giving a sermon in a tavern. All he needed was a tankard and an unruly table of listeners, ready to agree or disagree with equal ferocity. "And you are exactly the same as us mere lowerlines. You feel the same emotions, and you bleed the same colour blood." He thought for a moment. "And you can die just as easily. The difference is that you all are precariously extreme in everything you do." He wanted to laugh again. She was not impressed.

"Ah, fuk this." She started to rise and he took hold of her wrist. She shot him a look and he released her immediately. He could criticise her, he could mock her, he could even humiliate her for loving him, but that look was a warning; she was a threat and it would be best to remember that.

"Please stay," he whispered.

"Oh, fuk off, Emir."

"Please stay with me."

"So you can laugh at me again?"

"Probably."

Despite herself, she smiled at his punishing charm. *Good thing, too.* He knew he danced with fire. She held her closed fist in her open hand and he smiled at the memory. "Go on, charm me with your cruelty," she hissed.

"Love…" he said, as though it were a curse. *It is.* "Yes… Love is just attraction at its most extreme, and you can't see anything else. The extent to which I desire you is depthless, but I don't love you. I'll never love you," he said.

"Aye," she replied, feeling tight in her chest. What did he know of her emotions? She cursed herself and her loose tongue. It had felt like the moment. Love was humiliating. *Stupid, stupid, stupid.*

"I will love no one ever again," he said, sounding like a healer giving arrogant advice to a fool. *Just one slap.* She stared at him, hating with her eyes. "There does not have to be an extreme. There need not be black and white alone. Sometimes, there is calm. Sometimes, there is desire. Sometimes, there is the colour grey." Without warning, his lips were upon hers. She didn't expect the assault, and kissed him back for a wonderfully-stolen breath before drawing away. *A last kiss.*

"You are tormenting me, Emir," she hissed. "Little boy with all the wise answers."

"You're the most beautiful girl I've ever seen. Longing for you, tasting you, taking you should be enough for me, Roja." He took her hand in his and tore her apart. "But it's not."

"Aye," she countered gamely, fighting the torrent of emotions spinning through her. Sadness and confusion won out.

"You will do great things leading us in the years ahead." He placed his hand across her chest. "I bring no worth to your cause. You asked why I laughed? I laughed because you and I falling in love is an absurd notion." He still kept his hand on her chest. She could feel how rough it was. *And warm.* "The absent gods are cruel. Destiny will gift us no happy ending."

"Very well. I will wait for you outside your shack tomorrow morning, regardless."

"Aren't there better ways of spending your time?" he asked dismissively, as though she were a child without a clue.

"Don't presume I do it out of misplaced desire. I do it for myself."

"As you wish," he said, and perhaps he spoke some truth.

Perhaps she had chased an unattainable prize. Perhaps she needed to live within the greyness of the world a little more. She loved him, but if he couldn't try rising from wretchedness, it was his tragic loss. *Our tragic loss.* It shouldn't matter that she was queen and he a peasant. He could rise above; she could sink below. She wished she had the words to argue. She wished he could understand that she feared life as much as he. She wished she hadn't said the word *love*.

He shuffled in his sitting position as though he had more to share. Or worse, another attempt at wit. She didn't want to hear him speak. "I was—"

"Whisht," she hissed. "Let us sit in silence a while. Let us think of many grey things."

Her mind was awash with frustrating thoughts, and time slipped by without her notice. He must have felt the same. He said nothing more.

Instead, he looked into the dark, shimmering water below until a familiar voice called from the riverbank, a voice sent by the absent gods to distract.

"The Alphas have returned to the city," shouted Stefan, and Emir shrugged.

"Well, good for them," Emir countered, but Roja was intrigued.

"I thought you'd want to know." Stefan seemed disappointed. "A few of us will pay our respects."

"Which Alphas?" Roja asked.

Does Dia know?

Had she agreed to Magnus's demands?

Why wasn't I told?

She'd argued with the Primary in their quiet chambers several times on the matter. Perhaps the moment had come.

"Erroh and Lea from…"

Emir shook and she heard his gasp. He placed his hand to his mouth and sighed slowly. His eyes never blinked; they stared vacantly, and Stefan nodded.

"From home," Emir whispered.

"There's talk of a gathering. I… will be… speaker for Keri," Stefan said, and Emir nodded his head in agreement. "I have the sword. I think I should…" Whatever he asked without asking, Emir nodded. She'd never seen him freeze like that, even when a patient closed his eyes in his grasp.

"If you can't face them, I understand. However, I must kneel," Stefan said, turning around and walking away.

"We must attend this gathering," she said decisively. Lea had been an insignificant enemy once. That wouldn't matter now. *Would it?*

Emir remained statuesque. "I believed them dead."

"Is this not a great thing?"

"Aye. Still, I cannot face them."

"Why?"

"Whisht. Let us sit in silence. Let us think of many grey things."

"No, Emir, we are done sitting upon this rock." Music played from across the river and she had the sudden foolish urge to dance. *With him.*

She could already hear the shift of movement throughout the shantytown. People were whispering. It wouldn't be long before Mydame became aware.

He shook his head suddenly. "Even in a world this small, I struggle to make friends. They became friends. I was mad with her, and oh, I was so very mad with them too, knowing I should have stood with them all along that infamous wall." He sniggered. It could easily have been a wail. "A fuken wall of furniture. Hardly a heroic thing." She edged closer to him and laid her head on his shoulder, and he ran his finger along her cheek. *Strange behaviour for those not in love.*

"You are a coward, my Emir. Such a foolish coward."

"Perhaps."

"This world is vast, Emir. Take everything it offers."

"Including love?" he asked.

"Including a willing lover when they throw themselves at you."

"A fine point," he muttered, and something snapped in her mind like a keystone hammered fiercely into a bridge. It was all a ruin of rocks until it became something more.

She pulled her pathetic, needy head away from his shoulder. Her voice was strong, urgent, her own. "You are unwilling to grasp happiness. You would prefer wretchedness and regret over happiness. I see it now, dear boy. Oh, I see it clearly. And, I am the greater fool for not seeing it sooner."

"And what's that?" he mocked, and then froze as she slid onto his lap, facing him. He instinctively grabbed her arms but made no move to shove her away, to strike her from the rock. Everything about him was infuriating. No man ever made her feel so angry, so ashamed, so stupid and so warm in a single moment. She knew he was thinking about the dead female, Aireys. And he always would. She bit her lip. It was time to take charge. The role of humble, apologetic little waif had brought her little happiness. She was Roja: the city's ace of queens. She went all in.

"This is not about eggs or my reckless, foolish attack. I fuked up. I've bowed and pleaded for your forgiveness. I've been waiting for you to fix whatever this is. I say this now and you had best fuken listen."

"Aye," he mumbled, though she could see his expression. *Aireys had been strong.* This, she knew well. Aireys had taken what she'd wanted. *Kudos, girl. My turn.*

"I am not the dead girl, Emir, and I don't care. If you can't see what we could have, then I'll show you." She leaned in close and their lips met. She drew away before he could react, for she was not done. She pulled her arms from his grasp and he placed his hands on her hips. It was a fine manoeuvre on his part.

She wasn't done.

"At the tournament, I will introduce you to the Primary... to my grandmother. My only living family. Let her see the path I choose. Let you both see the path I choose, and whom I take."

"If you want," he gasped, and she thought it a perfect reply.

"Do I drive you crazy?" she whispered in his ear, and he nodded.

"Do you want me?"

"I've always wanted you."

"I'm not Aireys; I'm something else entirely," she cried. "So stop fuking around and claim me already," she shouted, sliding away from him and leaving him this final moment to prove himself worthy. She perched herself at the edge with her back to him. If he did not reach out and kiss her, she would drop to the water below and be on her lonelier way. She counted three breaths, and as she did, she sent a silent prayer to the absent gods.

Let him reach for me.

Let him reach for me.

Let him reach for me.

And he did.

32

IT ALL COMES TOGETHER

Doran searched for the words and, after a few careful moments, found them. Playful and enticing. He'd never been great with words, particularly with the fairer sex, but sometimes he nailed them. "You know what? For a Ranger, you are rather attractive." *Perfect.*

She didn't seem to take notice, and that was fine. She was rather skilled at refilling jugs of alcohol. He leaned closer to look down her blouse—hardly a chivalrous manoeuvre, but he was drunk and she wouldn't even notice. So, really, there was no harm. A few watching feet away, Wrek the bouncer took a step closer but made no manoeuvre of his own. *Let him try.* The last time they'd tangled over female matters, the bouncer had had the upper hand. His Wolfen comrades respected Wrek; that was the only reason he hadn't sought a little retribution. Doran couldn't respect anyone who struck an unaware opponent.

"You really are beautiful," he whispered, catching a sight of rounded skin a little lower, slightly paler in colour.

"I know." She didn't even look at him when she spoke. *Playing it coy, letting me see.*

Gracefully, she spun away from Doran's attention with two freshly filled jugs, and he watched her swaying hips disappear into the crowd.

Beautiful, indeed. The gathering of revellers wasn't enormous; she'd be easy to find later. Wrek stepped away and Doran spat on the ground, eyeing the bigger brute. *Did he think I'd misbehave with her?*

Doran watched the numbers sway as one comfortable collective. He'd never felt at ease around masses of people. He didn't trust them for a moment, either. Best to stay wide of their loose tongues. It's what any friend would do. *No, not any friends.* Many friends were likely to let friends down, particularly Alpha males.

Aymon's eyes glistened dangerously, and Doran knew he was raring to start trouble with a Ranger. *Any Ranger.*

"She didn't look interested," his best friend jested.

"Because you would know?"

They had grown up a dozen miles away from each other, and throughout their youth they'd never been far from trouble. Truthfully, though Doran would never admit it aloud, Aymon was a terrible influence on him. Tonight, Doran would have liked to spend the night drinking and perhaps seeking the company of a few girls, but Aymon's own frustrations with his lot in life usually rose to the surface. Aymon served the city, but would the city desire his pledge should he reveal his predilection for male lovers? Doran thought about the Cull and shook his head in disgust. *Fuken whores.* Living a hidden life earned Aymon a little relief, a little release. Doran's own predilection for females could wait. They appreciated scars and stories, anyway.

Erroh could see Wynn's irritation, though he tried to hide it. Lillium returned to the table bearing drinks and Erroh cheered, hoping to ease his friend's mood. Though he didn't know Wynn particularly well, he could see the unhappiness. *A far cry from when we last spoke.* Lillium appreciated Erroh's enthusiasm, raising the jugs in victory before bowing theatrically. She even offered a smile, and Erroh remembered her cruelty in the Cull. *Wynn suffers from it too.*

"Thank you, Hero," she said, smiling a dazzling smile.

It swiftly faded when Wynn spoke. He sounded less an easy-going friend and more a sulking mate challenged. Threatening, overprotective. *Possessive.*

"What was that about?" He cracked his knuckles, eyeing the Wolf. His hackles were up. Moreover, his drunken hackles were up. A perilous thing.

"Just another foolish male." She poured four glasses and offered one to Elise, who remained nestled upon the lap of Magnus, looking impossibly comfortable.

She offered the second to Erroh, winking as she did. Erroh was not impressed, but he nodded in gratitude.

"What was he saying to you?" Wynn had now begun staring at the bald Black Guard.

"It was nothing, Wynn. Go get drunk," she hissed, and after a moment forced a smile to ease the sudden silence at the table.

"That's a fine idea. I think I'll join you, Wynn," Erroh said, grabbing Wynn's shoulder and dragging him from the table. Wynn had more to say, but ever the diplomat, Erroh decided avoiding the problem was a finer idea. Holding the drunken Ranger tightly, he marched him through the crowd towards less hostile territory. *Away from howling Wolves, away from catty females.*

"How have you been, my old friend?" Erroh asked, and Wynn shrugged, keeping his eyes less on the ground and more on the bald brute of an Alphaline. *Was I ever as desperate to fight?*

"I'm having a fine time, Erroh. A fuken fine time. Look at that bastard over there... with the eyes. I'll show him." He turned to change course, but Erroh held him steady.

"You'll show him how controlled you are, Wynn, that's all. Leave him to it. You are mated with her; let him leer. It's hurting nobody. At least for now."

At least for fuken now.

They stayed the course, away from the warmth of bodies, excitable voices and volatile things. Every few drunken steps Wynn attempted to change direction, but eventually he fell into step with his driver.

"I see the freedom you've given Lea is working out really well. She's popular with those Wolves." He sniggered at his wit, and Erroh allowed him. Lea needed no watching. There was trust. There needed to be trust. "I've never known soldiers to adore their commander as they do her," he added, drinking a little too much of his drink. Erroh could see now the wear a year had inflicted upon him. His charming arrogance was absent; his infectious confidence was shattered. What remained was bitterness. Snapping at his rudeness would do little to pull him from his mood.

"Well, she had to keep morale up, I suppose. At one point, she considered fighting with no clothing," Erroh jested, and Wynn spat in the dirt. *So much for humour.* Their march from the table had brought them as far from the revellers, the musicians and the Black Guard as they could be without disappearing into the plethora of tents and supply carts. Besides, some of those tents were occupied. Rangers and wretches were falling in love all over the camp. Loudly, too.

The large fire at the centre of the gathering caught Erroh's attention. He watched its waving flames for a bitter moment and thought of Aireys. Many revellers stood around the fire laughing, joking and singing.

I couldn't save her.

He held on to the vision for a few breaths before replacing it with this sight of merriment. A difficult task, but he forced himself. Connecting every large fire with the trauma of a dead friend was a sure way to walk into madness.

"This seems like a fine place. Just us and a few horses," Erroh said, releasing Wynn to fall against a parked cart. The cart was part of a train of similar carts, drawn up in a circle around the gathering. All were long emptied of thirsty partygoers. It was quiet, save for the hobbled and settled mounts; Erroh reached over and patted the pair of beasts nearest him. From here, he could hear himself think. "Now, what has some careless fool left behind here?" he added, spotting an untapped barrel of sine sitting behind a cart wheel.

"I think our night has just become epic," Wynn said, grinning. The sight of such treasure returned some of his wit and excitement. "And isn't Magnus paying?"

Erroh recognised the handwriting upon the barrel. It was the same as the script on his map of the surrounding territory. *Small world.* He remembered a drunken bargain, right before everything turned on its head. "Looks like Sigi left a gift for us and us alone," he said, tapping the barrel and hearing the unmistakable sound of hidden treasures within.

"We need something to pop this beauty." Wynn began clawing at the barrel's edges, trying to remove the lid. "Perhaps Lillium will come sit and enjoy a drink with us, then."

"What happened with Lillium?"

"Nothing happened, Erroh." Wynn froze as he spoke, suggesting something very much had happened. "Besides, you are the one with interesting tales to tell."

This time Erroh froze. "I'll not bring down the cheer of the night with my story. It's the only thing people will speak about—until you win the tournament, that is."

"You should enter. It would look more impressive when I knock you out in the semi-final match. The final needs to be Ranger and Wolf."

"When we fight again, it will be without an audience."

"I look forward to it, Hero."

They watched the crowd. Beneath the roar of the party, Lillium and Elise's laughter rose.

"Lillium has a great laugh," Erroh said, watching his friend's face.

Wynn spat onto the ground again. "I am useless with words. Better with actions. Too many words. Words with connotations. Fuken females and their words. Sometimes, I just don't know what to say, but I say it anyway and it gets much worse." He lost some wine to the necessity of gesturing. A great speaker would argue it was a worthy sacrifice. Wynn stared at the ground, mourning the loss.

"Words are overrated and difficult after walking the road so long. It's easy to fall out of practice when you haven't spoken," Erroh said, remembering his own inability to say the right thing to Lea at the beginning. *And the middle. And the end. And yesterday.* Lea had forgiven his missteps, and he'd forgiven hers.

"I hurt her." Wynn drank deeply and spluttered and hacked up his breath. He went to throw his glass away but caught himself.

"Badly?" Erroh asked.

"Aye, badly."

"I hurt Lea along the way, too."

"They'll tell each other everything, won't they?"

"Aye."

"If I could turn back time, I'd do things differently, Erroh. I really would."

"If I could turn back time, I'd have thrown Lea in a river sooner," countered Erroh, and Wynn laughed.

"You both are a fine match." Erroh could see Lea embrace her comrades one last time before returning to their table. Even from here, he could see her smile, and he desperately wanted to charge through the camp and take her in his arms. They were no elder mated couple; they could still enjoy such actions. She spoke to Lillium, but Erroh could see her looking around, searching for him among the crowd. He could have waved, but it was nice to be wanted. *To be missed.*

"We weren't a good match at first, but we worked on it."

Some movement caught Erroh's eye as the bald Alphaline walked down towards their table. Behind him marched his equally despicable comrade. Both carried pints of ale in each hand. *That's nice of them.*

"Those idiots are stirring some brew," Wynn said, and Erroh didn't like that tone. Not one little bit. "Lillium wants nothing to do with them. She said that, didn't she? Unless she told them something different. But she wouldn't do that. Not with everyone here."

"Easy, Wynn. Let them talk; let her send them running." He chinked Wynn's glass and something in his words must have calmed him down.

"You speak like Magnus. You also have more nerve than me, Erroh," he said, leaning back against the cart. "I think I may have overestimated my understanding of females."

"We both did."

Wynn's face became serious. "They say you faced down an entire army alone in Keri."

Erroh could taste it in the air before it happened. A strange thing to feel the weather change, but he'd felt it change that last dreadful day, and he felt it change now. Above them, the clouds released the first droplets of rain. "Aye, it was all I could do," he offered weakly, knowing well the moment's importance. Moments like this were the turning of the tide. An army of fewer zealots might well have turned their tails after that event, realising success was not worth the consequences to come. They were believers, and if a mad god ordered that they run into a wall of spikes, they would do it. *Their Riders mightn't.*

"The songs are true, then."

"I ran at them before they could understand that they were actually being attacked." He shook his head, thinking of the foolishness. No song could ever describe the moment. Greatness had touched him for a few fleeting breaths. He'd never attempt something so stupid again.

The absent gods disagreed.

"Incredible," said Wynn, looking into the sky above. He spoke in awe, and Erroh almost turned on him. Almost spoke of the nightmare of bloodshed, but instead forced himself to speak as a leader would in times of war.

"We will both earn our legend, friend. What chance do the Hunt have when we raise our blades together?"

With a roar, the rain began to stream down in earnest. The fire flared in response to the assault, and in the fading light Erroh spotted the bald brute attempting to charm Lillium and Lea with outlandish gestures. In his defence, Erroh had never been able to walk up to a girl until the city. Mostly because he feared the expression that both Lea and Lillium were giving the bald man now. They had the good grace to nod politely at his words, though. A few drunken revellers held out their arms and stared up into the sky, taking in the refreshing torrent. A few less inebriated guests took cover under the many welcoming tents of the Rangers, and the gatherings there became that little bit more intimate. Erroh and Wynn drank and let the rain cover them.

———

Roja lay across Emir, clutching what warmth she could. She didn't know how long it had been raining, only that her dress was soaked through. The fabric stuck tightly against her shivering skin, but it didn't matter. She never wanted to leave, never wanted to stop kissing her wonderful wretch, either. It had taken only a decade to find him. He held her in his strong arms, and Roja hadn't felt this comfortable in a lifetime.

"I'm not taking you on this rock in the middle of a rainstorm," he whispered.

"But it's such a fine rock." In the shadows she could see his grin. He wore such an attractive scowl normally. This was nicer. She hadn't expected his passion. She felt his controlled hunger for her and took great pleasure in the prospect of further connections. How long had they kissed? Hours? Many hours? Moments? It didn't matter. Nothing mattered but now and however long to come. The world was ending, but not tonight. The music had faded with the rainstorm, but the rain's melody upon the river, the rock and themselves was just as beautiful. She slid on to his lap and kissed him again. It must have been hours, as her jaw ached. *Wonderful pain.*

His eager hands slid up and down her thighs. "Perhaps, if I found a pillow or two…" he ventured. "I could manoeuvre you into some interesting positions up here." He dared a smile, and she truly knew this was her mate; she'd always known. She could feel his willingness and she did not slip away. They had all the time in the world. Without warning, lightning lit up the sky, followed immediately by a roar of thunder. It boomed menacingly, like a beast of war seeking prey. He flinched with fright and she giggled.

"We are on a rock in the middle of a river in the middle of the storm," he protested, continuing to slide his hands up and down her. She could feel him shake in tandem with her own quivering, and she laughed again.

"You know much, but not lightning mechanics. We are safe enough out here, my… beautiful Emir."

"In that case, I think we should furrow like wildlings in a cave."

She tightened her legs around his waist, allowing her full weight to rest upon adventurous things. Nibbling on his ear, she whispered. "When you take me, it will be in silk."

"Would you accept some coarse wool on a few strands of hay? It's not the bed that matters; it's the warmth."

"Oh, but I'm so nice in silk," she whispered, before sliding away. Rolling like a graceful goddess, she escaped his warmth and dropped from the rock. He leapt up to catch her. *Silly Emir—as if I'd fall.* The water shook her as she hit, and she caught her balance. A few feet above, he gasped and she reached for him, beckoning him to follow her into the freezing river below.

"Let's go see your Alpha friends," she hissed, and after a moment, he leapt down.

———

"Where are you going with that barrel, Ranger?" The question sounded more like a threat, delivered as it was by the hulking figure of the Alphaline Wolf. *Aymon?* He still couldn't remember the brute's name. Asking would be considered rude.

"I think we've met, friend, though I cannot for the life of me remember your name. Is it Dayv?"

Aymon, definitely Aymon. The other is Doran.

The fiend named Aymon took umbrage, snarling a curse under his breath, and such predictable behaviour brought Wynn delight. The party was about to kick off. In truth, Aymon had brought it upon himself. As Erroh tended to natural events involving a wall of waste, silence had gotten the better of Wynn, who'd begun rolling his newfound wealth back towards his comrades. Until Aymon had stepped in the way and placed his heavy boot on the barrel, halting Wynn's progress.

"I asked you a question, Wynn." *Ah, good. He knows my name.*

"I'm just taking it for a walk."

His mud-covered fingers tingled. He formed a fist. Just in case. His eyes caught Lillium's. She still sat with her collection of females in the rain, the deluge not yet enough to quench her thirst. She drained her glass and stood up from the table. He tried to tell her with his eyes that he'd brought a fine barrel of alcohol as a prize for her. *I'm trying.*

"Are you being funny, boy?" Doran asked, and Wynn's eyes narrowed. *Big fuker appeared out of nowhere.* Perhaps Wynn's senses were as damp as the encampment. He left the barrel and stood up to both brutes just as Erroh appeared beside him.

"Good evening," Erroh said, patting Wynn's back before facing the two thugs with his "No need for violence" smile. With the numbers even, Wynn's caution turned to anger. Nothing like punches thrown to get the juices going. He and Erroh could take them. *No problem.*

"Two little lost eastern boys," muttered Doran, and Erroh held out both his hands in a disarming gesture. Wynn could see the tall bouncer walking across the encampment towards them. He sensed the massive figure was liable to add the final chemical to this hostile concoction. As with most explosive arguments at gatherings, the violence usually concluded before the first witness even noticed the first of the spilled blood. That was fine. Lillium could see from where she stood; Lillium could see just fine. He eyed both males and the oncoming bouncer. He popped his neck loudly and waited to strike. It was coming. He could feel it in his bones. He could also feel it in his churning stomach, where the hearty meal was mixing with the sweet alcohols.

"How are the ribs?" asked Doran, and Wynn gritted his teeth and clenched his other fist. The bald fuker was getting the first strike. *So much for secrecy of the Cull.*

If Erroh was insulted or embarrassed, he showed nothing on his face; Wynn was aggrieved for him. They had needlessly inflicted ruination upon Erroh that awful day. He deserved some reparation. Erroh held his side noticeably, pressing on his ribs.

"It's funny; they only really hurt in the rain."

A fine reply. Wynn sniggered. *Still, though, to the fires with false niceties.* He pointed at the bald bastard. "You've been eyeing my mate this entire evening. I've had enough, Doran." He caught sight of Lillium watching. He was lost using words, but actions he could master just fine. And then she turned and walked away from their table, dealing a devastating blow to his spirit. *Everything I do is wrong.* He wanted to scream, to curse, to beg for forgiveness, and also to condemn her cruelty and silence. He wanted to start afresh. Everybody had assured him this was possible. He wanted so many things, but mostly, in that moment, he wanted to knock out the grinning Wolf standing in his fuken way.

This is about to turn nasty, thought Erroh, feigning a smile. They should all have been brothers in arms, but until the enemy showed up, they were likely to fight among themselves. The tournament couldn't come soon enough.

"It's not my eyes you should fear going near your mate," mocked Doran, grabbing at the black metal plate protecting his manhood. Erroh was swift. He saw Wynn's shoulder drop suddenly, and he linked his elbow beneath his friend's arm before he could throw the intended punch. Smoothly, he spun him away, and Wynn turned drunkenly as though he were an old dancing partner.

"Calm down, Wynn," Erroh said quietly.

But Wynn had no intention of calming and tried a second time, this time throwing his full weight behind it. Again, Erroh predicted the strike and directed it away from the waiting Wolf, who seemed happy with the thought of being struck.

"Don't lose your footing there, Wynn," Erroh suggested, easing him away from the dull-witted Alphalines before he could attempt a third strike. *The first punch allows justified retaliation.* "Take it as a gift from the Rangers to the Black Guard," Erroh said, jerking his chin towards the barrel and keeping Wynn subdued with a firm hold.

"What?" Wynn spluttered. "It's our barrel! I rolled it halfway across the camp and these ugly shits are taking it?" He lunged drunkenly for the barrel.

"Why ruin a wonderful night?" hissed Erroh, trying again to drag him away.

Wynn went limp then, his face a stew of emotions. Grabbing his head in his hands, he dropped to a knee. "You heard her earlier—she hates the Wolves too. She wanted to fight them, but as soon as I try to do anything…" He punched the muddy ground, leaving a deep indent. "I hate the rain," he whimpered, and Erroh dropped beside him. Too much booze, too much fire in their veins.

"Pull yourself together, friend. No female desires a snivelling ruin of a male."

The victorious Wolves began rolling the barrel away towards a cluster of their delighted companions.

"Get up," hissed Erroh, and Wynn duly complied, though his eyes shot daggers of hatred upon Doran. Erroh could see the frustration; Wynn was volatile and dangerous. "You can prove your prowess in front of the entire city. She'll have no choice but to look at you. Impress her then."

Wynn nodded dejectedly. "I suppose the night needs no violence."

"Aye, those two are looking for it. Let's not dip to their level, friend."

———

Aymon crashed against an empty barrel but kept his legs under him. Grasping the barrel for support, he took the punch well and shook his senses clear. Wrek leapt back, his fist stinging with the fire of violence and the numbness of a sudden strike.

He should have fallen.

Aymon, spitting blood, returned with his own retort. Throwing wild combinations, Wrek blocked the first few before a stray right snapped his head back. All gatherings resulted in a few brawls. It was almost tradition. Truthfully, it wasn't at all like Wrek to instigate the violence, but the heart wants what the heart wants, and he really fuken wanted to beat the shit of Aymon.

"I wasn't doing anything," roared Aymon, following up with a flying knee, which Wrek caught easily. *Should have punched me more.* Heaving the brute back against the cart, Wrek pummelled Aymon's stomach with a flurry of his own.

"I saw you bother the girl. I fuken saw you." Wrek's frenzy was growing. He'd not vented his rage like this in a while. He'd made mistakes in rage-filled moments, but this time, here, tonight, he couldn't help himself: he'd heard Lara cry out, and suddenly nothing else mattered.

He leapt away now to see the damage he'd inflicted and it was impressive. Aymon gasped against the cart, one knee to the ground, hacking up blood.

"I have no interest… in the girl… I was just trying to…"

Wrek struck again, but his victim was fast and sneaky. He rolled away from the blow, his size belying unnatural speed. Wrek struck the wooden cart with a dull thud and he roared in agony. He'd heard crunching and prayed it was the wood cracking from the assault. His cry was cut short by another assault, and again Wrek leapt away from Aymon's strikes. He could hear shouts in his ears as the crowd reacted to the violence, some screaming for peace, others baying for blood. The legend of Wrek was marching again. *With a few broken knuckles.* Wrek knew he should have put the fuker down in one strike.

At last, falling into defensive poses, both warriors caught their breath.

Panting, Wrek mocked the cur. "I believed all you Alpha males respected women."

He'd seen Aymon corner Lara between the carts when she'd hopped down to remove an empty barrel. It was quieter between the carts; darker, too. She'd attempted to leave, but the brute had stood in her way. He had not touched her, but Wrek had heard his mocking laugh and her whimpered plea to step aside, and like a poorly ventilated sine vault, hidden deep in the ground, he'd exploded.

"We only respect the pretty women," sneered Aymon, and Wrek attacked again. *She is stunning.* They fell back against the carts, fists swinging wildly. It was said that Alphalines were capable of terrifying feats, but they'd never seen the depths to which Wrek would swim dragging a bully down.

He cared for Lara a great deal, and she cared for him. He believed. He caught her stealing glimpses of him when she thought he was unaware. He made her laugh, and when she spoke, her gentle wit enthralled him. She said she'd felt safe working the bar whenever he

337

worked the door, so he'd made certain to work every night. He always walked her home in the dreary hours of the morning, and it swiftly became the highlight of his day. From her words, from Emir's warnings, from his better senses, he knew she was a fragile piece.

And if anyone scares her…

Suddenly, Doran appeared, and then it wasn't as fair a fight as before—especially when he announced his arrival with a right hook below the chin, felling Wrek instantly. Distantly, he heard a girl scream. *Sorry, Lara.* As the muddy ground reached up to meet him, he wondered if this was how he'd die. A heavy boot struck his stomach, followed by a different boot to the head, and he suspected he had his answer as the world went dark.

Without a word of warning, Emir tackled the massive beast who was stepping all over his friend. There was no thought, no sound; he simply jumped. It was an effective tactic. His momentum knocked the brute against a standing barrel, and Emir went with him. Their combined weight was too much to bear, and the cask splintered loudly as limbs, armour and bodies collapsed everywhere. Emir reacted first, for he was at home in this mayhem. He climbed across the brute's chest plate and swung indiscriminately. By the third blow, blood covered his fists. By the fourth, Aymon was pulling him kicking and screaming from the fight, while another set of hands took hold of Aymon, who lashed back with an elbow.

There was a loud crack, and the melee ended as swiftly as it had begun.

"Enough!" roared Roja, with the authority of the city behind her. Aymon, realising his grievous error, released Emir and raised his hands in innocence.

"Forgive me, Mydame. I did not realise…" he muttered through bleeding, gritted teeth. His elbow had devastated her face. Her eye looked ready to swell, and her nose was pouring crimson down her face. Regardless, she stood among the melee as though in chambers. *They can control pain.*

Emir dropped to the slow-moving form of Wrek. The battered warrior opened his eyes and growled before realising Emir's intentions. "Easy, big man. Easy. You got kicked around a bit." Emir took the moment to slide Wrek's dislocated nose into place with a nasty crunch, an act he'd long since perfected after working so many Keri festivals. Wrek tried to climb to his feet and Emir held him down, no mean feat given the man's his size. "Not yet. Wait for the stars to settle. Tell me, Wrek, can you count them above?" Wrek looked up and muttered something about cloud cover. *A good sign.*

"You two are done for the night," Roja declared, as an unsteady Aymon helped an equally unsteady Doran to his feet.

"We never started it," Aymon protested. "That thick brute Wrek jumped me. I needed to pop a barrel, that's all."

"You should leave this place now," Roja told him.

"You have no authority," Doran retorted. "You barely have it in the city as it is," he added, and the gathering crowd, which had fallen silent, began to mutter. Some condemned his words; others nodded in agreement.

"She has all the authority," Magnus declared, nearing both Wolves. They shrank noticeably in his presence. Emir had never seen him more at ease standing face to face with Wolves. "Best remember that," he said. His tone was cordial, but a shrewd man might recognise the subtle threat. Emir imagined he could rip their fuken throats out in a moment's notice. "You are too valuable to lose for the fights ahead." *Ah, there's the actual threat.*

Dutifully, Doran turned to Roja and bowed theatrically. "My apologies, Your Majesty. We know our place."

The rest of the Black Guards formed up around their battered brethren now, and they retreated as one from the Ranger camp, triumphantly carrying the barrel full of sine with them. Emir sent them a rude gesture as they departed.

"You'll sit at our table," the Ranger Wynn said, stumbling over himself as he tried to help Wrek to his feet. Emir, too, tried to help, but two figures fell on him as one and nearly knocked him from his feet, embracing him. Two friends from Keri.

"I didn't come here alone," Emir said, as his friends dragged him to the table. Behind him stood the wretched Primary in waiting. She was watching her allies disappear back into the city, and Emir wondered if she'd ever cut a more lonely, detached figure.

"She is welcome to sit with us," offered Erroh, dragging Emir back to the table.

"Someone get these wretches a drink," Lea declared, eyeing the blood upon Roja's face, the mud upon her body, the rips in her dress. The rains above had ceased their hostilities, and the beginnings of the shattered moon appeared through the thinning clouds. A freshness filled the air, and a few hopeful notes from a drenched musician restored sweetness to the night. Wrek accepted a glass of sine and slumped heavily onto the bench at the table of legends. Lara busied herself with cleaning the mud from his long, matted hair, whispering unknown things to him and him alone. His only replies were slightly dopey smiles.

In all their many ways, they each took their place at the table of Magnus as though outcasts from the city and drank and spoke and jested among themselves without a care in the world. The alcohol flowed and the cheer returned to the entire encampment as the Rangers enjoyed playing host to the return of the Heroes of Keri. They smiled as if it were the last time they, as warriors, would experience joy and happiness. They celebrated like it was the last time they would know a peaceful night.

As, indeed, it was. Everything was about to change.

33

AURORA BOREALIS

Her name was Aurora, and she liked to kill. She was very good at killing. That was probably why Uden, her Woodin Man, was so fond of her. She was young, though she couldn't tell how young, for she had been born more than once. *Born in blood. Born on a special night when the sky was alight.*

She climbed from her bedding and stretched her thin arms out in the air. Her left hand brushed gently against the edge of her cell wall, her nails scraping harshly against the dark grey surface. *Wrong, unbalanced, wrong.* She instinctively slashed at the wall with her right hand. The grating sound was nasty to her ears. *Better.* Everything needed to be even. She didn't know why. She only knew. She stared at the wall for a few moments and listened to her breathing. She was bored, but her fingers stung with the same amount of pain. This was good; was how it should be. This was a good day so far.

She lifted her hood over her long black hair and sat on the satin sheets with her back against the opposite wall. She was beautiful. She knew she was beautiful, and she knew why she was beautiful. He referred to them as "her godly eyes." They were blue, strikingly blue, and when she stared at Uden, he held her gaze. Aurora turned her strikingly blue eyes towards the little open gap in the wall above her head. The bitter wind blew in through the barred window, night and day. It was the only light he gifted her in the cramped cell. When the sun set and shadow covered the white land in a beautiful, deathly grip, Aurora was left to sit alone without light. She deserved this fate, though, and besides, she was comfortable in the black.

She crossed her legs and rocked back and forth a few times. It was oddly soothing and a wonderful way to start the day. She had angered Uden far more than normal this time. He hadn't even met her when she'd passed through the gates. How long ago now? Long enough to him, therefore, long enough for her. *At least a week.* A week staring into nothing, thinking of blood. *Bliss.*

Gemmil had met her at the doorway and led her to her quarters. She'd known the way and had walked eagerly, expecting much penance for the many nights she'd spent wrapped around sweating, naked bodies that didn't belong to any gods. Uden must have seen everything for her to have earned this jealous punishment. Perhaps he'd heard her moaning all the way up here in the mountains? He'd always said that her screams carried farther than any he'd heard before. This had pleased her.

Aurora stared up at the gap, watching a little spider struggling to make its precious web in the biting breeze. *Wondrous creatures.* They lived to kill.

"Hello, little one."

The spider didn't reply.

She leapt gracefully from her cot, her powerful legs thrusting her high into the air, towards the little gap in the cold grey stone. He'd said that her body was perfect, and he was right. She was weightless and comfortable as she flew. Catching the two iron bars keeping her imprisoned, she slammed herself hard against the wall, as she did every morning. She dug her bare feet into smooth stone, finding her usual painful grip, and then, wedging herself impossibly high off the ground, she looked out across the landscape. It hadn't changed since she'd looked at it the morning before. Or the morning before that. It would never change. It would always be the same white-capped mountain range. She missed the warm soil of the north and the colour of green all around. She missed the slaughter. *Rivers of red and covered in blood.* The north called to her. It always had. She needed to see it again, before the fires of Uden's wrath burned it all away. She counted the little trees peering above the mountains of white. She counted the mountain ridges and made sure they were even. Nothing had changed, and this pleased her.

She ignored the rising pain in her shoulders and pulled her dazzling eyes from the frozen south to focus on her new friend. Her breath shook the little black and red spider's progress, and she leaned in closer and it froze. *It knows I watch.*

"There are no flies to gorge upon up here," she whispered lovingly. *Poor hungry little spider.* It listened to her and loved her voice. She knew this and blew gently and it swung loosely from one of its silken strands. It swung for her. Everything died in these conditions, even the birds. *Even the birds delivering messages.*

"You should eat your young," she whispered, leaning in closer to the spinning arachnid. It was all about survival. Aurora stuck her tongue out slowly. Would her little creature friend be bitter or sweet? Would it scurry away from her touch? Oh, how she wanted it to bite back. The spider's legs were sharp like blades. Or sharper, like her crossbow bolts.

Delicious.

The arachnid scurried up its web, and this delighted her. She released her grip on one of the rusted metal bars, and her muscles screamed. She endured the pain, for she had endured far worse, and held herself steady. She held a shaking finger in front of the hanging insect.

"It's time to leave here, little one…"

She blew the little red and black spider a delicate kiss and then flicked her finger. It flew out, out and away, but her dazzling eyes could not track it in the white. *Bye-bye.* She wondered, did it survive? Or was it a little spider corpse now, falling to the ground below? She would never know. She hoped it screamed a little, knowing its god had become tired of its struggles. She released the grip of her other hand now and fell, landing perfectly. *Soundlessly, elegantly.* Like any skilled murderer.

She spotted the little bowl of cold water at the doorway and smiled. Enough penance had been served; her god desired her today. Gemmil was silent, like Aurora. She wondered, could she kill Gemmil? *Probably not.* He might be one of the few wily enough to avoid her talents. He'd left the bowl while she slept, without her knowing, just to spite her. She hated sleeping. Vulnerability was overrated. Tossing and turning and open to a slitting of the throat. She'd slit enough sleeping throats to recognise sleeping's misleading shelter. What if another assassin slipped beneath her bed some tragic night? She picked up the little porcelain bowl and set it by the bed. The water was the icy summoning. She knew the routines.

Stripping off her black cloak, she took the soap from the bowl and scrubbed. Two strokes with her left hand, two strokes with the right. *Balance, perfect, so nothing feels left out.* The time had been unkind to her natural allure. He would desire sweet, fragrant aromas and honeyed goodness before he devoured her. Her enthusiasm to see Uden hastened the cleansing. She forced herself to calmness. She was her god's paramour, and it was her pleasure to claim such a title. She left the cloak where it lay and donned the leather dress she'd worn when she'd first stepped into this prison. She'd lost a little weight since she'd stripped last, but she was still strong, still powerful, still delectable. She dabbed a little paint to enrich her lips. But he rarely desired such things. She knew to enhance her eyes, though. He would bathe in her eyes.

She knew today would be good. Today he'd return her army to her. When he did, she'd ride north and spill tainted crimson all over the place. *Enough to cover me.*

The click of the heavy door's bolt drew her from her delirium. She barely heard Gemmil's footsteps walking away. Sometimes she wondered if he'd received the same training as she had.

"Not all the training," she whispered. Gemmil barely acknowledged her presence at the best of times. He probably spat in her food. It didn't bother her if he did. *More to eat.*

She slipped from her cell out into the dark hallway. She knew the route. The light at the top of the stairs, leading down to her divine destination. Her hands spread, gliding through the thin corridor. Her fingers tipping the black walls on either side. *Evenly.* It was very important she tip them evenly. *Otherwise.*

Thirty-three steps through the darkness into the light.

Twenty-seven steps down the old wooden staircase.

Sixteen steps into the room of history. The room of his beloved scrolls. The scrolls that told him the truths of the past. The scrolls that marked his path ahead in this world.

Her mind settled when she was in his company. The numbers in need of counting would sit and wait patiently. He gave her relief. He gave her what she needed. He would whisper his wishes and she would do his bidding. The world would be even, equalled, and there would be blood. Since her birth, he'd promised her so much blood. It was time.

Aurora counted her steps and on the last, spun in a perfect circle, serenading her Woodin Man; her leader, her keeper, her idol and her lover. *Why simply walk into a room when you can dance?*

"You called for me," she whispered. Her heart beat wildly; her body ached with urges and excitement. She might love in these next moments, might even die, too. What a death she would have. *Oh, to be nothing but convulsing flesh, bleeding over my vanquisher.*

He hid his face from the glow of the flames; he sat away from the fireplace and she worried the tales were true. The same worry that drew her back home to him without rest. And if the rumours were true, she would wail for her god but love him anew. *I will tear my right eye out and rest it upon a platter.*

She leaned back seductively against the wall of capsules; everything she did was seductive. Her fingers tapped against each of his precious scrolls. The gentle clicking of equally touched things. Only she was allowed touch them. So she did, and it pleased him. Today, though, he did not look up, and she wanted to run to him and love him, but she would not, for she was Aurora and Aurora showed nothing unless asked. If asked, she would show it all.

"Come to me, my love," she whispered. It was no request; it was a challenge. Games were afoot and she aimed to be beaten, battered, brutalised and eventually... bested.

She would make him work for her attention, god or no. So began their loving embrace. Sometimes, she was barely conscious when he pinned her down and entered her. Those were the finest times. Those nights her screams carried across the world.

She heard him sigh, heard him take an inhalation. "There will be no play today, my child." His voice resonated anger. Beautiful, powerful rage that usually meant death. Perhaps hers? Whichever way she died would be perfect, and after, carrion birds would peck her stunning eyes out. She bit her lip and waited for Uden to reveal his injuries.

"Show me, my love," she whispered. Floating across the room, she grabbed the open bottle of wine between the two empty plates. It was never too early to share a glass with a god.

"Show me," she demanded, her voice turning; less ethereally seductive now, and more the potent killer she was. Sometimes, she could be both. "No god should hide in the dark. No matter the wound. No matter the fear." She stood and waited. For how long, it wouldn't matter. She had beauty to stare upon. *Terrible, wounded beauty.*

He showed her. He leant towards the flames, displaying the wound given to him by another god. *A false god of fire that she wanted to cut up into little pieces and chew on and taste and swallow and vomit up.* Uden stared with his one remaining eye and arched his head sideways to reveal the damage, and for a moment she saw herself chained and wailing and begging and killing and moaning, and she tried desperately to shake that thought, because her god was wounded and she needed to be covered in blood. *Covered in blood.*

Covered in blood.

One more time, Fyre.

Covered in blood.

Aurora fell to her knees, gripping his feet, and wailed for him. His dazzling green eyes were lost forever. He had feared her seeing him, and so he had hidden in the dark from her. She wanted to destroy. *Covered in blood.* To tear to pieces all in her way. *All lost.* She felt the need to count her words.

"My Uden."

Two.

"Please, Uden, send me on my way. Send me to slay all who failed you that night."

Seventeen.

He reached down and ran his fingers through her hair, and she melted inside until he took hold and pulled the strands back violently. Under his strength, her head was no longer hers to control. It was his to hold and to break. Should he choose? *Wonderful.* Her long black hair whipped back in his grip and she writhed in pleasure and dominated pain.

"Do not pity me!" he screamed into her face, and each word reverberated through her chest, and she understood her mistake. He was not diminished. He was greater than that. She lost count and licked her teeth at him. He leapt from his chair and pulled her to the ground, and she didn't fight. His knees pinned both her arms to the cold floor and he clasped his massive fingers around her throat. She couldn't breathe and she didn't care. Her life was always in his hands. All the Hunt's lives were.

"Never pity me."

She couldn't respond even if she wanted to.

"Fight for your life, my love," he demanded, and though his tone softened, his grip tightened. She kicked out and heard the bottle of wine spilling its contents, somewhere far away. She slid one of her hands free, formed a fist, but resisted the natural urge to attack. *Why fight magnificence?* Tears escaped her eyes and she cursed their betrayal. *Why flee something pure?* She heard her gasping chokes. She stared into his beautiful eye as he slowly choked the life from her and smiled. *This is a fine way to die.* She reached up and ran her quivering fingers across the open wound of her god. The room faded to black. She was comfortable in the black. Her hand dropped heavily on the floor; it landed in a pool of fluid. It was probably the wine. She felt him kill her.

· · ·

347

Nothingness.

"You disappoint me," he growled from his place at the table. She still lived. *Interesting.* She couldn't remember waking up. Aurora tried to speak, but the bruising was too raw. She could only whisper. *Like a waif.* She sat on a chair opposite her god with a plate of steaming meats in front of her. She downed the new glass of wine accompanying the feast in one painful gulp. Her murderer chewed on a piece of steak with relish. Fat dribbled from his mouth onto the plate beneath. She poured herself another glass of wine and drank it just as quickly. *Who needs a glass?* She spun the little goblet a few times in her fingers and then flung it at him. The god just edged his head sideways and it shattered on the far wall. She was allowed to be angry. Either kill her or not. Don't fuk with her.

"Not as disappointing," he muttered, dropping the piece of meat on the plate.

"I'm glad I please you," she mocked, finding her cracked voice once more. She picked up her plate and flung it behind her. It was an easy shot, with a satisfying outcome. He jumped as the plate shattered against the wall of scrolls. A piece of slimy, blood-soaked beef stuck against a few unfortunate capsules. *Point made.* After locking her up so long, a kiss would have been far more pleasing than taking her breath away with a touch. His teeth clenched, and she prepared for his fury. This time, she might fight back.

"I will not give you your finger back," he whispered, louder than most men could speak. She drank her wine and seethed a little. What was a goddess of death without her army? How could she drain the blood without an army marching behind her? *I want my army.*

"At least for a time," he added, and she knew his tone. This wondrous, godly tone. He had something else for her. She could already hear the dying breath of her next victim. She hadn't killed a girl in a while.

Oh, let it be a girl.

A fat one.

"What would you have me do?" Her eyes flickered in the firelight, and she knew he craved her. The god stood up and walked towards her. She remained seated, drinking her wine. He stood behind her and it all felt so very familiar.

"Why do you furrow with those not worthy of your body, my beautiful, perfect Aurora?" he asked, and kissed her ear. She felt tingles run up her back. She felt tingles in other places, too. She closed her eyes and craned her neck back to him. It was painful.

"I have itches that you cannot scratch from so far away," she replied dreamily, keeping her eyes shut.

"Open your eyes, Aurora."

She knew her eyes pleased him too much. They remained closed. He would need to earn her favour to gaze upon him again. *This was play; this was finest play.*

"I ask, and you deny me," he said, sliding away, and she reached blindly for him but he was already gone. "Why, oh why do my followers stray from my touch?" She could feel his pain and it angered her.

"I will never stray from you," she whispered, opening her eyes and seeing him wiping a few smears from the wall.

"Not you, my love. Never my Aurora." He was back at her side in a graceful moment, rubbing his fingers through her long, black hair. "There have been disturbing gatherings, since word of my injury has spread," the god admitted.

She ran her finger along a crack in the table. She didn't remember seeing that crack before. She didn't like when things cracked and other things crept through the cracks. That's why she desired blood. "Those royal wastes. Those selfish few. A curse upon their houses."

"They do not see what leads them," Uden said, and she hated them. Hated them for their stupidity. For their ideals. For their misguided morals. They had had their time; they had doomed the south.

"Unbelievers," she spat.

"Oh, they believe in something," he countered, and she hated them more, but still, he used the tone she loved most. She desired the feel of metal in her hands. She missed her tools of war. She missed her silent friends. She already knew her mission. *Send me on my way.*

"What will you have me do?"

He knelt down to her and looked into her beautiful eyes. She looked back into his empty socket and almost reached out to touch it.

"Discover the ones who chant Erroh's name. Send the message of what awaits the believers in a false god," he whispered, and she moaned in pleasure. "And after, take the reins of what remains of the army Oren leads and wait for me."

Oren.

"Let me kill Oren for failing you," she roared. Oren should have fallen upon his sword the night the false god flew into the darkness with stolen flesh.

Uden appreciated her outrage. Dropping to his knees as though in prayer, he lifted her dress and kissed her inner thigh, and she sat back in her chair, allowing him to spread her legs. "I have charged Oren with two acts of redemption. He leads the first wave, and I've tasked him with delivering the gifts to the false god of fire: Erroh."

She felt fresh chills running up through her perfect body. "What if Oren lives after he delivers the gifts?" He kissed her other thigh. A perfect balance. He knew what she liked. *He always would.*

"Slit his throat and let his blood cover a mile of ground."

She howled at this command and wrapped her powerful thighs around his head. "And then?" she whispered.

"Kill everything you desire and cover yourself in blood," he growled, pulling her from the chair. He lifted her into the air and she felt weightless in his grip. *Lifeless.* She moaned with the pleasure of his touch. She moaned at the thought of the killing he had gifted her. She moaned at the thought of her god waking the Arth and bringing the end of it all.

As the ancients had written upon the scrolls.

"As you wish, my god."

34

THE INCIDENT IN THE CULL

The morning was not going well, because the night before had never fully ended. The stench of damp clothing, alcohol and an entire evening of extravagant revelry filled the cold air of the little room in the Cull. Everyone had been invited to the hangover of a lifetime, and Erroh and most of his family had accepted the invitation. Erroh and Lea stood side by side, with his parents on either side of them. They came to support; they came to be united; they came to hear what a failure he was—or at least the four figures watching from above might have thought so. The Primary stood at her podium; Roja stood beside her. They hadn't come alone. Two Black Guards stood watching over the proceedings. If it came to violence, the odds were hardly fair.

Erroh's tired voice echoed all the way up into the rafters, each word delivered with a haze of freezing white that caught in the light. They hadn't thought to set a fire anywhere nearby to stem the cold. They hadn't had the respect to illuminate themselves and those standing below.

Typical.

The room felt smaller, though no less impressive. Perhaps it was the comfort of having survived the event with his pride mostly intact that helped. He'd shared a silent look with Lea as they stepped through the heavy door.

Many miles walked since then.

Though he was more composed, some things hadn't changed; the cutting tone of a female was a familiar thing, the Primary's cutting tone even more so. She stared at Erroh mostly, but her cruel eyes were never far from Magnus. As though studying his behaviour was entertainment. Perhaps it was to her. His father had never been one to conceal his thoughts or feelings on any matter. Though she spoke to Erroh, it felt as though she engaged her rival.

"So, you might have finished the war... but you jumped to your death?" she asked from her privileged position upon the podium above his head. It sounded like a loaded question. He hated questions in this room. Beside him, Lea muttered a curse and he felt a little better.

Next question.

Magnus wasn't ready for another question. "You've learned of the massive numbers and all you've paid attention to is how he escaped?" he asked, and Erroh enjoyed hearing his father's warning tone. *Prey should be wary of that tone.*

The Primary was unmoved. "I've paid attention to everything your kin have said. I'll think on any matter I choose."

"Mydame, I—" began Erroh, but Magnus hissed him to silence, and for a hurtful moment, Erroh felt his father's shame at the thought of his cowardice. The memory of hiding beneath blankets in a frozen sanctuary surged through him. He wanted his cage. He wanted to hide from his shame. Instead, Erroh straightened up and fought the redness showing on his face. *These fuken lights hide nothing.* Magnus began pacing back and forth below the Primary's podium, and Erroh wondered if he wasn't about ready to leap up and attack her. *Maybe just throw a bottle at her.*

Magnus shook his head in frustration. Hangovers were a dangerous thing to an irate Master General. "There are a few thousand soldiers in the first wave alone. Many thousands following. We need to take the fight and keep on marching. Every day lost is territory lost. You must honour your word, Dia."

Again, the Primary was unmoved. "We will meet them from behind our walls. If you don't mind holding your tongue a few moments longer, I was still speaking to your little cub."

Magnus minded. "The entire south has a bone to pick with you, with the city, and probably with me. When a thousand foot soldiers come strolling up to your precious gates, what then will you think of inaction? When a few hundred Riders come charging down upon us, will your silent hopes cause them to lose heart?"

He stopped mid-tirade as though something had struck him. Something terrible and brutal. He took a breath before continuing on, and though his voice was strong, it lacked conviction. "Few things would make a charging army lose its nerve. Your silence will not be one of them."

"We can avoid war," she hissed.

"The moment they attacked the first towns, it became war. The moment they attacked my line, they declared war on me." As quickly as he'd lost it, Magnus's attention had returned. If Erroh's voice had echoed into the rafters above, his father's voice boomed and played its own menacing thunder. Magnus stared up at the Primary and Erroh recognised that exact stare from his youth, when he'd snidely mocked his training. A swift and deserved strike usually followed. The distance between Primary and the fuming, hungover legend was vast, though. Magnus was tall, but even he might struggle to jump up to the balcony above.

"Why fight me on this?" he demanded. "Why can't we vanquish this brute before he ravages the rest of the world?"

"If war comes to our gate, my Wolves will fight, but you have no claim to the rest," Dia roared, and Roja jumped in fright. She wasn't the only one to recoil. Everyone in the room recoiled. All but Magnus, who stepped forward in challenge.

"A thousand times we've argued back and forth; still you cower." He shook his head. Erroh could sense a caged beast ready to strike. There was something about this freezing, dark room that brought out the absolute worst in a hot-blooded warrior.

353

"Magnus, I am the one at the podium. I am the one with the crown. And in this moment, I am the one asking about Erroh's escape."

Erroh didn't like how she said the last word. He didn't like it one bit. He almost stepped forward, but Lea locked her warm fingers in his own.

"Be wary," she whispered. Fine unnecessary advice; he knew to keep his wits about him in this room.

"So, he just offered you a chance to strike him down?" the Primary asked, and Erroh nodded.

"Aye, Mydame, he did."

"Just like that?"

Just like that.

Magnus whispered to Elise loudly. "He told her all of this already. The years have stolen her memory. If that happens to me, make sure you kill me before I start drooling."

Dia didn't bite for an entire breath. After she took the breath, she bit hard. "You'd nearly blinded their mad god, but instead of finishing the task, you fled?"

He didn't like any of her words there either. "Aye, Mydame."

The room felt electric and dangerous. It felt like any Cull day, really. That said, whatever criticism Dia could throw at him, he'd already thrown at himself a thousand times over.

"The remaining Factions will not blame you, Erroh; it is simply that your master failed you." Her eyes were narrow slits; they watched her old adversary pacing. "I had expected great things of you, Erroh. The entire world had. The apple falls far, I suppose." Erroh thought her petty. The world was burning, and she took open shots at his father. *Because she's terrified.*

Someone muttered the word *bitch*. It may have been Elise. She may have been trying to scream it. The night affected her badly, and the room's coldness wasn't helping. Though their breaths were a heavy mist, hers were barely a flicker of hazy white. He'd asked her not to walk with him, but she'd insisted he have support. It was hard to stop any mother protecting her cub. Magnus had plenty of breath, though.

"I've had enough of this, Dia. I refuse to fight for the city. I refuse to send my Rangers into war."

"I allowed you to keep your army for such an event," she snapped.

"You allowed me to keep my army at a tenth of its numbers, and I, the fool, agreed with you. I owe this city nothing. My son has returned. We march tonight… home."

Erroh spun on his father and saw him eyeing Elise, who was in agreement. He wasn't the only one in shock from this statement. Even the Primary was staring, dumbfounded, her mouth agape as though she had been stabbed mid-breath. Only Roja appeared to hold her nerve.

"You can't do this, Magnus. You can't leave us to fight this monster alone."

Erroh could hear the terror in her voice. Lea released her hand and drew it into a fist. Even the two Wolves dared a cautious glance at each other. Enemies or no, splitting the army this late would bring catastrophe to the city.

"My apologies, Dia, but I cannot beat them alone. It's best I withdraw to the east and begin rebuilding an army big enough to counter the oncoming threat."

"Leaving us to stand alone?" Roja asked.

"Every single one of you is welcome to march this grand retreat with me. The more the merrier." *Fleeing like Keri.*

"Father!" Erroh cried.

This time Elise silenced him. "He is still your master. Be silent," she warned, and despite his outrage, Erroh held his tongue under the gaze of his disapproving mother.

Enough of this, thought Magnus. Matters needed to rest.

"To the fires with you, Dia," he hissed. He needed to scare her, to shake her confidence. If he needed to bow, he would bow having unsettled her. He silently dared her to threaten him. Dared him to curse his cowardice. "We march this very night. You have sturdy walls. Let's see how long they last." He spun away for added effect and stepped towards the door, not close enough to reach out and pull it from its hinges, but close enough to gain what momentum he needed.

"You can't," cried Roja. *Sorry, Roja. I can.* Magnus dared not face her. To look at Roja might unnerve him. Might crush his composure. Instead, he stared at the door and counted his steps.

Dia slammed her fist on the podium loudly. If it hurt her aching bones, she showed little pain. Instead, she hissed some fine threats. "You walk into this room and offer me ultimatums, as though I am a wretch wandering the Wastes? You believe I would allow you and your mongrel family to walk free of this room?" She leaned forward. "You think I would allow your Rangers to leave this city?"

Perfect.

He leapt despite his armour. He leapt into the air and kicked his foot against the frame of the old wooden door. He was far more agile than most would ever presume. Using the frame of the door, he grasped the edge of the walkway above. He swung silently in mid-air for a moment and then with a tremendous, painful effort, nearly dislocating every one of his fingers, he pulled his body onto the floor above. It took only a handful of breaths. The Wolves stared disbelievingly, when they should have been shepherding the Primary from the room.

Magnus could hear the desperate shouts from below, and he ignored them. Besides, Elise would keep Erroh from following. And if his son or daughter-in-law came after him, by the time they reached the upper level, it would all be over. It was time to make a point.

"You think you are safe behind the walls?" he roared, moving along the thin walkway. It was darker up here, warmer, and that made sense. The wall was a few feet in from the bannister; with a quick sidestep, it was easy enough for any disapproving girl to disappear from view altogether. A fine place to intimidate excitable Alphalines and dominant legends. The Primary had chosen well.

"You think I fear you, Magnus," roared Dia, desperately trying to get past the two Wolves whose wits had finally returned. With weapons drawn, they stood in front of their leader as thunder hammered down on them in the shape of Magnus's swift steps along the top of the Cull. "What will the people think when you add the Primary to your list of distinguished victims?" Still she struggled, and Roja held her back. Horrifying her young granddaughter brought her little pleasure, but it was best she learn the precariousness of dealing with a brute from the Savage Isles before she took leadership. It had taken only two decades, but Dia had forgotten his threat.

Instinctively, he reached for his sword, knowing well he was unarmed. *Good thing, too.* The first Black Guard made the mistake of charging forward and swinging wildly, leaving his companion behind. The upper balcony was far too narrow a battlefield for inept swordplay, and Magnus easily ducked away as though sparring. The blade struck the side wall, and the crack of steel on stone swiftly followed the crack of leather glove on unprotected skin. The second strike knocked the man out. He could have killed him, but killing any Wolf would have ended the matter. His dull sword clattered loudly at Magnus's feet, and better judgement won out. He stepped over the unconscious man as the second defender attacked. His technique was better. From a distance, he plunged forward; Magnus slipped backwards out of range, caught the tip in his glove and pulled the off-balance guard towards him.

It wasn't knocking an arrow out of the sky with a sword, but it was impressive.

"Come here!" he roared, as the Black Guard stumbled into range. He reached for his victim's wrist and twisted. The blade fell free and he took hold of the man's arm with both hands. "This will hurt," he whispered, and twisted a little more. There was pain; there were also screams, the straining of tendons, a few swift punches. Then there was silence. A typical outcome when any legend fought hand to hand without murderous intent.

"Don't do this!" Roja rushed forward, throwing punches, and Magnus held his ground. Instead of striking her, he blocked each attack and spun her away, using her own momentum against her. She stumbled against the wall and he slipped by. "Please," she begged, and he almost held his step. He'd done enough terrible things in taking away her family. He couldn't take her grandmother. *Adopted grandmother.* He wanted to tell her he was sorry. Instead, he stood over

357

the defenceless figure of Dia. To her credit, she concealed her fear. Her face was pale, but she did not run, and Magnus thought well of her.

"Kill me, but don't desert the city." Her voice did not break, and this nerve impressed Magnus. "Our race fades into the night. Don't waste their potential on fruitless war. Please, Magnus, only wield the Alphalines at the darkest hour," she begged, taking his hand and gripping it firmly. He could see the hatred, he could see the strength, and he could see her pride, and he remembered her from the Faction Wars. It meant little to his actions now, however, for he was resolute, he was assured and he had made his point. It would always come to this. He towered over the frail old woman. Her life was in his hands, and he did something nobody expected. He knelt down on one knee in front of her. Lowering his head in submissiveness, he surrendered. Their lives were flickering candles in the breeze, and he aimed to calm the storm. Elise, as usual, was right. Spending a moment longer bickering was a fool's gambit. It was time to declare himself allegiant.

He did it for those he loved.

He did it for the world.

"I pledge myself to you, Primary," he whispered, and the room went deathly still.

Dia took in his words for a few moments and then nodded, before releasing his hands and telling him to rise. "If you offer me loyalty, I offer you mine. You will never bow in my presence again. It is time to find peace between us," she said. "Perhaps we will do so by turning the tide of war."

35

TENSION

T he first whispers of an incident in the Cull brought about great interest, but as the days passed, they were dismissed as foolish gossip. Even whispers of Magnus leading both armies were met with scepticism; anyone knowing the Rangers' history knew this appointment would end badly. The people of Samara concentrated on fear and strife. The upcoming tournament was a distraction, but it likely would not be enough. Everyone in the city was on tenterhooks. Tempers were frayed and arguments broke out among the natives over minor issues. This same ill ease spread to the guests along the wall. Whispers of the marching army from credible sources grew to loud proclamations by uninformed peasants. Rumours abounded of great numbers, and the foreboding sense of certain death carried in the wind. Everyone had questions, and those few with answers were keeping tight-lipped.

Magnus hid away from most others in his war chambers. Every day, new scout reports occupied his time and tested his nerve. From morning to night, he sat staring down upon a fine collection of different maps, suggested options and hastily formed intelligence. He knew himself capable, but that did not stop the doubts from creeping in. They had enough soldiers to fight, for now, but the Hunt vastly outnumbered them. Though he was wary of stepping foot on the rich soil of the Savage Isles, the further he delved into his planning, the more he sensed an ocean journey was likely in his future.

But not quite yet; that would happen when both armies had settled upon disputed territory. Though the south would favour such an approach, they would not fight this war in a handful of skirmishes. He understood Uden's thinking, and it was naïve. *Dangerous, too.* A true leader would have led the charge, but no leader marched with them. The first wave were to erode away the city's defences and batter them back to the city gates, and the next wave would surround and crush them.

Delay their advance.

It was one thing predicting their moves; it was another taking advantage. Were it the east, he'd pick any one of a thousand points at which to assemble. As it was, he searched for an understanding of these northern lands, as though studying for a master's testing.

He turned from his notes to stare aimlessly at the grand battle map sitting upon a large mahogany table in the centre of the room.

"Talk to me," he whispered, running his fingers along the creases, searching for further inspiration. Any peasant would see pathways, rivers, mountains and settlements. Magnus saw brutal death and victory.

Only the best for the Master General.

The map was nearly as old as the world. Nearly, but not quite. Dia had assured him of its near perfect accuracy. *Near perfect?* A river incorrectly scribed or an unexpected break in the forest could easily cost them the entire city. His hands were a flicker of anxiety as he moved a few figurines across the stained, oily surface. Each figure represented battalions of lives to lose and enemies to slay.

"Talk to me," he demanded of the map, of his mind, of whatever faith he had in the absent gods. He feared battle, like any warmonger worth their salt, but this silence in the face of such urgency was harrowing. In battle he might decide upon a turning event, but these silent tactical moments were the making and breaking of legends. Though he'd never say it aloud, age was no friend to an old warrior.

Two decades before he had doubted himself, but with every battle fought and won, he'd eased himself into a routine of brutality.

"Tell me the way."

Magnus knew the danger every fist fighter faced walking into a sparring ring. It didn't matter how experienced or how skilled the better fighter was. It took just one unexpected punch to crush a champion. A wise fist fighter took a few strikes to understand the measure of his opponent. The wisest fist fighter didn't reveal their full arsenal in the first round at all.

The Faction War had been about power and dominance. A little taste of glory, too. This, though, was about the survival of humanity. The first skirmish would be controlled.

He picked up a small lead piece and looked at its shape as though it were a childhood possession. Truthfully, he despised these impeccably carved pieces. He hadn't removed them from their case in years. He'd never been outmanoeuvred using these cursed things, so that was enough reason to place them across the map. He wasn't superstitious, but you didn't fuk with the absent gods by laughing in their faces.

He placed the piece closer to a ridge. *It looks like a ridge; could be a rock face.* It was a devastating thing trusting in an unknown, dead soul who knew the Wastes better than he, but beggars couldn't be choosers. He'd always liked that saying. Beggars who'd chosen to march in his army always turned out to be his finest warriors. He took another couple of pieces from the case and placed them midway between the city and where he suspected the first battle would occur. Then he slid them deep into a section of forest closer to the marching army.

"Hiding and fighting like burgeoning legends."

The black and white pieces belonged to a game from the ancients. He knew the rules and felt it fitting to use them in strategy. He placed the queen behind the city wall. After a moment he moved her towards the ridge nearest the enemy.

Easier life.

Magnus wasn't worried about losing this first skirmish; no, he worried about the losses that would be accrued while attaining the first victory in the first skirmish. The test was in decimating the first line of southerners and then better preparing themselves for the counter-charge thereafter. *It might take weeks.*

"We aren't that lucky," he told the map. The map had few thoughts on the matter. It simply waited for the next three pieces to be placed upon its surface. His hand was still for a moment, and he jingled their heaviness in his palm.

He did not yet know these soldiers.

He did not yet know their ability.

He did not yet know their nerve.

He slid them into a line along his forces. All one line, all fighting for the city.

"Fuk it, brothers in blood."

Their heavy black armour was the sturdiest of any army he'd known, and their swords were balanced and sharp. Moving as one huge mass of black, the Wolves would be a sight capable of sending a shiver down any barbarian's spine.

Archers against Riders.

He needed to trust the city; he needed to trust Dia, and he needed to trust her army. If he could polish their hatred for each other and direct it towards the southerners, that would be his grandest manoeuvre in an already outstanding career. History and shared hatred were the only constant both armies shared, and he would most definitely make the most of that hatred. Aye, his loathing for the Wolves was fathomless, but if he could feign a little respect, perhaps there was hope. The tournament was upon them, and Magnus believed it could have come at no finer time.

Nothing like kicking the ever-living shit out of each other to help form bonds.

The tournament might well save the entire city. *It will just as likely ruin it, too.* Let them battle to the singing of the crowd; let them have a fine time. With over a hundred entrants into the tournament, Wynn would be the Rangers' favoured champion. He imagined there were two fierce Alphalines that would represent the city. Though it galled him, a win for the Wolves might suit the war effort best, but still, he hoped Wynn would emerge victorious.

More than that, he expected it.

He stretched his aching arms and looked back to the figures within the forest again. This war would rage with Rangers and Wolves, but hidden legends might win it.

"Enough thinking on these matters," he told the map, which had little to offer on the matter. Sliding the pieces back into the metal case, lest eager eyes come looking, Magnus walked out into the sunlight searching for reassurances of his fledgling tactics.

———

From the comfort of neutrality, Erroh watched Wynn block his opponent's strike with ease and spin nimbly away from the second combination. It was a fair manoeuvre, and it allowed him a precious moment to set himself up for his own counterattack. It wasn't the move Erroh would have chosen, but each to their own. Erroh had his own reckless style of fighting, and a shield would not be, nor would it ever be, part of his style. It seemed less dignified to block with a cumbersome piece of wood. A lifetime ago, when he'd used only one blade, his fist had assisted him. He knew his prejudice. His father had required shield bearers in war. If Erroh ignored the shield, he ignored the responsibility of protecting his father's flank. He had taken a different path and felt assured of it.

Wynn blocked a strike, abandoning his attack and slipping away from his opponent, looking refreshed and sprightly. Wynn knew how to handle a shield. Was he good enough to be a shield bearer?

"Hey Wynn, you are shit," Erroh called, mocking his friend, who ignored the jibe. Probably a good thing, too. His opponent charged forward and almost took his head off.

Magnus sat along the fence too, his dark eyes scrutinising every move. His thoughts were elsewhere. Possibly planning to charm the Black Guard into following him into battle.

Or brooding because I didn't react positively to his plan.

Wynn anticipated his opponent's ferocious speed. He chanced a kick at the warrior and met some success. Kicking was allowed in competition, and it was one of the ponytailed Alpha's better weapons. His foe stumbled over the boundary, and Wynn withdrew his charge.

"He's not shit, Erroh. He's just using different tactics to the more traditional ones," Magnus said, deliberately alluding to his plan for the war ahead. Erroh had always believed they fought wars on open plains with a chain of command. Orders were given and followed until an eventual victor emerged. His father was a master of this art, so why change now?

"I don't understand your plan. It'll never work."

Magnus shook his head. "I will have some trouble convincing the rest of the Alphalines, if I can't convince my son."

Guerrilla warfare.

"I understand your need to try new things, but couldn't Lea and I be better used elsewhere? How many warriors have seen bloodshed? A few little groups creeping through the forest are unlikely to merit much of a victory," argued Erroh, and Magnus conceded the point with a grunt.

"I'm thinking beyond the first battle, little one. In open warfare we might last a few months, but eventually, we will fall. Tell me, how many of these Hunt would fall under Garrick's blade were he released into the Wastes to kill liberally?"

"Countless."

"Aye, and if you and a few others like you had similar liberties?"

"At least half that apiece," Erroh said, nodding his head. He was slowly understanding his father's thoughts on the matter. Rangers and Wolves were built for open warfare, but a savage pack of Alphaline could hide deep in the Wastes and inflict what devastation they could. "Hardly honourable, though."

"It's not about honour or a fair fight. The Hunt lost that right the moment they attacked the innocent." Magnus's face darkened. He drew back from his place at the fence to stand closer, so eager ears couldn't hear. "How is Uden so ferocious that he bested you?"

Erroh had been fearing this confrontation. He'd enjoyed the slow preparation of warfare around him these last few days and had even ignored his own wretched feelings of failure. His father had lulled him into comfort with talk of war and brutality, but the question had remained unanswered. Why, indeed, had he failed? Anyone could ask, but only his master deserved an answer.

"He was incredible," replied Erroh, and found the words disheartening when spoken out loud.

"Are you not the finest swordsman to walk the road, Erroh?"

Erroh watched Wynn's opponent throw down his shield in frustration. Erroh knew how he felt. "I wasn't the finest swordsman that night."

"And what if Uden stood here now?"

I'd rip his fuken head off.

"I would let you slay him, Magnus," Erroh muttered, and cursed his own petulance. Even after everything he'd endured, it was easy to fall into bad habits.

"Three years and the same moody shit," Magnus spat back. "When you desire a discussion of proper things, come find me, and you will find a man willing to listen."

Erroh tried and failed to find an apology, so he muttered a few curses of his own. He could have admitted his fears to his father, or admitted how broken he'd become, but it wasn't in him to reveal his weaknesses. If he did, who knew how much he'd reveal.

Elise and Lea appeared from deep in the green and Erroh waved. They carried a brace of quail each and left them in the capable hands of the Rangers' cook as they passed. Erroh could see through the smile of his mother. She'd been at her strongest the night they returned, but every day since she'd grown weaker. He thought her brave for enduring the cool forests and the thrill of the Hunt, but really, it was an unbearable thing to watch a parent wither away. How could he admit the depths to which he had sunk in chains, when his mother and father fought desolation every day?

"I understand you wield two blades now," Magnus said, turning back to Erroh. "An interesting choice. Will you spar with Wynn?"

Erroh understood his father's attempt at manipulation.

Critique my skill.
Demand futile exercises.
Put me in my place.

"I would be very interested to see what habits you've picked up," Magnus added.

Erroh could have bowed dutifully, but instead he shrugged. "Wynn is no match for me. He is confident and ready for the tournament. Best I not shatter him in front of all these people."

"Maybe you need the practice," challenged the master.

"I practice enough." This felt like a lesson. Magnus must have thought so too. This type of uncomfortable conversation had occurred between them for years. His father smiled, and Erroh smiled with him before returning his attention to a struggling Wynn, who was backing away from his dual wielding opponent.

"Come on, Jeroen—batter him!" Erroh called out.

"Jeroen is skilled, but the shield will win out against double blades," Magnus warned.

"Not against a master."

"Aye, perhaps so. A fine point," admitted Magnus, and Erroh was unprepared for agreement. "Wynn could be a great warrior, but he lacks the experience of defeating a skilled opponent."

"He defeated me."

"He does not believe he got the better of you," Magnus countered. "Besides, I'm not sure defeating a little shit like you is very impressive."

"Aye, perhaps so. A fine point," conceded Erroh, and they both laughed. Something was different between them. Perhaps his father understood his march better than he expected. Perhaps the horrors he'd endured had earned him a modicum of respect. Regardless, it was something better. "If I couldn't beat Wynn, what chance did I have against Uden?"

"Not much at all, I suppose."

They stood and watched for a little time longer. Erroh thought on his father's words, on his questions, on his plans for the coming war. Erroh also thought of his own behaviour. Around them, the Rangers and Wolves prepared. The city was buzzing with tense anticipation and Erroh struggled once more to reveal fears to his father.

Pathetic.

His words came at last, and they came swiftly, in a rush, lest nerves get the better of him. "For a moment, I almost had Uden. He had weakened and on a better day, I'd have struck him down. On a lesser day, I'd have fallen to his blade." He took a breath. "Some might suggest cowardice, but leaping was my only chance. If I could stand on the edge of the mountain again, I would leap a thousand more times."

"I'm glad that you did, Erroh, and I'm proud of you for what you've become. Prouder for what you *will* become." Things had certainly changed between them.

Proud.

"It looks like you had success," Erroh said, as Lea and Elise reached them. Lea dared a swift kiss on his lips before turning to watch the battering Wynn was receiving at the hands of Jeroen. *Shame Lillium isn't watching this.* Lea's hands shook, as they had most of the morning. Spending time alone with Erroh's mother was as terrifying as firing a burning arrow into a sea of black.

"I am tired, my love," Elise whispered, and Magnus immediately lost interest in the skirmish. Her voice was weaker than ever.

"Shall I call for Emir?" Magnus asked, and she shook her head.

"I only need a little rest. Lea would wear out a young stallion." She took Lea's hand and kissed it before wandering away to her tent under the watchful eye of her mate.

To say Lea had been excited about marching through the wilderness would have been a lie, but having completed the precarious event, she realised she had enjoyed it immensely. Elise couldn't help but set everyone around her at ease. She was funny, smart and infectiously kind. It took a few hours of cautious conversation, but eventually they became comfortable with each other. All the females in the city knew her legend; she was as renowned as Magnus. It didn't take long to understand why. Despite her frailty, she was imposing in almost everything she said and did. She did not glide through the forest like a skulking hunter; she marched as though she owned it, and Lea had marched with her, laughing with her, confiding in her.

Impressing her?

Aye, Lea had puffed out her chest a little more. The time had flown swiftly, like their doomed prey, until the sudden exhaustion got the better of the older woman. Lea heard the deathly rattle of a cough. She'd never heard it in anyone so vital, so fierce, so worthy of better luck. The absent gods were cruel to inflict such a weakness upon her. Lea wanted a mother. She so desperately wanted a mother.

"You look troubled," Lea said to Erroh when they were alone again.

"You weren't there when I awoke."

"So I wasn't at your beck and call?"

"I didn't mean it like that, my beo," he muttered, and she knew this. "I just missed waking up beside you. I love waking up beside my goddess." She knew this as well; he'd foolishly fallen into her trap and escaped at the cost of a fine compliment.

They had made camp a half mile from the city, discovering that neither was ready to face the taste of electricity, stone and war just yet. They'd settled by a little brook, sheltered under the cover of a thousand oak trees. A camp fit for a king, a queen, or even a Primary. They took advantage of the solitude; they took advantage of the leisure, and they took advantage of the privacy too.

"After our games, you should still be asleep, even now," she whispered playfully.

"I'm still aching all over."

"As am I, my beautiful boy, as am I. Tell me, though, what really troubles you?"

"You and my mother out in the wilds plotting against me."

"Silly Erroh. It's Lillium I plot with, mostly."

He took hold of her and kissed her, and she returned the embrace with enthusiasm. With the march to the city completed, their passion had fallen upon them tenfold. War was in the wind, but they had each other. Nothing else mattered. She drew away and tugged at his hair. *Answer the question, Erroh.*

After a while, he told her of Magnus's intentions, and she agreed with her father-in-law. Hiding in the forest, killing the Hunt in silence, was an interesting proposition. Had she not stayed concealed for months in near proximity to them with almost no incidents?

Almost.

She offered her thoughts and he accepted them without argument. For a strange moment, she remembered walking from the city with him for the first time. He had treated her with the disdain she'd probably deserved. Now, though, her word held as much water as his. *Magnus's too.*

"It was so much easier before you started agreeing with him," he jested.

"He's the Master General. It's the smarter move," she countered.

"You just wait until I become Master General; then, you'll obey me without question. I will proclaim that you must dance for my entertainment whenever I desire. I'll have a special hat stitched up for you."

"Make sure there are ribbons. I'm a ribbon type of girl. Although I'm not sure Magnus will be thrilled with your appointment."

"If I held his crown, Magnus would likely be dead…" Abruptly, he went quiet and his smile faded. Perhaps jesting of such things brought about ominous portents. The way Magnus carried himself, though, she doubted anything would ever kill him, and who was to say a female wouldn't lead the Rangers in the years ahead, anyway?

The final clatter of blades ended the skirmish and drew their attention. Both exhausted warriors were bruised and bleeding, and Lea thought it a fine sight. The Rangers stepped from the ring as though they were close friends and shared a ladle full of water; she could hear the low mutterings of Jeroen in the early afternoon air. Wynn nodded as he received instruction. Looking at the scuffs in the ground, she craved a little violence herself. A few days had passed since she and Erroh had faced each other, and though certain primal itches were wonderfully scratched, the divinity of warfare was a powerful irritant.

"Come win my heart in violence," she whispered, taking him by the hand.

———

Her feet never made a sound as they slipped across the dusty ground. The sun's relentless gaze had diminished any memory of the rain. He didn't need to hear her feet to know they moved quickly and gracefully. Lea's feet were not the problem today, though. It was the glint in her eye that made him cautious. That glint meant terrible things, and it was just another reason he loved her. The sparring ring felt impossibly cramped. It was a small matter. Erroh calmed his breathing and let the world slow down. Spinning his blades, he challenged his one for life. A flicker in her eyes confirmed her acceptance, and the duel began. Nothing else in the world mattered.

Magnus watched from his tent as Erroh spun both blades theatrically. *Same show of foolishness.* Lea did the same, and Magnus shook his head. *Perfect match.* She lunged forward and missed wildly, and Erroh did not fall for her ruse. *Clever girl, clever boy.* The follow-up strike was the killing blow, and Magnus approved of her technique and his reflexes. A dozen warriors would have fallen for that manoeuvre before the thirteenth spotted the ruse.

"You have that face again, Magnus," Elise whispered from her bed. She was sitting up and the eucalyptus aroma was already filling the tent, and her lungs too. Her colour had returned, but the worry was still there. She knew his fears too. *All this way and unable to fight.* He dared not say it to her yet. Once he said it aloud, it became real.

"I'm watching our cub and his mate sparring."

"How are they?"

"Better than we ever were," he said, stepping out into the hazy light.

Erroh wasn't attacking now; instead, he was rolling away in the dust, escaping each strike. Even in that position he appeared impossibly composed, and Magnus knew he watched greatness. With every attack Lea laughed wildly, as though blood-crazed; Magnus hadn't seen such fierceness in his lifetime. Their bodies were a terrifying blur of motion.

He stepped out of the tent and approached the sparring arena, moving to their rhythms as if listening to a swiftly beating piece of music. He'd known Erroh was capable of incredible things, but this display was unexpected; despite his youth, the cub was inspiring. Walking the road had served them both well.

"Come on!" Erroh roared, and drew her near.

"If you insist."

Lea feinted and leapt beneath his guard and almost struck a killing blow, only to meet a counter of his own. Within a flash, the fight turned on its head as Erroh charged her down, battering her defences with flurry after flurry, and the clatter of wood echoed across the Ranger camp and drew notice. Magnus beamed with pride at the flickering figures, spinning and twisting in the dusty afternoon heat. They were divine, and he wished Elise could see. At least it would be a wonderful tale when they retired to bed that evening.

They spun and contorted their bodies in perfect unison, each master swinging with complete conviction and godly control. The strikes they suffered left marks, but neither slowed their assault on the other. A crowd gathered, and Magnus drew nearer lest he miss a beat. Time became still, but for the vision of stunning violence. Erroh spun and sliced; she parried and plunged. They engaged and entwined themselves in each other's flailing limbs, so close that they could have kissed. Then closer, to inflict pain.

Eventually, it was Lea who struck the deeper blow, a grazing strike across Erroh's forehead, and both Alphalines separated to gather breath. The crowd cheered, but neither warrior acknowledged the accolade. Instead, they stared at each other, watching and waiting for the next movement.

"That was my kill," she proclaimed, and a few agreed.

"A graze is all. I could fight on. It takes more than a girl in a ribbon-covered hat to stop me." There were a few snickers from the gathered crowd, but Magnus didn't care. He just wanted to watch the display.

"Perhaps so, but you'll find it hard to fight with blood blinding those pretty eyes."

"I've fought with blood in my eyes before."

"And you got kicked around," she warned, and he conceded the round and the battle of wits.

Magnus leaned on the fence and took in the watching crowd. They were as transfixed as he, and it was no surprise. Even Wynn could barely conceal his disbelieving grin. Perhaps he was relieved Erroh and Lea were not entering the arena.

"Are you two done with this extravagant spectacle, or must I allow my Rangers the day off to study your skills?" Magnus called, and only then did Erroh appear to notice the crowd watching. He looked around in mild surprise and, seeing his distraction, Lea took that moment to attack.

"We are just getting started," she roared, meeting her mate's blades as they began round two.

36

PRESTIGE

Wrek stared morosely at the beverage sitting in front of him. It was good; it should have improved his mood, but it only made him more nervous. Crystal clear, it numbed his tongue and went down smoothly. The finest batch of the year, from the farm of Mea and Jeroen. *A last honourable batch, too.* The Alphaline couple would have been aligned with their Primary. At least now he understood why Sigi desired to free himself from their partnership. Everything was changing, and Wrek was on the outside; a silent partner, a glorified bouncer. An innocent bystander. *Innocent?* The roar of so many distillers filled his ears, and the constant motion around him pressed on his last nerve. He wanted to hit something. *Someone.* His eyes rested on Sigi and then swiftly moved on. If he hit his intended, that would be the end of them both.

Choose your words carefully.

This was not the first time Wrek had sat at a table arguing for his life. Sigi had chosen this meeting place well, and Wrek wondered which trader had been "persuaded" to give up such a grand warehouse and what exact deal had been struck. Wrek had had little to do with acquiring the building, and less with setting up the massive brewery within. When you had all the money in the city, you could afford swiftness. It was thrice the size of any building they'd used before; only a few of its windows had been barred up, and it would take an army to penetrate the heavy iron outer doors. *Clever little Sigi.*

Sigi's smile was dangerous. Wrek imagined the same smile on a seductress learning the whereabouts of her elder companion's will. Wrek wondered how much value Sigi placed upon sentiment. *Very little.*

"Oh, Wrek, you aren't seeing the greater picture at all."

Wrek didn't like the dismissive tone. He hadn't heard it since Sigi had offered him employment, back when Wrek had been a wretched nomad searching for purpose, back in simpler times when he'd taken on any fool in need of a battering. He wasn't a nomad anymore, but he was in this room alone and he carried no blade.

Fooled again by a comrade, a brother.

"The greater picture, Sigi? Who have you been speaking with? Who has twisted your vision so spectacularly? I look around and all I see is a tyrant taking advantage during terrible times." Thoughts of taking another sip disgusted him, and he slid the glass away. Seeing this, Sigi corked the bottle he'd opened earlier, when they'd sat down as friends.

Were we ever really friends?

Sigi's usual easiness slipped away beneath a scowl, and Wrek was wary.

"If it weren't me taking advantage," Sigi said, "it would be someone else. Now that you play with your hovel companions, you suddenly have a conscience. We built this together, Wrek. I understand your hesitation, your attempts at redemption, but really, you are tainted like me." After a moment, his glare faltered. He almost looked like himself again. Almost, but not quite. "I thought my plan would please you." He looked hurt, but Wrek could see it was a ruse. How many words spoken in the last few months were just whispered deviousness?

And you the fool.

Wrek looked around at the dozen mercenaries standing ready, as though they protected the Primary herself. No, the Primary required no such protection. *Sigi will, though.* When his plan took its next turn, a dozen mercenaries wouldn't be enough. However, a dozen mercenaries and the entire Wolf army would keep him protected. "You think I want the Wolves? You think I want this city?" he said.

Choose your words carefully.

Wrek took a breath and bowed. He should have known something was amiss when whispered word reached him that Sigi hadn't paid his dues this month, especially when the one thing they weren't short on was wealth. He should have followed his gut sooner. He should have asked more questions.

"We agreed to take this city as ours, Wrek, or don't you remember?"

"I'm happy with my station, while you play with fire, Sigi. You know I'll never go against you, dear friend." Sigi smiled at hearing this. "But there are terrible things coming. These thoughts, my old friend, could be the death of you, the death of us all."

I said friend *twice. Will it be enough?*

"It will be no such thing. It is generosity on my part."

"Your generosity will evict how many people? How many people who've trusted you as a landholder will suffer? You take their money and allow them to be thrown out?"

"Oh, there will be harsh words spat both ways in the days ahead, but who will do the evicting? Who will enforce the laws? We are in this together, Wrek. We two generous partners."

Fuk.

He alluded to Wrek's name on every deed. Sigi had needed Wrek to stay afloat at the beginning, but now that Sigi had his own militia, he would have little need for a partner gripping at his coattails. *Running a tight ship meant little.*

Wrek looked at the mercenaries, but their attention was on the distillers brewing the city's ambrosia. *Poison.* A mercenary for every brewer churning out gallon after gallon of crystal gold. Long walk to the door.

"You just aren't seeing the greater vision, Wrek. Dia has brought ruin upon this city. I will prevent bloodshed," countered Sigi.

One mercenary left his place by a copper cylinder and stood behind

Sigi. He did so calmly, his face as serene as though he were out strolling, and Wrek recognised that dangerous nonchalance. He was up to no good. Wrek eyed the door again. A dozen steps and a dozen blades. He didn't like those odds. Wealth and power corrupted even the simplest minds. Sigi had never been simple, despite his simple methods.

"Have you spoken to Dia yet?" Wrek asked, keeping his tone as amicable as possible.

"She will not meet with me."

"Until you force her to."

"Aye, until I force her to." There was no denying Sigi's unquestionable blindness towards the better road taken, but he'd never thought him a bad man. Sigi could see only the gain, see only the opportunity. *Is this how dictators are born?* Had Dia taken the city in similar circumstances? Somehow, Wrek doubted it.

Sigi offered the corked sine. "Take this to the tournament. Think on what you want... friend."

"Wait until after the tournament."

"So you can whisper in Roja's ear as to my intentions? She'll have a blade put through my heart before the Wolves realise they aren't paid to commit murder anymore."

"Please, don't do this, Sigi," whispered Wrek, grasping his partner's shoulders. "Not with the killers marching towards our gates," he pleaded, knowing there was no changing his mind.

"That is exactly why I do this. It will be a better system."

Wrek watched Sigi's guardian carefully. He had not noticed his hand fall to the grip of his sword. He had not noticed there were fewer mercenaries watching over the distilling; he had not noticed at least three slip behind him, out of his sightline. *Everything can be corrupted.*

"You never see beyond your own nose, Wrek," decided Sigi, and Wrek climbed from his chair. Standing up, he was more imposing and he felt more in control.

Still, though.

"I cannot be a part of this, but I wish you no ill. My wealth is my own, and I need little from you," he said, backing away from the table. Sigi narrowed his eyes as though unaware what threat he was to Wrek. "You are on a different path, and I wish you well."

Bitten once, never again.

Get out, get out, get out.

Wrek's head spun and he wondered whether he was merely overreacting, but the expression on the face of Sigi's protector reaffirmed the danger. He grabbed the bottle and turned on his heels. Striding forward, worrying a blade would appear from somewhere behind him, he opened the door, slipped through into the hazy sunlight and disappeared into the crowd.

———

Sigi marched through the alleyways flanked by impressive mercenaries. It was all about timing; it was all about the whispered word. Mostly, it was about the frailty in humankind's desire for more. He passed a tavern and smiled. *This early, and already a queue of thirsty wretches pawing and scraping at the door.* He wondered if the tournament could become a monthly event. Perhaps Dia would take it under consideration. She would still be grand ruler; however, the city was big enough for another voice. A voice of the people. Someone who knew how to run it properly. *Give the people what they want.* He passed through the crowds and on through the winding streets, his step calm and steady against the rush. He was in no hurry. Soon enough, the crowd would part for him.

His flagship tavern was just as full as the many others, and he imagined hearing the tinkle of shiny pieces dropping from their little pouches into his depthless pockets. Everyone seemed to smile, and Sigi thought Dia a genius for arranging this tournament. He would not be in attendance, though; best he conceal himself away for the next few days until everything calmed itself. Until Dia was desperate enough. Seth had arranged the safest place in the city for him. Seth, too, knew the importance of keeping peace with the marching south. Seth knew the need for change. Dia had done many things right, but concentrating on Alphaline reproduction had blinded her to more pressing matters.

Seth was already waiting for him when they entered, and they embraced as any friends would; Seth had become a friend to him these past few months. Seth did not drink, and this made Sigi trust him even more.

"How did it go with the bandit?" Seth asked him.

"He will not be joining us for the meeting," said Sigi, and Seth appeared unsurprised to learn this. For a moment Sigi felt miserable at Wrek stepping away, but it was inevitable. Wrek had been his muscle working with the Wolves. Seth was the muscle working with the Alphas. The trio would have been impressive.

"I wish you hadn't told him."

"In a few hours, everyone will be aware. I had to know if I had his trust... I do not."

"I'm sorry, friend, but you have mine."

Sigi nodded approvingly and felt better.

As one, the two businessmen disappeared behind the bar and into Sigi's office. A tight squeeze with five mercenaries, but necessary. Sigi placed two chairs down in front of a solitary table and waited while Seth leaned up against the wall with the rest of his protectors. He would share no words, but his presence was necessary. It would have been cruel to deny him the opportunity of seeing such a momentous occasion, having broached the strategy of pulling the rug from beneath Dia on this day. *A good friend to me; a greater friend to the city.*

As they had done for the past few days, the Black Guard arrived at the tavern around noon, though this time they were directed to a more intimate setting. Sigi felt the energy as he walked through the crowd, but sitting here, he could taste the excitement of battle. *Who needs a tournament anyway?* Lara opened his office door, and Sigi gestured for a young Wolf named Gael to come in. He entered the office warily, looking every day of his young age, and Sigi almost asked how his stretching routine for his slight limp was going. He didn't care; it was just the usual remark Wrek offered most collection days. Best not show any pleasantness, thought Sigi.

"Take a seat, Gael," he said, and the Wolf eyed the watching mercenaries. His three accompanying Black Guards watched them, too, though none reached for their blade. *Good thing, too.* Unlike Wrek, Sigi insisted on punishing at the slightest sign of threat.

"What is all this?" Gael asked, easing himself down onto the chair. Sigi slid a glass of sine across the table, which the young man reluctantly refused, though not after a lengthy stare at the alcohol. *You will have all you want.*

"This is opportunity," Sigi countered. When the wealthiest man in the city offered opportunity, the shrewd listener paid attention. When the wealthiest man in the city removed his wealth from the economy in one fell swoop, what happened then?

Opportunity.

Gael either didn't understand or cared very little. He unrolled a large parchment and placed it in front of Sigi, as he usually did.

"On order of the Primary," the young Wolf said, "you owe three hundred pieces for the northern sector of dwellings, five hundred pieces for the southern sector dwellings, and seven hundred pieces for the taverns. And, unfortunately, you owe a fine of seventy-five pieces for late payment. This is your second request. Failure to comply in payments will result in immediate evictions from said premises." Gael tapped the names of faceless renters upon his scroll as though it mattered.

Sigi had spoken to every one of them at least once, and every one of them had been gifted glorious opportunity. Every one of them had signed their crushing agreements over to him. There was little love for Dia and her outrageous rents for a shack in the city. It could take even the most able trader half a month of bartering to cover her demands. To them, Sigi was a god for cutting their rents. They had never asked why he took their pieces and paid the rest owed to the city. Why would they? It was a splendid deal, and their contracts protected them. Those who did push were gifted the truth: "Someone needs to stand up to her." A fine answer. There was more truth to be offered, which he didn't.

A man of lower stature wouldn't have wasted so much money unless his funds were limitless.

A man of lower stature couldn't have amassed control of this much land were Dia in any way competent.

A man of lower stature shouldn't have learned how precarious the city's economy had become, but he had.

Was your Wolfen army worth the impoverishment, Dia?

Sigi was generous in his dealings, but he was not a generous man. In truth, the cost of covering so many rents was a substantial drain on his resources, but worth it if he had the patience to wait for his own bet. To say his hand was strongest, however, was incorrect. To say he held every fuken one of the cards was more precise.

Sigi took a breath. This was the final moment before he reached his zenith, and he wanted it to last. "There will be no payment today. Nor any day after. I will not pay another piece to the Primary under this current regime."

Gael inhaled slowly and took his words in. "Are you short of funds? Have your tenants not paid you yet?" he asked, and Sigi shook his head. The city needed his payments. They could survive a few hundred missing pieces here and there, but to lose all in one fell swoop? This was how a fragile economy collapsed; this was how shrewd bastards came to power.

This was how war was avoided altogether.

"My tenants have paid all that they owe, and business is good."

"I don't understand," said Gael.

"Who pays you?" asked Sigi.

"The Primary."

"Aye, and who fills her pockets?"

"The collections."

Sigi eyed Seth, who smiled at the unfolding events. *And why not?* Was Seth not charged with balancing the catastrophic finances these past few months? Was he not salvaging the city from ruin?

"Who owns nearly all the trade in this city, and who owns all the living quarters?" whispered Sigi. Two of the Black Guards had caught on; their faces had gone a little pale. One reached for a blade, but Sigi's companions stepped forward.

Best listen to events unfold.

"You own almost everything," hissed Gael, and Sigi heard the young man's stomach growl. He smiled and offered the drink again. Again, Gael refused. "You will collapse the entire city. Who pays the Black Guard?"

Sigi wanted to reassure him, but he dared not show kindness. "Until I meet with Dia, there will be no more funds offered. You will not be paid. I'm sorry, Gael, truly I am. This is the way of things."

"You can't do this. You can't—"

"How many of your brethren will work with an empty stomach, I wonder. If the Primary speaks with me, I will offer terms acceptable to all parties involved."

Counter-offer made.

Sigi was pleased with himself. He watched Gael struggle from his chair and limp out into the crowd with his companions beside him. Though he limped, his march was purposeful. Nothing like terror to heal a man's injuries. Or give him wings. "Your limp is looking better," he called, but the young warrior was gone.

"Well, things are moving," declared Sigi. His stomach was churning, having being unsettled all day from excitement. He felt like eggs and yellow soup and wondered if there was time for Lara to cook up a few delicacies before he disappeared to shelter from the coming storm. On top of Dia's outrage, he didn't fancy facing the wrath of Magnus, either.

"Remember this, friend: I and I alone will come for you, when Dia is ready to speak," Seth whispered. "In the meantime, I believe it would be best to steal you away from this tavern before someone comes knocking with some unanswerable questions."

"Aye, that sounds like a simple enough plan."

37

SPARK'S MOST MEMORABLE DAY

"*I hear the drums calling,*" muttered Wynn.

"*They're beating your anthem,*" said Erroh, smiling.

"*And away in silence from you.*"

Erroh knew the song well; he'd memorised it in times of war. Wynn had never seen war, and thus treated it with unwarranted admiration. Erroh didn't think any less of him for it, although he couldn't face donning armour for simple competition as Wynn was doing. Still, though, Wynn fought for Ranger honour, so the stakes were respectably high.

"*I am not done yet, not taken my last breath. I need no final meal*" he added, though closer to a mumbled hum than words. Even this far away from the walls, they could hear the buzz of movement. It was early yet, but the wretches were wasting no time in gaining access to the fabled city treasures. Apart from the crowds gathering, the drums from the arena were booming across the world, building the crowd into a frenzy of excitement.

Wynn stood in the middle of his tent, tapping his foot in time. "*I fear no rope, no lead or your steel,*" he finished, and Erroh remembered battle horns playing impressively.

Erroh pulled at the last buckle, securing both pieces of metal sheeting. Satisfied that he had done his duty, he stepped away. "There you go. You look ready for battle and honour."

Wynn's armour was unwieldy, heavy and glorious looking. He had chosen sturdiness and magnificence over ease of movement. Perhaps he'd listened to Magnus's advice too closely. Still, though, as the day progressed and the skirmishes grew in number and ferocity, perhaps he was wise to save himself a careless injury from lesser opponents.

"I look fantastic, don't I?" he joked, testing his movement loudly.

"Well, don't go fall in a river or you'll sink to the bottom. Terrible end for a legend, really."

Wynn spun and nearly knocked Erroh from his feet. "Ah, it's not that heavy. Just need to get used to it." It was one of Magnus's suits, stitched and reshaped. Obnoxious, golden and fabulous. To any uneducated warrior, it was impressive. To Erroh, it was distasteful.

"What do you desire, efficiency or flashiness?" Erroh asked, twisting his friend back around before attaching the golden cloak to some buckles along his back. The cloak was thick and as heavy as a leather helmet. Another needless weight on this scorching day.

"I wish to be both," declared Wynn, inspecting the golden garment carefully. Erroh knew he'd look amazing in the sand, his blade spinning in unison with his trailing cape. The crowd would be drawn in and enthralled with false spectacle. *That is the cost of entertainment.* "Too much?" he asked, and Erroh laughed before unbuckling the garish golden piece. As he did, Wynn spun an invisible shield and sword, and Erroh wondered if he'd ever craved attention like Wynn.

Perhaps.

Now that he'd attained unlikely fame, he found it wasn't what he'd expected. He could never repeat the exploits of Keri, and the weight of expectation crushed him. He looked at Wynn and saw a proud warrior desiring to touch upon greatness. Daring to reach out and steal victory where he could. Erroh just wanted to reach out and take his swords back. Maybe redeem himself while he was at it. *The little things.*

"I thought Lillium would assist me. Thank you." He sounded awkward, and Erroh shrugged. There weren't any real traditions to preparing for a tournament. Erroh would have expected Lea to assist him, though, and he would have been honoured to strap up her armour, too. She'd have chosen leather. *With added shielding around the shoulders.* "Lillium didn't even speak to me today." His eyes fell to the separate bundles of bedding on either side of the room.

Unsure of what words to offer, Erroh patted him on his back and then tried words, anyway. "She walked up with Lea to take in the atmosphere. She'll want you to win today; she'll be shouting your name." It was a lie, but it sounded a nice lie.

Wynn smiled. "Appreciate the effort, Hero. Will you walk with me?"

———

The city was alive. It was alive because she opened the gates and the blood that pumped through was enriched with reckless excitement. Wynn led the procession of Rangers through the busy little side streets, and he led them as any leader should. The Rangers talked excitedly among themselves, deciding tactics, making wagers, and taking in the atmosphere and revelling in it. They marched as an impressive line, and everyone in their path cleared the way.

The few Wolves they met begrudgingly stepped aside and eyed the passing procession with distrust and distaste. They eyed the few waving banners with outright contempt, gesturing crudely as they passed. The flags were unimpressive, little more than a solitary "R" painted on aged beige fabric, and despite himself, Erroh felt humbled watching them, just as he always did.

Beneath the shadow of the monstrous arena, the two friends halted their march. Their comrades marched on, some in towards the competitors' entrance, others to find a seat for a day's entertainment. Standing away from the swell beside the arena gates, Wynn took a moment. His eyes danced nervously across those who passed, be they Ranger, Wolf, wretch or citizen. Erroh waited with him, careful to control his breathing and disguise the unease he felt at so many passing bodies. *Too many, too many, too many.*

"Well, this is it."

"Aye, so it is, friend."

Erroh had never fought a tournament before, but he felt he should offer a few wise words. "Finish each round swiftly. Don't show off; don't do stupid things. It's hot out there. Every fight will be exhausting." Wynn nodded, and Erroh thought it finely made-up advice. "There are many arenas within. No one will watch you in the first few rounds. You can take your time, get the feel of battle."

"Unless they match me with a right bald bastard from the start." Wynn grinned, and Erroh believed this a good sign.

"Oh, I feel you'll be facing that bald bastard at some point, and that's when you can be flashy. If you face him in the final, I'll run back and get your cape beforehand. The ladies will love that, especially Lillium."

Wynn laughed. "I've won smaller tournaments before, just never anything like this. I'm a master at playing at war."

"Magnus battered you these past few months; he prepared you for what will follow." He watched as a stunning brunette Alpha female, dressed in a black and blue outfit, passed through the gates and eyed both warriors. She looked back a second time before disappearing into the masses of the crowd entering the arena, and Erroh smiled. "Lillium will fume with the attention you'll get after this."

"Aye, Lillium is embarrassingly overprotective of me. It's because she's such a jealous person."

Erroh leaned in close so Wynn could understand the weight of his words. "If you win, the honour is yours and she will think highly of you. If they batter you… make sure it's a good battering so you get her sympathy. It worked with Lea."

Wynn sniggered at this. "Maybe it's time to go searching for dazzling brunettes in blue and black outfits." As though gifted by the gods, another female Alphaline walked by and eyed both young Alphas before entering the arena. Her hair was black, her eyes painted dramatically.

"They really are loving me today," declared Wynn.

"She was looking at you? Oh, I don't think so. She was looking at me," countered Erroh.

Wynn reached out a hand, and Erroh grasped it tightly and shook it. *Enough words. It's time.*

"The sun is out, no clouds above. I'm going in to become a hero," Wynn declared, spinning on his toes and heading through the entrants' doorway.

"Don't fuk this up," cried Erroh, watching him march away in the awkward armour.

"Don't you worry, I have this."

What could go wrong?

Don't lose your nerve.

The day outside was bright and cheery, while the gloomy, cramped corridor was miserable. It also stank of sweat and waste. While the crowd were offered fresh air, the combatants were shunted through like beasts of burden plodding deeper into a salt mine. Far ahead in the darkness, the rest of his comrades waited, and Wynn's ears rang from the sound of a thousand stamping feet above him. He dared not look up at the ceiling lest its shaking unsettle him; he thought it strange to be unable to hear his own heavy steps over the noise. Probably a good thing, he supposed; his heart was probably beating as loud. Wolves could smell fear. Could their namesake hear it?

The entrance door closed heavily behind him and his first few steps brought him through a sea of black armour. Apparently, the Wolves were happy to hide themselves in the dark, while the Rangers favoured the light. He found it difficult to slip through unnoticed in this loud, bulky armour, and for a moment he wondered if he shouldn't have worn his traditional attire.

Less impressive, though.

Doing his best to ignore the jests and gentle exploratory shoves, he marched on, steeling his nerve. Rising to any ruse in these close quarters would end in tears. The Black Guard must have thought so too, as the mocking worsened the farther in he ventured. Magnus would be pissed if they beat him up before the event began, or, worse, manoeuvred his premature elimination.

"Look at the little golden god."

"Tug his ponytail—see if he squeals."

"He looks like he'd tug at a few things."

"Fuken Ranger piece of shit."

Get to the Rangers. Wait for your name.

Don't hit anyone, Wynn. Don't hit anyone.

Those who were unaffiliated with either faction and simply desired blood and sport filled the tunnel's middle section; passing them was less arduous. They smelled dreadful, and Wynn couldn't help but pity them. Some of their faces were nervously hopeful, others were cautiously excited, but all of them shared the same desperation. His winning might change their lives, might earn them permanency behind the gates. They allowed him through without issue, offering little more than a wary glance at his appearance.

They know my line.

Separating the wretched from his comrades were a few healing slabs. They were squeezed in against the side wall, and a few apprentice healers manned them with the indifference of spoiled youths. He touched one of the stone slabs as he passed and offered a prayer up to the absent gods.

I will not find myself upon one of these today.

Finally, he reached the Rangers at the far end of the entrance tunnel. Taking a seat among his brothers, he accepted some pats on the back and gentle jests. As the tournament progressed, he would likely face a Ranger or two, but since they were his brethren, there would be no ill will after the skirmish. As long as he won.

"We've got our champion right here," shouted one Ranger down towards the rest of the combatants, and Wynn straightened up as a few jeers of abuse returned from the darkness.

Hold your nerve and win this.

———

Erroh went with the surging crowd. Few were in any rush; most were satisfied simply following the rest, and Erroh just flowed along with them. This day belonged to the wretched. Those wonderful, brave few. War had touched them; they'd tasted horror and death. Their clothes were equally battered, torn and smeared. With his own shabby cloak wrapped around him, he felt indistinguishable from the rest. He felt more at ease with them than with the handful of goddesses and wealthy traders, who stood out like jewels in a god's blade. Listening to their jests, their excitement, their gratitude, he smiled. He did not fight for the city; he fought for these wonderful wretches. He believed they would fight for him.

The swell of people brought him up a thousand steps until he was as high as the city walls, where the crowded corridor opened up to fresh air and the vision of grandness. As he stood on the upper tier, the crowds behind him nudged him as they passed, while he took a moment gathering his senses. The arena was a structure from another time, and it unsettled him. It could hold the city's entire population, no doubt, all neatly settled in thousands of tiered seats running the length of the massive stadium to the sandy floor below.

Thousands were streaming in from many corridors throughout, and seats were filling up. He made his way down the stepped walkway in search of his companions, wary of losing his footing. There was an unusual energy to this place; to the people. Tripping only once and narrowly avoiding the wrath of an ale-sodden brute, Erroh moved through the crowd, hopping from one line of seats to the next, until he found the little boxed-off section reserved for the Ranger elite. For once, he was glad of privilege. Partitioned and roofed in wood and tarp, the private section was where royalty observed tournaments; it was a welcome refuge from the jostling of the burgeoning crowd.

In the level above, in a grander section decorated in the black of the Wolf and the Four Factions, sat the Primary. Around her sat a cluster of guards, a few females of higher standing, and Roja. Even Dia was smiling at the prospect of so much blood. Erroh bowed, but her attention was elsewhere, so he made his way up to join his parents at their seats. Instead of coming through the little security door provided, he jumped the little wall that separated them from the peasants and discovered another bonus to this kingly box. Sitting on each seat was an unopened bottle of sine.

"Thank you for this," he said, bowing to his father, who was smiling anxiously and looking out across the arena. The private box was halfway up: close enough to hear the crunch of bone; far enough away to avoid the splatter of blood.

"Though some of us enter this box like common savages, we feast like kings today," Magnus jested, raising a glass of his own. Erroh now saw that many of the Rangers also had bottles of their own. Magnus was ensuring his warriors enjoyed this day as much as possible.

Erroh leaned in to his parents and whispered, "Lillium never wished him well."

Elise merely shook her head in disappointment, but Magnus spoke. "How was he when walking up?"

"He'll do well today, broken heart or no."

"Do you know what happened between them?" asked Magnus, and Erroh shrugged. He knew some. Mostly whispered mutterings when dawn called and sleep called louder; when loose tongues couldn't wait a moment longer; when memories skewed the truth.

"It'll take time," Magnus suggested. "He was never trained beyond the sword."

Erroh understood his words as though taking instruction from a master. He had trained in the arts somewhat, but more than that, he'd never stopped learning. To understand a female and her grandness was a precarious thing. *Especially in this world.* Erroh had made mistakes, but he'd risen to the challenge. Perhaps Lea's testing him was another reason their mating was so strong. Erroh knew well that Magnus and Elise had their own interesting ways to survive the world, and each other, when simple love wasn't enough. Some might frown; others might pay attention. Erroh had little need for other enhancements, as yet. He was still a lovesick cub, excited every time she stripped off her clothes for him. Perhaps that's all Lillium and Wynn needed.

"Erroh!"

He started in surprise as a smiling Lillium leapt up from somewhere within the crowd below. She'd painted her face to exquisite sharpness and brushed her hair to a meticulously straight finish. She looked happier than usual, and Erroh suspected it might be due to the reappearance of Lea.

"I'm coming over," she declared, putting a hand on the low wall.

"There's a door. Use a little decorum," Magnus hissed, but she ignored him and climbed gracefully over the wall, as Erroh had. The similarly glamorous Lea followed behind, and Erroh offered his hand.

"Thank you for walking with him," Lillium said, bowing gently and almost stumbling over her long legs. She had donned her Ranger outfit, wearing her colours proudly. He hadn't noticed before how well army uniform suited her.

"Are you two already drunk?" Elise moaned, eyeing her nearly full glass. "It's a long event. Best you can remember some of it."

"I could drink for the north," Lillium declared, sliding into her seat and immediately reaching for her bottle. Erroh worried she might be too drunk for Wynn's finest moment. *Explains the smile.*

"I had a large breakfast," said Lea, sitting down beside Erroh and immediately taking his hand in hers.

The drums beat intensely and the crowd were clapping and stamping along with them. *Blood is coming.* A smithy could have made a lifetime of weapons from any of the hundred support beams standing throughout the arena, and every one of these monstrosities shook under the thunder of the crowd's excitement. Erroh felt the tremor through his seat, and he tapped along. He drank from his sine and coughed spectacularly, and no one noticed as the noise grew. Their section shook under the vibrations as countless feet stamped around them, and Lea wrapped herself around him in giddy anticipation. The world became louder and he felt the adrenaline of the crowd and suddenly he regretted not entering the tournament. His open hand became a fist and he saw the same spark in Lea's eyes, too. Even Magnus sat up straighter, his face grim as though preparing for battle. It felt like an absent god's thundering heartbeat, and Erroh slammed his fist down on the wooden balcony wall in front of him. Within a breath, Lea released him and slammed both her fists down in unison with his. They wanted blood; they wanted a fight.

Beside them, Magnus and Lillium joined in; only Elise's face was still and serene. Erroh had never seen his mother in war, but he knew her legend. While Magnus roared and moved like one of his hounds, Elise was calm and terrifying. *Saving her energy for killing.* He'd been told she'd danced through the enemy as though it were no matter at all. He could see a coldness in her. It was unnerving and comforting.

The hammering reached a crescendo and Erroh imagined the fervour the combatants felt, listening to this roar. Erroh's heart thundered, and he saw visions of the Hunt in his mind. Instead of shame and guilt, he felt a rage more terrible than he'd ever felt before. Visions of the sanctuary filled his mind like a poisonous cloud, and he silently cursed that terrible place away. He tasted a gelatinous substance in his mouth and he swallowed it down, and the rage was delicious. He could hear the fuken drums playing his anthem, and he was ready. Lea hissed and screamed along with the thunder of war and he loved her for the warrior she was. As though the absent gods whispered in his ear, he knew their part to play would be bloody, would be heartbreaking, would be dreadful. Suddenly he wasn't afraid of what was coming. In that moment, he renewed his oath of vengeance. He would make the southerners pay for all they had done. He wanted to kill them all. He hammered the wall and his hands stung and he took the pain. He would take whatever pain was needed, and the absent gods grinned, for they knew what was to come.

———

Dia could see wildness in the people. She could hear it in their cries, and she knew this event had been a shrewd manoeuvre to counter failing morale. Allowing them a day within the walls was a kindness, and the wretches were delirious with appreciation. Aye, it might be chaotic as the night drew on, and come the morning the prison cells might be fuller than usual, but it was all worth it. Despite everything, the city had survived these past months. It was time to unite. Like a seasoned master of beasts, she had battered them for long enough, and now, when they neared the moment of snapping back, she bestowed pleasure; she bestowed belief; she bestowed a marvellous day out. A day to spend those precious few saved pieces, to attain luxuries unavailable in the hovels. And the citizens enduring a flock of grubby unfortunates? Well, the pieces these wretches were pouring into their stagnant market would help the economy.

They can complain to Roja.

Dia lived for these moments, and she knew there were many more to come. Her heart was calm, for this was where she shone brighter than the lights of her city. Her city, nobody else's. She stood up from her throne and leaned out along the viewing balcony. The braying crowd had roared and cheered in anticipation, but now was her moment. *The city needs this.* She waited for them to notice, and she was patient. There was little wind; her voice would travel far. Her words even farther. *Maybe to the south.*

"I wish for silence," she called, and as though a steadying hand had passed over them, the crowd hushed, bit by bit, and then fell still. They feared her, they appreciated her, they followed her. *Even Magnus.* She held both her arms out wide and waited until every eye was upon her, every ear pricked to the words that would come, words she had at the ready. She stood high above them in her finest red gown and presented herself with such grace, they could only bow to her, waiting, holding their breath. The world was terrified. It was time to show how terrifying she was.

"Today, I gift you this tournament," she declared, louder than her frail body should have allowed. She heard her voice echo across the arena, right down to the abandoned sands below. In that moment, her pure, clear tones swept away any lingering doubt of her impressiveness.

"Tomorrow, however, I give you survival." She took a breath and watched those closest to her. No one blinked, and few breathed aloud. It was a good start to a brave speech. "The southern beasts intend to burn this city to the ground." Her voice was strong, and she terrified them, and this was perfect. "The first wave draws near, and we have no chance of fleeing." She spat this sentence out as though retreat disgusted her, and perhaps it did. She met the eyes of Magnus, who stood watching from inside his lesser private box.

Size matters.

She faced the crowd again and felt sorry for them. "You are right to be afraid. I have my own fears." She lowered her head and paused to take a shallow breath. The pause became a dreadfully long pause, so much so that some believed her speech finished. Like little worried sheep, they looked around warily as the truth of their fate struck them. Some muttered under their breath. Others looked to each other, to their lovers, brothers, sisters, family, friends and strangers, and their fear resurfaced. Fear could become action. Action could become violence. Dia knew full well that a few loose words or careless actions could erupt into a riot, one that would grow until the city was in ruins. *Not this memorable day.*

She took a deep breath and roared her next words, and they were inspiring. "This city will never burn!" She slammed her fist down on the wall she leaned against and the pain was immense. *Pain is controlled.*

"We have these walls, and everyone will be safe behind them." *Just not yet.*

"We have the Wolf to block their march." *Just not alone.*

"I promise you all of this." Thousands nodded in approval. A few even smiled. Some glanced at the massive walls towering high above them. How could these sturdy walls ever fall? she imagined them asking themselves.

The walls of Conlon burned.

Despite the threat, despite the terror, despite the whispers of discontent, Dia represented hope in the darkness. She faced Magnus once more, her eyes meeting his.

"We have the greatest warrior that ever lived, and we have his wild Rangers. How can we fail?"

She heard a few whispers of excitement now, and hearing this, she bowed deeply to the legend below. The crowd erupted.

"The Rangers and the Wolf, as one, will win this war!" she howled, and the city shook again with cheers. Magnus raised his fist and nodded respectfully towards the old woman in red. The hammering of feet began anew and Dia retreated from the wall, having stirred the juices of defiance. All around her she could see the excitement grow. It was one of her easier speeches, admittedly, but no less important than any before or those to come. The days ahead would be tough but the two fiercest forces had come together; and belief was as important as numbers.

———

On cue, the first of the warriors emerged to take their places at their designated sparring arenas. There were four identical sparring rings marked out in total, and each one hosted two eager champions. The crowd howled in ecstasy at the commencement, and each skirmish began simultaneously. The only sound audible above the cheer was the clattering of sparring weapons. The figures spun, thrusted, slashed and hacked, and they adored the violence. Blood was drawn by glancing blows, brutal strikes, and cracked bones, and each warrior revelled in the screams.

The one-sided rounds never lasted long; those least skilled paid for their foolish bravado, and to the sound of a thousand jeers were swiftly removed from the ring, usually unconscious. Those evenly matched combatants fought on to the sounds of wild praise until a victor emerged; then, to the sound of two thousand approving voices, they returned to the safety of the inner chambers to rest and recover for the next round, while the next few warriors ventured out to face the judgemental crowd.

A city close to collapsing needed these days. A city close to falling needed violence to soothe the mob's inner brutes. With the screams came bloodlust, and it was infectious.

38

BLOOD IN THE ARENA

Magnus could see that Lea was disappointed, and he could hear her sighing every few moments, each exhalation louder than the last. Wynn was beating the older woman comfortably; just not comfortably enough for Lea. Both warriors circled the little sparring ring before clashing again, and once more Lea muttered under her breath. Whatever she said was met with a nod of agreement from Erroh, and Magnus was perplexed. He was watching the same fight and believed Wynn flawless. His opponent had offered a fierce start, but now, in the blazing heat, she was faltering and Wynn was picking her apart, scoring freely.

"Ah, he did it again, Erroh," Lea hissed, and Magnus smiled. She held the same passion as Erroh for combat. *A perfect match.*

"Aye, sloppy," Erroh noted. Whatever they'd seen, Magnus had missed it, and this oversight was telling. He felt older than he ever had this morning, and suddenly he wondered when Erroh might challenge him to a duel. It wasn't Magnus's way, but some Alphaline traditions he embraced. He would welcome the challenge, as he did all others. Magnus had surpassed his own master by a far younger age, though that had been unavoidable. As had his master's death. When Erroh challenged him, it wouldn't be to the death. *Just to a battering.* Erroh had youth and reflexes, but Magnus had a lifetime of experience to call upon. Such things made epic encounters.

Lea cursed again, and Magnus pushed aside thoughts of challenge to focus intently on the melee. He watched Wynn for longer than he liked to admit and saw nothing but perfect form, fluid motion and disciplined manoeuvres. The weakened aggressor charged again, her body slow with age and fatigue, and he caught a flicker as Lea cursed again. A tell in Wynn's technique, but so slight that few would see. Had Lea not warned him of it, he might not have noticed. Wynn kept his shield up as though it was an extension of his arm, always deterring the attacker, concealing his movement and allowing him to dictate the attacks. And every strike was perfect—until he thrust forward. Perhaps he dropped his shield to allow himself additional reach. Perhaps he was overly confident in his ability. Whatever the reason, his shield slipped slightly behind him as he extended his arm, and as he drew back, it revealed a slight opening for any wily opponent with lightning reflexes. Magnus had sparred with him for months and never noticed the weakness. It had taken Lea and Erroh only a handful of manoeuvres to spot it.

Erroh was as concerned as she, and kept his voice low. "It'll take him a few weeks to lose that habit. Best we not tell him today."

She agreed, and so did Magnus. He wondered what pain they must have faced in their first year as a couple. What strength did they lend each other? It was no surprise they were inseparable. They walked a tragically similar path to him and Elise. Magnus smiled in delicate pride. *What trouble might they start? What wars might they finish?*

"Finish it," cried Erroh, as Wynn broke the woman's guard with his shield and struck her helmet in the same turn. The warrior without banner fell to the ground, sending sand flying. Her helmet rolled free and she made a half-hearted attempt to rise, but he held his blade to her cheek and she conceded defeat. The crowd erupted and Wynn spun around theatrically with blade and shield held out, every bit the Alphaline champion. He applauded towards all four sections of the stadium, before facing Magnus and Elise's box and bowing deeply once more. Lillium smiled and offered a wave of her own. It wasn't much, but it was something, thought Magnus. Sometimes war brought more than horror. Sometimes it brought the beginnings of healing. The right girl might like that thing, but an Alpha female devoured any victory dedicated to her and her alone. Wynn turned away again and won the rest of the crowd over by assisting his victim to her feet and raising her arm in tribute. After sharing a few brief words, they shook hands and went their separate ways.

"Looks like our champion is comfortably through to the next round," declared Lillium, clapping loudly, and Magnus wondered whether she was trying to disguise her own pride at her mate, or whether her satisfaction with a win for the Rangers was a sign of her growing allegiances. Both options were acceptable.

"Today will be marvellous," Magnus decided, and raised a glass to their champion, to the day, to his family, and to fuken Dia, while he was at it. Her words had stirred the crowd; they'd even stirred him somewhat. Something about today felt promising. The world was finally coming together. Aye, he and Dia would clash in the trying months ahead, but there was unity now.

———

Emir was late. This was a common occurrence for him, but an alarming trait for a healer. Perhaps his healing skills had grown because of his constant need to make up lost ground, having arrived late to countless gruesome scenes. He shuffled through the crowd, doing his best to keep his balance. Walking with him was his uninvited guest, Cass. It was the first time the broken regulator had emerged from solitude in months. The energy in the air was contagious; the drumming had stirred the man to action and movement. Emir had answered a knock on his door to discover Cass standing there, looking nervous and hopeful in his long coat; it was a moment reminiscent of Lara's unexpected and unlikely outburst, and Emir had embraced him as a friend, agreeing to accompany him through the city and crowds.

Roja will understand.

"How are you finding the crowd?" Emir asked, stopping at a gap in

397

the endless rows of excited revellers. Cass looked around apprehensively but continued to shuffle gamely along.

"It's a great day. I'm glad I'm out. Thank you for this, Emir—thank you."

Emir laughed. "Stop thanking me, friend. I'm honoured."

"And I am honoured to know you too, Emir."

Eventually, and with the competition in full flow, they made their way up to the grandest private box. He looked down to Magnus's section and felt a little envious. They were laughing, drinking and toasting the fighters in the sand below. They were having all the fun while he was about to endure some awkward conversation with a potential in-law. The box above was full of Alpha females, and he knew well the judgement he was to receive. It was a little rude on his part to ask entry for Cass, but he wasn't about to leave the fragile man behind as he struggled with his recovery.

"Let me do the talking," Emir suggested as they neared the door of the grand imperial box. Wary of confrontation and of the possibility of speaking with strangers, Cass nodded eagerly. From outside, Emir caught sight of Roja and thought her beautiful. Admittedly, he thought her beautiful every day, but today she was incredible. Even with at least seven bodyguards around the queen of the city and her entourage of judgemental sisters, the box had more than enough room for two grateful wretches, so he approached the two Black Guards manning the entrance, armed with his most charming grin.

"Hello—"

"Fuk off out of here," the taller Wolf growled, and Emir felt deflated. How many times had he heard these exact words when attempting entrance to anywhere in the city? Well, today he was an invited guest. *They can fuk right off.* The time he'd spent among the Rangers had clearly rubbed off on him. As if he needed a reason to hate the Black Guard already. He eyed them with as much silent disdain as he could muster before speaking again. "I am invited." Indeed, Roja had demanded he face judgement from the most powerful female in the world, so he had come willingly.

Smile, behave and bow where needed.

Don't be yourself at all.

Hearing his voice, Roja leapt up from her seat, showing her eagerness a little too readily. As she glided down a few steps, waving in excitement, he thought her a goddess of flowing red fire.

"He is my guest," she announced, and Emir did not recognise this smiling girl at all. She was happy and relaxed, and such openness was a fine look to her. "Let him in." Her tone was stern, but it lacked her usual disdain.

The first guard stepped forward and frisked him unsuccessfully for weapons.

"If he wanted to kill me, he'd have done it a thousand times already," she snapped.

"I don't know this second wretch, Roja. You never made mention of him," the Wolf argued, staring at Cass and shaking his head. He held his hand out as though to shove him, and Emir stepped between them. The crowd might be a welcome challenge to a recovering man, but aggression from a tall Black Guard was a step too far.

Cass hesitated and eyed the guard like a knowing deer in an archer's sight. Roja must have understood his apprehension, for she placed a hand on the guard and eyed Emir, silently asking why he'd brought company. Emir, ever the wordsmith, shrugged.

"We don't have to come in. We can watch from here," Emir offered, ignoring Roja's frown.

She stepped from the box, taking the wretch's hand. "Your name is Cass, isn't it?" Her voice was delicate, and he appeared to relax, even if his face was pale and his legs were shaking.

"I can vouch for him," Emir declared.

"I'm sorry about this," whispered Cass, and it pleased Emir that he stood his ground instead of fleeing.

"Let him in, Dane," demanded Roja.

If she intimidated Dane, he showed nothing. "I don't care what you insist, Mydame. I know of the healer. I do not know of this man."

"Let him in this very moment."

"Very well. Remove your jacket, Cass," Dane snarled.

Roja's face turned red, and Emir prepared for the scene she was about to make.

"He need do no such thing. He is a guest, and we afford guests respect when they sit at our table." *Any moment now.*

"I said, remove your jacket."

People were looking.

"Listen, Dane. When I give you an order—"

Cass stepped forward, interrupting the storm. "No, no, please Roja. The Wolf is right. I once stood as grand protector of a town. I understand the rules. I will do what he asks." He opened his long coat and spread his arms wide. His face remained pale but determined, and Emir felt the stirrings of hope. He'd never been Cass's friend, but he'd respected the quiet dignity with which he carried himself. He had stood beside Aireys when she fell. Returning his spirit to him was another way to honour her.

Roja tapped her feet impatiently as they searched him thoroughly. Cass did not try to fight their probing, and at last, satisfied, they stepped away. Roja took his hand and kissed it in apology, before loudly inviting him in as royalty. Cass gladly accepted with a bow, and Emir thought her wonderful.

"Thank you, Roja," he whispered.

"I understand why you brought him here," she whispered back, leading them through the doorway into grandness. The private box was imposing and lavish. While the stone stadium itself was hard and cold, Emir walked upon freshly laid carpets. The seats were cushioned, and servers slipped elegantly among the attendees with pitchers of wine and baskets of breads and cheese and fruits. From their elevated seats above the crowd, there was a fine view of the arena without the sound of a thousand wretches howling on either side. The two rows of females sitting with them were dressed in their finest silks, their radiant colours set off by the stunning, unnatural shades flowing through their hair. Only the ever-present shade of black, in the form of the Wolves, dimmed the gathering. Emir in his mostly scrubbed clothes stood out something awful, yet Roja looked at him with adoration as though he was as grand as anyone else.

400

"I want you to meet her first, Emir," Roja purred excitedly, and Emir nodded as though this wasn't the most terrifying meeting he'd been ordered to attend.

Cass, however, stopped and bowed once more. In his hand was a glass of sine, which he gripped for dear life. "It is not my place to speak with the Primary."

For a moment, Emir envied him. *Drink, friend. Enjoy yourself.*

"It isn't Emir's place either," Roja joked, taking Emir's hand. "I'm hoping she puts manners on my boy."

"Thank you for this, Emir, and thank you, Roja, for your kindness," Cass offered, then turned to watch the warriors batter each other in the sands below.

Roja pulled Emir close and kissed him swiftly on the lips before releasing him. "She is rather eager to meet the wretch who has ruined her granddaughter." Emir couldn't help notice a few nearby giggles from the Alphalines catching sight of Roja's display of affection. If she heard, she took no notice, and he allowed her to lead him towards judgement.

Dia sat upon a large wooden throne, sipping from a goblet of red wine that matched her fine, elegant dress. She gestured lazily for Emir and Roja to approach, and then looked him up and down with cold eyes. Roja made the introduction and he bowed as regally as possible.

"So, you are the healer with the magnificent touch?" she asked, apparently taking delight in his discomfort.

"I am… Mydame."

She must have been pleased he used her proper term. Emir knew few lowerlines understood the importance of terms. She stared into his eyes and Emir fought the urge to turn away, such was her intensity. Despite himself, he was impressed. She resonated power, dominance, assuredness. He wished he'd shaved; he wished he'd had a drink; he wished he'd scrubbed his clothing harder.

"Well, Emir, you really are beautiful, aren't you," she declared, and a few females giggled. Emir wondered if this was the only noise made in the Primary's presence. Beside him, Roja giggled too, and he held Mydame's stare. "You appear wretched, but those eyes suggest more.

She says you are kind. My Roja hasn't seen enough kindness." Strange words, thought Emir.

"Roja is a kind soul too," he countered, and a smile formed on the older woman's face.

She leaned forward and whispered, "I'm pleased to meet you, Emir." She made a gesture and a glass appeared in his hand almost immediately. "If I find you sober by the event's end, I'll be most disappointed in the both of you."

"Very kind of you," he murmured, sipping the wine. It was rich, bitter and warm. Only the best for Mydame.

Roja tugged him gently away. *Task done marvellously.* She pointed to the small figure of Linn standing at the edge of the box. Her face was clean and lightly painted, her hair brushed straight with a few thin strips of red running through. It matched her dress. *All matching generations of crimson.* In a few months she'd gone from wretched to Alpha kind.

"Hello, little one," he offered, and she bowed regally but barely acknowledged him; this pleased Emir. *Already trained.* He thought on her lineage and the entitled future to come. As swiftly as she had arrived, another adopted sister led her away, and Emir allowed himself a healer's smile. He had dragged the child upon her first step, but her saving was Roja's accomplishment.

"Let's watch the wonderful violence, Linn," the female declared, and Linn nodded in near understanding. *Start them young.* Only then did he recognise Lexi as her guardian. Done up with paint and grandness, she looked transformed. Just like Linn.

"The little miss has come on," Roja whispered, taking his hand. "Thank you for coming."

"It was nothing, Roja," he lied.

They leaned against the box wall, far enough away that they could share whispered nothings. She leaned against him, and for a few wonderful moments Emir felt less wretched. He watched the group of females and thought them a river of colour in a forest of wretched greys and browns. They were more at ease standing out than hiding their beauty away. Unlike their grand leader, however, they mingled throughout the imperial box, talking excitedly amongst themselves, grabbing at their Black Guard protectors and dragging them into conversations. All the while, their eyes were on the brutal battering in the sands below, and Emir thought they behaved no differently to the girls he'd grown up with. Once again, he marvelled at the power of whispered superstitions. He looked upon Roja and thought her a deity, standing proudest and most imposing among them, but she was as human as the rest of the wretches on the other side of the box.

Just better at it.

"First Linn, then Lara, and now perhaps Cass," he muttered, and she rested her head against his. "I seem to have the best success when you are around."

"We make a fine team, my beo."

"For now."

She kissed his cheek. "You still believe me a foolish girl discovering feelings for the first time."

"Perhaps after the war we might speak on these matters."

She pushed him away gently but held his rope belt; he wavered, and she pulled him close again, close enough to kiss. Instead, she whispered. "You fear a foolish girl from the city following a wretched healer all the way to Keri?" He hadn't thought of them beyond the city. Beyond this dreadful feeling of unease.

"You wish to leave the city and live a pauper life?" He turned and scrutinised her.

"You know I do. With or without you… my love."

He held her firmly for a moment. Heavy words spoken in jest were still heavy words. "Would a life like that suit you?"

"I have uses. I can make a life whichever way I choose. You speak of Keri, and I wish to see it for myself." Her eyes were alive as though revealing aloud her greatest secrets. "I could become mayor easily enough. Their current one is rather disastrous." She dared to kiss him, and he enjoyed it. She spoke of things he'd never considered; he thought of Aireys and knew she might even approve, and his stomach churned. Roja must have read his thoughts, for she returned to watch the violence in the arena below. His heart was hammering, and he loved this moment. Fuk it, but he loved being around her. "But, let's just wait until after the war," she jested, before draining her drink. Her hands shook ever so.

For a leisurely time, they watched many skirmishes played out across the arena, until the gates opened and Emir gripped the box wall in anticipation.

"How was he today?" called Silvia, appearing from within the group of females. In her hand was a glass of red wine which she held out at arm's length while making her way over to them. Though her dress was simple white, she was no less dazzling than the rest of her silken-gowned sisters. She had tried for her champion today.

"Stefan was fine when we spoke. He is a fantastic fighter, a former Keri champion. I'm not too worried," Emir said, smiling. He felt the opposite. This wasn't Keri's competition; this was something else entirely. Stefan had no illusions that he would earn victory; he'd been humbled by an Alphaline in combat before, but the thrill of competing was something Emir couldn't talk his friend out of. And really, why would he? It was an opportunity to feel like himself again. It was also a moment to earn respect for the wretches.

As he emerged in his simple leather armour, he lacked any of the bravado he'd shown as Keri champion, but he looked charming, and Silvia cheered loudly for him. And then, his opponent appeared from the other gate and Emir's heart dropped.

———

Cass leaned against the box wall watching Stefan and cursed the coward under his breath. Even with the blazing sun, he felt no warmth. There were many Black Guards around him and they made him feel nervous, until one of them drew away from the adoring eyes of the Alpha females, marched over in his clinking armour and leaned up against the wall beside him. Immediately Cass felt very much at ease. He ran his fingers through his hair and embraced his friend and the calming gift he gave.

"I am glad you came, my dear friend," Azel of Keri whispered, and

Cass smiled, enjoying the kindness. He owed Emir a blood debt, but he owed Azel so much more. Even now, on this wondrous day, when the crowd unsettled him, Azel's compassion and strength were reassuring things. Sometimes, late at night when he finished his shifts marching as a Wolf, Azel came to him and drew away his tears and held him until the night no longer terrified him. *Why does the city frown so bloodily upon such things?*

"It is unsettling, being around so many. Today is a great day," Cass said.

Azel removed his helmet and smiled that pretty smile. He waved across to Emir, who returned the gesture, despite the goddess demanding every bit of his attention. *Isn't that the way with the females? Obsessed with making stronger children.*

"Seeing you here gives me hope for better things, Cass. Remember that."

"Better things would be nice."

Azel patted him gently. "Shall we watch Stefan's ruination?"

"Perhaps I shall watch it alone."

"As you wish, Cass."

———

Doran grinned, stretching for battle. There was blood in the air and he aimed to spill the next drops. It hadn't taken a fortune to get his name placed against Stefan's. He wasn't the first to search for retribution in legal combat, nor would he be the last. It wasn't Wrek or Emir, but it was a good start to besting the trio. He had little intention of killing the wretch, but beating him within an inch of his life in front of the crowd —and Silvia—would be a task well done. Thinking of her was the perfect muse for violence.

He heard his name announced, and his brethren cheered loudly as he punched the air.

He had little love for the flail; he did, however, have love for the arena's pathetic attempt at recreating a safer version of the flail. While most flails were heavy pieces of metal chain and spike, this rope-and-wood monster was still devastating. He thumbed the little wooden ball with its puny stumps that should have been vicious spikes and sniggered. Even neutered, this beast would break bones. Against a finer opponent he would use a sword, but he would take his time with Stefan, the wretch of Keri.

Stefan suppressed his fear, recognising his larger opponent, but the fear returned tenfold as Doran charged across the little sparring ring with unexpected speed for one his size.

"Oh fuk," he yelped, and distantly, he heard a few bouts of laughter erupt from those watching. He had never felt further away from Keri.

"Come here, you little shit!" roared Doran, swinging wildly as Stefan slid away from each charge. Stefan had always believed himself knowledgeable in warfare, but he'd never encountered a flail in combat and struggled with its unpredictability. It was an ugly, awkward weapon, but Doran wielded it like a master. He tried to watch his opponent's shoulders for clues of attack, but it was unnatural. He matched Doran's dancing steps, but the form used was too bewildering, and twice in a matter of moments Stefan almost tripped up on himself. This too was met with laughter, but fighting for his life, Stefan cared little for their mocking. Those strikes he couldn't slip away from, he blocked with his shield. Each heavy battering strike was loud and nerve shredding. Doran was impossibly strong, and Stefan, well, Stefan felt a wretch.

When defence became too precarious, Stefan attempted a few counter-blows, but he couldn't put enough distance between himself and Doran to strike back. When he returned with a lunge or slash, Doran leaned effortlessly away from the attacks. Only luck saved him from having his head split open all over the sand once Doran grasped the timing of his clumsy attacks. Around him, he caught sight of scuffles between traditional combatants, and for a moment he envied them and pitied himself. It was a terrible thing to know he was vanquished so early in combat. Doggedly, he resorted to frustrating his superior opponent by keeping his shield out in front, hoping the absent gods allowed him a quick defeat without too much humiliation.

Soon, they became an awkward dance of nullified violence, and Stefan swallowed his fear and exhaustion and instead focused on outlasting Doran. It wasn't much of a plan but he stuck to it, and for a time it almost worked. Retreating across the energy-draining sand, he used his leather armour to counter the weight of Doran's heavy black armour, and soon enough, the swinging, the battering, the ducking beneath blows lessened, as Doran tired faster than he. Distantly, he heard the crowd change their focus from surrounding battles. Ridicule slowly turned to appreciation. Thousands gasped as Doran charged in and nearly took him out, only to cheer wildly as Stefan somehow escaped certain defeat by dodging and slipping away. His arms became nothing more than tools to block the strikes, and his sight narrowed to everything but the spin of rope and the thud of wood. He didn't know how long the battle lasted, only that soon it was Doran who panted first whenever they separated. Every time he swung, Doran spat a curse and Stefan answered it with a curse of his own. It was all he could think to do, and his stubbornness won the crowd over and frustrated Doran even more.

"Meet me like a… warrior," gasped Doran, as though he'd consumed a barrel of stolen sine.

"I'm fine right here."

"Coward."

"A skilled one, at that," Stefan countered and couldn't decide if the growing red of his opponent's face was burgeoning sunburn, desperate rage, or sheer exhaustion. It didn't matter. He was exhausted himself, but he wasn't the one swinging away every ounce of energy he had.

Sweat dripped from Doran's forehead now; he wavered as he marched forward and suddenly the previously unused sword in Stefan's right hand felt heavy and assuring. He met the next lazy strike and charged forward with his shield, battering Doran across the sand.

"Oh fuk," yelped Doran, falling away in panic. The crowd cheered, and Stefan pounced with glory on his mind and swung at the brute's unprotected face. It would have been a killing blow, or at least enough to earn the win in this round, but Doran caught his wrist and struck him fiercely in the face with a fist.

Almost as fast as Erroh.

Just as cunning.

Stefan felt Doran handle him as though he were a beast being wrung from this life. He twisted Stefan's wrist, and his unused sword took flight. Before he could swing the shield, Doran spun away, slinging the flail fiercely as he turned, and suddenly Stefan fell down to his knees, clutching his throat. It felt like it was bleeding. It felt like it was torn open. It felt like looming death in a river. He tried to scream, but he couldn't breathe and he couldn't concede the victory. He vaguely heard the judge award a point in his opponent's favour, and saw Doran standing over him, watching him gasp for life. He reached for his vanquisher and felt a last wisp of air stream into his lungs.

The crowd weren't cheering anymore; they weren't gasping or laughing, either. He could hear them beg for mercy, beg for murder, beg for blood and beg for more. He knew people died in tournaments; he just hadn't expected to fall like this. Everybody in the world would watch him die. Two steps away, the Black Guard swung and Stefan held out his hand in one last attempt at saving his insignificant life. *Should have died in Keri.* The flail struck his hand and his fingers shattered. It was a scoring point, and he collapsed in the dirt as shards of agony streamed through him. The crowd roared, and he cursed them silently. It was said not one of his comrades from Keri had cried out as they died, so neither would he. He gasped again and no air came. He could see bone splintering through muscle, jutting through the skin of his hand. He watched almost dreamily as his blood spilled into the warm sand and saw Doran walking away with a triumphant arm raised. The world fell silent, and Stefan closed his eyes.

———

Cass stood away from the wall; he'd seen enough.

———

The judge pronounced the victor, but the crowd quietened as a few healers ran from the edge of the arena towards the body. The warriors in combat had not observed the devastating incident, but from the silence they knew something had gone terribly wrong. *At least it wasn't them.* They fought to the sound of eerie silence, and for a few moments the air filled with the clatter of blades, a few cautious whispers, and a few thousand silent prayers to the absent gods who favoured war.

Stefan's eyes suddenly opened and he took a breath. It was a very painful breath, but it tasted finer than any he'd ever taken. He could feel the damage around his throat, but the reassuring whispers from the healers suggested survival. Other whispers suggested he wave to the crowd, and this he did willingly and received the loudest roar of the day.

———

"I have to see him," screamed Silvia, pulling away from Roja. "He's ruined." Behind her, the crowd began cheering louder than ever before. Emir held his breath as he spotted the waving arm, and he praised the absent gods. He suddenly heard another shrill scream, something wild and primal and full of horror and terror. It sounded nearby. He looked around and saw Silvia sprinting down towards the lower step and then halting as though stabbed by an invisible pike. She spun around, grabbing at her eyes, and Emir saw blood splattered across her face. A second fresh splatter of blood suddenly appeared across her white dress, ruining it completely, and the screaming continued.

"This is all on you," Cass hissed, continuing to stab violently into the old woman's stomach. Her screams were lost in the day's celebration and he thought it wonderfully fitting. She struggled with frail, withered hands and he hated her for her sins, her betrayal of Keri being but one, her betrayal of those who loved their own being another. He made certain to stare into her eyes as his hand continued its relentless plunging. He still had his elbow pinned across her neck, and listening to her shriek was like an homage to a skilled artist. It hadn't taken a master assassin to slip in beneath the careless guard of the Wolves. Even now, as he murdered, they still stood like statues, only a few feet away, staring at the dying Stefan below. Cass was skilled with his little blade. This was not the first time he'd stabbed a female with it, and like his previous victim of war, this one too had no armour. *Like cutting into a swine.* He sliced across her throat to silence the wailing, but someone else took over.

Emir had no tools; he knew a technique, but Dia was too old for such a procedure. Painfully late in the tragic moment, the Wolves realised that their Primary was in peril. Roja screamed louder than everyone. A begging, pleading scream.

"Please, leave her alone. PLEASE!"

Cass kicked and punched at his attackers, waiting for one of them to strike him down; he was prepared for the darkness. He knew Jeremiah waited there for him with a fine glass of wine. He would ask for white. He'd seen more than enough of the red today. He felt an arrow pierce his chest and the grips lessened. He tried to pull the black arrow free, but his hands slipped because they were wet. He met the eyes of Azel, who notched another arrow. He tried to say something.

Azel fired again, sending the bolt through the assassin's head. The body fell backwards over the edge of the partition. It didn't fall very far. It landed on a few drunken revellers below and then the real screaming began.

39

THE END OF THE WORLD

She tried to reach Dia before she rolled from the chair and down into the widening pool of crimson beneath her. All around her was chaos, and Roja only wanted to reach her grandmother. Bodies blocked her way and screams deafened her. Her own screams were louder than any other, and she pushed through the crowd, trying desperately to catch her grandmother as she fell from her chair. Dia shuddered in her throne, her body convulsing, her mouth gasping silently. *Too much blood.*

Roja pushed her screaming sisters aside and, reaching Dia, she fell to her knees.

"I'm here. I'm here," she cried, taking her grandmother's hands, and Dia's eyes met hers, but they looked beyond her in panic, in terror, in knowing; in madness. "You aren't alone. I'm with you," Roja cried, hoping she heard, hoping she understood. Around her people shoved, crowded, fled. Wolves roared, sisters wailed, and the crowd beneath them surged. It was the end of the world. Everyone knew it. Roja most of all.

"Somebody, help her." Warm crimson covered her hands, spilling thickly over her dress. Through Dia's torn and shredded dress, she could see the damage within, and she knew no kindness from the absent gods could save her. Yet still she howled for a miracle, for help, for this nightmare to fade. *Wake up, Roja.* "PLEASE HELP HER."

It was Emir who broke through the madness and fell beside her. Her first thoughts were his roughness as he pulled Dia from her chair, laying her out along the carpeted ground.

"I need healing tools—get me tools!" he demanded of those watching this madness. Tearing his shirt into strips and roughly stuffing the rags into the biggest hole along Dia's stomach, he took Roja's hand and forced it down over the cloth. "Tight!" he screamed, as it turned a deep red immediately and he cursed in defeat.

"Save her, Emir," Roja whispered, though it may have been a scream. Her body shook, and he grabbed her hand and held it a second time. His force was rough and painful.

"Hold this tight," he roared, as though they were not in love, as though they were enemies.

"As you wish," she cried, though it may have been a whisper. She pushed with the red strip of bandaging and felt the warmth in her fingers. *Save her, Emir.*

He tore and placed fresh strips over her many gashes, stopping every few moments to scream for "A fuken healer's kit." No wonderful bag of miraculous healing tools appeared in his hands, but he continued on, regardless. Grabbing any spectator nearby, be they Wolf or Alpha, he took their hands as he had Roja's and placed them upon the many wounds, and soon strangers surrounded the fallen woman, leaning in, holding the blood at bay. They screamed, they wailed, they prayed to the absent gods, and Roja fought unconsciousness.

"Oh, come on," he hissed to the body, and Roja could see the inevitability in his eyes, could see it in the open eyes of her grandmother. He ripped another piece of his shirt. It didn't come away properly and he struggled, he even stopped and looked to the sky and moaned incomprehensibly before tearing the piece free and wrapping it around her grandmother's throat.

"Save her, Emir," she begged, and this time it was a primal roar. An order from the Primary in waiting. A warning to the gods, and to him. He eyed her for a breath before shouting for a healer's kit once again.

His hands were a blur attempting to stem the flow. He was a spinning dynamo, moving from each wound to the next, grabbing blood-covered hands and pressing each down upon futile dressings.

"Hold them tighter," he kept shouting before climbing over her grandmother's body and pounding on her chest and Roja screamed as he did. Still, though, she held the wound sealed. He counted aloud as he pushed with all his might and Roja understood his desperation to pump life through her body, but he cursed louder than before. He wiped his forehead and left a long smear of red across his brow. She might have wiped it off, but dared not free her hands from her task.

He leaned against Dia and listened for a miracle within her chest, and Roja wanted to scream that they would hear no beat above the commotion, that they must continue the fight regardless.

A healer's bag dropped beside him and he did not reach for it. Instead, he sat back, turned and embraced Roja. He was stronger than she expected and she let go of the rag. She didn't mean to let go. He'd told her to hold the rag. He grasped her and she heard his sorrowful pities, whispered into her ear. She screamed in reply before placing her hands back on the wound.

Not dead, not yet.

"I am so sorry, my love," he whispered in his southern accent. *Love?* She hated him for the word. How could he say such a thing? What good was claiming love when she was alone now? She could not take this sorrow. Would not take it. She looked into the dead, staring eyes, the deathly grin, and hated everything.

Everyone.

A maddening grief took her and she allowed it. Slapping Emir across the face, she pulled away from his grasp. She condemned his failure, again and again, and still he tried to hold her. The Wolves around them fell to their knees, ashamed for their failure. They wailed for her loss, too. Roja's sisters, now her daughters, screamed their own agony and it almost matched hers. She climbed to her feet and stared at her ruined hands, at her ruined dress. She saw her grandmother's blood drip to the stone floor as though from a boar drained for a feast, and it was too much. She could only hate now. There was nothing left but hate.

Her voice was cold; it was resolute, despite her brokenness. She stared at the man she loved and loathed him for the sin he had committed.

"You pledged for him," she growled. She raised a hand, almost languidly, and then, as though needing a victim on which to vent their own horrors, the Black Guard fell on him and she enjoyed it.

———

Erroh looked up towards the commotion in time to see a man fall from the Primary's box, followed swiftly by three Black Guards, who leapt on him like beasts of prey. To his horror, they hacked at the body with swords and axes.

They've murdered a spectator.

Those nearby scrambled away, climbing over each other in their haste to flee from the grisly spectacle of Wolves tearing their victim to pieces. Their terrified shrieks ignited a spark of fear that threatened to engulf the entire arena.

Waves of screams filled the air, beginning in the upper tiers of the stadium and cascading violently downwards. The crowd, hundreds and then thousands of them, surged into the aisles, some fearing unseen horrors, others seeking to know the cause of the chaos.

The first, and fiercest, charge came from above the Primary's box, and Erroh heard the sound of thundering feet rushing in a wild stampede towards Magnus's box. The air rang with wild cries.

"The Primary is slain."

"The Wolves have started a coup."

"The Rangers are killing."

"There is a fire."

Then somebody screamed that it was the southerners. Another screamed the city was besieged.

They surged down and struck the box head on. The creak and groan of heavy wood splintering drowned out the melancholic howls of the fleeing. On both sides, Erroh could see people streaming towards the exits. He tried to grab a young cub, carried along helplessly in the river of people, but the current took him. He struggled to keep his footing as the box wavered and groaned under the assault.

Then, at last, the world shook and their platform shuddered a few feet forward. There were further screams of terror, of pain, of panic, followed by an ear-splitting crash as the entire section shattered into a million jagged pieces. Everything collapsed around him as fleeing revellers trampled the stand to splinters and continued surging forward as though a dam had broken. He saw Lillium thrown clear of the crush; he saw Elise caught underneath a falling wooden partition. He saw Lea spun and swallowed up by crashing debris. In his ears he heard his father roar, and then he heard nothing but the end of the world as he, too, fell into nothingness.

———

They could not think; they only charged. Those in the upper seats sprinted for the gates at the top of the arena, where they bottle-necked immediately, while the majority surged down towards the larger gates below. It took only a handful of breaths for a crush to occur. The first wave made it through the thin corridors into the city beyond. They were the luckiest. The second wave pushed through after them, but in such numbers that they slowed their own exodus. Behind them came thousands, chased by phantom attackers, chased by frenzy, chased by their own terror.

In those few terrifying moments, the city would have known disaster were it not for the Primary. Even after her death, the Wolves followed the orders she had given long ago should such a dreadful event occur.

Now, they took control. Only a hundred, but that was all it took to change the tide of catastrophe. They roared, they cursed, they howled and they calmed, and they dove into the crowd as Dia had insisted they be trained to do. They cut through the panic with bitter aggression, striking where needed, saving where possible and directing as they had been charged to do. They kept their heads and saved lives. Like seasoned shepherds, they directed the surging bodies down towards the open plains of the arena, away from the exits, and in so doing, they relinquished death's hold upon the masses. Suffocation was eased as the people fell over the walls, out onto the arena sands below, and breathed air—albeit stale, sweat-and blood-scented air—into their starving lungs.

They howled for calm, dousing the fevered frenzy of the spectators with controlled aggression.

Their voices led, and the terrified little lambs followed their path. The Rangers, too, were quick to follow their lead. They roared and cajoled; they fought the current and demanded a slowing of pace. Enemies lost their bias and worked together as brave heroic champions, and for one moment in the worst day the city had ever known, there was no difference between the black and the beige.

———

Darkness.

Pain.

Little bit of panic too.

Get up.

Half-deafened by a high-pitched squealing in his ears after the roar of devastation, Erroh emerged from the rubble first. He shoved a panel of wood clear and felt breathable air again. Stumbling free of unconscious bodies, broken timber pieces, and shredded pieces of tarp, Erroh tried to remember what had happened but the images flitted away like moments of brilliance in a wretched drunken stupor. He tried and failed to gather coherence. "Is everyone all right?"

He looked around wearily. It had been a fine private box only moments before, and now it was a fine mound of debris. Around him, the sound of moaning increased as those who'd crushed and those who'd been crushed woke to their shared horror. Somehow, Lea was beside him, her face ashen, her yellow dress ripped and ruined, her face a grimace of barely controlled fear. She was helping Elise, who clutched her chest with a shaking hand, and they shuffled upon unsteady feet.

"We are all right. Where is Lillium?" Lea gasped, frantically looking around. "She was here."

Erroh's head pulsed with jagged pain as he tried to remember what became of Lillium, and he felt blood dripping down his cheek. Before he could check the gash on his head, Magnus was beside him, pulling half-conscious spectators away from the suffocating mound of rubble. Ignoring the dizziness, Erroh bent to the task and helped. It was something to do; it was all he could do. His thoughts were disjointed, his footing careless; he wanted to sleep; he wanted to throw up. He wondered how long he had been unconscious. Dimly, he reckoned that it was long enough that people were no longer trampling over them, and though the terrified spectators kept coming, the numbers had lessened.

He pulled a weeping old man to his feet, who tentatively looked around in shaken disbelief before scrambling down towards the arena floor to join the rest of the injured. No better place to riot, with so many healers present, Erroh thought bitterly, watching a dozen healers tend to what injuries they could. A few were climbing the levels, tending to the handful of unconscious victims still lying where they had fallen.

Bit by bit his head cleared, and he realised just how fierce the surge had been. Though much of their box lay crushed around them, many of its wooden panels had been dragged downward and left flattened among the abandoned seats. He hated to think of anyone crushed beneath them.

"I think I cracked a fuken rib," cursed Elise, gasping heavily. Erroh could see the strain on his mother's determined face.

"We have to get you home," Lea muttered, looking around desperately, but Elise shook her head.

"Just get me down to the sand and I'll walk the rest myself. Where is Lillium? Where is Lexi?" She looked back up the slope to where the dead man had fallen, from where the screaming continued, from where Lexi had insisted she watch the bouts.

"We will find her," Magnus hissed. He turned to Lea. "Get Elise safely home."

Lea shook her head slowly. It was a rare thing for any person to defy a legend. She looked to Erroh. Though they needed each other, their family needed them more. "Please Lea, stay with Elise. Protect her," Erroh said softly, and she nodded acquiescence.

"Be safe," she growled back at him. She looped Elise's arm over her shoulder, taking the taller woman's weight fully upon her, and the two women began picking their way down towards the sand and safety beyond.

Nobody stopped them as they hopped over the butchered remains of the man. Not even the few Black Guards kneeling around the bloody corpse, staring in shock at the riot they'd brought about. Nobody even noticed them as they climbed over the remains of the box's wall. Within a terrible moment, Erroh discovered why.

"Where is Lexi?" demanded Magnus before falling silent at the sight of such horrors.

This was the end of the world. This was desolation in the frozen south a thousand times over. *Dead, dead, dead.* There would be no recovery from this. Somehow, Uden had gotten to her. Among an army of protectors, Dia had been struck down. There was nothing they could do.

The city will burn tonight.
The city will burn to the ground.

He'd felt this before, back in the dead town when the horrors had first emerged. Some females wailed; others stood silently, too shaken to move. Erroh's head spun in horror, in terror, in hopelessness. He looked to his father for comfort, but Magnus was as lost as he. Shaking, the old Ranger roared aloud as though he were a wolf in the wilderness. His voice was lost among the wretched sobbing of Dia's mourners. None howled more tragically than Roja, who sat by the deep pool of spilled crimson. She held the torn ruin of her grandmother in her arms, rocking back and forth. No Wolf or Alpha female dared reach for her; instead, they stood helpless and allowed her lamentations. Erroh stood with them, still scanning the group for Lexi's face. He wanted to cry out for her, but his breath had been taken from him as though he had been struck by an ambushing brute.

He did not know how long he stood beside Magnus, only that the sight of a pack of Black Guard battering Emir pulled him back to the wakened world. Emir was covered in blood, and a fierce anger overcame Erroh. He wanted to join in, to kill his wretched friend for having a hand in Dia's murder. For playing his part in dooming the world. He pushed Magnus aside, his hand a clenched fist. He looked at Roja again and marched upon the melee.

Not like this, something whispered in his mind, and he hesitated. Emir moaned pathetically and Erroh remembered the giant Quig protecting this wretch, for that is what best friends did.

"Stop this," he cried weakly, and they did not hear, nor would they have heeded him, for he held no power over them.

"Not here," he roared, jumping in between the four brutes and the battered man. A wild fist caught him in the face, dazzling him, but he did not retaliate. "The city will need justice." Another swinging fist struck him. This one stunned him, but he saw that his words had given them pause, and Erroh fell upon Emir, covering him from further assault. "Not like this!" It wasn't his finest plan, but it was all he could think of doing. Fists drove into his head as the Wolves roared their hatred anew.

"Mercy," he wailed, expecting none, and he dimly saw that Magnus also threw himself in between the Wolves and their prey. He, however, had authority.

"Enough of this, fools," he ordered, shoving them away. It was his first official order as unchallenged leader of the Black Guard. His words were cutting, and they pierced the Wolves' desire for vengeance.

Now Roja released her grandmother and rose slowly to her feet. She pointed accusingly at the semi-conscious healer, but before she could condemn him, Magnus embraced her as a father would a child; and, like a child, she screamed into his chest, hammering at his arms, and he allowed her.

"Was this your doing?" she wailed.

"No, little one," he whispered and stroked her hair.

"Did you kill her, like you killed my kin?" she howled, and he held her tighter.

"I'm so sorry for your loss, Roja."

Her strikes soon subsided to a desperate grip upon his shirt as she wept. He whispered in her ear and she whimpered in reply. Erroh heard the words "proud," and "strength." He thought he heard her moan, "I can't."

Beneath him, Emir coughed and rolled on his side, and Erroh left him where he lay. His face was a tortured mess of blood. His eyes were turning red where bruising was to appear. "I'm sorry for this," he croaked, trying and failing to sit up. Roughly, Erroh pulled him to a sitting position.

Oh, Emir.

"What did you do?" Erroh demanded, feeling his hand become a fist again.

One of Emir's assailants spoke for him, his words cold and condemning. "He vouched for the killer. Let the fuk stroll in and gut her. He's as much to blame."

Roja drew away from Magnus on hearing this. Her face was marred with her grandmother's blood; Erroh hadn't noticed it until this moment.

"Is this true?" demanded Magnus.

Oh, Emir.

Emir nodded his head slowly. He might have shrugged, but one of the Wolves became enraged again and lunged for him. Only the fiery glare of Magnus halted him in his place. That and his outreached hand. The Black Guard was older than most. A captain of the Wolves, no doubt. He stared at Magnus disdainfully. Swiping the Master General's hand away, he moved no further, but his glittering eyes betrayed his intention to commit a little retaliation.

"Who was the killer?" Magnus asked.

"A wretch from the hovels," the older Wolf spat, stepping away from both Emir and Magnus as though anger would get the better of him.

"Place Emir in chains," Magnus ordered.

"The city needs vengeance," countered Roja, her tone broken and unforgiving. As though her own heart had been torn apart. Perhaps in the melee, nobody had noticed that it had. She shook noticeably but no female came to help her.

"There will be vengeance if he played a malicious part," Magnus countered.

No Wolf attempted to place Emir in chains. Murdering a chained man might lead to questions. There were a few disgruntled mutterings, and Erroh suspected they desired a nice quiet act of retribution. Nothing nastier than a trial to blur the bloodlust.

"Now!"

As roughly as possible, they placed heavy manacles around the healer's wrists. They placed another around his neck, and he gasped for air. Roja watched on, her face grim at seeing him in such a pathetic state.

"The Rangers will guard him in the cells tonight," declared Magnus, eyeing the ill-disguised intent in the faces of his jailers. Erroh saw it too. Emir wouldn't last an hour in their care, never mind the entire night. There would be no trial. He was culpable, and so he would die.

Deservedly so.

"Where is my sister?" Erroh asked.

"She fled with Linn," Roja mumbled, pointing to a discreet hatch near the box's entrance. "Better she not see these horrors." She took a breath, then wavered and collapsed clumsily to the ground; finally, her Alphaline sisters emerged from their stupor and came to her aid.

"Take the prisoner," ordered Magnus to a couple of Black Guards. He grasped Erroh and whispered, "Go with them. Do not leave him alone for a solitary moment."

"What about Lexi?"

"She will be fine. Worry of other things." He looked away to the crowd below, to the devastation leading up to where they stood. "Protect Emir… We will need him in the war ahead."

With that, Magnus embraced Erroh and then turned and began ordering the few Black Guards into action. Erroh could see the concealed horror in his father's face; the old man could clearly sense something in the wind. Erroh could sense it too. This, all of it, had been one step too far.

Beyond the arena's walls, he could hear a deep rumbling roar as those now free of the gate continued to surge down through the city streets. Fear was a powerful, destructive thing. Anger and resentment were just as hazardous, especially when they were released.

"A good soul might turn to wicked ways while reeling with demons," muttered Magnus, looking to the crowds surging out.

"Perhaps things will settle, once they are free of the arena," Erroh offered.

"Aye, these terrified few thousand wretches, drunk with passion, with misery, with fuken fear, will stroll home this very hour without incident; without release," Magnus growled, his voice heavy with sarcasm. "What reason could they ever have to riot in these streets tonight?"

Erroh smiled grimly. "I will come find you after, Father."

"No, Erroh. Protect Emir tonight. Terrible events are afoot."

———

There were many tunnels hidden throughout the city to serve the Primary's needs. It was whispered she could travel to the four corners of Samara without detection. She would use these tunnels only once more, carried by her guardians. Better the citizens not see her broken form, anyway.

Rolling away the heavy stone hatch to reveal the dark tunnel and its steps, which had been cut into the arena itself, the three jailers stepped from the sultry heat into cooling darkness. Two Wolves led the clinking prisoner, and Erroh walked warily behind the trio. He carried no blade and wondered if this had been a foolish decision.

The steps were endless, illuminated by only a few lights above their heads. The roar of panicked footsteps, of cursing voices and of burgeoning rioters lessened, but even as far down as they went, there was a constant hum of noise above their heads. Only when they reached a level deep below the city did an unnatural silence fall upon them. Erroh could see his breath in the subtle light; it reminded him of the Cull.

"What is this place?" he whispered, and his voice echoed as though he were alone in a massive salt mine. A light above them flickered, and Erroh could see it wasn't a salt mine at all; it was a tunnel of white glass, and it went for miles.

"This is our chosen path," one Wolf muttered. His voice carried unnaturally in the vast, echoing stillness. "There are a few hidden tunnels beneath the streets of Samara. It is a way for us to move unseen between its parts."

"I didn't know of such things."

"Why would you know of such things? These are things only the Primary…" The Wolf hesitated in the dark and Erroh understood his pain.

Still, though.

"What else don't I know?"

"There's absolutely nothing else the citizens are unaware of in this city," the Wolf replied neutrally.

This was the type of competitor Erroh liked to face when playing cards. He didn't bother to ask any further questions. Bad liar that the Wolf was, there was a dangerous, traumatised stubbornness to him.

As though an absent god had spent an eternity hollowing with godly tools, the tunnel wall was a perfect, smooth half circle, leading from one side of the city to the other. A man could fit an impressive house within it, yet Erroh still felt claustrophobic walking through. It felt more like a tomb, and he could feel the cold grip of panic in his chest.

This is a place of the dead.

Their feet crunched loudly on the strangely loose rock surface, and as Erroh moved to the side of Emir, he tripped up on a long piece of rusted iron bolted into the ground. A few feet across from it lay its twin, and he realised they were the corroded rails of a track, running parallel into the distant darkness. Somehow, this made him feel even worse. This was an unknown, ancient thing. Suddenly, thoughts of marching through a rioting city were far more enticing than spending another moment down here.

"Does anyone have any water?" Emir asked, and Erroh shook the unease away. He'd never heard a voice so broken and lost. Well, once, from his own mouth. He'd been in chains, too.

The talkative guard turned and appeared as though he would strike Emir for making a request. "Shut up, murderer."

"I'm not a…" Emir whimpered, and though he didn't know why, Erroh reached out and squeezed his shoulder. Emir coughed in reply and continued marching.

Eventually they came upon a stone staircase, and the guards roughly marched their prisoner up to the top, where there was a little-used door. Erroh followed, and one of the Wolves opened the door to reveal a concealed entrance to the Samara jail cells.

"Where is everyone?" one of the Black Guards muttered, realising the jail was unmanned, desolate, abandoned.

Riots.

The jail itself was unimpressive. A few open cells, a few desks, chairs, and four sturdy walls. The main room held three open steel-barred cells. They were likely used for minor offences until sobriety returned. Further in, down a little corridor, there lay a small dark chamber containing a handful of dreary cells. He could smell the misery and waste within. They were disgusting and fit for no beast. The Wolves didn't care about such niceties, however; their only concern now was why no one stood guard, and why the doors were standing open.

They tramped back out to the main entrance.

"Lots of people running around out there," the less talkative guard observed, peering out into the streets. His hand was on his sword. "Stirring some brew of trouble."

"Best you leave the keys with me," Erroh said, grabbing Emir by the scruff of his neck and shoving him into one cell. They approved of this decision.

"Aye, we should be out there with our brethren," the talkative Wolf said, throwing the keys across. "We will check in a little later," he added, and Erroh didn't like that tone at all.

"A fine plan, friends," he replied.

Erroh allowed himself a sigh of relief watching the two Wolves march away. His relief was short-lived, however; the Wolves had taken no more than a few steps when a dozen thugs appeared from nowhere and ambushed them. It wasn't much of a fight. They thrashed the less talkative Wolf against a wall before sending him through a window in the building across the road. Erroh never learned the fate of the talkative Wolf, who was swiftly dragged down the street and out of view. He wanted to believe the piercing screams didn't belong to the unfortunate man, but he knew better. He almost leapt into the skirmish himself, but better judgement won out. Shutting the heavy iron door with a slam, he hurriedly locked the heavy bolts.

"We are in trouble," he said to Emir. "Wait here," he said, and then set off to search the small building for weaknesses—a short search, considering its use. *Good place to be in a riot.* The windows were barred, and the rear door was solidly bricked up. Only a battalion could break through. That said, an entire battalion might come running once they learned of Emir's whereabouts. Perhaps the Wolves getting battered wasn't the worst event to occur.

"We are in a fuk-load of trouble," Erroh added, wishing he'd asked the Wolves for a sword.

Emir didn't seem as concerned. Perhaps he understood his fate was already settled. Perhaps he wanted a little more comfort before the end. "Can I get some water, Erroh?" he whimpered, eyeing a jug just out of reach from where he sat. He looked as wretched as the day he'd led the convoy to Spark, and Erroh felt a wave of pity. He unlocked his manacles and let them clatter to the stone floor. Emir nodded in thanks but made no move to leave the cell, so Erroh poured some water into a little mug and passed it across.

"Are you okay?" he asked, and Emir shook his head.

425

"I'm pretty fuken far from okay." His voice was dangerously close to breaking. He took the water and drank deeply. After a moment he poured some over his hands, and diluted droplets of crimson fell to the ground below. The wretch was a good man. He also knew well the sin of pledging for an assassin.

"Tell me everything," Erroh whispered, "so we might save your wretched life."

40

THE LONG NIGHT

Elise gasped, and a few loose drops of crimson fell from her mouth. *Not good, never good. Still, though. Just a scratch.* Nothing more than a cracked rib or two, she imagined. She'd broken ribs before; this felt no worse. *Not really.* She leant against the arena wall where they'd climbed down and searched for her breath. Her body shuddered. Just the shock of horrors, she told herself. She'd seen terrible things like this before.

"Just breathe," she demanded of her body, but it defied her. She felt the coughing fit draw near and she fought it off with will alone. She formed a fist and hammered it once against the wall behind her. Just once; just enough to hurt, just enough to defy her body as it disobeyed her. "Just fuken breathe, you bitch."

Beneath her, the sand warmed her feet and absently she wondered at how fine a day it had been. *Perfect for unsightly horrors.* She gasped, she challenged, she struck and she found breath again, though her head spun a little. Looking into the crowd, she fought her growing terror: Lillium and Lexi. Where were they? Everywhere she looked she saw blood-covered faces, heard voices crying out, swearing, roaring, surrendering. She could feel the panic give way to anger and she recognised this dreadful turning. She feared for the hours ahead.

Lea had left her for only a few moments, and already Elise missed the young goddess's support. Best they move soon, she thought, but better they find Lillium first. She could see Lea dance through the crowd, searching for the missing girl. Her voice was cutting and demanding, and every healer who spoke with her shook their head and Lea moved on. They'd not found her unconscious on the way down, not found her bloodied and battered among the sandy ground, either. At least not yet. She wondered if the wave of people hadn't just carried her right through, out into the city streets.

She watched the still bodies of a dozen revellers lying where only warriors should have fallen. Out cold, she told herself. Thinking any different was dangerous. She'd seen the crush, and the horror, but she'd also seen the treacherous Wolves at their best. Earning a little redemption, what with the new master watching, no doubt. She wheezed again and a strange coldness gripped her body. They'd heard things upon their slow shuffle down through the lines of seats, and leaning here with panicked words reaching her from every direction, she now understood the full horror of what had happened. If Dia's slaying was certain, the world might end tonight. She thought on this; she thought of the anguish to come, and she thought of those she loved.

"Breathe and march, you decaying waif," she told herself through gritted teeth.

It was a terrible thing to feel this helpless. Ten years before, Elise would have stormed up with Magnus and learned what terrible events had occurred. As it was, she could barely raise her head to the late afternoon sun as a thousand bodies moved around her as one panicked mob.

Lea returned alone. "There is no sign of Lillium. I'm sure she's well though," she said, drawing Elise from her melancholy. "Aye, they all say someone slew the Primary," she added sadly, and Elise placed a weak hand on the girl's shoulder. She looked to the exits and the destruction left in the crowd's wake. "What shall we do?"

Elise bit her lip, spat some blood and, leaning on Lea, shuffled towards the gates, which were almost clear now. "Let's get away from these horrors." Though the panic had faded, every step was a struggle.

428

She'd never felt this old, this broken. Maybe this was more than a cracked rib after all. Perhaps it was some other hidden nastiness at work within this shattered body. Was this how death stole up on legends? she wondered. Taking them under the guise of a lesser affliction when they believed all was well. When their minds were on other things.

"When we return, I think I'd like to see Emir." Her voice sounded drunk, lost, and fear took hold in earnest now. That was what happened when minds wandered.

Lea gripped her tightly. "I will get you home, Elise. I will find the healer. You will be fine. I promise this." There was such unexpected strength in the female's voice that Elise felt a strange comfort. There was strength there, she thought she'd seen it before when they were out in the Wastes hunting, but this primal fierceness was different. With the world around them shattering, Lea was strong.

"Thank you, little one," she gasped.

As they emerged from the arena gate, both women noticed that the mood in the crowd had shifted ominously. Where earlier there had been a palpable sense of relief at having survived the catastrophe, now there were murmurings about retaliation. Retaliation for the fear they felt. Retaliation for the months of heartache they'd suffered crouching by the walls, locked in behind the gates; for the stringent rationing they'd had to endure. Spark City, the City of Light, had become a miserable prison, devoid of any hope or joy.

"What is happening?" Lea muttered. She hid her fear and held her nerve.

"Terrible things."

They were terrible. She knew the word *uprising* even though it was an ancient term, spoken by those who'd burned in the fires. Uprising, revolution, rioting. All different, all born from the same emotion—and the wretches of Spark City were emotional this evening. Gangs, drunk on anger, shock and alcohol, were surging through the city now, destroying as they went. Contagious fury had overcome them and stolen their senses and whatever exhausted goodness they'd kept within. The cacophony of glass shattering, wood breaking, and ceramic smashing filled the air. Fights broke out on every street, down every alley, around every corner. Stalls were shredded and looted, and with each grievous act committed, the rioters grew in confidence and in daring.

Lea knew her Primary was dead, and all she wanted was to curl up in a ball and lament the old female's passing. She'd been no admirer, had despised her outright occasionally, but Dia had been their leader, their mother; she had deserved better.

Soon she became aware that it wasn't just rioters who passed them on the path. Sometimes she heard the lamenting of those loyal to the city, and she wanted to join them. Instead of despairing, she gripped her weakening mother-in-law and endured the next step and the one after that, for Erroh had charged her to get Elise home. Now was no time to be a pitiful whippet. She could cry all fuken night in her mate's reassuring embrace. Until then, she would remain vigilant, resolute.

It wasn't far to the Rangers' camp, but their pace was agonizingly slow. They shuffled along, sticking close to the walls, as wretches, citizens and curs surged past them. As the shadows behind them grew longer and darker, each alley became precarious, and voices of anger and restlessness became something more sinister. As though the darkness allowed for greater sins.

It was the shrill cry of a man in the darkness ahead that stopped both females in their tracks. It was a simple, tragic scream, like that of a man knifed for a few shiny pieces. A scream that fell silent with a few wet strikes. Lumbering footsteps neared them, and from beneath an archway appeared a male who froze like a statue upon seeing them. He was dressed like a wretch from the hovels. His white shirt was stained, his dark hair long and unkempt. The rank odours of sweat, alcohol, and waste struck Lea's senses. The man opened his bearded mouth to speak but no words came. Perhaps he knew the rule of the city; perhaps he knew his place within it. However, he eyed both females as though he knew no such rules, and Lea felt a chill run through her.

He made no sudden move lest he scare away his prey, and Lea's hand became a fist. Beside her, Elise stood straighter. Her tired breath became settled and she ducked slightly, lest she need to pounce. Lea thought her a goddess: even when weak, she was ready to kill.

They never discovered his true intentions. As fresh screams erupted from somewhere behind them, he slipped by, licking his lips, his excited eyes already searching for new prey. Watching him disappear into the shadows, Lea suddenly pined for her mate. She missed the quiet with Erroh. The city was no longer hers to miss. Walking the road was a finer life.

"I fear the night to come," Elise whispered, removing herself from Lea's hold. "I can struggle along for now. Better you keep your wits about you and assure our safety."

"The city will be all right. Everything will be all right," Lea countered, and her lie felt hollow.

It was a strange thing to be fearful walking the streets she'd grown up in. It was as strange to see so few Black Guards patrolling them. It was the lack of lights flickering to life which unsettled her most. It was the darkest of night by the time they reached their march's end, and the last few steps towards the gates were the worst. She was certain a dozen filthy hands would come from nowhere and pull them into the eternal darkness. She'd take a few with her, she told herself, and tried not to think of lakeside assaults.

"Almost there," Elise hissed, stumbling against a wall and breathing what air she could. Even in the dim light, Lea could see how pale she had become, how much sweat covered her strained forehead. *Just tiredness, that's all.* They stepped through the open gates and Lea felt the first glimmer of hope stir. *Not far.* With the massive walls no longer shadowing their every step, and with barely enough light to see around them, Lea took hold of Elise once more; now, she met little resistance.

"No Wolves watching the gate," Elise noted, eyeing the abandoned posts. Looking down the hovels, she could see only a few stirrings of movement. Lea wondered how many hid in their little shacks with treasures in their grasp and blood on their hands before cursing her own prejudice. *Easy to blame the lowerlines after seeing one glaring brute.* Still, she monitored the encampment as they shuffled by and only relaxed when she heard the barking of hounds as they stepped through the gates onto familiar territory. A dozen Rangers were at camp, those bitter, unlucky few having drawn the shortest straws on the grandest of days. With her voice a rasping whisper, Elise ordered them to don their armour, light the torches and stand guard at the Ranger gates. The loyal hounds stood beside their masters with ears pointed towards the city gates, knowing there was a threat in the air.

"I will leave you to rest," Lea offered upon reaching Elise's tent. She knew her duty was to her mother-in-law, but the night would be long if she sat with her, awaiting Erroh's return. If she could spend it searching for him and finding him even a moment sooner, it was worth the danger. As long as she had a sword.

Elise's face was pained with the effort of breathing as she crawled into bed, but when Lea turned to leave, her eyes shot open in alarm.

"Don't you dare walk back out into the streets tonight." It was a mother's tone. It had to be. That's what Lea had always imagined her mother had sounded like. Though disappointed, she was also comforted, and she took Elise's hand. It was weak, and she worried it might snap if she squeezed too hard. The older woman lay back against the pillow. "I know you would seek the healer, and then after you would go rescue my cub. I know you are skilled with these matters. I don't doubt that at all." Despite herself, despite everything, Lea smiled. Elise did not. She looked at Lea with the same seriousness as Erroh, and Lea's smile faded. "Tonight, you sit this march out."

"I fear for Erroh, and you need the healer."

"I need my loved ones. I need you here with me."

Lea thought of Erroh's request, and she nodded reluctantly. "I will sit with you this night." Her words pleased Elise, who smiled weakly before wrapping the sheets around her fragile form. Once she was settled, she began to speak, her voice soft but steady.

"I know all too well of Erroh's story of marching south in chains, but I do not know your story of that journey. There must have been many terrible times. Tell me, little one, so I may know you better."

Lea sat down on the edge of the bed. As she did, Elise unscrewed a little jar of eucalyptus and immediately Lea felt her lungs open up. She also felt impossibly tired from the day. Elise rubbed a little of the ointment beneath her nose, and her wheezing subsided. Lea closed her eyes and steeled herself to tell her ghastly tale once again.

"I thought I'd known miseries before, but I think it was my perfume that finally broke me," Lea whispered, eying the one candle alight in the room. "It's probably what pulled me from true desolation as well…"

———

Erroh unlocked the front door swiftly to allow the cloaked figure in, slamming and locking it immediately after. As night drew in, the streets became abandoned, apart from the roving gangs. Though they were few, they were enough to cause havoc. They'd shown little interest in the jail, but the night was young. Keeping the candles hidden had been a smarter move on his part. Without the city lights, a little flickering flame was an open invitation to drunken bastards looking for wealth, looking for trouble, or just looking for a fight.

"It's good to see a friendly face," Erroh said quietly as he glanced warily out a window. The distant glow of a few fires from other sections was visible in the growing darkness. Enormous shadows moved along the city walls, like giant creeping gods coming to lay waste to the city, and again he cursed the rioters. At least the city's stone would stop the fires from spreading, he thought.

"Have you heard any word of Lea? Of Lillium? Of my sister?" he asked the figure.

Wynn shook his head slowly. "It's chaos outside." He was shaken. His hair hung down around his grubby face and his eyes were wild with fear. He took a knee and tried to catch his breath. Removing his cloak, he revealed his tournament armour and a solitary sword along his waist. "The fukers attacked the Wolves and Rangers first. Everyone else after that."

Lea.

"What is happening out there? Are people dying?" Emir called from his cage. His face was in his hands; the heaviness of the world upon his slumped shoulders. He asked a question, but he didn't appear to desire any answer. He looked ready to break, and though Erroh knew he needed reassurance, no words came. These horrors were his doing, be they accidental or not. Sometimes it was right to reassure those who were hurting, and sometimes people deserved to taste some guilt. "They have starved and lived in squalor for months; it's no fuken surprise," he said after a time.

Erroh ignored him. "There are plenty of Black Guards to counter this madness. Why aren't they out there calming the storm?" he asked Wynn, looking back into the darkness as though speaking their name might bring them forth.

Wynn stood up and began retying his ponytail, and within moments looked more himself, apart from the strange glint in his eyes. "The Wolves retreated to their tower. Well, all those that didn't get kicked to shit, anyway," he replied.

Never trust the Wolves.

"They are charged with defending the streets from such things."

"I'm hearing there were… payment issues." He shook his head in disgust. "Rangers are the only authority in the city tonight, and it's not even our fight. Moreover, they're scattered. Magnus has his hands full, so he ordered me here." He offered a smile, but his eyes focused on Emir sitting defencelessly in the middle of his cage. "To assist you in keeping the prisoner… safe. Clever taking refuge in their jail—no one will never think to look here." It was a jest, but his tone was cold. Erroh let it ride. In truth, before hearing Emir's side, Erroh had been hostile. Wynn was allowed to growl a little.

"Did you bring weapons?" Erroh asked.

"Just my own."

"Well, I'm sure you can handle a battalion alone while Emir and I hide out in the back."

Wynn laughed—and then, in one smooth movement, he skipped past Erroh, pocketed the key and stepped into Emir's cell, slamming the gate behind him. Emir didn't struggle as he leant down, grabbed him by the collar and slammed him up against the far side of the cage.

This will end bloodily. Erroh winced as the sudden crash rang loudly in the quiet room. *Like the rattle of chains.*

"Did you do it?" Wynn demanded, punching Emir across the chin. The cell echoed loudly with the crack. He lifted his fist to strike a second time but hesitated to allow an answer. Erroh could have replied, but silence took him. Emir shook his head in shame, awaiting the punch, and Erroh saw a tear rolling down his cheek.

Though it felt like an eternity, it was only the space of a solitary breath before Erroh found his voice.

"He had no part in this!" he shouted, reaching through the bars and taking hold of Wynn's collar. Wynn pulled himself free and struck the healer in the stomach; it was a half-hearted blow, but it sent him crumpling to the floor, where he lay broken. Defeated.

"Ah, leave it out, Wynn," Erroh pleaded. Wynn stared at his victim for a moment, then, with a sniff of disgust, he strode over and unlocked the gate. That done, he returned and crouched down beside Emir, his anger seemingly gone as quickly as it had come.

He offered a hand and pulled the healer to his unsteady feet.

"Come on. I thought you Keri wretches could take a few punches."

"I'm not the one bleeding all over the floor," Emir countered, staring at the split knuckle on Wynn's punching hand.

Wynn held it in the candlelight and gave a rueful smile. "Thick Keri skin," he muttered, though not unkindly. Emir had refused to fight back; there was no sport in surrender. Wynn might well have continued attacking had he met resistance.

Emir's face was devoid of colour, apart from the fresh welt on his chin and the blossoming marks from his earlier assault. He dabbed at his chin absently and Erroh saw the weight upon his shoulders. It was a strange thing to carry a death sentence. They all knew his fate. It just wasn't official yet.

"I have ruined the world," Emir said.

"No, Emir, it was Cass who ruined everything. He is the one who has shamed the name of Keri. Don't wallow; be furious."

"He and his brethren have every reason to despise this city and the Primary. Has she not spoken of his kind's wicked ways throughout the years?" Emir pointed out, and Erroh suddenly understood Cass and his frustrations a great deal more. How had he not seen it before?

"Did he favour the company of males?"

"Aye, he hardly hid his desires."

Wynn spat on the ground. "So he favoured a male lover? What matter is it? It's a fuken decade since they punished anyone for these acts of desire. It's only frowned upon nowadays. Another decade and people might even rejoice in it. Do you really think this Cass slew the Primary because of her archaic beliefs?"

"I don't know why he slew her. I didn't ask him," Emir snapped.

"Well, killing her won't do his kind any favours."

Emir looked at the wall. "'His kind,'" he muttered, shaking his head.

"Yes, Emir, his kind. Those who can't reproduce. You aren't an Alpha; you'd never understand our duty."

"Of course I wouldn't. When all you are told is to get angry, get swinging, get a fine mate, it's easier to live inside black or white."

And make stronger children.

Both of them were on their feet, and Emir now appeared willing to fight back. It was a better look to him. Still, though, Wynn wasn't the enemy.

"Friends, be still." Erroh stepped between them before they raised fists. Emir fought the right fight for the wrong reason at the really fuken wrong time, while Wynn argued practicality over compassion. No one would come out of this shining. "Regardless of reasons, he took her life. The city is rioting, Emir is fuked, and we have no idea what to do."

It was a fine speech and both parties nodded. Tensions were strained during the longest night at the end of the world.

"I'm sorry I made your knuckles bleed."

"I'm sorry you are so fuked."

"And I'm sorry the two of you are the closest thing I have to friends," Erroh mocked, and Wynn laughed. After a moment, Emir sniggered too.

"No better company for tonight," Emir said after a time, and finally left his cell to sit down with his comrades. "I am to die come the morning. In the meantime, does anyone have cards?"

———

The sounds of footsteps ruined their game before it really began. The unmistakable thunder of regimented marching drew nearer until it came to a halt outside the jail.

Magnus?

Rangers?

"Sounds like the Black Guard have marched tonight after all," Wynn said, sidling up below the window. Torches shone some light in, and Erroh slid up against the far wall.

The Wolves are at the door.

Oh fuk, oh fuk, oh fuk.

If they began charging through, there was always the hidden tunnel to retreat down into. As long as no Wolves awaited them once they unlocked it, he thought. Regardless, Erroh didn't fancy that march just yet, and he really didn't like the sound of becoming an outcast from the city over the minor issue of helping a prisoner escape.

"Kill the candles," he whispered.

There were voices, muttered curses and the clinking of weapons against armour until silence fell among the group outside. Erroh looked to Wynn, who was counting under his breath. They numbered many. *Like facing down an entire army.* Erroh's fingers twitched. He longed for the sword at Wynn's waist, but to snatch it, even out of necessity, was a crime not worth being killed over. Besides, blood hadn't been threatened just yet, and Wynn still believed himself the better swordsman.

There came a heavy knocking at the door. Wynn ducked down. "Don't answer it," he hissed, and Erroh shook his head. He almost grinned. What type of idiot would answer to a battalion come calling? Oh no, they were sitting tight behind the steel and stone this night.

"How many?" Erroh mouthed, looking around the dreary room for any weapon. He'd searched a thousand times before, but now, faced with genuine threat, he saw potential in everything. A broken chair leg? A ceramic water jug? The rest of the chair? A hanging pipe caught his attention: long, thin and likely to have weight to it. He'd once bettered a thug with a poker; another time, he'd felled an attacker with a heavy boot full of stones. That was some tale. He'd like that boot right now. What he had was a pipe. He would have been happier with two pipes, but it was a small matter. He leapt for it.

Wynn continued counting. Better than answering the door. "At least three dozen," he said under his breath. "All loyal to Dia, no doubt. Those willing to risk coming out tonight just to do a little murder... Erroh... why are you hanging from the ceiling?"

"I found a pipe." There was a loud screech of metal, followed by a low thud of an Alpha dropping to the floor, and the sound of someone hammering the door again.

"Well, they seem to know we're here," said Wynn.

"Sorry."

"Open the door, friends," a voice from outside called. It didn't sound friendly at all. Suddenly a brick came through the window. *Definitely not friendly.* It crashed against the far wall and the room filled with loud cheering from the mob outside. They cursed, challenged and chanted for the warriors to come out to play.

"Windows break easily enough; steel bars less so," Erroh countered. Reassuring words that meant little to trapped rats.

"Now what?" Emir asked.

"I suppose we should stay away from the windows for a while," Wynn said blandly.

"Sounds like a simple plan."

Lillium opened her eyes and saw little more than darkness. She lay on her stomach with a heavy load pinning her down. She struggled to move, to shrug away her blindness, to discover how badly she was hurt, but all she could do was throw up, and the heaving delivered thunderbolts of pain through her body. She turned from the mess she'd made and felt fresh searing pain in her elbow. Blinking rapidly, she could see a blurry image and focused on it until her vision returned. Part of her wished it hadn't. It was dark; she was alone, and her elbow was twisted unnaturally to the right.

What happened?

Where is Wynn?

Where am I?

She called out for help but could only manage a dry, broken croak. It took her breath, and she fought the urge to fall unconscious once more. It was an overrated skill staying awake. She could see that now as it called her back to its reassuring clutch. The bitter stench of warm bile kept her conscious and she shifted again. Instead of her elbow, she now felt a different agony through her leg. Reaching down, she could feel where a burning steel shard had gone through and held firm. There were finer ways to wake up. She imagined the pain of a broken finger and stifled the scream forming in her throat as she leaned on her dislocated elbow. With a heavy crunch, she eased it back in. She allowed herself a dry moan before weeping and surrendering to despair.

"Get yourself together," she hissed after a painful few moments. She couldn't remember anything beyond a rush of people, her seat collapsing and being thrown through the air. Nothing but blackness after that. "To the fires with it," she whispered into the darkness, and pushed herself free of what pinned her down.

The large, thin panel of wood slid free of her as she rose, then kept going like a sledge upon a snowy mount. She watched it gather momentum as it glided down level after level until it came to a crashing stop at the wall separating the seating from the sand. She looked to the shattered moon above and the countless stars and felt alone.

"They left me here…"

She felt panic. Deep, sorrowful panic at the thought of lying here alone for so long with no one coming for her. *Erroh? Wynn? Lea?*

She tried desperately to recall anything more beyond the pain, but nothing came. Sitting awkwardly a few levels below the ruined box, she realised the wooden panel had likely saved her life from the rampaging crowd. It had hidden her, too.

They didn't look for me.

The arena was deathly silent, and she felt the breeze in her ruined hair. Distantly, she heard screams and thoughts of a southern siege filled her with dread. She'd recalled the sun and the crowd. Now there was darkness and solitude. She'd never seen the city as dark as this, and she sat up straighter as though intending to run. To run from this lonely place, to seek those she needed most. Those who could save her. *Would* save her.

"Hello?" she shouted, and her voice echoed miserably. *Alone, alone, fuken alone.*

She pulled her wounded leg close and her body howled in reply. The pain passed and she took a few deep breaths. Sitting up was better. Leaning against an abandoned seat, she unfastened one button of her Ranger's coat and carefully propped her injured arm in the V it made. *Better.* It wasn't the finest sling, but enough to get her home.

Reaching gingerly into her coat, careful not to jostle her arm, she tore off a strip of her undershirt and used it as a tourniquet on her leg.

Her injuries thus seen to, she got to work freeing herself from the remains of the viewing box, cursing the carpenter who had insisted such long nails be used in its construction. Gritting her teeth, she began pulling the long metal piece free, using her good hand. It was an arduous, painstaking process; she moaned every time the terrible, burning pain shot through her body, and more than once she cried aloud. Finally, she pulled it free, and with a cry of triumph she flung the offending nail down the steps.

Then, testing the tourniquet one last time and holding her elbow carefully, she climbed to unsteady feet and steeled herself for the long walk home.

41

I AM ALPHA

I am Alpha. The three most powerfully spoken words in the world. Even at its end. Words all young females were taught before walking the streets of Samara for the very first time. Lillium remembered emerging from their tower in a neat little line of Alpha sisters. A dozen at a time, they were shepherded through the city in their finest little silken gowns. For all the world to see, to recognise; to avoid. She remembered her older sister watching over them, walking with them along the cobbled streets. A beautiful guardian whose very presence caused the bustling crowds to separate as she stepped. As they stepped after her. Lillium also remembered Lea, only a few sisters ahead, marching this march as well, her unblinking eyes full of fearlessness and anger. Back before the city had gotten its claws into her nerve.

I am Alpha.

She remembered muttering those powerful words under her breath as though in prayer to the absent gods. She had feared being left behind as they marched through the bustling marketplaces, the tight shadowed alleys, to the city gates and back. She wasn't alone in whispering those words, for they all knew that should any of them stray, their lineage guaranteed them a safe return. Why? Because Dia made it so. The

Primary's law was as permanent and as definite as the surrounding walls. Any Alpha female hurt under her watch? Well, they'd all heard the stories.

I am Alpha.

Those three words guaranteed protection in the city and as far out into the Wastes as the Wolves' claws could reach. Those words guaranteed that the full might of vengeance would fall down on any brute who dared lay a hand on them, and Spark City's threat was recognised, respected, obeyed.

I am Alpha.

Aye, Lillium was a Ranger, but she was still an Alphaline. She limped through the unlit corridor and out into the madness and felt safe despite the signs of violence. The streets were blood-soaked now, tattooed in the shapes and hues of death. It would take a storm to wash it all away, or else a fire so fierce the stone itself would melt. The screams in the darkness shook her to her soul. They came from unlit walkways, winding alleys, places out of sight. The desperate words were the worst. People begged for help; they begged for mercy; they begged for anything at all, and she could not help.

Blood seeped from her bandaged leg, dribbled into the many pools she shuffled past. Perhaps pulling the nail free had been a mistake. Perhaps it was one mistake too many. "I am Alpha," she muttered, as though a prince in black would appear at her summons and whisk her back to the tower and safety and warmth and happiness and hope. She shook her head and tried to block out the screams. No Wolf would save her this night. No heroic mate, either. She would do it herself. She slipped quietly through the dark, claustrophobic streets. She didn't fear attack, but she feared both what her eyes had already seen and what dreadful, unknown vision waited around the next bend.

———

Perhaps, had the Black Guard attempted to take the jail, they could have stormed it with a ram, but they made no attempt. Instead, choosing threats and jeering over actual advancement, they swung their torches in the air, never once attempting to burn those who waited within. The moments became hours, and they howled like the Wolves they were. Frustrated, yet never enough to chase blood. As the city fell, those most loyal to the Primary gathered and waited for her killer. Desperate for vengeance, desperate for wretched healer flesh. Unsure of what to do beyond drink and share countless bottles of sine, they waited for orders from whoever led them now, whoever had a voice loud enough to shout orders. Whoever had the will to calm their bloodthirstiness.

Long after midnight, a tall figure emerged from the night. Behind him scampered a hooded wretch. Covered in blood and reeking of guilt, the figure saw the gathering of Wolves and instead of fleeing back into the night, he marched right on towards them. He wore no armour, he served no banner and he carried no blade. It was a small matter. His presence sent rioters fleeing; his furious strikes were more than enough to put down any defiant fool up to no good.

And his guilt was deep enough to keep him out in the city this night.

————

"I can't see what's happening," muttered Erroh from his seat below the broken window. He could see the crowd stir as someone approached them. *Father?* His eyes stung from peering into the dim light and his body ached from disaster at the arena. He'd expected a fight, or a lynching; instead, despite their bravado, the Wolves had done little more than hammer the door and cover the jail floor in glass these past few hours. It was something to do, he supposed. He could see the decorations on some of their armour. These were no fresh idealistic recruits or desperate wretches earning a little crust of bread; no, these were the Wolves who believed in their master, alive or dead. So they had come by for a little murdering. They had no better plan.

Emir climbed up beside him to look out. The swelling in his face was darkening; each eye was merely a thin slit now. "I think it's a male," he said of the tall figure. "Perhaps two."

Taller than Magnus.

The tall man offered a bottle into the crowd of Wolves, and a grateful hand took it. Swiftly after, Erroh heard laughter. The tall man's bearded features caught the light of a flickering torch, and with a start, Erroh realised he knew that face.

"It's Wrek," cried Emir excitedly. "Dealing with another mob."

"Are you sure about that, healer?" Wynn said, sidling up to look out. If any of the Wolves looked back at them now, they would have had a clear shot at three gawping idiots staring out, asking for trouble.

"He's a friend," countered Emir.

"So was Cass. Friendship is overrated," retorted Wynn flippantly.

The tall man's words carried in the night air; they were imposing and assured. He spoke like a leader.

After a time, the crowd stepped away from the jail, but did not leave. Wrek and his hooded companion marched towards the door. The smaller man hid his hand beneath a rough wrapping of bandaging. Wynn looked to Erroh anxiously as they approached. *Friend or foe?* Opening the door was asking for trouble. Erroh shrugged. It was a fine answer.

Wrek didn't knock; he didn't have to. His voice boomed out like thunder.

"Open the fuken door."

Erroh shrugged again.

"I'll not ask a second time," Wrek warned, and looked back at the waiting Black Guard. He held his hands aloft, showing his lack of weapons.

"It's on my head," Emir said, and before Erroh or Wynn could stop him, he stepped away from the window and unbolted the door. At once he was knocked back as Wrek stormed through, Stefan close on his heels.

"Is this the only way in?" Wrek growled, slamming the door closed and bolting it again swiftly. Ignoring Emir on the ground, he moved hurriedly around the room, searching for weakness.

"Only a small passage, locked from this side," Erroh offered, wary of Wrek's intentions now that a steel door no longer stood between them. He was bigger, but Erroh could take him. He had his fine pipe. Even if the grip was worn, the balance a little off.

With a lifetime of experience behind him, Wrek read the mood in the room. He eyed the pipe and Wynn's drawn blade. "I came for my friend," he offered, looking at the glass on the floor and then at the Black Guards out in the night beyond. "It looks like he'll need all the help he can get."

If it was a Wolf ruse, it wasn't a strong one. Erroh did not drop his pipe; he merely rested it on his shoulder and watched as Wrek pulled Emir to his feet. Stefan stood away, still clutching his hand where Doran had ruined him.

"Who did this to you?" growled Stefan, peering at the three of them in turn.

Keep eyeing me, friend.

"It was nothing. A little retribution from the Wolves is all. I've had worse during most Puks."

Wynn shuffled his feet. "I might have been rough," he muttered, and Stefan faced him fully now. His eyes were cold as he dropped his injured hand and formed a fist with the other. Erroh thought this strange. Time heals all, Elise used to say. *Not heavy lung, though.*

Ever the ambassador of peace, Emir laughed. "You call that rough? I call it a good night at the Sickle."

Wynn shrugged. "I don't know what that means." He dared a weak grin. "Does it mean there are no further grudges?"

Emir offered a hand. "It means the next time you take a swing, I'll swing back."

"I'm glad you have been making friends and all, Emir, but there are a few dozen brutes out there, just desperate to hang you from the gallows," Wrek said sharply.

Wynn sat up by the window again and looked out. "Why did they let you waltz on in without question?"

Wrek smiled. "I promised I'd talk you into seeing sense."

"And they agreed?"

Wrek looked around the room once more. His eyes suggested approval of their defences. "Gut feeling. They want bloody justice, but

I'm not sure they want it tonight. Stringing up Roja's beloved in the middle of a riot might not earn them acclaim."

"Friends in prominent places," quipped Erroh. But Wrek's words made sense; the Wolves would sit waiting this night outside a cage full of prey, unwilling to dig their claws in or to slink away. Waiting for dawn, waiting for the shock to wear off. Erroh knew the feeling; he, too, had waited for prey in his time. Still, he wasn't opening the door again until the Rangers were knocking.

"How long do we have?" Wynn asked.

"I promised them a few dozen bottles of sine for their trouble. Especially if it took all night." He shrugged. It was a convenient solution; Erroh had learned never to trust convenient.

"You look ruined, my friend," Stefan muttered, looking beyond Emir's bruising to his clothing.

Wrek agreed. "Aye, too much dried blood. He must be presentable for the trial come dawn."

"That is sooner than I would have liked," Emir said in dismay. Nonetheless, he sat down in front of Stefan and rolled up the man's sleeve. "Show me," he said.

"No, best get it done sooner," Wynn offered, in a fruitless attempt at reassurance. Riots or not, the city would demand retribution. And dragging the torn remains of the assassin in front of a crowd wouldn't sate their blood-lust. They needed to see the body twitch its last, needed to hear the gasps.

"Not even a last meal," murmured Emir, examining Stefan's destroyed fingers.

"Not going to be elite, am I?" Stefan mocked through gritted teeth. Erroh could see the pain on his face, but he held it in. A fine test of will.

"You'd best get good with the other hand."

"It'll take a year with some fine sparring," Erroh suggested, grimacing as Emir popped a finger into place. Groaning, Stefan spat on the ground. Tears fell from his eyes as a second was manoeuvred painfully into a more recognisable position.

"I'll not live that long," countered Stefan, grimacing as Emir rooted in his healer's bag. "Just do what you can with it," he said, biting down on a leather strap as Emir went to task repairing unfixable things with thin wooden splints.

Erroh watched Emir work and thought of the drunkard attending to Lea in better terrible times. Even with death hours away, the condemned man still helped those in need of healing. In between the loud cracking and the gentle wrapping of bandages, they attempted distracting conversation, but their words were heavy and disheartened.

Finally, Stefan spat out the leather strap and silenced them with perfect words. "You can't save everyone, Emir, but the fact that you try makes you a hero. I'm sorry Cass betrayed your trust. I'm sorry you face this nightmare. I pledge this to you, brother: you will not face this alone."

Erroh couldn't believe this was the same pompous coward who'd skulked away on that sunny morning in Keri a lifetime ago.

Hearing this, Emir looked down at the floor. "Now that I see the end, I don't want to die."

————

Lillium's hair drooped down across her face as she shuffled through the darkness. Sweaty, tangled, bloody strands obscured her vision even more in this eerie gloom, and every time she whipped her head back, she thought about cutting them all away. She would settle for a brush and hair tie, for now. She needed a change; she needed a new outlook; she needed a fuken rest.

She had opted for caution over haste. Her eyes watching for shadows, her ears listening for threat, she made her way slowly along. She knew her bloodline assured her safety, but she wasn't foolish enough to believe there was no risk to her, moving injured and alone through gloomy streets. As darkness drew in, the savage roar of violence no longer rang in her ears, but still, now and then, she was reminded of the terrors of this dreadful night. The route she took was darker than most; long, twisting paths, away from the shuffling of unseen feet. Tight walkways where no right-minded wretch would dare to venture. She knew the lesser-used paths, had known them since she was a child, slipping out with Lea in tow. *Rioting all ladylike.*

Though injured and hobbled, she was still carefully graceful. Her wounds hurt with every step, but she was unwavering. She couldn't remember when she'd stopped hoping Wynn would come find her, or any others, for that matter. Instead, she remembered her teachings; after a time, she remembered her strength, too. It had faded while she'd waited for love; it had vanished when she'd found love, but in the dark, in agony, she found herself again. She'd always been angry. Anger was a gift.

Avoiding any fires, she stuck to the dark and embraced its concealment. She whispered a silent prayer for all she came upon. Those who had died in fear, blood and pain. She prayed to the absent gods to end this wretched night and deliver the dawn.

She should have prayed for herself, but she did not.

She didn't know how long she shuffled, only that, in the second hour, her dressing had opened up leaving a thin trail of crimson seeping out behind her. She wasn't bleeding to death, but it felt as though she were. She stepped away from the path and rested against a splintered doorway. Squinting into the pitch black of the abandoned building, she convinced herself no beast lay in silent ambush within. Though her elbow was weak and painful, the sling had gifted her enough relief that she could stretch it out somewhat. More importantly, she could now work the dressing on her leg with two firm grips.

"No problem," she muttered to the wind, pulling the bandage back over the seeping gash and slowing the flow. "Miles to walk."

Without warning, without a sound, someone slipped up behind her and took hold of her neck. She knew it was a male touch from the hairs upon his powerful hands. From his bitter stench, too. He squeezed her throat, then clutched her hair in his other fist and pulled her through the doorway into darkness. Her leg exploded in maddening pain as he dragged her across the room. She could hear his eager grunting and she staggered beneath his forceful grip.

He does not know his prey.

He does not know my lineage.

448

He has no right to handle me as he does.

Dragged across the dark little room, she felt furniture knocked aside and her anger rose. She was no fool; she knew his intention, knew the consequences for his sin already. She fought his powerful grip and he clutched her hair more tightly, pulling her head back. Then, releasing her hair for just a moment, he struck her once in the stomach, hard enough to take a pugilist's breath, and she gasped. He spun her to face him as though she were a plaything, then clutched her throat again. She could not see his face in the darkness, and he could not see hers, but this wasn't about sexual desire, anyway.

This was a show of dominance, of cruelty, and it was repugnant; it was everything wrong in the fuken world. His face came near as he grunted again in her ear, delighted with his treasure. His face was bearded, but he was no man. Not anymore. He had relinquished his right to be called a man the moment he'd fallen upon her. He loosened his grip and made a move to lick her, and beautiful air streamed into her lungs.

"I am Alpha," she wheezed. Her warning. Her plea.

"I do not care, whore," he growled, and struck her a second time back against the wall.

"I am Alpha," she roared, fiercer now. He would understand. His hand fell upon her again, gripping her throat, attempting to squeeze the life from her, and a coldness ran through her. He would kill her after he had his way, for he was a beast of nightmares.

"Don't do this," she moaned, and he held her upright. Her anguish fuelled his desire to destroy, and she reviled him more.

"Shush, little girl." He released her and she spun on her good leg. A fresh pain, fiercer than his assault, shook her and she stumbled. She tried. Oh, but she tried to avoid this bloodshed. He fell upon her and her elbow popped again, and the tears stung her eyes. He looked out through the doorway for any sign of a guard or unwanted citizen, and she saw his cruel eyes glimmer in the night.

They were all alone.

Again.

"I am Alpha," she whispered, as tears streamed down her cheeks.

This was not how the world should be. His hand reached beneath her coat, searching for her flesh. "I am Alpha," she warned again, though she knew the futility of her words.

At last, she could take no more, but she knew that once she began, she would never stop. "I don't want to do this," she begged, taking hold of his wrist as his clawing fingers ripped her torn vest wider. "I DON'T WANT TO DO THIS!"

It was a plea for mercy.

It was also a warning, unworthy of such a brute.

She had warned him.

I am Alpha.

Those words had meant more when she had come of age.

She twisted his wrist now, and he froze. She twisted it further and his hold broke. He reached up to stop her with his other hand, but it was far too late. She didn't hear the wrist snap, but she felt it. He squealed like a swine at market.

"Fuken bitch!" he roared, falling away from his prey and grasping his wrist. Stumbling, he turned for the doorway, but she was already on her feet. Already hunting him. Her kick was as swift and silent as his first assault had been, and it separated the cartilage behind his knee. He screamed again and she stepped over his fallen body and, without hesitation, stamped down on his ankle, feeling the satisfying crunch as it popped in upon itself.

"Am I your first?" she growled, as a coldness came upon her. There was no answer he could give to ease her hatred or soothe her lust for retribution, so his cursed reply meant little. He was no longer a man, no longer worthy of her restraint. He began crawling, and she took a moment to enjoy his misery.

"You deserve to die," she declared. Using his one good arm to carry his impressive mass, he resembled a dying snake, slithering away from its toying vanquisher. When he was halfway to the door, she dropped down, ignoring the distant ache in her leg, and sat upon his back. He cursed her again, so she grabbed his head and smashed it once against the stone floor. Not enough to concuss or kill, but enough to knock his fuken teeth out.

He deserves this.

She slammed his head down a second time and his nose split. She could kill him, she thought. No one would know; no one would care. But taking life was no small matter. She had donned her Ranger uniform believing her first kill would be justified, would be honourable, would be earned. But this felt like murder. Even for a vile piece of shit like this. Besides, his crime had already condemned him. Regardless of whether she was Alphaline or not, he would die this day. All she had to do was wait until her comrades found her come dawn. Soon after, he would swing from a Ranger's chosen tree and fine justice would be meted out.

He wept openly now, feeling with his one working hand the gaping ruin of his face, and she revelled in his pathetic sobbing.

"Do you think if you reach the doorway, you might slip from my grasp?" she hissed, and he kept slithering forward. A ruin of a beast desperate to escape. He left a smear of crimson upon the floor where his nose and mouth bled all over it, and she almost found mercy in his agony until, with rasping, slurred words, he assured his own fate.

"I'm glad your queen bitch is dead."

This held her in her tracks. *What?*

"Who died?" she demanded, as he slipped out through the doorway. He rolled forward a little and she screamed a second time. "Who is dead?" Her body shook with adrenalin, pain and sudden fear.

"Your Primary, whore. Struck down like a beast," he howled back with his ruined mouth. He began laughing, knowing the horror he inflicted, as she fell to her knees and broke apart like bone driven down upon unforgiving stone. She shook her head in the darkness as he slid away from her, his pathetic scraping growing quieter with every breath she sobbed out.

He would recover.

Will I?

The world spun, and she felt herself rise as though some absent creature from another realm took hold of her limbs and did what she desired. And oh, she desired retribution. Those phantom limbs brought her to the doorway and returned control to her, and she was grateful, for how else could she make something right again in this world? He wasn't far from the doorway. Pulling him back into the darkness took little effort. Turning him over, she straddled his chest and set about making him pay for his sins. Her screams were almost as loud as his as she struck down fiercely, repeatedly, upon his face until he stopped trying to stop her; until his screams became wet moans; until they fell silent altogether; until he went still; until her throbbing fists broke through bone and into the wet softness beneath.

Eventually, when her broken body could show him no more justice, she rolled aside and lay among the debris of the little room. She wept loudly for the city, for herself, for what had become of her life. At last, spent, she rolled up in a ball beside her fallen attacker and prayed to the absent gods for dawn.

42

DAWN

E rroh watched the figures sparring from his perch by the side of
the window. A cool breeze blew through, the same breeze that
carried rain. He hoped rain might discourage the Wolves from their
vigil. They still waited in muted dissatisfaction as dawn approached.
They waited for Wrek, no doubt. Their eyes returned to the jail every
time the loud clanging of metal rang out in the early morning air.

"There's no point. He's fuken useless," Erroh muttered, looking
back at the combatants standing apart in the middle of the room. A
strange arena, but an arena.

"I am not."

"Ah, you really are."

Wrek held the pipe in sweaty hands as though it were a trusty
blade. "Whether he's useless or not, he needs to do something." He
charged once more, and Emir clumsily defended with Wynn's blade.
Again, the loud crack of mismatched weapons filled the room and
beyond.

Wynn also watched, as much to see their collective attempt at
training a doomed man as to monitor the fate of his sword as it cracked
loudly against a sturdy piece of pipe. A lesser man might not have
allowed his sword to be used so carelessly. "I think letting the wretch

sleep might be a finer way to prepare," he said, in an attempt to get his sword back while it still had some sharpness.

"They'll convict me; they'll sentence me. Better I have a chance at the end," countered Emir. "If I'm to die this day, I'd rather not sleep the last few hours away." His grimy forehead was sweaty, his shoulders were slumped and his feet barely moved. The hours of careful sparring had taken their toll. "I'm desperate at this point."

He took his inevitable slaying better than most. Not once had he begged them to allow him to slip back through the dark tunnel and search for escape there. He was smaller than most, but Erroh saw a giant.

"Staying awake in combat is a good first lesson. Second rule, protect your belly," Erroh offered, and Emir gave him a puzzled glance before taking his turn to charge.

Within a few haphazard strikes, Wrek had knocked the sword to the ground. Emir recovered it with quivering hands, taking only a moment to catch his breath. He was trying. Everyone in the room knew he was trying, but he was failing miserably. They had tried too. The first few suggestions were beneficial. Hold yourself at more of a standing angle; watch the opponent and not yourself; don't punch your way out. They were the basics; his opponent would be superior. *Alphaline.* No miracle would stop a sword being thrust through his gut, and they would thrust into his gut first. An injury like that would take longer to drain. *Cause more pain, too.*

They'd spoken of his charges, hoping to find any adequate counter-argument, but this was no room of legislators. The law was definite. He'd pledged for Cass; the blame was on his sweaty, shaking hands. Erroh wondered if Roja might sway the vote, but dared not say it aloud. She had the ability to rescue him; pardon him, even. Such a move would have dreadful repercussions, however. He'd heard kings were hanged for less.

"Ugh, let's just keep going," Emir said, spinning the sword in his hands and nearly decapitating himself in the process. Without trying, Wrek continued to disarm Emir until eventually, Stefan halted the sparring. Stepping between both fighters, he took the sword from Emir.

"It would take a year of this to get anywhere. Best you drop your weapon, Emir. I've got this, brother. Should they condemn you, I will fight for you." His words were heavy and filled with steel. Fine words.

Distantly, Erroh heard a murmur of voices, and he caught sight of the Wolves suddenly becoming alert. Above their heads, rays of burning amber and ocean blue filled the sky. Dawn was breaking, and the Wolves were stirring to action.

"I'm honoured, but you can't fight for me," Emir countered, reaching weakly for the sword with heavy arms. "I will not cause another person's death. There has been enough bloodshed."

Stefan was unyielding. "You are more important alive than I could ever be. You can still do marvellous things."

"According to Magnus, some wonderfully ghastly things too," muttered Wynn, shrugging.

Stefan gripped Emir's shoulder with his good hand. A pathetic, noble sight. The road had taught him the value of life and honour. He might not cower from this pledge, either.

"And when you die in the arena, they'll kill me anyway," said the healer. "I will not doom a friend to death just to save my skin."

Erroh dropped from his window ledge, strode over to Stefan, took hold of his injured hand and squeezed. The man yelped and fell beneath his grip, and Erroh stood back. Lesson learned through pain. Magnus would have approved.

"All apologies," he said, helping Stefan to his feet.

"Fuken Alphalines. Want to squeeze my hand as well?" Wrek asked, stepping close, pointing the pipe at Erroh's forehead, and it felt very familiar. Erroh could see the muscles on Wrek's powerful arms twitch with every word he spoke. The giant's adrenalin was pumping and he looked ready for war. *Excellent.*

"Making a point was all, friend. No meagre words would stop Stefan from pledging for Emir." Erroh held his hands up, smiling his best "don't pummel me," smile. He had no pipe; it might be a fair fight. Wrek was unmoved until Erroh looked to Stefan. "We aren't friends, but we aren't enemies either."

"It's a start," agreed Stefan, pushing Wrek's hand down.

"Erroh is right about Stefan's injury. Truth is, I pledged for you, Emir. So, it's my right to defend your honour," Wrek said.

"You can't," replied Emir. "I can't watch another friend go into battle without me. I cannot be left behind again."

Erroh knew he spoke of Keri, knew well the guilt he felt at surviving Aireys and Quig and the many others. Still, he was meant for greater things, like giving life, not taking life; not like the warriors standing around him. Distantly, Erroh heard the rumble of marching, and he feared the Wolves were gathering their pack for a dawn raid.

———

With a hundred gathered Rangers in tow, Magnus was the threat in the city this night. He wore a determined grin, as he always did upon battle, but he felt the weight of devastation around them. That did not slow the march, however, and it didn't stop him bringing calm to the chaos in the darkness. How many streets had he calmed already? Each one was now littered with fiends who had had thievery and murder on their minds. *In their actions.* This was his justified way of dealing with the bastards. Accidental tragedies rarely stemmed from one mistake. Usually it took many fuk-ups before devastating repercussions brought an entire city to its knees. Aye, Dia's assassination had begun these dreadful events, but it was the slow retreat of the Wolves that guaranteed catastrophe. Word travelled quicker than any Rider, and word of the city's financial collapse had brought about their cowardly retreat into their tower. All because of one bastard with ideas above his station. From between the gritted teeth of those he would call allies, he had learned of Sigi and the power he wielded. Tonight, he would carry the burden of this man's sins. Tomorrow, he would sit cordially with Sigi, look into his eyes and ask him to undo his calamitous act. If Sigi did anything less than kneel to the city's cause, Magnus would strangle the life from him that very moment. Those who replaced him could expect the same bargaining. This was not business being wielded recklessly. This was war.

They marched on through the alleyways, no longer needing to flex their muscles to calm the storm; their thunderous footsteps were enough now to settle the violence. Like a serum to a fever, they worked through each section cleaning the infection, and now, as dawn broke, this was another battle under his belt. He looked at his hands and the blood upon them. He thought of Lillium, and his anger festered. A terrible night.

A youth named Theo marched with him. His inexperienced eyes were wild with rage and exhaustion. Magnus did little to calm the youngster or offer any respite. The boy had done well amidst the violence and horror. A good Master General spotted these things. Magnus had come upon him first, still dressed in his week-old beige armour, tackling three brutes and standing firm down near the city harbour. He had been steadfastly keeping the sun at his back, avoiding their strikes, plunging his fists as though they were sharpened blades. With sword in hand, Magnus had charged into the brutes assisting his comrade, but Theo hadn't accepted his rescue silently. Instead, turning with the battle and putting a man down with his hands alone. They were bonded in blood now. Many of the recruits were.

Lillium, too.

"A pack of Black Guards, Master General," Theo said in a low voice, seeing the gathering of black outside the jail. In the dawn's light he saw the shattered windows and a fury overcame him. His son was inside, as was the most important man in Samara. Though most Wolves had sat out the violence, there were a few whose sense of duty rose above petty things such as payment. These were the bastards he knew from the Faction Wars; these were the bastards that would resist Magnus at every turn. These were also the bastards that would fight their hardest. He hated them, but respected them for the bastards they were.

"Lower your swords," he warned, leaving his own sword nestled in its scabbard. They raised their weapons in reply. *Perhaps they can't count.* At midnight, Magnus would have been outnumbered, but having spent the night roving the streets gathering and distributing his comrades, the momentum was very much with him now. It was still a miserable return. At least a dozen Rangers had perished this night, struck down in the roving frenzy of madness. Some had died at his side, others alone as the stampede and rioting had carried them into menacing territories. At least a hundred still roamed the streets, searching for peace, searching for control, doing their duty. The rest stood watch at various junctions, keeping the growing peace with the brutalised prisoners they guarded. They were the luckier ones, having seen only a taste of the horrors meted out by civilised brutes. *And I wage war for their lives.* He wondered if the southerners had ever shown such brutality to their own kind.

Probably.

It was on nights like this that Magnus regretted his decision not to rule. How might the world have been then?

As wild as the Savage Isles?

Wild, but stable.

Magnus held both his arms out to calm his brethren as they spread out in a wide arc, filling the street as they marched up. Only a foolish young Wolf would consider attacking, but still, he was wary. His eyes fell upon the glow of candles within the jail, and he clutched the slender hope for what it was. The Black Guard huddled together, seeing Magnus approach. Torch-bearers stood on either side of him, and he knew how impressive he appeared. Sometimes wars were won with extravagance and games of the mind. Any fool who argued differently had never seen combat.

"Lower your swords, or I shall raise mine!" he bellowed. His voice rose high above the Rangers' heads, loud enough that the clouds above must have taken heed and opened up. The first raindrops fell tentatively, and some Wolves lowered their swords.

"I know you rage and seek vengeance, but they slew the assassin." Rain spattered down upon his armour. After the march, the violence, the blood, it was a welcome thing. Any fires they hadn't extinguished would fizzle out in this downpour. Sometimes a little rain changed everything.

A brave voice erupted from somewhere within the wall of black. "You come for Emir, the healer. We charge him with crimes that must be answered for."

Around him the Rangers stood poised, and Magnus held them steady with a raised hand. He stepped forward slowly and in a few elegant strides, he was among the sea of black, standing taller than most. Hate him or love him, there was no Wolf brave enough to strike down a legend.

"Oh, don't you worry, my friends. Emir will answer in trial. He will face judgement. You have my word on it." He was calm. He met the eyes of every one of the gathered Wolves and he looked right through them. When Magnus spoke, most listened. "This is not the way," he added. Still, he walked through them and the Wolves were impressed. As were his watching comrades. As were the three faces peering through the jail window. He recognised his cub and almost smiled.

"Do not deny the city its spectacle," he called. He was tired of delivering speeches. "Do not deny the city a vision of blood." It was a warning, and those few who hadn't sheathed their swords did so. "I promise you retribution," he pledged. His throat was raw. How many promises had he offered to the masses tonight? How many was he capable of keeping? How many would he bother to try keeping? "I swear to you all that there will be blood in return." Another loosely offered pledge. Despite what most honourable people would say, Magnus believed words were made to be twisted. If people were held to their every word, some men would have an ocean of deceit to answer for. Some women, too.

There were mutterings, and Magnus hid his frustrations that these guardians had sat idle this entire night, waiting for unlikely justice, instead of attempting to return civility to Samara. Still, though, better that than hiding away over money matters. The mutterings turned to acquiescence and the Wolves dispersed as a beaten company back towards their tower.

Magnus turned to the jail. He wasn't certain how to get Emir out of this one. He knew only that he needed him alive. It wasn't a strong enough defence that Emir could be the difference between victory in the battles to come. Only a fool would announce such a thing, regardless of its truthfulness.

———

Emir scrubbed at his shirt, but it had little effect. No amount of bathing or cleaning would ever wash the stains away from his clothes, from him. Still, he scrubbed away because he'd nothing else to do. Dawn arrived, and with it salvation, albeit temporary, in the form of Magnus. Between soapy scrubs he looked to the doorway, where Magnus stood whispering to his son and his lieutenant. Emir hadn't the heart to face him. How many of his warriors had lost their lives because of his stupidity? Even if Emir had tried listening to their words, most were lost in the downpour's hiss. Most, but not all. The rain wouldn't last. Living in the hovels had given him a knack for recognising the changeable weather. He could taste a sunny afternoon ahead.

"I will do it," muttered Wynn, loud enough that Emir heard. Magnus placed a hand upon his shoulder and Erroh shook his head in disappointment, and Emir felt his stomach lurch. Wynn was to be the vengeance. The beast to slay him should the trial have a dreadful conclusion. The city and Wolves would demand blood. *Savour it.* It probably made sense to have as impartial an executioner as possible. *Less punishment.* He looked across at Wrek and wondered if he knew his opponent's skill as Emir did. At least Erroh hadn't agreed to do it. That would have been too much.

A few Rangers entered the jail and stood at attention, awaiting orders. Emir knew their orders. He threw the soap down and cried as quietly as possible in the corner. He dipped his head and hoped nobody could see. *So tired and no last meal.* He thought of Aireys and thought about dying in battle with her. Holding her hand as they passed into the darkness together. He wondered would she greet him in the world beyond. So far away, yet close enough that a thin shard of steel could hasten the distance. He wiped the tears away and sniffed in disgust. If nothing else, he would die honourably today.

———

Lillium lay in the darkness, her only companion her own wretched breathing. She couldn't hear her attacker's breath, and the bile in her stomach churned once more. She'd thrown up a few times already; this was now part of her murderous routine. Her mouth was bitterly dry. She couldn't remember the last time she hadn't been thirsty. She glanced at the body and shuddered. *Dead? Dying?* If she climbed across, she could search properly for signs, know for certain how enormous her deed had been. And if she discovered no heart beating? Well, she would know forever that she was a murderer.

What a fine goddess you have become.

Her own decisions had brought her to this place, this moment. She couldn't even blame Wynn anymore for their unhappiness. Truly, she could never have been happy after the Cull. Her decisions since then had brought her to this bed of heartache with a dying rapist.

Or a gathering of slaughtered, cooling meat.

Lean over and know for certain.

Lillium leaned over and vomited for the fourth time, then lay back down and wept into the dark. She closed her eyes again and gave up ever so.

The sound of heavy boots woke her from her slumber and she struggled to rise, but her body surrendered to the traumas she'd endured. She tried to rise a second time, only to collapse again beneath her betraying injured leg. She heard a low moan and realised it was her own voice. Somewhere out in the walkway she heard muffled voices and she tried to crawl backwards into the darkness. Moving, she felt the agony once more and she cursed her own weakness. A torch passed across the window and she froze.

Hide.

Honouring the memory of her victim, she dropped to her belly and crawled across the room searching for cover, for blankets, for anything at all to conceal her. She wasn't ready to fight again; wasn't ready to take another life; wasn't ready to roar futile words at indifferent ears.

But I will.

She reached the corner and found nothing. Sitting up, she waited for her next assailants. She would allow them three steps, she told herself. Just three and then she would attack, but her body would not move for her. She could not rise. Not yet.

Perhaps it's Wynn, she thought. Maddened with worry and searching the city high and low for his beloved. The voices turned to cautious concern as the light from the torches shone over the blood streaks in the doorway. *Oh yes, the blood I spilled.* More voices emerged, more than she could take, and she felt herself dig into the unmoving wall. Trying to slip through brick, like some illusionist's deception, before coming out the other side to a resounding applause. She almost screamed as a tall figure stepped into the room. A brightly burning torch stung her eyes as he waved it over her handiwork and then its light touched her face. Panic became uncontrollable terror and her strength ebbed away and she hid her eyes behind her hands as if blinding herself might better conceal her.

The figure stepped closer and she wanted to cry into the night. She wanted to beg for rescue from this nightmare, pardon for her deeds. *Murderer, executioner, slaughterer.* The figure knelt down beside her, but said nothing. Her lips trembled and she uttered no words of warning. She could see the torch's light from behind her fingers, but she couldn't face the world. *Better to stay in the dark.* The figure called to her, using a term she recognised, and after a few moments she opened her eyes to her Master General.

"It's all right little one," he said. "You did well."

He reached for her and she drew back sharply against the wall. Magnus reached a second time anyway and pulled her close and she allowed him. *Not alone.* After a few breaths, she relaxed and rested her heavy head on his shoulder.

"You did well," he repeated. When she was a cub, her father had silenced her wailing with simple words. Lacerated knees became nothing more than scrapes when she was reassured. Magnus's strength and words were as infectious, and she felt braver in his warmth. She wept quietly on his shoulder. She heard him hiss away those who'd come in behind him and she was grateful.

"He tried to…" she whispered. "I had to…"

"Fuken animal," Magnus growled, releasing her and shining the light over the body.

"Is he dead?" he asked. "He looks dead." She liked the tone he used.

"I think so," she mumbled. "I warned him to stop, and then he didn't… and he said the Primary was dead… and I couldn't stop," she gasped, as panic returned. *Murderer.* She was no longer Lillium; she was an animal. "And Wynn was nowhere, and…" And then she sobbed again. "I tore him apart," she wailed, remembering the pain in her hands. It had felt good to kill him; it felt good confessing her deed.

"I'm so proud of you, Lillium. I'm so fuken proud," Magnus said loudly. He took out a small dagger and held it across the body before slitting its throat. He slit it a few more times and wiped the blood on its dirty white vest. He called for one of his waiting Rangers. "Grab this piece of shit and dump its body with the rest."

He held her until it hurt a little less, while the Rangers went back out to search the surrounding alleys for fiends and other victims. Magnus stayed with her and whispered more soothing words. To hear him tell the events of the arena was easier than hearing it from the bile-filled mouth of her first victim. A victim she now shared with Magnus. She listened as he spoke of the stampede that had almost killed her; the chaos in the streets after; the fear, the blood, and the dead.

"Please Lillium," he said warmly. "Do not blame Wynn. He found me after the crush and I sent him with Erroh to protect Emir. It is my fault he is not out there looking for you. It is my fault you found yourself alone."

Hearing this, she felt her strength return and with his help, she climbed to her feet. She could see the pain in his face. The guilt, too. She wiped her eyes and saluted her Master General.

"Nothing to apologise for, sir," she offered, and he embraced her again. She leaned on him the entire walk back to the Rangers' camp, gathering confidence and strength with each step. As they walked, she begged Magnus not to tell Elise or anybody else what she had done until she was ready. She vowed to keep that silence with Lea too. The absent gods alone would know the guilt Lea would feel, knowing she'd left her closest friend behind.

They passed through the chaos of the city, down past the hovels, and at last Lillium fell into the arms of an overjoyed Lea. Before she was taken to the infirmary to have her wounds tended to, Lillium watched Magnus refill his tankard before marching off into the night. This was the behaviour of a legend, she told herself, and remembered herself crouched alone in the room as monsters surrounded her. She spat that memory away and vowed never to show such weakness ever again.

In the infirmary, she lay back with her elbow propped up on supports as a young apprentice healer hovered with needle and thread over the gaping hole in her leg.

"Just fuken stitch it up," she demanded, biting down hard on a leather strap.

43

A LESSER SANCTUARY

A Black Guard escorted her through the corridor in silence. His head was bowed, and his hands shook. Whatever pain he suffered, hers was tenfold. Her mouth hurt from grinding her teeth; black tracks around her eyes betrayed tears she had shed privately. She could only stare ahead as she walked along the gloomy corridor, not daring to look down at her dress. She could feel the dampness of her grandmother's blood. *So much blood.* Somewhere outside in the world below she heard a faint scream and she slowed to look out the nearest window into the unsettling night. *End of the world.* A stronger female would have taken to the streets, calming the natives and driving back the wretched refugees. A stronger female would have gathered her closest allies and assured the world that, come morning, the city would still stand. Instead, she hid away. To the fires with this life, she thought. She just wanted her nana back. *She was more than that.*

As she turned from the window, her feet gave way beneath her, and she fell painfully against the wall. Her waiting escort leapt forward, catching her with strong but shaking hands before she collapsed completely. His eyes were dark in this light. Pretty, too. She liked his jawline and the thin veil of stubble. She imagined bedding him, writhing naked and forgetting the pain. To be the carefree goddess again, even for a few fleeting breaths. If she took him, she could furrow away her feelings for her wretched love.

My Emir.

"I'm fine," she hissed, shoving him away. "I'll walk the rest of the way by myself." It was Emir she wanted to catch her in the dark, to catch her and love her, take her to a bed of silk and, afterwards, wake her from this nightmare.

"Aye, Mydame," the Black Guard said, allowing her to pull free of his clutches. He bowed and turned away without question. *Why wouldn't he?* Her word was law now, wasn't it? Providing she became Primary. She was younger than Dia had been, and had seen far fewer horrors, but who cared for age in such precarious times, anyway? She would have become a young leader, regardless of her grandmother's brutal assassination. She walked the last few steps towards her sanctuary without stumbling, and then stood outside the door, sobbing silently. She was alone in the world. Dia would never offer counsel, ever again. She felt a fist grasp her chest and tear away what air she had.

I cannot do this.

Twisting the handle quietly, she glided through the doorway and met the wonderful aroma of cofe and apple honey. Such comforts almost crushed her. Instead of succumbing to fresh emotion, she slipped into the room and felt her grandmother's absence anew. She could see it in the unkempt ledgers on her desk, in her cardigan still hanging on its hook, even in her near empty mug, its contents as cold as her bones. Only stubborn strength of will kept her standing.

She took a calming breath and looked at the sleeping child upon her chair. She didn't want to wake her, didn't want to explain that everything was changing, but Linn was a clever little one. She'd seen horrors long before a beast had taken a knife to her grandmother. Roja had seen similar miseries as a child and grown stronger for it. Perhaps Linn would rise to Primary in waiting. Perhaps she would be better suited for the task.

"Hello, little one," she whispered, and the young girl's eyes widened in shock as she woke. Lexi spun around from the stove, grabbing her chest, and she scowled for the fright. For a moment she almost looked to embrace her but returned to her cooking instead.

"Roja," Linn whispered, and Roja opened her arms for an embrace. After a moment, Lexi abandoned her cooking altogether, hugging Roja too. In this sanctuary, Roja could be herself, with those she loved dearest. She could gain strength from them. She could do what was needed most.

———

The night was long for the city. For Roja it was everlasting. Mourning for her grandmother in near silence was devastating. Seeing the city fall on her watch was soul crushing. Dooming her love to death was no small matter either, but doom him she would. For that was the way of the world. Those were steps a Primary should take. Lexi forced soup down their throats and sat down only when Linn was tucked up in bed in her chambers, and Roja was eternally grateful. Lexi had rarely come by in the days before, not since the heated argument over Erroh. Lexi was right, but none of that mattered to a Primary or her second-in-command.

Roja had missed her little companion a great deal these last few months. She'd convinced herself that watching over Linn had taken up Lexi's time, just as Lexi had taken up her time when she was a cub. Lexi was wilder than most other adolescent Alpha females, but she was a fine choice as guardian over Linn. Today had proven as much. While her elder sisters and guards alike had reeled at the horror, Lexi had swooped up Linn and fled the chaos through the Primary's entrance. What horrors had she saved the young one from with her quick actions? Yes, she was a fine female, from a fine family.

"Do you want more?" Lexi asked, leaning over the little stove and the saucepan of honeyed apple and roasted tea leaves. She dropped a little cinnamon in, and its aroma filled the room, covering the damp stench of blood.

Roja suddenly wondered which gown they would bury Dia in. She wrapped her blanket around herself, draining the remnants of her sweet tea. She would have one specially made. Cost be damned.

"I'd prefer a little cofe."

"Not tonight. You need to rest."

"As if I could rest on a night like this," she snapped, and Lexi nodded. She wasn't done speaking. It was easy recognising when Lexi had more to say. It was more difficult to find silence with Lexi around. Tonight, she needed distractions. Tonight, she needed her little sister to protect her from the monsters in her thoughts.

"As if any of us could." Lexi left her bubbling tea to cool and sat down with her mug of cofe opposite Roja. She took Dia's seat. She always took Dia's seat, and when she did, she usually claimed it would be her seat in a decade or two. "If you do not rest, you'd best make use of this time. Write the names, Roja."

"Aye so, I will have tea," Roja whispered, trying and failing to change the subject. As Lexi stood back up, she slid the parchment across the table. The quill lay waiting in its pot already.

"Write the names, Roja," Lexi repeated, and the quill scraped loudly as she scribed the first name along the top. She thought she would feel a cold relief in setting terrible things in motion, but she did not. Every time she closed her eyes, she saw Emir's look of shock as she'd set her Black Guard on him. It was better than the sight of Cass cutting her grandmother apart, she supposed. Her quill stopped for a moment before beginning again.

Lexi refilled her tea. "I know you love him; I know this cannot be easy, but you are the Primary in waiting." Her eyes were cold, hard. She looked like Magnus in that moment. It should have felt reassuring. Instead, Roja felt even more alone. "You mishandle this event and you risk ruination."

"This morning, we had a city, we had an army, we had a fuken leader," Roja hissed, pushing the parchment away as the absurdity of her situation struck her.

"Magnus marches. Come tomorrow's end, we will have all three again; this I know," Lexi countered and her childish enthusiasm almost brought a smile to Roja's face. Almost, but not quite.

"If he can find Sigi…"

"Oh, Sigi will face a separate judgement," Lexi whispered, holding up a second parchment. It was blank. "This one right here will be his. Put my name down first, will you?"

Roja laughed, and her laughter turned abruptly to sobs. Instead of comforting her, Lexi shoved the condemning parchment towards her. "Write the fuken names so we may be done with this matter."

Roja hated when Lexi was right, because it usually meant that she, Roja, was wrong. The sooner Roja condemned Emir, the better. Lexi knew well that Roja's love, her need, her foolishness, all conspired against her. These were the moments when revolutions were born. *Show strength.* Anything less begged for rebellion. Knowing the city shook this night was a stark warning of how far from favour her tenure might become.

Run from this.

The tea quelled the churning bile in her stomach, but no amount of tea could counter the nausea of writing her own name in among the names on the list. Then she wrote Erroh's name and Lexi's head turned slightly. After a moment, she scribbled it out. Erroh would vote for Emir's innocence. Everyone would see that. Was he not the Hero of Keri?

"You need to put Dane's name in," Lexi said, and Roja nodded. Hard not to allow the leader of the Black Guard to pass judgement.

He will suggest he be the executioner in battle.

A knock at the door stirred Roja from her miserable task. Without waiting for a reply, Silvia slipped in. She was dressed in unfamiliar dark clothing, her usual white dress no doubt steeping in a soapy bucket somewhere. After briefly embracing Roja, she hissed at Lexi to move, before sitting down in Dia's chair, taking a moment to look around as though imagining herself in such a position. It was unlikely Silvia could ever amass enough support or goodwill to get elected. For all Roja's flaws and misgivings, she was still a more favourable candidate.

"I suppose I'll take the stool then," said Lexi under her breath. Saying both females disliked each other was the grandest type of understatement. Lexi was higherline, but far younger. If Silvia didn't find herself a fine young mate in the next few seasons, she would be the one taking the stool. Silvia was well aware of this fleeting advantage, and Lexi had suffered under her snide behaviour these last few years, but a day of reckoning was coming. Both females knew it. Like her unpopular father, Lexi played her part perfectly. She even offered her rival a steaming beverage.

"Don't fight, not tonight," Roja begged. Shrugging, Silvia leaned across the table and eased the parchment gently from the Primary-in-waiting's hands.

"So, you are writing the names?" she asked coldly. She grimaced as she read through the names. "Put my name down," she whispered.

"I won't condemn you to this vote. People know your ties to Stefan. You will face as deep a criticism as I will."

"Dia would have wanted me on the tribunal," she retorted, and Roja hadn't the heart to tell her how Dia had frequently referred to her as "the rat". It had been Dia's way of condemning their salacious behaviour without ever coming out and attacking both females.

"How will you vote?" Lexi asked from her stool.

"However Roja wants me to vote. You love Emir, but justice might not be favourable to him. I can be the telling vote. I can handle the repercussions, Roja. I'm a big girl now." She slid the page back to Roja who, with a heavy heart, added her name to the list.

Lexi eyed Silvia and gave a half smile. It was the closest thing to geniality she could offer. "How is Stefan after his injury?" On any other night, their usual screaming arguments would echo around the tower by now. Roja could see the attempted sincerity on the younger female's face and appreciated it.

"I cannot be with Stefan knowing his comrade had a hand in Dia's murder," Silvia said evenly. "He is a fine boy, but a boy, nonetheless." Roja could see the pain beneath Silvia's lie. Perhaps that was her way to deal with her own mourning.

"His friend condemned, his hand ruined, and now discarded by a goddess. Awful day for the boy," said Lexi. Silvia shrugged and hid her sorrow behind a thorough third reading of the names.

"I hope his hand heals," Roja whispered, but Silvia wasn't giving much away. Instead, she stood up with the parchment in hand.

"I don't know these people, but I will see to it," she said, rolling up the list. She smiled coldly and spun on her heels to leave.

"Ask Seth for their location. He knows the whereabouts of everyone in this city."

"Come dawn, Emir will face proper judgement," Silvia said.

"Wait!" Roja leapt from her seat and took hold of the parchment. She unrolled it, set it on the table, scribbled over one unfamiliar name and replaced it with another. The name of someone more sympathetic to Emir's cause, no doubt.

"I do not know either."

"Seth will."

"As you wish, Mydame," Silvia said, bowing deeply and heading off into the night to attend to life-and-death matters.

Lexi wasted no time recovering her seat. "Know this, my sister: Emir treats my mother, but I will not judge you for sentencing him to death in the arena," she whispered.

"Would I care if you judged me, little one?" Roja snapped, and instantly regretted it. Lexi nodded and bowed her head, and Roja felt even worse. Lexi's deference went beyond everything intrinsically natural to her. Roja wanted to crawl into a ball and weep until this nightmare was done. More than that, she wanted Emir to hold her as she did.

"I'm sorry, little one," she said softly. "It's not every day I doom my love to death."

"I will make a fresh brew. Tell me again of when you first saw Emir, all those years ago."

44

MY VOTE WILL COUNT

"Oh, fuk me, this never ends well," muttered Erroh, leading Emir through the old doors into the freezing room of black. Emir knew this place as the Cull. A place where bitter accusations were cast like weapons. Where Alphas fought their greatest battles. He knew a little, but nothing beyond a few pages scribed in a journal, and any time he'd asked Roja about the event, she'd been cryptic in her replies. He knew the treasure gained at the end, but doubted there would be any such reward coming his way. At least he wasn't alone. Flanked by Alphas on all sides and moving beneath the banner of the Rangers, they had crept from the unspectacular jail into the most infamous building in the city. Erroh had led, while Wynn and Wrek had followed behind, muttering under their breaths many secretive things. He wondered if Wynn was warning Wrek of his burden. Better his friend escaped with his life, he supposed. Magnus entered the room last and now stood far off in the back. He was support, albeit the quieter kind.

The room was an unnatural black, as though a demented artist had painted the very night upon its surface, and only one solitary light shone upon him from somewhere above. One light in the dark, segregating him from his companions. Emir's body ached from the long night and the many beatings throughout. His eyes stung in this low light and though he endeavoured to savour every breath, he couldn't help but feel a few hours' sleep might have made his doom altogether more bearable.

The crowd already waited. Standing in a line, side by side; the entire fuken city. Or so it seemed. They wore their finest gowns. He'd never seen so many women in one room, and Emir desired to look upon only one. This, he refused to do. For shame, but for anger too.

He could hear his own breathing and his pounding heart. The delicate creak of angry iron echoed into the rafters far above as he shifted his wrists in the manacles. Wrek had locked them far too tightly. He gazed up at the five figures directly above him. They stood apart from the silent gathering. He understood these five would cast their votes upon his life. He could have knelt deferentially, but there was little point. It wouldn't matter what he said or did. There was no way in the Wastes he would leave this room without chains.

It was Silvia who stepped forward first. Her face was cold, her glare condemning. He resisted looking back at Stefan, lest he give something away. He called her an ally. That was one in favour. He'd need two more. And then he'd need to move to another sanctuary. *Perhaps Adawan?* He shook those foolish thoughts away. He wasn't surviving this.

When Silvia spoke, her tone matched her glare. "Emir of Keri, you know me as Silvia. My vote will count towards your judgement." She stood back, linking her arm with Roja's. Sisters to the end.

A second Alpha stood forward, older, yet no less impressive than any he'd met before.

"My name is Mea. My vote will count towards your judgement."

Beside him, Erroh took a step forward ever so. She seemed to offer a slight bow to him in reply. Perhaps it was a trick of the light? She stepped back as the next one stepped forward.

"My name is Dane, and my vote will count towards your death," growled the Black Guard. He was in full armour, his breastplate decorated in discreet insignias. He gripped the balcony bannister tightly, spitting each word venomously. He gave the distinct impression he would not favour Emir.

An elderly woman with tanned skin stepped forward. As old as Dia. Now she would grow older. She had a kind face, and Emir recognised her from the little building of books. "My name is Massey. My vote will count towards your judgement," she whispered, but her words carried in the air.

Last of all, Roja stepped forward. She wore a gown of blue; it lacked the majesty of her usual garments. "You knew me as your lover, Roja. My vote will count towards... justice."

Despite himself, he met her eyes and he saw the depthless sorrow in them. Mesmerised, he couldn't look away. His hands shook as he fought tears of regret. He wanted to fall at her knees and beg forgiveness; to offer his own life as recompense. Instead, he stayed silent, willing the absent gods to save his life this day.

It was Silvia who was overseeing this court, and she revelled in it. "We charge you with assisting in the Primary's assassination. You will die for your crimes; they will bury you in an unmarked grave in the Wastes. We will strike your name from this world—unless you convince us of your innocence."

Her words cut through him and he nodded his understanding. He waited for the next person to speak at him, twisting the uncomfortable manacles absently as he did. He fell still until Erroh appeared beside him.

"This is when you speak, Emir," he whispered, and Emir tried to remember the instructions his comrades had suggested. "Tell them your tale. They will not interrupt until you declare yourself finished."

He took his time. And why wouldn't he? His voice quivered, but at least it never broke. He spoke of trauma and a young girl named Lara and how time and care had returned her to the world. He was eloquent. He even successfully used symbolism at points. He spoke of Keri, its brutal sacking, and of a traumatised regulator named Cass. He counted the months of slow rehabilitation he'd attempted, and strangely, it was Dane, leader of the Black Guards, who nodded in understanding of his recounting of the devastating mental wounds inflicted; this gave Emir further foolish hope.

Finally, he spoke of an invitation to meet a grandmother to the one he cared for most. He spoke of his shattered patient, who was so eager to see the arena. He admitted his good faith had been misplaced, before facing Roja and offering words of sorrow, regret and apology. With nothing else to say now, he stood straight and waited for judgement, but no one stepped forward to condemn him. After a few moments, Erroh leaned into the light and whispered that he needed to declare himself finished.

"I have spoken," Emir whispered, and again, it was Silvia who stepped forward. Her eyes were warm and she tilted her head sideways slightly.

"Stirring words, Emir. Words that prove how big a man you are, despite your stature."

He nodded; the chains rattled a little.

She continued. "I believe your intentions were pure. You had no ill hand in our Primary's death." He felt his heart stir in hope. A good start would be a positive vote. Fuk that—it would be an incredible start. "However, intention or no, you pledged for him. I judge you to die in the arena." He felt weak in the knees, as though a blade had been plunged through his belly. He almost stumbled, but a hand shot out and held him upright. It was Stefan's. Neither could face the other. Roja looked at Silvia and dropped her head as though she were crying. And perhaps she was. It was no small thing to endure revenge so openly.

"Aye, death to the healer," added Dane, unable to wait his turn. Another knot in the swinging rope. Two down and three remaining. *Dead man marching.* Dane struck the bannister's edge. "Death at the hands of my finest Wolves," he threatened, and the silent, watching crowd found their voices in muted mutterings of approval. They hissed, they hated, and he dared not look around, lest they see how much it stung.

Instead, he offered yet another silent prayer to the absent gods, although he doubted they'd listened to any of the hundred he'd offered before; again, they made no reply. They didn't even whisper the plans awaiting him beyond this tragic day; plans he might forsake outright.

The librarian Massey waited for the murmuring to die away. She was old enough that she had learned the skill of patience. She raised her hands, but no one fell still. As though protocol had been breached beyond repair, their voices grew with every breath, every hissed curse. Magnus, who had not learned the value of patience, could take no more.

"Shut up," he roared from the darkness. A terrible bellow built for war. His voice carried and they fell silent as though answering a disapproving master. A few Black Guards shuffled nervously against the bannister. Some had seen his violence first-hand. Those who hadn't had learned of his deeds.

Massey offered a slight smile, a courteous bow, before dooming Emir to a bloody death in the arena. "You are a principled man, Emir, but you pledged for the killer." Her voice was apologetic and each word weighed her down. Her eyes pleaded with Emir for forgiveness; hers was the telling vote. "I judge you to fight for your life in the arena," she offered.

Oh fuk, oh fuk, oh fuk.

Emir wanted to run, to tear free of this unfairness; to rage against it. He also wanted to weep, to beg for mercy, to scream, to curse, and finally he wanted to pledge vengeance upon them all. Also, he wanted to stay silent, hold the tears and accept his fate.

Mea hissed them all to silence as easily as Magnus had, though she did so with less threat and more majesty. She wore simple garments, yet exuded grandness. "This court has not concluded sisters, daughters. Find your silence." When she spoke, she spoke like a true Primary-in-waiting. Even Roja stared at her.

"My heart goes out to you, Emir, as you stand nervously among a pack of Wolves." She eyed Dane. "There is far more fault in those who were charged with protecting her. Why has nobody questioned the appearance of the blade used?"

A fine question.

"Why has the Master of the Black not offered other guilty parties?" Mea challenged, and Emir felt a glimmer of hope.

Dane couldn't hold his tongue. "Who are you to question my Black Guard? They searched Cass and found no blade. There is no blame on any of my warriors for unpreparedness, and I resent such an implication."

"And Emir carried no blade inside?" Mea asked, and Dane appeared to realise his misstep.

"Aye, they searched Emir," he muttered. "They swear there was no weapon on him… either."

Her reproachful tone changed to a more patronising one, as though she were teasing out a reply from a confused child who had neither studied nor grasped the importance of their answer. "There was no hidden pocket on the killer's body?"

Dane stared at her the way the Wolves stared at Emir, and she was magnificent.

"There was no pocket or hiding place for a blade," he admitted, listening to the indistinct murmurs growing around him.

"So then, fine sir, I have one question," she said, addressing less Dane and more the entire room. "If neither man entered with a blade, how did it appear in Cass's hands?"

"We will question those who were in the box," he mumbled, sounding like a man trying to hide something. Without moving, he seemed to shrink beneath the scrutiny of the watching audience, and all Emir wanted was for the votes to be recalled. "We will investigate the knife, eventually." It was no answer.

This time Mea struck the balcony as he had. "This man will die today. That is all you offer?"

"I have plenty to offer. I will take no order from a farmer girl trying to incite outrage," he countered.

"Know your place, Wolf."

He was a man used to giving orders. He was not a man used to defending himself. "I know my place in the world. I guard this city." He took a deep breath as though planning a coherent counter-argument. "Fuk off back to your home in the forest. See to your family." Another breath. "Like a good little woman." The room went silent. Even the dead man raised an eyebrow.

She knew her place; she was fully in control. "Do you think words offend me, Dane? Do you think outrage serves me?" The narrow balcony they stood along was tight, yet she slipped past Massey gracefully and stood closer to him. He was taller than she, dressed in his armour, but she looked fit to punch right fuken through it. Despite himself he took a step back at her sudden dominance, her sudden challenge. Primary or no, she was Alpha female. *Hear her roar.* The guarding Wolves, standing among the audience, dared not move. They knew their place, too, and it wasn't standing by their leader.

With no warning, Mea's hand shot out and fastened upon his neck. With her other hand, she took hold of his wrist. A fine manoeuvre she must have learned in her youth. She squeezed, and the Master of the Black immediately collapsed to one knee. He tried to break her suffocating hold, but she just squeezed tighter. He struck at her and she twisted his wrist further to the point of snapping. She did it effortlessly and he gasped. "You think only Emir should suffer for a mistake?" she hissed, and he stopped struggling, conceding defeat. He was powerless in the face of her dominance. After a moment, she released him and shoved him away as though he was little more than filth. The Alphas were still the dominant species.

As two Black Guards helped him to his feet, Mea turned to Emir. "Others are far more culpable than you, Emir. I judge you guilty of foolish kindness. You do not deserve death." She bowed her head and stepped back from the edge. Even so, they both knew her words weren't enough. It was all formality, and as a sinking man knows his watery grave, Emir realised his fate was already sealed. He let go of hope and sank.

Roja stood forward. She looked ready to shatter and Emir thought her beautiful. "I judge you innocent. Despite this, you will fight for your life in the arena," she declared, and the crowd gasped as one. As though struck by an invisible fist, she stood back away from him, away from the condemning circle of women and their growing outrage. The very room was alive now with damning vitriol spat her way. She looked ready to faint. Grabbing her chest, she almost collapsed and only Mea, stepping forward and taking hold, kept her upright.

Sensing the growing hostility, Silvia stepped forward again. "Emir of Keri, we have sentenced you to die." She looked to Dane, who nodded for her to continue. "But as demanded, we will allow you to fight for your life. Against two Black Guards of Dane's choosing."

Two Black Guards?

"You will face the Alpha males Doran and Aymon," Dane declared, staring into the darkness to where Magnus stood.

Things were afoot that Emir had no clue about, but he couldn't think beyond the terror of facing two Wolves. Surely that was an overreaction. One vanquisher was more than enough. From that same shadowed corner, he heard a bitter curse, as though someone's simple plans had taken a nasty, unexpected turn.

"You will choose the weapons," Dane continued, "and combat will end only through their submission or your death."

The crowd roared its approval and Emir nodded his head dumbly. Even Wrek could not defeat two Wolves.

"Is there a champion from your clan to come forward?" asked Massey loudly, struggling to be heard against the noise.

A clan? Emir had no clan. He had Wrek, though, who was a clan unto his own. A few moments passed and Wrek made no move to put himself forward. He just dropped his head in quiet shame, and Emir felt a strange relief alongside a sense of terrible loss. Following that, a tempest of sweeping terror.

"I am my own champion," he said quietly. His voice didn't even crack. He had a simple plan for the arena: to die messily.

A voice emerged from the darkness—a Master General's voice, at that. "He is a Ranger." Emir stared into the gloom, perplexed.

"And I will fight for my brother," declared Wynn, stepping forward into the light. He bowed magnificently as though he'd prepared for this eventuality and though he was confident in his pose, Emir couldn't help notice the shaking of his comrade's hands. He'd seen shaking like that before. Usually in his own hands, right before he bolted for the nearest escape.

45
I'VE MADE A HUGE MISTAKE

He didn't mind how raw his wrists were, only that the relief of being free from manacles was wonderful. He continued to massage each wrist as he marched up towards the arena. *Ranger.* A fine move on Magnus's part. People might have argued against an Alpha defending a guilty wretch, but a Ranger defending his comrade was just fine. At least he had a place to go if Wynn emerged victorious. How bad could life under Magnus's banner possibly be? He suspected his skills as a healer weren't the only skills Magnus would call upon. He lamented this, but took comfort in the fact that his loose tongue had earned him a respite. More than that, he had hope again.

They marched to the beat of a drum. Each strike was loud and intimidating, delivered by a young soldier marching at the rear of the Ranger line, and it drew the citizens from their hiding places. Even with the smell of scorch so prevalent in the air, Spark's grey stone was mostly untouched, but it was only the eternal stone that had survived unmolested. He could see the devastation in the billion and one shards of glass at their feet; the forest of broken wood, all charred and splintered at every bend. Mostly, though, he saw the horrors in the crimson-tinted puddles of rainwater that they stepped over.

I caused this.

The few people they passed were as shattered as the debris around them, and his longing to tend to their wounds was overwhelming. Oh, how he wanted to make what amends he could, but he was a prisoner; an outcast. He did not—could not—try to lessen their anguish, and they glared bitterly at him as he passed.

Leading the procession was Magnus, dressed in his finest flowing gold cloak. A golden beacon of hope after a dreadful night. He resonated strength, power and resilience. All the things the city needed. Declaring his allegiance openly to the culprit responsible for this mayhem was no small matter, but subtlety was not the legend's forte. Wynn marched behind the impressive Master General. He too wore a shimmering outfit that was almost as garish. *Almost, but not quite.* Still, though, Emir thought him impressive in the glistening sun. He wore a smile as though enduring a victory lap, but Emir could see the terror in his eyes, and it was disheartening. Every time he caught sight of the Alpha's face, his bravado appeared to diminish. Emir knew overconfidence was as deadly as a misfiring crossbow. He hoped a little apprehension might temper the wild young warrior this day.

Lea and Erroh marched, behind muttering schemes of their own. Whatever they spoke of was heated, albeit quietly so. Lea's allegiance would be to the Primary, and it stung him to think of her condemnation.

Behind the two bickering Alphas marched an impressive line of Rangers. Their previous night's deeds having earned them renown and pride, they were boisterous considering the circumstances. Perhaps it was easier to be loud and heroic, even in the face of their own comrade's demise. Emir still felt every death while leading the Keri convoy; they stamped in time with each pounding beat, they sang, they jested, they cheered as they marched. They believed in victory today. Perhaps he should too.

It was the Black Guards, marching their rounds, who moved quickest from their path. Those paltry few valued honour over payment, and to these few, under order from Magnus, the Rangers bowed as they passed. Any brute who had stood his ground while his brothers had fled around him was a comrade to respect, if not particularly like. The Rangers were valued highly in the city, and the Wolves knew their place. At least for now.

Emir had finally learned of the crush, but did not know how many had perished. He believed few would venture back into this dreadful place to view his execution, but he was wrong. Word of his death sentence had stirred the people. That or the drums, he thought, seeing more and more eager citizens peering out from broken doorways and windows as they passed. Closer to the venue, some joined in the parade and followed, eager to be part of the retribution. Vengeance was in the air and delicious blood-sport loomed ever nearer. At least he'd had a hand in treating their trauma, Emir supposed bitterly as they followed the procession into the arena.

The drums ceased their beating at the gates, and Magnus led the handful of chosen comrades through the doors into the long, dark corridor, leaving the rest of the Rangers to take their places as spectators in the stands. Emir looked back at the city once more and thought again of the horror he'd inadvertently inflicted upon her, upon her citizens, upon Roja. This was his penance, he told himself. Offering a prayer to the absent gods that justice might be served this day, he stepped from the afternoon light into the dreary darkness. He dared not say it aloud, but it felt like stepping into a graveyard in search of his crypt. As Magnus guided them along, Emir met the eyes of his Master General and for a brief moment he believed again, until the door slammed loudly behind them.

———

"Okay, does anybody have any fuken idea what to do instead of going through with this?" hissed Magnus, suddenly throwing his helmet aside and kicking it to the corner where Erroh and Lea were taking their seats. Emir felt his feet taken from beneath him. Gone was the golden warrior of legend, replaced by a shaken old man. The abrupt change in Magnus's demeanour was as disheartening as staring at Wynn, and Emir felt suddenly lightheaded. A cold veneer of sweat covered his body in moments, and suddenly this little dark corridor became a little too tight. *Calm yourself.*

Fighting his panic, he stared out through the arena door to the battlefield beyond and tried catching his breath. He could see a few dozen figures hurriedly attempting repairs to the stands and the arena floor, and he willed them to complete their tasks magnificently because dying among the debris would be a little too poetic for his liking. Dying anywhere was a little too poetic for his liking. Mostly, though, dying sober was a fate worse than death. He thought about a glistening bottle of sine and held that vision like it was his newborn child. Perhaps, as a dead man, he was entitled to a last drunken dance?

"I need a drink," he muttered, gripping the bars on the window and silently cursing the absent gods. He'd prayed to them and they'd repaid his faith with impossible odds. Beside him, Wynn sighed as though carrying the entire world upon his shoulders, and to Emir, it seemed he was.

"I wish Lillium were here," Wynn whispered, more to himself, before digging his hands into his knees and taking quick deep breaths. This didn't appear to work, as he suddenly sprang up from his seat and began pacing. "Fuk... fuk... fukety fuk fuks," he said under his breath.

Erroh noticed too and whispered in his mate's ear. She nodded gravely.

I'm fuked.

"Calm yourself, Wynn," Erroh said, then turned to Magnus. "Father, perhaps your talents might best be served earning the Rangers' favour with the Primary in waiting, instead of terrifying Emir's champion."

"I am as calm as I can be," hissed Wynn, before displaying his calmness by kneeling down against the wall and throwing up onto the sandy ground. The stench immediately permeated the room, and he had the good sense to cover his waste quickly. Magnus stood over the young Ranger, valiantly attempting to conceal his unease. "I need a few moments to collect myself," Wynn croaked, wiping his mouth, "but I'm not terrified."

There was silence until Magnus kicked his helmet again. "We were played a fine game by Dane. Wynn could defeat either Alpha, but besting both is a different matter. Costly too."

"You could match them in combat, Magnus," Erroh muttered, and his father spun on him angrily.

"It is not the Master General's place to attempt such an endeavour." He stood over Erroh commandingly. "Now is not the time, little cub."

"You know my feelings on the matter, Master General," Erroh countered, staring up at his father coldly. Magnus intimidated everyone he spoke with, yet Erroh was undeterred. Beside him, Lea wore a similar expression, and for a strange moment Emir imagined the two side by side upon the siege wall of Keri, bringing the fight to the Hunt. How ferocious they must have looked. *Is it too late to choose champions?*

"Why did you become my champion if it was a lost cause?" Emir asked, trying and failing to conceal his anger. He knew how ungrateful he sounded, but still. "Why offer a liar's hope?"

Wynn looked ready to apologise, to forsake his burden, but it was the Hero of Keri who had the answer.

"Because there's always a chance," he said, and Magnus spun away. "Better to claim a champion, and claim it boldly, and worry about it after." He looked at Lea, their eyes spoke of different matters.

"Aye," muttered Magnus. "Erroh is right. There is still a chance. There is always a chance." He placed his hand on the shaking shoulders of his lieutenant as though he were his father, but Wynn looked ready to collapse.

"I will fight them so," Emir said in a voice not his own, and immediately felt the urge to relieve himself. Who knew volunteering for a little bit of self-slaughter brought such a need? Well, Emir knew. He'd studied the phenomenon.

"You will die in moments," muttered Lea, as though it were a small matter. After what she'd seen and endured, perhaps dying swiftly really was a small matter. "Better a warrior fights those thugs."

"Perhaps my cub has a point, rare as that is. I could fight for Emir," Magnus said. He reached down and recovered his helmet and dusted it off absently.

"The Master General has no place in such issues," Lea countered, and Emir again felt that cold sting. He could have spoken with her, offered another useless apology, but he didn't have the heart to see her stare through him.

Wynn pulled himself from his stupor. He drew away from Magnus, shaking his head. "What are you all talking about? I will still fight. I refuse to bring shame to this outfit, to myself. I pledged for Emir. I know the weight of this burden."

"No, fuk this. I'll fight them and be done with it. I need no champion," hissed Emir, formulating a foolish plan. "Can I bring a crossbow?"

"No projectiles allowed," Erroh said.

Oh well. Whatever. Never mind.

"You need to live. Elise needs you… The war needs you," hissed Wynn.

"There are finer healers in the city," countered Emir, lying through his teeth. He wasn't the worst with a sword, especially after a few bottles of wine. Quig had been the same. He wondered had Quig drunk wine on the last day. He'd ask him later. "My mind is made up. I will not doom another man to die for me."

"No Emir, it is no longer your decision," said Wynn with finality. He would fight for him, regardless of his fear.

Erroh saw the events to come as clearly as steps in the sand. The larger-than-life Wynn he'd known from their first meeting might have had a chance. He'd have needed some luck, but he'd have had a chance. But now, this shell in shimmering gold was marching himself and Emir into bloody death and it wasn't fair. While Erroh had grown colder, fiercer and sadder too, Wynn had fallen to near ruin. Only now did he see it, in his walk, his movement, even the way he sat; Wynn was many miseries thrown together. They probably kept him afloat. Sometimes self-indulgence was a finer path than seeing one's own shortcomings. Perhaps Wynn would find his true self, eventually. Perhaps he might find it in a fight to the death in an arena. Was it worth the risk, though? And at the cost of two lives?

"I will fight. I will win," Wynn hissed, practicing his routine, repeating his words like a mantra. As though he were at breaking point. Each time he spun in the flickering candlelight, his shadow on the far wall mimicked his motion, and he was impressive. The absent gods could see how lost he was, though. He used just one sword, his naked arm held high as though bearing a shield. He gasped with every manoeuvre, working himself into a frenzy. With each spin, he hissed his mantra aloud. "I will fight. I will win."

He turned towards the wall now, as though confronting his shadowed opponent, and thrust low and swift. It was a fine thrust with one sword, but exhaustion, terror and doubt allowed his weakness to show through the bravado. "I will fight. I will win."

He retreated, blocking imaginary opponents who countered as he did with impressive moves, moving on gliding feet, and Erroh could see that his speed bettered both Aymon's and Doran's; he had the ability to beat them. Still, Erroh knew he would fail.

"Rest yourself, Wynn. Save it for the arena," Lea implored him. She watched as Erroh did, her eyes betraying little of the concern they both shared and the dreadful decisions that needed to be made. Wynn ignored her and continued his assault on his doubts, and Lea eyed Erroh again.

I know, Lea, I know.

Magnus leaned against the wall, watching with arms folded. His forehead was creased in apprehension; his eyes flickered with every slice, thrust, counter. "Be swift. Be ruthless," he urged him. "Concentrate on their heads. They'll wear no armour; they'll want no anonymity for this deed. Especially for killing another Alphaline." He winced as he said these last few words.

Don't mention Wynn getting killed. Still, though, fine advice.

"I will fight. I will win."

Erroh had his own tactics, were he to be the one facing two brutes. It began with wearing light armour that fitted properly. He absently tapped his own chest plate and closed his eyes. *A long night.* He felt

Lea's head rest on his shoulder and he relaxed despite the shuffle of feet, the hissed words, and the heavy pall of inevitability that hung over them all. He felt delicious sleep come upon him, tempting and sweet, like a slice of roasted boar to a starving hunter. He allowed it tickle his nausea and settle his nerves.

"I will fight. I will win."

Emir's voice faded into the background, and Erroh leaned back against the wall and felt his heart settle as he fell asleep.

The thunderous march of footsteps above them stirred Erroh from sleep. He didn't know how long he'd slept, only that he felt a thousand times better. Lea still leant against him, her shallow breaths swift and comforting. He wondered if she dreamt of easier times, back when they'd marched the road alone together. Back when it was easier; when the world had felt smaller. She had had more nightmares these last few weeks, ever since the homestead. He stroked her hair and tried to forget their miseries for a few moments, but as he did, her eyes shot open. She sat up straight, reaching behind her back for a blade that was not there. Just like the road. *Easier times.* The room shook around them, and only Wynn and Magnus seemed unperturbed by the noise. The crowd were coming out in force to watch the show, it would appear.

"Not long," Magnus murmured, looking out into the arena.

"Aye," Wynn agreed, sitting with his head in hands. "They're beating my anthem."

With the footsteps came the buzz of conversation, and its rumble filtered down through the stands to the outcasts hiding beneath. The spectators were without cheer, and rightly so; this would be less entertainment for the mind and more of a cleansing of the soul.

"Small enough crowd, a fraction of yesterday's. Just enough to fill a few rows," Magnus observed.

"Ah, good. Fewer people to watch me... attain victory," Wynn said, shrugging his shoulders. He was paler than ever; whatever blood had been flowing into his face had all but drained away.

"Lots of Black Guard out from under their rock, too," Magnus said, still looking out. He cursed them a few times under his breath. If a Ranger defended the guilty man successfully, whatever goodwill the Rangers had earned would swiftly be forgotten. The Wolves knew this and were working to recover what grounds they'd lost. Promises of payments must have reached them.

"I march to my doom and still Lillium is not here to wish me well," Wynn said unhappily. He held his blade out in front of him. Its tip shook as though in a struggling child's grip.

"Tradition. No mate is allowed to view combat, whether they be man or woman," said Magnus quickly.

The sound of catcalls filled the arena now, and the group exchanged uneasy glances.

"Do not feel intimidated by the booing," Erroh said quickly to Emir and his champion. Emir smiled grimly, but Wynn blinked rapidly.

"Well, I'm sure I'll be booed as I enter," he declared, standing up and stretching. "They'll adore me by the time I'm done." He dared a smile to steel his nerve.

"No, Wynn," said Lea. "If you win, you will be an outcast for the rest of your life, shamed for defending the guilty, and they will revile your name as much as they do Cass's. As much as Emir's."

"Quiet, Lea. Now is no time to shake him," Magnus barked, and Lea glared at him. Erroh had been on the receiving end of such a look many times. He almost smiled.

That's my girl.

"He should know all of it, Magnus," Lea countered determinedly. "Confidence will not save him this day. Holding his shield properly when attacking would help, though."

"What about my shield?"

Magnus shook his head and muttered under his breath. "Fine match, the pair of ye."

"Sorry, what about my shield?"

"Don't drop it when you thrust forward. Apart from that, you have a solid defence," she told him, and Wynn looked freshly shaken. A fine tactic by Lea, if not a little crude. She stared at Erroh, her meaning clear. Aye, she was unhappy about it, but some things needed to be done. She too had recognised that Emir probably had just as good a chance of defending himself.

"Well, I couldn't care less about my name," declared Emir stoutly.

"It's a shit name anyway," mocked Erroh, laughing, but his eyes were upon Wynn. Everyone could see he was close to breaking. Everyone but Magnus.

———

Erroh noticed Lillium first. She might have knocked, but it was difficult to hear anything beneath the stands. Standing in the doorway, she looked a complete ruin. Her usually immaculate hair was wild, and her face was gaunt, pale, streaked with running paint. Bloodstains covered her clothing. Leaning on a crutch, she shuffled out of the burning sun into the gloom.

"He wasn't to see you like this, Lillium," Magnus hissed. "I told you to stay away until after the event."

"What happened?" demanded Wynn, speaking to Magnus rather than Lillium. "What fuken happened to her?"

The room had suddenly become charged with pent-up Alpha emotions.

"I'm fine, Wynn," Lillium assured him. "I came to show support." Her voice was weak and she hobbled forward, but Wynn wasn't looking. His eyes were upon Magnus, and Magnus's eyes were upon the ground. Something terrible had happened.

"I'm sorry, Wynn," the legend said. "I didn't want you distracted."

"*Distracted?* Fuk you, Magnus."

Holding out her hand, Lillium invited him to her. "I'm fine, Wynn. I just got hurt. Magnus took care of me." She offered him an embrace before battle, but Wynn abruptly turned from her and stormed towards Magnus.

"She's my mate. You should have told me," he roared. He leapt upon the older man, knocking him to the floor. "What happened to her?

What did you do, old man?" He gripped the legend's shoulders in trembling hands and shook him as a hound would its kill.

Magnus let him. Erroh did not. Within a breath, he was off his seat and upon his friend. As easily as removing a blade from its scabbard, he pulled Wynn away, using his own weight against him before slamming him against the far wall. Not enough to hurt, but enough to warn.

Stay away from my dad.

"At least there's a little fight in him," said Lea scornfully, reaching down and offering a hand to Magnus. The legend needed no help. He simply lay in the dirt, waiting for a resolution.

"Get away from me, Hero," Wynn hissed, turning on Erroh. Each breath was a frenzied pant. His eyes were wild, and spittle dribbled from his mouth. *There's fight left in him, all right. Not enough, though.* He clenched his fist to strike, and Erroh calmly shoved him back against the wall.

"Easy, friend. We aren't enemies. But if you come at me, I'll show my teeth."

"Wynn," roared Lillium, finding her voice now, and finding it in fury. "You attack a comrade in my name?" She shook her head in disgust. "You are a child. You disgrace us both."

"Direct your hatred at your opponents," Magnus said, raising himself to a sitting position and pointing to the sands and the filling arena.

Wynn did not strike again. He looked for support and met only contempt. Mostly from Lillium, who spun away and took comfort from Lea, who saw openly a horror she concealed.

He fell to his knees, grasped his head in his hands, and moaned. "I'm sorry, I'm so sorry."

Whatever doubts Erroh had had about Wynn's ability were now confirmed. He was still a child, bending dangerously under his burden. It was no small matter knowing a life would be taken within the hour. If ever Lillium were to cast a line and pull him ashore, it would have to be now. Instead, she accepted Lea's hand and stared in loathing at her suffering mate. In that moment, Erroh almost expected her to step forward in his place. She was a Ranger, after all, injured or no.

I've got this, Wynn.

Though Erroh had argued in the jail, Magnus had still denied him the opportunity to defend Emir; his son attending to such an unpopular task would be costly to the war's cause. This, though, was an entirely different matter.

"I will fight for Emir," Erroh said.

"We spoke of this," growled Magnus, climbing to his feet.

"As did we," Lea said.

"You have no right," muttered Wynn half-heartedly, staring out at the arena as though it was ready to swallow him up.

"I am the Hero of Keri. Emir is of my clan. I have the greatest right to defend him," Erroh said staunchly. "I'm taking this burden, Wynn."

"I am no coward," hissed Wynn, but the words felt empty. He stormed away from the watching eyes and sat at the far end of the room while Erroh went to Lea. He kissed her hand and she allowed him.

"I must do this, my beo."

"Remember the Cull. Remember the beating each one gave you," she whispered, and he remembered it all too well. "Use that hate and come back to me, Erroh. Don't you fuken dare leave me. If it takes killing them both, you kill them both."

He kissed her on her perfect lips and pledged in silence that he would return to her.

———

When the thundering boots fell silent, there came a knocking on the arena door, announcing the stirrings of battle.

Emir walked to the doorway beside Erroh. "There are no words, friend," he said quietly.

"Consider this a step towards an unpayable debt," Erroh countered, looking back one last time at Lea. He held two unfamiliar blades in his hands. Though he'd picked up many swords since Keri, no blade felt right in his grasp anymore. It was a small matter. Mercy and Vengeance were not meant for acts like this. He spun the blades in his hands, testing them. Then, satisfied that he could cause absolute chaos with them both, he turned to Wynn, who still slouched in the corner.

"If I die, rescue Emir and kill both those fukers out there," he jested. "Pledge it to me," he warned, and this sounded less a joke.

The drums began to beat the rhythm of a coming execution. A few brave fans cheered, a few even stamped their feet in time, and the door opened.

"They're beating your anthem, Erroh," said Wynn, getting to his feet.

46

MISSING THE FIGHT OF THE YEAR

When Erroh spoke of life in chains, Lea listened. For that is what good mates did. Even if it tore her apart. She knew what horrors he'd endured. She knew it all. She had sought truth, and it had revealed itself in all its ugliness. *Like lying with a whore goddess.* He had failed her, but under the circumstances, he had behaved better than most. *If not all.* When Lea thought of Erroh in chains, she never pictured him alone. *That beautiful whore, Nomi.* She knew that her time might have been better spent imagining the suffocating feeling of imprisonment her beloved had endured; then, she might understand his agony more. But no. *Blinded by a dead girl.*

She ran her finger along the barred window of her cell and was disgusted by the brown slime that stained her fingertip. This was not like marching chained to a cart, she thought, but it was close. It was a fine cell; she supposed. As spacious as a hut from the hovels and, from the mush she wiped along the wall, probably as sterile. She wished there was better light, instead of the solitary, eerie flame burning outside the door, but a prisoner had few privileges. Lea was a prisoner, and this torment matched Erroh's.

She dared not think of how many prisoners must have despaired down here, awaiting their call to the sands of judgement. *Barbaric times.*

The flame caught a breeze and cast disturbing shadows down along the damp walls. Her mother had once spoken of portentous things in a candle's shadow, but Lea didn't believe in such notions. Perhaps it was a flickering candle that had burned down her home, she thought dispassionately. Her mother might have seen such a thing and allowed it to occur. Lea remembered loving her father, but she also remembered his brutal strength, his fierce wrath. Mostly, she remembered fearing him. Perhaps it was Uden himself who had killed them. Perhaps, as she took his head, she might ask about an insignificant homestead set ablaze, about an old, bitter man larger than life and brothers she couldn't remember at all. She rarely thought of her blood family any more. She thought of them now because she had a second opportunity to lose her entire family this day.

Whisht with these thoughts.

The fight had not begun, yet the uncertainty was already killing her. This was how any great downfall could begin, she imagined. A female could go mad in this room. She vowed to endure Erroh's talk of imprisonment with a fairer mind from now on. It was the little things. He had spent months in chains. Hers would be a swifter stay.

An hour, no less.

Lea drew her eyes from the flickering candles and looked to the straw bed and its dweller. "How are you feeling?" she asked.

Lillium lay on her back, staring at nothing, indifferent to the stains in her bedding. The stains probably explained the stench in the room, but Lillium didn't seem to care. She seemed so weak, so beaten, so very angry too.

When no answer came, Lea tried again. "Do you think they've started yet?" She looked up to the ceiling. If Lea spoke aloud her true terror, it would become real. Distantly, she heard a scream, and ignored it as a trick of her mind.

"No, not yet," Lillium whispered.

"Why not?"

"We'll know by the noise. Even down here." Their chambers were deep below the arena. Deep down, where Lea couldn't scale the wall and fight with Erroh, should the inexplicable occur. *No, no, no.*

Suddenly the crowd's cries reverberated deep down into their cell, right into Lea's soul. Lillium nodded, as though she'd expected as much. A drumming beat reverberated and Lillium tapped her finger against the wall in time. Though she rarely prayed, Lea bent a knee and whispered a few prayers to the absent gods. She laced them with subtle threats, exhortations not to bless her mate, but to stay clear of him.

"The absent gods aren't real," whispered Lillium distantly. She was far from her usual self. "I called to them many times and they forsook me when I needed them most. Fuk them."

Lea nodded in agreement. They probably weren't real. Still, she finished her threats in silence. She knew Erroh had to fight for Emir, and she was proud of him. But her banishment was a cruel form of torture. She could take watching him fight—after all, she'd watched him wither away for months and held her nerve. What was one brutal act of retribution after such a torment? Truthfully, she had a greater right to defend Emir than Erroh had. Had Emir not dragged her from the night's deathly grasp? But Erroh's insistence on who was the better master of the blade had been the telling blow. She scowled; he was a better master, but she was the better warrior. He wouldn't dare argue that matter.

"And if the gods are real? I want nothing to do with them," Lillium spat. She looked to the ceiling again. A solitary tear spilled from her eye and disappeared into the stained straw. A chorus of booing rumbled from above and both females stared up, listening intently. "It sounds like Erroh's introduced himself."

Lea felt the familiar panic course through her. Once again, useless to help.

No Nomi, either.

"Your beautiful mate is elite. I'm sure everything will be fine," Lillium muttered.

Lea felt her stomach turn. She felt a dreadful dizziness take hold, and the room spun as though she were upon a dance floor in the middle of a dead festival. "I feel sick."

Tell me it'll be fine, Lillium.

Tell me the crowd will wail in dissatisfaction.

Tell me my Erroh will return.

Hold me in my darkest moment, Lillium.

Whisper loudly so I don't hear the crowd cheer as they strike my Erroh down.

She needed to flee this dreadful little cell in the middle of the world. Far from light; far from life; far from everything she loved; far from her only family.

"Everyone left me to die in the arena last night," whispered Lillium. "And I am a ruin for it." Her voice was as cold as a southern lake, and Lea saw the ravages of pain in her friend's face. She could barely move, yet still, here she sat with her oldest friend. Her eyes flickered as the crowd first went silent and then gasped, and Lea saw the anguish tearing Lillium apart. Throughout their entire childhood, had Lillium not cared for her? Spoken for her? Protected her?

"Oh, my Lilli," Lea whispered, collapsing next to her, embracing her as the tears spilled freely from her broken friend. "I'm so sorry for failing you." Lea cried with her. "I'm sorry for leaving you." Her own tears would not stop.

"You were protecting Elise." Her tone was neither condemning nor kind. It was eerily unemotional. What devastation had befallen her?

"I didn't know... you said nothing... I thought Wynn would find you," Lea whispered, and Lillium hugged her in return. *Sisters in agony.* "I thought someone had injured you during the riots. I should have known... Oh, Lillium, I should have known."

"I pick my moments to fall apart," she whispered.

"We always fell apart together."

Lea felt the earth shift, and screams of terror grew deep down in a place where she kept her love for her mate. Lying beside each other, they listened to the shouts from the crowd, but to wonder how the fight progressed was to invite madness.

"You brought Elise home. That matters," Lillium blurted. "And I…
found my way home, eventually." Lea knew there was more. She
would not push. Lillium would say everything when she was ready.
"The blame is not with you, my friend. It is with the worthless wretch I
call a mate."

Though she did not know Wynn, she fought his battle. "Had he
known, he would have—"

"Attacked his master for rescuing me," Lillium snapped.

"He is an injured male."

"He is a bastard," hissed Lillium, and Lea nodded. Had Lea
appeared at the doorway as Lillium had, Erroh would have leapt to her
aid. Soothing, loving. Doing a mate's proper duty while Wynn turned
to anger.

After a time, Lillium withdrew from Lea's embrace. She swiped at
her glistening eyes and the paint running down her cheeks. "Erroh will
be fine. I know it in my aching bones," she whispered, taking Lea's
hand and kissing it gently. "Know this—for a strange moment, I was
proud of Wynn when I learned of his burden." She shook her head and
snorted away another tear before it fell. "I'm sorry. How vile a wretch
am I to turn the subject to me at this time?"

"It's fine."

"I am a better friend than this." She wiped her nose and the
unwanted fluid at its tip. "You brought me here as support." Above
them, the crowd stirred nervously as one. It was a strange sound. Both
Alphas looked up to the cracked ceiling above them. It sounded like
Erroh was winning, or else he had struck a telling blow, at least. Lea
felt dizzy again; her hand formed a fist. In that moment, she vowed to
kill both Aymon and Doran should they slay her love. And then Wynn
after, just because.

And then?

Well, then she would traverse the south alone one more time and
cut the Woodin Man's fuken head off.

A sudden, deathly silence fell upon the room, the sort of quiet that
fell only once the killing blow had been struck. Somewhere above, a

warrior was stepping into the darkness. Despite herself, Lillium muttered a few words of prayer to the absent gods she claimed to have no faith in. Now there were murmurs overhead, muted and emotional. Then suddenly the crowd roared and Lea strained her ears, trying to discern its emotion. She searched for outrage, for hatred, for any hope, really.

"Maybe Erroh is winning," Lillium said. Her eyes were wide in terror, but she grinned in excitement. Lea felt it too, until the crowd cheered raucously, a victorious roar, and Lea felt herself falling. Lillium stood up and placed her palms on the walls of this little cruel cell as it vibrated around them.

He's dead.

He's dead.

He's dead.

How can I live?

It felt familiar and sickening. The stamping returned. Louder now, like battle horns descending upon a doomed town. As though a worthy champion had been crowned after three decades of waiting. These were the cries of the victorious masses, and Lea was ready to lose her mind. The cheering never stopped. It never would, in her mind. She prayed again. Loudly. Beside her, Lillium dropped to a knee and matched her every word. But these were not prayers of blind devotion, eager pleas for mercy. Instead, both females challenged the absent gods to defy the inevitable tragedy, to work a miracle, or to fuk right off to the fires with them. Their voices rang out loudly in the cell, but no prayer was loud enough to silence the rumble of death above.

Eventually, Lea heard a key turning in the lock and she silently begged the gods that Erroh would be in the doorway smiling his mischievous, perfect smile. The door creaked open and an amused-looking Wolf entered, with Magnus a step behind him.

"What happened?" she whispered, as the panic grew in her heart. She knew, oh, she knew. Magnus looked pale. Paler than any man should. He shook his head in shock and reached for her. He didn't have the words.

She stumbled away from his grip and fell against the wall. She could hear the screaming above her. It was closer than before. All around her. It was a tormented wail, like none she'd ever heard before. It was coming from inside her, and it would never fall silent.

47

GREATNESS

"Keep your head up, brother," Erroh muttered, as they stepped side by side out onto the warm sands. The glare after so long in darkness was jarring, and he shielded his eyes from the early afternoon sun for the first few steps. Fear was festering in Erroh's stomach and he embraced it. Let the adrenaline follow, his father had insisted. Another wonderful lesson. Erroh had learned a few more in the years since. He took a deep breath and drew upon him a warrior skin, a skin born in Keri, a skin capable of godly things and much brutality, and he felt the fear fade. Not diminished completely, but enough to give him the edge. He'd done this dreadful waiting for death before. It was difficult to forget such things.

Out on the sands, he could see the crowd was larger than he'd expected. Many of his Ranger allies were lost in the sea of black and grey. Among them, standing out like jewels, were the vibrant colours of the Alpha females.

He and Emir began to walk. They needed to cross the wide expanse, and they did so alone. It was no small matter to feel the vitriol of a thousand spitting voices, and Erroh held his head high, despite the glare of the sun.

Pay us no heed. Just two outcasts, out for a stroll before some killing.

Every time Erroh allowed a mocking jest to catch his attention, the terrible weight he carried felt heavier. He believed himself and Emir inherently good, but to the city, they were the theatrical villains. Come nightfall and their freedom, they would be pariahs.

An insignificant price for an eternal debt.

Fuk Spark City.

It wasn't fear, or the weight of responsibility, that worried Erroh most. It was the burgeoning overconfidence that he well knew could doom him. Doom them both. No longer was he a wretch shuffling around in unfamiliar armour with nothing but a club in his hands. He was something else entirely. Aye, both Alphas were formidable foes, but had their paths this last year hardened them as he had been hardened? Erroh had endured war, tasted death, seen much misery beyond today's scene of controlled brutality. Moreover, he had been born for it. Had these two opponents faced an entire army down and charged forward? Had they faced a dynamic god with barely a breath left in them and still lived?

He shook his head, willing his arrogance away. Overconfidence was a slippery slope to a gruesome death. He didn't want to die today. He didn't want anyone to die at all today. If he played his cards correctly, he just might manage both tasks.

"Everyone has come out for the fight of the year," Emir muttered as they walked.

"All but two," Erroh said, feeling the sand crunch beneath his steps; he felt it shift underfoot, putting him slightly off balance. He hadn't thought about the sand, had never fought in it, either. In his youth, though, Magnus had charged him as part of his training to run miles on such surfaces, so he knew how little things like this could play their brutal part. He imagined his home for a few blissful breaths and felt himself relax.

Ahead of them the members of the tribunal stood along the edge of the stands, as though judging another Cull. They stood alone but for a few Black Guard on either side. In the levels above, the ruined seating for the Primary and her entourage remained untouched, as it had been the day before. The people weren't ready to clean the stains away. However, they were ready to return for a show.

"No matter what occurs, show your pride, Emir," Erroh warned. Around them, the sound of jeering grew louder.

"What pride?" Emir muttered, and Erroh laughed at this. As did Emir. Brothers in death, laughing at the darkness as it formed up around them. "Is this terror similar to what it was like when you stood with my friends?"

"Aye, this is what it felt like."

"Somehow, this comforts me."

They reached the group and fell still. Far below, he knew Lea was listening, and knowing she was close was both reassuring and agonising. If he'd told her his plan, though, she'd have hit him. He kissed the pouch at his wrist and cleared his mind of her as Silvia stood forward and addressed them both. Her words carried in the early afternoon air. She played to the watching crowd and she played it well.

"We have come for justice. We will receive it." She was imperious, and the crowd agreed like the loyal peasants they were. "For your part in our Primary's death, we charge you to die." She stopped speaking then, suddenly realising that Emir's champion had shrunk a few inches and wore plain armour. She turned to Emir. "Erroh has no right fighting for you."

"He is of my clan. He is the Hero of Keri," declared Emir. His voice was lost in the fresh howls of the spectators' wrath. Mea tried to speak but caught herself; Erroh could see the concern on her face, and he wished he could ease her worry and conscience. All he could do was bow deeply.

Silvia appeared unhappy with this, but a few hushed words from Dane silenced her. Then, the heavy slam of gates from the arena's far end announced the champion's opponents, and this ended the matter completely.

Side by side, they marched in to triumphant applause. Neither man wore a shirt, and their brutish strength was visible in their impressive frames. It was a challenge they were offering, and Erroh accepted it without hesitation.

No armour. As you wish.

He tugged his own shirt off to reveal the body of a fighter who had rebuilt himself from ruin through arduous training. They were impressive; he was godly.

As they neared, Erroh felt his heart hammer and he willed it to peace. Doran led, his eyes staring through Emir, his fingers twitching in anticipation. He grinned and Erroh wondered if he hadn't freshly shaved his head this very hour for the special occasion. Aymon followed behind; his long curly hair had been tied up in a ponytail and braided. His eyes never left Erroh or his naked chest. Perhaps he was choosing which area to pierce first, and Erroh remembered his speed. Of the two fighters, Aymon was better. On they marched, to the roar of the crowd, raising triumphant hands, playing the part of honourable executioners perfectly. The war effort would lose two fierce warriors this day if Erroh wasn't careful.

As if there weren't few enough Alphalines already.

"I should have eaten before this," Erroh whispered to Emir, whose face had paled a little. Truthfully, it wasn't just a distraction. He really was hungry. It was foolish fighting with a full stomach, but he wouldn't have minded a little breakfast. As it was, he imagined the taste of boar on his lips and pledged he would scour the city to find some when he emerged victorious. *Dried, salted boar, fit for a king.*

"I'll hop back to my hovel and pick us up something, shall I? I might have some eggs," Emir jested. He tried to smile. Tried to have hope.

It's all right, Emir. I have this.

"Your choice of weapons is the blade?" enquired Silvia. Along the wall was a wide selection of unique weapons, all hanging neatly, and Doran ran his finger along a perfectly constructed flail as he walked by before removing a long sword. After testing the edge for sharpness, he settled himself in front of Erroh. His eyes were cold and focused. He wasn't here to play now, and Erroh offered his most disarming smile.

Aymon picked a shorter blade with intricate designs and a heavy grip. He spun it a few times for balance and after a moment's pause, inspected a few more to be certain. The crowd held their breath. They were loving the routine, loving the expectation, loving the event entirely.

"Fuk it," Aymon muttered, returning to his first choice. Disappointment in a chosen weapon was a splendid start, thought Erroh. He held his own less impressive blades, gifted from the dungeon of the doomed. They were sharp, which was something.

"They've both beaten me before," Erroh whispered to Emir. He patted his friend on the shoulder. "I'm better now, though," he added, thinking of Keri and the camaraderie that lay in shared horrors. He took a few deep breaths and steadied his shaking hands. A Black Guard appeared and led Emir up to join the tribunal members as the three warriors waited in the sands.

Erroh bowed and backed away towards the centre of the arena, and the crowd erupted into a fresh cacophony of booing. Neither of his hunters followed him into the centre. They had all the time in the world; there was tradition to follow. They knew their place in the world. He caught sight of his father and his companions standing at the edge of the arena, enjoying a fine view of the battle. He offered them a bow and tried to clear his thoughts of everything except his opponents. Erroh knew they weren't respected by the females of the city, but sometimes these points were lost in the grandness of protocol and retribution.

"Emir is to die, and you are the tools of the city's vengeance," Silvia declared, earning another roar of applause with her commanding performance, and Erroh wondered if she spoke for Roja. If she spoke the words Roja couldn't bear to utter. He had always understood a Primary should rise above such things. "Make him yield or cut him down," Silvia commanded, and both Alphas nodded an acceptance to her challenge. They raised their swords, then turned and marched towards the doomed Hero of Keri.

"He looks relaxed," said Wynn quietly.

"He will win," whispered Magnus, radiating the same aura of calm that had served him so well at the worst moments of his life. It was better that Elise, in her weakened condition, be unaware of this skirmish, but he knew that he would pay for it afterwards. She would castigate him for not telling her. This he knew. But were she to have learned of this, nothing would have stopped her charging onto the sands and bringing ruin upon them all.

————

The two Alphas moved well together. In war, they would be formidable allies. They never moved too far apart, yet never appeared to interfere with each other's line of movement. If Uden was watching, he would smile at the city's finest protectors slaughtering each other.

Erroh knew they were irreplaceable. But he had a plan. A simple plan. He prayed it would work.

Doran led first, breaking left and kicking up sand in his haste, his eyes frantic with bloodlust. Such a desire was invaluable in war. The Hunt would fear this bald bastard something fierce. They would speak of his brutality. Who was Erroh to deny the Hunt such an enemy?

Aymon moved wide and swung first. Erroh caught the strike with his own less impressive blade and stepped casually away from Doran's killing blow on the other side. Aye, they were fast, but they had not improved this past year. *Don't kill them.* Erroh retreated and Doran followed, swinging wildly. Behind him, Aymon searched for openings and Erroh countered by stepping out of range. The clink of clashing blades was lost in the roar of the crowd. Their approval for the hunting Alphas' aggressiveness was deafening. They were oblivious to the defensive masterclass they witnessed. Aymon and Doran were not, though. They knew from the first blows that they had already lost.

Sparring with Lea had been nothing like this, Erroh mused, even as his body spun and twisted. Every time they had drawn swords, it had been more than practice and they had revelled in it. For anything less was to invite defeat in the titanic days ahead. They had held nothing back, offered no quarter and shown little mercy. In battle, they'd found acceptance and comfort. In violence they'd found desire, love.

This fight was something else entirely. Erroh's opponents couldn't hide their sublime skills behind elaborate feints or graceful manoeuvres as Lea did. Theirs were aggressive, powerful and telling; they announced their assaults loudly. Erroh saw the way their eyes searched for openings, how their favoured feet pushed forward, how the angles of their shoulders shifted before every attack. They screamed their intentions, and Erroh lay in wait like a patient trapper nestled in deep cover. It only took him moments to learn their traits, and he mastered their impressive strengths a few moments after that. The greater challenge on his part had been avoiding killing them both in the first few attacks. Instead, he retreated behind an impenetrable wall, always aware, always watching, always moving.

Aye, there were dangers. A foolish mistake on his part could end in tears. Stepping into a strike too early, or blocking when he should step away, could mean his own doom were he not careful. So Erroh trusted himself and kept his breath controlled, listened to his reflexes and waited for his moment. It didn't take long.

Aymon stepped in close and unleashed a flurry, but frustration diluted his effort. It was a loose combination, and Erroh met his eyes as he deflected each strike easily. Doran, suffering equal frustration, lunged in next, hoping to find an opening that wasn't there. It was a fine lunge, a debilitating blow with perfect form, but Erroh spun away, allowing both his spinning blades to touch unprotected skin as he did. Feeling flesh tear and seeing blood splatter, Erroh finished his perfect manoeuvre with a theatrical roll away from the duo's counter-strikes.

The crowd's enthusiasm dropped as the thin spray of blood marred the sand's pristine surface.

"Do you yield?" Erroh cried, digging his swords into the ground. Leaning on them, he looked impossibly relaxed and perfectly impressive, while both his opponents carried identical streaks of crimson along their chests. The wounds were not deep, but they would leave scars worthy of a tavern tale.

In reply to Erroh's question, they charged him again, and once more the clashing of metal filled the arena. They pressed home each strike with the force of all their rage and hatred, but every time, Erroh glided out of reach or effortlessly parried away their attempts. He never allowed them a step in the fight; any time they believed they had the upper hand, he delivered minor cuts across their naked skin as a painful reminder. They carried more weight than he, spent more energy swinging fruitlessly, and suffered more beneath the afternoon's unforgiving rays than Erroh ever could.

In the intervals when they stepped away to catch their breath, Erroh would ask them again, as gently as though he were standing over inept amateurs. "Do you yield?"

"To the fires with you, Erroh," they would retort between gasps.

Don't kill them.

Erroh continued to dominate, and bit by bit the disbelieving crowd fell silent. The longer the fight went on, the easier it became for Erroh to inflict what minor gashes he could. Eventually, it was a deep cut across Aymon's face that decided the course of the battle. Enraged by his friend's injury, Doran charged laboriously forward, swinging and cursing loudly as he did. He ignored his defences completely and Erroh easily disarmed him with a flick of the wrist before delivering a second burning strike across his cheek. Doran howled in pain and hatred, and Erroh followed through with a kick, which knocked him to the ground once more.

"Do you yield?" Erroh demanded, but neither man climbed to his feet. Erroh could see the fear and pain and humiliation in their faces. The crowd looked on, hushed and waiting, as all hopes of bloody revenge for their beloved Primary disappeared.

Erroh stood over them, and still they didn't raise their swords. "Do you yield?" he asked again, more quietly this time so that no one might hear their shameful surrender.

"Fuk off," Doran muttered. It was a fine reply under the circumstances. Erroh could see how deep his breaths were, how his head glistened with sweat.

"I will continue to ask until I am satisfied." He looked to the burning sky above and the surrounding blue. "I can do this all day, friends."

At this challenge, both Alphas picked up their weapons and struggled to their feet. They were brave, Erroh thought. Or else stupid. There was only so much any brute could take before fatigue and agony won out over bravery alone. Stupidity, on the other hand, was eternal.

Don't kill them.

They charged forward and the cub met their attacks as before. Erroh closed his mind to the outside world and the murmurs of unrest growing in the crowd. The world slowed to his will; he turned and twisted his body away from each strike and struck with a power that no warrior had ever faced. *Apart from Lea.* Every attack ended the same way. When the moment called for it, Erroh would lure them into a mistake upon which he pounced; then, he would draw away with his bloodied sword and repeat his question. He glided effortlessly around the now wildly swinging duo and blooded them like a Wolf upon a charging mount. It was no longer a sport. He had bested the champions. Erroh was the executioner, should he choose. Sublime and untouched, a god of the arena.

At last, when the duo were once again bent over, gasping for breath and examining their many wounds, Erroh drew away from the fight and spun towards the crowd.

"I will not kill these fine warriors," he roared, so all would hear. Now the crowd came to life as one, spitting venom in reply. The cub held out his hand to calm the onslaught.

"Why should I sacrifice these souls, these two fierce Wolves who will bring war to our enemy? I cannot afford to kill them. Our joint cause cannot afford to lose them."

The crowd, however, could not see the value in his mercy. Could not see beyond their own fury. It was a mob, now, and they were on their feet, bellowing their displeasure like an unstoppable, cruel machine.

His battered foes, however, heard something else in Erroh's grand pronouncement: his words of mercy had inspired them anew. Magnus had once said that a warrior who hesitated to deliver a killing blow was a beaten opponent. Perhaps they understood this too. They climbed to their feet and charged Erroh with a fury born of contempt. They leapt forward with the vigour of maddened steers and forced him under the edge of the balcony, where the tribunal stood motionless.

Erroh, his back to the wall, suddenly felt a tremor of fear; a rivulet of sweat trickled down his back.

Don't kill them.

Don't kill them.

Unless you have to.

His opponents came on as one, now, and suddenly Erroh felt the day's efforts catching up with him. His movements slowed, even as Doran and Aymon drew upon his mercy as though it were sizzling meat to feast on. Doran led the attack, and Erroh parried his fierce strike, sending his blade into the sand. He struck out with his fist, catching the bald brute squarely in the jaw and sending him to his knees. Erroh knew he could take the fiend's head clean off with one slice, but he stepped away, leaving the man reaching blindly for his sword as his senses searched for clarity.

Aymon stepped in now and attacked awkwardly, and Erroh drew him in close before ducking wide and tripping him as he charged past, sending him careening into the wall of hanging weapons. His sword joined Doran's in the sand beside Erroh's feet.

Before Erroh could ask his question again, another voice rang out in the arena. Strong, assured. The voice of a fit leader.

"I will not watch this anymore," Roja declared and the crowd fell silent once more.

Erroh stabbed the ground again and bent to a knee as though pledging to a king.

"Emir's champion has shown mercy," Roja roared, slamming her hand down on the edge of the arena wall. It looked like it hurt. She didn't react. *A Primary wouldn't.* "I declare mercy in reply," she called. A low murmur of dissatisfaction rose up in the crowd, while a minority —likely in the beige section—clapped in appreciation.

Panting heavily, Erroh bowed deeply, feeling relief flooding through his quivering body.

But before he could rise to his feet and salute his Primary, he heard the subtle crunching of sand behind him and turned to see the shadow of a swinging war hammer above his head. He rolled deftly away from the strike, but Aymon was ready. The brute kept swinging, hammering thunderous blows down around him. Erroh struggled to rise and made it to one knee before a sickening blow knocked him aside like a rag doll. He landed heavily against the arena wall. His body convulsed and he cried out in pain.

Again, he tried to rise, but his body shook and betrayed him. *Don't give in.* He'd felt this pain before. Dashed against rocks and spinning helplessly in an unforgiving current. He had no one to save him this time, though. *Goodbye, my beo.* Someone pulled him roughly to his feet. It might have been a mountain; it wore a beard. The bearded mountain head-butted him; stars exploded in his head, and he collapsed in the mountain's hold and awaited a hammer blow to send him into the darkness.

"I command you, stop this Aymon!" Roja shrieked, and Erroh tried to speak, to mock their cowardice, to earn himself a few moments to recover, but the words wouldn't form.

"You have no authority here," shouted the bearded mountain known as Aymon. He held Erroh aloft like a toy before striking him again with his forehead. The world slowed and darkened. Erroh knew this was the end. He looked to the sky through a haze of his own blood and winced as the sun burned his eyes. His vanquisher dropped him in the sand to recover his war hammer, and with his last ounce of strength Erroh looked to those who had condemned him to this death. Around him he heard roaring as the crowd eagerly awaited death.

———

It was an easier leap of faith than Wynn had imagined. The fear had been the hardest part to overcome, but once he'd taken the first forbidden step, the rest were easier—and faster, too. Lillium would hate him anew for the shame he would bring upon her name, but sometimes, the wrong thing done at the right time was the only thing to be done.

It's okay, Erroh. I've got this.

Wynn had started running the moment Aymon had recovered his hammer from the wall. It was quite a distance, but Wynn was swift on his feet. The crowd booed him as he sprinted, but he ignored their outrage and kept his eyes fixed upon the bastard accosting his friend.

He covered the distance in a few breathless moments and sped past Doran, who, to his astonishment, was upon bended knee, pleading with Aymon to release his prey. Who knew the bastard was capable of honour in battle? Or mercy?

Aymon was capable of neither, however. The brute stood over the unmoving body of his victim, hammer in hand. He had a right to this killing, Wynn knew. Neither he nor Doran had surrendered, and the law was to be honoured. So Wynn intervened in the only way a shamed outcast could: by leaping on him from behind. The momentum took both Alphas into the stone wall, where Aymon's head struck the arena's boundary with a sickening, hollow thud.

Doran, seeing his friend unconscious, forgot mercy and rushed in to save him. He met an effortless spinning kick for his troubles and collapsed unconscious in the blazing sand. Wynn heard the outraged howls of the mob above him, and he embraced it. *This is a fine way to die.*

Now the masses of Black Guards swarmed forth, summoned by Silvia's cry, spilling onto the arena sands from their places among the crowd.

"I'll batter you all," Wynn warned, standing over the unconscious body of Erroh. He used no blade, instead kicking out at any Wolf who stepped in close to him. He fought them as they rushed forward, but all too soon he was outnumbered and his great rebellion was ended as quickly as it had begun. They thrashed at him with foot and fist, and he tasted blood and then he tasted sand. He felt chains being clamped around his wrists and then watched in horror as they chained a helpless Erroh.

A manacled Emir was dragged up beside them both. "Fuk you all!

I'll fuken kill you, you fuken fuks!" he spluttered. The wretched healer took every strike as though it were welcome, grinning maniacally, spitting in their faces and condemning the watching crowd for good measure. He was fearless, and Wynn was proud to die with him, snarling his own hatred right back at his assailants. He stayed conscious as long as he could, but at last the battering became too much. A pair of arms wrapped themselves around his neck and squeezed the breath from him.

"Ah, fuk you," he wheezed, as the looming darkness took him and delivered him into the respite of unconsciousness.

48

PARANOID

Garrick fell against the tree trunk, gasping. Grasping his head in shaking hands, he allowed himself a moment's agony while gathering his frantic breath. Wiping the sweat from his brow, he cursed his luck. Cursed his failing mind, too, and the foulness festering in the wound he'd suffered.

Can't stop yet. The old scout took a moment to calm his breathing and gather his scattered thoughts before facing the unforgiving Wastes once more. He could feel his pursuer stealing up behind him, and he shook the thought away. *That shit got you into this state.* He leaned against his tree and peered into the silent forest behind him, and as expected, heard nothing, saw even less.

"Stupid fuken fool," he told himself, but held off blinking lest he miss something. Paranoia had driven him to this lunacy. Oh, how he wanted to stop this frantic run through the Wastes, but until his race was done, until his spirit was shattered, he would keep on. He would serve his Ranger brethren this day. "There's no one there."

His paranoia had worsened the weaker his decrepit body had become. "Trick of the mind," he muttered, cursing his blood loss. *Delirious imaginings of the demented.* He could feel it now: the fresh burn of infection. It was a different pain to a clean wound. Like salt

513

and fire, but without the cleansing. He was better than this, he reminded himself. But was he?

The old Ranger pushed himself away from the tree and stumbled on through the endless green, each branch slapping at him and grazing his face. He staggered like a drunk in this serene, beautiful landscape. This was Hunt territory now.

A mile on, he felt the tourniquet fall away and he cursed aloud again and then swiftly cursed his loose tongue. *Go silently.* Take the pain, he told himself, pushing on, ignoring the wound. Ignoring the warmth dribbling down his skin. A few more miles and then he'd see to it properly.

You've had worse. Keep going. Stay ahead of whatever hunts you.

"No one hunts you, Garrick," he told himself, and this he believed, but still, he could not stop. Prey never rests until it is sure of safety. His mind was a broken line of frenzied thoughts. Some real, some wild. So he ran from them, as he had from the beginning.

Reaching down, he touched the open wound below his knee. Deep and volatile. He'd done enough to stop the constant flow of blood, but the pain almost felled him again now and he moaned in misery. Don't fall down. *Do that, and you won't get up.* Determined, he kept running. One foot in front of the other. For just another mile more, he pledged. He almost believed himself, too.

Distance became nothing but pain. He did not know how long he ran, only that it wasn't far enough from his own imaginings. From his own terror. The sun had moved across the sky to near evening now, and beneath the canopy of green it was darker still. He chose a worn path despite his better judgement. He was far from their main encampment, but he knew that some of those sneaky bastards marched patrols through the forest, looking for prey, looking for victims. They didn't always stick to rivers, either—an insignificant detail but information Magnus would desire.

It's not them I fear, though, is it? It is something else.

This would be his last march. Most warriors knew when the end drew near. Even if he survived, he would be of little use to the war. Who needed a Ranger who'd lost his nerve and mind? Slowing beneath a gigantic oak with a wide trunk, he found a seat of moss to rest on. *For a few breaths is all.* Dropping like a stone upon a slope, his body crumpled beneath him and for a moment, he enjoyed the earned relief. He sniffed the air and listened again, but found only silence and the smell of damp and moss. There were worse things. If he died here, the Wastes would take him; he would be part of this untouched land forever. A comforting thing, though he'd have preferred a grave with a view.

His pack felt heavy on his aching back. There wasn't much under its flap. No silver trinkets or stash of wealth. His only riches were his study of enemy numbers and his tactical suggestions. They were everything to him, but really, they were just scribbled thoughts upon parchment for a Master General's eyes alone. He would die a pauper.

Drop them now and you'll move more swiftly.

He reached for the wound again but held his silence this time. His breathing was desperate. His body understood and savoured each one while it could. *This is a suitable way to die.* The gash ran from knee to ankle. No healer from the city would say it was a mortal blow, but he was days from being among healing hands and foul-smelling tonics. He listened to the deep silence around him as he refastened the strip of cloth around his bloodied wreck of a leg.

Any wanderer would be wise to know a few tricks to stay alive in the Wastes, and Garrick knew them all, but he had no trick to slow time and grant him safe passage through these hostile lands. He listened for anything in the forest, but nothing moved. He could feel the phantom gaze, though.

Maybe it's death that hunts you this day.

He cursed his mind again, pulling the bandage tight and knotting it as shards of agony shot through him. *Pain can be controlled.* An Alphaline mind-set, but no less effective.

Garrick knew he was the best scout in the Four Factions. Until this dreadful mission, he'd taken pride in claiming this to any apprentice who would listen. The best scouts found employment in the best armies with the best Master Generals too, and Magnus knew the value of Garrick's word. Garrick had never imagined he'd have a last report.

He'd never thought he'd fail with his last report either. *Interesting report, too.*

Watching these last few days, he had learned their numbers, and he knew they were preparing to charge. Magnus hadn't been too far off in his predictions. The world believed the Hunt almost undefeatable. Garrick did not. A skilled scout could spot these things a mile off. They marched and gathered more like an aggressive family than regimented soldiers. Erroh and Magnus knew this custom too. *Fuken southerners. Greater numbers, but same shitty behaviour.* Perhaps, with Uden leading them, it might be different, but Garrick wasn't certain.

How could one general possibly steer so many willing soldiers without the advice of lieutenants? Aye, councils slowed down decisions in the great machine of war, but decisions argued by many were usually the better option.

Though he knew better, he lay down in the moss and immediately his body began whispering to him a perilous lullaby, and the days of marching caught up with him. A most terrible and wonderful exhaustion came upon him and he gave in to sleep, to infection, to whatever hunted him. Instinctively, he dug into his knee again and the pain woke him anew, but only momentarily. His body became heavy and his desire to struggle on faded into the surrounding silence. *Give in.*

"I brought this on myself," he muttered, closing his eyes and feeling the relief of emptiness draw around him like a soothing blanket.

The last few days watching the Hunt had unnerved him, though he couldn't understand why. He was no believer in divine intuition, but what had begun as a feeling of being watched had swiftly become something more. Even when he'd been concealed perfectly, watching them from his vantage point, he'd felt a presence. In the way a deer senses a hunter's gaze, he had become certain he was no longer alone. A patient man, he'd waited a day for the fiend to reveal themselves, but night had fallen and no fiend had come forward. The forest spoke a unique language to him, as it did to others. He needed no print embedded in the mud, no broken branch, to understand the movements of his quarry. Moving swiftly and soundlessly, he'd spoken to the forest and searched the area for signs, for tracks, and found none. This should have brought him immediate relief, but the uncertainty returned the following day in a second hiding place. Again, he'd told himself it was paranoia, but the feeling grew the more he searched. He had allowed his unease to become painful wariness. Instead of observing the Hunt, he constantly searched the unmoving green. Like a tiny crack draining a dam during a drought, he lost his assuredness to obsession. He had flirted with old age during the Faction Wars, but never truly had he felt as old as he did now.

He thought he'd feel better once he'd gathered enough information and begun a swift march towards Spark, but the nervousness increased. As he jogged through the forest, his every step was poisoned by visions of a clawed hand appearing from behind the next tree, dragging him towards doom. Every stop to quench his thirst became a patient wait for a blade to punch through his ribs from somewhere behind him. He took no comfort in sleep either. Lying huddled up beneath a bush with his cloak around him, he'd feared silent assassination for two sleepless nights before, on the third day, he'd emerged from a cluster of trees above a slope and doomed himself.

Had he had his wits about him, he might well have chosen his path better, but paranoia had stolen his sense like heavy lung took the breath. He'd heard a twig break from a distance behind him, and, certain his many days of suspicion were now coming to fruition, he'd fled on down the slope and stumbled on the very first rock in his path. As he spun, he remembered blue sky, muddy brown and the dull grey of a second, unforgiving rock as it rose to meet him.

Awaking with his breath a haze in the starlit sky above, Garrick knew his doom. His body burned painfully and it took all his will to gather enough wood and kindling to light a fire. The race was done. His body shook as though he were lying in a lake of ice, and only once the flames were burning brightly did he tend to his leg once more. Cutting the bandaging, he wept. Not for the pain, but for relief. In the flickering flame he could see the thin line of pus seeping from the edge of the gash, and it was an ugly sight.

"I'm sorry, Magnus," he whispered to the wind. Fine, fitting words and they set his mind at ease. Wrapping his leg once more, he climbed to his feet. He would die in a grander place than the clustered forest. His mind betrayed him yet again as he stumbled painfully through the night, but even when his paranoia begged him to turn back around and face the demon that hunted him, he increased his feverish pace. *A fine hill with a finer view.*

Near dawn, he stood upon a steep ridge overlooking green as far as the horizon, and he thought it perfect for his needs. He lit a second fire effortlessly and lay down beside its comforting heat. He had given up, yet his body fought bravely to keep him alive, and he thought life a beautiful, natural thing. With an amber sky above him he considered conjuring a little poultice to ease the pain as he slipped into darkness, but such an effort was of no interest to him. All desire to survive was absent now, taken by the growing infection. So, he looked into the distance in the direction of the city, and wondered how it would all end.

He closed his eyes and waited for sleep, but a slow, growing rumble of thunder pricked him to wakefulness. He felt it in the ground around him, and he realised even in his delirium that it was the marching army in the valley somewhere below. He cared little if they saw him or his fire; he lay back, too spent to count their terrifying numbers. His pack, with its cargo of scribbled thoughts and suggestions, observations and predictions, lay discarded by the fire and he wondered if he could use some parchment for kindling. With the Hunt marching towards war, his notes were useless.

Failure, failure, failure. Such thoughts should have saddened him, but there was a cold comfort in relinquishing effort. He would not be missed in the days ahead, nor would many remember him fondly. Only now did he regret not having family. Who didn't want a legacy? For some, children were the only gift they brought to the world. Others, like him, desired something more.

He looked down again; he could see the southerners now, and he hated them. They wore their finest armour. Hardly impressive, really, but their wildly swinging banners looked terrifying. Such things mattered in war, he knew.

He wondered which scout was rushing towards Magnus with word this very moment. The first battle for Samara would begin today. Magnus would find a way or he would not. The city would fall or it would not. The Primary would die or she would not. He could offer nothing more to this warring world. Garrick watched the last group of thundering beasts disappear from view and he sighed a dead man's sigh.

"Not long now," he whispered to nothing, before crawling slowly back towards the fire and its warmth. His brow was a river of sweat. His body was drowned. The shakes would come next, he knew; the coma sometime after that. Drinking from his tankard, he thought this a fine death. Not hunted, not captured and not felled by a knife's cruel edge. There were better deaths, of course; he'd have preferred to die in the arms of a beautiful girl after acts of devilish pleasures, but that was an unlikely ending for him.

"I did my best," he whispered.

He was at darkness's doorway when the angel came to him. Without a sound she emerged from the forest, bearing a smile of such loveliness that he wanted to weep. Instead, he reached for her as his eyes grew heavy, and she took his hand and bent down to him. Her stunning eyes held him in her gaze as she kissed his hand, and Garrick felt such desire as he'd never known before.

"You are an angel," he cried.

"You and I must talk, Ranger," she whispered in his ear.

49

THE DARK

T*hirsty.*

Erroh opened his eyes and, for a wonderful moment of numbness, forgot where he was until the pain woke with him. *Pain means alive.* He lay flat on a bed of stone in near perfect darkness. It might have been night, morning or somewhere in between. Without windows, he couldn't tell. Wherever he was, the air was dry and stale. It felt like indoors. It also felt like death. A terrible stench hung around him, and he tried to sit up and cover his nose and mouth, but was held by chains attached to both his wrists. *Not chains; anything but chains.* A larger, longer chain keeping him in place hovered across his vision like ship's rigging. It hung from a heavy hook in the wall above his bed, looped through a crude iron ring hammered into the rock. He could move, just not too far and always carefully. *In chains again.* His breath caught in his chest and panic coursed through him. He imagined the painful pull of a cart and his body trembled. Gasping, he took in a lungful of the fetid, dry air and gathered his nerve. Steeling himself, he tried to piece together where he was.

I'm in chains, but I live.

If I live, there is hope.

There is always hope.

With this familiar mantra ringing in his ears, he began examining his injuries. His back was a dull furnace of aching. Reaching down to where the last blow had landed, he half expected to find a chunk of muscle and skin torn free, or a few bones protruding out at awkward angles. To his surprise, he discovered tight flesh, albeit bruised and tenderised like boar's meat. It was wretched agony, but in a few days he might feel better. He sat up straight and swallowed the pain. As he did, he became aware of the aroma of Lea's perfume cutting through the stench. He touched the pouch strapped to his wrist, kissed it once and then kissed the ribbon fastening it. He felt better, albeit not much. *Imprisoned again after failing in battle.* He fought the panic again and searched for distraction by looking around the dreary cell. It was long and tight. A man's height in width; twice that to the door. He sighed loudly and realised his mouth was as dry as the Adawan sands. Again, fresh clutches of panic took hold, questioning him like a bitter foe. And, oh, he allowed it.

Thirsty? You want a drink? Well, go drink. What's stopping you? Chains? You can't go anywhere now? But what if you die of thirst? Are you thirsty? If you weren't in chains, you'd not be thirsty. Shit for you. Chains, Erroh. Chains. You are in fuken chains and you can't fuken drink because you are in fuken chains.

Thirsty.

Fuk.

Chains.

He shouldn't have struggled. Months in chains told him he shouldn't, but suddenly escaping from the chains became important. No, more than that, it became critical. He jerked and twisted. The chains held, and he grunted in frustration. With panic picking at his nerve, he stared into the darkness and imagined forests and rivers and no chains anywhere, and somehow he took hold of himself. *Chains, thirsty. Dead alone in the dark.* Shaking his head in defiance, he stood up carefully and caught sight of a bucket of waste at the foot of the bed, a foot from the doorway. It was a fine bucket, with no leaks. It was a popular bucket, too. It was half full from the previous tenant, and his stomach turned as he caught sight of the mushy contents within.

Carefully he edged the reeking container away from the door into the far corner, where he would become more acquainted with it at a later time.

The cell door itself was ancient and heavy, as most cell doors were. At least there was a hole to look out. However, his keepers had barred it over to stop a slim prisoner slipping out into the next room. That room was three times larger than his cage, and just as dark. With a start, he realised he was in the jail from the night before. Or the day before that. He'd been asleep for a while.

The vision of Aireys flashed in his mind. "Fuk it anyway," he muttered, resting his head against the bars. She had been so brave as she burned. He had offered a last gift, and it had been for nothing. She was dead, and he was in chains again. Heavy, unbreakable chains.

A voice disturbed his melancholy. "Hello?" It sounded familiar. "Emir?"

"Oh, fantastic. I thought you were dead... Hero."

Erroh turned toward the voice and felt a spasm of pain in his shoulder; it knocked him to the ground with a clatter of chains. Biting his tongue, he tasted blood in his mouth and he howled. *That won't quench my thirst.* Forcing the claustrophobia down, back into its cage, and taking only a moment to spit the blood from his mouth, he struggled to his feet again.

"Did you just fall, Erroh?"

His eyes were growing accustomed to the gloom now, and Erroh peered back through the bars. There was a cell door on either side of his own in the little circular room; a fourth door led out into the outer jail, where they'd plotted and failed. Through it there shone a faint light; whether it was from a torch or sunlight, Erroh couldn't say. Either way, it was just enough to show the enormous barrel sitting in the centre of the chambers. Erroh could almost smell the water concealed within.

"Aye," he croaked. "My body betrayed me." He licked his lips and thought of the barrel tipping and spilling over him. "What happened?" he asked.

"You lost," came Emir's reply from his right.

He could hear resentment and disgust in his friend's voice, and it stung. But despite his many missteps with his mate, Erroh was unskilled in the art of contrition. Besides, how could he apologise for failing as he had? What if Emir denied him? That would make this imprisonment a thousand times worse.

"I was winning," Erroh protested, and decided it a fine reply. The blades had never come close to him, he told himself. He'd been in control until Roja had called an end to matters. It was her fault. *Bitch.* He thought about blaming her, but fell silent. Emir might argue that gambling both their lives in a game of impossible odds was where the blame lay. When adding everything up, Emir might well have had a point.

"Aye, you were winning, and then... well, you weren't," came his angry reply. Erroh could hear the rustle and clinking of chains, and Emir's battered face appeared at the little window. He looked more hostile than normal, but his expression changed swiftly to concern once he glimpsed Erroh's face. "They battered you. Are you all right?"

Erroh touched his face gingerly and felt the damage around his nose straight away. He stepped away from the doorway and felt the panic attempt to drown him once more. *Stay afloat, little cub.* He felt swelling and dried blood. His face was his favourite thing about himself. He wanted to scream, to weep, to curse, to give up and crumple into the dirt with his knees in his arms and shiver for a while. After a breath, he did exactly that.

"Erroh?"

Not now, Emir. I'm having a moment.

The chains rang in his ear again and he closed his eyes and felt snow at his feet. The thunder of the carts deafened him. The pull of his restraints stole his will, and then he heard Nomi's voice in his mind. It was as though she called to him from beyond the grave, and perhaps she did. *Ah, Forerro.* As a prisoner, he had had pride and fight, cold comfort as that had been. This was something entirely different. There was no honour in this captivity, nor any liberation in his resolve. This was worse; this was only the beginning. He was a pariah: hated forever and destined for the gallows. His body shook as he wept. Thankfully, the rattling of his chains cloaked the sound.

"It's not that bad," offered Emir, breaking the silence a few hours later. It might have been hours. Without light, who was to know? Emir had been thinking. There was nothing else to do. He didn't know what demons plagued his friend, only that his smile disguised horrors. He tried to stay angry. Fuk it, he tried, but to hear Erroh weep was a sobering thing. *Drink.* Oh, Emir wanted a drink something terrible. He shook that thought away swiftly. It wouldn't help matters.

"I've woken up in worse places," he added, running his fingers along the three bars in front of him. He wondered whether he could make a tune from the clinking noise. Maybe clink his manacles up against them to make harmonies. A few hours in and he was already losing his mind to boredom, to wretchedness, to the unfairness of his life. Truthfully, he'd shed a few tears himself in the first hours after they'd dragged him in here. Before Erroh woke. The tears had been welcome, and no one would have judged him for their release. He just would not admit to his own weeping.

Emir took a dry breath and waited for the shamed Alpha to answer. Maybe silence was the better move. He felt cheated by what had happened; Erroh had not lost. At least not technically. That was the likely reason they were simply chained and not already hanging from a tree. For all he knew, as they waited here, there might be a Ranger coup occurring. Or else a city riot. Perhaps there was another trial taking place. He might ask for another champion. He'd insist on Lea this time.

"It feels somewhat bad right now," replied the technically undefeated champion at last, appearing back at the bars of his cage, looking like an aggressive drunk during the festival of the Puk.

"I don't think they broke your nose, but it has taken a fine battering." He was a friend in pain and Emir couldn't stand that. "Give us a smile? Any lost teeth?"

Erroh smiled weakly.

"No broken teeth. You still have your good looks. And here I was thinking if they beat you enough, I'd have a chance with Lea." He forced a laugh, hoping Erroh would join him. His champion did something else entirely.

"I'm sorry, Emir."

Emir's eyes opened wide and he allowed a moment of bitter venom to course through him. He was entitled to scream at him. Had the Hero of Keri not doomed him with his idiotic notion of mercy? *Fuk you, Erroh.* The moment passed, and with it his anger. Had Erroh not given enough already? Was Emir not the one responsible for his own miserable fate? Should Roja's commands not have settled the blood lust of Aymon without question? "Mistakes were made by all of us, Erroh. You sought mercy. They punished you for it."

"Well, I still doomed us both." The chains jingled as he shrugged.

"Cass doomed us. Not you."

Erroh fell silent at this. Perhaps with contrition attained he could focus on more pressing things, like how uncomfortable the bedding was. How long moments felt in this darkness. How thirsty he was.

Emir remembered being thirsty in the sands. Hungry, too. He could have asked for something—a dead man's last meal, perhaps. Alas, his mind was on other brutal things.

"Well, you were winning until Roja told you to stop winning. It all went downhill from there," he said. "You dropped your swords in honour. Probably shouldn't have done that with Aymon around."

"I remember getting hit by a hammer."

"As though you were a nail."

The sound of chains came again, followed by a light yelp as Erroh tested his injury. "I thought I was dead from that blow alone."

"Aye, your reflexes saved you. He caught you like a mount's kick. But it was only a glancing blow. I've seen a lot worse with swifter recoveries. Besides, Alphas heal quick, or so they say."

"It's our stubbornness," Erroh said, sighing as he rested his head against the bars.

Say this without panicking him. "Hey, Erroh, if you piss blood, let me know. If you vomit, let me know too? You can expect a fine bit of pain, so don't bother me with that. Let's call that your penance for dooming us."

"I remember little after that."

But Emir did. He remembered the battering he had taken. He remembered the screaming, from all involved. Through the fists and feet, he remembered seeing Roja once more as they'd brought him to the ground, her red hair flowing around her as she stared down at him with undisguised hatred. And what were his parting words as they took him?

Goodbye.

"Wynn jumped in like a glorious idiot, and now all of us are rightly up the creek," Emir said, sitting back down on his bed of stone. Thinking of Roja was like receiving a punch from Quig. Or Wrek. He could feel himself falling into his own pit of despair. He had never liked the dark. Perhaps if they lit just one torch in the centre of the room, it might feel different. Less disheartening. He was not a strong man. He never would be. Before he died, though, he wanted a drink and he wanted silk for his bed of stone.

"Is Wynn dead?" asked Erroh.

Emir hesitated. There were three cells, and he was certain they held only two guests. "I don't know. I knew you were in here, but I don't know what became of him. Brave bastard."

"There are three cells. Perhaps they…"

"I called for him, but nothing stirs within that third cage." Emir imagined Wynn already put to death. Out in the wilderness, hanging from the finest tree; crows dining upon his flesh and the worms waiting eagerly for his carcass to be cut down. "It was a fine sacrifice on his part."

When Erroh spoke again, his tone was distant. "When I face those brutes again in combat, I will show no mercy. It will be swift."

It was a good oath, thought Emir, smiling to himself ruefully. As if they would allow him to fight for their lives again.

"I owe him a debt," Erroh continued. "Entering the arena was lunacy, but the bravest act I've seen since…" His voice trailed off and Emir knew what place he spoke of.

There was a sound of chains again, and a few loud groans, and Emir wondered if Erroh wasn't crying again. Or else having a seizure. That would add to the day. Hearing his champion convulse and die while he unable to do anything about it would be a fathomless torment. He stood up, listening, but there was only silence.

"Are you okay?" Erroh called.

"Aye." *Not a seizure, so.*

He turned and peered at the little light in the main jail; it glowed dimly, barely a respite from the dark, but it was something. He knew how darkness tore into a man's mind and also his soul. Hadn't Jeremiah preached on this many years ago, back when he was far younger and searching for meaning after his many sins? He wondered, did he have a soul or was such a gift a transient thing? Was it used up like water in the body? Had he smeared his so much that all the goodness in the world couldn't remove its taint? Were souls brighter than light? Was his soul brighter than Erroh's? Was it dimmer than Wynn's for sacrificing himself? He imagined his soul glowing in the darkness, looking pretty with a blue tint. Emir whispered a prayer. To dead friends; to opportunities lost; for mistakes made.

Erroh stirred, interrupting his strange imaginings. "I could not have shown the heroism Wynn did, had it been me. A brave, brave warrior. A genuine friend."

There was another clash of chains and Emir leapt up. The sound had come from another side.

"I entered the battle to finish you off," declared a voice from the third cell. It sounded like Wynn, but lighter than before. "It's just you looked so peaceful, all asleep and ruined in the dust, that I thought it would be a shame to wake you up with a blade to the stomach." His chains rattled again as he put his bruised and bloodied face to the bars. His bruises weren't as bad as Erroh's. His face hadn't landed against a wall.

"You are only talking now?" yelped Emir in excitement. Or in anger—he wasn't certain himself. He certainly was embarrassed at having wailed for his champions, believing himself the only one alive. He'd gone quiet when they'd carried Erroh in. Wynn must have entered long before. How long had he lain there listening in the dark, in silence?

"I have no words," Erroh said, looking towards the third cell. Towards his friend. *A debt I owe.*

"Either I've lost my sight, or we're back in the jail again," Wynn said flatly, groaning ever so. "Oh, those Wolves really beat the shit out of me." Despite his injuries, he looked calmer than he'd ever been. Perhaps a concussion was all it took. Or else he looked better with darkness. Whatever it was, Wynn laughed now, a sound probably never heard in this room before, and as welcome as a torch's glow. "You should have seen the looks on the faces of those two brutes," he said between chuckles. "It felt good. You know, dooming myself."

"They looked rather confused at the sight of you running across the sand, all golden and honourable," admitted Emir, laughing with him. There was a strange, demented ring to their cheer.

Their mood was contagious, and at last Erroh chuckled along with them and felt the surging relief after clenching every muscle in his body for what felt like days. "You would have looked impressive with a cape streaming out behind you. For the full pompous effect," he said gamely. Somehow, this felt better. Misery took company well. There were worse things, he supposed.

Wynn knew jesting might get them through this. However long "this" might be. All his life, humour had kept him afloat in harsh times. His father, Marvel, had taught him the value of an excellent joke; it was the only true thing his father had ever spoken. Wynn could have told them he'd woken a few hours before now, but listening to Emir's laments had broken what remained of his will. At the start, it was his inability to face either of them. For how could he face the man he'd stood for and abandoned so easily? Fear wasn't a strong enough reason, even if it was a fine muse. So he'd hidden in the darkness, thinking of many things, mostly of Lillium. He knew that his ultimate act of betrayal to the city would give her the excuse to dissolve their coupling. His sacrifice would give another the opportunity to lie with her. A day before, such a thought would have torn his insides asunder, but now he took the pain and dedicated it to her. The wretched darkness had stripped him of everything he thought he understood. He saw himself for who he was, how he behaved, and the mate he was. Aye, she was not without her sins, but his hands were dirtiest. He knew now it was all his fault. It was childishly selfish to imagine winning back her favour. As soon as he had stepped onto the sands, they were over. *Beautiful Lillium, beautiful Wynn. The perfectly mated couple.* Not that he loved her any less; in fact, he loved her with all his broken heart, but it was this love that had slowly killed her. Taken her fire, taken her will, even taken the fuken colour from her hair. She deserved a life of love and warmth. She deserved a mate with a kinder tongue and better nerve.

As the darkness rang with sounds of a lamenting healer, Wynn had given up on Lillium and accepted his mistakes for the cruel acts they were. If she faced him again, he would kneel at her feet and wait for her judgement. More likely, though, they would spare her ever seeing him again, and that was all right. As they placed the noose around his neck, he would think fondly of her. Then he would think of nothing at all.

The other two captives were still laughing about the sight of him racing across the sand, and Wynn took pleasure in their joy. "I knew I should have brought my cape," he added staunchly, "but your heroic champion thought it was a little too extravagant."

"Some fuken champion he turned out to be," Emir mocked, and the laughing stopped. Too soon to laugh in the face of doom? Too soon to mock the absent gods for the bastards they were?

Erroh mocked them first. "If I'd believed you innocent, I might have tried harder," he said, and Emir exploded in laughter. Wynn felt the darkness lift ever so, just enough to stop him hiding away in silence again.

"Imagine if I hadn't made it in time," Wynn said. "Imagine if they'd killed Erroh, and I'd run all the way over just to doom myself for no reason."

Emir imitated Aymon. "What are you doing over here, Ranger cub?" he growled. Then, with his companions' laughter ringing, he switched to Wynn's higher, eastern tones. Terribly, in Wynn's opinion. "I came to help! Here—let me kick his mushed-up corpse a bit. Fuk the healer. Didn't even give a shit about him."

They roared for a few breaths more, and then suddenly Emir announced, "My chains won't let me reach the far end of the cell. Where they've left the bucket of waste."

There was a clanking sound from Wynn's cell, and then he cursed loudly. "I can't reach mine either."

As if to mock their predicament, suddenly the lights went out in the main jail and they found themselves in complete darkness. A last trick by the vengeful gods to break their minds, no doubt. Wynn sighed and lay down on his stone slab.

"At least there's no breeze," he called out, stretching out uncomfortably. He would not give in to despair. He was not alone in this cage; he had two brothers in the dark.

"I guess this is good night," said Erroh, his chains clinking loudly as he lay down. "I would kill for some water."

"As long as they don't need to be Wolves," mocked Emir.

50

THE HOWLING TOWER

M agnus loathed this room as much as anyone could loathe a room. Perhaps it was unfair loathing, but he couldn't help himself. It was a charming enough room, admittedly. Long stained-glass windows sent sparkling colours against the bright walls. His feet creaked loudly on the oak flooring, varnished to perfection. He liked good varnished flooring. It matched the shine of the Black Guards' armour. He'd always liked their armour. Not much else about them, though.

Aye, this was a fine entrance hall to the Wolves' tower, and it was as far as he would dare step. The long spiralling staircase hugging the wall was another striking feature, but he had little interest in ascending it. Or passing the Wolves standing on each step. The tower held many hundreds of Wolves, and they stared down at him with hostile eyes.

Their Primary in waiting, too.

He sniffed the air, and the stale aroma of sine and sweat turned his stomach. The tower shook with the noise of their gathering. They laughed and sneered at the Rangers below them, and Magnus reminded himself they were his to command. His to feign respect for. With the Hunt moving, it was time to take these bastards by the throat and lead —if he could find a tight enough leash.

Roja stood beside him now. She looked shaken, but when she spoke, it was with authority.

"I demand silence," she roared, and her voice echoed all the way up. Those nearest, those of the older breed, fell silent immediately, but those above resisted the request. *Too many ruts in the ranks.* They did not know the rich history of their name.

Brutal, cruel and bloody as it was.

They'd gathered with word of a march, but these beasts were still reeling from Dia's passing. The world suffered, but there was no excuse for ill-discipline. *Mourn with swords, Wolves.*

The jeering was low, but it carried in this tower, and Magnus glared in silence. Dia's forerunner had created a strange machine in the Black Guard. These brutes were a pack. All male, answering to one female Alphaline. Their queen. The Primary Wolf. He didn't quite agree with their practices, but the world was full of injustices; full of thinking and behaviours different to his own. If women wanted to fight, well, the Rangers were always hiring, and when anyone joined the Rangers, they fuken learned their history.

Brutal, cruel and bloody as it was.

Roja tried again, but Magnus sensed the mood turning. "Silence!"

A few levels up, they fell still. Those above, though, still resisted openly, and Roja visibly faltered for a moment. Long enough to lose the room. A few Wolves nearby hissed them to silence, and to Magnus, this spelled her doom. No Primary should be denied respect. No Primary should ever need help either.

Magnus distinctly heard the term "City whore," and he snarled, eager to challenge them himself now. This tower had one entrance. It wouldn't take more than a bottle of their cursed sine and a little flame to shut them up. Instead, he remained motionless. This was her fight. A true Primary would need to recover her grace unaided.

"Open your legs for us."

Don't react, Magnus. He did not envy the girl for her position. Any Primary might struggle, particularly a Primary who'd bedded the city's most reviled outcast. Not to mention having to contend with the lack of payments was crushing as well. Magnus sighed, listening to the growing rumble. Little could silence them now. He eyed the door and the comrades he'd brought with him.

An awful start to a shitty day.

He had hoped to see a stirring of comradery, but events had torn both sides further apart than ever. *Well, almost ever.* Dane would lead them out, come the dawn, and what would follow would be cruel brutality and a dreadful amount of blood. He heard the words "Ranger fuk" spat like poison now, and he formed a fist. This was no day to test him. Though Roja needed to find her feet, Magnus's footing was more than assured; speaking ill of his army this day would cause him to take a few steps.

"Fuk the Alphas."

Magnus took another breath, eyeing the door. Enough of this fruitless gathering. He had greater worries. So did the Wolves, although they hadn't allowed Roja to worry them yet. His heart was heavy. Garrick was long overdue and he feared the worst. In all the years he'd known him, he'd not once failed to return with his report. Others had reported in, though.

"And Fuk Magnus, too."

Don't react. Don't tear their fuken heads off.

When Magnus addressed them, it would be upon the battlefield when jests and overconfidence gave way to terror and realisation. When the enemy appeared, they would look to Magnus. What alternative was there to bedding down with beige beasts?

"Show us your gifts."

"We've earned a bonus."

"Who here has furrowed Roja?"

Roja stared hatefully at each mocking male above her. Their point was hardly subtle, and they made it loudly. She stood proud, though she cracked inside. Despite herself, she felt more at ease with the four trespassing Rangers than those who had bowed and served her for her entire life. Dia had warned her of the resistance she would receive when she came to power. This was normal, Dia had reassured her. The sooner she was ordained the better. That said, with coffers nearly empty and an invading army at the gates, she faced greater disadvantages than any Primary before.

"I did," jeered a voice. "She was terrible. Never moved at all."

Clasping her hands behind her back, she stuck out her chest. A fine move on her part; she had a fine chest and no one would see her hands shake. Unsure of what else to do, she stood motionless while a tempest of abuse rained down on her. After a moment, she felt a gentle pat on her back. Looking behind, she met the tired face of Lillium. In a den of devious allies, how strange that her only support came from her oldest enemy. Roja was suspicious. Did she patronise her? Had she become even more of a smug bitch since they'd last spoken? They could have been friends; should have been friends.

The torrent of abuse continued, and Roja wondered if Lillium didn't derive a modicum of pleasure from hearing it. *Aye, I have taken men to bed. Not all of us waited like a damsel for divine love with a ponytailed god. Some of us desired writhing in the murkier depths.* She offered her a curt nod and looked back to her abusers. Fools, she thought. She came with worrying news, and they hissed and spat like spoiled brats. *Oh, Dia. You left some dreadful mess behind.*

"Fall in line, Black Guard," she screamed, a piercing cry that Dia would have approved of, and they met it with violent giddiness. As though she were a young stepmother to children already of age. They knew their place and stepped beyond it. "I command you!" She was fierce and determined, and they laughed in her face. Someone from the upper echelons threw a bottle, which came to a crashing end at her feet. A warning shot, no more. Those loyal to her and the city hissed and cursed, they issued threats, they raised fists, and the wild pack snapped at each other.

And Roja gave up. Stepping away from the shattered glass and the loud jeering, she felt her body quiver in fear, in anguish, in rage. Beside her, Magnus leaned in close.

"You will not win this day out. These brutes are untrained, unprepared. Come dawn, all will change. You have other matters to attend to, do you not?" With that, he stepped away, and Roja felt alone.

534

Though not without purpose. Everything was about to change. It didn't take a Primary in waiting to know that. It didn't take an outcast either.

"Sort this shit, Dane," Magnus roared, and Dane, who had remained stoic throughout, now offered an apologetic nod. Dissent was one thing, but incurring Magnus's wrath was lunacy. He might set the place alight in a fit of rage.

"To the fires with this," he hissed, and Lillium spun with him, taking her place in storming away from the hostile eyes. *Fuk it.* Roja followed. Preferring the company of Ranger over Wolf, she marched to the ringing of even wilder taunting as the Wolves lost themselves completely.

But before she reached the outer doors where the Rangers waited, the tower fell silent. Looking back, she caught sight of the elusive Sigi and Seth stepping out into the centre of the room. Sigi slid a few shards of glass from his path and stood as though about to address an army of zealots. A great fury came upon her. He'd dismissed every attempt both she and Magnus had made to restore control to the city. All the while, he'd hidden with a rat she'd once trusted. *To the fires with you, Seth.* She stood in the doorway as they all bowed as though he were a god, as though he was their Primary, and fury overcame her. She almost charged him. What would her Black Guard do then?

Was he here to apologise for denying them payment? Was he admitting fault? What was his plan, apart from starving the city?

"This is the business of the Black," declared Dane, inclining his head slightly to her. "You need not be here... Mydame." His smile was warm but his eyes were full of hate, and Roja felt a shiver run down her back.

"As you wish," she replied, turning from her Primary Wolf pack.

———

"Walk with me," called Lillium from the main gate, as Roja slipped away from the tower doorway. "Rangers would never treat you like that," she assured her. *Is this bitch mocking me?* Roja knew Lillium needed something. That was how she'd always worked. It was the City way.

"They need someone to blame," Roja replied weakly. It was a dreadful, humbling thing to be torn asunder in front of an enemy. Regardless, she did not look back as she followed Lillium out into the quiet streets. Though it was a blazing sunny day, Lillium carried gloomy clouds above her. In her walk, in the way she spoke. A gentle, patronising pat was not enough to smooth a life of friction; not enough to make Roja ask. Despite her demeanour, Lillium appeared taller than she remembered, although that might have been the boots she wore. Her armour was polished and ready for battle too. She matched her beige comrades. *Ranger Lillium. Who'd have expected such unlikely things?*

"How are you, Roja?" Lillium asked, and something in her tone demanded truth. Kindness?

"I'm humiliated… heartbroken… scared too," whispered Roja, and to her surprise, Lillium hugged her suddenly and Roja fought the urge to cry. Any kindness left her on the verge of collapse these days. She hoped it was a fleeting affliction, a side effect to her world shattering like a bottle on an oak floor. She broke the embrace and saw the misery upon Lillium's face.

"How about you?" asked Roja in turn, finding cordiality a strange thing. Dia's passing had affected all Alpha females in Samara, something Roja should have noticed more. It was hard seeing the truth of the world through heartbreak, though. Lillium made no reply; she continued walking in silence, and Roja followed. Magnus was right: she had greater things to concern herself with. Like tending to funeral arrangements, preparing the city for the war to come. The little things. She also needed to see to the prisoners.

Lillium halted while the rest of the Rangers marched on, and the two women watched them leave.

"I need your help, Roja," she whispered. *Of course you do.* "I need to see Wynn." *Of course you do.* It was hardly surprising that she wanted to see her lover.

Roja spat in the dirt. "You know you cannot see him until there is another tribunal." It wasn't the first time the extravagant Alpha had tried to charm her into getting her way. *Well, Lillium, I can't see Emir, so fuk right off.*

"I march at dawn," she pleaded. Roja shook her head. *War or no, this is no time for whispered words between lovers.*

"I must offer a final kiss," Lillium whispered, reaching for Roja with shaking hands. It was a compelling argument. Roja sighed.

"It will be done," she whispered back without hesitation.

51

VISITING HOURS

itch-black boredom. It felt like weeks since sunlight had warmed Erroh's face; infused him with life; hurt his eyes. It might have been only a day, but who could count hours in darkness? Time moved at its own pace in darkness. The outside room's torch was unlit now. Their faceless jailers had ignited and snuffed it out at seemingly random times since he'd woken here, and Erroh suspected it was a subtle way of playing with their minds. Hunger and thirst weren't enough, it would appear.

He lay on his bed of stone, wondering if the others were awake. He had once believed boredom consisted only of monotonous tavern tunes butchered by unskilled bards for an entire sober evening, or the grinding practice of a sword form performed daily, a thousand times over. Either of those things would be more interesting now than this tedium. Erroh turned restlessly on his bed; he was bored, he was thirsty and his head ached.

Sitting up, he tried stretching the pain from his limbs and again met the clanking of chain. That noise always shook him, bringing back memories of marching beside a cart, just like fire evoked memories of Aireys. They clanked again as he stood up carefully. Standing made the

538

rest of his body hurt, but standing up was different. Standing up was an adventure in itself. For a few breaths at least. Afterwards, he might lie down and sleep away this nightmare some more.

He slid quietly up to the doorway. No point disturbing his comrades if they'd found solace in oblivion. "Anyone awake?" *No harm in asking, though.*

"Oh, thank the gods," came the voice of Wynn, then the clang of his restraints as he leapt to the door.

If Emir was asleep after all this racket, the absent gods themselves might have asked for his secret. But Emir was not asleep at all. "Is it morning already? I slept wonderfully." There was a stumbling crash, another ringing of heavy chain, followed by a distinctive thump against the door and a colourful curse.

"You slept in late, Emir," Wynn called teasingly. "Erroh and I had a fine feast altogether. We could have woken you, but you were sleep-talking about a girl named Sheep. We thought it best to leave you be."

"Ah, Sheep. Wonder where she is now? Probably still living on that mint farm. Tell me, brothers: were there eggs served in this feast?"

"I couldn't tell. It was very dark."

"If there weren't eggs, I missed nothing."

"Wait—I think there were a few, but I smashed them on the ground."

"Too soon, Wynn. Too soon," Emir chided him, though he was smiling. "It's probably midnight on the fourth day. I suspect those fukers are playing with the lights." He scratched at a thin patch of grizzle on his cheek as he spoke. It didn't look four days old, but that could have been the light. "I hate you ugly Wolf bastards!" he roared suddenly, and Erroh watched the outer room for movement. Unsurprisingly, he saw nothing. He could spend a year in here growing accustomed to the light and still barely see anything. Still, he saw better now than three days ago. Or was it five days? A day and a night? Who knew? Apart from everyone in the city.

"You know what?" Emir went on. "I bet we've only been here a day. Two at most. I can't even spit in disgust." He sighed heavily instead. It wasn't as effective. "Oh, to have the luxury to send my phlegm on a merry adventure."

Though perfectly awake, a weariness came upon Erroh. He knew this feeling well. A desire to slip away and hide in wonderful nothingness. Looking back to his unappealing bed of stone, he shuddered. He was dying of thirst. They all were. His chest was heavy; his throat felt like a shard of glass was cutting into him every time he swallowed. And oh, the alluring call to sleep was intoxicating. He wondered if this was some unusual survival mechanism of his body. Shutting down everything in a desperate wait for dawn. *Any day now.*

Wynn would not let him rest, though. The sound of metal chain rubbing against metal bars was grating, and Erroh realised with surprise that Wynn was trying to file the bars down. The grating sound became piercing as he went to work. If he had a year, he might wear all three bars down. *Then what?*

"Who thinks we'll make it?" Wynn called cheerfully.

Emir made disturbingly accurate strangling sounds from his cell. In his defence, he'd had a longer time to imagine his death than the others. "I do," he gasped.

"There is always hope," muttered Erroh hopelessly.

"Aye, they might only castrate us," agreed Emir.

"Lea might never forgive me if that happens," argued Erroh.

"Lillium might be thankful, though," added Wynn, laughing, and they joined him. "Right, my friends. Here's one I just made up this very moment. Stop me if you've heard it." He cleared his throat, and it sounded painful. "A poacher, a mount and the Primary all walk into a tavern…"

———

Conversation helped pass the timeless hours away, despite the pain of conversation. The torch remained unlit and Erroh knew each man kept his eyes on the door, waiting for illumination.

It was Wynn who braved the dry, rasping act of speech most. When he wasn't telling jokes, he regaled them with humorous tales involving hapless warriors, monstrous beasts and unique worlds. He knew countless tales and were he not an infamous Alphaline built for war, disgrace and a little bit of death, he might well have enjoyed a life as a bard or storyteller. He claimed he made each tale up as he went, but Erroh suspected his household contained a book from the ancients. Perhaps, after these dreary days, Massey might find a place for him scribing such tales for the city. There were worse professions.

When Emir spoke, however, he usually complained, and he had an uncanny ability to delve deep into the wretchedness of each complaint. It didn't matter what he complained of; his gift for lamentation was perfectly entertaining, be it the unfairness of their situation, be it the quality of ale during wartime. His anger brought smiles, and Erroh suspected he knew this and played upon their miseries for the sake of distraction.

Erroh, though, had neither stories nor complaints to offer. His guilt still played upon him, and his misery dragged his mood to worrying depths. Put him in battle and he was a hero, magnificently delivering death and violence. Render him immobile and he was a peasant. He tried to stay with them, to lighten their load, but he was a wretch in the dark. Slowly dying.

———

A light flickered to life outside the doorway and illuminated their chambers.

"Wake up, friends," called a voice.

"Who is out there?" Erroh called to the moving light; it burned his eyes. It was the most beautiful thing he'd ever seen. The torch bobbed around in the darkness and he heard the sounds of locks clinking. Muffled voices emerged from the room beyond. Heated exchanges over their combined fates, no doubt. *Is this it?* He heard a female's voice. *Lea?* He couldn't see her. The disorientating light grew brighter as the door opened with a heavy clunk and the room exploded in dancing fire as the torch bearer entered.

"Wynn?" whispered the female voice.

Why does my Lea call Wynn? He knew the truth. He fought it a moment more.

Wynn sounded nervous. "Lillium? What are you doing here?"

The flames spun around towards his voice, and Erroh saw Lillium's face in the flickering light. She was stunning, graceful and nowhere near perfect like Lea. Crushed, he turned his face away; it was cruelty by the absent gods to deliver hope like this and then snatch it away.

Lillium slipped the torch into a copper holder above the doorway, allowing the room its first dawn. Now Erroh could see that there were wires along the wall, with long-broken bulbs attached. Their jailers had chosen darkness after all. The flame danced in a little breeze and Erroh watched, mesmerised, as if in a dream. He would have preferred Lea in the dream. Maybe in her yellow dress. Or not in her yellow dress? If she brought a tankard of water, that would be fine too.

Wynn's chains rattled loudly as he shuffled to the door to gaze upon his beloved.

"Hello, Wynn."

"Hello, Lillium…"

She looked around and grimaced at the conditions, sniffing the air distastefully.

"Did you bring water?" Emir asked, ignoring the awkwardness between the two mates.

She shook her head. "They allowed me nothing."

Erroh almost begged her to lift the lid on the barrel. She must have read his mind, or followed his pleading eyes. She tapped the barrel, and Erroh didn't like that hollow sound. Not one little bit. Painfully slowly, she pushed at its side and it teetered as though light as air; as light as a hollow barrel.

"Empty." She turned to Erroh, placed her hand across her chest and bowed lightly. He had a thousand questions, but her eyes swiftly returned to her mate and it was not Erroh's place to speak.

"What are you doing here?" demanded Wynn again. He kicked his cell door fiercely and she flinched. "You shouldn't see me here. Have I not shamed myself enough as it is?"

She tried whispering, but the room echoed her words. "We must speak."

Erroh wanted to look away, to give them both their privacy, but he couldn't retreat from the flickering light or the shadowed goddess standing in its wake.

"I'm sorry, Wynn. I truly am." She found no words to continue, and he nodded. "I march out with the Rangers at dawn."

Still, he said nothing. His face was pale in the light, paler than when he had knelt in the sand, forsaking Emir.

"I understand," Wynn said at last, and Erroh resisted the urge to interfere, to demand a word of those he loved. If she marched, who marched with her? Lea? Elise? Magnus, for certain. "You come for one final kiss?"

"Aye."

This was the end of them, Erroh knew now. Whatever had occurred between them was too painful and dreadful to save. To do this now was pure malice. Doing it before war was tenfold the cruelty. *If you die, you still punish him from beyond the grave.* Wynn would not recover from this. Emir must have known the term just spoken aloud and was wise to offer Wynn the dignity of silence.

Wynn tapped the bars gently, searching for anything to counter her words. There was nothing. "Keep to the trees," he said at last. "Don't stand still. An archer is only as effective as their nerve."

"I will, Wynn."

Erroh could hear the relief in her voice, and he shook his head in silent fury. How could she inflict such dreadfulness? What cruelty had he inflicted upon her that he accepted her retribution so gently? *Fight for her, you fool.*

"Be strong throughout the horrors," he said, and his concern was pitiful.

A better friend might have looked away. Erroh didn't. Emir, however, disappeared from his doorway.

"I will, Wynn. I will." She stepped towards the cage door and Erroh thought of the two young cubs ruining his day with glances of love and excited whispers, while he was the useless brute ready to flee the city.

She looked into his eyes and waited for him. Waited for his final kiss that might change her mind, might warm frozen hearts, might undo dreadful sins.

"Is Lea marching?" Wynn suddenly asked.

"No. She will not fight without Erroh. Will not rest until he is free. She stays by Elise's bedside," she replied, glancing towards Erroh's cage. "Elise is weak." Erroh's stomach lurched with pangs of both relief and sorrow.

"Has Elise fallen any worse?" Wynn asked.

Erroh heard a gentle rustle as Emir leaned forward, trying to learn of his patient's troubles.

"The bruising makes her breathing difficult," Lillium said aloud. "She takes her eucalyptus, but all she does is sleep." Her voice quivered with a terrible finality. "What else can we do?"

Emir spoke now. "The body knows what to do. Sleep heals all wounds and fatigues. Let her sleep."

From beyond the chambers, the female voice argued once more.

"Do you know of our fates yet?" Wynn asked. He knew this visit would end soon. *Enough of the niceties.* There was one more act to perform.

"Be brave, be patient, all of you."

"How is Roja?" Wynn asked, and Lillium looked directly towards Emir's now-empty doorway.

"She suffers for her vote in the tribunal. She suffers more for those she keeps close to her heart... *kept* close to her heart." Words like that might stir Emir. Might keep him warm. Or might tear him apart. "I need to leave, Wynn. I'm... I'm sorry." She leant closer to the bars of his cell. *Beg for forgiveness and fight for her!* Wynn stuck his fingers through the bars and ran them through a few strands of hair. She allowed him to. He looked ready to shatter, but he kept his eyes upon her. Did not blink, did not shy away. Silently, she allowed him to try and win her heart one last time. To search his soul for one shred of love and offer her every single star in the sky. To remember their first kiss. To reignite the passion from the Cull; to erase all the mistakes; to be young and foolish again. "I remember, Wynn," she whispered, and he nodded.

He looked upon her like he had the first night and whispered his own goodbye. "I will not abuse you any further by kissing you with these ruined lips." He eased his face away from the grimy metal bars, touched his broken, dry lips and offered his most tragic smile. Instinctively, she reached and took his fingers in hers. There was still warmth between them, but it was hidden so deep that neither could find it. Erroh ached for them both; they should perform this act beneath a starry sky or a burning sun. Anywhere but in these miserable chambers.

"There were no others, only you," Wynn went on. "I will spend the rest of my days regretting how greatly I failed you, my love." He pressed her fingers to his broken lips. "For what you endured, I will not dare attempt to sway your heart with a pitiful kiss. You deserve so much more." He kissed her hand and released her from their joining forever, slipping away into the darkness of his cell, where she could not follow.

"Thank you, Wynn," she whispered. She could have shone the torch into the cage, but she knew he had earned his peace. Suddenly she felt both bitter relief and tragic levity. She had expected a dreadful scene, the opposite to what occurred. She'd expected dreadful weeping. Pleading. Shouting, too. She had not expected such humble behaviour. For the first time since she couldn't remember when, she saw his goodness. "Goodbye."

She stepped back out into the main central room and pushed the heavy door to the cells closed behind her. She was lighter, fiercer. She was Alpha female again. She was Lillium the Ranger, and such a title was an honour. She turned to the Primary in waiting, who had made this visit possible.

"It is done," whispered Lillium coldly. She recovered her weapons from the jailer who had held them and re-armed herself before facing the city streets. "They need water," she hissed, then strode through the stuffy room and opened the door out into the night. At the doorway, she turned back briefly.

"Should they not receive any, I know your faces." There was something in her tone; both jailers nodded swiftly. She held the door for Roja to follow.

52

QUENCHED CONFESSIONS

Wynn remembered her hair, radiant blue in the warm sun against the natural beauty of the surrounding green wastes. She had glided through the world alongside him. She had smiled. She had been alive. He'd quickly taken the fire from her eyes and the blue from her hair; more than that. *He'd taken everything.* In turn, she had dressed in a soldier's attire and torn his heart apart; he thought her no less stunning without paint, dye or silken gown. He closed his eyes and pined for his beo. *This is our last goodbye.* He would never see her again; never make proper amends; never win her favour.

Gone, gone, gone.

It shouldn't have happened, he told himself, but it especially shouldn't have happened in this grim place. His comrades remained quiet and he appreciated their civility. Had he been able to weep, he might have, for though he knew her reasoning was more than fair, he still loved her; still desired her; still ached in her absence. He had never felt further from her than he did now.

Resting his weary head upon his stone pillow, he imagined the two of them together again, still racing east, towards a legend. Hand in hand and still in love. He thought of blue against green, and soon enough he slept.

. . .

"I hear you need water," the jailer growled, marching into the room with a jug. Emir heard the unmistakable melodic swish of perfectly cooled water. *From the Great Mother, no doubt.* He thought of his rock. Thought about sitting upon it and leaping into the blue beneath. Cool, wet imaginings. Stumbling from his less impressive bed of rock, he fell up against his door, his fingers clawing pathetically at its rusty surface. He could hear the water singing and he desired a duet. *Just a few notes is all.* His throat was raw, and speaking had become an excruciating experience. How many days had it been? Enough to torture. Not enough to kill. *Clever little Wolves.* Keeping them barely alive to meet their deaths. They had treated them as beasts. He wondered if this was just. But perhaps they were not the fine, honourable people they believed themselves to be, but criminals who had sinned against the laws of the city. A brute never believed himself a bastard. He never said this aloud; after all, it was his foolish tongue that had placed them here. The jailer swished the jug and Emir almost squealed. If offered, he would drink it all and demand more. His comrades would do the same.

"Aye, if you're offering?" Erroh said, and Emir heard the caution in his voice. Erroh had marched in chains. He knew the routine better than either of them, so Emir said nothing, allowing the Hero of Keri to conduct business. His eyes never left the Black Guard or the jug. Emir had imagined their jailer to be a brute with cruelty in his eyes and bitterness in his step, but this Wolf had no such clichéd traits. He was younger than Emir, with a kind face. At worst, his armour might have needed a coat of polish. A station guarding the jail as opposed to daily marches around the city bred bad habits, it would appear. Emir wondered if mocking him would help matters and decided against it. Instead, he watched their keeper produce a wanderer's canteen. Grinning, he poured a stream of crystal-clear ambrosia into it, spilling only a few drops as he did. Emir tried to lick his lips, but the cracked surface made it too painful. That would soon be rectified. The Wolf filled it to the top and swished it again wonderfully. It was nasty bravado, but Emir would gladly clap the encore should the bastard demand it.

Just give me the fuken water!

"Healer?" the Wolf said at last, producing his set of keys and unlocking the door.

Emir reached desperately for the water and his chains halted his grasp. He yelped with pain and the Wolf laughed.

"Every time," he sneered, stepping close and handing it across.

With a deep gulp, Emir drank and almost drowned in his first mouthful. It was the finest drink he'd ever taken. Sweet, cool and perfect. In the annals of time, few would have endured such a grand experience as drinking this liquid, and Emir would gladly tell the tale.

"Trusting little wretch, aren't you?" the Wolf mocked, and Emir shrugged and continued drinking. He felt his body revitalise, felt his aches disappear as his body tingled with pleasure.

"Not worried we didn't relieve ourselves in it, no?" Emir shrugged again, and kept drinking. Any toxins were worth this quenching. His indifference displeased the Wolf. A steel glove shot out and struck Emir fiercely across the face.

Emir's limp body collapsed in a heap beneath the doorway and his vanquisher stood over him, unsure of what to do next. Wynn and Erroh screamed. It was one thing pissing in a man's drink; it was another knocking him out cold. Erroh forgot his own aching throat, his thumping head, and screamed what profanities he could. They were many. Of course, the brutes would offer no gift without payment. They were not honourable; they were animals. Both Alphas threatened with the wrath of an entire army. They challenged him to attempt the same with them. Silently, though, they hated him for not offering them water. Even though Emir lay beaten on the ground, he had got the better deal.

"I didn't hit him that hard," the Wolf hissed, and Wynn cursed his mother, his father and his ugly children. "I didn't mean to knock him out cold," he added, and Erroh informed him he'd had his wife one drunken night and she was shit. With Emir still taking breath, the assailant gathered his wits and kicked his protruding legs back through the doorway before locking him back in. He held up the jug. "Who still needs water?"

"I'd barter a strike to my jaw," Erroh said, forgetting the abuse he'd offered his keeper almost immediately. He squeezed his face against the bars in desperation. *Give me a drink and you can hit us all day long.*

"If you think I would open a door to a feral Alpha, you must think me a fool," the Wolf mocked, and Erroh's stomach churned some sand.

Wynn countered in a strangely unemotional tone. "If you think there will be no reckoning for accosting our friend, then you, sir, are a fool." He'd just received a final kiss. The Wolf should have taken heed. "I will remember your face," he added.

The Wolf thought on this threat and threw the contents of water through the bars over Wynn, and Erroh almost cried. Shaking the jug and its last dribbles of life, he cast the last few drops at Erroh. He couldn't help but be cruel, and Erroh couldn't help himself but drink what he could from the few drops upon his face. Those on his shirt he sucked on pathetically. Tantalising relief surged through his mouth, but he craved more. A wild, maddening fury came upon him. *More.* He licked at his fingers and distantly, beneath the haze of satisfaction, he heard the shuffle in Wynn's cell as his comrade mimicked his actions. They had no pride, but it was a small matter. Grabbing their torch on leaving, the jailer stormed off to think about Wynn's threats for a while, but Erroh barely noticed. He dug his fingers into the ground, hoping to recover blessed moisture, and felt wretched.

"I regret nothing," declared a jovial Emir, awake once more. "And I gained everything." There came the most beautiful sound of wet swishing. He tapped the metal canister against the bars. "As if that bully had anything on a Keri punch. Next round is on me, gentlemen."

Erroh saw his wide grin in the dim light, and the waving tankard was a thing of beauty. Slowly and carefully, Emir squeezed his arm through the thin bars. "Wynn, stick your arm out," he whispered.

"I'm nearer," hissed Erroh, sticking his arm through. He was gripped by a desperate fear of getting left behind. Wynn was drenched; he was not.

"Whisht, Erroh—I can't get to you from this angle. Best this water takes the long route around." Begrudgingly Erroh had to admit he was right. Emir's cage was just slightly closer to Wynn's, and Wynn would have a better angle after his turn. *Still, give me the fuken water.*

Wynn reached through and waited nervously as the healer lined up his trajectory. Erroh couldn't watch, but still watched. His lips stung and his mouth ached for more water. *More.* He could still feel little bits of grit and sand in his mouth from the floor.

"Are you ready, Wynn?"

"Aye."

"Are you sure?"

"Aye."

"…"

"…"

Dry, nervous silence.

"Emir?"

"I'm no great thrower of things."

"Just throw the fu—"

It spun in the darkness, and Erroh watched it as though time stood still. A divine, popping arc. Fine speed, too. Emir may have doubted his ability, but it was a near perfect throw. A master thrower would have seen the flaw, though. The tankard was over half full. That was a lot of water weight. It descended towards the doorway a little too quickly, a little too short.

"Oh no," Emir cried, but Wynn adjusted his waiting hand as though it was nothing and snapped it from the air effortlessly, like catching a ripe apple in an orchard. Erroh wanted a ripe apple.

He flipped the cap and sipped gently, groaning in pleasure. Taking a second mouthful, he swirled it gloriously around his mouth. Erroh watched this and were he capable, he would have salivated. Wynn took a third deep gulp before replacing the cap, lest he drain the lot.

"That was the greatest moment of my life," he purred. He took a moment to plan his trajectory and Erroh waited eagerly. "Where?" he asked, and Erroh pointed to a spot in his sightline. Within a moment the canister floated in front of him and Erroh snatched victoriously, removed the cap and gulped.

"To you both," he whispered, taking a second mouthful, which he held without swallowing. Finally, he let it trickle down his throat, sighed in pleasure and thought of a sunny blue sky, a tranquil brook and a rock to call his own. He couldn't stop licking his lips in happiness. He felt such joy that tears sprang into his eyes. He took one more mouthful and teased it down his throat. He closed the cap and shook his head resolutely before leaning through the bars and offering it back to his companions.

Wynn shook his head defiantly. "I don't want that temptation, brother. I'm already sick that I gave it to you in the first instance."

"Emir?"

"Best keep it from me, but if I hear some midnight guzzling going on, I'll come over there and batter you."

Erroh lodged the tankard in a slight dent in the wall as far from the doorway as possible. If they came looking for it, they'd need to step into his domain.

"You took that punch like a champion," Wynn said. "They must be ferocious fighters in Keri altogether."

"Aye, Keri folk are tough," he muttered, and Erroh thought fondly of the mass brawl in the tavern during the festival of the Puk. Truly, he'd fallen in love with the town's charm that night. *Brave fallen heroes, the lot of them.*

"Had I known you could take such a punch, I wouldn't have felt bad striking you," Wynn said. "I am sorry. I was reacting to the moment."

"No need to apologise, Wynn," offered Emir. "For an Alpha, you don't really have much of a punch, do you?" It was hard to hold a grudge in the dark, and in moments, all was forgiven.

———

Eventually, when talking hurt no more, Wynn told them exactly why he was a single man again. It felt fitting to admit his shortcomings, less they judge Lillium a little harshly. It would pass the time, and it would help him to finally begin the painful journey of moving on. He spoke slowly, honestly, and they listened to each word. He left nothing out. They queried his actions, critically, brutally, and at other times, favourably. Friends did this when showing support. Even if they'd fuked everything up. He broke the rules and spoke of the Cull and everything after. He did not rush and they never tired. He delivered the great tale over many hours, and he felt a significant burden lifted. When he at last reached the moment of her final kiss, Wynn felt weak at the knees. His mistakes were out in the open. He clutched the bars and waited for the verdict.

Erroh spoke first. "I too have made horrible mistakes. As has Lea. Truthfully, we all make them. Some we get over; some drag us to the depths of wretchedness."

"She earned some fine vengeance and you rightly deserved a kicking, but there was love between you once," Emir said solemnly. "When she kissed you goodbye, I thought there was still something there. That said, my first great love exiled me to this shithole city. The other one condemned me to death."

"Technically, she revoked that condemnation," Erroh countered.

"Ah, it's not the same after your future wife orders your death. Call me old-fashioned. I'd say Wynn has a greater chance of earning Lillium's favour then we do of forgiving each other."

"Oh, I think Lillium has earned a reprieve from my advances," Wynn said, looking at his unused fingers in the dimness. "Even if I could take Magnus's advice and she would allow me to take her to bed."

"My father is full of advice."

"I bet it served you well, though," Wynn mocked.

"It was an awkward conversation. I suppose I am grateful, though."

"Spoken like an Alpha with the perfect mate, the perfect adventure. Fuk off, Erroh, with your perfect life," Wynn mocked, and both he and Emir laughed with only the slightest hint of jealousy.

. . .

"In my sleep, sometimes I call out for another girl," Erroh said into the darkness, and two sets of chains neared their respective doors immediately. Fresh troubles and fresh conversation were on the table, and they intended to play.

Emir couldn't hide the delight in his voice. "Oh, that sounds like an interesting problem. Not for you, but for us hearing about it."

Even Wynn sounded amused. "Unburden yourself with us, brother. You will feel better."

So he did. He told them about Nomi, sparing no detail. He knew he called less for her, but there were still mornings when he missed waking up with a goddess wrapped around him. He did not love her, but the guilt of their bond weighed heavily on him, as did the guilt for inadvertently causing her death. Keeping these thoughts secret weighed heaviest on him. He adored Lea, but he could not hurt her with words of another. Speaking of Nomi within this darkness was a tonic, if only for a few moments.

"I wish I could have thanked her a thousand times more. I wish I could have repaid a little of what she did for me."

"Well, I don't think she's dead, at all," decided Emir, and his words shook Erroh with cruel hope and terror in the same moment.

"Aye. After we win the war, ride south and seek her out," agreed Wynn, as though hopping down south was a small matter.

"Aye. Guilt taken care of," added Emir. It sounded like a plan, albeit a stupid one. Neither one had a clue about the opposite sex. One had a lover who preferred battle over staying mated another day. The other awaited a death sentence given by his lover. They were idiots.

"You both are idiots."

"Aye, we are," agreed Emir. "What a problem to have. Two stunning women wanting to keep you warm at night. A man stuck in the dark might spend it wisely, fantasising about a predicament like this. You poor bastard."

Wynn laughed. "Erroh might be right. Lea might not take kindly to him riding south to seek a stunning blonde with such alluring traits.

I'm single at the moment, so I could keep her warm for you while you are gone. I pledge to you in the darkness, brother, that by the time you return it'll be her suffering the guilt."

Emir had a better solution. "No, no, Wynn. Lea will insist on coming. Now, if I know anything about females, which I don't, I think when you rescue Nomi and journey back, things will take a wonderful turn."

"Emir, shut up."

"No, no, I've been thinking this one out. There must be one night that's colder than most. Like, real fuken cold... and you must take shelter... together... and you must huddle in close for warmth... real close... because the fire won't light... and..."

They laughed for long enough that both Alphalines at last felt better about themselves; as always, Emir took pride in playing the fool.

"I suppose this is where I shed my heaviest problems on you both?" he asked, stretching in the darkness. *Enough talking for now.* He knew they had an interest in his sins, but he wasn't ready. With thirst satisfied, hunger gnawed at his insides. This enduring stay was becoming an education in keeping firm their morale. "I have little to offer, for I live a devout existence."

His head softly hit the pillow of rock and he smiled, hearing the low chuckling from his brethren. It was nice to have friends again. He felt a strange ease in this horrible room. Though he desired freedom, this camaraderie reminded him of life in Keri. He could speak freely without fear of perilous consequences. The world no longer rested upon his shoulders. Aye, there were terrible, regretful things on his mind that came easier in the dark. Foolish actions by a cub determined to create concoctions that would save the world. *Doom it, too.* He desired to speak aloud his regrets to people who would offer comfort. Those who would not see advantage in his mistakes. *Important mistakes.* He fell silent, and they never pressed.

After a time there came the sound of delicate snoring. It sounded like Wynn. Dry, raspy breaths that would disappear in a few moments when he found a more comfortable resting position. Did he snore himself? He wondered if he had the strength of will to stir his sins again. He did. This was why he belonged in the dark. The shamed mayor of Keri thought about his life choices and finally decided that he had done his best with what had been offered. Aireys's request had been granted, and the moment had come to cease his charge. To end his march and stop fighting the good fight for the refugees of the dead town. He imagined he could hear her dead voice in his mind as sleep called, and it was comforting.

"Thank you, Emir. Your pledge is done," the dead girl whispered, and Emir smiled sadly. He had tried. The absent gods could attest to that. Emir slipped into sleep and snored softly. After a few rasping breaths, he turned over on the hard bedding and his breathing settled. The cells became deathly silent, and another hard-fought day ended.

53

CALM BEFORE THE STORM

It hadn't taken Magnus long to realise Jeroen's life as a farmer hadn't diminished his prowess. He had a glint in his eye for war; a glint many warriors never found. Even Alphalines. Upon first meeting him, he'd thought him an impressive brute; built tall and muscular with a taste for violence, but a mind for strategy. He carried himself with composure, fierceness and a kindness rarely seen in predators. Like Magnus, he was a leader in every action he undertook, and in a few short weeks the Rangers took to him quicker than they had Wynn.

It hadn't taken long to see his potential; it took even less time to integrate him into his counsel. However, it seemed Jeroen had been born in the wrong era, and he suffered for it. Were he a couple of decades younger, he would have stamped his name into legend in the battles to come without the weight of family and responsibility holding him down. Were he a decade older, he might well have been a giant of the Faction Wars. A mundane life of tilling fields, raising beasts and brewing fine alcohol would have softened most Alphalines, left them to languish into irrelevance, but not Jeroen. He was still imposing, the type of warrior who could serve the Rangers long after Magnus hung up his mighty Clieve. The type of warrior with a build sturdy enough to wield his gloriously outrageous weapons. And they were outrageous.

Impractical, too, but that didn't stop the enemy from falling beneath their wrath like wheat beneath a thrasher. For now, though, Jeroen would stand on Magnus's right as his shield bearer, learning the art. There were worse stations to serve. Some would argue there were better.

Some, like Erroh and Elise.

He could feel the energy in the air. The buzzing of insects fell silent in their wake, as did the gusting of the leaves. It was Magnus's march, and the world fuken knew its place. Both warriors waited atop a steep hill overlooking the procession of Rangers marching through the valley below. A thin line of beige, all in step, waving their banners proudly in the morning air. And, oh, the clatter of their armour and weapons filled Magnus with pride. The finest soldiers the world had known. They led the line and they would hold fast against the great numbers to come. *Who needs an army of Alphalines, anyway?*

Far behind flowed a sea of black. Their stride was just as impressive, their marching tunes boisterous and intimidating, but they marched without duty, without enthusiasm, without determination. Their banners had been long since cast aside and it was a strange thing to see. Without a Primary, their hearts had been cut out. They answered to no master. Nor would they until the next Primary was ordained. It was tragic to see the Wolves humbled as they were. A lesser Master General may have worried about discipline, but they marched and that was enough. He needed them only to charge when needed. His Rangers would take care of everything else.

His fingers did not ache today. They knew better than to offer distraction. His heart hammered as it had done since the night before, pulsing warm adrenaline through his body like fresh water down a parched throat. He had not slept but was unworried. He'd never slept on the eve of battle in his life. He took this as a fine omen. It was in these last quiet hours that he always took notice of such things.

He'd studied the maps, he'd learned the numbers, agonised over every tactic and planned for every eventuality. He had four hundred Rangers to stand at the front, and at last count, at least a thousand of the city's finest protectors. They were outnumbered twice over, and he was untroubled. Any Ranger was far greater than any zealous, undisciplined barbarian serving a madman. Any Ranger with a plan was tenfold that. Aye, southerners were ferocious warriors, but they bled like any other. He'd met greater numbers of their kind in battle and beaten them back. The Hunt would charge the Rangers first; such a charge would favour them. He'd ensured they held the better ground, had the sharper blades. Battles turned on many things, and he'd prepared for them all. Sometimes it was a bold strategy that won the day. Sometimes it was a foolish young legend running at them with swords raised. Other times, it was an early retreat that settled matters.

A foolish retreat could ruin everything.

He shook that last thought away lest he curse himself. Were the Hunt to retreat too early, without their numbers diminished, the city would face a second, greater battle. Those with tactical acumen would state that a warrior should see only the battle in front, but Magnus couldn't afford such a luxury. Today would belong to the Rangers. They would lead, they would impress, and fuk it, they would inspire the Wolves to show their teeth.

He missed Garrick's calm head at this moment more than ever. Looking around at the surrounding eternal green, he felt his absence anew. Somewhere within, his old friend lay as cold as stone. His death would never be avenged or honoured, either. He had suggested this region and it was a fitting last gift, along with the numbers of soldiers he'd given. Those many Riders, those few crossbow wielders.

Exhaling, he stared down at the lone figure of Lillium leading the soldiers. It was no surprise Elise thought highly of her. He believed she'd crumble under the weight of melancholy, but it had made her stronger. She'd taken Wynn's place at the head of the line for now, but she would not lead them into war. Hers was a different calling. Her mission more precarious. He could have had three more Alphalines to call upon, but fate had deprived him of such riches. Still, it was enough.

"With the sun at our back, we'll have a fine advantage," said Jeroen, watching the sun flirt with heavy clouds above. He sounded less nervous than Magnus had thought he would. A fine recent recruit, pushed to the front of the line. He liked Jeroen; he approved of his teachings, even if there was a taint of jealousy that he'd instructed his son so well. *Got through where I couldn't.* That was the way, wasn't it? Fuken Alphalines always stuck together, and Magnus, well, he was just a savage.

"I welcome every advantage," agreed Magnus.

Jeroen took a canteen of water to his lips and drank, before offering it to Magnus. "The Wolves are taking their time. They must not desire to march into war today," he mocked, but his eyes were serious. It was a fair point. What had started as one impressive march was now two. They placed one boot in front of the other, but they weren't in any rush. Every mile or so, they dropped farther behind.

"Excellent thing we are leading this little line. Otherwise, they'd get there and the fight would already be over," Magnus said, stretching in the saddle before urging his beast forward. The Wolves below would have seen him watching, seen him waiting. Jeroen followed alongside, matching his mount's pace. *Putting in the practice before taking up his shield.* The last few miles were the worst. *The quiet before.* That's when soldiers began doubting themselves. It was also when he found a place in his heart for fear. Having Jeroen nearby was a tonic for nervousness, though. Jeroen believed implicitly in Magnus's legend. Believed in the plan, too. Such things could reaffirm a legend's misgivings.

"They probably weren't ready to rise and march towards battle so early, Master General. Most probably didn't get any sleep. I know I didn't."

Magnus felt the weight of hours marching before dawn, too. Setting themselves in place long before the Hunt realised their position was crucial to winning the day out. A few yawns never made much difference come the clashing of blades.

"Ah, they had long enough. Slow marching or not, we've still made fine time. They can catch up on their beauty sleep tomorrow. They'll have earned it."

They brought their beasts along the top of the hill and looked to the little speckles of death in the far distance. Every mile they walked was a mile closer. Somewhere in between both points was a plain that would be the grave of many warriors today. Though he'd never traversed these lands, he'd memorised the entire region. His Rangers had too. They would fight the battle in the open, but he was leaving little to chance.

His pack of hounds sprinted along with them. They had little knowledge of war, but they sensed the energy in the air. They growled low amongst each other as they bounded along. Psyching themselves up for duty and bloodshed. *A perfect pack of killers.* They devoured the ground beneath them with impressive strides. Their garments, dark leather to match their fur, with thin metal plating, ran the length of their massive bodies from tail to head; light enough to grant them speed but still durable enough to protect from arrows and brute attack. They looked less like hunting hounds and more like demons from ancient tales.

They charged along, ready to answer his whistle. Like Lillium, theirs was not to stand in the centre of the battlefield. Some might see it as a weakness that he protected his hounds more than his Rangers, but there was no weakness in a master's love. Rangers could think for themselves. Hounds could not, and he would not train them to run willingly into death. His hounds were greater than some bastards of his own race. Besides, why slaughter loyal magnificence like these wonders, when their training could be put to better, more brutal use? Magnus was a brutal warmonger, but he was no monster, and the absent gods approved of this.

Both Rangers trotted down towards the marching armies. Swiftly, they brought their mounts to the front of the first line.

"Did she wish you well, as you left?" Magnus asked, and Jeroen took a lengthy breath. For the first time since they'd embarked from the city, his companion looked shaken, and silently, he cursed himself for saying anything.

"No. Mea offered no kindness. She offered a few interesting words on the matter, though," Jeroen quipped, daring a wry grin. "Truthfully, our argument did not match yours, Master General."

Elise's anger at Magnus for leaving with Erroh still chained had spawned one of their fiercest arguments. Though she barely took breath, she still had the lungs to scream when she needed. Magnus never retreated, even when wrong. Especially when wrong. Their arguments had been heard throughout the camp and out to the city walls, no doubt. As if he would leave his son to die in a cell for no reason. Things were afoot; matters were at hand. He could not hesitate a day or two more, hoping to bring his son into war, even if he'd have felt better with Erroh marching too.

"You know, a smarter lieutenant might have ignored an argument between a mated pair of crinkled old warriors." Though his words were a warning, he grinned at Jeroen's boldness. The younger Alphaline gave little ground, and such things were important in the company of legends. "Mea will come around, my friend. Give her time."

Jeroen shrugged, as though hopeful thoughts would serve him little now. They took their places at the head of the congregation and entered the valley in which the warring tribes would finally meet.

"I might offer the same advice to you, Magnus. Elise will come around."

She is dying. There is nothing I can do. She might be dead when I return.

Magnus pushed away the panic and searched for calmness. He found it in a few carefully taken breaths. He even feigned a smile. "Thank you for saying as much, Jeroen." Leaving Erroh behind was one thing. Leaving her was another. "This is the first time she will not fight alongside me as a Ranger."

This time, Jeroen spoke respectfully, and this too endeared him to Magnus. "I'm sorry, sir. I know the tales of both your legends."

"We will miss her blade," Magnus muttered, and meant it. Oh, she was as divine in war as she was in bed. She would have slain a hundred of the barbarians in the hours ahead—or claimed as much. Even broken, she was worth dozens of Black Guard.

He heard the thunder of hooves and it pulled him from thoughts of Elise. A scout raced through the far end of the valley towards the Rangers' front line. She rode aggressively, as though an entire army were in pursuit. Perhaps it was. All the better, he thought.

The surrounding forest was deep for miles each way. It was strange
what rough terrain did to morale. Only a fool would ignore this open
path, and Magnus counted on it. He'd feared a cartographer's loose
scribble up to this moment. It was an unfounded fear, he realised, and
he was in fleeting love with it now. The land was smooth and
appealing to southern eyes. Open enough to charge, but tight enough to
offer an advantage to their fewer numbers. In a fair battle, the Hunt
could ride from either side. However, this valley was narrow; Magnus
had enough numbers to gain advantage, albeit imperceptibly. It was a
fine gamble he played. Had Magnus chosen to fight in a bottlenecked
region with an obvious advantage, the Hunt might not engage. This
valley was appetising enough that the brutes would surrender the
higher ground, trusting their superior numbers. It was a fair strategy,
but Magnus had never lost a battle against fair strategies. It was the
unexpected that kept him awake at night.

"Halt," Magnus roared, and the Rangers fell still. Some eyes were
upon the nearing scout, the rest upon him. The Wolves continued
marching, their camaraderie lessening as the reality of war came upon
them. *You aren't in your tower anymore.*

The scout slowed her horse in front of him. She was as old as
Jeroen but with a drawn haggardness to her. He recognised the face,
but he couldn't remember her name. She had been a Ranger for only a
couple of weeks. He knew her mate had died in the hovels. Many of
the newer recruits shared similar tales. They needed a place to direct
their suffering; they remembered the charity of the Rangers. Did she
have a son? he wondered, and was disappointed in himself. She knew
the land well and rode a horse like the wind. Either would have made
her an excellent scout. It was a lonely task and she performed it well;
he should have known her name.

"What's the good word, Corporal?" he asked.

"They march two miles back. Following this path, Master
General."

Magnus nodded and dropped from his horse smoothly. "Fall in line;
take up arms. Exemplary work, soldier." He offered her a smile.
Vengeance was a potent device, but, approval was always appreciated.

"Prepare," he roared. His order was repeated down the line, and Rangers charged out along the length of the valley in a wave of movement and he was proud. Behind them, the Wolves took to their orders under Dane, and he was pleased. Rolling his crunching neck loudly, he stretched the muscles in his shoulders. "Time to strap myself into the machines of war," he declared. "Bring me my Clieve."

54

THE PERFECT CRIME

"Nomi!" He could see her in front of him. Warm Nomi. He reached for her, but she was away from him now, standing over Lea with blade in hand. She offered a smile. Stunning and kind. For him and him alone. Then he saw the dagger of gold and jewel. She plunged it into Lea. "No, stop! Lea!" His mate did not fight or block the strike. And why would she? She was long since dead. *Dead.* Rotting with the other corpses in the fields of ruin, filled with torn limbs and soaked in crimson. *All dead.* He was alone and lost, and he screamed again and distantly he heard his name. It was soothing; from his brothers, too.

"Erroh."

He reached for the voices as though he lay at the bottom of a lake. *A frozen lake.* Reaching harder, he touched a frozen, icy stone and it ached and he searched for a better spectacle. Some vision not filled with horrors. Everyone was dead and he was alone. *Not real, not real.* Nomi continued stabbing, muttering obscenities in her southern tones, and he hated her for her cruelty and he was alone and Lea was dead and nothing in the world mattered beyond going mad.

"I can't take this!" His body shuddered as though struck by a stampeding mount and suddenly, the images disappeared like raindrops in the sun. He couldn't remember the sun, but he remembered the taste of raindrops and they were divine. His mind spun and he twisted painfully, all to the symphony of holding chains, and he wailed aloud again. "Help me!"

"Erroh, wake up, brother, please."

Waking from a vivid nightmare was no easy task, and flashes of horrors stuck with him as he climbed from unconsciousness into the waking night. *Lea is not dead.* This settled him, though gruesome memories from the nightmare returned. He saw Uden; he saw snow; he saw countless bodies fallen in war, bodies of those he loved. He closed his eyes and kept screaming, but the horrors were etched into his mind like prophecies. *I am no god seeing things to come.*

"Erroh, wake up." The voices were harsher now, trying to cut through his mania. Alphalines did not sleep like lesser beasts; they dreamt of the end of the world. And they did so loudly.

He stopped screaming and opened his eyes. He was lying flat on the floor, his arm wrenched at an awkward, painful angle. Slowly, he gathered his wits and struggled upright. *Am I awake?* The pain in his throat suggested as much. He wanted to vomit and his back ached from where he'd landed. He could hear the soothing tones of his friends trying to calm a savage in the cell beside them.

"Everyone was dead," he moaned.

"It's okay, brother. You are safe."

"Safe in prison."

"I fell out of bed." He felt embarrassed, trying to remember what he'd screamed.

"Who was dead?" asked Wynn. It was a fine question. Erroh knew the answer but had no desire to speak on the matter. Or admit how heavily the guilt of missing the battle weighed on him.

"It was nothing. I had a bad dream is all." Carefully, he climbed back upon his stone slab and laid his head down again. The chains felt more uncomfortable than normal, and he wondered if he hadn't snagged them as he thrashed. The fresh, stinging grazes at his wrist suggested there had been quite the violence to his actions. He wanted to sleep, but he feared dreams. He wanted freedom from this place. He wanted water too. And some food. He wanted everything, but also, he just wanted his fair share.

"Was I in it?" asked Emir. He sounded sleepy. It was late at night. Or late in the afternoon. It could have been breakfast time. Erroh really wished it was breakfast time. "Did I get killed? Was it at a redhead's hands?"

"It was about the battle," Erroh muttered, and winced. He'd shouted *Nomi*; he was sure of it. Nomi, death and a lost battle.

"They lost?" Wynn asked.

"Aye,"

"Was Lillium struck down?" Erroh could hear the fear in his voice. Easier to believe in prophetic visions in the dark. Perhaps it was just tiredness.

Despite himself, talking on these matters brought him relief. "I could not see," he muttered, but he did see. He saw her dead. He saw Emir dead too. He needed them to laugh off this bad dream and mock him for his foolishness. That would help; that would put his mind at rest. *This is your moment, Emir. Make us laugh.*

Wynn stepped away from his cell door, his voice muted behind stone and thick with worry. "It was only a dream." Hardly the levity Erroh craved. Wynn sighed heavily. "I'd gladly take a noose if I could fight on the battlefield with her."

Erroh understood his anguish. He might have felt the same once. However, he had seen the dreadfulness of war. Most of their lives they had trained for conflict, been drilled in violence to become masters of warfare. Theirs was a destiny of heroism. Hearing of a march stirred the lunacy in any Alphaline. Being denied their calling was like cutting part of their soul out with a holy man's blade. Erroh feared war, feared killing, but that fear did not quench his desire to fight. It just drew away the veneer of poetic heroism.

"I never usually remember my dreams," muttered Erroh, and Wynn said nothing more. Erroh's shrieks had struck a dreadful blow to their morale, and try as he might, he couldn't undo it. Even sleeping, they were unsafe from wretchedness.

Erroh shifted on his stone slab and tried to rise above melancholy, but found only a dreadful desolation. His chains felt too tight, the darkness closed in and the bitter panic returned. His dreams tore at his courage, and he remembered them more clearly now. He searched them for meaning, but all he met was misery and death. He swung his feet to the floor and reached for the canister of water before he realised it lay discarded somewhere in Emir's cell. We are beaten, he told himself, and it had a fine ring to it.

Emir had something on his mind. Twice before he'd almost said it, and twice they'd pulled themselves from the gloom's hold. This was different. Something in Wynn's desolate tone suggested as much. Admittedly, this was the safest time to say terrible things. It went against everything a healer should ever say or do, but in the darkness, with morale at its lowest, Emir stirred a brew of trouble. *Fuk it.* He licked his dry lips and coughed his throat clear. He would take the punch when it came, and it would deservedly come, but really, sometimes a man just had to set a treasure alight, just to watch it burn. He leaned against the cell's opening so he might deliver the words clearly.

"Erroh's mother has incredible breasts."

There was a stunned silence.

And then came a snigger from Wynn's cell. It quickly turned to guffaws, and then to hoots of laughter, and it was almost infectious— the deep, booming tones of a cracking man feeling comfort for the first time in an age. Erroh might have laughed, too, but he was likely working on the simplest, most painful way to remove a male's tongue.

Emir wasn't finished. "They're lovely to touch." *Oh, Emir.*

Erroh appeared at the bars. He looked fit to kill Emir for his crimes.

"I will kill you, Emir," he warned, but there was humour to his tone along with the menace.

"Please, go on," cried Wynn, laughing, and Erroh eyed him.

Emir sniggered uncontrollably, an irritating sound at best, a charmless cry at worst. He was making everything worse and making it a thousand times better at the same time. "I'm a gentleman. I won't betray my patient's trust by describing her talents. Impressive as they are." He nodded as though recalling a wonderful memory. "Of all the breasts I've tended to, they were my favourite."

Wynn could barely contain himself. "I've not seen them as you have, but I agree to their exquisiteness." This admission brought yelps of fresh delight from Emir. At least when Erroh came to kill him, he'd have Wynn standing in his way.

Even Erroh smiled now, but it was a terrifying sight. His eyes were cold, as though he thought of dark things. "Emir, a blunt rock will be my weapon of choice."

"Oh, I really don't think Elise would like you getting rid of such a plaything," warned Wynn cautiously.

Emir wasn't finished. "Lillium is next on my list. The next time she gets a chest infection or a scratch on the knee, even a fuken headache, I'll attend to her properly," he declared sincerely, and this time Erroh laughed. *A little too soon, but the best jests are the devastating jests.* "Guilt free, too. Because she left you. Remember?"

Wynn fell against the door laughing, and it was a wonderful sound. Erroh joined him in earnest now, and the darkness was once more beaten back by camaraderie. "Oh, you are a fuken bastard, Emir."

"Is it any wonder Roja wants you dead?" Erroh mocked, fully joining the cheer, now that it was directed at both Alpha males and not just him. *That won't last.* "After all the ladies you've… treated?" he added, and Emir hoped the blunt rock was heavy enough to knock him out with the first blow.

Emir still wasn't finished. "I have another confession, Erroh." He neared the doorway again and his companions forced their laughter down. "We had to remove Lea's clothing when I treated her." He knew he shouldn't have said that. They all knew. It didn't matter; they'd forgotten Erroh's dream. Gone like Wynn's desolation. The echoes of wonderful laughter had seen them off swiftly. "Sorry, brother." It didn't matter that he had barely glimpsed her talents, or that nothing beyond tearing her from death's grasp had stirred him that dreadful night.

"Oh, I hate you, Emir," hissed Erroh, through clenched, grinning teeth. He kicked the door loudly and cursed at the pain.

"Did you hurt your foot? Take your shirt off and I'll have a look." Emir could see Erroh grin devilishly in reply. Like a terrible card player who had over-bet on a dull hand, he could sense the counter. *Excellent.*

"I won't kill you, Emir, but I will let Lea know how you spent your time healing her. Then after, I'll tell Roja about it. Then after that, I'll tell my mother that she has competition for your attention. And then Magnus after that."

Emir took great delight in the threat. "You will tell tales on me? Wow, great fuken hero you are."

"Now I really am worried he will see Lillium," admitted Wynn, wiping the tears from his face.

"When it happens, I'll sit down with you both and give my professional opinions on their builds, on what stirrings they caused, on what fantasies I stole from them." *Oh, Emir.*

"Were I a lesser mate, I might find offence in your words. As it is, knowing the ruin the females will make of your face sustains me," quipped Erroh, wiping his eyes.

"Best we get him back with Roja before it's too late," Wynn suggested.

Emir offered them both his warmest grin. "It's my calling in this life, brothers. You two are great at stabbing people. I am the one with memories that keep me warm at night."

His brothers continued laughing in the darkness, and none of them noticed the sound of a key turning in the main door.

———

It was Erroh who finally spotted the shuffle of movement from the corner of his eye. A massive figure moving smoothly, as if born to steal through pitch black. He stopped laughing. The figure stepped through the doorway, leaving the heavy door swinging behind him. A small lantern from the main jail illuminated his movement, and Erroh's eyes stung wonderfully. The only sound was the delicate clink of a bunch of jailers' keys.

The guards didn't like good cheer, Erroh thought in alarm. *Oh, no.*

"Ah, whisht," hissed the phantom clinking figure, and the rest of the laughter died out suddenly. *Coming for Emir.* This large brute would take no chances facing a caged Alphaline, but a diminutive healer was no problem at all. Emir watched fearfully from his door. He knew he was the easiest target.

"Don't you fuken touch Emir," Wynn warned, and the figure stopped in place; his keys continued to jingle.

"Face me instead," Erroh added, kicking the door in challenge. "Come on." A man his size might see challenge if insulted enough. *Think quick.* "You big, ugly brute."

"Well, hardly the welcome I expected."

Erroh recognised his gruff tones and his heart leapt. "Wrek?"

"Aye. Had I known prison was so much fun I wouldn't have spent my life avoiding the iron chains." He found the desired key and began unlocking the nearest cell. With the skill of a man who had opened many stubborn doors in his time, he clicked the lock, stepped in and began working on Emir's chains.

"What's happening?" Wynn demanded, craning his neck to see. "Are we free?"

"In a way. Just keep on laughing, fools, and let me do my work," Wrek hissed, taking hold of Emir's chains and examining the little locks. Nobody said a word. This was obviously a dream and it was crueller than any nightmare. Wrek cursed as each key refused to turn, and then at last came the wonderful moment of success. They all heard the click and it roused them from their stupor. "Oh, thank the gods. I'd no idea what to do if that hadn't worked." After a second click, the heavy chains clattered to the ground. "Stop hugging me, Emir."

Wrek moved from cage to cage with the jingling keys, unlocking as he went. As his manacles fell free, Erroh fought the rising urge to weep aloud. Instead, he offered a firm hand to his liberator. Wrek took it, and Erroh couldn't help but embrace him anyway.

"Enough of this hugging shit," Wrek said gruffly. "We have miles to walk yet. You can hug me after."

He led them through the doorway, back into the main jail. It had changed little since that first horrible night. Two jailers were unconscious in one cell, their arms and legs bound and their mouths gagged. The companions realised as one that Wrek hadn't accomplished this daring task alone. Lea stood over them, casually watching for any movements, one of her blades at the ready. Seeing Erroh, she dropped all calm, leaping upon him and entrapping him in a perfect embrace.

"My beo," she whispered, and her voice was a tonic after his terrible trials. He tasted her kiss and he knew he was home. Her momentum carried them clumsily against the far wall. It was divine pain. He hugged her with all of his strength. He didn't have much, and she knew it straight away. She struck him across the cheek.

"Why did you do this to me?" Her eyes blazed with anger and love and horror and need, and he fell painfully against the cell bars and almost toppled over, but for Wynn catching him. She had every right to violence. He'd deceived her when they'd spoken on matters, when he'd assured her of success. She wouldn't have given a damned spit for his mercy had he spoken his intentions aloud. They both knew it.

"Guess there are advantages in not mating with an Alpha female," muttered Emir under his breath.

Lea decided to direct her anger towards other things. "They've been treated dreadfully," she growled.

Wrek nodded and kicked one guard's foot. Lea looked fit to do more damage. Instead, she pulled Erroh from Wynn's grasp and rested her forehead against his.

"I love you, Lea. I'm so sorry," Erroh said softly.

"Better," she growled, kissing him again. *Her Erroh. Nobody else's.*

Wrek would countenance no further moments of passion. "Can you wretches walk?" he asked, dousing all but one of the jail's lights, and the cursed darkness returned. Perhaps he, too, knew the sting of light after imprisonment. "Were you fed? Watered?" He poured a mug of water for each, which they drank swiftly.

"More," gasped Wynn. A fine idea altogether, and they each drank a third and fourth mug.

"We should have brought food," muttered Lea, as though she had failed them all. "Why didn't we think of food?" She spun towards the sleeping jailers willing them to hear her words and see her clenched fist. "Why didn't you feed them?" They did not hear her words. They no longer saw her threat.

A swift search resulted in success. Wrek recovered a few chunks of stale, dry bread from a sack and eyed them suspiciously. Before he could discard them, Emir snatched the bag from his hand, cast his brothers a chunk apiece, and then bit into his own hunk as though it were a boiled egg.

Each golden slice was hard like wood. Little speckles of mould lined their surface and none of them could have cared less. It just added to their flavour. The sound of joyous crunching filled the air as the first moments of recovery began. Between ravenous bites, Erroh smiled as Lea touched his cheek and gazed at him, unable to hide her heartbreak. She knew his agony. *Chains.* He offered her a piece of his feast between bites and she smiled.

"This banquet is all for you, Erroh. Enjoy your last ever meal in the city." Leaving Erroh to gorge the last of his bread, she recovered her blade and bent down in front of one the jailers. Her hands shook with anger.

"Wake up. Try to escape," she whispered; it was less a threat and more a plea.

"The way you beat them, I'm not surprised they do not try to regain consciousness," Wrek observed wryly, and Lea shrugged as though battering two Wolves into oblivion was a small matter.

"Had to be done."

"I'd happily have disarmed them," he offered, shrugging. "Small meals at first," he said to the three prisoners. "Just a few bites now. No point in throwing it all up." He spoke as if he knew what it was to starve, as if he knew how to feed after a lengthy period of fasting as well.

Finishing the greatest meal of his life, Erroh allowed himself a contented burp. His eyes fell on Lea and the depth of her sacrifice struck him. Her crimes matched his; they would revile her name

ROBERT J POWER

throughout Samara. A small matter for Erroh, but it had once been her
home. "I know the cost of your actions, Lea. Thank you," he
whispered, touching his forehead to hers. He wanted to slow time and
embrace her, but with food and water in his belly, his mind was clearer.
He could see Wrek nervously watching the night sky through the
broken windows. "Thank you both," he added.

Wrek nodded and began pulling cloaks from his pack. "We have to
leave, my friends."

Lea began unlocking the impenetrable front door while the outcasts
covered their wretched garments.

"Through the tunnel?" Emir asked, eyeing the hatch from which
they had entered.

"Not at all. The last thing we need is to journey further into the
city," Wrek said, donning his own cloak.

"So, what's the plan?" Wynn asked.

"It's simple enough. Hoods up and walk as though you belong in
the city," Wrek said.

"But we *do* belong in the city. We belong in its jail."

"Shut up, Emir, and tie up your belt. It appears to have come
undone."

Lea led them. Stepping out into the chilly night, Erroh tasted fresh air
and drank it in as though it were water.

"Wait a moment," Emir hissed, stepping towards the two
unconscious guards. He stood with his back to the others and, instead
of tying up his trousers, suddenly tensed his body.

"We have to go," hissed Wynn.

"Not enough water," muttered the wretch to himself.

Wrek sighed and shook his head before turning back and following
Lea. Erroh, too, delayed a few moments. It was petulance, but he
sincerely hoped Emir would attain a little of the retribution he
deserved. All of them did.

"Everybody stop talking a moment. Come on. Think wet thoughts,"
Emir muttered to his appendage.

574

Nothing happened, and Erroh slipped into the night. Behind him, Wynn hissed one more time for Emir and followed, leaving the healer behind. The sudden fear of being left behind served him well. He appeared out in the street a few moments later, looking thrilled with himself.

They walked as one lengthy line through the winding paths. Never rushing, never talking, just five wandering souls, out for a midnight walk. It felt like Lea's first city walk all over again, though far less conspicuous. She took in the city's glow. Should she never see the lights again, she wanted to remember everything. She had few regrets.

They passed under a deep archway and headed towards the city gates without a solitary soldier blocking their path. The Wolves had left only a handful of guards to maintain peace in the city, and they took advantage of it. There had been more adventurous jail breaks in the world's history than this, but not all of them required violence, bloodshed and unlikely scenarios. It was a fine plan delivered onto their plate and they took advantage.

They passed the place where she had first set eyes upon her beo, a lifetime ago, when he had been but a brazen Alpha with a fine walk and no clue about the world. Perhaps she had been just as wild and foolish. Perhaps she still was. A lifetime from now, would she regret this act? *Probably.* She took his hand, enjoying its warmth. "Worth it," she whispered, and he kissed her.

They walked through the heavy gates of the city one last time. The two figures in black barely took notice of them as they left. They appeared to be lowly wretches returning home to sleep in the hovels. Emir courteously wished them well.

"A fine night, friends."

Neither Black Guard saw the clip across the ear he received from Wrek a moment after.

· · ·

"They must not find us in the Rangers' camp," warned Lea, as they walked away from the welcoming glow of the city lights. Erroh was more comfortable in the low light. The feel of soil beneath his feet was comforting; the breeze on his skin was a delight. *Freedom.*

Five fully packed mounts awaited them on the outskirts, far enough from the Rangers' camp that no fault for the jail break could be placed upon Lea or Wrek. A solitary figure in a black cloak stood over the beasts, staring out into the water. Lost in thought, she appeared like a statue. She spun in alarm at hearing their footsteps and swiftly drew a sword. She did it more smoothly than most, and Erroh recognised her proud stance despite her weakened state.

"My cub," the woman whispered, dropping the blade and embracing him.

In the distance, the first shouts of alarm rang out. *So much for effortless escapes.*

Wynn gripped the reins of his mount and hoisted himself atop the beast.

Emir looked questioningly at Elise, but she dismissed him with a glare. She needed no further healing. Grimacing, he climbed atop his horse, watching the gate as he settled himself.

"Mother… I…" Erroh began.

"Whisht—take flight. Go find your father and join the Rangers. Make sure they know victory."

"Was there word of the battle?" Wynn asked.

"If they fought, there is no word yet," Elise said quietly, looking to the gates. In the light, Erroh could see the worry in her face. "Ride through the night."

Time was a cruel thing, a candle burning swiftly. He had a thousand words to say to her, with no way to begin. No time, either.

"We might not be too late," Wynn cried, and then cursed his outburst.

"Please, come with us," Lea said to Elise, as though this was an argument they'd battled for long hours already. Elise shook her head and kissed her daughter-in-law. The effort took her breath, and Erroh's heart dropped. Her hour drew near; this, he knew.

Fresh shouts erupted, closer now, and he imagined the Wolves at the gate suddenly taking notice of the hooded figures that had passed through just a little while before.

"When did they march?" asked Wynn.

"Three days ago," whispered Wrek.

So, whatever the outcome, the battle had been fought and won or lost. Now, they would ride either towards victorious Rangers or an unstoppable enemy.

Where are the scouts with word? There are none...

"Thank you, Wrek," Elise whispered, bowing deeply to him.

Climbing onto his mount he shrugged as though it were a small matter, but he smiled.

"We will get word to you," promised Lea, climbing atop her horse. Erroh recognised the beast.

"Is there food in these supplies?" Emir asked, looking at the packs upon his mount. "I will not eat it yet. I'll just like to know. For when we get there."

Elise ignored his question and patted Lea's horse gently. Her voice was painfully frail, and Erroh longed to embrace her one more time and then return her to bed. Demand Emir discover a cure, right fuken there and then.

"See that you do," she said.

A clanging of alarm bells rang out into the night, placing further haste upon their desperate flight. He hugged his mother one last time. "They're playing our song," he said, climbing atop a familiar-looking beast. *Highwind.* The mount immediately reared at his weight and he barely clung on. "Shush, you fuk," he cried, and hearing his voice, it settled. He hadn't seen the beast since Keri, had presumed it had been sold off for riches by the convoy. He should have felt emotional about the reunion, but he was too exhausted and weak.

The magnificent animal responded eagerly to its first master. It turned on its hooves and faced the road and the imminent doom awaiting them.

Elise bowed at the companions one more time before gracefully stepping away to find rest in the comforts of her warm bed. The shattered moon was alive above them, and Erroh was free of chains. He knew the path; he knew the land. They all did. Magnus had insisted they memorise the routes.

"Let's ride," Lea hissed, kicking her beast forward. Behind her, the outcasts of Spark City followed as they disappeared into the Wastes.

55

WAR

Magnus had not created the Clieve, despite the many claims. No, he had merely refined the mechanics of the unique beasts. Any bulky thug with muscles could attach its long reaching blades to each arm and wade into battle, but with the right spring loaded mechanisms, the right balancing of weight, a clever warrior would have enough strength to swing these beasts more than a dozen times before exhaustion overcame them. In fact, Magnus did not need to swing these mighty blades at all. He merely needed to wave them as though greeting an enemy, and the blades answered his effort by decapitating his target.

Magnus held the blades out in front of him now; strapped upon his back, the connecting mechanics clicked loudly. *Never a great sign.* He stretched both arms out wide and each six-foot blade extended menacingly. Immediately he felt their dreadful weight along his shoulders and down through his legs. The first moments controlling these monstrous weapons were the worst. Then he acclimatised to the weight, their counter weights and swallowed his exhaustion and savoured the adrenalin.

On either side of him, the Rangers kept wide. Those unfamiliar with the mighty Clieve watched in awe as Magnus swung them in practice. Again, they clicked, and he cursed his useless, arthritic fingers. Perhaps he could have allowed another warrior with tinkering fingers to tend to their maintenance these last few months, but only a bearer of the weapons had any right to understand their workings. Some uneducated, superstitious peasants claimed these were superstitious contraptions blessed by the absent gods, and he never argued differently. It all added to his legend. Letting go of his left weapon, it remained frozen in the air; held tight by steel and leather.

Carefully, he tightened the straps at his chest and took hold again. *Better.* He could breathe less easily, but at least they had stopped shifting between manoeuvres. He stretched his neck muscles and grimaced as his vertebrae popped. *Old fool. Warring is for younger, stronger legends.*

"Fuk it," he muttered.

They heard the southerners now, only an hour from their camp; it was barely a march for the bastards. For years after the Faction Wars, he'd heard armies marching in his dreams. The boot steps differed in volume, but the warriors always chanted the same words of death. Around him were the stirrings of readiness as his Rangers stood watching. Behind him, though, the lines of Wolves were skittish. Dane charged through their ranks upon horseback barking out orders, and Magnus grinned. Ordering the Rangers to hold the first line was a cruel blow to their pride, regardless of their nature. They might have shuffled towards this war, but come blood, come horror, come victory, the Wolves would want to play their part too. They would fight, and their charge would be the defining blow in the moments before the battle turned. However, they would know—the world would know— that the Rangers had earned the victory. As would every bard. As for the battles to come? Well, the message would be clear. They would never hesitate under his march again. They would fall in line and do their duty. They would win this war for him.

"Be still, Rangers," he ordered, stepping forward. Two hundred warriors stood on either side of him. One beautiful, beige line of menace. All prepared, all eager. "You know your places." His words echoed up and down the line, and he offered a prayer to the gods of war, be they absent or no. *Make today glorious. Make it bloody. Let the southerners know the distance they've come.* They stood ready in the centre of the valley, and the first line of southerners emerged as the dark clouds formed overhead.

Their banners were striking: impressive and barbaric and predictably southern. There was no grace in their art. They stood for savagery, and to their credit, their banners spoke loud their intentions. Beneath their banners came the leathered brutes, all intimidating and evil and wonderfully ill-disciplined.

"I didn't batter you hard enough in the Factions, so you had to come back," he roared, steeling himself against the growing unease. "You just had to come marching again." *Fine fighting words.* He smiled so his comrades might see. *Time to play the part of legend.* Around him, they feared as he did, but that was usual; no Ranger would retreat from battle today. Though most were unproven, those older few stood brazenly enough. *Fine leaders.* By day's end, all would be tested. All would be leaders.

The southerners formed up at the far end, and Magnus slung the blades of the Clieve into their clasps behind his back, before releasing his hold. The relief as the weight shifted was wonderful, and he took a breath. Carefully, he walked along the line of Rangers, meeting each warrior's eyes where he could. He walked with his head held high and his broad shoulders straight. It made him look taller. *Casual, too.* He smiled ruefully as he strolled, avoiding the few hundred cavalry poles that lay in the wild grass at their feet. Each man and woman stood proudly in reply, poised for battle. The early afternoon wind gusted and he knew speeches would be lost. Still, though, there was no rain. At least not yet. Battle was always worse in the rain. How many fantastic warriors had he seen fall to a slippery surface? Wind was good, though; they would take the crossbow bolts a good distance more. With so many crossbows to call upon, accuracy was a small matter in this swirling wind. *Except to a goddess alone in a tree.*

"A fine day for a bit of murder," he barked, and the Rangers cheered. War was rarely won with numbers. Only fools depended on greater numbers swallowing the enemy. Why waste needless life? Such leaders rarely lasted long in power before they had their throats slit—usually by their replacements.

He strode further into the thick grass. Knee height. A good height. Within the hour they would trample it to nothing. It was a small matter. He could not see their faces below him yet. Only their scurrying movements. Like rats emerging from a sinking yacht. *Like rats.* His fingers tingled. His breathing relaxed. He could taste the fight to come and his savage blood pumped. The king was marching into battle. He licked his lips in anticipation, and as the masses gathered below, the last of his fear gave way to hate. He wanted to kill them all. He thought of Erroh and his capture, he thought of the women dying in the flames, and he raged. He fought the urge to throw away his strategy and charge them down alone.

Unsheathing the Clieve, he pulled them free and they were magnificent. Lighter than before. They were a part of him. A beast with elongated talons, stretching out, offering death to all. He stood and pointed them upon the Hunt. They could not see the fury that stirred behind his eyes; they could not hear his primal, panting breaths of excitement, but they saw the blades' grandness as he stared the army down. He growled aloud and spat on the ground and hated them for all they were. His savage heart beat in excitement.

———

Lillium sat in her perch and tried to swallow her third bite of the apple. The Hunt were so close she could hear the low mutter of their language. It was ugly and cold and nasty to her ears. Her southern vocabulary comprised only a few courteous sayings. Listening now, she tried to remember a few of the cruder phrases, thinking she might utter them as she went to work. She chewed the juicy apple but derived little pleasure from it. Two more bites, she told herself. Enough to keep still her churning stomach. *I am Alpha.* She peered across the battleground and watched for her intended. They were so close she could see their eyes now, and strangely, they appeared scared. Why wouldn't they? All factions knew of Magnus, the savage warmonger.

Were Lillium on their end, she might well fear this day too. Her eyes darted from southerner to southerner.

Where are you?

The breeze worried her ever so. The layers of dried and painted leaves stitched into her concealing gown of green wavered in the draft, and she watched them rise and fall. "Fuk it," she whispered bitterly. The first thing any archer learned was that gusting, constant wind was better than gentle, sporadic wind. "You'd love this moment, Lea," she whispered, suddenly sorely missing the only female capable of besting her in these conditions. She wished her best friend was lying prone on another tree branch beside her. They would be unstoppable. Truthfully, Lea was exactly where she needed to be. Doing what needed to be done. As if to mock her solitude, the wind whistled in her ear and the branch she lay upon rocked her gently. This high up, she could remain invisible for as long as she desired. It would take a sharp-eyed cur to spot her. She was Alpha, but in this moment, she was also tree.

"Where are you?" she said to herself, scanning the ranks below her.

The only thing that would move her from this place now was an entire battalion setting camp beneath her, but she doubted the Hunt would set camp any time soon. She was less fearful than she'd expected, and she wondered if this was shock, madness or warmongering on her part. Maybe all three. Her polished bow hung from a branch above her head and she strapped her quivers to her waist. *Soon.* Her eyes darted from the enemy back up to Magnus, who stood waiting, ready. *I will gladly kill for that man.* Beside him, she almost expected to see Wynn standing proudly with shield in hand, and her stomach lurched. *I'm sorry, Wynn, you beautiful bastard.* She despised herself for thinking of him. Missing him. Hating him. Needing him? *No, not anymore.* She forced herself to chew the last piece of apple before swallowing. She knew this battle's path. A few others did too. The creaking branch swayed gently in the growing wind, and she felt a storm coming. Magnus had asked her to use her own judgement and take the shot at her own leisure. His tones had been fierce, but his eyes had been warm and protective. She was closer to their enemy than any Ranger, but once the madness began, she would be safest. *And deadliest to the Hunt.*

———

Jeroen and Theo watched the legend carefully as he walked the line of Rangers. If he were to step into battle, he would need them at his side. Their large shields strapped to their arms, their blades unsheathed and wrapped to their hands.

"I'm excited and terrified," confided the younger man under his breath. His eyes were wide, watching the world and the amassing army, lest he miss something. Jeroen had little comfort or experience to offer. He was afraid, but the emotion faded beneath his pride at standing with Magnus. *I am shield bearer to the legend.* His heavy armour plating reassured him as he took each step. *Delightfully over-dressed for the occasion.* As the rumble grew, he thought of his mate, of her touch, and swiftly, he shook her from his mind. Thinking of her now was a torment.

"You'll do well today, Theo," he offered, patting the young Ranger's back. It was a strange decision to let an inexperienced youngster stand at his left flank, but Magnus trusted his ability. He was tall, well built. *Just like Wynn.* An adequate swordsman, too.

"Aye, fuk it," Theo muttered.

Perhaps taking lives during the riots had granted him this privilege. The allure of a peaceful resolution tugged at Jeroen's own soul whenever a bandit apologised for having been caught thieving. He always accepted their contrition, but he still never hesitated to kill them, regardless. It wasn't in his nature to take a chance. Looking along the line now, Jeroen thought the Rangers both fierce and inexperienced. A terrifying prospect. Killing was a treacherous business of the soul. A warrior who could kill and remain on the line was a trusted warrior. Perhaps in Theo, Magnus had chosen well.

Theo smiled at Jeroen's words and stood prouder, despite the crushing steel weight he carried. *My shield brother.* At a distance, no brute could compete with a Clieve's strike. Swords broke beneath its power. Each strike was a killing blow, or close to it. But get in from either side and the Clieve wielder was defenceless to even the feeblest dagger.

Jeroen's shield was heavy and durable, better than most others, and oh, he would need it standing at the flank. He would be only a foot from accidental decapitation as Magnus surged forward, killing indiscriminately. Their task was bloodier than any other. On top of protecting Magnus from side attacks, they were charged with slaughtering those few still offering fight having taken a Clieve and lived. The two shield bearers were only currents in the tempest of Magnus, and it was a glorious station to have. They were to be baptised today in war, in blood, and it would be spectacular.

———

With the Clieve hanging again at his back, Magnus allowed himself a moment to rest. The last thing he needed was to exhaust himself before the first swing. He marched along the line to its far edge and stepped behind his last Ranger to meet the eyes of the first Black Guard standing far behind him. Without breaking stride, he marched back up through the second wave, eyeing the Wolves as he went. *I am Magnus. Hear my fuken stomp.* He could have offered the waiting Wolves some fierce, warmongering words, a poetic speech suggesting honour, battle and camaraderie, but his words would have been lost in the wind, lost in the retelling as they were repeated. They knew their orders. Showing an interest is enough, he told himself.

They looked away as he marched through them, and he thought it strange. They had been brave mocking Roja, but now, standing upon the battlefield, they could not even face their Master General. The man taking their burden. All of this will change come tomorrow, he reassured himself. In time, they would believe in allegiances unquestionably. Next time, they would stand alongside the Rangers, not behind them. *Because they want to.* This wasn't the first hostile band of untrusting curs he had commanded, either. He smiled almost savagely as he recalled his younger years.

Looking through the Rangers' line down to the gathering brutes, he saw their numbers swell like a tide coming ashore. The bards would exaggerate the numbers, but the tales would be impressive without embellishment. Those same tales would help enlist those few still unsure of their duty. As he marched, the wind blew hard and it carried the sound of the Wolves' arguing further down the dark line. A few steps on, he could see the disturbance grow and he cursed under his breath.

Not now, you fools.

He recognised the three warriors arguing, and his fists clenched.

Why always them?

He strode up closer and could hear them clearly now.

"Know your place, Alpha," warned Dane, pushing Doran, who'd stood too close to him. Aymon took hold of Doran and pulled him away. Their tempers were clearly frayed.

Around them, Wolves pretended to ignore the quarrel, and Magnus understood their predicament: favouring the Alphas was a likely hanging. Favouring Dane would bring the wrath of an aggrieved Alpha onto the interloper's head—not to mention his swords.

"You fool, Dane. Do not allow this," Doran warned, ripping himself free of his friend's grip. He made to swing at his commander, but caught sight of Magnus and returned his fist to his side. He bowed hastily, and Aymon did likewise.

"An honour to fight today with Magnus," Doran bellowed, so all around him would hear. "Apologies for my outburst, sir." He eyed Dane coldly. "This is Wolf business." He sounded almost genuine, almost respectful of Magnus.

Dane, for his part, looked fit to hang the insubordinate bald bastard for all to see. *Not the worst idea.*

When Magnus spoke, his words resonated with authority. "War brings out the worst in us—including fear and stupidity."

"This matter is done and settled, Master General," Dane assured him. He stepped up next to the seething Alphas, and Magnus knew it was wisest to leave the Wolves to settle matters themselves. If they were ever to answer to him, he needed to show respect in kind, meet them at least part of the way.

"See that your brave warriors are settled and prepared," Magnus said briskly, before giving his inferior, a deep, respectful bow. A fine move on his part, and he could see the relief appear on the old warrior's face. Perhaps this moment was as important as waging terrifying blades in battle.

"Sir, the matter is not settled," Aymon hissed.

"Settle it," he snapped.

"Sir, the men are scared. They have every reason to bolt," Doran hissed.

Hearing such spineless words spoken aloud enraged Magnus. "No coward flees today," he roared, so that even with the wind, they would hear him down the line. "Any man who retreats faces the rope." Without another word, Magnus spun on his heel and strode back up the line.

Behind him, Dane finally found his voice.

"You heard the Master General's threat," he shouted to his troops. "There is no peace brokered under Ranger rule. You have your orders."

———

The Hunt waited. They could see the tainted army and it was as their god had pledged. Uden had seen this; Uden had promised them victory today. They couldn't see all who faced them, but they knew of Magnus. As they gathered and awaited Oren's divine word, whispers grew. The fabled one was among them. The false god of fire waited, but before terror reared up and showed itself, Uden himself placed upon them a blessing of rain. Fine, heavy showers that lashed their smiling faces. How would the false god burn them with rain dampening his will?

All hail Uden. The Hunt fell silent despite their numbers, and stood like sentries, waiting to be unleashed. They would not attack until the first line had led the assault. Suddenly, they heard another rumble, and their pulses quickened as the Riders charged from beyond.

Hooves tore across the landscape with the thunder of a thousand storms. The wet grass danced and the Hunt licked their lips with glee. The Rangers drew nearer now in their hundreds, and the world prepared itself for war. The Hunt knew these moments; they'd all seen this charge before—upon settlements, upon fleeing cowards. The Riders would charge through them, smashing their defiance. So they signalled their intentions: they blew the great horns of war.

———

Magnus had listened to Erroh's grim description of the horns on the first day of the siege, and now, at last, he heard them play. His son had spoken of their crushing, disheartening tones and had done them no justice. Their wailing anthem played on, carried on the wind, and Magnus's stomach turned. How horrific had that sound been to a little doomed town? It was a tactic devised by a great mind, one that understood the importance of morale and inspiration—and how to batter it down. It was a fine first blow struck by the Hunt. There would be few more—Magnus would see to that.

From their places at the edge of the treeline he heard his hounds bark and whine, and he smiled. His boys would repay the Hunt for instilling a taste of fear in them, and he had trained them how best to do that: with a sharper bite. He took a moment to marvel again at their grandness. He'd never lost a hound in battle. Today would be no different. *The absent gods agreed.* Their tails wagged watchfully and Magnus could sense their eagerness from here. They stood at the ready, sniffing the air, sniffing their comrades both beige and black. Probably sniffing the enemy's scent, too. *A sniff before a nice bloody mouthful.*

"Soon," he muttered aloud, and excitement took hold of human and hound alike. *Enough of this music shit: let's get to killing.*

Beneath the call he heard the cavalry's thunder, and he gripped the handles of his blades firmly and the horns fell silent.

———

Lillium notched an arrow and sought the perfect shot. "Where are you?" she whispered, scanning every soldier. Waiting for inspiration. It was a fine mission, seeking and taking out their leader, whoever the fuk he was. Unconsciously, she looked for a tall, godlike fiend with an eye missing, but she knew she wouldn't be that lucky. Necessity dictated that Magnus march into battle first, but Uden had no such obligation. No scout reported of their foe either. *Not yet.* "Strike him down with an arrow and lose yourself in the green," Magnus had told her. A fine mission; a fine day for it. Few would notice a stray arrow once the fighting started. She bit her bottom lip and watched the two parting sections of the army. The Riders were close now; the surrounding leaves rustled gently as the hundreds of hooves beat to one constant war drum, louder than any thunder. She felt terror, but also exhilaration. Scanning the line again, she searched fruitlessly for any brute barking orders. Be still, she told herself.

———

Suddenly, the group of Riders dashed through the opening. Without breaking stride, they fanned out swiftly across the width of the battlefield, charging towards the waiting warriors. The horses screamed as they were kicked and urged forward. How terrifying an enemy they were to gaze upon, and for a moment, Magnus admired them. Mounted upon such fearsome beasts, they sacrificed a quicker pace for terrifying power. No cavalry assembled could match their fury.

They howled their hatred loudly and drew their weapons as they rode. They pierced the sky with raised swords, axes, maces and pikes, and Magnus watched from his centre place among the Rangers as though gazing upon a tournament of skill. Behind him, he heard the Wolves shouting among themselves, and he cursed them under his breath. *Show daring, you fools.* He could feel the shield-bearers on either side of him tense. They had not held their blades aloft and he had not raised his Clieve. None of the Black Guard or Rangers had done so, either.

Halfway out, the ground shook and it was perfect. Magnus grinned.

"Now!" he roared, and his word carried far along the line of defenders.

The Rangers did not reach down to the grass as one well-oiled machine, nor did he want them to. Their movements were laboured and obvious, and every single Rider watched them as they charged forward.

"Let's see how much faith you fukers have in your god!" he mocked. He knew they feared anti-cavalry spikes. Had he not seen enough of southern warfare? Had Erroh not exploited that very weakness defending Keri?

Each spike was long and beautiful, and he thought them splendid as they hoisted them high into the air for everyone to see. The Rangers dug them deep into the ground for support. They were thinner than Magnus's blades, but they were ten feet long, thin and sharp enough to penetrate a charging mount's sternum and keep going. And of course, it wouldn't be the horses alone that would die. Any fool with the slightest understanding of warfare would understand this. *Aye, you face death in every charge, but this is certain death.* Magnus watched the entire line of Riders slow ever so as the open field suddenly became precarious to those on unstoppable mounts.

You thought you had a clear run, didn't you?

"We showed them too soon," spat Jeroen, reaching for his blade.

Magnus just smiled. Aye, he could have waited and raised them a few moments before the brutes fell upon them and it would have been brutal. The Riders would have been decimated with an acceptable loss of life to his Rangers. However, should they falter their impressive charge in any way, he might save the army from more losses than needed. *Just slow down a little, you fuks. Just enough to be easier targets.*

He knew the southerners. Zealous or no, he would bet on them attempting to save their own skin, every fuken time.

———

There was still a significant distance between the Riders and the line of tainted, and time enough for every warrior to think dark thoughts. Knowing that inevitable death was moments away tested every soldier's resolve. Their war cries lessened, but still they drove their beasts forward instinctively, and the tainted waited patiently. Riders cursed and hissed in fear. The tainted enemy still did not stir. And why would they? Were they not in the far greater position? Did they not have devastating anti-cavalry weapons in their grasp?

The leading Rider was the first to lose his nerve. He slowed and tucked in behind his neighbour, allowed him the honour of taking the lead. The new leader slowed too. This began a devastating chain reaction as Riders slowed their mounts and loudly challenged their orders. A few continued on, those with stronger resolve or demented beliefs, and the rest gathered up behind them. In moments, Magnus's army had slowed the first wave by doing little else but showing them their weapons. To turn upon a charge was no simple task for a line of mounted warriors, either. The Riders pulled wide to break the line in a clustered group along the outskirts, only fifty feet from the defensive line. As they did, they argued and forgot themselves while trying to make amends for their cowardice.

———

Watching the sudden change in direction enraged Oren. He called for the horns of retreat, vowing to take the first faltering Rider's head. The second head would be that of his chief scout for insisting there were no anti-cavalry spikes lining the battlefield. He had expected a devastating assault to show his leadership in a good light, to earn him favour at Uden's table, but such a pathetic display under his watch was yet another embarrassment. It was all the more troubling with Uden's most trusted lieutenant at play in the region. Aurora would not be best pleased.

"We will do this ourselves," he roared to his foot soldiers, and they approved of his order. He raised his blade and prepared to spur his brutes, and a delicately crafted arrow with a nice quail-wing flight appeared from nowhere and struck his stomach.

———

The dishonourable call of the retreating horns must have stung the Riders' pride. Though most pulled wide, forming into a group, a dozen of them charged onward and died brutally upon the spikes. The Rangers plunged and stabbed, and in a breath the deed was done. Their dying wails brought further disheartening cries from the remaining Riders who reared, spun, and turned to answer the lifesaving retreat, and Magnus offered them no mercy.

"I can't believe that just happened," Jeroen hissed in disbelief, and Magnus smiled. If he had a coin for every time the southerners had blinked first in the face of adversity, he'd have heavy pockets. This was only half the task, though. Little point in allowing them to regroup.

Hard to strike down a rushing target.

Easier in a group.

Perfect.

"Take up arms," he roared. The Rangers dropped their spikes and reached for their fully cocked weapons, still lying in the grass. Lifting their crossbows, they loaded each magnificent weapon in calm silence. "Now!" Magnus roared, and each warrior fired. The collective clicking and whooshing was louder than Magnus remembered. As was the squeal of hundreds of killing bolts released into the air.

56

NEVER FORGET

They screamed as they died, and it was dreadful. Beautiful to the ear, but oh, so dreadful. They fell covered in arrows, still gripping the reins of their mounts. Their thick armour was no match for the crossbows at such a range. Their slow, ill-disciplined charge had been a gift from the absent gods to the inaccurate, inexperienced Rangers. He'd hoped for favourable consequences from his own imaginative thinking, but he'd never expected such success. *Another chronicle in the legend of Magnus.* The land was a blood-soaked vision of horror now, and he approved. He'd feared their cavalry charge above all others. Feared a later charge too when both groups were engaged in the melee. But the absent gods had favoured them, and he offered them silent thanks. *Amazing how swiftly some faith returns come wartime.* With a bitter, warmongering grin, Magnus surveyed the murder he had created.

Let the fukers know their failure.

Let them know the cost of their sins.

Let them know this land is under Magnus's protection.

"Again," he roared, and the archers dropped to their knees, reloading their weapons. He drew his eyes from the massacre and watched his lines of Rangers go to work. He counted the breaths and waited for them to rise, and they did so even more swiftly than they had raised the anti-cavalry poles.

"Fire!" A second deadly volley of bolts took flight, bringing a second deadly round of hissing and screaming and killing. The bolts struck down those attempting to retreat, and the others, wailing in their own ruination, fell still. Distantly, the horns blew desperately, but it was too late; they were already decimated.

"Again."

"Fire!"

The third volley was the most accurate. It usually was with those who were untested. Anxiety won out, always, until they found their composure, their taste for butchery. Nothing like a slowing, confused gathering of clustered Riders to settle the nerves. He stood with a fine line of experienced killers now.

Nearby, Jeroen nodded victoriously, watching wounded Riders struggle to pull at the barbed bolts. Hundreds stepped into the darkness in those first wonderful moments. Magnus knew this battle wouldn't last. By the fourth volley, only a few dozen remained. Most were too injured to crawl, let alone fight. They wailed and prayed to Uden and died slowly.

A few Riders eluded the carnage, escaping grievous injury through good fortune alone. Those few made it back to the Hunt's assault line, and the horns fell silent, and Magnus sent a few dozen Rangers out into the ruins of the Riders carrying massive war axes. The Hunt watched in outrage as the Rangers put the wounded out of their misery. They hacked the defenceless Riders apart with glee, for such were Magnus's unsavoury orders. They cheered, they mocked, and they directed every suggestion of merriment at the southerners watching on.

Magnus struggled to watch; he never looked away. These gruesome murders were his sins to embrace. This is war, he told himself, and it meant little. *Magnus the Bloody marches again.* In front of him, he watched a brute plead in his native tongue as his executioner stood over him. The Rider wept and crawled, a bolt sticking from his back. *You brought this on yourself.* He howled incomprehensible words, but Magnus didn't speak the language of mercy. A few breaths later it didn't matter, anyway. *I am foul and it is necessary.*

He would dream of this day a thousand times more in his life. He would wake up with their pleading cries ringing in his mind.

Finally, the last forlorn scream fell silent and the blood-soaked Rangers dropped their heads and their axes and slowly trudged back across the tarnished ground to stand the line. The scattered bodies were too numerous to count.

Slowly, with less discipline than a coward's retreat, the Hunt began charging up the line in separate groups. Beaten fools, unable to forsake a demented god's wishes.

————

The second arrow sent Oren crashing against one of the massive carts. It pierced his shoulder and he roared in pain, pulling it free. Nobody heard him above their own screams. Their eyes were upon a massacre. Why worry about a doomed leader? He reached for the arrow at his stomach, expecting the worst. Pulling it free, he saw its tip had only pierced the skin. His armour had taken most of the force. *I'll live to see execution.* Blood came streaming out, but his anger granted him a better threshold for the pain.

A comrade finally noticed his injury and knelt over him in shock. She reached for his wound and a third arrow went through her throat, pinning her to the cart. She gasped in shock, bled all over him and whimpered. Within a wet breath, her beautiful brown eyes stared into nothing.

"Erin," he whispered. Despite his panic, his anger, his pain, he reached for her. He'd bedded her before. She was gentle, wonderful. He pulled her corpse against him as another arrow embedded itself in her body. Blood seeped down upon him and her heavy weight pinned him. He cried out for help, but the horns blew fiercely. He alone was under attack, he alone the target.

Aurora? He knew the arrows came from the forest. Nearby, somewhere high. A distant kill suggested nothing of Aurora's flair.

His lover took another strike through the back of the head and her hair fell loosely in his hands. Terrified, he slid from her cover under the cart, roaring orders as he did. On the other side, he heard one more arrow embed itself in the cart and he knew he was safe.

"Killers in the green," he howled, tearing his armour free, tending to what healing he could. "I will survive this," he growled to himself, shoving a rag against the tiny wound. His shoulder bled more, but one thing at a time. "Counter their charge," he roared, unsure if any heard his outburst. On the other side of the cart, where arrows now appeared uninvitingly, he heard the Riders return, screaming, cursing, lamenting their losses. He should have met them, should have slain the first returning and sent them right back out. Instead, he hid from invisible assassins, searching for his pelt.

A few began charging up towards the defenders and he knew disaster was in the wind. Ill-discipline had caused the disaster in the town, and he sensed it here now. His stomach quivered, although that may have just been from the blood it now leaked, and he wondered was he dying?

"Help me," he cried, watching feet run back and forth in panic on the other side of the cart. They weren't listening; they had taken action for themselves and it was another insult to his leadership.

Those first hundred charged forward, and the rest followed. They engaged in war without thought, and without belief, either. They sought revenge with the instincts of an unruly mob. Oren accepted that losing the Riders along with heavy Ranger losses was a fine bargain. Taking the first line would have resulted in the grand retreat, but the Rangers held firm. More than that, their nerve had been shaken. Might they have stayed the course if he had ridden with them? Might he be lanced upon a spike, but the day already won?

"Everyone attack!" he roared from his place of hiding. He dared a glance out from cover to try spot his attacker. *Attackers?* He watched the trees for shapes and then slipped back swiftly lest another arrow take him. *Might hurt less than Uden's wrath.* He stared at the still body of his lover and cursed in anger. A tragic day, indeed.

———

"Prepare yourselves, Black Guard," howled Magnus triumphantly. He watched the beasts charge recklessly towards their line and he couldn't believe his luck. Aye, southerners preferred the feel of steel in their hands as they took their victims, but what type of fool sent their entire infantry charging up towards a line of waiting archers? With the Riders eliminated, the battlefield was a glorious killing ground to those who were prepared. It was almost too easy. *And Magnus the bloody took no prisoners, for they were not worth his gaze.*

When he spoke, he addressed both waiting armies. "Take up arms!"

Behind him, with the first attack countered, the Wolves had their orders, simple as they were. He knew their distance; knew the wind; knew what the moment required. There was a wave of motion as they prepared and alongside, his Rangers dropped to their knees, reloading their crossbows. They did not rise. *Why take chances when a thousand arrows were about to take flight?* Magnus ducked with them, his eyes on the nearing Hunt. Oh, they outnumbered them, oh, they carried shields, oh, they had a bone to pick, but oh, the defenders of Spark City were only getting started.

Give the order, Dane.

They waited as the stirring behind increased, and Magnus could not blink. His breath caught in his throat. He watched the many hundreds in the first line. The hundreds behind them. Spread out invitingly. A terrifying sight to those unprepared. He gripped his Clieve.

Give the order, Dane.

No arrow was released, and the world went silent but for the sound of arguing Wolves, and Magnus gave the order. *To the fires with you, Dane.*

"Now!"

Still no arrows took flight, and Magnus spun around in horror. Like a few grains of sand through a sieve, a handful of Wolves stepped from their ranks. More followed. The newest recruits were swiftest to turn. *Oh, no.* As the Riders had learned, once rips appear in formidable

597

forces, gaping holes follow. The rear-guard collapsed in a few terrible moments and Magnus was too shocked to cry out. *Betrayed.*

Dane led the retreating charge. Upon his horse, he roared for retreat and it was a miserable sight. A few older Wolves challenged. Gathering up in a cluster, they screamed their outrage as their comrades fled around them—not through fear, for this battle was already won. The charging Hunt, buoyed on by fleeing cowards, cried out in victory. They believed as though whispers of a possible Black Guard retreat were true.

———

No man forgot Sigi's words on the field that day. His pledge to them. His incredible generosity and his careful, dreadful threat. They could never forget. It was an excellent speech, given by a simple man with grand plans. He had no time for the Rangers. He had no desire to assist those refusing peace. He was no grand Primary, blind to the world's workings; he was no embittered warmonger marching for one last taste of glory, either. The Hunt desired peace. And peace was good for all. But Magnus was in the way.

"All who return from the march will receive a hundred pieces," he declared in the howling towers, and his soldiers had cried in joy at such a gift. He was a generous man and they loved him for it. Had Wrek not treated them well, these last few seasons? Had Wrek not ensured their loyalty?

"To every man marching at dawn: you lose no honour in fleeing at the right moment." *The right moment.* Finishing, he warned them once and it was cutting. "Any Wolf who dies upon the field will continue to suffer. No payment will reach your family ever again; no payment will be made upon your death to those starving few who need it most."

Aye, it was a cruel pledge, but a necessary one. They understood his meaning and Dane ensured they acted on it. Privately, he assured Sigi that no Wolf would retreat until the Rangers were committed, and he kept his word.

———

The younger enlisters had nearly bolted as the Riders had charged down on them. Dane had seen their terrified faces and held them fast as they braced themselves for the clash. He'd trusted Magnus's plan to reveal the spikes. *It was genius.* The Wolves had only one part to play in this skirmish: stand firm against the Riders. If they fled beforehand and the Riders broke through, they would have been charged down with little effort despite the whispered agreements already made. It never came to that. A fine day, indeed.

———

Doran and Aymon stood against the roaring wave of deserters. They grabbed out at their running brothers, trying desperately to stem the impossible tide. *Not like this.* This was the moment to place honour above wealth. Instead, their kind were treacherous. They screamed, they pleaded, and they cursed each man for ignoring their call. Three-quarters in total fled in the first few moments, and it was a catastrophe.

———

There was sunshine earlier. Magnus sprinted along the line, screaming in disbelief, in horror, in fury. He used no words but instead uttered only primal cries. The changing of the day was upon them all, and death loomed. His Rangers stood firm, and they were gloriously outnumbered. Without the rear-guard's arrow assault, little would affect the thundering brutes charging toward them now. Behind him, his Rangers fired off their crossbows as the Hunt charged into range, and the land seemed to collapse beneath their feet. They continued to fire, but the numbers were too great, their nerve too shaken by the retreating bastards. It was all they could do, for they knew that darkness loomed. Unlike their sullied comrades, they would not flee. They could not flee either, lest they be struck down swiftly. They knew tragic things. These were their last moments. Not one Ranger followed the Wolves' cowardly example. They stood their line as the approaching army set upon them, and they suffered for it.

Magnus screamed one last time, but none listened, and he cursed them all to the fires. He pondered retreat, but such an action would doom them all, and create fewer casualties among their vanquishers.

"My brave brothers," he said, his voice nearly a sob, and both his shield-bearers understood. *Lead us to our death, Magnus.*

"No finer way to die," Jeroen said stoutly.

"An honour, sir," Theo barked, gripping his shield and sword. His eyes were terrified and alive. A fine warrior.

Goodbye, Elise. I will wait for you in the darkness. Goodbye, Erroh. Goodbye Lexi. Make me wait even longer.

With his Clieve raised in anger, and taking long, purposeful strides, Magnus charged first into the unsurmountable numbers. His shining golden armour was spectacular against the dull grey land. His weapons swung and he waded through wood, steel, leather and flesh. Those he did not kill received a swift stab through the heart from Jeroen and Theo as they surged along beside him. Onward the trio waded, always moving, always forward, deep into the enemy as the sudden counter-charge brought a bloody, savage end to the day. Around them, the Rangers formed up tightly and charged, but they met a wall of hate and violence and in moments, any Ranger unlucky enough to be on the outside was swallowed up by southern hate and swiftly sent to darkness. Aye, they were superior swordsmen, but the massing army were relentless and they drove swiftly through the few hundred beige warriors.

Despite the panic around him, Magnus showed no fear, nor any humanity either. He was a god of war, a deity of such ferociousness that his victims feared his step. They scattered around him and he struck them down. His blades were a flash of silver and crimson and they never stopped swinging. He became once more the beast of the Faction Wars, and his path of destruction was terrible to behold. Around him Rangers screamed, killed and died, but he never slowed, never offered a step back. Instead, he strode deeper into the Hunt's oncoming wave and killed them all.

He was not alone. To his left, Jeroen was a legend. Easily, ferociously, he brought the fight to every fool attacking from the side. There was no better shield-bearer. He matched Magnus's step, his body twisting and complementing every savage strike of his leader as though they'd marched a decade together.

On his right, Theo howled in fear and bravado as he too fought the line like a seasoned veteran; he threw everything into the violence, and Magnus was never prouder than he was now to stand alongside such a fighter.

For a few wonderful, tragic moments as the Wolves fled the war, the Rangers held firm, but like a wall of fire giving way to torrential rain, they could not last long. The Rangers tried to move with their Master General, but as the legend stepped further into the sea of menace, they beat the Rangers back. Their killers surrounded them and stabbed mercilessly into their huddled groups. They fought until they died; they did not beg for mercy; they did not give up the fight. They died bravely, like magnificent heroes. Were any to have survived this day, their heroism would have been celebrated, but the Hunt killed them. Every single one of them.

———

Lillium continued firing, for she had plenty of arrows and she wished to be free of every one. The general lived, but he hid from her reach. Already, she had claimed the lives of a dozen brutes, in particular the fools who'd come searching in the forest for a grounded soldier. She'd liked the noises they made as they fell. Easier to listen to their howling and gaze upon their quivering bodies than to witness the horror upon the battlefield. *Was this what Lea endured in Keri?* Watching brothers and sisters butchered? *All safe and hidden.*

Another member of the Hunt broke through the treeline, searching for her. Unlike most other comrades, he carried a crossbow and scanned the branches in the trees above. He was dead long before he spotted her perch. Then, to her dismay, she realised he hadn't been alone. She heard a twig break behind her, and then felt the sting of a bolt as it passed her ear. Without a thought, she dropped from her branch and rolled before she knew what was below her. Three killers waited, and they fell upon her. She dodged the first attack, but felt a second blade's steel pierce her chest as she leapt away. Stung and stumbling, she fell against a trunk and took hold of her attacker's wrist as he tried to push the blade in deeper. They wrestled fiercely as the two others danced around, awaiting their chance to kill. *Or rape.* Screaming in his face, she pulled her sword free and slashed. His struggle lessened and her face became wet with crimson spray, and her assailant fell to the ground clutching a shredded throat.

With stable ground beneath her and a moment to pick her stance, she met the next attacks. She knew she was already struck down, and though terrified, she chose violence as her parting gift. The second and third attackers charged in with blades swinging, and she met their attack. She imagined them as beasts from the dark, and terror became fury and it was easy. Within a few manoeuvres, the remaining attackers fell. Her blade spun and she allowed herself a moment of triumph, an entire breath. But all too soon, there came the heavy rustling of leaves, the breaking of twigs, and more searching groups of fiends. She knew her orders to flee, and surviving these horrors was a tempting thought, but she caught sight of the last dozen Rangers offering their lives as their vanquishers tore them apart and she wailed silently. She had spent months with these friends, understood their peasant ways, and appreciated them more now that she was free of the city's whispers, the city's prejudices. Side by side, they were slain, but they took many with them; the bodies of their victims still lay in the southern line, and she was proud of her kin.

She caught sight of the magnificent battle hounds on the outskirts of the battle, the pride of their legendary master. They worked their routine as though it were a game, a savage pack taking down prey. They surged as one, avoiding the masses, running up and down through the forest cover, all the while seeking any southerner careless enough to have strayed from the herd. There were dozens, all too concerned with warring.

Further down the slope she saw a few Wolves fight against the unending tide of brutes. They had not fled as the others had, and they paid for the sacrifice. They were no longer rivals; they were brothers. Dia would have saluted them. So would she. They fought well; they fought like true relics of a city's pride, and she gripped her blade tightly.

Her attackers drew close, and Lillium did not move. Instead, she looked at the three warriors now giving greater fight than all the others. Magnus was a near unstoppable force, striding into unbeatable numbers. Even from this distance, his victims' screams were piercing. Stunning weapons swung and drew blood, broke and shattered all that they faced. He marched as it had been told in the tales, a tempest of fury and majesty. He was more god than man.

She did not desire death, but she could not run from this battle. There were worse ways to die. *Wynn will avenge me.* Gripping her sword, she charged towards the searching killers, aiming to take as many as she could before she stepped into the darkness.

———

It was Theo who fell first. A fine death, with brief pain. It was a rarity to find a southern archer on the battlefield, but find one Theo did. Only the killer knew how many bolts he fired blindly into his own comrades, hoping to strike down Magnus, but it must have been many. One of his strikes missed the flailing blades, the mass of movement, and struck Theo through the one chink in his armour: beneath the armpit. Onward it tore, and somewhere deep it took out his heart. His body dropped to the blood-soaked ground in mid-swing, resting forever beside his last victim, who dropped a moment after.

Two bolts struck Jeroen in the back, and he fell to his knees. Suddenly alone, Magnus spun back towards the fallen Jeroen, swinging recklessly, and cleared himself a path. An arrow went through his knee and he stumbled, breaking off the wooden shaft as he did. Hatred overtook agony and he stood again and took off the head of the bastard who'd struck him, but swords jabbed from all sides, attempting to pierce his tough armour, and Magnus knew this was the end. A few southerners took hold of his blade and held him fast. He struggled, but his body betrayed him. He fell to a knee, releasing his hold on the Clieve, which remained pointing skyward like an ominous fin protruding from a wave.

Instinctively, he pulled the clasp from his weapons and rolled as the Hunt took hold of the Clieve. Perhaps they thought it a living beast, for they surged around the weapons in a churning mass, treading over him as they did. He drew a ragged breath and waited to die, and suddenly Jeroen took hold of him.

"Come on," he roared, and Magnus saw his chance at impossible escape as a gathering of crossbow-wielders fired indiscriminately into the Clieve-bearing crowd hoping to strike him down. *Ill-disciplined.* Southerners collapsed around them, screaming their agony. Some turned on the attackers, slaying them for their foolishness, and the colour green filled Magnus's eyes as the land opened up for them. Instinctively, Magnus grabbed the whistle around his neck and blew hard. Its shrill note rang across the battlefield, delivering the order to retreat to those still fighting—to Rangers, to Wolves, to hounds too. He could not see their losses nor those they'd inflicted upon the enemy. He could only see his shield-bearer, who grabbed him as a fresh volley of arrows took flight, killing more Hunt, clearing their way, and striking both him and Jeroen again.

Screams erupted all around them. Bodies flailed and a second bolt pierced his knee and he howled in pain. Jeroen took three more bolts through his armour, into the chain mail beneath. He howled as loudly as his leader, but still dragged Magnus towards the treeline. Venting their wrath upon the remaining crossbow wielders, the Hunt turned on their own and allowed both Rangers to slip free of the devastation. They slipped into the peaceful green and brown of the forest, and despite the crippling pain, they kept moving, seeking escape.

Magnus's mind was wild, his hatred alone fuelling each step. *Live and find revenge.* Beside him, Jeroen struggled; crimson drops seeped from beneath his cuirass. Behind them, the thunder of violence had stopped, replaced by the wails of the dying. This too kept Magnus moving steadily towards retreat. He did not know how far they trudged, nor how swiftly, only that it was Jeroen who collapsed first and when he did, Magnus could hear their pursuers not far behind. It was a dreadful sound.

———

Doran stabbed, he killed. He dodged, he swung, he killed again. It was easier to kill than he'd ever thought. *Easy, aye, but soul crushing.* Just in front of him, another Wolf brother fell, and he lamented the loss before taking his killer. Another swing, another death. *Easy.* They'd ruined his hand. Torn in half by an axe, it hung in two parts and the pain was dreadful. Still, he took the pain, blocked the strike and killed again. They were near the treeline now, all nestled up, killing and dying all in the same breath. He wondered, would they all meet again in the darkness? Would it be awkward? Would they continue the fight? Would they be able to? He'd pissed himself in the first few moments. How brave an Alphaline was he? Beside him, Aymon fought fiercely on; dying beside his friend was probably a fitting end.

Picked the wrong army.

Not getting paid, either.

No one will lament me.

Suddenly, the shrill, piercing cry of retreat filled the air, and hope stirred in him. They were not the last alive. Somewhere among the horror, there still stood a general demanding a regroup, and Doran would need every comrade to exact revenge for this horror today. *Forget the Hunt.* It would be Dane who would die at his hand. *That fuker Sigi, too.* And every one of those cowardly Black Guards after.

"This fight is lost," cried Aymon, and Doran drew up beside him.

"Let's get the fuk out of here!"

Aymon charged towards the treeline, dragging comrades as he went. "To cover," he cried, and Doran followed, cutting, dodging, swinging and killing. They fled over countless bodies in red and beige, and Doran's shame was depthless. He'd tried. Fuk it, but he'd tried. Seeing the devastating first wave crushed under Magnus's tactics should have reaffirmed their call. Put to rest any suggestion of retreat. *Stand ground this day and send a message to the invaders.* He'd argued and failed. He'd lost many brothers because of it, too. Those honourable few left nothing behind but starvation for their families. Aye, he would spend quite a time on Sigi the Bloody. *Ruler of Samara.*

Ahead, he saw Aymon reach down and pick up a heavy burden. It was the same shape as Azel. Doran was unsurprised to see him unable to leave the pretty young boy behind. Azel bled from his neck, his face already pale. But that wouldn't stop young love.

Doran charged ahead of Aymon, killing as he went. Desperate to keep his best friend safe, and his burden. *And why not?* Doran owed a debt to the young Wolf, too. Were it not for his cold composure with the bow, they might not have struck down so many. It was his Keri blood. He always spoke of Keri, and fuk him if it wasn't a little endearing hearing such barbaric mutterings out of one so unimpressive in stature. He'd stood with them this day from the start, and they'd moved as a different type of trio to Magnus's troop, and they had been fierce. Azel had calmly notched his long bow and fired as if he were in a field with straw targets. On either side, the two warring Alphas had cut, pummelled, stabbed and battered the group of Hunt and it had been easy. *Easy and terrible.*

"Just keep running," Doran howled, and many of his surviving brothers charged with him. Ducking into the green, they took flight and never stopped running until their pursuers were left far behind.

———

There was little point trying to hide. The trails of blood from Jeroen's wounds were too plentiful. They lit the way for their pursuers. All around them, the forest was alive with death. Those pursued, and those tired of the pursuit.

"I cannot step another foot, Master General," gasped Jeroen, tearing his armour free and revealing the wounds beneath. They would be fatal if left untreated, and they were debilitating now while they attempted to flee from a pack of murderers. He lifted his hand up in the light and was distraught to see the wide, gaping hole in the middle of his palm. "When did that happen?"

"That's not a good injury at all," Magnus sniffed, resting against a tree. His decision was clear: he would not let Jeroen stand alone, and he knew Jeroen had no desire to allow such foolishness. "But I've seen worse. Some bandaging and a bit of rest and you'll be fine." It was a fine lie, and the crashing of southerners grew closer. Cursing under his breath, he snapped the second arrow in his knee and began wrapping his wound with a rag. He hissed quietly with the pain. "A king's region to have had Emir in this battle," he muttered.

"I'll be ready to fight soon enough," lied Jeroen, already counting his breaths. The pulsing pain along his back where'd they'd gutted him was agony. A tragic end, but perhaps not a fruitless one. He held his hand out, but it would not answer his request to clench. *I'll never wield two blades again.* He gasped a few breaths, spat some blood and stood up. There was one more act he must do as a Ranger. Pulling a large, discarded branch from the ground, he passed it across to his Master General. "Tell Mea I thought of her at the end," he whispered, unsheathing his dagger.

"We can survive this nightmare together, brother."

Jeroen shook his head and bled a little harder for the effort. "I'll not last another day," he said, offering his hand. Seeing his determination, Magnus nodded. "Delaying another moment longer is an insult to me," Jeroen said. Fine last words, too. At this, Magnus gripped the temporary crutch and hobbled into the green. *May the gods bless your journey.*

Jeroen waited for Magnus's footsteps to fall silent before sitting down upon a low-hanging tree branch. It was almost comfortable after such efforts. He thought of his pride in Tye and lamented that he would miss seeing him grow to manhood. He thought of Mea and loved her as he had the moment they had first kissed. He whispered his apologies to the wind in the hope the gods would grant them flight and deliver them to her sleeping ear. Every breath was hard, but after a time he stopped noticing. His exhaustion left him, though that might have been his mind gifting him a softer passing.

It didn't take long for his hunters to come upon his little resting spot. He must have looked so pathetic, bobbing with the gentle sway of the tree, with his life blood dripping into the dirt underneath. Coughing weakly, he waited for the last strike as they stepped in closer. When they did, he leapt at the nearest, stabbing the bastard right through as though he were butter. Blood filled his vision, and he wondered could he borrow some for the night.

He was not strong enough to take the dozen remaining southerners, and they fell upon him and trapped him like a Puk in a net. He still did not go quietly. He stabbed beneath the punches and kicks and cut deep another screaming cur. He kept stabbing and they kept striking until the world went dark and the screams became silent.

———

They discovered Magnus when his heart was as low as a beaten leader's could ever be. Hours had passed; who could rightly tell? Not him. Every laboured step was agony, yet still he pressed forward, like a god's forgotten child pursued through the forest. He'd never experienced exhaustion like this, but somehow, he persevered.

It was the clearing in the forest that finally beat him. Up to the clearing, he'd believed, but hope was a curse to any doomed man. It just prolonged the tragic moment longer than needed. Halfway through the clearing, he finally heard his pursuers steal up from behind. He scrambled onward, hoping to reach concealment, but he knew well a few remaining Riders had caught his scent. Every step became too slow, his burning knee tore at his will and he roared in frustration hearing their victorious jeering. Turning mid-step, he saw them charge down upon him, not with swords but high upon their southern mounts and he hated them.

Never forget their sacrifices.

Buoyed on by those whose spirits ran with him, he drove towards the treeline, making one last effort to save himself. But at the edge of the clearing stood a wall of stone, and it ended his race. The Riders roared mockingly as they formed up around him. On either side of the massive rock there lay a steep climb of mud and green that he hadn't the heart to attempt.

"Now who would place a rock face right in the middle of a forest?" he growled. It was a prayer, a threat, a concession. He knew this land. The mound of rock hadn't appeared so impressive upon his map, but up close, it was a remarkable thing. He fell against the overhang and stared to the level above. Tapping the smooth grey surface a few times in defeat, he turned to face his conquerors. The weariness of battle and the frantic flight had taken all of his energy. His body ached. It was time to sit down.

And so he did.

The five killers dropped from their beasts in triumph and stood over him. They were wary, though. They'd learned the perilousness of an injured Ranger feigning deathly exhaustion. Magnus had no fight, though. He couldn't even growl any longer, although he heard growls all around him. Bitterly, he dropped his crutch against the mound and sat back. The sun had broken through again. The flash storm had dissipated to nothing.

"I'm a finished soul," he whispered as they closed in around him. He was ready to join his warriors in the darkness. He'd led them well. They'd marched admirably. He allowed only one regret to stir his last few thoughts, and it was for the Wolves. He should have known the measure of their honour. Should have known the depths of their betrayal. He had counted on cowardice from the southerners; he hadn't expected it from the Wolves.

Again, he heard the growling and he wondered if it was the gods' disapproval of his actions today. The Hunt hovered and held their attack as a chorus of menace grew, and this time Magnus heard it properly too. Primal. The sound of a pack eager to serve their master.

The growl was steeped in the blood of the southerners and it was delicious. As one pack, the master's mighty battle hounds emerged from the forest. They came slowly and with lethal purpose. Only the absent gods themselves knew how long they had tracked their master.

Only the absent gods knew how many southerners they'd killed to get to him. *There were many.* They were trained as a pack, and this hunt was no different. They carried injuries, they ached, they were exhausted, but every one of them was still marching, still hunting. They understood the movement of man-beasts; they understood the threat of blades, and they understood their teeth were far more effective. They took their time, for he had trained them to do so, and they waited. This was no savage gathering of too many man-beasts, shuffling and cutting while they, the pack, preyed upon those careless few along the outskirts. No, this was closer to home. This was natural.

One Rider spun and swiped at a hound. The beast leapt backwards, snarling, and the true attack came from his left. A savage, spitting smile of jagged teeth covered in saliva and blood took hold of him. He screamed as the beast tore apart his throat, and the younger hounds growled and barked in yearning. They wanted to play. A second Rider went to help his fallen brother. He dropped his guard for the smallest of moments, and two of the beasts struck him down, tearing into him as though he were fresh bait. They knew how to fell a man. They sought juicy and pink, the throat, mostly, and Magnus's years of rigorous training were rewarded.

The remaining Riders charged at the pack, but the beasts were wise enough to stay clear of the sharp blades. Always circling, they edged backwards and then pounced the moment after a blade was swung and missed. The Riders never understood they were sport after a vicious day. The hounds knew how to kill, and kill they did. In a few savage moments, the battle was concluded and the hounds, answering their master's whispered call, fell around him, desperate for praise, desperate to feast upon their spoils. This blood was different. This blood was sweeter.

When the forest settled, Magnus lay with his boys and loved each magnificent beast with all his fading energy. They surrounded him and tried to lick at his wounds, to will him to rise, and eventually, he rose, and it pleased them greatly. He pulled himself up and grasped the reins of one of the dead men's mounts. Climbing atop the beast, he felt the weight of the world upon him and it was crushing. From deep beneath the desolation, he drew strength. He found menace. The cuts would stop bleeding, the wounds would heal and the pain would eventually leave him.

But the time of the Rangers was done. He knew this and it was tragic. He had marched his last, but as long as he lived, there was hope. His heart ached for what had been lost this day. He felt the tears flowing down his cheeks and he allowed them to fall.

"Let's go," he said gruffly, and the hounds dropped their spoils of war and barked in excitement. "There will be plenty more, my boys," he assured them, kicking the massive beast forward. The hounds followed loyally behind, eager for the next hunt.

57

OUTCASTS

The water was cool despite the blazing sun. Refreshing after such filth. *A necessary detour.* Erroh's body ached, exhaustion slowed his every thought, but he refused to sleep. He'd slept enough these past few days. The water was worth an entire day's delay; one solitary hour was a small matter. Everything around him was vibrant and alive. He'd missed colour. Missed freedom, stolen as this was. The little secluded area was a fine place to bathe. He dipped his head under the surface, listening to the roar of the current. He allowed its pull to take the last of the city's stains from him. Surfacing, he sighed in pleasure.

Lea watched from the edge of the bank. Her feet dipped, swaying in the water's pull. This felt like the road had felt, when it was them alone. *Alone and in love.* She scribbled a few notes in her journal and he thought about warning her as to the dangers of water upon leather-bound paper but remained silent. She was likely aware; she knew the road as well he did.

"This is wonderful," he said, spitting water from his mouth and revelling in its reviving coolness. He always thought it amazing how swiftly his body recovered once rested.

"You should put your shirt back on. You are a distraction, beo."

"You could join me," he suggested, grinning and raising an

eyebrow. Because that's what over-stimulated males did when left alone with the most beautiful girl in the world.

"I'm sure the others wouldn't mind waiting a few more hours." She smiled and blew him a silent kiss. He could see her desire hidden beneath the mocking. Neither wanted to leave. Horrors lay beyond this transient sanctuary. They could have kept charging, should have, but trauma needed tending to. *A brief rest is all.* He should have insisted on longer. They wouldn't fit much into an hour's play, so he floated in the water, thinking salacious things instead of contemplating how much of a ruin his life had become.

She distracted him with food. "Here—eat this," she whispered, leaving an apple to float over to him.

She watched the apple float gently towards him; he watched it languidly, and she knew he was deep in thought. Thinking of darkness, thinking of terror, thinking of the weight of their actions. She thought on these matters too. Still, she accepted them. She had stolen the son of Magnus as her mate. How smooth had she expected life to be after that? He stirred a fire inside her, a desire to bend the world to her will. She thought of the little lamb that had once hidden among the darkened corridors of Spark, and she despised that female. She'd found her true self in the green with her mate, in facing dreadfulness and suffering horrors alongside him. She was that type of girl now. She closed her eyes, listening to the swish of water, and for a wonderful moment she pretended they were wandering alone.

That's not enough, is it?

She was content, but something stirred deep down. It had stirred since she had come upon her burned homestead and begun remembering glimmers of dreadfulness. She desired something more than what life gave her. She wanted it for them alone. When she discovered what that was, she would reach out and take it.

Her hand followed her thoughts, and she blew on the ink and the words she'd scribed. They were ramblings; most of her scribbles were. She never read back over them, choosing to look forward, instead.

"You missed my birthday," she muttered, closing her journal and returning it to her pack. She looked back over the water at where Erroh floated. His eyes were wide and bright. Thankfully, his imprisonment had not permanently quenched his fire. She watched him try to count the days in his mind and become embarrassed at forgetting. He stood up in the water facing her; only his chest remained in view, and she desired him. She knew that, someday, gazing upon his naked chest would not affect her as it did now, and she did not fear that day. When it came, she would have him grow a beard for a few weeks or cut his hair. *Maybe paint it a wild green for a few nights?* She knew of many tricks. An Alphaline was wise to know the tricks when mated so young. He stretched his arms out and she almost melted. They had been mated a year. They were still new to wild yearnings. Sometimes, in the green, in the water, they remembered these things.

"I'm sorry."

He waded closer to the bank, and she reached across and touched his cheek. "I missed your birthday in the snow." Why remind him of the night a stunning blonde first took him to bed throughout a storm. *A fine birthday gift?* She slipped into the water gracefully and linked her legs around his waist. It felt wonderfully familiar. She gripped the bank and pulled him closer. He raised an interested eyebrow, but she smiled and shook her head. "We have no time for games," she whispered, kissing him gently. His lips were wet and healthy, no longer dry and discoloured. They were perfect, and somehow, she refrained from tearing at him.

"When we reach the Rangers' camp, we'll find the most suitable river," he pledged to her, laughing at their joint frustrations.

They both turned as, distantly, Wynn's impatient voice called to them from within the green. He'd argued against any rest, and truthfully it was a fine argument.

"I like it here," she whispered. She wanted to savour the moment. To love him for a while, lest it be their last coupling for a long time. *My Erroh, only mine.* He kissed her forehead before footsteps breaking through the foliage disturbed their sanctuary.

"We've waited too long," declared Wynn, whipping the branches clear and marching through the trees as though disturbing two young enamoured Alphalines was a small matter.

Lea understood his urgency, even if she did not completely approve of it. No longer mated to Lillium, Wynn had little right to worry after her welfare. Still, his concern was telling, if not a little favourable. Were Lea apart from Erroh, she might never stop caring for him either.

"Oh, I've disturbed something, haven't I?" He sounded both irritated and contrite. *More irritated.* He looked to the sky above as though looking away from some unmentionable act.

"A moment more, is all," Erroh said menacingly.

She liked this tone. Liked the threat. She wrapped her arms around her mate and decided to never let go. Let the others ride on and they would catch up. She'd stared at his chest for too long. These things happened when two cubs were in love.

"Well... we were supposed to be leaving... now," muttered Wynn, thinking on this more. He kicked a pebble into the water beside them. "I suppose you both could take... longer..." He looked around, searching for escape. "The mounts need more rest, as well... Emir mightn't be so grouchy with another hour's sleep either... I could eat a little more too..." he added. Then, he bowed grandly, pleased with the gift he had given them, before disappearing back into the green.

Lea smiled giddily and unbuttoned her blouse as Erroh pulled her roughly against him.

"I can offer you a late gift," he said, and she thought it a perfect recovery.

————

Nobody complained as they charged through the green. Not even Emir, though he wanted to. His rear ached and his teeth chattered loudly. He rode in the middle of the group. Wynn and Wrek led, while Lea and Erroh followed behind. Emir kept his eyes ahead. A lesser brute might have found distaste in the couple's saccharine behaviour. But every grin they gave each other, every silly, affectionate expression between them, brought a smile to his face until he heard a marching army on the road ahead.

Wynn pulled up suddenly, his beast rearing with fright, and those behind slowed and drew up beside him. The winding path ahead was sloped, and a suggestion of terrifying marching things lay beyond the bend.

Get off the road.

Their horses whinnied in alarm at being so suddenly clustered and Emir wondered if they didn't sense their riders' sudden unease.

Get off the road.

"What is it? Rangers? Southerners? Wolves?" Wrek hissed, listening as he tried to control his mount. The mount was having none of this. She spun in circles, deliberately stamping the ground beneath; the nearing thunder of feet was louder now without the rush of wind in their ears.

Get off the road.

Emir was disinclined to chance his freedom until he was standing in front of Magnus. He knew Magnus's desire for his skilled hands. Knew his value to war, too. "Hide?" Emir asked bravely.

"Aye, let's get off the fuken road," agreed Wrek, dropping from his horse and pulling it off the path into the forest. It was a strange thing seeing a fearless man cower. Only in that moment did Emir understand his future. *Hiding in the green as loud noises pass.* A fitting life.

Erroh and Lea in turn slipped from their mounts and led them soundlessly into the trees.

Wynn, however, did not. He watched the road ahead, listening as the march grew louder, and now Emir recognised his intention.

"Wynn, let's play the game of hidden seekers," he said nervously. "Let's get off the fuken road."

"No, brother, I'll wait here a moment longer. If it is the Rangers, I wish to see them first, but if it is the Hunt, then my comrades are dead."

"And if it is the Hunt?"

"Well, I'll be dead a few moments from now, but many will suffer beneath my blade." He sounded determined and brave—and idiotic. He touched the Ranger crest across his chest and his hands shook as though he had pledged to defend a condemned man.

"And what if it's the returning Wolves and your glare is the first thing they see? Their victory is unlikely to erase their memory."

"Aye," he muttered, but still sat upon the horse. "They won't see me disappear into the green. I'm swift like that."

Emir dragged his horse off the path and stood at the treeline. He wasn't swift like Wynn, but he wasn't blind to signs of danger either. "This is where I should suggest you hide with me, brother, or I won't hide at all," Emir hissed. The army were moments away now, and he was far from getting off the fuken road. "And then we'll all find doom together."

"Is that what you intend on doing?" he asked, finally looking away from the road ahead.

"Not at all. Stop acting the spitting fool and follow me, idiot."

Ahead, there came a flicker of movement as a banner appeared, and Emir dragged his beast further into the trees. Within a breath Wynn was behind him, grinning warily. "Well? Is it the Rangers?" Emir whispered.

"I couldn't see. You took my nerve," he whispered, and they moved further into cover. "Let's hope they don't recognise recent tracks though," he added, intending to worry Emir. It worked, and Emir suddenly realised the gaping indents his mount's hooves had made upon the muddy ground. He led his mount in further, wary of a keen-eyed enemy peering in and catching sight of a watching criminal.

At last the marching army drew into sight. "Black Guard marching in formation," Wynn whispered. They stood still, holding their breaths.

"They wouldn't be in formation if they were vanquished," whispered Wrek.

The army came alongside their hiding place, and the outcasts pulled further into camouflage. How odd, thought Emir, that they were now hiding from those they had once considered allies. *Magnus will smooth things over.*

If the Wolves noticed the hoofprints, they showed no interest in following them and seeking the fugitives out. Instead, the world darkened ever so as the first line passed the spot where the five and their horses had stepped in. They marched past in groups of ten, taking up the entire width of the path; their heavy boots sent tremors through the forest and birds took flight in terror. *Keep walking.*

Emir peered through the undergrowth, studying them, watching for a clue as to the outcome of the great battle. The Wolves looked beaten, exhausted, but their numbers were still great.

"No Rangers," whispered Wynn, and a sick feeling stirred in Emir's stomach.

"Perhaps Magnus has sent the Wolves alone back to Samara, while the Rangers watch the line," Erroh suggested, and it sounded reasonable. A fine tactic, and one guaranteeing them safety in the Rangers' base.

Still, though.

———

When the last Wolf disappeared around the bend in the road, Wynn was first to emerge from cover. He wasted no time in charging forward; no meandering wanderings in a river would prey on his better nature this time, either. Knowing the battle was fought and won was a potent inspiration, and the rest of the group followed eagerly now. They attacked the road, spurring their beasts on to greater speed. They rode at a steady pace for many hours, until they caught sight of little beads of smoke on the horizon.

Erroh had almost forgotten the comforting sights of villages and the warm glow of campfires. He knew that most people had fled to the City of Light as word of the Hunt spread, but he wondered how many still lived unseen out in the vast, green wilderness, in settlements that were unknown except by those with accurate maps. *As if there were such a thing.* It was an enormous world; there were many places to hide. Not all could fit into Spark City, or suffer along its wall. Those of the east wouldn't bother to march. They'd take their chances under Magnus's watch. He suddenly thought of the east and the thousands of miles he'd marched alone. The people he'd spoken with, the curs he'd faced. *Simpler times.*

The path became narrower as it succumbed to the cruel ways of the Waste. The twinkling lights of the city faded away behind them into the darkness; they were only halfway to the little trails of smoke they had seen in the far distance. The shattered moon above faintly lit their way. In their eagerness, they passed the Black Guards' abandoned campsite without seeing it at all; they thought only of reuniting with their chosen comrades.

A darker part of Erroh's mind worried about the losses they had incurred. That darker part also worried after his father, but he suppressed those thoughts swiftly. Whatever would be, would have to be. A man might go mad worrying about things unknown.

They found no need to speak as they pushed on along the increasingly overgrown pathway. Highwind fought Erroh's every order. *If you were loyal, we could do substantial things together, beastie.* The horse, however, did not trust his lead; it seemed to fear the dark, and he cursed its cowardice.

At last, they saw the little lights of the campfires glimmering through the leaves, and it was a most welcome sight. Erroh could almost taste the boar and sine Magnus would have waiting for them. Perhaps the celebration was still going on, he thought, and then realised that all was nearly silent. At first, it sounded like the encampment was humming with low conversation, but their joy swiftly turned to horror as they realised they heard the low groans of dying warriors.

Oh, no.

Erroh's mind reeled. Dropping from his mount, he managed a few steps before he felt Lea's hand on his shoulder. For a moment he thought she was offering him comfort, supporting him at his time of need, for she was stronger than he. But she gripped him harder and he realised she was the one faltering; she felt the devastation as he did. But only for a moment. She took a breath, squeezed his shoulder once more before releasing it and stepped assuredly. Even in the campsite's low light, they could see the bodies, lined up and still. Most had been cut to shreds and bled dry. Most were clad in Black, but a few wore beige. All were butchered and broken. The Wolves had left their injured behind. *Why?*

The stench of infection, waste and death struck him like a fist to the face. Erroh's stomach turned, and he heard Wrek vomit beside him. Wynn slid from his saddle and collapsed to his knees, weeping.

This was a camp that should have served as a rest spot for a thousand; now it numbered fifty living souls at most. No tents had been erected. There were only grubby strips of sheeting stretched out here and there on the ground. The Rangers had been defeated. The world was falling to darkness. This was the beginning of the end.

On either side of him, his comrades wept, gasped and cursed, and Erroh barely heard them now. His arms felt weak. His fight was gone. His heart was broken.

Only Emir seemed to retain his senses. Dropping from his horse, he grabbed his medical bag in one fluid motion and sprinted into the camp. Erroh watched with numb detachment, unable to move, as the wretched healer went to task among the many bleeding soldiers.

The healer's energy seemed to jar Wrek and Lea from inaction. As though inspired, they took off after Emir—a brave thing considering the company. But if the Wolves noticed their presence, they gave little indication. Those who were uninjured sat in the fire's light, gazing upon the flames as though searching for relief. Others walked restlessly among their wounded and slain comrades, and Erroh's heart ached for them.

We should have been here.

Then, beside a small fire crackling at the edge of the camp, Erroh saw a weary figure that he recognised at once. Magnus. Covered in blood, the legend gazed blankly at the dancing flames. His hounds were huddled in close beside him. He turned, almost languidly, to watch Emir working over the battered bodies, but he made no move nor offered a gesture of recognition. After a moment, he returned to staring at the flames, and Erroh watched him in silence.

———

"Shush," whispered Emir gently, kneeling by the fallen warrior. He took the broken man's hands in his own and slid them slowly away from the bloodied hole they tried desperately to cover. There wasn't as much free-flowing blood as Emir had hoped. *Never a good sign.* The man's intestines spilled out, and Emir knew now there was little hope. He offered him some dream syrup from a little spoon and held a cloth over the foot-long gash below his navel, ignoring the moaning around him.

"What's your name?" he asked, but the wounded man fell swiftly asleep from the pain and the syrup. Perhaps he had administered too much; this would not have been a bad thing.

"Is he dead?" Wrek asked, clasping the injured man's shoulder gently. "I know him. A terrible card player, but good for a jest. Never caused an ounce of trouble either. Those things matter, you know?"

"Aye, they matter. He is at the door, Wrek," whispered Emir, gently sliding the man's innards back through the gaping hole. Pouring some disinfectant around the wound, he took a needle and thread and sealed a few inches along the edge with a few swift flicks. "Better a man dies intact," he whispered, as though it were nothing. Inside, he wailed. Grasping Wrek's wrist, he offered the needle and thread. "He's out cold, regardless. Practice the stitching on his wound, while I see to the rest of these boys."

His voice was firm, reassuring, and Wrek began his grisly task, while Emir moved off with Lea in tow offering more syrup to the next man in line. The wounded man stirred only a few times as the behemoth sealed the wound, and Emir, glancing at him from time to time, thought he'd done a fine job. *Better than Roja.* Finally, Wrek patted the sleeping man gently and Emir directed him to the next wounded.

———

"Father?"

Magnus looked up from the fire. His face was pale and lost. "Forgive my lack of cheer that you somehow escaped the city," he whispered, and Erroh could see blood seeping through a heavy bandage on his knee. The wound looked a few days old. *Untreated, too.* "But it pleases me, Erroh."

"What happened?" Erroh asked after a time. He looked back into the night and spotted Emir handing Lea a needle and thread. Whatever directions he gave, she nodded and carried them out. Erroh knew that soon enough he, too, would be taking instruction and tending to the dying with nothing more than his own inadequate healing skills to call upon.

"My Rangers have stepped into the darkness."

"I'm sorry, Father." He could see that Magnus was weak, broken. His words were powerful, but there was little behind them.

"There will be an awful vengeance placed upon every man that betrayed them to die." He stared into the fire.

Unsure of what to do, Erroh opened his canister of water and offered it to the old Ranger.

"What of Jeroen?" he asked, already knowing the answer. Magnus shook his head and Erroh felt a strike to his stomach. *This is just like Keri.*

"Lillium?"

Magnus sighed heavily, as if the world's weight was upon each shoulder. "Perhaps she will show up at a later hour," he said dully. "We knew to rendezvous at this camp." He took a breath, as though it were the most gruelling task he'd ever endured. "Some Black Guards are still filtering in; some of them return with fallen comrades."

Erroh nodded. "How long has she been missing?"

"Two days," he whispered, and Erroh nodded again. *Little chance at all, then.*

"Tell me of the battle, Father," Erroh said, and slowly, Magnus told him the tale of betrayal.

58

LOST GIRL

He needed no sleep or rest. Such petty needs affected only mortal men without purpose; his purpose lay in saving the girl. His girl, his former mate, his Alpha female. She was alive, and Wynn would find her. It mattered little how long it took. Gripping the reins tightly, he charged on through the darkness, leaving the camp far behind. He had all the directions he needed. *A few hours west and I'll reach it by dawn.* Leaves slapped his face, branches tugged at his body, but he would not stop. Could not stop. Erroh's words had been tragic and kind; delivered delicately. He'd heard nothing beyond where she'd hidden in the battle. She was Alpha and she was a Ranger. She would survive this. He knew it, as he knew his own failings. This task was of love, duty and honour. Their tale was almost concluded, but there were a few pages left to turn. She was out in the Wastes alone, and he would find her and bring her home. Lillium deserved him at his best, and after far too many miles walked badly, he could—would—do this right.

Marvel had been tough on him as a cub. He'd believed religiously in the value of a jest, but he'd also believed in knowing the skills of tracking a path. Marvel was no master instructor like Garrick, but he had enjoyed the torturous tests and trials he'd set, and they were brutal. How much of his own blood had Wynn shed? How many tears? All to hone his craft, understand the way; all for moments like these. *You prepared me for the road and little else.*

Magnus had taught him more about other things in their brief period together. Tonight, however, he ignored his guidance. Tonight, he rode into enemy territory regardless of the danger. No army could stand between him and the female whose life he'd ruined. Saving her this day would hardly redeem him, but it was a start to earning forgiveness. *And love and mating soon after?* He spat into the night. No, he would never drag her divinity down to his wretched level ever again.

The forest opened up, and the light of the moon shone down through the tree branches. He rode steadfastly along the path, keeping an eye out for hunters and listening for predators. Towards dawn, he spotted a few groups of the enemy, setting up camps along the edges of the Great Mother, but he rode on, unmolested.

As the sun touched on noon, Wynn stepped at last upon the battlefield where the Rangers had fallen. Their bodies had not been burned; instead, they had been left to rot in the long grass, and the carrion birds feasted heartily. He walked the length of the field and cried for his brothers and sisters, but he would not, could not, pray. Such scenes of horror would take any man's faith.

When he could take no more of the devastation, he bowed a last time to his fallen comrades and led his horse into the green along the edge of the field. According to the Master General's instructions, she had taken her position somewhere in here. After a few hours of searching, he discovered more dead southern bodies, but no sign of Lillium. Looking closer, he saw that they had been struck down by a Ranger's arrows.

She has been here.

Circling the bodies once more, he now saw a set of small boot-shaped prints on the ground. *Yes.* Like a hound on a scent now, he followed the little tread marks beneath the leaves and the tale began to reveal itself to him. He saw everything that had happened here in the wilderness as others saw letters upon a page: twigs broken as she limped and stumbled. Lighter steps on her right where she'd avoided another attacker. Little speckles of crimson left behind. *Why would a southerner march like this?*

He moved further into the Wastes, searching for the lost girl. In a patch of undergrowth, he saw the marks where another skirmish had occurred, and the bodies of his quarry's next victims.

"That's my girl," he whispered proudly, still watching for movement.

The distance between the blood spatters increased now, and he suspected she had been moving quickly; perhaps she had been chased. *Why else would she leave her injuries untended?* He wanted to run now, to find her sooner, but he made himself walk slowly and carefully: haste could make him miss her tracks and he dared not lose her scent. He would not fail her this one last time.

He followed her trail for several hours more; his heart broke as her story unfolded. *So much blood.* She had been pursued by three more hunters; he could only imagine her panic. A few miles on, he discovered signs of another melee in a break in the trees. She'd waited for them. Struck one down with an arrow. The second shot had gone wide; grazing a tree as it did. *More scuffles, more blood.* She must have been terrified, and he had been a hundred miles away, locked in an unlit room.

He discovered the other two bodies of her pursuers, butchered. Even cornered and weak, she had made a last stand and taken their lives.

At a cost.

The ground was thick and dry. It was hard for him to read her movements now, for they were frantic. How long had the fight taken? How long had they chased her only to meet their end? She had truly earned her place as a Ranger.

He stepped over the bodies, marvelling at the savage wounds they had received—some after they'd died. He stepped back into the forest and saw larger drops of her blood; she had suffered at least one more terrible wound.

He discovered the point where she had collapsed the first time. He wanted to hold her and love her and earn his place as a companion. He knew he was tracking a wounded girl's last steps, but he could not stop.

She had climbed to her feet and continued on; she was brave and he was so proud of her. Even so terribly wounded, she had tried to make it back to camp. With a heavy heart, he discovered where she had fallen a second time. The marks in the ground suggested she had lain in the soft grass for a while. *Given up for a time.*

Then his breath caught in his throat as he realised she'd never climbed to her feet. He wailed aloud as he read the ripped-up tufts of grass, torn free of the dirt as she'd pulled herself forward. Despite her legs betraying her, she had still fought on. The path was too easy to track now, and he knew there was no redemption waiting at its end. Still, he trekked on through the green, steeling himself to find the body of his goddess of beauty and war, his Lillium, struck down before her time.

I have failed her again.

Again. Again.

Always.

A frenzy took him. He needed to end this story, no matter the outcome. He climbed back onto his horse now and galloped wildly through the trees, ignoring the noise they made. Let the Hunt attack. He could barely see the path for tears, but he pushed himself faster and faster and faster.

And then an arrow struck him down.

It pierced his shoulder clean through. A fine shot taken from a great distance. The force knocked him from his mount and sent him crashing to the ground in a heap. The arrow snapped painfully in the tumble and his horse bolted in terror. He was dragged beneath it for a few dreadful moments, and then fell free and tumbled to a stop. Terrible pain tore through his shoulder and he groaned aloud, cursing the shooter to the fires. It was no honourable thing dying without taking a life. *Not in war.* He hissed again and waited for his Alphaline vanquisher to finish him.

. . .

As the arrow left the bow, she caught the glimpse of his hair and immediately recognised her victim. *Oh fuk.* She tried to scream, but no sound came. She stood there as her arrow pierced the man she had once loved. She had known her shot was true; she'd judged the pace and the distance. A little wind might have blown it wide. He fell and thrashed, then was dragged by the fleeing horse and then dropped, and she wanted to die for her act. Too numb to move and too scared to call out, she listened and prayed to the gods who had abandoned her.

"Wynn?" she called out at last. There was no response. Her heart pounding, she leaned upon her bow and shuffled towards her dead mate and discovered that her dead mate was very much alive.

"Lillium?" He gave a pained grimace, which quickly turned to a weak smile.

She nodded, barely able to speak. "You came for me?" she asked at last. Perhaps his presence here was a blessing from the absent gods.

"You are injured," he whispered, looking to the many wounds upon her. The healing she'd attempted in her campfire's glow had done little more than stave off death a few hours more. She could barely stand; her vision was blurred and marching would be an impossibility. He struggled to sit up, then unhooked his canteen from his belt and offered it to her. She took it and drank blissfully, then sighed contentedly.

"You have no idea how thirsty I was," she gasped. She sat down beside him and drank again, and he sat quietly beside her and bled a little down his shoulder at her.

A pang of guilt struck her and she drank one last gulp before offering the canteen back. "Where are the others?"

"It's just me," he whispered. He looked down at the shard of broken wood protruding from his shoulder as though seeing it for the first time. She touched it tentatively, though she knew the barb had torn him badly.

"Just you…" She'd been alone in the Wastes, certain of death; she had never before endured fear like this. She'd seen such horrors and committed such brutal acts that she had feared her mind would never return. She'd needed saving, and fuk him, he'd come searching for her and she'd almost killed him for it. She should have felt warmth, gratefulness, but she could not. Not yet. "It wasn't your place," she hissed, and saw him wince at her sudden spite. "This earns you no favour with me."

He was crestfallen but offered a smile. "I'll always come for you." Gripping her hand, he looked into her eyes—not the last act of a desperate lover, but something else entirely. It was a pledge that he would never fail her again. Never let her down. Wading out into enemy territory, tracking her down, had been just a means of demonstrating this.

She liked it.

Rather than kiss her hand, he simply bowed his head. *Enough said.*

Using each other as support, they struggled to their feet and made their way slowly toward the now-grazing mount that would take them home.

59

GIFTS

Erroh watched the camp stir as another day came upon them. It was his third morning waking with these wretched undesirables. Warriors without a banner, without direction to follow. None had died the night before. They clung on, preferring to spend hours in agony rather than slipping into the darkness. That stubbornness was both a blessing and a reminder of their will. The harrowing wailing still rang in his ears, however; it always would, he knew. A sense of grim acceptance had replaced it. The world was ending, and there was no plan to counter that, no hope. The only gift was the morning after. The wretched gift of survival.

He worried about Spark City and thought that a strange thing. He was its enemy now. His allegiance was to the east, although that was misguided. Would the east go to war against all others, despite his attempt at mercy? He wasn't that important. He was no king. He was just a savage wanderer of the road. *You really fuked this one, Erroh.*

It wasn't all bad. He sipped his cofe and savoured the flavour. There was no boar, but the camp was flush with supplies. He appreciated the cofe most. If sine was the fuel of a city, cofe was its potent antidote. Someday, he'd find himself a cofe bean tree and plant it and think of Jeroen. The thought of Jeroen struck him deeply; visions of him and the other fallen Rangers he had known flooded through his mind in miserable waves.

No hope left.

He walked among the dusty wretches now as though he were their watching master. He was no leader like his father, but his tone was cutting enough to hold order until his father recovered his strength; his anger. A few orders were all they'd needed. Once they'd grown accustomed to the outcasts' presence, many had answered his simple commands. *Set a watch; erect a few tents; eat some food and bury the fuken dead.* They wouldn't gather their weapons and charge into battle upon request, he knew, but now was no time for battle.

A Wolf marched past offering a nod, and Erroh returned the gesture.

Truthfully, it was Emir whose dedication to healing had earned them the most grace. He had slept no more than a handful of hours in the few days since they'd arrived. From dusk till dawn, he had walked from tent to tent, treating the wounded and the dying with tenderness and expertise. An Alphaline of a different sort, he knew the body like Magnus knew a battlefield. He ignored screams and pleading and pulled life from nowhere. Where Erroh or Lea or Wrek believed they saw mortal wounds, Emir saw only challenges, a chance to cheat the darkness. He had worked miracles in this wrecked camp of the fallen. To Erroh they nodded; to Emir they bowed.

Distantly, he heard Emir's laugh coming from one of the larger tents in the middle of the camp. *What torment does he inflict upon Wynn now?* Erroh ducked under the flap as fresh laughter erupted.

"Shut up, Emir," hissed Wynn from his bed. Emir was bent over his shoulder, inspecting the wound and laughing again about the infamous arrow wound he'd received while saving Lillium. "And stop talking about her chest—she's healed enough," he warned, flinching as Emir prodded his back where the arrowhead had poked through.

Lillium lay in a little cot across from her former mate. Sitting up now, she covered her naked chest with a few bedsheets and thin strips of bandaging. She stretched as Erroh entered, barely keeping her shame hidden, and didn't appear to care.

Erroh bowed, averting his eyes, and she gave a gentle wave.

"Until I know her wounds are free from infection, I will gaze upon her as much as I desire," Emir told Wynn. He grinned at Lillium, who found little insult in his jest. Perhaps seeing Wynn recoil was a pleasurable experience for her. Shooting him had certainly elevated her mood.

"You both look better than before," Erroh said, seeing the fresh colour in Lillium's face. She was glowing. Perhaps it was the syrup. Or else she was enjoying the fact that she'd felled Wynn so neatly. Nothing like violence as a tonic. Emir had offered her private quarters, but she'd opted for the cot beside Wynn's. Perhaps it was the guilt of having struck him down. Maybe it was love? *No, that ship has sailed.*

"Oh, wonderful. Have you come for the show too, Erroh?" Wynn muttered, grimacing as Emir left him.

"I heard joy; it was only reasonable to assume Emir was at work."

Emir turned to Lillium now, scrutinising the bedsheets covering her chest. "Fresh bandages?" he suggested with a wink, before stepping out of the tent with mischief in his eyes. He would enjoy the torment as long as possible, Erroh knew. Wynn could have silenced him with a harsh glare, but no glare came. Brothers of the dark could only mock these tasteless ways. Even though the mood was low in the camp, after the chained dark, they all found humour in their shared wretchedness.

Erroh stepped out of the tent after him. "You look rougher than both young lovers in there," he said, offering Emir his cofe.

"I'd murder a sine if you offered it, brother. As for our couple? Aye, they are healing well. I'm not sure either will stay another day in bed. Fuken Alphalines can't even rest up like the rest of us."

"I can think of no worse way to spend time than on my back waiting for my body to heal."

"What about chains… darkness… thirst?"

"Aye, that is shit too."

"Look at the big man. He's in his element," whispered Emir, pointing across to Wrek, who was checking a younger man's wounds for infections. "Saves a few lives and he thinks he's a god. That said, everyone he tended to survived. Maybe he is blessed." Erroh watched him kneel over and inspect a long, untidy line of stitching stretching across the man's lower belly. "He is burdened with guilt for the sine merchant's actions. This is a fine distraction."

"It wasn't his fault. Fuk the sine merchant, and fuk the Wolves."

Emir shrugged. "Power corrupts the simplest souls, I suppose. Whatever Wrek's reasons, I'm just grateful for the help." He dropped his head, and fleetingly Erroh saw the dreadful exhaustion Emir suffered: the weight of each life; the fear of mistakes. Emir exhaled slowly and recovered his façade of strength immediately, and Erroh was in awe of his will. How far had he come since the day they'd first met? Erroh could have said something, could have embraced him, told him his acts were godly, but he did not. Emir would shy away in embarrassment at such notice, he knew. That's what heroes did.

With no words to offer, Erroh pushed the steaming beverage into Emir's hands. The weary man drained the cofe as though it were some healer's tonic. And perhaps it was.

They walked through the camp together, checking on patients. Without the rows of dead, without the misery of indecision, it flourished. There was a strangeness to the stillness, though, like the last act in a dreadful piece before another miserable play began. It was the silence between battles, Erroh thought uneasily. Whispered by outcasts without a banner.

"How is his knee?" asked Erroh, looking over to Magnus; the legend was engrossed in conversation with two Alphaline Wolves.

"Few warriors survive an arrow to the knee. He took two and insists in walking on it."

"It's no straightforward task arguing with him, is it?"

"He should be done with battle, but what do I know?" Emir whispered, and Erroh noticed the brace strapped to Magnus's knee. It almost resembled the Clieve in its makeup. He'd seen Wrek working on the beast the night before. Rebuilding a legend might lessen his burden tenfold, Erroh thought.

Suddenly, cries from their sentries broke the serenity of the morning. Erroh's eyes shot to the treeline, to the surrounding hills beyond. Like hornets taking flight, the Wolves emerged from their sombre state and sprang into action. Yells echoed throughout the camp; the threat was genuine.

"Above the trees."

"There—up there."

"They found us."

And then he saw the flicker of movement along the lip of the valley. One, two, then a dozen brutes appearing above the treeline, looking down at the little recovering camp.

Oh fuk, oh fuk, oh fuk.

More appeared; dozens, all in a line. All southern in appearance, all intently watching the camp.

Magnus was first to take up arms. Beside him, both Aymon and Doran drew their swords and the Wolves, too, swiftly followed their master. Aye, they were some force all right, Erroh thought. A hundred more and they'd have had some army.

For a moment, he felt the stirrings of panic at a nearing enemy, and then he remembered Keri. Remembered the warrior he'd been. Challenging them all to a fight. *Winning.* A sudden calm took hold of him. Moving with purpose, he strode towards the tent he shared with Lea. If there was to be a battle, he wanted to fight alongside her. He would not allow himself to become separated from her.

Never again.

She was in the middle of the tent, hastily fastening her armour, her face flushed with rage and excitement. Her fingers were a shaking blur as they moved.

"This is it," she growled, her eyes wide and fierce, and maddened with grief. Tending to the dying had left its hateful mark. "Those fuks wouldn't even allow us time to regroup." They were fine, aggressive words. *Anger is a gift.*

He clipped her last strapping and she helped him with his own heavy piece. Behind the cover of their tent it almost seemed still, but that's how it always was until the horns blew and the fighting began.

"We fight together, no matter what," he said softly.

"We will not die today," she pledged, and he nodded in agreement. Leaning close, lest it be their last kiss, they tasted each other and savoured the moment. This was their life. A few brief moments of joy between terrible violence and death. *Are you sure you made a fine choice in me, my beo?*

"Stay beside me," she said. It was not a question. There was no vantage point where he could place her. She would fight alongside him, and truthfully, he felt better for it. She strapped the two blades across her back and stretched a muscle in her neck. She was grim, composed, and beautiful in war. *A fine choice.*

They emerged from their tent, and then stopped in their tracks. They were greeted not by a charging army and the hushed silence before bloodshed, but by a grand surrender. One lone southerner bearing a white flag waved from the hill. Without awaiting a reply, he shuffled down towards the Wolf camp, and it held its breath as he approached.

Lillium and Wynn appeared now beside the two Alphas, their beige armour already donned. Wynn looked terrified, but Lillium had fight in her eyes. Behind them marched Magnus. Without his mighty Clieve, and hobbling slightly, he appeared diminished. His brace clicked in the stillness with every step he took. Aymon and Doran stood watching, tense and ready for warring. As one, they waited for movement, for Magnus's word; he was still their leader.

The scrawny southerner bearing the flag took his time approaching them, meandering through the trees as though he were enjoying a pleasurable stroll and not about to face the remnants of a battered army itching for retribution. At length, he reached the boundary of the camp, waving his white flag as though it would protect him. Had he heard of the Keri incident?

Azel, limping and unable to move properly due to Wrek's stitching, shuffled towards the visitor. Azel remembered the fate of Jeremiah, the holy man.

"Let's just lop off his head," he muttered, and Lea hissed him to silence. He nodded but his eyes were cold, his bow already loaded.

Magnus approached the flag-bearer now, and the world held its breath. There would be no surrender from the Wolves today; no retreat, either.

Seeing an intimidating monster approach, the newcomer waved his flag once more before dropping it at his side. He bowed before dropping to a cautious knee as Magnus stopped in front of him. He looked terrified, but also in control.

"We... kill not," he announced loudly, gesturing to the camp and then to the killers above. Magnus stood with arms crossed, his face fierce and deadly. Erroh knew that expression. The chances of this bastard leaving this encampment alive had dropped ever so. *Terrible opening bet.*

After a moment, the smaller man continued. "In fire... yes, but not... the now." He looked to Magnus, to the listening crowd. *Am I making perfect sense?* No warrior said a thing and the silence grew more uneasy. This was the same unease that brought about slaughter.

Erroh looked around. The Wolves wore the same fierce expressions as Magnus. They sought violence. There was something in the air. Absently, Erroh reached for the swords at his back, but not to draw them; gripping their hilts braced his nerve. They offered less reassurance than his old blades, but still, they were decent blades and decent blades were a rare thing to come upon. Mercy and Vengeance were swords reserved for gods alone, and with a threat so near, he missed them tenfold. *Oh, to scour Keri one more time and seek out either one.*

"General?" the southerner asked warily, and raised his arms, swishing them in the air. It almost looked like he was impersonating the wielding of the Clieve. Magnus nodded and offered nothing in return. Erroh could see the muscles in his jaw tensing. The southerner pointed at his chest. "I hold... word... Uden, the Woodin Man, god of south, destroyer of tainted... um... walker of world... destroyer of Spirk... um..." He took a breath. *Do you know him?*

Aye, we fuken know him.

"... he sees all?" the messenger asked hopefully. *Sees less with one eye.*

"Aye, we know Uden," Magnus hissed, stepping closer. In reply, the messenger stood up.

"Gift, word, message for false god," the messenger declared. He looked hopefully at Magnus, as though wondering if he'd pronounced his words correctly. The general just raised an eyebrow. "God of north, gift of Uden the Woodin Man... gift... um... gift?" The killer struggled and compensated for his lack of grammar with a few hasty nods. The tainted language was hard for a barbaric tongue. He looked around, sighing in frustration, and then waved his flag absently as he searched for a way to explain. "City," he suggested.

Silence.

"False god of City!" he declared loudly.

More silence.

"Spark City?" asked Magnus, his fingers tapping the pommel of his blade, and Erroh knew his patience was wearing thin. The messenger needed to do a better job of explaining himself. Hearing Spark brought a smile and he almost cheered. Were there not a few hundred southerners standing above them, it might have been a humorous moment.

"False god of Spirk City!"

Magnus seemed to find this funny. He grinned dangerously. "Spark City has no god, but if you wish to speak a message to a person in power, you may do so here. Tell me this message from Uden, southerner. Tell me so I can offer a swift reply. Tell me so I..." He paused and stared at the man. "Are you understanding anything I'm saying?"

The southerner nodded as though it made perfect sense. "Eeeh row."

Magnus glanced at his son.

Erroh felt a dreadful coldness draw around him.

"Errrr oh?" the man repeated, then muttered something else under his breath in southern tongue. It sounded like something about the false god having a stupid name.

Erroh began to step forward and Magnus shook his head.

Don't let them know.

"Ero?" the flag-bearer asked the crowd, blissfully unaware that everybody was already staring curiously at the false god of Spirk City.

All except Lea, whose eyes were on the messenger.

"Kill Erroh in gift?" asked Magnus. *Good question.* His fingers strummed the pommel of his sword like a musician. It was best the next answer appeased him.

"No!" the horrified messenger countered, eyeing Magnus as though he'd just defecated on his boot. "No... no..." He spoke in his southern tongue again but this time he sounded angry, and Erroh understood his insanity. He believed his words. "How could you suggest that brutal act? The false god is incomplete. He will be blessed with Uden's gifts."

"Tell me of the gifts," Magnus demanded.

"No... kill gifts... tainted." He shook his head and Erroh stepped forward. Lea stepped with him.

"I am Erroh."

The southerner shook his head and sighed in frustration. *One more time, from the beginning so.*

"I am Erroh, of Spark City," growled Erroh of Spark City, and the messenger waved him away dismissively before butchering their language once more.

"Small."

Erroh hissed his retort in their brutal tongue. "I took Uden eye. Eat as food."

"Small," the man repeated, but his face creased in worry, as though he were struggling to imagine a small man toppling his giant of a god. He stretched his arm over his head, indicating someone taller. *Tall like a mad god at least.*

"What is the gift?" growled Magnus in the southerner's language. He pulled his sword free and held it down by his side.

The messenger shook the flag once, backing away. "Tomorrow, we offer the gifts to Erroh, false god of fire, false god of Spark City. We will bring gifts; we will offer safe passage." He pointed to the hills above and then turned to leave, clearly anxious to exit this surreal scene as quickly as he could. Then he spun around to face them again, his face serious and threatening. "Bad... run..." He waved an arm, indicating the entire camp. "All... dead... um... die... if... run?" With that he fled, leaving the flag behind.

Lea followed him for a few steps, then returned to Erroh's side. "Gifts?" she said, staring at him in puzzlement.

Erroh, badly shaken, said nothing. His fingers tingled and his stomach churned with bitter bile. His mouth went dry and he felt the eyes of every Wolf upon him. For a moment he missed the safety of the dark, or even a cage in the frozen south.

"I'm not sure I desire to know these gifts," he said, aware that his voice quivered. But as fearful as he was, he knew he needed to understand these gifts. They likely wouldn't favour him, but not knowing was a dreadful weight suddenly placed upon him.

Lea eyed him as though his lies were not worth the effort, and he suddenly wanted to flee with her and worry about the repercussions after. He also wanted to follow the messenger and accept the gifts this day.

———

At nightfall, the garrison remained on the hill. They waited and watched the camp but showed little sign of aggression. Erroh, the false god of Spark City, now found himself to be very unpopular among the Wolves. They never left him to wander alone for long. The threat of his vanishing was too great a worry. They argued and strategised. Few spoke of retreat with any enthusiasm, and even fewer spoke openly of fleeing in the night. Those others got as far as grabbing a pack and stepping to the boundaries before giving up on their plan. They hadn't the heart to follow their cowardly brethren.

Erroh had long since discovered his life would be full of terror, and this was just another tale in his saga. Terror would not stop him meeting with the Hunt. He only wondered if Uden would be among those offering the gifts. That wonder quelled his fear, for he had met that beast before and desired to meet him again. Be it in Uden's realm, on the battlefield or upon the very walls of Spark itself, he would show no fear. He would mock that fuker and he would draw his sword.

If Uden appeared, there would be no discussion of retreat, peace, or gifts. He'd tear his second eye out and then begin the real punishing.

638

Of course, it was easy having these imaginings the night before with a goddess at his side. She would march with him come dawn. He had tried to argue differently, but met with her resolute stubbornness. Such single-mindedness had got her to the south and back. How could he deny her this moment?

She took him to bed once more; her kisses were passionate, her touch was loving, and he found such comfort in her as the hours passed by that he almost forgot of the morning to come. He slept only a handful of hours, as did she. If this was to be their last night, they would enjoy it.

At midnight, their hunger for each other satisfied for now, they left their tent in search of camaraderie and found it.

———

Emir was first to notice the breaking dawn. Sitting at the table flipping the cards to each player, he stopped and watched the first rays of the sun warm up the land.

"Time for at least one more hand," he whispered.

"I'm all in," announced Erroh, pushing in his cheated pile of pieces. Lea matched his bet with the dozen pieces she'd borrowed from his little fortune. Aymon sighed, folding. Doran looked at his cards and then at the sky. He threw his cards away and stood up from the table muttering about "sharpening his sword." His best friend cursed softly and followed. Erroh had not run and their watch was done. Though Erroh loathed them, they were fine company at the table. There were worse ways to mend matters, he supposed. Perhaps knowing he walked into death had lessened their aggression towards him.

"Wait, no—this is so unfair," protested Lillium, pushing her own little pile in. She'd just got her grip on the game and now she was forced to play the last hand.

"Erroh, you have the wildest, most wonderful fortune," said Wynn with a laugh, turning his losing hand over for all to see. He pocketed the few pieces he still owned and patted them loudly. "I know I'm beaten, but I will rise again," he declared.

"Something seems real fuken familiar here," Wrek muttered, looking at his cards. "I think someone has been cheating me all night."

"Ah, you are just playing bad cards, Wrek. Sure, it's all luck anyway," mocked Emir.

Suddenly, the harrowing horns of war filled the fresh morning air, killing the mood entirely. The Wolves, rising to meet the horrors in the day ahead, froze collectively as the terrible memories returned to them.

Magnus emerged from his tent, already clad in his armour. Around his knee was an improved version of his brace. Two heavier strips of metal dug in on either side, holding him upright, ready for either the violence or the peace talks to come, and Erroh felt less nervous than before. Lea would stand with him, but Magnus would be at his back ready to charge. Ready to kill them all. *Dodgy knee and all.*

"They're beating my anthem," Erroh whispered, getting up from the table. Nobody noticed him pocket a card.

"Let's go get some gifts," agreed Emir.

Erroh sighed. They'd been through this already. It made little sense. "I'll walk alone."

"Never," hissed Wrek, slamming his fist down upon the table. "I've lost too many friends. I'm not sitting here waiting for more murder."

"We aren't really friends."

"If we live through this, we could be."

Wynn stood to face Erroh. "Why should you get all the shiny gifts, anyway?" he demanded, sobered by the knowledge that his comrades were ready to step into the darkness. He searched for words of gratitude at such selflessness. "You incredible idiots."

"Well said," muttered Emir, reaching for his crossbow.

———

He led them up through the forest. As the day grew into itself, he savoured the smells and the taste in the air. His stomach was sick and he wondered if he would be able to hold down his last meal. *At least it was savoury. Not boar, though.* The crashing and breaking of trees behind him grew in volume, and glancing back, he watched as each able Wolf followed him on his pilgrimage. They wore shining black armour; they marched for war. He was no friend to them, but they thought as his friends did. *Not alone.*

When they reached the hill's crest, they found the Hunt waiting for their glorious guest in the open valley beyond. At the far end, as though ready to march into battle, a large gathering of southerners stood still. A hundred at least. They were not the remaining forces, but they were impressive enough. They stood watching, waiting for a false god to appear. There were no waving banners; no raised blades. The only movement was the horn blowers lifting their instruments to their lips to announce their intentions. *Could be a fair fight.*

At the midpoint of the valley there stood a large tent erected in honour of a false god. Erroh stared at it in surprise, wondering whether Uden waited within.

Erroh stepped out ahead of them. Behind him, the last of the fifty Wolves watched him like a hound watches its master, their weapons at the ready. They had come for an event. Gifts or no.

He motioned Lea and Wynn forward now, and together the three companions began the walk across the valley to the tent. It was a large valley. The walk took a time. Erroh's heart hammered, but as he drew nearer his fear dissipated; he had heard this happened to doomed men as they stood alone at the gallows.

The Hunt ceased their movements, softened their call and fell into a defensive line. *Better to be safe than sorry.* Magnus raised his arm, and fifty Black Guard halted their march and waited. The legend took a few more steps forward and then stopped in the grass to watch the line of Hunt, should they suddenly charge forward.

Erroh, Lea and Wynn walked in under the tent, to speak with a bearded general of Uden's army.

———

It was a very nice tent, ornately decorated with the finest embroidery, and the hastily erected furnishings were overly lavish. The oak table was varnished to a perfect finish with chairs on either side padded with bright golden cushions. A family of eight could live happily in this tent, and for the briefest of moments, Erroh almost forgot that he was in the middle of the Wastes between two lines of hateful enemies, and that he was face to face with his captor from a lifetime ago.

Oren's smile was bitter. His crooked nose added to the nastiness of his grin. Upon seeing this foul brute, Erroh almost sent a blade right through his throat. Instead, he counted a few times in his head. Oren was not worth an aggressive act that might doom the rest of a beaten army. If Uden popped his head in, however, things might swiftly change.

Erroh stepped to the chair but would not sit.

"You, no god. You man," Oren hissed, taking his seat. His eyes betrayed his contempt.

Erroh could see the bandaging beneath his vest. Lillium had spoken of the leader she had failed to strike down. Knowing she'd bled Oren endeared her to him ever so. He looked less the impressive jailer he'd been and more a wretched remnant of a dozen brutal skirmishes. There was also a dreadful stench emanating from him. Not sweat, or waste; something else. Something rotten and aged.

"Just a man," Oren grunted. His accent was heavy with the southern taint.

"I am Alpha," Erroh offered in southern tongue. His pronunciation was better. Nomi had mocked him every time he'd erred. "Maybe a god too." He shrugged as though it wasn't out of the question, and Oren grimaced. At his waist hung a long blade. Erroh wondered uneasily if his bravado had been misplaced. Perhaps the Hunt were not here under honourable intentions. Such a thing should have worried him, but now, among the enemy, he felt strangely at home. A little violence would suffice.

Remember, Oren, I'm not in chains anymore.

"You are difficult... god to find."

"Well, I'm here now."

"Sit," he whispered. It was no request; it was a threat, yet still Erroh did not stir.

Wynn did. He sat down, staring at the southern general with cold, unwavering eyes.

Oren glanced at him once and found little to impress him. "Uden marches. Wait for him in Spirk."

Erroh could smell the horrible, rotting stench again. It was closer. Something in the wind. He sniffed the air and exhaled quickly. "Now, why would I wait for a mad god when I could do far greater things?"

As Oren translated the words in his mind, he smiled. "As you wish. I bring gifts. I bring…" He searched for the words and shook his head as he lost them again. "A challenge," he hissed in his natural tongue.

"A challenge?" Erroh countered in his own tongue, so all would understand. Oren nodded as though remembering the word. *A challenge sounds interesting.*

"I ask again, why should I please a one-eyed mad god?"

"Know place, little pet." He looked out past Erroh to the numbers waiting beyond. "You have no hill of spike. No valley of fire to bring. You have no army. You have no… Black Guard."

"I still have my laugh, you murdering piece of shit," Erroh hissed in southern speak. Swiftly he turned around to his comrades. "I just insulted him."

"Aye, of course you did," Lea said from behind them. It wasn't a criticism. She sounded approving of a little insult.

Oren sighed, and the stench in the room was dreadful. Slowly Erroh reached for his sword's grip. *Fuk it.*

"We are done, Erroh, false god… of Spirk City," he muttered, smiling as he did so, and Erroh allowed himself another fantasy of stabbing him. This time, through the eye. "You leave, we have no fight." There. The message was delivered. *Not much of a gift, really.*

Distantly, Erroh heard the rumbling of great carts upon uneven ground. He'd lived with that groaning beast for months. It sent shudders down his spine, but he held Oren's gaze.

"Gifts," Oren hissed, rising and stepping away from the chair, leaving Erroh a tragic sword and a half's distance away. One of the general's protectors stepped towards Erroh and presented some old friends to him.

His blades.

Oiled, sharpened and cared for. Erroh lifted Vengeance, and fell in love all over again. A perfect weight, it fitted perfectly into his hand. *A fine gift.* Sharper now than when last he'd fought with it. He took Mercy, and felt comfort in the magnificent blade's heavy weight. His eyes lit up and he stared across at Oren. The beard could not disguise the grin on his captor's face. The Hero of Keri didn't care at that moment. The gifts would come to fine use striking down Oren's brothers and sisters, no doubt. Uden wanted to face him with his godly weapons of choice, it would seem.

"You are complete now," Oren hissed, and oh, Erroh felt real fuken complete. Oren stepped away from the table, laughing, as Erroh slid free his lesser blades and replaced them with the finest swords he'd ever held. Lea gripped his shoulder. He knew she'd searched the battlefield for his blades only to fail miserably in her task. It didn't matter now.

"Uden give gifts, so you meet him in Spirk." Oren spun around, addressing a southerner standing outside the tent. "Others," he muttered, offering a careless bow before disappearing from the grand meeting altogether.

Within a breath, a second guard walked through carrying a little sack, and the stench grew to ten times what it had before. It was sealed with a tight knot, with a dark brown finish dyed into its bottom. Whoever had dyed the fabric had performed the task carelessly; there were many brown splatters in its finish. It was the size of a young man's head. Or a woman's. Swiftly, he placed it at the centre of the table and Wynn recoiled away, knocking his chair back as he did. It clattered loudly and Wynn stepped back, covering his nose. With the gift offered, the last guard quickly withdrew from the tent to join their greater numbers at the far end of the valley. The rumble grew and Erroh's head spun.

Nomi is my gift.

They had tied the knot a little too tightly, and Erroh struggled with the task. In his ear, he heard Lea's desperate whispers, but nothing made sense to him. All he could see was the sack. All he could hear was a faint drumming in his ears. It took a few dreadful moments to complete the task and only Lea dared draw near. He felt her hand still upon his shoulder, her breaths deep and sad despite the stench. Finally, he pulled the last thread free and shuddered at innocence lost.

Through the door of the tent Erroh could see a solitary cart rolling out across the valley. It came to a stop among the gathered Hunt. He remembered the little boy who had died in the first town long ago. Remembering his pledge in this moment mattered more. The last bit of the sack's rough fabric fell away and his heart sank as he released the little head from its resting place. It was soft and rotten with decay, but the broken face was easily recognisable. Beside him, he heard his companions gasp in dismay. He felt the tears forming, and the terrible rage, and he hated Uden with all his heart.

Little Mish had deserved a finer way to die.

You fed me and taught me and almost drove my sanity from me.

As is the way of any child.

You will never grow up.

In Uden, you trusted.

Erroh covered over the grinning skull and peeling skin and left the gift where it rested. His stomach lurched, his body shook as though struck by an arrow, and Erroh fell to his knees with a howl.

"Don't touch me," he screamed, as Lea tried to comfort him. Pulling away, he stumbled to his feet as though drunk and staggered backwards from the horror. His mind recoiled at the butchery. At the cruelty of it. A terrible rage came upon him and was swallowed by grief. He stumbled back out into the brightness of the day and looked to where his comrades, his allies, his army waited. He faced them as though defeated.

"Erroh," Lea whispered, her eyes upon the Hunt beyond.

He didn't want to turn. Didn't want to show them his torment. *Little annoying Mish.* The child deserved better. No child deserved that. "Erroh, please."

But Uden had one more gift.

The Black Guard stood waiting. Poised, terrified and full of wrath.

"Turn around, Erroh," hissed Lea. She dropped Baby from her
back, leaving it in the grass, but her swords remained in place.

Slowly, Erroh turned around to see the Hunt busy preparing Uden's
last gift. Some worked feverishly upon the large cart; others stood
nearby with flaming torches, and Erroh thought of Aireys.

No more.

Seeing Erroh gazing upon them, they went to work on the dead
body of a woman. Erroh recognised her, and he thought his heart
would break. He recognised the structure, too, from the pendant
favoured by Jeremiah: two wooden beams crossed over in honour of an
ancient god. These were the old teachings, and the Hunt spoke their
language. They nailed her hands to each end of the beam and Erroh
thought it a dreadful way to die. Her blonde hair was dyed brown like
the burlap sack, and Erroh's mind shattered. *Too much.*

The Hunt, thoroughly enjoying their bravado, their own
performance, lit the pyre around her and slowly the flames caught and
began to leap upward. Even from here he heard their laughter, and
Erroh collapsed in the warm grass.

Beaten.

"I could not repay her," he whispered, and guilt tore at his mind.
He remembered the cage and clenched his teeth, allowing hatred to
overcome him because sorrow might swallow him alive. Distantly, he
heard Magnus's roars, and they matched his own anguish. Magnus was
entitled to roar; he'd lost his army. Erroh, though, had lost something
else entirely. He couldn't look, yet he couldn't look away. He'd seen
this horror before. A burning body, and him unable to save her. With a
colossal effort, he rose from the grass and watched as the fire grew
beneath the cart.

He remembered Aireys; he remembered his gift to her. Suddenly,
he could no longer hear laughter. The sound of drumming replaced it.
The sound of defiance. The sound of blood rushing through his fuken
ears. He hated them. But more than that, he needed to destroy them all.

Every one of them.

He felt a dreadful itch in his arm. His scars needed one more
murderer worthy of remembering. He felt the world slow down and he

646

watched the flames grow around the beautiful ruined body of Nomi.
She had been something special and he had loved her. Not like Lea, for
their love was a divine gift. This had been an entirely different love.
Magnus's roars filled his ears and he tasted the same fury. They were
invaders; they were burning the world; nothing could stand in their
way. No city wall would hold back their attack. No blade was sharp
enough to pierce their collective breasts. Everyone would die. Nothing
could stop the Hunt, and he wanted to take the fight to them.

Lea gripped his shoulder and silently pleaded for stillness, but all
he could hear was the drumming and the hatred. His eyes were on
Nomi. Her beautiful innocence had led her to this horrible downfall.
He eased his beloved Lea aside and soundlessly screamed his
intentions. Lea already knew. Lea stood with him.

Magnus's roar was the call of a man who knew hatred and madness
were fine tools for revenge, and he stirred at the sight of Erroh's
madness. Erroh wanted to scream with him, but instead he walked
towards the flames.

Who would stop a god, anyway?

"Yes," shouted Magnus, following slowly after him. "Yes!"

The Wolves followed too. They did not understand, but they did
not need to. They needed leadership. They demanded blood.

Erroh's steps were strides now.

Every one of them.

The Alphas walked behind him and he heard their hissed words.
They knew they walked into death. They, too, were frenzied. If they
charged, the world would know no vengeance as brutal. *Lead the way,
Erroh,* they hissed. He knew this because the absent gods whispered in
his ears.

"No finer way to die, my Erroh," Lea said, and he looked to her as
they drew upon the watching Hunt. "Don't let them burn her body,
Erroh."

A fine plan.

Behind, Erroh heard the first of the Wolves' battle cries and he
turned to face the paltry number of the defiant and they waited for him.
They would never be brothers, but at this moment, when they were at

the Hunt's mercy, they all became warrior brothers in arms. Comrades in impossible odds. They watched and waited for anything. He reached behind his head and grasped the terrifying blades once more. He took a breath and listened to the screams of war. They were his own, louder than anybody else's. He pulled the blades free and the warriors in black roared and rushed forward as one. Erroh turned and sprinted towards an entire army. This time, he brought an army of his own.

The Hunt charged out to meet them and they covered the distance in moments and Erroh felt alive. He felt his warriors behind him and knew victory was theirs. He raised his blades and felled the leading southerner with ease. The soldier ran a few steps more before falling dead. By then, Erroh was already cutting into a handful of his doomed southern comrades, his fury and hatred spurred on by his drive to avenge the dead girl. He felt Lea at his side. He spun and she feinted and all died beneath their deadly combinations. Blades were swung, blades missed, and each time, Erroh and his mate twisted their stunning bodies to punish with glorious proficiency.

Desperate and reeling from the unexpected attack, the Hunt surrounded them, and Lea had never felt more relaxed. She closed her mind and concentrated on killing. With every stroke, she accomplished this task. She and Erroh fought back to back and blocked the never-ending swipes of blade and axe. It was almost too easy, and she began counting her victims as though she defended a falling town. Erroh's numbers were greater, but this war could last awhile. They charged into death and suffered no killing blow, and their Wolfen comrades joined them in their wrath. Spurred on by burgeoning legends, they struck each foe down and suffered little. It took only moments for the Hunt to retreat.

Wrek tore into the beasts with suppressed rage, like no beast had attacked before. He killed many, but it was not enough to quench his thirst for revenge. He would never stop trying, though. He was not alone. Beside him stood the wretched healer from Keri, wielding his impressive crossbow skills. The numbers disappeared in front of them, and Wrek roared in triumph as the battle turned to their favour.

"Kill them all!" he roared, and Emir roared hateful challenges of his own, and the Hunt fled further from the battle.

Lillium moved more slowly than usual, but she was fierce. Wynn would not stray far from her side, and it was a beneficial partnership. *Their first since a foolish female had taken a leap.* She killed without remorse, but her wounds soon halted her own vengeful assault. She tired quickly and could kill at only half the pace of her Alpha comrades. Still, she waded in deep, remembering her Ranger comrades with every devastating strike. Her body soon became covered in crimson and it was a fine colour, indeed.

Wynn watched the life leave his first victims and his heart ached for them. He bit back the remorse and continued to attack, trusting instinct to overcome misery. He would mourn the brutes later. He was a killer. A skilled killer, at that. He smiled as he struck every killing blow and hated himself for it. Deep within, he felt his soul burning away to nothingness.

Magnus was under protection from two fierce Wolves. Unable to move freely, he still pushed forward and struck down all who stood in his path. The powerful Alphas on either side were under the illusion that his life mattered most. They never strayed. Ahead, he watched his son charge into battle with the new generation of legends and knew how this war could still be won. The victory would begin with brutality as savage as this.

· · ·

The Hunt scattered towards the forest, but Erroh did not give chase. He left that to Lea, Magnus, his entourage and most of the army. He had other plans. Standing below the burning cart as flames grew all around Nomi's body, he cursed the time it had taken him to get here. Cursed his own weakness too. She would not burn to ash, he told himself, gripping the edge of the cart and pulling himself into the flames. As though he were a god of fire.

———

"Aim for the god!" roared a frantic Oren from atop his steed. The few crossbow wielders he called upon answered his order, despite those many retreating around them. To those scurrying many, he barked out orders, threatening their lives, but they were deaf to his voice. They knew the turning of the tide. They did not fight for him as they did for Uden. Months without a rousing godly speech were enough to crack the veneer of any zealot. The Riders' cowardice was no rarity. Oren was not yet old enough to be aware of southern history, southern temperament. As he watched his soldiers flee from paltry numbers yet again, he knew at last the cost of this march; he knew he would likely die at Uden's hands for this defeat. Their attack had been too quick, too violent, and the burning of Nomi had been their ultimate mistake.

———

The flames scorched his hands as he tried desperately to release Nomi from her restraints. The rope holding her body in place was too tight. Still, he tried. His fingers seared in the heat. Sparks ignited on his clothing and he slapped at them, fearing sudden immolation. The thick beams holding Nomi's body aloft had kept her safe from the worst of the flames and he leaned against her now, tearing at her bindings as the flames surrounded them. In the flickering orange light, he could see the abuse she had suffered. They had battered her face almost beyond recognition; the bruises along her arms were deep and ugly. Who knew how many covered the rest of her body?

The first rope came free, and with a ghastly hollow noise, he pulled one of her hands from the long nail holding it. Her dead arm fell limply and he lamented her fate anew.

Below him, Magnus drove the Wolves and Rangers onward upon the last of the southerners. Erroh had never seen his father march in pure war, but he saw it now. The Hunt saw it too. Saw it from their victorious pedestal before it burned beneath their feet. *They shouldn't have set this battle alight.*

He pulled Nomi's other arm free and began undoing the great knots at her waist. He could no longer hear the rest of the battle. All he could hear was the roaring of the flames and he felt no fear.

———

Darkness.

Pain. All the pain in the world. And a terrible, aching darkness. Warmth and the burning smell of fear all around her. Her eyes would not open. *Beaten shut.* Far too many wounds, yet still she felt her body dragged and attacked by some unknown aggressor. *Please, no more pain. Too much already.* She opened her battered eyes and inhaled heavy black smoke and wondered whether these were the fires her false god had warned about. She tried to blink and saw him, her one for life, and the world was torment. The world was pain, and she was dead. She felt burning sorrow and begged without words for kindness at an arrow's tip to end this nightmare. End this pain. End this wretched existence.

"Erroh?" she whispered through cracked, broken lips, and he stopped struggling and stared into her eyes as the last piece of rope fell free. A terrible weight pressed her down. It was her own, and she fell, straight into the glittering cinders at her feet. A horrible way to die. But her Erroh caught her, held her, and she loved him and she ached. Oh, but she ached.

He tried to speak and she saw the worry and pain in his face. Then he jerked painfully and fell back. She reached for him, but she was not strong enough. The arrow pierced his chest and he fell in slow motion away from the flames. She followed him. She'd travelled this far. Through the wall of fire, she saw him fall. His arms were on fire and an arrow pierced him.

Then she, too, fell to the ground and unconsciousness quickly followed.

———

Had he imagined her speaking aloud, or was he dead already? Was this the darkness beyond? It was brighter and much warmer than he'd expected. More painful, too. Erroh pulled himself to his unsteady feet and walked aimlessly through the carnage. His mind was awash with blurred thoughts, wild hatred and utter confusion. He'd saved Nomi, saved her from burning. *Did she speak? Did she look him in the eyes? Am I dreaming again? Does it matter? Who shot an arrow into me?*

"Gifts," he muttered, and he held that thought. He sought Oren amidst the chaos. Killing Oren would quench his fierce hatred. And killing every other fiend too.

Fine gift for Uden, too.

The Hunt were being slaughtered all around him, and he tried to walk clear of the thick smoke. It was so thick the sun was shaded and that was fine because his hands were sunburned. He stumbled forward and spotted a brute atop a mount a great distance away. The end of an arrow bobbed in front of him, bouncing with every step he took, but he paid little heed. He'd hit his fuken head again. Harder than he thought. Pulling the arrow free was a fine notion, but that seemed like an awful amount of pain to go through before he died.

Let's go kill Oren, Erroh.

Okay, Erroh.

He couldn't see anybody he loved, so he decided they were dead. It wasn't a very productive thought, but it drove him forward. This was his last march. He was sure of it. He shook his head to clear the dizziness, but the act almost sent him to his knees. He knew they were winning. He could see Hunt fleeing all around him and heard his father's impressive war cry instilling terror in their retreat.

"Oh fuk," Erroh muttered, seeing the flames on his gloves. The leather was burning through on both hands, and he walked as though bearing two fierce torches. *Probably explains the Hunt running in terror from you.*

Suddenly the notion of fire shook him to his senses, and he began to run up through the treeline towards Oren, who was still waiting upon his mount. A few warriors with crossbows stood out on either side. At least one fired, and Erroh felt another arrow pierce through his thick armour and he fell to his knees. It hurt less than the first, but still, fuk off archers.

"Again!" roared his quarry, as Erroh climbed to his feet. The leather on his forearms had burned away now and he felt searing heat upon his skin. It hurt less than two arrows sticking out of his chest, so he ignored the pain and instead reached for the swords upon his back. *Gifts.* He charged towards Oren and watched in dismay as the general turned his horse from the fighting.

"Fight me, Oren!" he roared, as his prey kicked his beast and charged away.

Fuelled by hate and pain, Erroh could not surrender the chase. He surged forward as the nearest archer knelt down and fired, catching him in the chest once more. This one hurt most and took his wind. Mad with frustration, he pulled the arrow free. He felt blood pour down beneath his armour and this infuriated him.

"Oren!"

The archer swung his bow around, and Erroh swung Vengeance in a graceful spinning arc and removed the man's head as he charged by. It rolled a few feet. *Like Mish's might have.* The ground opened up under him, and he caught sight of Oren galloping away and there was nothing he could do. He roared fiercely and they fired another arrow. In his fury, he knocked it out of the air with a swipe of his burning blades. Screaming, he tore the remaining arrows free and broke into full chase. He didn't notice the remaining archers fall to the ground in fear and awe as he ran by them. He tried, oh, how he tried, but Oren disappeared behind the tree line and out of Erroh's life forever, and finally he ceased his assault. He was done. The pain overcame him, and with it came the terrible need to rest. There was nothing more he could do.

Erroh did not hear the calls from the smoke-covered battlefield, as each of his friends and loved ones thanked the absent gods for victory.

He did not hear Emir's angry rant at Wynn and Lillium for opening old wounds.

He did not hear the boasts of Wrek among his Wolfen brothers.

He did not hear his father's contented sigh as he counted the dead of his enemy and remembered the Rangers and offered each victim as a pledge of vengeance.

He did not hear Lea's exhausted grunts as she pulled the unconscious body of Nomi away from the growing fire.

He heard only his own laboured breath as he patted the flames on his sleeves to reveal the bubbled skin underneath. He pulled his ruined armour free and loosened his chain mail vest so he could breathe easier. He counted the arrow marks and the little streams of blood coming from each wound. *I will test Emir this day.*

A terrible exhaustion took him, and the desire to call out for his victorious comrades became too much effort. He looked to the blue sky and thought it a beautiful day. Lying down in the long grass, Erroh, the Hero of Keri, the Outcast of Spark City, closed his eyes for a little while and rested.

———

HERE ENDS THE SECOND BOOK OF THE SPARK CITY CYCLE.
THE STORY WILL CONTINUE IN BOOK THREE: THE OUTCASTS

THANK YOU FOR READING MARCH OF MAGNUS

Word-of-mouth is crucial for any author to succeed and honest reviews of my books help to bring them to the attention of other readers.

If you enjoyed the book, and have 2 minutes to spare, please leave an honest review on Amazon and Goodreads. Even if it's just a sentence or two it would make all the difference and would be very much appreciated.

Thank you.

EXCLUSIVE MATERIAL FROM ROBERT J POWER

When you join the Robert J Power Readers' Club you'll get the latest news on the Spark City and Dellerin series, free books, exclusive content and new release updates.

You'll also get a short tale exclusive to members- you can't get this anywhere else!

Conor and The Banshee
Fear the Banshee's Cry

Join at www.RobertJPower.com

ALSO BY ROBERT J POWER

The Spark City Cycle:

Spark City, Book 1

The March of Magnus, Book 2

The Outcasts, Book 3

———

The Dellerin Tales:

The Crimson Collection

The Crimson Hunters, Vol I

The Lost Tales of Dellerin

The Seven

ACKNOWLEDGMENTS

All the thanks in the world to Jill, Jen and Poll for all the love, the laughter and the incredible support. Also, for putting up with my ranting opinions so no one else has to. To say you've done the world a service is an understatement. And another thing…

For Cathbar and the constant reassurance you provided throughout the frustrating times when the pri*k keyboard became my enemy and the last chapter seemed so far away. I'll need you for Outcasts. I really really will.

For Jean and Paul and their endless support. I cannot thank you enough for all your kindness shown throughout. May the book be worthy of your praise. Can't wait to raise a toast in honour of the greatness of me. They always make the best toasts.

Special shout to Tristan Burke, who made a song and dance about not getting an acknowledgement for Spark City despite doing nothing to help. Well, you still did nothing to help, but your site was a wonderful escape when I needed it these last few years.

For Eoin who got me in trouble with my editor for an in-joke. Next time you make the style guide! Thank you for the constant support and all the times you didn't get me into trouble with my editor for an in-joke.

For Ant, who walked me through the intricacies of the Clieve. After which a wonderful friendship has grown. Such things are appreciated from my cage. Because you are Australian and I'm Irish, I can't share any in-jokes suitable for the written form. Stay classy, mate.

To the DNF THIS crew who were with me during the good and mostly bad days. From all four corners of the world, I am lucky to call you friends. However, I'm still not sure Pigeon Armour and iocane cake are the answers to all life's questions (only most of them.) Plotters for the eternal win!

From the bottom of my heart I wish to thank The Army of Ed for the endless amount of abuse I've received over the last two years since Spark City's success took off. Without you guys, I might think I'm good at this writing lark. Despite what the record sales have suggested- we make pretty music and I'm proud to be a brother. See you at practice. Don't be fuken late.

Last, I need to thank my amazing fans. Look at you all. Beautiful and demanding. My type of people. I hope it was worth the wait. I hope this book makes you smile.

ABOUT THE AUTHOR

Robert J Power is the fantasy author of the Amazon bestselling series, The Spark City Cycle and The Dellerin Tales. When not locked in a dark room with only the daunting laptop screen as a source of light, he fronts Irish rock band, Army of Ed, despite their many attempts to fire him.

Robert lives in Wicklow, Ireland with his wife Jan, two rescue dogs and a cat that detests his very existence. Before he found a career in writing, he enjoyed various occupations such as a terrible pizza chef, a video store manager (ask your grandparents), and an irresponsible camp counsellor. Thankfully, none of them stuck.

If you wish to learn of Robert's latest releases, his feelings on The Elder Scrolls, or just how many coffees he consumes a day before the palpitations kick in, visit his website at www.RobertJPower.com where you can join his reader's club. You might even receive some free goodies, hopefully some writing updates, and probably a few nonsensical ramblings.

www.RobertJPower.com

facebook.com/authorrobertjpower
twitter.com/RobertJPower
instagram.com/RobertJPower

Milton Keynes UK
Ingram Content Group UK Ltd.
UKHW010155190124
436280UK00005B/71/J